PRAISE FOR THE D

"Well researched, well th
ten, these books repres
'alternate Earth' story. . .
highly."

—*New York Times* bestselling author David Weber

"Taylor Anderson . . . [has] steamed to the forefront of alternative history."

—national bestselling author E. E. Knight

"Pick up the Destroyermen series and kick back and enjoy." —SFRevu

"Anderson has a gift for complex plot and dialogue and a fabulous sense of humor." —*North County Times* (CA)

"Action sci-fi doesn't get significantly better than this."

—*Booklist*

"Simply put, this is great stuff. . . . Read it—you won't be disappointed." —Fresh Fiction

"Taylor Anderson is . . . a solid and imaginative storyteller." —SFFWorld

"Combines a love for military history with a keen eye for natural science. Reddy is a likable protagonist, epitomizing the best of the wartime American military."

—*Library Journal*

"Pay[s] homage to such tales as *A Connecticut Yankee in King Arthur's Court*, *Robinson Crusoe*, and William R. Forstchen and Greg Morrison's *Crystal Warriors*."

—*Publishers Weekly*

The Destroyermen Series

Into the Storm
Crusade
Maelstrom
Distant Thunders
Rising Tides
Firestorm
Iron Gray Sea
Storm Surge
Deadly Shores
Straits of Hell
Blood in the Water
Devil's Due
River of Bones

DESTROYERMEN

DEVIL'S DUE

TAYLOR ANDERSON

ACE
New York

ACE
Published by Berkley
An imprint of Penguin Random House LLC
375 Hudson Street, New York, New York 10014

ISBN: 9780451470669

Ace hardcover edition / June 2017
Ace mass-market edition / June 2018

Printed in the United States of America
1 3 5 7 9 10 8 6 4 2

Cover art by 3DI Studio

To Silvia, for . . . everything. And in case I left something out, thanks for everything else.

ACKNOWLEDGMENTS

Thanks to Russell Galen, as always. Simply put, I wouldn't be doing this if not for him. (Some might curse him for that, I suppose, but I'll always be grateful.) Thanks also to my amazing editor, Anne Sowards, who really went above and beyond on this one, to my eternal appreciation. She's the best. As usual, I have to thank Fred Fiedler, my "alpha" reader, for helping me keep things straight. (I hope you appreciated the bugs, Fred. All for you.) And there's still a fine bullpen of technical advisers as well, including Mark Wheeler, William Curry, "Cap'n" Patrick Moloney—to name just a few. Then there's Matthieu, Clifton, Joe, Charles, Alexey, Brian, Lou, Justin, Don . . . Shoot, I can't remember all the great, supportive minds that visit my Web site and help me wrangle improbable ideas, but I'm grateful for your input. If I missed you, I'll try to catch you next time. As usual, some of my particular buddies' antics/expressions/personalities have been "memorialized in literature," but I won't be specific. I've mentioned most of them before and there's no sense in encouraging them.

A *very* special thanks goes to Ms. Kelley Ryan, a fine young man named Andrew, and to all the great people who work so hard to preserve USS *Kidd*, DD-661, in Baton Rouge, Louisiana. My wife and I just showed up there one day, and they treated us like family. Before we knew it, we were crawling through the engineering spaces and seeing whatever we wanted. I just wish we'd had more time. We'll be back, and I urge everyone to visit her. She looks and feels ready to fight—again.

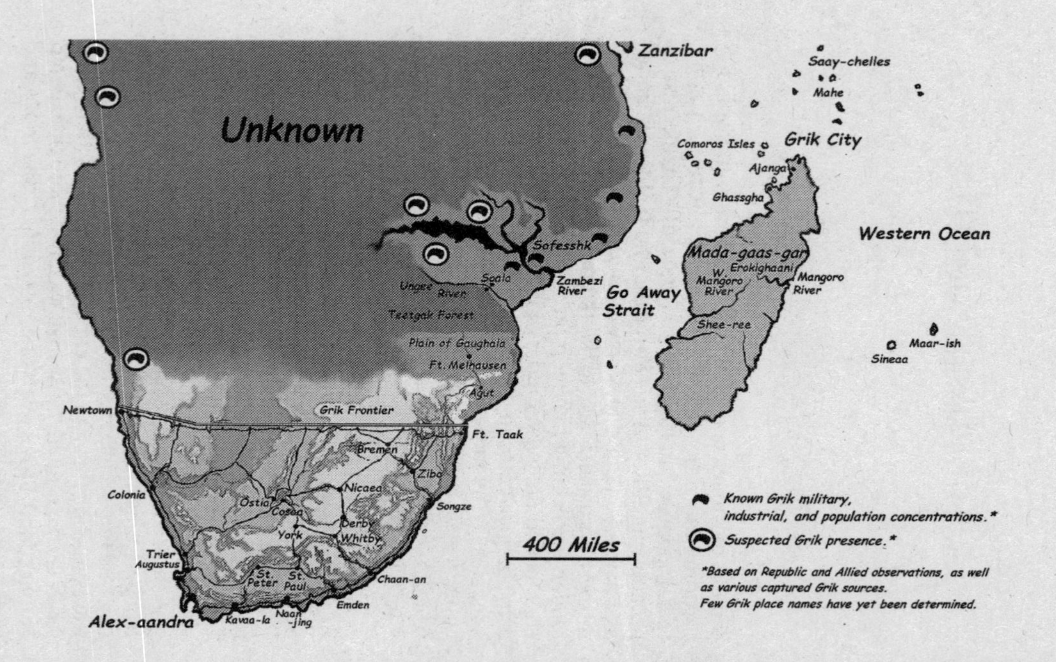
Zanzibar
Saay-chelles
Mahe
Unknown
Comoros Isles
Grik City
Ajanga
Ghassgha
Western Ocean
Sofesshk
Mada-gaas-gar
Erokighaani
W. Mangoro River
Mangoro River
Saala
Zambezi River
Ungee River
Go Away Strait
Teetgak Forest
Shee-ree
Plain of Gaughala
Maar-ish
Sineaa
Ft. Melhausen
Agut
Newtown
Grik Frontier
Ft. Taak
Bremen
Zibo
Nicaea
Colonia
Ostia
Cosca
Songze
Derby
York
Whitby
Trier
Augustus
St. Peter
St. Paul
Chaan-an
Emden
Alex-aandra
Kavaa-la
Naan-jing
400 Miles
Known Grik military, industrial, and population concentrations.*
Suspected Grik presence.*
*Based on Republic and Allied observations, as well as various captured Grik sources.
Few Grik place names have yet been determined.

Recognition Silhouettes of Allied Vessels

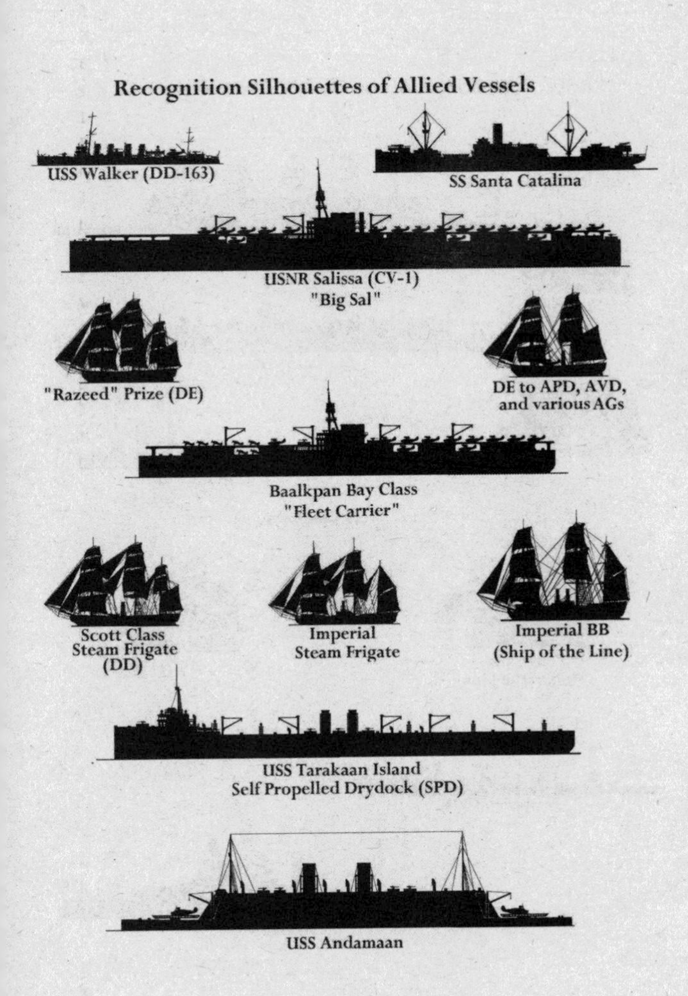

Recognition Silhouettes of Enemy Vessels

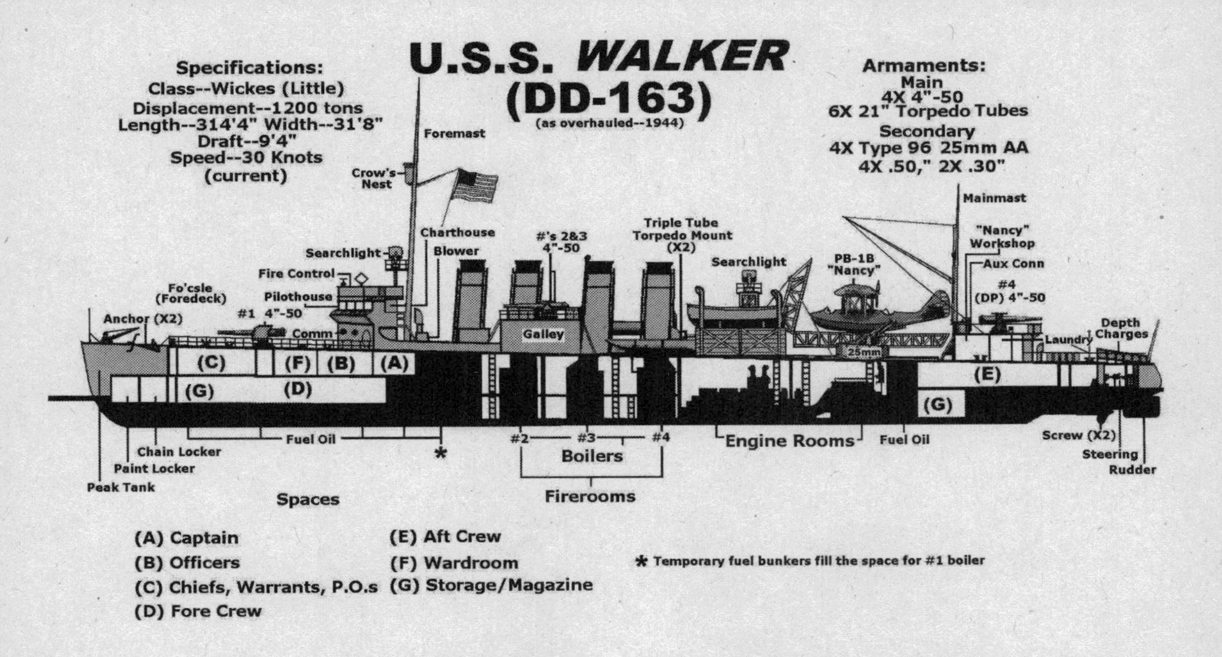
U.S.S. WALKER
(DD-163)
(as overhauled--1944)
Specifications:
Class--Wickes (Little)
Displacement--1200 tons
Length--314'4" Width--31'8"
Draft--9'4"
Speed--30 Knots
(current)
Armaments:
Main
4X 4"-50
6X 21" Torpedo Tubes
Secondary
4X Type 96 25mm AA
4X .50," 2X .30"
Foremast
Crow's Nest
Charthouse
Blower
Searchlight
Fire Control
Pilothouse
Fo'csle (Foredeck)
#1 4"-50
Comm
Anchor (X2)
#'s 2&3 4"-50
Galley
Triple Tube Torpedo Mount (X2)
Searchlight
Mainmast
PB-1B "Nancy"
"Nancy" Workshop
Aux Conn
#4 (DP) 4"-50
25mm
Laundry
Depth Charges
(C) (F) (B) (A)
(G) (D)
(E)
(G)
Fuel Oil
*
Chain Locker
Paint Locker
Peak Tank
#2 #3 #4
Boilers
Firerooms
Engine Rooms
Fuel Oil
Screw (X2)
Steering
Rudder
Spaces
(A) Captain
(B) Officers
(C) Chiefs, Warrants, P.O.s
(D) Fore Crew
(E) Aft Crew
(F) Wardroom
(G) Storage/Magazine
* Temporary fuel bunkers fill the space for #1 boiler

AUTHOR'S NOTE

A cast of characters and list of equipment specifications can be found at the end of this book.

OUR HISTORY HERE

By March 1, 1942, the war "back home" was a nightmare. Hitler was strangling Europe, and the Japanese were rampant in the Pacific. Most immediate, from my perspective as a . . . mature Australian engineer stranded in Surabaya Java, the Japanese had seized Singapore and Malaysia, destroyed the American Pacific Fleet and neutralized their forces in the Philippines, conquered most of the Dutch East Indies, and were landing on Java. The one-sided Battle of the Java Sea had shredded ABDAFLOAT, a jumble of antiquated American, British, Dutch, and Australian warships united by the vicissitudes of war. Its destruction left the few surviving ships scrambling to slip past the tightening Japanese gauntlet. For most, it was too late.

With several other refugees, I managed to board an old American destroyer, USS Walker, *commanded by Lieutenant Commander Matthew Reddy. Whether fate, providence, or mere luck intervened,* Walker *and her sister* Mahan, *their gallant destroyermen cruelly depleted by combat, were not fated for the same destruction that claimed their consorts in escape. Instead, at the height of a desperate action against the mighty Japanese battle cruiser* Amagi, *commanded by the relentless Hisashi Kurokawa, they were . . . engulfed by an anomalous force, manifested as a bizarre, greenish squall—and their battered, leaking, war-torn hulks were somehow swept to another world entirely.*

I say "another world" because, though geographically similar, there are few additional resemblances. It's as if whatever cataclysmic event doomed the prehistoric life on our earth many millions of years ago never occurred, and those terrifying—fascinating—creatures endured, sometimes evolving down wildly different paths. We quickly discovered "people," however, calling themselves Mi-Anakka, who are highly intelligent, social folk, with large eyes, fur, and expressive tails. In my ignorance and excitement, I promptly dubbed them Lemurians, based on their strong, if more feline, resemblance to the giant lemurs of Madagascar. (Growing evidence may confirm they sprang from a parallel line, with only the most distant ancestor connecting them to lemurs, but "Lemurians" has stuck.) We just as swiftly learned they were engaged in an existential struggle with a somewhat reptilian species commonly called Grik. Also bipedal, Grik display bristly crests and tail plumage, dreadful teeth and claws, and are clearly descended from the dromaeosaurids in our fossil record.

Aiding the first group against the second—Captain Reddy had no choice—we made fast, true friends who needed our technical expertise as badly as we needed their support. Conversely, we now also had an implacable enemy bent on devouring all competing life. Many bloody battles ensued while we struggled to help our friends against their far more numerous foes, and it was for this reason I sometimes think—when disposed to contemplate destiny—that we survived all our previous ordeals and somehow came to this place. I don't know everything about anything, but I do know a little about a lot. The same was true of Captain Reddy and his US Asiatic Fleet sailors. We immediately commenced trying to even the odds, but militarizing the generally peaceful Lemurians was no simple task. Still, to paraphrase, the prospect of being eaten does focus one's efforts amazingly, and dire necessity is the mother of industry. To this day, I remain amazed by what we accomplished so quickly with so little, especially considering how rapidly and tragically our "brain trust" was consumed by battle.

In the meantime, we discovered other humans—friends and enemies—who joined our cause, required our aid, or posed new threats. Even worse than the Grik (from a moral perspective, in my opinion), was the vile Dominion in South and Central America. A perverse mix of Incan/Aztecan blood-ritual tyranny with a dash of seventeenth-century Catholicism flavoring technology brought by earlier travelers, the Dominion's aims were similar to the Grik's: conquest, of course, but founded on the principle of "convert or die."

I now believe that, faced with only one of these enemies, we could've prevailed rather quickly, despite the odds. Burdened by both, we could never concentrate our forces, and the war lingered on. To make matters worse, the Grik were aided by the madman Kurokawa, who, after losing his Amagi *at the Battle of Baalkpan, pursued a warped agenda all his own. And just as we came to the monumental conclusion that not all historical human timelines we encountered* exactly *mirrored ours, we began to feel the malevolent presence of yet another power centered in the Mediterranean. This League of Tripoli was composed of fascist French, Italian, Spanish, and German factions from a different 1939 than we remembered, and hadn't merely "crossed over" with a pair of battle-damaged destroyers but possessed a powerful task force originally intended to wrest Egypt—and the Suez Canal—from Great Britain.*

We had few open conflicts with the League at first, though they seemed inexplicably intent on subversion. Eventually we discovered their ultimate aim was to aid Kurokawa, the Grik, even the Dominion, just enough to ensure our mutual *annihilation, removing at one time multiple future threats to the hegemony they craved. But their schemes never reckoned on the valor of our allies or the resolve of Captain Matthew Reddy. Therefore, when the League Contre-Amiral Laborde, humiliated by a confrontation, not only sank what was essentially a hospital ship with his monstrous dreadnought* Savoie *but took some of our people hostage—including Captain Reddy's pregnant wife—and turned them AND* Savoie *over to Kurokawa . . .*

Excerpt from the foreword to Courtney Bradford's
The Worlds I've Wondered
University of New Glasgow Press, 1956

PROLOGUE

Sovereign Nest of Jaaph Hunters
Zanzibar
October 18, 1944

Sandra Tucker Reddy had been inwardly terrified when that fascist French *weasel*, Victor Gravois, handed her and her companions to the Japanese after the League of Tripoli battleship *Savoie* sank SMS *Amerika* and brought them here. She'd seen what the Japanese on her old world were doing to prisoners of war when *Mizuki Maru* and *Hidoiame* . . . arrived, so she'd known how bad it *might* be. Instead, for now, it certainly could've been worse. She and her young companion, Diania, had been separated from Chairman Adar, Kapitan Leutnant Becher Lange, Gunnery Sergeant Arnold Horn, and the three Lemurian sailors she'd never even come to know, and locked in a small wooden shed, taller than it was wide. It was obvious by the streaked droppings that the structure was built as a nesting coop for lizardbirds to lay their eggs for human harvest. The vicious, duck-size flying reptiles were like the akka on Borno and could apparently tolerate one another long enough to jumble their eggs together in enclosed, shady places before abandoning them to hatch. The first to do so feasted on the others until large enough to fly—and reenter the food chain outside. Attrition was horrendous, of course, but lizardbirds had no mating season and there was a constant flow of careless mothers. Even now, they often darted through gaps high in the walls beneath the thatched roof and fluttered around inside. Finding the nesting shelves removed, they usually painted the place—and Sandra and Diania—with more foul-smelling excrement before flitting somewhere else to dump their eggs.

At least the gap allowed daylight, and a slight breeze to stir the stifling heat, lizardbird-shit stench, and sour sweat reek pervading their prison. Sandra and Diania were both small women, and even standing on each other's shoulders they couldn't reach high enough to peer outside, let alone escape. And if they did, where would they go? Sandra knew they were on an island—probably Zanzibar—completely controlled by the Japanese and their Grik allies. She couldn't imagine how they'd get away. Meals came twice a day, delivered by a young Japanese sailor flanked by two fearsome Grik carrying wickedly barbed spears. The young man never met their eyes, wouldn't speak, and acted almost ashamed. He also seemed resentful, even terrified, of the reptilian Grik accompanying him. That surprised Sandra, since she thought the Grik here served the Japanese. But the sailor was just a kid, and Grik *were* very frightening. It was probably as simple as that.

Their meals were always the same tasteless glop of unidentifiable vegetable matter mixed with gobbets of meat she didn't *want* to identify, but they weren't being starved. She and Diania even had enough energy for light exercise and practicing some disabling moves that Diania's lost love, Chief Gray, had taught her. And as bad as they smelled after weeks confined aboard *Savoie*, plus another week here—with lizardbird crap in their hair—they kept the cell as clean as they could. The single refinement easing their captivity was a box seat for them to do their business, with the waste dropping to the sand below. Even that was periodically removed by Grik fatigue parties, so they didn't have to endure that rising stench as well. Diania had seen the Grik tasked with the chore through the hole in the seat, and the women had shared a rare giggle at the thought of "bombing" them.

Fortunately, Sandra supposed, though she remembered

plenty of reports of atrocities in 'forty-two, the Japanese who had them now arrived when they thought they were winning the war back home, before it degenerated to a level of savagery that could fill a *Mizuki Maru* with living skeletons under the "care" of men who, in their postarrival panic, actually considered eating them. Most of those men, along with *Hidoiame*, and even *Mizuki Maru*—which had been given a chance, at least, to redeem herself—were dead. And some of the "skeletons" had survived and recovered. *Gunny Horn was one,* Sandra remembered. *Wherever the others are, he has to be in a special hell right now.*

Unfortunately, however, regardless of the prevailing circumstances when Sandra and so many she cared about aboard the old Asiatic Fleet destroyer USS *Walker* were hounded—and somehow followed—to this world by the massive battle cruiser *Amagi* and *these very Japanese*, the wars raging here had achieved their own unique barbarism. *Walker* and her people had sided with the then relatively peaceful Lemurians—Catmonkeys, some called them—who'd fought and eluded the dreadful Grik for hundreds, if not thousands of years. Voluntarily or not, *Amagi*'s commander, Hisashi Kurokawa, united with the Grik. What was more, he apparently blamed everything that had happened to him, from being marooned on this strange world in the first place and the loss of his *Amagi*, to all the ordeals he'd endured since, on USS *Walker*. And the greatest measure of blame was laid more specifically at the feet of her captain—Sandra's husband—Lieutenant Commander Matthew Reddy.

Sandra stirred from where she'd been sitting, just staring at the wall, and looked at Diania. In contrast to Sandra's tanned but fair skin and sandy brown hair, the tiny expat Impie gal's hair was almost black, her skin dark. Most of her people had spent the past two hundred years intermarrying with subjects of the terrible Holy Dominion in Central and South America with whom the United Homes and their allies were also at war. She—and most women of the Empire of the New Britain Isles, where the Hawaiian Islands ought to be—had once been practically a slave. That system had ended, but her previous condition probably helped her cope with the situation better than

Sandra had. Diania was staring back, concern and compassion in her dark brown eyes. Sandra forced a smile. "We'll be okay," she managed a bit hollowly.

"Aye'm," Diania dutifully replied. "Though I do wish we knew what they done wi' Adar . . . an' the lads," she added.

"They won't hurt them—yet," Sandra said, the qualification slipping out before she could stop it. "They'll use them however they can, even if it's just to make use of *us*. And they'll wonder if Adar's really as useless to them as he claims to be."

Diania looked down, and Sandra berated herself. She hadn't been as encouraging as she'd planned. She forced a smile. "Gunny Horn likes you, I think."

Diania looked up, searching. "Ye do?"

Sandra was stunned by how intensely her friend reacted. She'd *wanted* Diania to begin clawing out of the shell of grief she'd built around herself when Fitzhugh Gray was killed at Grik City, but hadn't really expected it so soon. Certainly not under these circumstances. *Hope is a very strange thing,* she told herself, *and comes at the strangest times. Here we are, helpless and surrounded by enemies, and her fondest wish is that some guy she barely knows might've noticed her. Maybe that's how she copes so well? She just thinks of something—someone—else.*

"I do," Sandra assured, her tone lighter. Then she managed a genuine smile and put her hand on the battered medical bag full of clothing and a few medicines she'd managed to keep in spite of everything. The Frenchmen on *Savoie* had been too rattled by other events—and her distracting performance—to search it when they took her aboard. The Japanese likely assumed the French had already done it, and passed it off as what it appeared to be: a bag full of nothing useful to them. *They'll regret that,* Sandra swore to herself, considering the amazing luck that had allowed her to conceal a certain deadly object for so long. General of the Sky Muriname, despite badly disguised hungry stares, had been true to his word to protect them from hundreds of sex-starved Japanese. At least until Kurokawa returned. Sandra's smile faded. *But Kurokawa's back now.* The planes that flew in and landed and all the noise coming from the docks that morning had practically confirmed it. *So,* Sandra thought, *maybe we'll know something soon.* She looked intently at Diania. "Horn's a good man," she assured her. "He didn't have to come, but he did. And I bet that was largely because of you."

Granted, she told herself grimly, *he'd probably be dead now if he* hadn't *come, along with maybe three thousand wounded men and 'Cats who went down with* Amerika. *But if it helps Diania pass the time, why not encourage her to think about other things, hope for something else?* She patted the pack beside her. *It makes me feel better, imagining what I can do with what's in there, and hoping I get a chance to use it.*

The lock clattered and the door banged open. Outside, a Japanese officer stood in the light of the setting sun. He was holding a white handkerchief over his nose, and instead of Grik guards, he had a pair of armed Japanese sailors. If they had Grik with them this time, they'd stayed out of view. Brusquely, the officer motioned the women to their feet. "You come!" he shouted.

Sandra glanced at the bag and picked it up as she stood, berating herself for not hiding its important content on her person sooner. *Perhaps I still can? All I can do is try.*

"Stay that *here,*" the man stressed. "Not change place. Come back."

Sandra nodded exaggeratedly, turning slightly away and staring in the bag as if wondering if she'd ever see it again, regardless of what the officer said. Finally, she took what she hoped looked like a wistful breath and tossed the bag on the wooden floor. No one saw her secret a very small .380 Colt pistol in her waistband as she made a show of tucking her filthy shirt in her dungarees. For once, the gloom in their cell and the sharp, bright sunset worked to her advantage. "Let's go, Diania," Sandra said, her tone dripping scorn at their captors. "We may as well do as they say. No sense *frightening* them by resisting."

Apparently, the Japanese officer understood more English than he spoke because his eyes narrowed and he drew back a hand to strike Sandra across the face. With a supreme effort, he controlled his impulse and grabbed Sandra's wrist instead, wrenching her bodily out of the cell. Diania crouched to spring, but Sandra quickly shook her head. "No, Diania!" She had no doubt the tiny wildcat could disable one guard, maybe two, who'd be caught completely by surprise. And Sandra was pretty confident she could take out the abusive officer quickly enough to assist her friend with the third man, but now wasn't the time. It was still daylight, men and Grik were watching, and they had no plan at all. They'd be recaptured, if not killed, and any future attempt would be far more difficult. Best let their captors continue to underestimate them. "Let's just find out what they want, sweetheart," Sandra said more softly. Reluctantly, Diania stepped forward and allowed herself to be seized by one of the sailors. Sandra was interested to see that the man took Diania's wrist much more gently than the officer had taken hers.

Their escort marched them briskly down a tree-covered path toward the harbor, the same they'd used when first taken to their cell. The first thing Sandra noticed—besides *Savoie*'s huge, brooding shape secured to the pier, its big guns bristling in what seemed all directions—was that the force Kurokawa had apparently brought back was considerably smaller than Muriname told her he'd set out with. Several more of the former Grik ironclad battlewagons were still under conversion to aircraft carriers at the extensive shipyards Kurokawa had established here, but they'd been there when Sandra and her friends arrived. None appeared much closer to completion. Their armored casemates and guns had already been removed when Sandra saw them last, leaving their hulls floating high in the water. The framing for their flight decks had begun and they rode a little lower, so she assumed their engineering plants had been the focus of alteration. Either way, they clearly remained weeks, at least, from readiness, and only *one* of the three finished carriers Kurokawa had taken to strike TF Alden was moored in the bay. Several of the returned ironclad steam "cruisers" looked a little battered as well. She prayed that meant TF Alden, with all its planes, new weapons, ammunition, and reinforcements, had bulled through to Matt on Mada-gaas-gar and decisively kicked Kurokawa's ass.

She shook her head to clear her mind as they passed

through a palisade surrounding a large building, carefully camouflaged from the sky, and stepped on a rough-hewn porch. She suspected she'd need all her wits to leave this building alive, and, just as important, steer the enemy's thoughts in the direction she wanted them to go. A door stood open, allowing the evening breeze to cool the interior, but the senior guard stopped and knocked respectfully.

"Bring them in," came an almost . . . *cheerful* voice Sandra didn't recognize, touched only lightly with an accent. Muriname had warned her about Kurokawa's mood swings and volcanic temper. She'd watch for signs he was losing it—and would redirect it if she could. She couldn't help wondering what had him in such a good mood, however, and the possibilities made her wary. The guards pushed her and Diania into the room and Sandra was surprised by the contrasting decor. The walls were rough wood, like the rest of the building, but a richly woven rug, probably a tapestry taken from some seagoing Lemurian Home, covered the timber floor. Colorful curtains swayed with the breeze beside broad, glassless windows on the seaward side of the room, and a great, carefully crafted wooden desk dominated the space in front of smaller windows in the wall to landward. General of the Sky Hideki Muriname stood to one side of the desk, peering through wire-framed glasses perched on his nose, his prematurely bald head glistening in the light of lamps spaced around the walls. He was frowning, his hungry leer no doubt tempered by how filthy they were. He actually raised a white handkerchief of his own near his nose before he caught himself.

They sure have a lot of those white hankies, Sandra thought, distracted by the notion, but her gaze went to a short, roundish man with an equally round face sitting behind the desk. His uniform was immaculate, and though reminiscent of those worn by naval officers of the Japanese Imperial Navy, was decorated with all sorts of fanciful medals, devices, and colorful ribbons. It was so ridiculously ostentatious, in fact, that she had to force herself not to snort with amusement. *Surely even he can't take all that seriously,* she thought. *But maybe he does,* she reconsidered. *He probably did it to impress his Grik allies, at first, but by all accounts—even Muriname's—Kurokawa is quite mad. Best not antagonize him. At least over something like that,* she amended.

Kurokawa alone seemed immune to their reek and appearance, and his expression was almost . . . benign as he stood from the chair behind his desk, regarding her and Diania with keen interest. His slightly bulging eyes focused on Sandra. "Ah," he said. "I finally have the honor of meeting the 'great healer' of the Alliance." He spoke with a growing note of sarcasm, lips stretched in a thin line across his small teeth. "How unfortunate that you cannot heal the reverse your cause recently suffered north of Mahe Island, or"—he actually began to *smile*—"the apparent loss of *both* your husband's puny destroyers."

Sandra felt her bones turn to fire. *He's lying!* she screamed inside, but managed to control herself, even affecting a confused expression. "I've no idea what you're talking about. My companions and I were confined by murderers representing the League of Tripoli, as you know full well"—she jerked her head toward the battleship docked less than a quarter mile away—"and then by your people here." She glared at Muriname. "If you fought a battle against my husband's fleet, this is the first I've heard of it." She stood straighter. "And it looks like *your* fleet needs a little healing," she said, then added, "so I'm not sure I'd be so confident you achieved all you think you did, if I were you." With that jab, she saw the flames of fury flicker behind Kurokawa's eyes, but he retained his composure.

"In that case, I will happily describe the action," Kurokawa said, turning to pace behind his desk. "It's not as if you can make use of the information, after all." He abruptly stopped and regarded her anxiously. "Would you like refreshment?" When Sandra didn't reply immediately, his lip curled in a satisfied sneer. "I apologize for not asking you to seat yourselves, but I must preserve the furniture. It's so difficult to obtain these days. In the future, you'll take better care to come before me more appropriately attired." The impossibility of his demand seemed to amuse him and he began to pace once more. "True," he continued. "We lost two of our carriers and a few insignificant auxiliaries, while your husband lost not only *Baalkpan Bay*, a heavy fleet carrier, if I'm not mistaken, but also some sort of immense seaplane tender built from one of the Grik dreadnaughts we abandoned at Madras. Those sinkings are *confirmed*, as are those of at least a dozen support ships—vessels whose loss will leave your forces on Madagascar feeling a distinct pinch, I assure you. Particularly with General Esshk and his Grik hordes preparing to cross the channel from the mainland of Africa and crush your ridiculously overextended force. Esshk's new swarm is so numerous it makes all his previous armies pale to insignificance! Furthermore, as I said, I have reliable reports of grievous hits made upon both your husband's 'modern' destroyers, *Walker* and *Mahan*. At least one couldn't have survived, given the extent of her damage. You'll pardon me if I choose to revel in the possibility that it was your husband's *Walker*."

Sandra's mind whirled. *Mahan* was still laid up at Madras, the last she heard. And *Walker* couldn't have been with TF Alden; Matt wouldn't have seen the need to meet it with his own damaged ship when the task force was protected by two *brand-new* destroyers, just delivered and virtually identical to *Walker*. So, despite all the intelligence the League of Tripoli leaked to Kurokawa, he—and they—hadn't known about the new DDs. She felt sick to think they might already be lost, in addition to *Baalkpan Bay* and the rest, but at least she was morally certain Kurokawa was wrong about *Walker*—and Matt.

"I wouldn't count on that," she whispered.

"I won't," Kurokawa snapped, his tone deadly serious, no longer gloating. "Despite the fact I must destroy him, your husband has earned my grudging respect for all he has accomplished with so little." He waved around him. "As have I. And I will never underestimate him again. But the balance of power, in this theater at least, has finally shifted in my favor. Yes," he added, noting Diania's surprise, "I know all about your war with the Dominion in the Americas."

Sandra did snort then. "We still have *two* carriers to your one, with more on the way, and whether our destroyers were sunk or not, our steam frigates are a match for your so-called cruisers. I didn't hear all that many planes fly ashore this morning either, so you obviously lost a lot of those, as well as pilots. How do you figure you're on top?"

"Simple, my dear Lady Sandra," Kurokawa said, using the title the Imperials had given her, probably as yet another means of showing how much he knew. In fact, Sandra got the distinct impression this entire meeting was little more than an opportunity to boast to her, the next best thing to having Captain Reddy himself. "Your forces on Madagascar will soon have all they can deal with once the Grik attack in earnest. My air force is . . . depleted, but I'll soon make up my losses in quantity"—he smiled—"and quality. Lastly, I noted you didn't mention the converted freighter, the *Santa Catalina*, your people armed and styled as a protected cruiser. Do you honestly believe she can match *Savoie*, after my people have time to familiarize themselves with her? You're not that stupid." He bestowed a gleeful smile on Muriname.

"And how long will that take?" Sandra glanced at Muriname as well, gauging his reaction. "How many of *Savoie*'s people stayed behind? Not many, I guess. And how many *Amagi* sailors do you have left, not flying planes, supervising factories and shipyards, or commanding ships? They must be spread awful thin. I don't know much," she confessed, "but I imagine properly operating *Savoie*, with her sophisticated equipment and modern weapons, will be a lot harder than your crude ironclads with muzzle-loading guns."

She could tell her shot hit home with Muriname, at least, when he frowned and blinked rapidly behind his glasses. Kurokawa's eyes bulged slightly more and his face reddened, but he didn't respond. "So," Sandra continued, getting down to it, absently adjusting her shirttail with one hand—near the Colt—while resting the other on the bulge in her belly that was finally beginning to show, "what will you do with us? Diania and I, and the two men and four Lemurians you're holding?"

"That depends a great deal upon you," Kurokawa said simply. "I have uses for you all, of course. Not all equally pleasant. For instance, it's been a great while since I, or the more than *three hundred* real men it remains my honor to command, have enjoyed the company of a woman."

Sandra took a step back, horrified, but Kurokawa nodded at her belly. "You're pregnant. And though you carry the child of my greatest enemy, I'm not a monster." He swiveled his head to regard Diania. "Your servant, on the other hand, is *not* pregnant, is she?" He glared back at Sandra and she saw the fury in his eyes again. "To preserve her and your friends from any number of unpleasant fates I might imagine, you'll tell me what I want to know."

"You *are* a monster," Sandra breathed softly, noting that Kurokawa actually looked strangely disturbed to hear her say it. For some reason, possibly because of his expression, she left the little Colt where it was and allowed her hand to fall to her side. "I have no illusions about that," she said more loudly. "But you already know as much as I could tell you. More, probably, with the League whispering in your ear. What else is there?"

"The League," Kurokawa spat, "cares nothing for me except insofar as I might advance their own murky agenda. They give me information and they gave me *Savoie*, true. There are even . . . other ways in which they'll still aid me. But what I want to know is, if Captain Reddy still lives, what will he do when he discovers I have you?" He leaned forward expectantly.

Sandra glanced at Diania, frowned, and finally shrugged. "There was a time when he would've started a war to save me. He kind of *did*, in a way. That's how we wound up involved in the Imperial's war against the Dominion—all because I was incidentally abducted along with the heir to the throne of the Empire of the New Britain Isles, and Matt *thought* certain people were holding us." She looked Kurokawa directly in the eye. "The thing is, he would've done the same even if they'd only taken the Governor-Empress, because she was under our protection"— she shrugged again—"and I would've absolutely supported his decision. As it turned out, we'd already escaped. But that didn't stop him. Not even a brand-new war, while we were already up to our necks fighting you and the Grik, made a difference to him, because it was the right thing to do. If *that* Matt Reddy knew you had us, and Adar and me in particular, he'd come at you with everything he had." She shook her head. "I doubt that's any secret to you. Now?"

she said quietly. "He's changed. He's changed a *lot*. He loves me just as much, I don't doubt that, but he's grown . . . harder than that."

"Harder?" Kurokawa demanded. "Like me?"

"He's *nothing* like you," Sandra snarled contemptuously. "The difference is, now he's hard enough *not* to drop everything and come right after us. After you. He's grown hard enough to lose us, to take the hit and keep on fighting, regardless of the cost to me or any of the others." Her blue eyes turned as remorseless as the sea. "And if you hurt us, *any* of us, he *will* kill you, make no mistake. But he'll do it in *his* time, and won't waste lives. That's the most important thing to him now. This war's cost him—cost us all—so much that he just wants it over. But he also wants it *won*. So he'll leave me here until it is, if he has to, but then he'll come for me." She gave Diania a gentle glance. "He'll come for all of us. But most important, he'll come for *you*, even if all he gets is revenge."

"And if I *tell* him I have you? That I'll kill you if he does not come?" Kurokawa demanded, eyes searching hers.

There it was. Unknowingly, he'd finally confirmed her suspicion that, despite all the battles fought across half this wildly mysterious world over the past two and a half years, no matter how many other enemies—and friends—joined the struggle, regardless of how many murky threats loomed on the horizon, the whole vast, impersonal war he'd helped fuel and feed with blood remained profoundly *personal* to Hisashi Kurokawa. There'd been little question in Sandra's mind that he'd try to use her and their unborn child against Matt, to bring on what he apparently wanted most: a final confrontation between them. Unfortunately, despite what she'd said, she could imagine nothing that would focus her husband's rage more destructively and perhaps disastrously at this critical time, and Kurokawa was likely to get his wish.

"His retribution will only be more terrible," Sandra said, staring back with all the defiance she could muster. "But killing us won't bring it any quicker," she lied. "You just don't get it, do you?" she asked, her tone filled with wonder as she returned to the absolute truth. "You fight only for yourself, to destroy. He's fighting to save a race of people, maybe the whole damn world! He's *idealistic*, don't you see?" Tears welled up in her eyes and she wiped them with her grimy sleeve and looked away. "Next to that, my fate's nothing in the short term," she whispered with as much conviction as she could summon. "But in the long term, whatever you do to me, to us, it won't be as bad as what he does to you."

For an instant, Sandra thought Kurokawa actually was going to lose it; order the guards to kill her then and there, and maybe march out and shoot all her friends with the pistol at his side. With tremendous effort clear to see beneath his purpling face, however, he slowly brought himself under control. Finally, he nodded. "I believe you," he ground out. "And that's fortunate for you"—he nodded at Diania—"and your servant as well. I must consider this for a time. All you have said. Until then, at least, you'll not be harmed. Or molested!" he commanded, raising his voice so his order would carry to the guards who had brought them. "I gave my word," he added under his own breath, "and I'm *not* a monster!"

Suddenly striding around the desk, he beckoned at someone in the adjoining room. There were words, then a rustling, scraping sound. To Sandra's astonishment, two more guards dragged a third form into the room by its arms and seated it on a chair. There, apparently unable to rise or do more than hold his head up, sat Chairman Adar.

"Oh my God!" Sandra cried, rushing to him despite the efforts of her guard to hold her back. She knelt in front of the Lemurian leader, a new fury rising that threatened to explode when she saw her friend's face. Adar was about forty, the same as his lifelong friend "Ahd-mi-raal" Keje-Fris-Ar. That wasn't particularly old for Lemurians, who generally lived about as long as humans, but Adar looked *very* old now, to Sandra's searching eyes. Always thin, he'd become practically emaciated, his gray fur matted and silver eyes dull as he regarded Sandra without apparent recognition. He still wore what his Amer-i-caan friends had dubbed his Sky Priest suit, with silver stars embroidered on the hood and shoulders, but it was just as torn and dingy as the Lemurian wearing it. Sandra wheeled to glare at Kurokawa.

"What've you done to him?" she roared. Kurokawa actually blanched, but his face purpled again and his eyes bulged enormously. "Only *I* demand here, *Minister* Reddy," he snapped, using her medical title within the United Homes and the Grand Alliance. He glanced at Muriname, however. "But the General of the Sky assures me nothing has been done to him—beyond subduing him and the others' continuing, misguided resistance. Other than that, he simply won't eat. Nor will the other ape-men. Gunnery Sergeant Horn and Kapitan Leutnant Lange both say his people"—he nodded at Adar—"cannot thrive in captivity. Is this true?"

"Of course it's true!" Sandra stated, and it was—to a degree. But she'd never expected *this.* She immediately decided Adar was literally starving himself to death to keep the Japanese from using him against his people, and the 'Cat sailors were doing the same to corroborate his excuse. In a way, it was brilliant, and she suddenly wished she could get away with something similar. *But that won't work with us,* she knew, *or for Horn and Lange.*

Kurokawa frowned. "I find that difficult to believe. The League has held ape-man prisoners before," he informed Sandra, startling her, but he hesitated before going on, an uncertain expression joining his frown. "At least *some* survived to teach League spies their speech." He pointed at Adar. "He was the leader of your alliance, after Captain Reddy, of course," he said harshly. "And though I'm inclined to believe, as he insists, he's of little value as such now—no doubt *my* radio operators can learn his language as easily from you as him," he threatened, "I may yet make use of him and do not want him to die. You're his doctor. Save him."

Sandra was still absorbing the implications of the fact that the League had Lemurian prisoners. The Allies transmitted in code groups, but had always felt secure using Lemurian for voice communications. No wonder the League knew so much! Her mind whirled. "You're keeping him—all the others—in the same kind of cell as us?" she demanded of Muriname.

"Yes, but . . ."

"Then that's your answer!" Sandra snapped scornfully.

"The League must've kept their Lemurians confined in the open. They can't stand the kind of captivity you've had them in for long, and *will* die no matter what I do! Why do you think the Grik never keep Lemurian prisoners, or eat them as quick as they can when they get them?" She felt fairly safe asking that. Kurokawa must've seen that for himself when he commanded all the Grik in India. Still, he snorted, and even Muriname looked skeptical. "*Look* at him!" Sandra thundered. "Do you think he's *faking*?"

Kurokawa clasped his hands behind his back and appeared to think furiously. Finally, he barked at Muriname in Japanese.

"We will prepare a . . . compound," Muriname said grudgingly, as if trying to envision how that would work in his mind. As far as Sandra had seen, they didn't have barbed wire. "Your men, Lange and Horn, will construct a shelter within a fenced area we will build," he continued, "with space out of doors." He frowned. "We'll have to put you all in it together," he warned. "Such a place will require constant guards, and we can't spare enough to watch you separately."

Sandra shook her head. "I don't care. They're our friends. *They* won't take advantage of us," she added, knowing Muriname, at least, might very well attempt it. He might even have been counting on their isolation to facilitate that. Sandra shuddered at the thought that three hundred other men probably had the same idea. Much as she loathed him, Kurokawa was hers and Diania's only protection from that. For now. She looked back at Adar and finally saw a spark of recognition in his eyes.

"No," he rasped, barely audible. "You must not do this. I love you, Lady Saandra, but I want to die. I *need* to die!"

"What more do you require?" Kurokawa demanded, thankfully misinterpreting Adar's meaning, and possibly alarmed by his determination. He'd helped create the Grik suicider flying bombs, but apparently even he considered Lemurians to be more like people than the Grik. Or possibly the fact that four of them obviously preferred a terrible, lingering death to what he must've considered a benign incarceration even appealed to his ideal of the

Bushido Code he expected his men, if not necessarily himself, to follow. Or maybe he really did hope to use Adar.

"Fresh air, food, sunlight, and at least the illusion of space around them. That's the only thing that'll save them now."

"Very well," Kurokawa grunted, looking at Muriname. Then he repeated Sandra's own earlier thoughts, almost to the letter. "See to it. After all, they cannot escape. Where could they go?"

"Let me die!" Adar groaned, slightly louder, and Kurokawa thrust his round face near the drawn Lemurian's.

"If you die, *she* dies, ape-man," he snapped. "I have little enough reason to keep her alive as it is, apparently. So if you care for her, you'll recover."

"Lady Saandra," Adar gasped as they carried him into the darkness. "How could you? I was *so close*!"

"Shush, Mr. Chairman!" she said sternly, then lowered her voice to a whisper when she kissed the matted fur on his cheek. "We're not finished yet!"

The guards took Adar away, and Kurokawa and Muriname stepped back inside. For just a moment, there was no one within earshot. "What you said," Diania hissed at Sandra, "aboot Captain Reddy. Ye didnae mean it?"

"I wish I did," Sandra answered, her voice the merest murmur. She sighed silently. "No, he'll come," she said with sad certainty. "He'll have to, and not just for us. He'll do it for *Baalkpan Bay*, and however many other ships and people we lost." She nodded at *Savoie*'s malignant shadow in the gloom. "And he can't leave *that* behind him, in the hands of a maniac, to come after him at its leisure. But I was right about the other part. He'll do it smart. And he'll *end* Kurokawa this time, no matter what it takes. Or costs."

CHAPTER 1

Baalkpan, Borno
October 20, 1944

"God, I miss Idaho," mumbled Alan Letts, the newly appointed Chairman of the United Homes, staring at the sloshy, muggy Baalkpan afternoon. He'd never thought he'd miss how cold it got in Stanley, or Grand Forks, North Dakota, either. That was another place he considered home after spending half his childhood there. But it was rarely anything but hot—and wet—in Baalkpan, the capital city of the new Union he'd helped build. The daily shower had finally passed and he and his wife, Karen, the assistant minister of medicine, stepped outside the main entrance to the Allied Naval Hospital east of the Great Hall. That was Karen's principal domain, and between her long hours and his crazy schedule, Alan sometimes gloomily suspected their little daughter, Allison Verdia, was the only child they'd ever get the chance to make. But at least he could see *his* "youngling" and "mate," which was a hell of a lot more than most could say these days. So many younglings had at least one parent deployed, sometimes both. Alan tried to prevent the latter, but that had been a losing proposition from the start. Lemurians made no distinction between sexes when it came to military service, and that was probably the only reason they'd had the numbers to survive.

But new regulations decreed that pregnant females returned home, period, and he tried to keep them as trainers as long as possible.

Even so, there were a lot of orphans running around. The youngest went entirely naked, scampering about on all fours as often as not, their frizzy tails held high. A pack of them dashed through a puddle, splashing water and mud, before rocketing up a heavy wooden pier supporting an old-style aboveground structure built in the time before genuine fortifications protected the city from large predators—and invading Grik. The younglings flowed through a window, raising alarmed, angry voices, then skittered down another pier to vanish in the bustle of the city. Alan laughed at the sight, but supposed it wasn't really funny. Lemurian younglings were boisterous by nature and their antics were well tolerated by adults. In the past, however, they'd been equally well supervised. That was no longer the case, and they now ran in packs almost as wild as Griklets. Alan tried to be philosophical about it. At least they didn't swarm all over people and *eat* them like Griklets. But even as they were losing an entire generation to the war, Alan feared they might lose the next one too. Culturally, at least.

"Mind your shoes," Karen scolded as Alan carefully negotiated the planks laid down to the paalka-drawn carriage outside the hospital. "And at least *try* to keep from making mud pies in your best whites! Maybe I don't have to clean them anymore"—she flapped her own clean but dark-stained apron for emphasis—"but somebody does. And it's a chore nobody needs!"

Alan had been caught by the rain while visiting wounded 'Cats and men, something he did every week. And he didn't mind that the deluge had delayed his busy schedule, heartrending as it often was to speak with the shattered victims of this terrible war, or to simply view those who couldn't even hear him. It also filled him with hope that, despite their pain, so many Lemurians—and humans from the Empire of the New Britain Isles, for the most part—remained so dedicated to the cause. Indeed, most were *eager* to return to the fight, regardless of how . . . unlikely that might be in many cases. *They'll get back in somehow,* Alan promised himself—as he'd promised them—*even if they never see the front again. We need instructors, engineers, and shop foremen who've been at the pointy end and seen what works. We may've lost their direct combat skills, but we can't afford to lose their experience. God knows we need them.*

"I'll try," Alan assured, stepping into the carriage and nodding at the 'Cat Marine on the front seat, holding the reins. The Lemurian made a curious chirping sound and whipped the reins. Moaning rebelliously, the paalka squished forward. Alan swayed, still looking at Karen and the hospital behind her. The hospital wasn't as large as the great factories now crowding the Baalkpan waterfront, once so charming with colorful, bustling bazaars and brisk commerce, but it was the biggest building past the Great Hall in Baalkpan proper. That was a source of pride, as well as sadness. It said a lot about how committed "his" people were to helping those who served them. His expression turned stony then, because as much as his visits to the hospital inspired him, they also renewed his resolve to exact vengeance against those who'd caused so much suffering in the first place. *All of them,* he secretly swore, with a fresh stab of furious grief over the sinking of SMS *Amerika*, and two-thirds of the wounded she carried, caused by the shadowy League of Tripoli. Some of *Amerika*'s survivors had finally reached Baalkpan, and between their accounts and what Matt sent from Grik City, they had a better idea of what happened—and of what the League was, even if its motives remained obscure. Three *wars now?* Alan mused grimly. *No, not yet. Not if we can help it. We can barely handle the two we've got. But there'll be a reckoning.*

"And put on your hat!" Karen admonished, raising her voice and gesturing at the sky. The sun was stabbing through the clouds, raising steam from the sodden ground. Alan Letts had a very fair complexion and burned easily. He didn't spend much time outdoors these days and sometimes forgot to protect himself.

"Yes, dear," he called back dutifully, quickly adjusting his high, tight collar and plopping the white hat on his head. "I'll see you and the girls tonight," he added, finally sitting as the carriage lurched onto the main, gravel-mixed street. For all the younglings running loose, even more had been adopted by females working in the shipyards or factories, both Lemurians and expat Imperial women. Some families with the wherewithal, still intact because they ran businesses essential to the war effort and weren't *allowed* to fight, had adopted half a dozen or more. Alan and Karen had taken two themselves, both female, and treated them as their own. They would've taken more, but their duties already required that they have a nanny—a young, one-armed Marine veteran of the Battle of Raangoon named Unaa-Saan-Mar—with three younglings of her own. For the first time, he noticed the many furry Lemurian faces watching from the newly built ground-level shops and porches lining the road, their amused but respectful blinking still coming as a surprise.

They actually enjoy *that I'm henpecked!* he realized with a mental snort. Then he reconsidered. *But maybe that's why they've accepted me. It makes me more a person to them, regardless of what . . . species I am.* Alan still found his official status as the leader of the new, wildly diverse nation they'd built a bit overwhelming, and more than a little unbelievable. True, he'd been accepted as *acting* chairman during Adar's absence, and the members of the Grand Alliance, including the Empire of the New Britain Isles and the Republic of Real People, which hadn't joined the Union, were accustomed to that. He even thought he'd done a good job, under the circumstances, managing the logistical side of the war effort in particular. But he'd never dreamed he'd be practically *drafted* into the job for real after Adar fell into enemy hands.

It might've been easier to understand if he'd just been acclaimed High Chief of Baalkpan. He was well-known there, and even—as were all his surviving shipmates from USS *Walker*, USS *Mahan*, and S-19, to various degrees—beloved. They'd *saved* the city, after all. But the fact they'd also, literally or by extension, saved Aryaal, B'mbaado, B'taava, North Borno, Sembaakpan, Sular, Austraal, Chill-Chaap, the Shogunate of Yokohama (which included the tragic village of Ani-Aaki), and all the Filpin Lands—not to mention the eleven seagoing Homes that had joined the Union—apparently hadn't been lost on anyone. Though still amazingly fractious (particularly in the case of Sular, which still argued over representation after all the seagoing Homes joined as a single, relatively high-population state), the various Homes had apparently recognized the validity of some version of the old axiom "Never change horses in the middle of the stream." Or war.

It also probably helped that Alan came from the one Home or Clan that every other had to materially support and considered most impartial: the "Amer-i-caan Navy Clan." It not only protected everyone, but most of its members now came from *every* clan or Home. They swore allegiance to its flag and a constitution that had served as a guide for the one adopted by the Union, but though their loyalty to its high chief—Captain Matthew Reddy—was unquestioned, everyone knew they remained loyal to the United Homes as well. In addition, every Union warship belonged to the Amer-i-caan Navy Clan except those designated as reserve, such as *Salaama-Na* or *Salissa* (CV-1), and an increasing number of auxiliaries entering service. It was no longer required that all sailors join the Amer-i-caan Navy Clan forever, but officers must in order to be commissioned. Regular sailors' oaths would be allowed to expire (if they wanted) when the war was over and they went home. But the Marines practically *belonged* to Captain Reddy. The Navy Clan also had a few land possessions, such as the islands of Tarakaan, Midway, and Andamaan. And there was a "daughter" colony being built at a place it called Saan Diego, so far away that it was literally on the bottom of the world as far as most were concerned. Even that didn't cause disputes, because all contributed solely to the maintenance of the navy and would never become independent Homes.

Alan often wondered to himself if the mishmash they'd put together would survive the war. He also worried that the unusual powers he'd helped reserve for the Navy Clan might be abused by some future high chief after they were gone. He hoped not. He *hoped* the tradition of selfless service Matt and the others had established at such a terrible cost would last a very long time. Either way, though, for now at least, the Amer-i-caan Navy Clan—as the one most responsible for the conduct of the war—had to remain a very slight "first among equals," even as it truly was viewed as the most neutral when it came to disputes among other Homes.

He stuck two fingers in the collar at his neck and pulled. *Damn thing's getting* tighter *as I sweat!* he grumped to himself. *What the hell was wrong with my khakis?* It was his wife's idea that he always wear his best whites in public. Despite his complaints, he supposed it made sense. He *was* the chairman—*practically* president, *for God's sake!*—after all. He should try to look the part. *And at least whites don't show sweat like khakis,* he conceded. *But maybe most important, the uniform's a good recruiting tool. We need more people than ever to crew the ships and fly the planes we're building, and fill the ranks of our armies.*

Conscription had been instituted in the Empire of the New Britain Isles, and now in the Republic of Real People as well. But nothing like that had been proposed in the Homes forming the new Union simply because, once the war practically surrounded them, there was no place left for "runaways" to go. Particularly after the battles of Aryaal and Baalkpan. That was when it was driven brutally home that there weren't any noncombatants and it became understood that every person, male or female, capable of bearing arms and living under the protection of the Alliance from the Malay Barrier to the Filpin Lands was a member of a local guard. Even factory workers attended daily drill sessions (usually at work) and fell in for larger unit instruction once a month in the open killing grounds beyond the ever-expanding earthen walls protecting the cities. Armories stocked with old-style muskets were conveniently situated and factory and yard workers were assigned defensive positions close to where they worked.

That was all well and good, but though anyone was theoretically subject to being called up and sent to an Advanced Training Center and assigned to a building regiment, or shipped off to replace casualties, it almost never happened. They needed *workers* as badly as troops. The addition of the Great South Isle, or Austraal, to the Union would help a great deal—eventually. The populous Homes there had remained an untapped reservoir of potential sailors, soldiers, and labor for most of the war. Now they were in it, and though most had to stay and build their own factories and defend their cities, many wanted to fight for their people—and their new nation. Getting them here—or anywhere—was a major problem, however. The Allied sea-lift capacity was stretched to the breaking point, supplying forces in the east *and* west, halfway around the world. And Austraal didn't have the same nautical mind-set of other Homes in the Union. Their huge island was lush and fertile (on this world) and never depended as much on the sea. They had a few decent shipyards, but it was taking time for them to gear up—and there was no point in building more old-style ships like they were used to, in any event. They'd agreed to focus on heavy haulers and auxiliaries, based on the hull design of the Scott class steam frigates, but half again as big. In the meantime, Allied seagoing Homes ponderously freighted steam engines down to Austraal shipyards, and just as tediously returned with loads of volunteers. Alan considered it his duty to, by example, get those recruits to choose the Navy or Marines. *Besides,* he thought, *wearing the uniform lets me remind everyone that I belong to the Amer-i-caan Navy Clan, and, chairman or not, whether I currently outrank him or not, Captain Reddy's still* my *high chief.*

The carriage slowed as it passed the growing military cemetery on the shady grounds surrounding the Great Hall, and finally stopped. The Great Hall was once supported high in the air by the massive Galla tree growing up within it, but had "expanded" down to the ground. Alan was running late for his rendezvous with Lord Bolton Forester, ambassador from the Empire of the New Britain Isles, but the tall, gray-haired man with a huge mustache stood from a bench on the hall's porch and smiled up at Alan. Forester's aide, Lieutenant Bachman, had been pacing on the carefully fitted timbers, watched by a relatively short and wiry, and also apparently amused, man named Henry Stokes. Stokes had been a leading seaman aboard HMAS *Perth*, and was now Director of the Office of Strategic Intelligence (OSI). Alan remained in the carriage as a pair of Lemurian Marines escorted the men to join him, ready to assist them up if necessary.

"Good afternoon, Mr. Chairman!" the Imperial ambassador said through a grin behind his mustache, climbing up with an agility that belied his years.

"It's still just Alan, unless you want me calling you Lord Forester again," Alan replied dryly.

"Oh, no. Bolton's the name." He sat opposite Alan and leaned forward. "I confess some difficulty resisting the urge to rub it in, as it were, however. I apologize."

"You shouldn't be sorry," Stokes said, hopping up and sitting next to Alan. He was quickly followed by Bachman, who stiffly folded himself on the bench beside Forester. "He needs to get used to it an' quit maunderin' about, wishin' he was just a simple sailor again. He ain't," Stokes continued. "Bloke's the bloody *chairman*, an' needs ta act like it. Includin' lettin' folks be polite to 'im."

Alan shook his head and glared at Stokes, wondering if the Australian could read minds. There was no doubt he was well suited to his intelligence role. Probably better than Commander Simon Herring had been. Herring had always seemed more interested in the process of his "game" than achieving results. With one possible exception . . .

The two Marines climbed on the back of the carriage and Alan instructed the driver to proceed. The paalka mooed, and the carriage trundled forward. "I let people be polite," he defended. "Hell, *I'm* polite! But it'll take time to get used to all this."

"With respect, *Mr. Chairman*, you ain't *got* time," Stokes stated simply. "Not any."

Forester frowned. "I doubt it's of any great importance how we address one another as friends, but Mr. Stokes has a point. My own Governor-Empress was thrust into an arguably more difficult situation than yours. At least you enjoy a measure of domestic stability, after all. She"—he nodded at Alan—"with the help of Captain Reddy, of course, survived an attempt on her life, the loss of both parents, and the destruction of her entire government. This, immediately after our country was plunged into wars both foreign and domestic." He rubbed his chin thoughtfully as they moved into what remained of the old commercial district. "She kept things together largely by insisting the proprieties be observed—even as she fundamentally reworked the Empire around her. She couldn't have succeeded without help from our allies," he conceded, "or if she'd shown the slightest indecision. Or, frankly, flexibility."

Always objective when it came to analysis, Stokes nodded at Forester. "Not to be a knocker, but that hasn't worked as well lately, if you'll pardon me sayin'."

Forester grimaced. "Combined with the . . . impetuosity of youth, she did perhaps allow her inflexibility to overrule the better judgment of more experienced minds," he allowed, acknowledging the debacle that led to the naval Battle of Malpelo, against the twisted forces of the Holy Dominion. In hindsight, the battle had been a great victory, as had General Shinya and X Corps's desperate defense of Fort Defiance. It even appeared a turning point may have been reached in the war against the Doms. But that was *in spite of* Governor-Empress Rebecca Anne McDonald's decisions, not because of them. She'd done a great deal to rectify her errors, helping the situation do perhaps a bit better than simply stabilize, but her inflexibility had undoubtedly cost lives.

Alan threw his hands up. "So you both give me hell about being too familiar, then tell me I'll lose us the war if I'm too imperious. Which is it?"

"Both, I suppose," Forester said. Stokes nodded agreement.

Alan avoided rolling his eyes in frustration and changed the subject instead. "So, *Bolton*," he began, stressing the ambassador's first name, "how was your visit to the lovely, friendly paradise of Sular?"

Forester rolled his own eyes, and began relating his latest discussions with the most recalcitrant member of the Union. He may not have been a citizen of the United Homes, but it was in his nation's best interest that the Union thrive, and Alan often used him as a trusted, "objective" go-between. The carriage slowed again as it moved through crowds of workers coming off shift, even as others headed in the opposite direction. Most were Lemurians, of course, their furry coats dingy from long hours at machines or forges, their large-eyed faces slack with fatigue, tails hanging low. Quite a few were human females, however, generally dark-haired and -skinned, averaging about five feet, five inches tall. They were the expat Impie gals, who'd come to Baalkpan and the Filpin Lands before Governor-Empress McDonald "emancipated" them, nullifying the indentures many labored under. Some went home after that, but most remained. *This* was home now, and they were just as much citizens of Baalkpan, the Filpin Lands, even the American Navy Clan, as anyone else. They were weary too, often performing work difficult even for Lemurians, but they were free, and helping the cause with determination.

The thing that struck Alan most was, in spite of their exhausting labor—and the prospect of more for those heading to work—everyone's morale seemed good. Many even tiredly *cheered* when his carriage passed! This after word had already spread about the sinking of SMS *Amerika* by yet *another* potential foe, and the terrible losses they'd sustained in the battle with Kurokawa north of Mahe. *They still trust us to pull this off, to win, in the end,* Alan thought. *They still trust* me. *One way or another, I'll earn it. No matter what,* he swore.

"I don't know how you've done it," Forester said softly, interrupting his discourse on Sular and apparently echoing Alan's thoughts about the people here.

"What?" Alan asked, falsely cheerful. Many Lemurians spoke some English now, but they'd never hear his words over the ruckus, regardless of how good their ears were. They'd hear his tone, though. "How we've killed a *generation*—and sparked a population explosion of another that'll never know the culture we destroyed, or even their own parents?"

"No," Forester said. "How you *saved* them—despite the rest. They're fully aware of *that*, I assure you," he added. Alan said nothing more.

Past the old ropewalks—now a factory making thousands of wooden barrels and hundreds of wheels for heavy freight wagons and artillery pieces every week—they turned right to parallel a loud, smoky battery of oil-fired steam generators providing electric power to a pair of huge machine shops on either side. As sad as it genuinely made him that they'd turned this almost idyllic city into a massive industrial complex, Alan could never suppress a lurking sense of wonder at all they'd accomplished. What began as his own little Ministry of Industry and Sonny Campeti's Ordnance Division, which attempted to manage a wide variety of relatively small enterprises—with the exception of the refineries, shipyards, foundries, and ammunition works they'd geared up at once—had morphed into a blossoming, if chaotic, manufacturing infrastructure. Not only here, but at Maa-ni-la, and in the Empire as well.

The shipyards were the most evident example of that, and from the vantage point of the carriage, they'd grown to encompass nearly everything. And the Baalkpan Metal Works was now inextricably combined with them. Under the ownership of two brothers, it had expanded from its prewar capacity of making crude, nonferrous castings to pouring complex iron castings for every manner of thing, and was getting tolerably good steel from Madras. It had multiple divisions of its own, including steel mills, rolling mills, and tubing and pipe mills, as well as facilities for making wire and wire cables. The Baalkpan Boiler and Steam Engine Works made arguably *better* boilers and engines than they'd first copied, and they'd been *surpassed* by similar works in Maa-ni-la and the Empire in terms of output, as had the Baalkpan ICE houses, which made internal combustion engines. Those here were still amazingly productive, but focused more on innovation than quantity. This was where they'd pioneered the new radial aircraft engines and steam turbines, for example, because Baalkpan had made the longest strides in specialty steel production and treatment.

That had been a conscious planning decision, not only to spread the load, but also to build in future competition. With the ratification of the constitution, it was agreed that all manufacturing facilities would—someday—be broken into competing companies. Letts had worked hard for that, since the labor and treasure of *all* the people had gone into making them. Those same people who'd worked so hard for so long—before they were even *paid*—would have shares they could keep or sell. It would be a nightmare to implement, but it was the right thing to do, not only for the people but also for the future. Competition was good. That would have to wait, however.

The powder mills and magazine complexes (now situated

on the other side of the bay, northeast of the Baalkpan ATC), were frighteningly monstrous, but there was redundancy now. Most industrial Homes or land-based "states" in the Alliance had powder mills of their own, and numerous secure magazines. The Grik zeppelin raid on Baalkpan hadn't hit the one they'd had at the time, but that was sheer luck. They'd never risk such a devastating blow again by keeping all their explosive "eggs" in one basket.

The only exception to that was the Smokeless Propellant Works on Samaar. There weren't enough Sa'aarans, a race of Grik-like Pacific Islanders that Saan-Kakja, the high chief of the Filpin Lands, had taken in, to expect them to contribute troops. Only one, with the unlikely name of Lawrence, was currently under arms for the Union. But in their gratitude to Saan-Kakja, the Sa'aarans desperately wanted to be of use and actually lobbied to have the dangerous installation built in their midst. The fact that Samaar was overrun with a kind of plant that produced an ideal type of cellulose for the project was advantageous. And there'd be other installations of the type soon, in Sular and on Respite Island, importing the "guncotton" plants from Samaar. But the demand for regular gunpowder still surpassed the need for the "smokeless" variety, and probably would for some time to come.

The Baalkpan, Maa-ni-la, and now Imperial naval arsenals were responsible for making everything from small arms—such as the "trapdoor" Allin-Silva breech-loading rifles, carbines, and shotguns—to torpedoes, mortars, bombs, and ever larger naval rifles. With the associated heavy lathes required, they were also tasked with making other large machined parts such as propeller shafts. Each of these endeavors, and those devoted to making the new automatic weapons, pistols, bayonets, cutlasses, and even canteens and helmets, was under the supervision of various division chiefs, as was the production of the thankfully small variety of fixed ammunition for all standard weapons. Alan imagined dismally that they had several *regiments'* worth of division chiefs alone, scattered around the Alliance. *Napoleon was wrong,* he realized. *Armies don't move on their stomachs. They slide along on the slippery heaps of paper that bureaucrats excrete like brontosarry shit. How the HELL did we manage all this before we even* had *paper?*

In addition to reporting to Ordnance, each division made duplicate reports to the Ministry of Industry and Supply, which coordinated the production of all other combat gear, from shoes and sandals to field smocks, cartridge boxes, rations and medical supplies, transport wagons, and field-comm gear. And then, of course, there were the thousands of "little" things that troops needed in the field—like shelter. Alan still managed to find a measure of ironic amusement that all their 'Cat soldiers and Marines slept under shelter-half pup tents. But each of those had to have stakes, ropes . . . The list was endless. Finally, Supply had to figure out who needed what, when, and where, and arrange to get it there. That'd been Alan's primary job before his acclamation to chairman—and the one he missed least of all.

The only reason any of this is working, he thought, as Ambassador Forester continued to describe the self-serving shenanigans of the Sularans, *besides the fact we're in an existential war, is because stuff is so cheap.* He'd helped institute a financial system more than a year before, the first the Lemurians had ever really known. Before that, their various economies were based on barter and carefully tabulated indebtedness founded on numerous standards. The closest they'd come to the gold standard in use in the Empire of the New Britain Isles, and that Alan had roughly copied here, was a barrel of gri-kakka oil as a reference for relative value. But with so much dependent on petroleum now, gri-kakka oil was in the tank. It still made better lamp oil and flux for a wide variety of natural lubricants—including bullet lube—but the *industry* was probably almost as dead as the sea monsters they killed to get it. But metal, *any* metal, had real value, and gold, being the most durable of all—and least useful for turning into bullets, blades, and airplane engines—set the standard for the relative, *representative* value of other metals that could be made into things. Copper, iron, zinc, lead, *all* had value relative to their weight in gold, and gold was the "money" they exchanged in their place.

The most valuable metal in the world, for example, was

aluminum, worth ten times its weight in gold. They needed it for a number of very specific things, primarily to do with aircraft, and simply couldn't make it yet—if ever. All they had was what remained of the old PBY Catalina, a few wrecked P-40s, an old "Betty" bomber they'd found crashed in the jungle of Borno, and a few other curious relics that turned up from time to time. Not long before, for example, a prospecting team recovered the carcass of a P-40 lost in the raid on Madras. They'd been looking for it specifically and had a good idea where it was, but then another team discovered the wreckage of a Japanese dive-bomber on the southwest coast of Java, near Chill-Chaap. So there was always hope that other "leakers" from another war-torn world might appear.

And, as Alan noted, things were cheap. At least for now. The economy of Forester's Empire of the New Britain Isles had been pretty much in the crapper, and it would've been virtually impossible for them to go on if not for a number of factors. First, they were in an existential war as well, and that tended to make people more flexible when it came to what they were willing to sacrifice for the cause. Second, Rebecca Anne McDonald had assumed almost dictatorial powers in the wake of the treachery of the so-called Honorable New Britain Company, and members of her own Court of Directors and Court of Proprietors. The mass murder of most of the loyalists within her government had left her little choice. She'd seized the assets of the Company, and all those implicated in the treason. Then, as a gift, the Western Allies informed Her Majesty where large oil and gold deposits might be found within the bounds of the Imperial colony in North America, centered near a bay city they called Saint Francis. That reserve gave the Empire much-needed credit to draw upon.

Most Lemurians, on the other hand, had always considered themselves well-off if they had enough to eat. Now there was plenty. The great seagoing Homes still brought in gri-kakka—for meat, primarily—and many sold their huge fish harvests on a daily basis. The great ships themselves were virtually independent of land and needed money only to replace things that broke or to make necessary repairs. As reserve navy ships, they had access to the repair yards for things like that. Hunters scoured the wilds of Borno for rhino pigs that never seemed to decrease in numbers, and some Lemurians had actually begun raising them and other wild beasts. The vast killing grounds beyond the fortifications had been planted with crops as well, initiating the first large-scale agricultural effort Lemurians had ever attempted. A lot of food went to the war effort, of course, but there were no shortages at home. Luxuries weren't unknown to Lemurians, but they weren't very important just now. That would change, eventually, Alan suspected, especially after the war was won. But in the meantime, there was little for anyone to spend their pay on, and no reason to complain that it wasn't greater.

Beyond the waterfront machine shops, incongruously, was a long, open-sided tavern called the Busted Screw. Over time, it had become as much a fixture on the Baalkpan wharf as the teeming bazaars had been. The place was packed, as usual, with yard workers, sailors, and Marines, but few were there to drink. The Screw's principal owner, a 'Cat called Pepper, charged more than the factory commissaries, but his chow was better. So was the entertainment, for 'Cats and men. The Screw still served beer and seep, but only to workers showing timecards proving they weren't due back at work for more than six hours, and sailors and Marines had to show their liberty cards. The Screw's personality changed considerably after dark, but food was still available for the night shifts.

Alan shook his head. Pepper was a character who'd been one of Earl Lanier's cook's mates on *Walker*, and Lanier remained an absent partner in the Screw. But Pepper had other business interests, not all entirely savory. His partnership with Isak Reuben and Gilbert Yeager, for instance, to make the nasty, waxy Aryaalan tobacco fit to smoke, would probably get them all lynched if word got out that they stripped the leaves with a process involving the urine of the pygmy brontasarries indigenous to Borno. Alan arched his eyebrows thoughtfully. *Then again, probably not. Too many people, 'Cats and humans, are already too addicted to their vile PIG-cigs to shut down supply.* He'd have to have a word with Pepper about modifying his process, however.

Finally, they worked their way past another engine powering the first of many heavy cranes along a busy dock, and for the first time they had an unobstructed view of the old fitting-out pier and Baalkpan Bay beyond. The bay was packed with shipping of every description, some under sail and others coughing smoke from tall funnels. Small feluccas darted to and fro, carrying passengers or small cargo from one part of the harbor to another. But dominating the scene were three monstrous seagoing Homes. Two were moored some distance out, while the third had maneuvered past them with its great sweep oars. Its three massive "wings"—semirigid junklike sails rising up tripod masts, enclosing the pagodalike quarters of its people—were starting to draw the midafternoon breeze. Soon, the sweeps would be secured and the whole thousand-foot-long monster would move—slowly—under wind power alone.

"A stirring sight," Forester said, loud enough to be heard over the engine noises and voices around them.

"Yeah," Alan agreed, embarrassedly aware he'd tuned out Forester some time ago. No doubt the ambassador knew it and understood why. Alan was barely twenty-five and had an awful lot to wrap his head around. Just then he was remembering the first time he'd seen one of the immense, seagoing Homes. "*Big Sal* was one of those once," he said a little sadly. "So was *Arracca*. Now they're aircraft carriers. The biggest ones we have, along with *Makky-Kat*." *Maaka-Kakja* was the Maa-ni-la-built carrier that had been damaged at Malpelo while fighting the Doms. Though a purpose-built carrier, she had the same hull form and dimensions as a Home. "And of the four first-generation fleet carriers we built, *New Dublin* and *Raan-Goon* are finally heading east from Maa-ni-la to join Second Fleet and help High Admiral Jenks against the Doms. *Madras* is steaming west to join First Fleet." He took a deep breath. "And *Baalkpan Bay*'s on the bottom of the sea," he said, then added to their driver, "We'll stop here." When the carriage swayed to a halt, the four men and two 'Cat Marines stepped out.

"*New Dublin?*" Forester queried, surprised. That was the name of a once-rebellious city on the Imperial island of New Ireland. "Don't misunderstand; I'm not ungrateful for your country's generosity! And two carriers—and the escorts we've completed at Scapa Flow—will give me greater confidence we can hold what we've gained against the damnable Doms, but perhaps I don't understand your naming conventions."

"We name carriers for battles," Alan told him.

"An' destroyers for bloody heroes," Stokes adjoined. "We didn't in His Majesty's navies, but it seems fittin'."

"Ah." Forester cleared his throat. "Indeed."

The pier they stood on was the old one in name only, having been badly damaged once and rebuilt three times. The newer fitting-out piers and shipyards to the north were larger, but were still almost entirely devoted to building wooden hulls. Some were quite large and would become the latest—again, slightly smaller—class of Fleet Carriers, as well as cargo ships, oilers, and essentially everything they wanted Austraal to start making. Bigger, dedicated steam-powered auxiliaries would help with many things. They'd require smaller crews, carry heavier loads, and get them where they were needed faster. Only that would help get a handle on their supply problems. But while the Empire of the New Britain Isles was finally hitting its stride building screw-propeller, iron-armored wooden warships, the western Alliance had gone all in with steel-hull designs for combat vessels. And now that they knew how, and materials were available in larger quantities, they were quicker to make. Not only did they require less skilled labor, but it also wasn't necessary to cut the wood, freight it in, trim it, and lay it up to dry—or dry it themselves, which, on the scale they were building, required a process nearly as extensive as making steel in the first place.

Three steel ships were currently fitting out, floating high in the water at the pier, and the skeletons of more were rising on the ways nearby. The closest two hulls looked just like *Walker*'s and those of the two other new destroyers that had already deployed. Unfortunately, one of *those* was already lost as well. And hulls were about all these were, as yet. The closest had been decked, and the foundations for the bridge structure and aft deckhouse stood incongruously square atop it, but the skylights over the engineering spaces gaped empty. Workers operated windlasses and heaved on taglines secured to a large, complexly shaped object suspended from a crane. The next ship seemed slightly farther along, and a couple of hundred yards down the pier was yet another similar, larger shape that looked almost complete. Two Lemurian naval officers practically ran to meet them, but Alan smiled and waved them away after returning their salutes. "As you were. We're just here to gawk."

"Ay, ay, Mister Chaar-maan," one said, "but peese waatch you steppings." He waved at the crane and the extremely heavy-looking iron . . . thing . . . hanging from it. "Is stuff sqwaash you all ever-where. Even in aar!"

"We'll be careful," Alan assured. "Don't let us distract you."

The 'Cats nodded skeptically and backed away, leaving the four men watching the object sway down toward the closest hull.

"That's one of our reduction-gear boxes," Alan told Forester proudly. "And you'll be hard-pressed to imagine anything requiring more precision. Maybe a gun director or TDC. But reduction gears take a *lot* more abuse. They're what transfer the rotation of the turbines to the screws."

Forester shaded his eyes. "It seems a rather crude housing," he objected. "And I thought the, ah, turbines were the most difficult part of copying *Walker*'s power plant?"

"The geared turbine *drive*, Lord Forester," Stokes stressed. "An' the turbines themselves were tough enough, even with examples to look at. We had to make good nickel steel first—which we needed for proper automatic weapons and naval rifles, anyway—an' then we had to relearn how to heat treat the stuff." He grinned. "You've been watchin' us go through *those* labor pains, and we've given you reports on everything we did, to share with the Empire. Suffice to say we made 'em. But you can't *use* 'em as efficiently without reduction gears. Unlike reciprocatin' engines, they get all their torque from their high speed." He saw that Forester still looked unconvinced. "Don't let that casin' fool you. There's nothin' crude *inside* it."

"They're what took us so long to get the first new DDs out to the fleet," Alan confirmed, then shook his head and held his hand up, thumb and forefinger almost touching. "Even with the rest of the first ships already built, we were *that* close to starting from scratch on their power plants, trying turbo electrics, or something like that. Some wanted to go direct drive and take the efficiency hit, or put reciprocating engines in 'em and settle for twenty knots. But Captain Reddy told us we might as well do it right. And he *was* right. We needed the technological kick in the ass making those things gave us. We've been building guns, engines, even torpedoes, and our tooling still wasn't precise enough. We lost our best metallurgist, guy named Dave Elden, in the battle out there." He pointed at the bay. "Fortunately, he'd already written down a lot of stuff. But our people still had to relearn it. And Courtney Bradford and Ben Mallory helped too," he added. "Both were engineers in fields that use special metals—petroleum and aeronautics." He shrugged. "But when it came to actually making the gears, we had an ace up our sleeve we didn't even know about: a guy named Charlie Murphy." Forester raised his eyebrows. "Another prisoner who survived *Mizuki Maru*—and the Japs," Alan explained. "He'd been a machinist on the sub tender *Canopus* in Manila Bay. The *old* . . ." He stopped. Even Stokes had only recently learned the story of how, bombed out and listing, *Canopus* and her machinists fixed or made everything imaginable, not only for her subs sneaking in and out, but for anything else needed on Corregidor before it fell. And she did it all at night, setting smoke pots and pretending to be sunk and abandoned in shallow water during the day. "Anyway," Letts said, "Murphy's one hell of a machinist. Even so, he had to do a lot of hand turning and milling, constantly checking his work with calipers—all while teaching others to take the same care he did. He designed jigs. . . ." He stopped again. "Long story."

"I'd love to meet him," Bolton Forester said.

Alan waved east. "He's back in the Filpin Lands now, helping with other stuff." He smiled. "Maybe you can borrow him in the Empire someday, but that guy's never getting close to anything that'll shoot him, stick him, or eat him, if I have anything to say about it." He nodded back at the gearbox. "Building the first of those was like making giant watches." He gave an exasperated snort. "And then we had to torture them to death! I don't even want to think about how many units we shredded before we got the bugs worked out. But we've got the tooling now, for them and other stuff, and a whole shop dedicated to making one complete unit a week. Just like the ICE houses make nothing but the same engine they're contracted to build, one after another." He waved at the crane and chuckled. "Funny thing is, ordinarily, you'd install something like that before you even launched a ship, but we had so much trouble with the first ones—taking them out and putting them back so many times—the yard apes like it this way better. They're even kind of superstitious about it."

Bachman surprised them all by speaking, rather hesitantly. "But will that thing, designed for these"—he waved at the narrow hull the crane was lowering the gearbox toward—"work in a larger ship?"

Alan smiled. "Interesting you should ask, Lieutenant." He nodded down the pier and began to walk. "Watch your 'steppings,' gentlemen."

The second DD had the amidships deckhouse nearly finished and the aft searchlight tower erected. It also rode lower in the water, and Alan explained that was because all her machinery was in place. As on the first one, 'Cats romped all over it, pulling air hoses, driving rivets, and grinding rivet heads amid great yellow, sparkling arcs. Forester and Bachman appeared amazed by how fast the new ships were going together, and Forester even said as much.

"They built USS *Ward*—one of *Walker*'s sisters—in seventeen and a half days, at the Mare Island Navy Yard . . . back home," Alan told them. "And it took less than three months from keel laying to commissioning. That was a big deal at the time," he conceded, "and they weren't even fighting monsters that'd eat them if they lost the war. They *were* going as fast as they could, though, to see what they could do. So are we, and our shipyard workforce, at least, is almost unlimited." He frowned at Stokes. "Maybe *too* unlimited, at the expense of other projects. That probably sounds strange coming from me, but we'll see." He nodded back at the DDs and his frown faded.

"Still, we haven't already built a hundred of the damn things, to the point where the guys can slap 'em together in their sleep, and we're still making stuff—to make stuff better. I'll consider it just as big a deal if *these*'re ready to go in three *more* months."

"That will still be quite a feat," Forester agreed with a touch of envy as they continued on. But then their eyes fell on the third ship secured to the pier and Forester barked a laugh.

"Your cruiser!" he said gleefully. "I haven't seen her since the launch!"

"You weren't in Sular *that* long!" Alan objected. He started to say that she could be seen from the Great Hall, but that hadn't been true for quite a while. Only a small sliver of the bay, due west, was visible from there anymore. There was simply too much in the way now. "And we were *on* the bay together two weeks ago when we visited the ATC," he said, remembering. "You didn't even look this way?"

"No," Forester confessed. "You may recall we were all a bit . . . preoccupied that day. And otherwise"—he held his hands out at his sides—"between one thing and another, I just haven't been down to see her. My, she's a lovely thing! And nearly complete!"

"Well, almost nearly," Alan qualified. "There's still a lot to do."

To a casual observer, the new cruiser looked almost identical to USS *Walker* except it was bigger, with a higher freeboard even than the empty DD they'd first seen. But the pilothouse looked similar; there were four stacks and an amidships deckhouse, and a rather large aft deckhouse as well. A more careful look revealed the pilothouse was higher than *Walker*'s and rested atop another deck. Two gun mounts squatted in front of it instead of one, with *pairs* of muzzles protruding from splinter shields. The second mount was higher than the first, just forward of the pilothouse. Ordinary-looking DP 4″-50s stood on either beam atop the amidships deckhouse, and another pair stood in tubs behind the quadruple torpedo mounts flanking the aft two funnels. A tall crane with a searchlight platform on top jutted behind the fourth funnel. Two empty seaplane catapults dominated the space from there to the aft deckhouse, which was crowned by yet a third protected two-gun mount. Finally, a fifth DP 4″-50 poked up from the cramped fantail between a pair of depth-charge racks. Probably the most obvious difference between the cruiser and its inspiration, however, was a tall tripod mast forward where *Walker*'s foremast would've been, with what looked like a smaller version of the square-windowed pilothouse high in the air. Topping that was another pair of searchlights—and the obligatory crow's nest near the top of the mast.

"Oh my," Forester murmured, peering upward and imagining what it must be like in the small tub all alone, so high above the ship.

"You used the same, ah, reduction gears in her?" Bachman asked.

"The very same," Stokes confirmed. "Only she has three of 'em, an' three turbines to drive her. Two outboard an' one on the centerline. She can cruise on that one an' save fuel. Gives her longer range."

"I saw she had three screw propellers when she launched," Forester remembered aloud. "Will that truly make that much difference? And with the same engines as the smaller ships, will she not be considerably slower?"

"We *hope* it'll make a difference," Alan hedged. "*James Ellis* sustained thirty-six knots on her trials, with engines built in Baalkpan. That's faster than *Walker* ever was. Will her engines last as long as *Walker*'s have?" He held his hands up, then dropped them. "Who knows? We *have* identified a lot of inefficiencies we think we fixed on those." He nodded toward the DDs under construction. "Either way, except for some nagging quality-control issues with tubes, I believe we've built better boilers than *Walker* or *Mahan* ever had." He blinked fondly at the Lemurians working on the ship. "Those little guys can be awful imaginative when you give 'em a chance. They're never satisfied, now they've got machines on their mind. They seem to constantly think, *Well, if* this *works good, why don't we do* this *too?*" He arched an eyebrow. "Sometimes it works. Anyway, once *Walker*'s repaired, she should still work up to twenty-eight knots or so. I'd *love* to get her here and put brand-new boilers in her!" He glanced at the cruiser. "She's got *eight* boilers spinning three turbines. Should make twenty-eight knots, at least."

"I'm glad to hear it," Forester said, still somewhat skeptical, Alan thought. "But how can that work?"

Alan shrugged and began to recite the cruiser's specifications by way of explanation. "Her hull shape's almost literally an up-scaled version of *Walker*'s. She'll probably roll just as bad, but they're damn clean lines. She's four hundred and forty feet long, with a forty-five-foot beam. Fully loaded and ready to fight, she'll displace around four thousand tons." He nodded at Forester, anticipating his next question. "Yeah, three times as much as *Walker*, so it'll take her longer to start and stop, but it won't put much more strain on her engines to keep her at speed. At least that's the theory. And with that centerline screw right in front of the rudder, she'll turn even tighter. One of the limiting factors on *Walker*'s speed has always been her boilers more than her engines." He rubbed his nose. "And age and hard use, of course."

He nodded at the new ship "The math comes out like this: We're figuring on between twelve- and thirteen-thousand-shaft horse power. We don't have the instruments to measure precisely, but it's close, based on what *Walker*'s engines were rated at and the performance of the new DDs. Add three shafts together and we come up with around thirty-nine thousand. The old Brit C Class CL's of the last war . . ." He hesitated, looking at Forester. Though somewhat British by descent and culture, it was pointless to describe a class of ships built one hundred fifty years after Forester's ancestors came to this world, possibly from *another* world entirely, where C Class light cruisers may never have happened at all. The multiple lines of history that seemed to have converged here often made things difficult to explain. Or comprehend. And trying to do either always made Alan's head hurt. "Skip it," he said. "Anyway, these other ships, of similar hull shape, length, and displacement, got nearly thirty knots out of about forty thousand SHP. . . ." He realized he'd lost Forester entirely. "Skip it," he said again, and sighed. "We're pretty sure."

Forester cleared his throat, then smiled and waved at the ship. "Well," he said, "she certainly *looks* formidable!"

"She is, by most standards," Alan agreed, but his enthusiasm was suddenly waning.

"By *any* standard, she's a hell of an achievement," Stokes stressed. He pointed. "She's got six five-point-five-inch guns, all tied to a calibrated gun director copied from *Amagi.* We went with the five-fives because we're already makin' ammunition an' liners for 'em, for the salvaged Jap secondaries on *Santy Cat* an' the others. They're bag guns an' won't shoot as fast as four-inch-fifties, but they'll shoot farther an' hit more than twice as hard. She's also got five dual-purpose four-inch-fifties, as you can see, which'll help against aerial targets. We're workin' hard to design a proper antiair fire-control system, after what happened to TF Alden. . . ." He frowned and looked at Alan. "*Nobody* saw that comin, an' it was *my* job to expect it." His tone sounded more scolding than contrite. He looked back at Forester. "She's gettin' the first new fifty cals as well, a full dozen of the bloody things, in six twin mounts. That'll help too." He gestured aft. "An' she'll carry eight torpedoes an' two Nancy floatplanes. The aft deckhouse has more space for a workshop than *Walker* ever had, for torpedoes, everyday repairs, an' aviation maintenance as well." He waved his hand back and forth. "She's got half a dozen depth charge launchers down her sides to frighten mountain fish"—his expression turned hard—"or kill subs, which she'll find as easy as *Walker* ever did, now we've matched the old girl's sound equipment." He shrugged. "An' her electrics are better than anything we've done. Commander Riggs's been bloody busy with all his contrivances. The only thing she hasn't got I wish she did is radar."

"What's that?"

"The holy grail, Ambassador," Alan answered wistfully. "Maybe someday."

"Well, then," Forester said, "I'm sure it must be amazingly technical." He nodded at the cruiser and the two other ships. "Have you decided where these will go? I hope you'll consider sending them east. I know the two, ah, destroyers can't be completed quickly enough, but the cruiser might be just the thing to tip the scale against the blasted Doms. General Shinya is going all out to chase that loathsome Don Hernan to ground before he can escape, and the Governor-Empress wants a push toward the Pass of Fire in support of that—perhaps even to break through at long last and join young Leftenant Reynolds and Ensign Faask and the friends they've made." He frowned. "I can't say I'm not disappointed to learn that the New United States were not as well prepared to support us as we'd been led to believe, but we've had steadfast assurances they'll now do their best."

"Believe me, Bolton," Alan said, with feeling, "I'd love to focus on kicking Don Hernan's sick ass. And you're right; this might be our best chance to get it done. But the situation's dicey in the west. We got *our* ass handed to us at the Battle of Mahe. Besides *Baalkpan Bay* and *Geran-Eras*, we lost a lot of auxiliaries. We have to get supplies, troops, and as many warships as we can scrape together out there as fast as we can." He regarded Forester with a worried frown of his own. "The fact of the matter is, despite everything, this may be our only chance to break the Grik as well—before they drown us in their own blood, if they have to. Colonel Enaak says the truce with General Halik is holding. He's busy tearing across Persia, killing other Grik. Enaak and Svec's cavalry aren't actually fighting alongside him, but they're acting as his eyes."

"How very strange," Forester mused. "Our forces and at least a band of Grik, apparently getting along . . ."

"Yeah. Bloody weird," Stokes agreed. "An' we're still not *sure* Halik won't link up with General Esshk," he cautioned, "but even Colonel Svec—who hates Grik mor'n most, by the way—considers that unlikely. Esshk'd probably want Halik's head after what he's done—an' become."

Alan was nodding. "But Esshk is up to something. He's got well-trained and well-equipped Grik *troops* ashore in southern Madagascar. They were obviously staging to launch an overland assault against Grik City, probably coordinated with another amphibious attack. They're on a string now, supply-wise, since Chief Silva and Colonel Chack messed up their scheme, and we'll cut the string completely when we get *Arracca*'s battlegroup and *Santy Cat* down there. But I have to stress these were *real* troops, well armed and disciplined. That's confirmed. Matt—I mean, Captain Reddy—always suspected the last attack was their way of getting rid of thousands of old-style Grik berserkers, while hurting us at the same time. We think they've got ten or twenty thousand new-style Grik already ashore, and *all the rest* of Esshk's forces are just as well trained and equipped."

"An' I don't like those rows of boat sheds Lieutenant Commander Leedom saw, when he flew past the Grik capital of Sofesshk," Stokes supplied. "He an' Jumbo Fisher took two Clippers down an' bombed 'em yesterday—along with a few dozen Grik zeps, I'm happy to say. Dodged a lot of ant-air rockets too, an' took damage to one of the planes. But they reported the sheds were empty." He shook his head. "Whatever was in 'em is gone, scattered up the rivers, most likely. But I think Esshk is gettin' ready for a big push of his own, an' we need to jump before he does."

Alan nodded. "Reports from Major Bekiaa-Sab-At in the Republic of Real People indicate Kaiser Nig-Taak and General Kim finally have their forces on track to advance on Sofesshk from the south. Bekiaa still has reservations about their preparedness, but everyone feels the urgency that we have to hit Esshk before he hits us." He took off his hat and rubbed his brow. "I sense it too. Based on everything we know or can guess, if Esshk gets all his shit in the sock at the same time, he'll have *three-quarters of a million* troops to throw at us. Generals Alden, Safir Maraan, and Muln-Rolak all agree we have to hit him first, before he consolidates, defeat his army in detail while it's still scattered. A surprise attack from the south should help with that, followed quickly by Alden's attack up the Zambezi with three full corps. It's all we can do," Alan added with a trace of desperation in his voice. "And I don't need to tell you what'll happen if we fail," he stated simply.

"It does seem a rather risky scheme," Forester observed somberly. "But I don't know what else you *can* do. When do you plan to go?"

"At the last possible moment," Alan answered fervently. "We'll keep up the harassing raids on Sofesshk, increasing them as *Arracca* and hopefully *Madras* get in place and add their planes to the effort. But the main point of those'll be watching for when Esshk makes his move. Maybe he *won't* gather his forces as long as we keep that up. We need time more than anything, time to get more ships and planes and people down there—and time for Captain Reddy to deal with Kurokawa on Zanzibar."

"I was wondering when you'd get to that," Forester said, glancing at the cruiser. "His possession of the battleship *Savoie* makes all this rather more problematic than would otherwise be the case."

"You can say that again. *Savoie*, and whatever else he has. At least one carrier, with planes as good as ours. If he goes down to join with Esshk and we can't stop him, he can shred *Arracca* and *Santy Cat*—and there won't be much we can do about it."

"So you, and Captain Reddy in particular, will deal with him before he can cause more mischief," Forester predicted.

"That's the plan. If *Walker* can be repaired in time, and *if* we can get our strike team assembled . . ." Alan smiled mirthlessly. "With their four puny tanks." The tanks had been Alan's brainchild, and there'd be no more in time. The assembly of representatives had decided to focus resources not already allocated to more shipbuilding. And Alan could understand that. But what happened when they weren't fighting on the sea anymore?

"And that's also your chief concern, is it not?" Forester asked gently. "You're concerned that with Captain Reddy's wife, Lady Sandra, in his hands, Kurokawa will attempt to use her in some way that will prevent Captain Reddy from doing what he must?"

Alan sadly shook his head. "No, Bolton. I'm sure he'll do exactly that. And I'm just as sure that nothing'll keep Captain Reddy from his duty. I'm just worried what that'll do to *him*. To all of us."

Forester coughed, then turned to face the cruiser. "Indeed. Well, perhaps this will help."

Stokes snorted, and Forester looked at him in surprise. "Oh, we'll do our damnedest to get her there," Stokes said, "but it ain't bloody likely. She's still a few weeks from her trials. As she sits, she might not even *make* it there! She's the most experimental thing we've ever done."

"Yeah," Alan agreed, his voice grim. "And that's with shifts going around the clock to finish her." He shook his head. "All for nothing."

"What on earth do you mean?" Forester asked, troubled by Alan's tone.

"He means she's no match for *Savoie*," Stokes replied. "When we laid her down we thought the worst she'd ever face was a Grik dreadnaught or two, or a flock o' Dom ships o' the line. She'd serve them up proper without breakin' a sweat, from farther than they could even hit her. But we never dreamed there was anybody out there like the League, with somethin' like *Savoie* they could afford to just *give* away. What the hell *else*'ve they got? I'm the sticky beak around here now, an' I'll find out," he said forcefully. "An' there's a fair go I will pretty soon," he added cryptically. Then he waved at the cruiser. "She's a fine ship, an' we learned a lot makin' her, but we'd o' been better off makin' four more of those"—he pointed at the DDs—"with the same steel. Now, if we had her to do over again, gave her bigger guns an' a bit of armor, it might make a difference. As she is, by herself she's little more use against somethin' like *Savoie* than *Walker* is—except she's a bigger target."

Forester blinked. "I fear you may have been overly influenced by recent events and allowed yourselves to grow too gloomy," he scolded. "Particularly if that ship can do all you say. And it strikes me that unless you want to send her east after all, where she'll be quite welcome indeed—and all she'll have to face is a flock of Doms—then the key is *not* to use her by herself. And, if necessary, *let* her be a target. I don't know Captain Reddy as well as either of you, but I know him well enough to be quite certain that's what *he* would do." He looked back at the cruiser. "Whether she's complete in time to help him against *Savoie* or not, Captain Reddy *will* find a most excellent use for . . ." He paused. "What is your naming convention for ships of her type?" he asked at last.

"Cruisers are cities," Alan replied, his tone now thoughtful as he turned Forester's words over in his mind.

"But a lot of our cities are 'states' in the new Union." A ghost of a smile appeared on his lips. "And what about the seagoing Homes? Can't name a cruiser after them and have two ships with one name! And since so many cities have hosted battles"—the smile turned ironic—"their names usually go to carriers." He shrugged. "Public sentiment being what it is, though, there was never really any choice. She's USS *Fitzhugh Gray*, CL-1." Alan managed a genuine smile. "The Super Bosun's probably spinning in his grave, with his name on a cruiser. But at least she's a *light* cruiser. Maybe we can get away with classing her as a destroyer leader?" He shook his head. "I guess it doesn't make any difference."

"Oh, but it does," Forester objected, turning to face him. "The name does, at any rate. Can you imagine any member of your Navy Clan who wouldn't do his or her very best to ensure she's worthy of that name? I can't. And I'll tell you something else: names are important. They *mean* things. And if any part of Chief Gray's spirit went into that ship, along with his name, I'm confident she'll perform with the same resolve and commitment to duty he embodied—and sell her life just as nobly and dearly as he, if the time ever comes."

Stokes actually chuckled. "I didn't know Gray well, but who's gettin' the ship might make him spin even faster." He shrugged. "We'll skipper the new tin cans all right. Plenty of 'Cats have experience in *Walker* or *Mahan*. But we've damn little choice when it comes to handlin' large steamers. Most're goin' to the new carriers, even the big freighters an' oilers. An' *Gray* needs a skipper with experience handlin' an' fightin' a fast, big ship like she was a destroyer, while rememberin' she ain't—an' we only have one of those just hangin' around right now."

Forester looked at him questioningly. "Who did you give her to?" he asked.

"Lieutenant—well, I guess he'll be Commander when I tell him—Toryu Miyata."

Miyata had been a junior navigation officer aboard *Amagi* when she came to this world. Disillusioned by Kurokawa's madness, and even sympathetic to the Allied cause after their heroic defense of Baalkpan Bay and

Amagi's destruction there, he'd defected to the Republic of Real People when, considered expendable, he'd been sent to deliver an ultimatum to the Republic to join the Great Hunt or become prey. Distracted by reverses at the hands of the Alliance, the Grik never pursued their threat against the (to them, frigid and undesirable) land of the Republic, and had apparently practically forgotten it, considering it a negligible threat. Hopefully, they'd soon be disabused of that notion. But after he warned the Republic, Miyata came east with *Amerika* and ultimately joined Laumer's and Silva's attack against the Celestial Mother. He'd been the most badly wounded member of the team to survive, nearly losing a leg to the jaws of a huge, terrible beast unleashed to guard the lower levels of the palace. Finally, accompanying his new friend Gunny Horn, he'd been one of the wounded aboard *Amerika* when she was sunk by *Savoie*. Immediately upon his rescue, he'd begged an audience with Alan Letts—and made his oath to the American Navy Clan.

Alan still remembered the sincerity—and intensity—of the interview, and shook his head now. "I may be wrong, but I don't think Miyata's being a Jap would much bother the Super Bosun anymore. He made his peace with Shinya, if you'll recall, and knew Miyata had volunteered for the Cowflop stunt. That was a suicide mission if there ever was one, and it's a miracle anyone survived." He removed his hat again and ran a hand across short, sweaty hair. "And you know? I like to think Chief Gray was listening when I interviewed Miyata. If he was, I doubt he'd have any issue with the man's motivations for joining us, after all he's been through." He grimaced. "And he damn sure wouldn't doubt Miyata's resolve to get even for *Amerika*—and the other stuff Kurokawa's done. *I* don't." He looked at Forester. "So maybe you're right. If Gray's spirit *is* in that ship, combined with Miyata's determination, I probably have been selling her short."

CHAPTER 2

Occupied Grik City
North Mada-gaas-gar

"This is, hands down, the goofiest damn place I ever been," Chief Gunner's Mate Dennis Silva growled at Lawrence, his Grik-like Sa'aaran pal, as they strode along the top of an earthen berm on the southeast side of Grik City Bay. Silva was looking around at the modest fortification they walked on, the harbor to his right, what remained of the city and the huge structures ahead away from the waterfront. As usual, though the sky was relatively clear for once, it was hot and oppressively humid, without the slightest breeze. And being just below the equator, apparently a kind of spring was trying to kick in, as far as the local fauna was concerned. So in addition to the uncomfortable environment they'd grown accustomed to, new clouds of swarming insects had emerged to torment them wherever they went. They reminded Silva of mayflies—that *bit*—and there were different-colored ones almost every day. The annoyance they caused was balanced, however, by the fact that Petey absolutely loved them.

Petey was a weird, colorful little tree-gliding reptile—as much like a parrot as a lizard—that liked to ride the back of Dennis's neck, draped around it like a loose bandanna. He was constantly snatching insects from the air with darting jaws and munching contentedly, making happy chomping sounds and dropping twitching legs and membranous wing fragments in their path. The endless buffet helped Dennis and Lawrence cope with the muggy climate and teeming bugs, because Petey had redefined gluttony, in Silva's estimation, and anything that kept him fed—and quiet—was a blessing. What made Dennis uncharacteristically grumpy, however, was that he'd been ordered to clean up. Even that wouldn't normally have penetrated his customary "malevolent cheerfulness," as Courtney Bradford once described his personality. It was why, and for whom, that pissed him off.

Silva was tall, about six foot two, and powerfully built, and even his deeply tanned hands—the only visible skin besides what little of his face wasn't covered by a sun-bleached beard—were crisscrossed with the scars of many fights. His most obvious wound hid behind a brand-new "dress white" canvas patch over his left eye that matched the rest of his best shore-going rig. Those who knew him might suspect the white eyepatch was his little way of protesting the rest of his garb, particularly since he'd slightly reinterpreted the prescribed uniform of the day. He'd added leggings, a helmet, and his ever-present web belt, festooned with a hard-used 1917 Navy cutlass, razor-sharp '03 Springfield bayonet, and a 1911 Colt secured in a flap holster. Most of the rest of the belt was taken up by twin magazine pouches for the Colt. The only exception was space for a canteen and a small gap just large enough to accommodate an ornate, if somewhat battered, long-barreled flintlock pistol hanging by a belt hook. His philosophy was, dolled up or not, he'd needed each of those weapons many times and would never be caught without them. His sole concession to the spirit of his orders was that he'd left his primary weapon—a monstrous breech-loading rifle he called the Doom Stomper—in the tent he shared with Lawrence. The Doom Stomper was similar in appearance to the Baalkpan and Maa-ni-la Arsenal Allin-Silva "trapdoors," except it was built around a turned-down 25 mm Japanese antiaircraft gun barrel. That made it just about twice as big as the standard .50–80 caliber Allied infantry arm in most dimensions, including bore diameter.

"It is 'ery strange," Lawrence agreed, his tone less than cheerful as well, as he flapped at the mayflies with his tail plumage or tried to shoo them from his face with his dangerously clawed left hand. He kept the claws on his right hand carefully trimmed so he could handle cartridges for the Allin-Silva rifle slung over his shoulder. He spoke English and Lemurian almost perfectly, as long as he avoided words requiring the lips he didn't have. How he managed many other sounds remained a mystery. He wasn't Grik but was of the same species, if not race, and the long, sharp teeth lining his jaws should've made almost all human or Lemurian speech impossible. Somehow, he did it with his tongue or even in his throat. Courtney Bradford wasn't sure, and Lawrence wasn't about to sit and hum—or whatever—while the Australian naturalist stared in his open mouth. His unhappiness was inspired by the fact that he was also wearing whites. Others like him, the Khonashi from North Borno primarily, had joined the Alliance and even the Union, but *they* were all Army and wore the standard tie-dyed, camouflage combat smock he preferred himself. There were no standard-issue whites to fit his form, and Juan Marcos had quickly knocked out a set. If anything, the one-legged Filipino was too good a tailor, and the uniform covering Lawrence's orange-and-brown-tiger-striped feathery pelt was considerably tighter than he preferred. *Much* too tight to fight in.

Silva stopped a moment to stare, shaking his head and swatting at bugs. To the south, beyond the nightly bombed, daily improved dockyards, was a razed area that had been the warrenlike maze of wood-and-mud huts housing tens of thousands of upper-class Grik Hij. All that was gone, the materials used to construct defensive works. What remained, except for the scars left by zeppelin raids, was a great green grass field, well fertilized by eons of Grik dung—and the blood spilled to take the place and keep it. There was grass everywhere now, in fact, which everyone found curious. There hadn't been a single patch this side of the Wall of Trees when they conquered the Celestial

City, and even Hij Geerki couldn't get a satisfactory explanation from the several thousand civilian Grik prisoners he had laboring around the city in exchange for food—and life. The closest he'd come was to note a general consensus among his workers that the Celestial Mother—killed by Isak Reuben during the fight to take the "Cowflop"—didn't like green. That may've been true. Courtney Bradford, also the closest thing they had to a sociologist (among so many other things), theorized it was probable she'd had her subjects pluck each blade of grass as it emerged as a constant, daily reminder to obey her every whim. That made the most sense to Silva. Picking grass was her version of having the hands chip paint whether it needed it or not, or make a constant "clean sweep down, fore and aft." It had been busy work, to keep the masses in check.

Protruding over four hundred feet above the fresh sea of grass was the Celestial Palace, irreverently dubbed the Cowflop. And it *looked* more like a stupendous heap of manure than anything anyone should call a palace. In reality, it was more like a huge, dark granite pyramid, with rounded corners and a mashed-down top. The interior was like a warren as well, or some nightmare maze. Silva and Lawrence (and Petey too, though he'd literally just been along for the ride) had been part of the team that took it, and that had been a rare fight indeed. Both were wounded; Silva too badly to go on, and Lawrence enough that he'd been unable to help much at the end. They were fit for duty now, largely due to the analgesic, antiseptic paste that was one of many things made from the ubiquitous polta fruit. Silva's favorite was an intoxicating fermentation called seep, though he still preferred Lemurian beer for "wettin' his whistle." They'd also recently returned from a lengthy rehab tour, consisting of a jaunt across central Madagascar, where they met new Lemurian friends among the Sheeree, a tribe left behind during the ancient exodus of other 'Cats from the island. And, of course, they'd capped off their convalescence with a fierce battle against a support base for an army of infiltrating Grik.

In the distance, past the Cowflop, was a wooden stockade out of an opium dream. It was practically a mountain range made of thousands and thousands of monstrous Galla trees that walled off the city from the amazingly hostile jungle beyond. Galla trees had become an almost holy symbol to Lemurians since they'd been forced to flee their ancestral home, and many considered their use for such a thing the height of sacrilege. Others, like Chack's sister, Risa, were more philosophical. The barrier had saved them from a recent Grik attempt to retake the city, and she considered it fitting that all the stupendous effort the Grik exerted to erect the great wall, who knew how long ago (Galla trees were extremely resistant to rot), had contributed to the slaughter of thousands of Grik.

Grass was growing on the wall of trees now too, and thousands of canvas pup tents were arrayed at its base. Indeed, tents were everywhere—far more than they had troops to fill. Safir Maraan's II Corps had been cutting and sewing them like crazy out of huge stores of canvas captured in Grik warehouses. Hopefully, they'd need them eventually, and that was one thing, at least, that wouldn't have to be shipped in, taking the place of more vital cargoes. The tents surrounded the bay on every hand, even providing shelter for their Grik prisoners on the west side of the bay. More important at present, however, the surplus tents more than doubled their apparent numbers. The ones closest to the harbor each sheltered two men or 'Cats. Those farther out might be occupied by one, and the farthest probably had only a company of troops to stir the fires and be seen moving among enough tents for a battalion.

Long, narrow trenches were everywhere as well, in addition to the more extensive fortifications, carefully arranged along company streets to promote drainage when it rained and give troops a place to ride out the frequent raids. There wasn't much danger from those anymore. Not only were fewer zeppelins attacking at last, their lashed-together formations sometimes consisting of fewer than fifty airships now, but the extra planes that recently arrived, crated in the holds of fast transports, meant they had nearly enough for all their pilots again and they'd savaged the latest zep formations with the new, faster, and more heavily armed P-1C Mosquito Hawks, or "Fleashooters." Besides, oddly enough, after an initial apparent reluctance to bomb the palace, most Grik bombs now fell on or near it. That made no sense to anyone, unless losses among Grik aviators had left the rest so poor that all they could be trusted to hit was the biggest target they could see—or the raids truly were meant primarily to gall them and remind them that the Grik hadn't forgotten them. The palace was practically impervious to Grik bombs.

The works they stood on were the most lightly defended of any surrounding the city. Heavy batteries of captured Grik guns, carefully protected from the sea and sky, now guarded the mouth of the bay and should be sufficient to keep them secure. These works were just in case the enemy somehow got past. In that event, reserves would quickly fill them. At least that was the plan. Their greatest fear was that the Grik might manage to attack *everywhere* again, with a larger, more capable force than before. If that ever happened, there'd *be* no reserves.

Dennis and Lawrence had been heading toward the great, long docks on the south side of the bay, and Silva waved at mayflies and pointed. "Looky there," he said. Not far away, where the docks began, a huge, counterbalanced wooden crane was hoisting iron plates off the wreckage of a half-sunken Grik battlewagon, while the exposed carcass swarmed with Lemurian yard workers, troops detailed to help, and even a few civilian Grik. The latter were performing the most dangerous tasks, but Hij Geerki, General Muln-Rolak's pet, was acting as the Grik "mayor" and had assured Safir Maraan they'd volunteered. Silva kind of doubted that. *Ol' Geerki's a slippery little lizard,* he thought, *tryin' to make the nasty critters he's responsible for seem worth feedin'.* Either way, he didn't much care. Grik were murderous animals, as far as he was concerned, and he genuinely enjoyed killing them. It even struck him as ironic that he'd learned to discriminate Grik from Grik-like so well. After all, Lawrence was one of his very best friends, and he liked I'joorka and the Grik-like members of the Khonashi in northern Borno just fine. But killing "real" Grik had become his very favorite thing to do, and the fact that they'd slaughtered such a high percentage of the relatively few people he ever cared about was enough to make him want them *all* dead, even if that resulted in an end to his calling. *Oh well,* he consoled himself. *I'll find a new hobby. Wherever you go, somebody always needs killin'.*

A multiton plate cleared the wreckage, the crane swiveling to the side to lay it on a stack piling up on land. Beyond that, several more cranes were doing the same, and another erected on a massive, flat barge was salvaging a wreck farther out from the dock. And the bay was crowded with more than just wrecks. The great Home-turned–aircraft carrier, USNRS *Arracca*, was moored in the center of the bay, surrounded by what remained of her battlegroup, consisting of four steam frigates (DDs) of Des-Ron 9, and more than a dozen auxiliaries. Hopefully, she'd soon be joined by *Madras* and her brand-new air wing and battlegroup. Two fast transports were alongside *Arracca* now, sending crated aircraft aboard, while one of the first of their big steam oilers waited to top off her bunkers. The former general cargo hauler and now protected cruiser *Santa Catalina* crouched between *Arracca* and the shore, her still slightly unusual "dazzle" paint scheme distorting her lines. Four PT boats of MTB-Ron 1 patrolled inside the harbor mouth, and what remained of Des-Ron 10 sailed offshore, keeping watch, their engines secured.

There was an unusually large number of planes overhead today as well, flying in formation back and forth, ostensibly practicing maneuvers. The primary reason for that was the two "strangers" in the bay. The first was a small, nondescript Spanish oiler, looking considerably worse for wear. But the second was long and sleek, with a sharp, straight-up-and-down bow lying just inside *Santa Catalina*. She was the Leone class destroyer, *Leopardo*; a third longer than USS *Walker*, twice as heavy, and armed with twice as many, bigger guns. More unnerving, not only did she most assuredly *not* look like she'd been beaten apart and patched together several times, but in addition to the flag of the Kingdom of Italy fluttering at her fantail, the bizarre fascist banner of the League of Tripoli stood straight out from her foremast, high above the first of her two stacks. The only consolation, such as it was under the circumstances, was that *Leopardo* couldn't be anxious for a fight. Her decks, and those of the oiler, were crammed with what was reportedly the majority of *Savoie*'s crew.

"*Santy Cat* could take her," Silva said, nodding at what he considered an enemy ship. "Close as they are, just sittin' there," he qualified, beginning to walk again and picking up the pace. He could see the group he'd been ordered to join assembled on the dock. "She's got bigger guns—those five-fives—and can probably take more hits. But if that *Leopardo* gets on the loose, with her speed—an' prob'ly torpedoes too—I wouldn't give a chicken's ass for *Santy Cat*'s chances."

"Then us should sink her now," Lawrence said simply. "'Hy not us just sink her?"

"Beats me, little buddy. But the Skipper's got a reason, sure. You know he *wants* to." Dennis could tell who was who now. Captain Reddy was there, as was Colonel Chack-Sab-At and his beloved Orphan Queen of B'mbaado, General Safir Maraan. Courtney Bradford was holding another wide hat, practically a sombrero, on his balding head, and Silva realized he must have a dozen of the things, as many as he'd lost. Major Alistair Jindal of the Empire of the New Britain Isles stood beside him, acting prepared to catch the hat if the breeze took it. A number of guards stood a little back. These were Lemurian regulars and Marines, a couple Impie Marines, and even a few "Maroons." Maroons were distantly related to Impies in the sense that all their earliest ancestors had been part of a three-ship convoy of East Indiamen brought to this world in the middle of the eighteenth century. After they arrived, the Maroons sailed west, trying to make their way back to England, and wound up here. The other two ships went east and founded the Empire.

Facing the Allied delegation was a tall, dark-haired man named Capitaine de Fregate Victor Gravois, dressed as a French naval officer. The slightest mustache, grown a bit unruly of late, adorned his upper lip, and he was clearly making an effort to appear undisturbed by the swarming, biting insects. He'd been joined on the dock by several of *Leopardo*'s officers, dressed all in white, and Silva finally understood why he'd been told his usual

T-shirt and dungarees wouldn't do. *If the goombahs are gonna get all duded up, I guess we should too,* he thought, smoldering. *And then there's that Gravois bastard. . . . He's slippier'n Geerki, in all the worst ways. At least Geerki's kinda one of us, an' he's tryin' to help. Gravois's a* bad *frog, just out for himself—an' his goddamn League.* Silva still hadn't figured out which enjoyed the Frenchman's greater loyalty.

His eye went to Captain Reddy, searching for a clue as to what was going on in his skipper's mind—and maybe a hint about how the captain expected *him* to play this. *Ol' Gray always knew what to do or say in situations like this,* Dennis lamented. *Whether to rant an' rave, threaten, or poke—to throw a scare at whoever he was talkin' to—or keep his damn trap shut.* He smirked. *Or do somethin' to crack 'em up an' break the tension. I don't know if I'm cut out for that, even if that's prob'ly why the Skipper wants me here. I'm just used to gettin' pointed at what needs killin.'* But try as he might, he caught no sign from Captain Reddy as he and Lawrence approached. *He looks tired, sure. We all are. He still looks mad too. Well, he ain't alone in that. That bastard Gravois an' his League* gave *Kurokawa a goddamn* battleship*! I don't care how he says it happened. There's no way it* could *have if he didn't want it to.* Silva also knew his captain was desperately worried about his wife, but nothing of that leaked past his fury. He'd never let them see that. *Guess mad's the order o' the day,* Silva decided, *so I reckon I'll poke.*

Gravois finally swatted at a mayfly that landed on his nose and took a bite, but turned the motion into a gesture encompassing the bay. "But where is your poor little ship, your *Walker*?" he asked. "I'd hoped to bid her farewell myself—and show her specifically to Capitano di Fregata Ciano, of course." He nodded at one of the Italian officers. "Ciano is always trying to distinguish himself," Gravois explained, "and your ship's example cannot help but make an impression on him, regarding how he might accomplish that."

"It's none of your concern where USS *Walker* is," Matt snapped. "In fact, the only reason we're letting you go instead of *hanging* you as an accessory to the murder of thousands of wounded troops and the sinking of three of our ships—not to mention the intelligence and material aid you've given our enemy—is so you can personally convey our 'greetings' to your leaders"—his lip twisted—"your triumvirate in Tripoli. And you'd better tell them that we finally know exactly what you've been up to out here." If possible, Matt's expression hardened. "We don't give a damn what you do in the Mediterranean, but you'd better quit sneaking around and sniping at the edges of our fight, here or in the Pacific. From now on, you stay the *hell* out of our war—unless you want in it. All the damn way."

Gravois raised an eyebrow, but nodded. "In all honesty, Captain Reddy, that's precisely what I will tell them." He gave a long-suffering sigh. "It's what I've told them from the start, in fact. The League has concerns enough of its own, as I've alluded to; the very reason we've been unwilling to lend greater resources to either side in this—please pardon me for characterizing it so—backwater struggle." He shrugged. "As you now know, it has merely been our desire to ensure that neither you nor the Grik—with Kurokawa's aid—grew strong enough to become a threat to us." He paused thoughtfully. "That strategy was perhaps misguided. Particularly in respect to the 'horse' we bet on." He shook his head sadly. "That couldn't have been made more abundantly clear than by Kurokawa's sinking of the hospital ship you refer to and the abduction of . . . certain members of its company." Chack bristled, and Courtney Bradford took a step forward, his face turning red. No one believed Kurokawa had already controlled *Savoie* at that point. The fact that there'd been *some* survivors was sufficient evidence of that for most. And then to refer to Sandra and the others being in Kurokawa's hands . . . It had to be an attempt to rattle them. But if he'd meant to get a rise out of Matt, he failed.

Gravois continued. "In any event, your tenacity and industry in the face of such adversity"—he paused, smiling slightly at his choice of words—"proves we should've pursued amity between our peoples from the beginning, and"—he waved again at the bay—"even depleted as you are, and confident of victory as I would be, I must concede that full-scale hostilities between us—which we do not desire—could weaken the League at a time it can ill afford it. Even if destroying you only required the redeployment of sufficient assets to accomplish the task."

"I guarantee a fight with us'll take more than just a redeployment," Matt said with complete conviction, leveling a piercing gaze on *Leopardo*'s captain. "And USS *Walker* has accounted for more enemy tonnage than we can calculate, including a Kagero class destroyer and a forty-odd-thousand-ton battle cruiser, either of which could've turned *your* 'little' ship to scrap. So I wouldn't go looking for distinction at her expense, if I were you." A predatory grin slashed his face. "I can't deny *Walker* may need a touch of paint and a bolt tightened here and there, but she and her people know how to take down heavyweights. They've had a *lot* of practice. Have you?"

It was Ciano's turn to bristle, but Gravois touched his arm. "Nothing could be farther from our intent than a confrontation of any sort, I assure you."

"Good," Matt replied. "Because we'll be watching. You and your oiler will have safe passage down the Mozambique—I mean, Go Away Strait—and around the cape." He paused. "And I wouldn't expect a friendly welcome at Alex-aandra, if I were you, after the way *Savoie* behaved there. If you've got the fuel, I'd highly recommend you just keep going." His expression went blank. "But if you deviate in any way from a least-time course to the Atlantic, you'll think you kicked a hornet's nest. You might knock down a few of our planes," he conceded, "but the rest'll shred your ships. Our pilots've had a lot of practice too." He glared at Gravois. "And the same goes for the Kraut U-boat you've got sneaking around. When we find it, we'll sink it on sight. Period."

For the first time, Matt appeared to have broken Gravois's self-possession, but the Frenchman quickly recovered. "I have no idea what you mean," he said, eyes narrowing, suddenly darting, searching. "Even if the League had a submersible in these waters, how would we supply it?" He waved at the Spanish oiler. "We're taking everything away—that is in our power. And speaking of what is in whose power, where is my pilot? Oberleuitnant Fiedler?"

"Just now worried about him?" Matt asked dryly.

"Maybe Chiss-maas Island wasn't the only base they had in this ocean," Chack said aside to Safir Maraan, speaking for the first time, and Gravois goggled at him.

"Yeah, our people out of Ja-vaa found it," Matt told him, "while searching for survivors from *Amerika*. So now we know at least one of the ways you've been spying on us for Kurokawa. The base was abandoned, but it's clear it was recently occupied by your League. It's ours now, including the intact fuel-oil tank batteries you were kind enough to leave behind. But if we find another—and we'll be looking now—whoever's there will get just one chance to surrender before we bomb it out. Clear?"

"Of course," Gravois answered distractedly. "But where is Fiedler?"

Hardly noticed until then, except for appraising glances when he and Lawrence—and Petey—had joined the group, Silva suddenly slapped his own face. "Goddamn it! There's a *bug* in my eye!"

Nearly everyone jumped, but Matt kept watching Gravois. His reaction to the fact they knew about the submarine had been revealing, for a number of reasons. "Shit!" Silva cursed, bending low, and mashing around his eye with a finger.

"Shit!" Petey shrieked in alarm, spewing sticky, chitinous fragments. Disturbed from his perch by Silva's antics, he launched himself at the nearest person—Gravois—who frantically twisted away, swatting with his hands, terror rising on his face. Petey landed on the dock, glaring at Gravois for refusing him refuge, and then quickly scampered up Chack's leg, over his rhino-pig armor, and settled on his shoulder.

"Bastard's kickin' an' floppin' all around!" Dennis snapped. "Damn it! He just took a *plug* outa my eyeball!"

"Here, let I see," Lawrence said solicitously, trying to pry Silva's hands away.

"The hell with that! Get your damn, poky claws away from my *one* damn eye! Are you nuts?"

To his credit, Gravois quickly collected himself. Straightening his tunic beneath his belt, he smirked. "Ah. The inestimable Mr. Silva!" he said, his tone ironic. "Brought low by a meager insect!"

Silva slowly straightened, still pawing at his eyelid, but the eye inside was steady—and hard. "An' *you* nearly pissed yerself at the sight of a little lizard, no more dangerous than a mouse. You ask where's Fiedler. *I'll* ask one more time where's Lady Sandra an' the rest. They'd better be safe."

Gravois's smirk disappeared and he took a step back. "I have done—and will continue to do—all I can, by radio, to our, ah, embassy at Zanzibar, to ensure she and the others remain unharmed." He turned to Matt. "You *must* trust me, Captain Reddy, in this above all else." His voice had taken on a tone of pleading sincerity. "If in *nothing* else," he added bleakly, then shook his head. "But Kurokawa is mad. There is no telling what he might do."

"Well, I'm mad too, by anybody's lights," Silva assured Gravois, his one eye slightly reddened by the rubbing, but even hotter and deadlier for it. "An' *I* blame you *personally* for Kurokawa havin' 'em in the first place. So, if anything happens to any of our people you left with that crazy bastard, I'll hunt you down wherever you go, no matter how long it takes, an' take it outa your ass." He brightened. "Hey! That's an idea! I'll pull your wormy spine right *outa* your ass, an' beat you to death with it."

"Indeed," Courtney said, a serious, contemplative expression narrowing his bushy brows. "You know, Monsieur Gravois, despite the apparent physiological impossibility of Mr. Silva's promise—and I *would* consider it a promise, if I were you—I suspect he'd somehow accomplish it. He's actually quite imaginative about things like that, and I've seen him do a great many unlikelier things."

Gravois went pale. "Where is Fiedler?" he challenged Matt once more, though somewhat weaker than before, his eyes flitting at the big chief gunner's mate.

"Here he comes now, actually," Major Jindal said cheerfully, nodding at a guard detail escorting a sullen-looking man in rumpled, blood-spattered khakis. He looked like he'd been beaten half to death. His lip was broken in several places and one of his eyes was swollen shut. "I'll be honest," Jindal said, as the guards shoved Fiedler at the League officers. The German stumbled but kept his feet. "I offered Oberleuitnant Fiedler asylum in the Empire of the New Britain Isles in exchange for information." Jindal shrugged. "He refused."

Gravois's eyes bulged. "He has been *tortured*!"

"He tripped," Jindal countered. "And we may have asked him a question or two after we picked him up and dusted him off. But if I were you, I'd worry less about what we might've learned from him and more about whether you've told us everything you can regarding aid you've given Kurokawa—or any other way you've hurt our cause—because we'll find out for ourselves."

"I told those bastards *nothing*," Fiedler snapped and spat blood at the guards.

Gravois glared at Jindal, then turned back to Matt. "I demand you arrest this man at once and punish him severely!"

Matt held his hands out helplessly. "Can't."

"But you are supreme commander of all Allied Forces!" Gravois protested sarcastically.

"Yeah, and Major Jindal's under my *military* command. But he's the senior representative of the Empire in the west, and even if it's part of the Alliance, it's still a sovereign nation. Jindal offered asylum; I didn't. I wouldn't want Fiedler as a gift; he's a Leaguer, like you. A *Kraut*. And if I ever took my eyes off him, he'd probably throw another wrench in the works. But I can't fool with any *state* decisions Jindal makes, or any . . . associated activities. You'll just have to take that up with Her Imperial Majesty, Governor-Empress Rebecca Anne McDonald." Matt appeared to consider that. "Which might be hard, considering *all* Allied military forces are under my command, and they're under standing orders to sink anything flying your stupid flag in the Pacific too." He shook his head and held his hand over his heart in mock solemnity. "I'll mention his behavior to the Governor-Empress in my next dispatch, though." The incongruous grin that appeared on Matt's face looked more like a snarl without the sound that came with one. "*Trust* me."

"Trust me! Goddamn!" Petey hissed at Gravois.

* * *

"Good riddance!" Courtney practically stomped as *Leopardo*'s barge carried the Italian officers and Gravois out to the crowded ship. "I've always liked the French, y'know—oddly enough—but that twisted bugger proves a sharp exception!"

"What *did* haappen to Fiedler?" Chack asked, grimly blinking at the departing boat as well, while trying to untangle Petey from the long, brindled fur on the back of his neck.

"Yeah," Silva chimed in. "Last I saw, he was at the airfield, workin' on that junk heap they flew in on. Seemed like a right enough guy—for a Kraut. 'Specially since the plane ain't as bad off as he made out to Gravois. Fiedler *wanted* to come here, an' knew the frog'd never risk his sorry ass all the way back to Egypt if the plane sounded like it was gaspin' its last." He chuckled. "Buggered it up just enough, well enough, over long enough, he even fooled his Spanish copilot into thinkin' it was crappin' out for real. Him an' the rest o' Gravois's toadies're either on that ship"—he motioned at *Leopardo*—"or still at Zanzibar. Hey, maybe they're who Gravois meant by his embassy."

"Possibly," Safir agreed, blinking her silver eyes. "But I think Graa-vois came here specifically to secure *Leopaardo*'s escape past our forces, and personally take our measure. Fiedler only ensured he would not desire to continue on in a faltering aircraft."

"He came to spy," Jindal spat.

"You get that outa Fiedler?" Silva asked.

"It was obvious," Matt agreed, sidestepping Silva's question and looking at Safir. "He came for all those reasons, but spying is the main reason we let him go." They all looked at him in surprise. "Sure," he said, "we *know* he'll blab. Definitely to his League, and probably to Kurokawa. And if Kurokawa gets it, General Esshk might as well. But what did he see?"

"That we got damn little at sea to stop anybody," Silva growled thoughtfully.

"True. Or to move what's here. And that *is* true. But not as true as they think, based on what they saw in the bay. What else?"

Safir waved at the sea of tents. “That we are strong on the ground?”

“Also true”—Matt smiled—“if less accurate. But mostly he saw what I wanted him to—that we're *all* here, including both corps that made it through the Battle of Mahe.”

“But . . . ” Safir hesitated. “Only *Second* Corps is here. First and Third are still at Maa-he.”

“Exactly,” Matt said. He gestured the Maroons closer. One was named Will, and had seen fierce fighting at the Wall of Trees. His regiment of Maroons had since doubled to brigade strength as more of his people filtered in to be armed with “maskits” and join the fight. “Based on Jumbo and Leedom's recon flights to Sofesshk, we may have an opportunity—and not much time to take it,” Matt explained. “Maybe our only—and last—chance to win this war,” he added soberly. “That's why Chairman Letts”—Matt couldn't hide a slight, wistful smile at the memory of the gangly, sunburned lieutenant (jg) who first reported aboard *Walker* in Cavite before the old war back home—“gave the go-ahead to our plan. Colonel,” Matt said when Will stood before him and saluted.

“Cap'n Reddy.”

“You're now in direct contact with Corpor—” Matt smiled. “I mean, Colonel Miles, to the south, both by radio and runners.” Miles and his Shee-Ree had found a nice, level place along the bank of a wide spot in the West Mangoro River, upstream from where they'd engaged the Grik, and fashioned a passable airstrip simply by scything down the tall grass. Since then, several Fleashooters had flown down, laden with a few small arms and their own machine guns, which had been removed before they returned to be rearmed. And one of the Clippers had made two trips full of muskets and ammunition, landing and taking off from the river. Matt wanted their new Ju-52 trimotor to carry much more—once it was deemed airworthy. “What's your assessment of his reports?” he asked the Maroon officer.

Will frowned. “Aye, an' thar's a heap'a Gareiks a-camin', as ye saed. Miles an'”—he shook his head almost unbelievingly—“the mankey falk”—he glanced apologetically at Chack and Safir—“them Shee-Rees, is nippin' at 'em an' the march. But tha'll lakly git hare in a manth er sae—thaugh twixt the nippin' an' the jangle buggers tha'll hae laft half thar army's banes fer tha rats tae gnaw."

Matt looked like he'd followed Will's tortured English fairly well. "And if they arrive with, say, fifteen thousand, can you and your men—and the Shee-Ree training here—hold the wall alone?"

Will's brows arched but he nodded. "Aye. We's may hafta abandon tha two cities alang tha coast we's gardin', but wit' maskits an' big gaanes—an' tha trainin' ye've gave us—we's'll kill that many Gareiks wi-oot nae trabble." He paused. "Ye's . . . ye's abandinin' us?"

Matt shook his head. "We'll *never* abandon you," he said with sharp finality. "The Maroons, and now the Shee-Ree, are as much ours as anyone we brought with us, as far as I'm concerned. And several companies of our best troops will remain to give you a hand, just in case. But it's time for us to go on the offensive." He looked at Safir Maraan. "So though we're not abandoning Grik City or our friends, most of us *will* be leaving when First and Third Corps arrive here, and embark Second Corps." He looked back at Will. "But we're not leaving the fight. After we finish some . . . other business, we're taking it where the Grik live. Up the Zambezi, all the way to the enemy anthill. Sofesshk itself."

"Than tayke us tae!" Will objected, but Matt shook his head.

"We still have to defend this place, and who better for that than the people who *live* here?" Matt regarded Safir and Chack separately, with an expression deeply apologetic. Silva realized it was the first time he'd seen the Skipper radiate anything but fury in many days. And he also understood the emotions at its heart. "I hate to split you two up again," he said simply. "God knows you've spent enough time apart. But I need you in different places. Hopefully, it won't be for long this time."

Chack blinked understanding and, with a nod from Jindal, stood slightly straighter. "My First Raider Brigade will be ready for whatever you require of it, Cap-i-taan Reddy," he said.

"As will Second Corps," General Queen Safir Maraan assured. Then she blinked fondly at the mate she outranked on so many levels, but the heirarchy couldn't have mattered less to either of them. "You brought us together in the first place, and always reunite us. Chack will help return that favor to you and Lady Saandra while the rest of us prepare to make a world fit for us all to live in."

Matt could only nod. "Very well," he said briskly. "We all have our assignments, it seems. Second Corps and the indigenous forces detailed to defend the city will remain here, while Chack's First Raider Brigade embarks aboard *Santy Cat* and *Arracca* for Mahe. Just as soon as that thing"—he nodded at *Leopardo*—"is well underway. Within the next few days at the latest. *Arracca* and *Santy Cat* will then steam south to the mouth of the Zambezi and start raising hell." He smiled at Safir. "Some time after that, we can't know exactly when, the Republic of Real People will begin its offensive in the south. It may take Esshk a little time to get word of that and try to respond, but when he does, General Alden will come down here with First and Third Corps to get you, and you'll proceed with the invasion of Sofesshk together. You'll be in complete command here until then, but after that"—he turned to Will and nodded slowly—"you'll command the defense of Grik City. *You*," he stressed. "Not your cap'n or anyone else who might try to pull clan rank. Is that clear? You've learned our ways, and I trust you to get along with *all* our people here. You can let others advise you, and by all means make use of the Shee-Ree and their unique communications network. But *you'll* be the senior Allied officer. Is that understood?"

Will gulped and glanced at his swarthy comrade, a seasoned warrior named Andy. "We'll git nae guff," Andy assured. "Ye're tha *one*, Will. Sance ye farst met that'un." He nodded at Chack. "Nay'n tha cap'ns'll buck ye."

With a deep breath, Will took a step back and crisply saluted Matt as he'd been taught. "I unnerstand, sar, an' ye hae me sacred oath."

"Thank you, Will," Matt said, returning the salute.

Chack nudged Jindal, finally peeling Petey loose and holding the clearly resentful but suddenly limp reptile by the scruff of the neck. "In that case, Cap-i-taan, if there is nothing else, I will begin preparing the First Raider Brigade to embark."

"And Second Corps has much to prepare, even if its departure will be considerably more delayed." Safir grinned and blinked at Chack. "It is somewhat larger than Chack's Brigade, after all."

Matt managed a smile. "Then by all means, consider yourselves dismissed. And, Chack," he added, "you have capable subordinates. Majors Jindal and Galay, as well as your sister, Risa. Let them do most of the work. You still need rest from your latest adventure. Take some time with General Queen Safir Maraan. I'm sure you have a lot to . . . talk about."

With a wide grin, Chack tossed Petey at Silva. The tree glider squalled and latched onto Silva's arm before scrambling back to his customary perch.

"Asshole," Dennis muttered amiably at his friend.

Finally, the only ones remaining on the dock, within a wide bubble reserved for them by the yard workers, were Matt, Courtney, Silva, and Lawrence. Silva was watching Matt very closely, suspecting he'd planned it that way. "Well, I guess me an' Larry'll be sankoin' along. We ain't Chack's Raiders, but we'll be taggin' along. Ol' Larry won't wanna forget his favorite toothbrush. Gotta keep them nasty choppers o' his nice an' bright!"

"Just a moment more, if you please, Mr. Silva," Courtney said in what, for him, was a no-nonsense tone. "Several other . . . unresolved subjects remain."

"About Larry?" Dennis asked innocently. He glared at his Sa'aaran friend. "Did you take a dump in the chow line again?" he demanded, shaking his head with exaggerated scorn. "I swear. Can't *nothin'* stop you?" He looked at Courtney apologetically. "It's them Shee-Ree that's been such a bad influence on ol' Larry, Mr. Bradford, pissin' all over everything they take a fancy to. Mighty covetous critters. Thank God the rest of our 'Cats don't do that!"

Lawrence hissed at him. "I not *e'er* do that!"

"Then where *did* you take a dump? Or did you get caught sniffin' around that female lizard Geerki's pet Griks've been hidin'?" It had been discovered that the civilian Grik in the city had been protecting a single breeding-age female in their midst. She'd been comfortably confined in the Cowflop, not only as further leverage to ensure their cooperation, but so Courtney could study her. He hadn't learned much beyond the fact that she was somewhat duller even than the average Uul. A broodmare, he'd called her.

"You oughta be ashamed!" Dennis continued, warming to his diatribe. "Why, you're not even the same *race* as her. I can just imagine what our Grik workers'd have to say about your schemes to mis-eggenate with their only broad!"

"Mis-eggenate!" Petey hooted scornfully.

Lawrence hissed again, a growl in his throat. "I *not* sniphing! And you're to talk? You and Risa . . ."

"That's quite enough," Courtney declared, rolling his eyes. "My dear friends," he told Dennis and Lawrence, "you've both contributed far more than you know to our cause, and might've even saved it more than once. But *just* for once, *will you please stop playing silly buggers and pull your heads in*?"

"What did you say to Fiedler?" Matt challenged. Silva's imaginative smoke screens usually amused the Skipper, but he obviously wasn't in the mood. "The last time I spoke to him, he was still working to fix the plane. Said he owed us that much, but was sticking to his 'I'm just a pilot' line." Gravois had "generously" allowed the German to attempt repairs to the Ju-52 they'd arrived in, but he'd been confined to the airfield.

Silva looked genuinely surprised. Whatever he'd expected to be raked over the coals for, this wasn't it. "Not much," he replied, concentrating. "I went an' talked to him, sure. I was at the airfield to see if they'd fixed my zep." He'd captured a Grik airship with the help of some Shee-Ree and somehow flown it all the way to Grik City, barely arriving before practically crashing it. It had been mended to a degree, but the Grik hydrogen-manufacturing facilities had been damaged in the battle to take the city and hadn't been a priority for repair until now. "Kraut bastard seemed kinda lonesome, though, an' I guess he'd been by himself a lot at one of the airfields on Zanzibar too." He shrugged. "I know he's a Leaguer an' a Kraut to boot," he said, then added, "but I felt kinda' sorry for him, y'know? Still, we didn't go on about our favorite childhood toys er nothin'." He brightened. "I *did* tell him he oughta stick with us, an' told him we got lotsa dames. He kinda hinted they had plenty in the Med. Didn't ask where they got 'em—figgered that was the sort o' thing *you'd* ask." He scratched his bearded chin. "He did seem to appreciate me suggestin' he stay on, though. Got all quiet-like, and I almost thought he'd go for it. Who knows? Maybe he's got a girl." He glanced at Courtney, then back at Matt, and swatted at a bug. "But if I'd'a known you were gonna squeeze him, I'd'a done it."

Matt shook his head. "As it turned out, squeezing him wasn't necessary." He was talking to Dennis, but seemed to be explaining to Courtney as well. "He asked to see Major Jindal and me early this morning, saying Gravois and others like him heading up the League are nearly as crazy as Kurokawa. He claimed to be against that. He's still loyal to the German contingent within the League, though, and wouldn't spill anything that would hurt them directly, but he still gave us a hell of a lot." Matt pulled a folded page from his pocket and handed it to Silva. "Part of it was this map he drew of Kurokawa's layout. He claimed it was the same one he drew for Gravois when he flew observation missions around the island. It's Zanzibar," he said, "showing rough positions of everything from airfields to industrial facilities, to whatever shore batteries he saw from the air."

"Do you trust it?" Courtney asked, skeptically.

"I think so," Matt said.

"Indeed," Courtney said, brows furrowing. He knew intellectually that Fiedler's Germany wasn't the same his son had gone to fight in 'thirty-nine, but the man still remained a variety of Nazi, apparently. They needed to learn more about that. "Why?" he asked simply.

Matt sighed. "Why not? He knows we'll check it, and clearly hates Gravois. Why make stuff up? And he told me more, mostly about what the League—and Gravois—were up to out here in the first place. He preferred not to go into the other problems the League faces, or get too specific about how heavy an opponent it would be if we tangled with it head-on. He's not a traitor, to his own people at least, and feared too much information might kill Germans. Said that was too much to ask. But he does think they're done with us for now." He waved his hand. "We'll get into that later. We have plenty to occupy us now as it is."

"What's the gist of it?" Courtney pressed.

Matt frowned. "Only that the main reason the League's pulling out is that Gravois already accomplished his mission to do everything he could to promote the mutual annihilation of everybody in this region: us, the Grik, and Kurokawa." His frown deepened. "I don't intend to oblige him to the extent he hopes, obviously, but we're in a hell of a jam."

Silva cocked his head to the side. "The whuppin'. It looked convincing enough. Fiedler's idea?"

"Yeah," Matt confirmed, and exhaled, like he'd just set down a heavy load. "He's a tough guy, and knows he's been on the wrong side, I think. At least out here. He wasn't happy before, but the whole situation with *Savoie* pushed him over the edge. And he knows Gravois will figure he spilled *something*, about the sub if nothing else. So the beating was probably necessary to keep them from just dropping him over the side. Who knows? If he lives and keeps losing faith in the League, we might wind up with somebody on the inside someday." He looked at Silva and his expression changed to one of challenge. "We'd have to go with the operations we've already got in the works, no matter what. Both are risky as hell, and the raid on Zanzibar has to come first. If it flops, the assault on Sofesshk could go really bad, particularly if the Republic doesn't do its share." He stopped and looked at Courtney. "Which reminds me—I want you with Bekiaa. She's been on her own long enough, and we need a real, official representative with the Republic army. You'll go?"

Courtney's face flushed with protest, but resignedly he nodded.

"Good," Matt said, turning back to Silva. "Because we've got to win this war as fast as we can, *if* we can. So we can start getting ready for the next one."

"We'll get it done, Skipper. And we'll get Lady Sandra

back too," Silva pledged. "Then we'll make the damn League sorry they ever muddied up our war!" He started to turn away, but Courtney stopped him.

"One final thing, if you please." He glanced worriedly at Matt before returning his gaze to Silva. "Do you have it?" he asked simply.

Silva's good eye widened in confusion, then narrowed just a bit. "*Have it?*" he asked, and a gap-toothed grin began to spread. "Nah, Mr. Bradford. Ol' Doc Stevens got rid of it for me before we ever wound up here, God rest his skunky, Yankee soul." His grin faded at the sight of Matt and Courtney's intense expressions, and he realized they had no patience at all for his evasions that day.

Matt took a deep breath. "Do you or do you not have the thorn weapon Adar and Bernie cooked up and Commander Herring smuggled out from Baalkpan? Herring told me with his dying words that he'd given it to the 'perfect person,' undoubtedly someone he thought would use it without hesitation if the appropriate opportunity arose."

Silva's face lost all expression—he couldn't help it—even as he knew Matt and Courtney both would see it as a sure sign they'd caught him. Despite his tendency to evade indirect questions, he'd promised long ago he'd never *lie* to his Skipper again, and Matt had accordingly made his question very specific. An equally specific response was required.

"Captain Reddy," Silva said very formally, "I don't have Mr. Herring's kudzu bomb. Sir."

Strangely, Matt nodded with relief. "Kudzu bomb" was Bernie Sandison's term for a weaponized version of the thorns of a profoundly sinister plant found on Yap Island. Even dried and stored for long periods, the thorns could be resuscitated if exposed to blood, sending roots into the capillaries and veins of an infected host at an astonishing rate. The infection was extremely painful (as the newly promoted Captain Abel Cook of the 1st North Borno could attest), but also came with an insidiously sedative fever that made the host practically indifferent to the fact. Eventually, enough of the victim's circulatory system was compromised to cause death, and the kudzulike plant would emerge from the nourishing corpse to spread and bloom—and make more thorns. Realizing this, while he and others had been stranded on the island, Silva helped, under less than ideal circumstances, cut off one of Cook's fingers. Bradford was later horrified to learn of the weapon's development, fearing if the plant ever got a foothold beyond its native isle, entire continents might be rendered uninhabitable. For that reason, no one, except possibly Herring, had seriously contemplated using the weapon.

And it wasn't really a very *good* weapon. Its tactical applications were limited because it couldn't work fast enough to decide a battle, and even the strategic value was questionable. One couldn't easily occupy territory where it had been used, even if it killed anyone the thorns pierced relatively quickly. The thorns lying all over the ground or the plants sprouting from the enemy dead would be equally dangerous to friendly troops. It might deny territory to an enemy that knew about it, but then they could collect enough thorns to grow plants for their own use. The only practical value it seemed to have was as a revenge weapon and when the initial intent of their attack on Grik City had been a mere raid in force. Herring had probably meant to sow the thorns as they pulled out, killing Grik City and making capture unnecessary. Things hadn't worked out that way and now, of course, they *couldn't* turn it loose even if they abandoned the city back to the Grik, because it might spread all over the island, eventually threatening Maroons, Shee-Ree, and other "worthy prey" the Grik had allowed to live there for their amusement.

But Matt was relieved because, by using the term "kudzu bomb," Silva confirmed, at the very least, he knew *what* it was, and therefore probably knew *where* it was. Unfortunately, his half answer wouldn't cut it this time.

"Okay," Matt allowed, "you don't have physical possession. I can see that, unless you keep a handful of thorns in a snuff can in your pocket. But you're obviously Herring's perfect person and know where it is. The time's come to spill it. Maybe literally."

Silva's eye went wide. "Really? Damn!"

"Indeed," Courtney agreed with supreme reluctance. "Other than the four of us here"—he sent Lawrence a small, quick smile, knowing whatever Silva may have done with the thorns, Lawrence had almost certainly been in on it—"Bernie Sandison, and, apparently Ian Miles, Chairman Adar was the only one in theater to even know it exists. And Adar is in the hands of the enemy." He shook his head. "Though I'm morally certain he'd die before revealing anything detrimental to our cause, he may not be allowed that choice. Therefore, at the same time we may face a 'use it or lose it' scenario, we may also have identified a pair of valid applications." He frowned. "I do, of course, remain opposed to using the weapon for ecological reasons. But even I recognize the mitigating circumstances of the situation we're in."

"What applications do you have in mind?" Dennis asked, curious how Courtney—the same man who'd practically wept with fury when they scorched part of the giant, horrifying briar patch covering Tarakaan Island—could justify such a momentous change of heart.

"Only if we can't neutralize the enemy by other means," Courtney qualified insistently, "I can, perhaps, imagine a scenario for deploying the weapon at Zanzibar." He sent another worried glance at Matt. "And should our expeditionary force meet insurmountable difficulty in the campaign for Sofesshk, and *if* we devise a way of dispersing the thorns widely enough, we may contrive a strategic use for the weapon."

Matt and Silva both goggled at him. "We talked about Zanzibar, but now you're proposing we turn it loose on the continent of Africa!" Matt said.

"Yes, damn it, I am," Courtney snapped back. "It's a tropical plant and shouldn't thrive in the land of the Republic. Conversely, everything we know about Sofesshk indicates it's the very hub of Grik civilization." He took a long, shuddering breath, but his voice was firm when he resumed. "If it comes down to victory or defeat, the very survival of our civilization, our people, and all we hold dear, balanced against the ultimate triumph of the Grik—even if that means infesting a large percentage of a *continent* with that confounded weed . . ." He stopped and mopped his forehead, refusing to meet their gaze. "God help me, even I'm willing to make that trade, with the stakes so high."

"It's in the Cowflop," Silva said quietly. "In the basement—the lower levels where I went lookin' for that other poodledragon, like the one Isak killed with a heartburn pitch." He grinned. "It's in copper drums marked FISH MASH, or some such." He shrugged. "Hid as rations for Grik prisoners—like we ever thought we'd need such a thing, an' if it ain't been found and served up to 'em already."

"Very well," Matt said, still watching Courtney and pondering what he'd said. Finally, he looked back at Silva and took a deep breath. "One last thing. Did you mean what you said to Gravois about what you'd do to him if, well . . ."

Dennis snorted. "Hell, Skipper, when did I ever not do somethin' I said I would?" Everyone just stared at him, even Petey, and Dennis rolled his eye in exasperation. "I mean that I *promised* to."

Matt canted his head slightly and nodded. "Good enough. Of course, I mean to do it myself someday. But if something . . . happens, and I can't get it done, I'll be counting on you to make that bastard *pay*."

CHAPTER 3

Maa-ni-la
The Filpin Lands
October 23, 1944

Lord Meksnaak hurried down the long dock past the "pee-tee" factory, where motor torpedo boats were built, toward the inlet where the big Clippers flew in from all over the Alliance. His closest diplomatic advisor, a young 'Cat named Heraad-Naar, scurried to keep up. He was also accompanied by half a dozen guards in Saan-Kakja's livery; black and yellow kilts with gleaming gold-washed breastplates, platter-like helmets similar to those the Alliance had settled on as standard, and the traditional short, stabbing blades at their sides. Meksnaak had been forced to accept the guard for his protection by Saan-Kakja's direct order. One couldn't be too careful these days, it seemed, and Meksnaak wasn't just High Sky Priest of all the Filpin Lands anymore; he was acting governor of the Filpin "state" until Saan-Kakja returned. He rather hated that. Unlike Adar, he'd never been the High Sky Priest of multiple Homes—no one else had—but all the hundreds of islands constituting the Filpin Lands, large and small, were united as one Home, one "state," and he had authority over the various provincial Sky Priests. That allowed him to wear the somewhat unusual title of lord. He looked like a shorter, slighter, younger version of Adar as well, with silver-gray fur beneath the purple cape flecked with silver stars.

Personality-wise, he couldn't have been much more different from the captive former chairman of the Grand Alliance and the Union that grew within it. While Adar became more open and tolerant as the world around him changed, embracing the monumental transformations required to face their enemies and combine the diverse cultures within the alliance into a national union, Meksnaak seemed to grow even more dour, suspicious, and (inwardly at least) isolationist. And though his hatred for the war in general didn't necessarily set him apart, the intensity of his antipathy toward everything associated with it was more unusual. Above all, he hated what it had done to his people, society, and beloved city of Maa-ni-la. It seemed that all anyone talked about, worked for, or prayed to the Maker to help them with was the war. And so many had been lost! Not only in combat, but also industrial accidents, killed or maimed by things that never should've touched them. And they were *different* now. An innocence, a . . . *sweetness* he'd always treasured had been swept away.

They still played, but they'd grown utterly absorbed by an invasive game called baseball that, though he had to admit was entertaining, practically encouraged participants to deceive one another to gain advantages! That disturbed him on a visceral level. He wouldn't come out *against* baseball, but often preached against its subversive, corrosive effects on morality. And when he officiated at games around the city as an "um-pire"—something else he grudgingly enjoyed—he leveled many dark looks upon anyone who "stole" a base. The rules might allow it, but that didn't make it *right*. There were five large ballparks around the city now, and countless little ones wherever space could be found to cram one, and they were constantly in use by younglings or off-duty workers.

And that was another thing! Maa-ni-la had been *destroyed* by the war! Maybe it hadn't been attacked or damaged by their enemies, as had Aryaal, B'mbaado, Chill-Chaap, B'taava, even Baalkpan itself, but it had been just as surely ruined by the unimaginable scale of industrialization. The bay was always full of ships, many belching dark smoke that choked his lungs or burned his eyes. Factories were everywhere, spewing just as much bitter smoke or the foul stench of disagreeable chemicals. The new glues reeked horribly, and even the fresh-wood smell in the aircraft, boat, and gunstock factories disturbed his sensibilities because so many trees had fallen to make the things. Metal shops were the worst, he thought—foundries, mills, and hearths that spewed frightful chick-ashish sparks and gouts of smoky flame night and day. Machine shops stank of hot metal and oil, and were so dreadfully *loud*! The people (foreigners, most of them, and many not even Mi-Anakka) worked too hard, drank too much, debauched, and used foul language. Worse, they were so *rude* to one another!

And the Chiss-chins! Most humans from the Empire, and the few survivors of *Mizuki Maru* still in the city, openly espoused heretical doctrines similar to that misguided, if not otherwise wholly offensive, Sister Audry, who'd gone to the war in the East. Adar had battled that himself, Meksnaak knew, but had decided that the middle of a war wasn't the time to push divisive restrictions. Meksnaak reluctantly bowed to that wisdom. It took time for faith to find the truth, particularly if it came later in life and competed with set beliefs. But it was bewildering and disturbing that so many people—*Mi-Anakka*—had veered from their own enlightened faith to embrace the *new* doctrines! It was difficult to bear, on top of everything else, and he hated how intensely that affected him personally, how . . . betrayed he felt.

Because of all this, by extension, he didn't particularly like the Alliance his people had joined, and more especially the new Union. He even disliked the original Amer-i-caan destroyermen to a degree, who'd forced so much change upon them. Their arrogance grated and they were always in such a dreadful hurry. Not to mention, they—and all humans, to his sensibilities—were so very . . . unsightly. They had no tails, which he simply couldn't approve of, and their practically furless, naked bodies revolted him, as did their stunted, malformed ears and tiny, beady eyes. He knew they considered his people unexpressive—utterly ridiculous—and their bizarre face moving meant almost nothing to him. Many had learned to interpret it, just as some humans could observe deeper meaning in Mi-Anakka faces now. Meksnaak had forced himself to try. His suspicious nature left him no alternative but to learn the language called English extraordinarily well. But the face moving . . . The only straightforward things about it were that a grin was a grin and a frown was a frown. That was all he could tell with certainty. Sometimes he guessed right, but a guess was all it was.

And of their various allies, he disliked the Empire of the New Britain Isles the most because they constantly *wanted* things! Their prewar industry had been impressive; broader based in many ways than all the Mi-Anakka combined. But they'd been late to gear up to make all the disturbingly modern things like lex-tricksy, and even *flying machines, for the Maker's sake*, that this war required. They were finally starting to carry their weight, but the Filpin Lands had borne a disproportionate burden for them, and still did in Meksnaak's view. And the vast majority of Filpin Lands' troops and ships were still in the impossibly distant East, fighting Doms instead of Grik—which even Meksnaak recognized required opposition. And that was what he hated most of all: that his High Chief, Saan-Kakja—to whom he was utterly devoted—had chosen to fight *her* war against the Dominion, alongside Governor-Empress Rebecca Anne McDonald of the Empire of the New Britain Isles.

Only recently had Meksnaak figured out exactly why she'd gone in the first place, why she'd chosen East over West, and specifically why she left him, of all people, in charge. The last was easy; *because* he was so committed to her and hated her absence so much, he was the perfect person to be her steward in the Filpin Lands. The clan councils couldn't object, nor did they dare defy him as they might once have challenged her because of her age. For the same reason, her presence in the East was useful to the war effort there because he couldn't refuse anything she or the allies protecting her asked of him. It was terribly unfair, of course, to use his loyalty so, but at the same time, deep down, he couldn't help feeling a measure of pride in her for how well she was manipulating him. His high chief, still hardly more than a youngling in years, had grown up most agreeably equipped to lead her people—if she could only manage to survive.

He and his guards neared a group of men and 'Cats who'd obviously just arrived on the big, four-engine, weather-beaten Clipper. The flying boat's hot engines ticked as they cooled after the long flight from Respite Island, and lizardbirds swarmed and skirmished along the leading edges of its wings, feeding on dead insects. The visitors noticed his approach and smiled wearily. He could tell that much as well, he noted; the body language of fatigue was also universal. One of the men, a very large one, in Meksnaak's estimation, with the huge tuft of upper-lip fur so common among Imperials, but with only one arm, advanced toward him, holding out his hand.

Oh, by the Heavens! Meksnaak thought with dread. *He wants to do that thing they do . . . shake hands, I believe. How can I avoid touching him without seeming rude?* Saan-Kakja had been quite clear that she'd never tolerate rudeness toward their allies. He stopped several paces away and raised his own hand, palm out, in the sign of the empty hand. That almost-universal greeting among the people had diminished in use, probably because so many went about armed all the time. *Another fundamental cultural change,* he thought bitterly. *Unless perhaps it has only temporarily faded due to a sense of hypocrisy among those who refrain,* he reflected. The big man stopped as well, as did his companions, and all raised their hands in return. *Quite ridiculous,* Meksnaak grumped. *Most are obviously armed with* something. *A blade at least. Then again, there are my guards. Perhaps* I *am being hypocritical?*

"Lord Meksnaak!" the big one boomed. "I'm glad indeed ta' make yer acquaintance at last."

"*Sir* Sean Bates, prime factor and chief advisor to the Governor-Empress, Lord," Meksnaak's assistant whispered in his ear. "Your, ah, counterpart in their government, as he has been left to rule in her stead as well."

"I know who he is," Meksnaak hissed back. "They *said* he was coming!" He looked to the delegation and switched to English. "Welcome, Sir Sean, to Maa-ni-la. Welcome to you all," he said, managing to keep his tone cordial. "Sadly, you will never see my city as it once was, but I hope you enjoy your stay regardless. There remain a few distinctive diversions, and the martial activities at the Advanced Training Center on the far side of the bay must rival those at Baalkpan, though I've never seen the other. This is my foreign advisor, Heraad-Naar. I assume he is the one most of you are here to see."

Sean Bates grinned. "Not at all, though he's the one most'll end up with, no doubt. Yet our priority is ta thank ye, yer city, yer state, an' yer nation for yer commitment ta the cause." His grin turned to a knowing smile. "The Governor-Empress an' yer own dear Saan-Kakja herself both said ye were a prickly one, opposed to what we do. Yet that only makes me gratitude to ye personally all the more profound."

Meksnaak was taken aback, both by the boldness of the statement and the apparent sincerity of the compliment. "Indeed," he said, with a creeping trace of genuine warmth. "But since we're being so forthright, so quickly, let me ask the question foremost in my mind: Why else are you here, aside from a desire to extend your gratitude? In short, what do you want now?"

Sean grinned broadly again. "Can we nae at least refresh ourselves an' have a drink, er even a wee morsel, before we get down ta business?"

Meksnaak actually barked a spontaneous laugh, completely astonishing everyone, particularly himself. He'd heard Bates was an engaging man, but he'd never instinctively *liked* any human on sight. He was uncomfortably suspicious that might be the case in this instance. He quickly controlled himself, however, and gestured toward the city, and the great hall at its heart. "Of course," he said, a genuine smile touching the lips still tight across his teeth. "Forgive me. And to think I was once the one most given to promoting delay when it comes to getting to the point!"

* * *

If Maa-ni-la had been destroyed, in Meksnaak's estimation, a theme he harped on as they wove their way through busy workers and mooing paalkas pulling heavy carts all the way through the factory districts, at least the Great Hall had been preserved. For one thing, it hadn't been burned to the ground around the sacred Galla tree it encompassed as the one at Baalkpan had. And apparently, all the new offices required by the burgeoning industrial and military power of the state had been erected elsewhere and not allowed to intrude. Sean Bates (as the fugitive Sean O'Casey) had seen the Great Hall of Baalkpan in all its glory, and this one gave him a powerful sense of déjà vu. The tree, barely two hundred feet tall, was not quite as large, but, then, Maa-ni-la was a younger city. And the hall itself, massive and high, with a broad porch wrapping completely around, might've been transported directly from that older city and earlier time. And it brought back other memories. True, he'd been a fugitive of sorts from the Honorable New Britain Company and forces striving to supplant the throne, and a great battle had been looming that no one seriously thought they'd survive, but it had been a simpler time as well. He'd been just Sean O'Casey, a one-armed but quite capable protector of then Princess Rebecca, before she'd endured all the torment to come and accepted the mantle of Governor-Empress of a nation at war. He and Meksnaak were sitting on comfortable cushions on the west side of the hall, watching the sun descend toward the distant isle of Corregidor across the bay. Both drank nectar from large tankards, though Bates had flavored his with rum from a flask in his weskit pocket. Meksnaak had reverted to his earlier reserve to a degree, as they waited for a meal to be brought to them. Sean sighed deeply.

"I understand yer bitterness far better than ye may comprehend," he said at length, and Meksnaak glared at him, blinking astonished denial. "Aye," Sean assured. "This is me first time here, o' course, though Her Highness spent a good while among yer folk, an' described the city—and you—quite well. An' ye fergit I lived in Baalkpan before it became like Maa-ni-la now is, so I know well what's been lost." He took a long sip of nectar while Meksnaak absorbed that. "The beauty of the New Britain Isles has been spoiled just as surely in many ways, by the same rapid industrialization. Its major isles, New Britain, New Ireland, an' New Scotland—all part of what Captain Reddy called the Hawayee where he came from—have all been torn by war as well. Both against the bloody Doms an' ourselves. Count yerself fortunate that, from that at least, Maa-ni-la's been spared."

Meksnaak rubbed his chin, blinking thoughtfully. "I knew all that," he confessed, "but had not much cared, to be honest." He waved a hand. "The Grik are terrible and must be stopped. I know that now. Even before we joined the Alliance, the city was flooded with refugees. A sure sign that war snapped at their tails. I finally agreed we should aid Baalkpan, lest we stand alone in the path of that scourge." He looked intently at Bates. "But refugees also came from the East, to escape *your* nation," he emphasized, referring to the women fleeing the indentured servitude that had prevailed. "And war pushed them as well. So I've reluctantly concluded that your fight is one we cannot ignore either, Sir Sean. It is just . . . much harder to fear a threat as unimaginably distant as the Dominion—on the very bottom of the world!—or to summon the same urgency to confront it in my heart." He snorted. "Particularly since we never believed it possible to even *stand* only as far to the east as your islands lie. I still find that a wonder. How can 'down' change directions?" He shook his head. "Courtney Braad-furd once tried to explain, but it seems so unnatural!"

"I understand how ye feel. Ye should travel. I believe the notion grows easier to accept with experience. But the war—our war against the Dominion, as ye've referred to it—has only remained distant because we've kept it so," Bates reminded gently.

"That is what my dear Saan-Kakja insists," Meksnaak agreed, then stiffened on his cushions. In that moment he reminded Sean more of Adar than ever before. "But I *cannot* travel. I wonder that you can. We are both in much the same boat, as you say."

"I cannae follow my Governor-Empress ta war, as I long ta do," Sean agreed, "but in her stead, I can an' must keep the alliance strong. Comin' here ta meet ye at last is part o' that, as I see it."

"I have no desire to see the war my high chief rushed to join." Meksnaak almost shuddered. "But my soul understands why she went. Her people are in it, so she must be with them, sharing their perils and hardships. It is one of the things that will make her a *great* high chief—if she lives."

"Me Governor-Empress feels the same, no doubt, an' if we win, her line an' rule'll never be challenged again. If *she* survives," he added grimly, echoing Meksnaak's sentiment. His gaze had drifted out to sea as he spoke, but now turned back to the Lemurian. "Sure," he said, "I want things, above an' beyond what ye've already gifted: more of the new gasoline engines ye use in yer torpedo boats, to start. We havenae made 'em yet, an' there may be weapons o' mutual interest they'll let us build. An' more ammunition for the machine guns we're startin' ta build on yer patterns. We're makin' some, but we're just now gettin' production of fifty-eighty ammunition for Allin-Silvas an' forty-fives for the Blitzers runnin' smooth. We havenae enough thirty caliber ta even test the guns we make as yet. I need a *thousand* things, Lord Meksnaak, an' have a lengthy list. But most of all, with us both 'in the same boat,' left behind to fight the war at home against sarpent-tongued skuggiks, wi' interest for naught but themselves . . ." He finished his nectar and frowned. "An' with the lasses we care about most in all the wide world beyond our protection, it just seemed ta me that ye an' I have far too much in common not to be great friends."

CHAPTER 4

Mahe Island
***Aboard USS* Tarakaan Island**

Three utterly massive ships were securely moored in the center of the picturesque bay on the northeast side of Mahe Island. One was USNRS *Salissa* (CV-1), the very first aircraft carrier in the Allied arsenal. Rebuilt from one of the great, thousand-foot-long seagoing Homes after her near destruction in the Battle of Baalkpan, she could carry up to eighty aircraft and had been the backbone of Allied naval aviation in the West. Her high chief and the ranking naval officer at Mahe was Ahd-mi-raal Keje-Fris-Ar, a bearlike Lemurian with a dark, silver-shot, rust-colored pelt. He was also Matt Reddy's dearest Lemurian friend.

Anchored beside her was the nearly as massive USS *Sular*, a protected troopship rebuilt from a captured Grik ironclad battleship, or BB. She didn't look much different than she had under her previous owners, except she had only two funnels now, all that was required by her better boilers and engines. And her armored, angled sides, once pierced for many huge muzzle-loading smoothbores, were now covered by a hundred stacked, gasoline engine–powered landing dories. Four DP 4″-50s squatted in tubs at the narrow peak of her casemate, as did several protected machine gun nests.

Between *Sular* and the busy docks, still under hasty construction, lay the SPD (self-propelled dry dock) USS *Tarakaan Island*. Not as large as *Big Sal*, she was bigger than *Sular,* even longer and displacing as much as a fleet carrier. And she represented still greater technical ingenuity. At a glance, from abeam, she most resembled a Great Lakes ore carrier, which some of *Walker*'s human crew might've remembered, but any similarity ended there. She was, essentially, an 820-foot-by-150-foot wooden hull built around a massive 100-foot-by-650-foot repair bay large enough to accommodate anything in the Allied inventory—except a fleet carrier, or seagoing Home. And *Big Sal* herself, of course. *Tarakaan Island* and her sisters had been *meant* to handle fleet carriers, but they wound up just a tad too big. The *next* class of Allied flattop, and everything else under construction in Baalkpan, Maa-ni-la, and the Empire of the New Britain Isles, should fit just fine.

Lemurian shipbuilding techniques, particularly considering they'd always relied almost entirely on wood, had been a source of astonishment and respect. Their system of diagonal, cross-laminated planks laid on heavy, lattice-like frames most closely resembling those of a monstrous Wellington bomber made their hulls incredibly strong and allowed them to build on an otherwise impossible scale. As the Alliance eased into the construction of iron-hulled ships, Lemurian structural designs had been evolving as well, combining lessons learned from the strengths and weaknesses of both materials into plans for hulls that were, though admittedly complex, probably stronger than anything of similar displacement ever to cross over from another world. *Tarakaan Island* was one of only three of her kind likely to be built, however, and after the loss of *Respite Island*, one of two in existence. There'd be more SPDs, made of iron and built along the same basic lines and dimensions, but they'd be lighter, faster, and probably go together quicker.

Two tall funnels vented exhaust from four boilers in her hull on each side of the bay, and were surrounded by a forest of heavy, steam-powered cranes. The boilers themselves—a total of eight—were enclosed in narrow spaces on either beam and fed two powerful (but extremely cramped) triple expansion engines patterned after the one in USS *Santa Catalina*. That made her fast enough to keep up with a carrier, and her two screws and rudders gave her the agility, despite her size, to turn with the battlegroups. She wasn't helpless either, having been armed with five of the new DP 4″-50 guns—one forward, and two on each side around her funnels. With the introduction of copies of the venerable M-1917 light machine gun, she was heavily festooned with those as well—particularly in light of the new aerial threat. And *Tarakaan Island*—and the other ships in the anchorage—currently had even more protection than usual, with nine steam frigates (DDs) clustered around, numerous armed auxiliaries, the new USS *James Ellis* steaming back and forth beyond the mouth of the bay, and a constant air patrol probing outward from the island.

Unlike *Big Sal* and *Sular*, however, which appeared to be resting from their labors, gathering strength, there was tremendous, almost feverish activity aboard *Tarakaan Island*. For within her repair bay, slowly settling on the blocks that would support her tired, battered hull when all the water was pumped from the ballast tanks, was Matt Reddy's flagship of the entire naval effort to destroy the Grik—and Hisashi Kurokawa: USS *Walker*, DD-163.

Walker's one DP 4″-50 aft added to their mutual protection, as did her own machine guns, and they remained fully manned. Despite there being little threat from Grik airships this far from Madagascar, they were in waters Kurokawa *could* reach with his more formidable air power if he chose to risk his final carrier. They had little choice but to gather their strength and make repairs there, however. Chances were Kurokawa wouldn't risk it, and with Grik City menaced by mobs of zeppelins, Mahe was the best place to assemble all the troops, equipment, aircraft, and ships that had staggered through the gauntlet. It already had an airstrip of sorts, with more under construction on surrounding islands at the direction of Colonel Ben Mallory, and though they didn't have as many planes as they'd hoped to have, quite a few had gathered there—

almost certainly enough to stop one carrier. And Kurokawa's torpedo planes couldn't sink Mahe. *Savoie* was another matter. Stopping her with what they had might prove problematic once her new crew learned how to operate her. But that should take some time. Enough to put *Walker* back to rights again? They'd have to see.

Commander Brad "Spanky" McFarlane spat a long stream of yellowish Aryaalan tobacco juice into the swirling water of the repair bay and watched it splatter and surge aft in a string of pirouetting bubbles. He was short and wiry, with reddish blond hair and beard, but his personality was larger than his physique. He knew that, and carefully cultivated the impression, so he was particularly glad to have eliminated the one sign of weakness undermining his physical authority: the crutch he'd leaned on since the Battle of Grik City Bay had been tossed in *Walker*'s feeble wake as she steamed here almost a week before.

"Agh," he grunted grimly, pointing at rainbow hues beginning to appear, streaking *Walker*'s sides as more of her hull was exposed. "That ain't good."

Leaning on the rail around him, feeling the vibration of mighty pumps shake the ship, were most of the heavyweights of First Fleet and the Allied Expeditionary Force. Keje was to his left, blinking sympathetically to Spanky's observation, fully aware of what he was referring to. To Spanky's right was the leathery-tan, dark-haired General of the Army and Marines, Pete Alden. He'd risen to his exalted rank from a wounded Marine sergeant aboard USS *Houston*, who'd been in a hospital in Surabaya and missed his ship's final sortie against the Japanese. Limping and bleeding, he'd hitched a ride on *Walker* to escape . . . here. Beyond him was Colonel Ben Mallory, who, as a second lieutenant in the United States Army Air Corps, had also escaped Surabaya after USS *Langley*, loaded with the P-40 fighters he was trained to fly, was hammered down by that old enemy as well. He commanded all the army and naval air forces of the Alliance—which, ironically, included a rapidly diminishing number of P-40Es they'd discovered aboard *Santa Catalina* when they found her half-sunk in a swamp near Tjilatjap (Chill-Chaap). Both men were nearly as concerned about *Walker*'s condition as Spanky, and had their own reasons for considering her their savior.

Perhaps even more reverential toward her for that reason, even more than Spanky, was the seasoned Lemurian standing to Keje's left. Somewhat past middle age, his pelt gone almost entirely gray, was the commander of I Corps, General Muln-Rolak. One of the few true prewar warrior 'Cat commanders in the Alliance, he bore many scars on his body and soul. He'd been lord protector of Aryaal before the Grik came and still held that title in Aryaal as well as its traditional rival, the island of B'mbaado. The monarch over both city-states, once antagonists and now politically united, was his adored queen, Safir Maraan. As military commanders, however, they were equal, and Safir usually deferred to him due to his age, wisdom, and, frankly, more thoughtful nature.

"It's certainly a pretty color," Rolak observed in his usual urbane tone, pitching his voice above the thunder of pumps and rushing water. "What does it mean?"

"It means she's leakin' like a sieve," Spanky ground out. "That's fuel oil from the bunkers lining her hull. I expected that," he confessed, "based on how much saltwater's been gettin' in the fuel, but it still pisses me off to see so damn much of it. Shit, half the ship looks like a goddamn rusty trout."

"You think it's the rivets again?" Alden asked. They'd had trouble with them before.

"Who knows?" Spanky spat, disgusted, squinting. "Maybe not. She's taken a lot of hits an' near misses since her last overhaul. Not to mention a goddamn *grounding*. We'll just have to see. It *looks* like most of the seepage is in the vicinity of roundshot dents," he added hopefully.

"She's got a lot of those," Ben pointed out.

"Yeah. An' if just three or four had been naval rifle shells of the same diameter instead of shitty Grik cannonballs—even if they didn't explode—she'd already be rustin' on the bottom somewhere."

"You *patched* many more holes than that, some even larger, if I recall," Keje reminded in his gruff voice.

"Sure," Spanky agreed. "But her bones were stronger

then. It's gettin' harder to find sound studs to nail to, if you know what I mean."

Alden waved around at the huge ship and the swarm of Lemurians, already starting with their cranes now that *Walker* was firmly resting on her blocks. A number of things had been prepared for removal as soon as she entered *Tarakaan Island*'s bay, and the mangled number-two torpedo mount was already swaying up in the air as they watched. "They'll fix her," he consoled. "Look at *James Ellis* out there past the reef," he added, then pointed behind them at the low, sleek, distant shape, made fuzzy by the humid, hazy air. "They built her from *scratch*!"

"Yeah, they did. An' she's a dandy—aside from all the nigglin' little issues she has. Hell, we oughta put *her* in dry dock."

Rolak regarded him, blinking disdain. "You *are* determined to be unhappy today, aren't you, Co-maander Mc-Faar-lane?"

"Damn straight."

"Why?" Ben asked, honestly surprised. "You oughta be glad! The old girl's finally getting some real work done."

"Yeah," Spanky agreed. "A lot of it too. New torpedo tubes, boiler an' condenser overhauls, better searchlights than those first ones we made. *Finally* some decent-quality gear oil. They even brought out thick, bullet-slowin' mattress pads that can be brought up an' hooked on the stanchions so the guys'll have better protection than just those stupid wooden rafts, if we ever have to repel boarders again. There's better glass for the pilothouse windows that doesn't look like you're starin' through the bottom of a Coke bottle, lightbulbs, electric fans, all the latest luxuries, and even new liners for her main battery. The Skipper declined the new DP mounts for numbers one through three." He shrugged. "I get that. They're still a little twitchy an' tend to shoot loose, an' he wants *Walker* to keep bein' our sniper in surface actions. Figures, in addition to extra machine guns to keep planes away, she can still squirm out from under Jap-Grik bombs and torpedoes." He glowered. "But that didn't work so good for *Geran-Eras*."

"Did not *Geran-Eras* have Dee-Pee mounts?" Keje asked.

Spanky glanced at the sky. "Sure. An' they didn't save her either. Goddamn *planes*!"

Keje looked at the others. "I do not believe Mr. McFaarlane is unhappy about the overhaul, only the location. And that his ship is, as you say, a sitting duck just now."

Ben looked at him. "It's gonna to be okay, Spanky. Look, I've got a CAP over the island and there's picket ships in all directions with TBS sets. Kurokawa's *not* sneakin' up on us!"

"Maybe not in daylight," Spanky sneered at Ben. "An' that's what your damn MacArthur said, right before the Japs clobbered all our air in the Philippines and bombed the shit outa Cavite!" Spanky snapped his fingers. "*That's* for your damn air cover. We never had any before, and I'll never trust it."

Ben rolled his eyes and leaned on the rail, looking down. The sea had receded to the point that he could see the heavy timbers at the bottom of the repair bay beneath the shallow water. There were other things too: quick, wiggling shapes, darting over and around the great blocks supporting the old destroyer. To his surprise, he noticed a group of naked 'Cats armed with fishing spears advancing in a skirmish line from aft, against the flow of calf-deep water. They stabbed down and heaved up as they went, pitching skewered fish—and other things—into a long, wide tub that a pair of Lemurians pushed before them, chittering happily (or in occasional alarm) at what landed snapping and flopping so close by. And there, marching grimly behind, his legs protected by heavy leather waders he'd probably stitched himself, was the obese form of *Walker*'s irascible cook, Earl Lanier. He was brandishing his own spear and urging the party into the fray like some great, fat, sodden general of the deep.

"Swell," Spanky growled. "Now King Neptune himself an' all his pollywogs're here, to add to my misery."

The traditional "crossing the line" ceremonies had languished on this world, not because Lemurians were averse to them or amusing celebrations in general, but because most of *Walker*'s earliest 'Cat volunteers were seafarers themselves and, due to proximity, had crossed the equator countless times without taking notice of the unknown fact.

Besides, they'd spent so much time *on* the equator, there was nothing particularly special about it. Scuttlebutt was that Greg Garrett allowed King Neptune aboard when *Donaghey* rounded the Cape of Africa. Maybe the tradition would catch on to mark the passage into unknown seas?

"Cheer up, Spanky," Alden urged. "It'll be fine." He waved at Lanier. "And besides, maybe somethin'll *get* him this time."

Something almost did. In a sudden flurry of frothing motion, a shape about seven feet long, with a segmented shell, which had apparently crouched in the shadow of the ship, darted out from between a pair of blocks and right at Earl Lanier. Whatever it was—a roughly oval-shaped centipede with *way* too many legs and slashing mandibles sprang to mind—was dark, almost blue-black, and amazingly fast. Earl instinctively flung his spear, which bounced harmlessly off the thick carapace, and then turned to flee. He splashed frantically away for perhaps three steps before the thing was on him. With a high-pitched wail, Earl went down and the . . . bug—crustacean?—scrambled atop the flailing, sputtering mound of flesh and kept on going.

"Hold you fire!" a female Lemurian PO bellowed nearby at a machine-gun crew that spun its weapon around and was trying to line up on the galloping creature. "You shoot up you *own ship*, you stupid shits?" she demanded. Finally, the surging thing disappeared aft, into the deep, and Earl Lanier slowly stood. Blood stained his wet T-shirt, probably where the sharp, uncounted legs had pierced his back, but he didn't look seriously injured. Hesitantly, relieved Lemurian laughter began. Soon it became a high-pitched roar, joined by the throb of stamping feet. Shaking his head, Earl picked up his soggy hat and plopped it on his head, then retrieved his spear. Without a word to his fishing party (also laughing helplessly), he urged them insistently on and they resumed the hunt.

"Gotta give the dumb-ass credit," Alden grudged, still chuckling himself. Lanier had always been obsessed with catching—and eating—fish, and sought any opportunity to harvest his favorite food. It didn't matter that many ships in the fleet lowered fishing nets almost daily and there was never a shortage. He wanted to catch his own. "He definitely stays focused on *his* priorities."

"Somethin'll get him one of these days," Spanky predicted optimistically around a smile that had involuntarily formed.

Within minutes, Earl's party completed its adventure and dragged the tub to a hoist that lifted it from the basin. Earl and his fish warriors quickly followed and the entertainment was at an end. At no time had the cranes stopped working.

"*Saanty Caat* and *Arracca* and her battlegroup should be here tomorrow," Keje stated, getting back to business. "Have you prepared a place to put Chack's Brigade?"

"Yes," Rolak said, answering for Alden. "With difficulty," he confessed wryly. "Maa-he is not large, and is excessively, ah, hilly. In addition to the space required for the near forty-six thousand troops of First and Third Corps, not to mention the fit survivors of the ships we lost, even now training as infantry, few flat places remain. How we will manage when the First North Borno arrives, I cannot say."

Keje huffed. "We will deal with that when the time comes. They are still weeks away. The bulk of the army may even have sailed by the time they arrive." He blinked discontentedly.

"What's the matter, Admiral?" Alden asked.

Keje sighed. "Only, along with my concern over our friends in Kuro-kaa-wa's hands, I remain not skeptical, but . . . apprehensive, regarding *Arracca*'s and *Saanty Caat*'s initial role in the campaign against Sofesshk." He was clearly thinking about Tassanna-Ay-Arracca, the other Home-turned-carrier's high chief, slated to be commodore of that task force. Everyone knew a relationship was blooming between Keje and Tassanna, despite their age difference. Things like that mattered little to Lemurians. But risk to Tassanna alone wouldn't have made Keje express concern, either. "They will be very exposed," he continued. "Almost . . . bait."

"Maybe a little," Alden agreed somberly. "But if anybody can take care of themselves, it's Tassanna—and Russ Chappelle in *Santy Cat*. They *will* draw attention while they're hitting Sofesshk with *Arracca*'s planes, but that'll keep Esshk's eyes off the South, where the Republic's about ready to kick off. We *need* that," he said simply. "Besides, they'll also be keeping more Grik forces from landing in South Madagascar. There may already be more than Miles and his army of Shee-Ree and Maroons, or the troops we'll leave at Grik City, can handle."

"But will the Republic truly strike?" Keje asked gloomily. "We place all our hopes on an ally that has proven . . . less than reli-aable."

The Republic's representative, Doocy Meek, was at Mahe, but wasn't with them. He was aboard *Big Sal*, for his daily wireless consultations with his government.

Pete Alden spread his hands. "Doocy says so. We have to trust him. And taken with Bekiaa's word, I do."

Keje looked unconvinced.

"Don't worry," Ben said. "When the Republic crashes into the Grik's belly, it'll yank their eyes right off *Arracca*—and that's when Pete'll hammer 'em with three full corps." He considered. "Or vice versa, depending on the timing. Either way could work, and at least this plan has some flexibility built in."

"I hope so," Keje said. "My experience with plaans is that they rarely proceed as intended."

"Plans're for shit," Spanky agreed grimly, spitting at the remaining inches of water below. "And I'll tell you now, we maybe ain't planned enough time to refit *Walker*, or do a hundred other things." He pointed. Now that she rested high and dry on her blocks, far more oily water than could be accounted for continued to pour from her hull. "Open seams in her bottom, prob'ly from the grounding," he said, then looked at Keje. "But I want in on the plan to get our people back from Kurokawa—an' kill his sorry ass. Has anybody given that little thing any thought?"

"You can *aask* that?" Keje snapped, blinking angrily.

It was Ben's turn to frown, nodding at Keje. "The Skipper, Admiral Keje, and Chack are cooking something up. But we have to make sure about the layout. That League Kraut drew the Skipper a rough map of the harbor, airfields, and industrial facilities, but he didn't know much about what defenses they have. Apparently, none of his bunch had complete access to the place, and him less than the rest. But he saw a lot from the air, despite Kurokawa's attempts to hide as much as he could, and was able to infer a lot based on what was obvious. He was certain about the harbor, the location of three airfields, and their main airplane-engine assembly plant, but a lot of the rest is educated guesswork. Still better than nothing—assuming he's on the level," Ben qualified in a cautionary tone. "Anyway, we're sending the P-Forty floatplane up to have a look. It'll rendezvous and refuel with AVDs we've had cruising between here and Zanzibar ever since Gravois told us where the Jap-Griks are. The plane'll cross the enemy coastline just at dawn, catch the Jap-Griks by surprise as the sun rises, get a good close look before they react, and get the hell out."

"Risky," Spanky objected. "Not only for the plane an' pilot, but it'll ring the bell that we know where they are."

Alden nodded. "Yeah, but just like we're still piecing together what the AEF'll run into at Sofesshk, knowing where Kurokawa is won't do Captain Reddy much good if he doesn't know what the bastard's got waiting for him"—he looked at Spanky—"and *you*. And *Walker* an' *Big Sal* . . . Not to mention Chack's Brigade." He shook his head and grimaced at Keje. "Sorry. Still not happy about splitting our forces so far apart."

"I share your concern," Keje agreed. "But our enemies are in two places. We cannot allow them to combine. It could be dis-aastrous if Kuro-kaa-wa moved *Saavoie* and the rest of his fleet to support General Esshk. My prefer-aance would be to destroy Kurokawa first, of course, and then move against Sofesshk, all together. But that would leave General Esshk free to make his move against Mada-gaas-gar . . . or, worse, respond with overwhelming force to the Republic's attack in the South, while we are *all* engaged at Zanzibar. Believe me, Cap-i-taan Reddy and I have agonized over this straa-ti-gee, and see no other option."

Alden frowned, but nodded. "Okay," he said, looking at Ben. "But why the P-Forty? Last I heard, you were getting kinda low on those, and we might need every one you have."

"We can't use a Fleashooter," Ben replied. "Their range is too short and they can't land in the water to refuel. A Nancy would be easy meat for those Jap-Grik fighters. That leaves the P-Forty. Even with those dopey Jap floats stuck on it, it should be able to handle anything it runs into, or just run the hell away." He glanced a little resentfully at Keje. "I'd rather fly the mission myself, of course, but the brass turned me down."

"Do not be downcast, Col-nol Maal-lory," Keje said with supreme indifference to the oblique complaint. "The braass is blessed to have three *Salissa* pilots checked out in that specific craaft, so there's no reason for you, or any member of your Third Pursuit Squadron, to make the flight, regardless how many hours they have in Pee-Forties. None of your other pilots have ever taken off or landed on the sea." He blinked amusement. "And due to the solitary nature of the flight, I refused Cap-i-taan Jis-Tikkar's request as well. If I'm not prepared to risk *Salissa*'s Commander of Flight Operations on such a risky scout, I certainly cannot allow you, his superior, to go." Keje grinned. "It might wound Tikker's . . . fragile sense of self-value."

Ben snorted and the others laughed. Tikker was the first Lemurian Ben ever taught to fly, and he'd embraced—and ably earned—a hotshot temperament extremely difficult to bruise. Even Spanky laughed at the absurdity of Keje's defense . . . until his eye caught another group moving purposefully toward them. He groaned aloud.

The approaching delegation was led by Lieutenant Tab-At "Tabby," *Walker*'s gray-furred Lemurian engineering officer. He loved Tabby like a daughter, but she still cherished a different—and unnatural, in his rationally considered view—affection for him, which could be difficult to deflect. At the moment, however, she was blinking consternation mixed with alarm. Marching behind her was the former fireman and now chief engineer Isak Reuben. Isak and his half brother, Gilbert, were the "original Mice," once so insularly obsessed with *Walker*'s boilers that they almost never left their firerooms. This behavior left them singularly pallid, in an Asiatic Fleet that produced rather spectacular tans, and universally resented by their division. They got out more these days, making impressive contributions to the cause. First, they'd drawn on their pre-navy experience as wildcatters to design the rigs that ultimately produced the one material surplus the Alliance enjoyed—oil—to fuel the war effort. And while Gilbert was now in the East with Second Fleet, "King Snipe" and de facto engineering officer in *Maaka-Kakja*, Isak had won notoriety as the slayer of the Grik Celestial Mother—and an unlikely power hitter, considering his short, wiry frame, on *Walker*'s baseball team. He wasn't blinking as he approached, but his face was red with fury as he pounded the deck with an eight-foot section of shiny, silver-blue tubing with every step. Trotting behind the pair, eyes blinking alarm, were four 'Cats in colorful civilian kilts.

"Ah, better excuse me. This looks like trouble. Probably have to stomp out a mutiny or somethin'."

"Of course, Co-maander Spaan-ky," Keje replied, his gruff voice amused. The others nodded, also expecting something interesting.

Spanky strode to meet the interruption, limping only slightly, and stopped in front of Tabby, hands on his hips. "So, what's the deal?" he demanded. "Can't you see I'm busy?" In response, Isak smacked the deck with the tube again, leaving a round, waxy imprint on the gray-painted wood. On a ship like *Tarakaan Island* there was no point keeping the decks holy-stoned bright, like on the steam frigate DDs, and everything on her had been heavily painted the same "dazzle" scheme as *Santa Catalina*. That would likely become the new standard, Spanky reflected. It didn't conceal ships from the air as well as a dark gray or blue might, but foamy wakes pointed directly at ships underway, so such camouflage was questionable, at any rate. On the other hand, contrasting geometric shapes of different gray shades definitely made it harder to judge the silhouette and range of a surface target from a distance.

"This *here's* the damn deal," Isak announced, his reedy voice indignant as he thumped the deck once more. Tabby's division had torn down the shattered number three boiler as soon as it cooled. They couldn't fix it, so they might as well. And they'd started on number two as soon as *Walker* steamed for Mahe. It had been secured before it could also fail, but they'd been keeping it as a spare. Number four had been their sole remaining "healthy" boiler. While disassembling the boilers and condensers, they'd discovered a number of things, most significant being the quality—or lack thereof—of some of the tubes *Walker* received as replacements during previous overhauls. Tubes that were in every boiler of every steamer built in Baalkpan and Maa-ni-la . . . Captain Reddy had fired off warnings via wireless, as well as a demand that the tubes be improved. Alan Letts replied that the problem had already come to his attention and been addressed. To make sure *Tarakaan Island* had the latest tubes, four brand-new PB-5D Clipper flying boats, already loaded with everything from ammunition to the last reserves of parts for Ben Mallory's remaining P-40s, had been hastily stuffed with as many standard-length boiler tubes as they could carry. The result had been a grueling 5,400-mile, 40-hour (counting refueling stops) flight from Baalkpan via Sinaa-pore, Andamaan, Madraas, and La-laanti, all the way to Mahe. It had been one of the longest flights Clippers ever made, and was a testament to their design and durability that all arrived without mishap.

Isak didn't care about that, or that Walt "Jumbo" Fisher's Pat-Squad 22 had just been increased from three planes, with one down for repairs, to seven. What he cared about, when he and Tabby scrambled aboard one of the planes and stripped the oilcloth wrappings off several tubes with the anticipation of children under a Christmas tree, was what brought this diverse assembly to Spanky immediately thereafter. Spanky sighed. "And what's the matter with 'this' here?" he demanded, nodding at the tube. It was coated with a water-soluble protectant of some kind of wax, cut with gri-kakka oil, by the smell. Isak thumped the deck once more for emphasis and the tube slipped from his grasp to clatter on the deck, nearly rolling into the repair basin below. A civilian 'Cat with yellow-and-orange fur and a dark brown–and-red plaid kilt lunged to save it. With some fumbling, he held it up, casting a series of hateful blinks at Isak, then turned to Spanky.

"Is nutt-een wong wit it!" he proclaimed.

"And you are?"

"Laap-Zol-Jeks, Chief Ma-sheenits, Baalkpan Boiler an Ma-sheenry Works." The Lemurian pronounced his title very carefully. "I an' my mates"—Laap gestured at the others—"flyed all de lon'-ass way wit' d'ese fine toobs to make sure dey's in-staalled right."

Isak's eyes bulged, and Tabby grabbed him before he could jump on the 'Cat like a grasshopper. "You're gonna tell *me* how to install yer shitty tubes?" he snarled. "Why, I oughta install one right up yer fuzzy ass!"

"Shut it, Isak!" Spanky snapped. "*Walker* may not have a brig, but *Tarakaan Island* does. So help me, I'll throw you in it for the rest of the war. Control your division, Lieutenant," he told Tabby.

"I just did," she said, shoving Isak behind her, where he sputtered and glared flashing knives at the three other 'Cats.

"So what's wrong with the new tubes?"

"They're just like the last ones!" Tabby snatched the offending object from Laap, nearly dropping it herself, and held it up to Spanky. "See? The number painted on it's the same as the others. The color's the same"—she pointed it at the late-morning sun for him to peer down its length—"an' there's the same fat-aass *seam* runnin' the length o' this so-called seamless tubin'! It's no daamn different at all."

"*Is* diff'rent!" Laap insisted. "We maybe had . . . ish-yoos wit' some few toobs."

"Issues!" Isak hooted. "Why, the only tubes worth a shit left in *Walker*'s boilers're what's left of the ones she came with new. An' they been steamin' hard for *twenty-five years*!"

"*Shut uuuup*!" Spanky ground out once more, looking at Laap. "But he's right." He glanced at Tabby, then leveled his gaze on the other Lemurian. "Now, I know there's always a visible seam in unreamed tubing; it's the *nature* of the seam that makes it"—he shrugged—"well, seamless. But I taught the class on how to make the stuff, and it was going fine . . . for a while. More important, I had Tabby's job before she did, so I'm skeptical too." Deliberately, he paused long enough to add fresh tobacco from a pouch to the wad in his cheek. "And when it comes down to it," he continued, "*I'm* the one you gotta convince more than anybody." He pointed at *Walker*. "Captain Reddy's gonna steam that ship in harm's way again on *my* say-so, and if the new tubes *ain't* fine and cost a single life, I'll make you sorry you ever saw a piece of steel with a hole in it. Am I clear?"

Spanky never raised his voice, but it radiated such menacing conviction that Laap gulped and his companions took an uneasy step back. "Der *was* ish-yoos," Laap confessed again. "An' we din't know why. *All* naval boilers is de same now, all Yaa-row types, like *Waa-kur*'s. Only some is more aa-fficcint, wit' im-poovermints," he added with a trace of smugness. "But toobs is staan-dard—all same. Den, of a sudden, we start get bad stories; dis ship, other ships, an' even some . . . in-dust'ral boilers usin' de same toobs now. Dey gettin' cracks, when dey's rolled." He blinked furtively at Tabby. "Can't see 'em, hardly, an' nobody tinks to look, but dey there. We blame the Toob an' Pipe Division o' Baalkpan Steel Works. Dey say, 'No way. Dey all get burst tested wit' air.' Toob an' Pipe blames us fer not rollin 'em right, so we built a test boiler." He jerked his head downward in a traditional Lemurian nod. "We checked it hydro . . . hydro-saak-tic'ly, an' it o-kay. Tee an' Pee says, 'See? Not our fault.' So we fired it up an' raised the pressure to tree fifty pee-ess-ays." His eyes went wide and he held up his hands. "An', *shoosh*! Dey spyoo! De whole goddaamn teeng goes *boom*!" He shook his head. "We blame Toob an' Pipe back, an' dey say dey's drawin' toobs just like all'ays, wit' no *shoosh*. Dey blame billets from steel mill. Chaar-man Letts finally thowed a fit at buck passin'—whatever dat is—an' maked ever'body work togedder to sort it out. Go to find out, de mill's still usin' *Amagi* steel—the last teengs it goes to is toobs an' ord'naance—but dey thought all steel from it was same. Not so. De baatch dey use for bad toobs was maybe gunhouse armor—dey don't know—but it gots too much carbon, an' sulfur too, makin' it too hard an' brittle to give a good roll."

"So . . ."

"So, some was fine, an' should *stay* fine in low-pressure boilers." Laap blinked. "For tree hunnerd an' more pee-ess-ays?" He shook his head very definitely. "No fine." He waved at the tube in Tabby's hands. "Dese is made same as all-ways, but wit' 'proved billets dat make all fine toobs. Same way makes same color, an' we keep same number for same boilers, but dey *is* fine!" he insisted. "We *test* dis lot in anudder boiler to *four hundred* pee-ess-ays. Make *daamn* sure!"

Spanky looked at Tabby and saw some of the tension had left her. Isak remained sullen, but no longer had murder in his eye. "I guess the first step to fixin' a problem is admitting it exists," he allowed grudgingly. "But you gotta start putting *lot numbers* on stuff, besides just part numbers, to keep 'em from getting mixed up with the others. Again."

"But . . ." Laap looked worried. "We *aad* numbers to numbers, somebody maybe not know dey's the right toobs!"

Spanky took a deep breath and vigorously rubbed his eyes. "They use lot numbers at the ICE houses for everything that goes in gas engines. They use 'em on ammo too. God knows what else. It's *not* a new idea. Did it occur to you—to anybody—that anyone stupid enough to make the bonehead call to paint the same stock number on these has no business screwin' around with boilers in the first place? No? I hope it wasn't you." Laap frantically shook his head. Spanky looked skeptical. "Well, whoever it was probably needs to get his silly ass out in the fleet where he can wonder when *he's* gonna get steamed to death because he can't tell good tubes from bad." He looked at Tabby and Isak. "I'll shoot a-ah, polite request off today, for lot numbers on everything they can think of—I promise. It's really my fault—and maybe Chairman Letts's too. Should've demanded it from the start. But all the first boilers were one-offs when I was riding herd on Naval Engineering and inspecting so much of the stuff myself." He shook his head, putting his hands back on his hips. "Doesn't matter. We should'a, but we didn't. Now we will."

His gaze focused on Isak. "In the meantime, you're in charge of rebuilding the boilers. *Use* these guys"—he nodded at the civilians—"an' quit bitchin'. Especially to Tabby. I want her focused on the bigger picture. There's a helluva lot to do and we got no time to spare." He paused, tilting his head at the civilians. "And don't kill 'em. Maybe they'll learn something they can carry back—what it's like out here for people who have to use what they make." His gaze settled back on Laap. "Do as you're told, and I don't want any bitchin' out of *you* either."

"An' if the 'toobs' are *still* shit?" Isak insisted.

Spanky shrugged. "*Then* you can kill 'em," he said lightly, but frowned when Laap and the others recoiled in horror. "Jeez, I was foolin'. But there's nothin' for it, Isak. Just have to put the boilers back together an' pressure 'em up. I guess we'll find out." He glanced at Laap. "At least chances are *we* probably have good tubes, if what he says is true. It burns me that there's likely a lot of bad ones still out there, just waiting to pop like a dropped beer can. Have to warn every snipe in the fleet to keep their eyes extra peeled . . ." His voice trailed off as he tried to think of what else he could do; then he seemed to notice they were all still standing there, staring at him. "Well?" he barked. "Dismissed! Get with it! None of this work'll just miracle itself done!"

The assembly bolted, and Spanky turned to rejoin the others.

"Not as amusing as we expected, from previous experience," Rolak stated dryly.

"Nope," Spanky grumped. "Not very funny at all. I guess it's inevitable, though. We've been damn lucky so many things we've cooked up right in the middle of a war have worked as well as they have. Bound to be exceptions." He shrugged philosophically. "And lots of finger-pointing when there are. Thank God Letts is on the ball."

"Thank the Maker, indeed," Keje agreed. "Letts is perhaps better suited for this aspect of being Chaar-man than Adar was," he added, blinking concern for his friend.

"Maybe," Alden agreed, "but there's plenty Adar was better at." He huffed a laugh. "Taking the sunlight, for one," he said, then sobered. "Getting along with everybody was another. Letts may've done the legwork to put the new Union together, but it was Adar's dream, and it never would've happened without him. Don't worry," he told Keje, "you'll get him back. You and the Skipper'll get 'em *all* back." His neutral expression turned to a frown as he looked back at *Walker* and envisioned all it would take to get her ready for sea. He knew she was just one old ship, no better suited for what was to come than her new sister steaming off the coast. Not at all suited for standing up to the likes of *Savoie*, one-on-one. Yet she'd come to represent so much to so many, not least of which was her continued survival—even victories!—in the face of overwhelming odds. If she wasn't exactly the symbol of the Allied cause, she'd certainly become its talisman. And even General of the Army and Marines Pete Alden wasn't immune to the itchy feeling that they all stood a better chance if Captain Reddy was where he most belonged in a fight: on the bridge of USS *Walker*. "If we have the time," he added, his tone turning grim. "That's what it comes down to. We might still get licked, even if everything goes exactly right," he qualified, "but we're licked for sure if we run out of time to get ready."

CHAPTER 5

***Aboard USS* Santa Catalina**
October 26, 1944

A brilliant orange sunset closed a very busy day as USS *Santa Catalina* steamed past the heavy shore batteries at the mouth of Grik City Bay and into the purpling night. The guns in Fort Laumer were big, heavy brutes salvaged from the wrecked ironclad dreadnaughts near the docks. As observed before, they remained excessively heavy and crudely shaped, but their nine-and-a-half-inch bores, capable of hurling a hundred-pound solid shot clear across the mouth of the bay, had been bored disconcertingly true. Grik gunnery had progressively improved as the war dragged on, and apparently a lot of that had to do with the quality of their weapons. It was just as well they hadn't been forced to face these in an open-water slugfest like First Madras. That had been bad enough, and boded ill for the future. The Grik hadn't used anything like the Allies' primitive but effective fire-control system before either, but they couldn't assume they weren't incorporating something similar into the ships under construction or conversion around Sofesshk. The quality of their bores alone meant conventional Allied naval guns retained little, if any, qualitative advantage at close range.

Not for the first time, Matt and others had made the

decision not to waste time and resources on stopgaps such as rifling muzzle-loading cannon that would, hopefully, soon be replaced. Nor was it logistically possible to rifle existing guns of deployed warships, even assuming they could handle the additional pressures of the heavier projectiles they'd require, which was no sure thing. As usual, the choice to focus their limited industrial capacity on *next*-generation weapons, perfecting the metallurgy and manufacturing techniques required by things like the dual-purpose 4″-50, or copies of Browning MGs instead of Gatlings (which they could've made sooner) had prevailed. Allin-Silva rifle conversions were a stopgap by definition, but their land forces had more desperately needed a breechloader of *any* sort to counter enemy numbers. Besides, the conversion was a relatively simple matter and entirely new versions required minimal production changes. And there was no urgent need to replace them. They were light, accurate, powerful enough to kill "boogers" larger than Grik, which troops sometimes encountered, and none of their enemies (before the League became potential foes) had anything remotely as good. But they were stuck with smoothbore artillery for the most part, particularly on land, until supply for the new 4″-50s and 5.5″s could catch up with demand. And making *field carriages* to accommodate the big naval rifles presented formidable challenges as well.

Matt understood that the remains of *Walker*'s old 3″-23 antiaircraft gun had been copied in Baalkpan. It had been considered practically useless at sea, and would be totally so against armored warships, but Bernie had long proposed that they put *them* on field carriages. That actually made a lot of sense, and the carriage works was gearing up to accommodate them. But then they learned a similar weapon already existed, about to join the fight. The Republic of Real People was supposedly bringing quick-firing field guns related to the French 75 to the battle on land, and had offered the blueprints to its allies. That might help—someday. But, once again, in the upcoming campaigns, smoothbore artillery—and aircraft—would share the battles on land and sea. Matt was struck by the irony of that. Still, the true-bored Grik guns in Fort Laumer made him wonder if their decision to forgo immediate, slight enhancements—like rifling their existing muzzle-loaders—in favor of vast improvements down the line would bite them on the ass. The big guns protecting Fort Laumer and the bay were unfit for field use, but well-suited for mounting in ships or shore emplacements. And they had to assume the Grik at Sofesshk had improved them even more, and almost certainly had better field artillery now. By all accounts, they had a better *army*.

Matt had been watching the sunset and speaking with Commander Russ Chappelle whenever *Santa Catalina*'s skipper stepped out on the port bridgewing to observe the channel. Russ had started out as a torpedoman and wasn't a "born" officer. He had, in fact, once reminded Matt more of Silva than he was entirely comfortable with, when it came to giving him what was arguably the most powerful ship in their Navy. In appearance, the two men could've been brothers. Both were tall, blond, and bearded. But Chappelle wasn't Silva, and he'd become a fine officer whether he'd ever been cut out for it or not. *Santy Cat* was in good hands. Now, nodding to the lookout, Matt stepped down the long metal stair to the main deck below.

The sea was brisker past the point and the old ship took on a gentle, corkscrewing wallow as she shouldered the waves aside. He looked to the west again as he strode aft down the ship's port side, occasionally nodding at Lemurians and Imperial humans in Chack's 1st Raider Brigade. *Maybe it's just my imagination,* he thought, *but it sure seems like the sunsets are more spectacular ever since Talaud Island blew its top.* He'd been thinking about that a lot lately: the volcanic eruption that shattered an island and nearly killed his wife. He'd also thought about the circumstances that put her in danger in the first place—and how he'd behaved at the time.

He'd *thought* Sandra and the then-Princess Rebecca, as well as a number of other people of theirs, were in the hands of a madman. And it turned out that their alliance with—and the very survival of—the Empire of the New Britain Isles had been at stake. But he'd selfishly reprioritized a number of things, at least in his mind, to a dangerous degree. It may have turned out for the best, but it probably shouldn't have, in retrospect. Now, though the current situation was similar on its face, he was *sure* Sandra—and more of their people—were in the clutches of a maniac at least as diabolical, and even more capricious than Walter Billingsly and Harrison Reed ever were. And Hisashi Kurokawa was certainly more dangerous to the survival of the Alliance and the success of their original cause in the West: to defeat the Grik. But Matt was deathly afraid he was doing exactly the same thing he'd done before—possibly subordinating the war effort to his own personal ends—and this time that was precisely what their bitterest enemy wanted.

He eased through more of Chack's troops, taking a final glance at the sunset, a smile fixed rigidly on his face for the benefit of watchers. If it weren't for all the gray steel around him, the water—and the short, furry people, of course—the sunset might've reminded him of those he'd seen nearly every evening as a boy in the central Texas sky. But that old home was farther away—in so many ways—than he could even wrap his mind around, and he rarely thought about it anymore. *This* was home now, these people were his cause, and he had no time for nostalgia. Particularly when his mind was so busy planning, evaluating, and worrying about screwing everything up. And the most insidious thing of all was that he was just as concerned his "objective" analysis of his previous behavior might overly influence him toward misplaced caution, undermining his instinctive evaluation of the situation. His gut had often served him better than his untrained and imperfect strategic thinking, after all.

A full half of Chack's Brigade was aboard, choking the ship's upper decks, and they respectfully parted before him as he walked. The rest of the brigade was aboard *Arracca.* The carrier and her battlegroup would follow the old freighter-turned–armored cruiser out to the open sea, as she always did when nightfall—and the near-certain air raid accompanying it—loomed. But this time, they wouldn't be back at dawn. Nearing the rear of the armored casemate forming much of *Santy Cat*'s superstructure and protecting six heavy 5.5″ rifles salvaged from *Amagi,* Matt stared aft at the darkened city. *Arracca*'s huge form was getting underway, half her escorts dashing out ahead, but the city itself was dominated by the squat black form of the Cowflop. *Such an awful damn place,* he thought, *to cost so much precious blood. I wonder if it'll still be ours the next time I see it—*if *I see it again—or if we'll have to pay more to get it back.*

He shook his head and stepped into *Santy Cat*'s oddly incongruous dining salon, surprised to find it almost empty. Only Courtney Bradford and Juan Marcos, the peg-legged Filipino who'd proclaimed himself chief steward to the CINCAF (Commander in Chief of All Allied Forces), occupied the strangely decorative space. Courtney probably should've stayed at Grik City and taken a Clipper straight down to the Republic city of Songze, but he'd chosen to join Matt for this short voyage to Mahe first. Most of the Clippers gathering there were going down to the Comoros Islands, to stage for a series of raids against Sofesshk. He'd take one of those. Now he and Juan sat on a pair of rocking chairs, of all things, knocked up to the Filipino's specifications "for Cap-tan Chappelle" by the ship's carpenter. Every chair and stool on the ship had been replaced as the result of a recent prank run amok, and Matt was impressed by the craftsmanship. In her Old World role as a naval auxiliary, *Santa Catalina* often carried passengers, primarily naval officers, who expected a few comforts. The dining salon was one. During her rebuild, with an eye toward her possible role as a flagship, the salon was actually made more spacious, comfortable, and even ornate in the Lemurian way, embellished with fine tapestries and woodwork. The new chairs had to match.

"Oh. Good evening," Matt said as the Filipino stood, apparently horrified his captain had caught him doing nothing. Courtney stayed where he was, nodding with a smile, both hands wrapped protectively around a cup.

"I, ah . . . There's coffee," Juan said defensively, waving enthusiastically at the large silver pot standing on the table.

"Mmm," Matt said neutrally, regarding the pot with caution. One of the longest-held secrets of the war had been broken, and Juan finally knew Captain Reddy hated what he did to the ersatz coffee they'd been forced to use on this world. It tasted vile and produced a greasy green foam atop the coal-black brew. Some could make it palatable, but Juan never mastered it. Worse, he *thought* he had, and no one had been willing to hurt his feelings—until they just couldn't stand it anymore.

Juan straightened. "*I* did not make it," he assured glumly with a quick glance at Bradford. "And I do think you will find it interesting," he added. Then he brightened. "You wanna eat? I will bring you something to eat!"

"I'd love a bite," Courtney said. "Captain Reddy?"

"Sure, Juan. Whatever's handy." Matt nodded at Courtney. "And make sure Mr. Bradford and I have a few minutes, if you please. I won't keep Commander Chappelle out of his own wardroom"—he managed a real grin—"his dining salon. But you might ask anyone else who comes along for a little patience."

"Of course, Cap-tan Reddy! *No one* shall pass!" Juan hesitated. "And do sample the coffee," he added grudgingly.

"I will."

They waited a moment while Juan quickly poured a cup—it did *smell* different—and then latched the hatches port and starboard before clomping forward, up the passageway toward the officers' galley.

"Oh, sit down," Courtney commanded. "You look dead on your feet. Worse, you look like a flashy ate your puppy. Can't go around like that, you know. There's morale to consider, don't you see? Of course."

Matt lowered himself into the vacated rocker and it creaked comfortingly in its joints and on the wooden deck. Then he glanced at the cup. Shrugging, he picked it up and brought it near his lips. He stopped suddenly when the full force of the aroma hit him—and he saw the anticipation in Courtney's eyes. "This is coffee," he said simply. "Isn't it? *Real* coffee."

Courtney grinned. "Yes, as a matter of fact. It's still a bit odd, you'll see. Slightly, oh, I don't know . . . woody?" He seemed discontent with the description. "Perhaps a different grind or roasting technique . . ."

"Where'd you get it?" Matt interrupted in wonder,

taking a sip at last. "My God," he practically moaned, savoring the taste. Courtney was right: it *was* unusual compared to what he'd grown accustomed to, but it could've been exactly the same as what *Walker* brought to this world, for all he knew; it had been so long since he'd tasted anything like it. All that mattered was that it was real coffee—and it was good. "Can we get more?" he immediately demanded.

"We can have all we want," Courtney assured, "as long as we hold Madagascar," he qualified. "It grows wild in the lands of the Shee-Ree and they pick the little red cherries, eating them as they stroll along." His eyes widened in horror. "Such a waste! But it stands to reason, actually. Coffee was indigenous to the Madagascar of our world, and I may have seen the flowers of *vanilla fragrans*. I'll certainly enquire about *that*, I assure you. Just imagine: vanilla! For the present, however, for the sake of the war effort, of course—since even Lemurians are becoming such fiends for caffeine—I considered the introduction of this Shee-Ree coffee of primary importance."

"When did you find it?" Matt asked.

Courtney waved his hand. "While on our little trek down south. I packed a few handfuls away and arranged for more to be brought back whenever arms and supplies are flown down."

"Hmm. Then it seems Silva's not the only one who can keep a secret."

"No indeed. Not that I *meant* to, at all," Courtney hastily added. "Nor did Mr. Silva have any idea. I doubt it ever occurred to him that coffee begins its life as sweet little berries! Otherwise, I merely wanted to make absolutely sure to, ah, experiment a bit before revealing my discovery to the world." He gestured grandly.

Matt took another long, satisfying gulp. "My God," he said quietly again. Then, carefully, he set the cup aside and closed his eyes, massaging his forehead with his hand.

Courtney leaned forward in alarm. "Are . . . are you all right, Captain Reddy?"

Matt glanced up, frowned, then nodded. "Yeah. As well as anybody. It's just kind of pathetic that I can be emotionally overwhelmed by a good cup of joe."

Courtney's features softened. "Not pathetic at all. I was quite affected myself." His bushy brows furrowed. "And you're doing a great deal better than anyone else I can imagine whose wife and unborn child are in the hands of a murdering madman," he added gently.

Matt shrugged again, then cocked his head to the side, regarding the Australian. Aside from Sandra, Bradford was the only one he'd ever been able to unburden to, particularly when it came to things like doubt. That was probably because Bradford had been a civilian, and when they were alone, Matt didn't have to be the all-knowing, ever-confident CINCAF everyone else, even his closest friends, like Keje, must believe him to be. Chief Gray was never fooled, and had had a talent for bolstering Matt's self-assurance with an oblique comment or even a simple glance. But Gray was dead, Sandra was a hostage—at best—and that left only Courtney. And the Australian had gone through tough times of his own, which Matt discreetly shook him out of. That created a bond of perfect honesty and confidentiality both needed from *somebody*. Still, neither abused the privilege, and their private talks were rare. In Courtney's case, he'd significantly improved. His drinking had reverted from dependency to recreational status, and, frankly, he considered any lingering personal problems too inconsequential to add to Matthew Reddy's weighty responsibilities. Matt was equally conscious that, while never knowingly indiscreet, Courtney was affected by the apprehensions he revealed. They became his own, and not only was that somewhat cruel, Matt thought, but others might notice his guarded concern and guess the source. It could also push him back to drink. It had before. But Matt desperately needed an objective opinion. He sighed.

"I fired off a message to Chairman Letts describing what Fiedler spilled about the League strategy to get everybody to wipe each other out so they can, basically, march in and pick up the pieces. I also dispatched a Nancy to Mahe with a copy of the map Fiedler drew, complete with updates Silva added." Silva had hung on to the copy Matt showed him. He'd need to know it well. He'd drawn another, and doodled on it before handing it back. Matt snorted. "Silva titled it 'Objective Shithouse' and made up a bunch of goofy place-names that are actually pretty appropriate, and we can use them for code references." He shook his head. "That guy is so weird. I changed the name to 'Outhouse,' but left the rest. Nobody just overhearing one of the place-names, without Silva's warped mind, will know what they mean. Anyway, if the map's accurate, it'll help our planning. I have to confirm it, though, like I said, and told Keje to send a scout."

Courtney raised his brows in alarm.

"I know—it's a risk. But not only can it confirm what Fiedler told us about Zanzibar, but it'll help me decide if we can swallow the rest of what he said."

"That makes sense, I suppose," Courtney agreed in a skeptical tone. "But even if we confirm every detail, I doubt *I* could ever trust Fiedler. Everything having to do with the League seems so utterly warped, so false."

"I know," Matt confessed, eyes straying back to the coffee cup. "And I even catch myself wondering if Gravois *told* him to have Jindal beat him so we'd believe him! Everything the League does is so sneaky and underhanded." He puffed out his cheeks. "I keep telling myself that Fiedler isn't the League, and I don't think anybody could fake how much he hates Gravois, *but* . . ." He sighed. "So many shades of gray. I always hated 'em. Preferred everything nice and neat, black or white, and now there's different shades of *shades*!" He took another sip from his cup. "I guess it all has to come down to principle and what our gut tells us in the end. I *think* Fiedler hates Gravois, and what's behind him just as much. My gut tells me he doesn't like what the League's been up to out here, or his German contingent's place under its triumvirate. I *feel* that he hopes if we win, we'll wreck Gravois's strategy to kill us off and the triumvirate'll fall, maybe paving the way for a more rational leadership we can deal with. Coexist with, anyway. It's a big world. Assuming that, maybe it really was Sandra's capture, and what *Savoie* did to *Amerika*, that forced him to make a choice." He looked back at Bradford. "That would be the right thing to do, the honorable thing." He chuckled darkly. "The black-or-white thing."

Courtney tightened his lips but didn't respond, and

Matt paused, considering. Finally, he raised a finger to his chin.

"And maybe it's that he *wouldn't* spill much that'll hurt his German contingent that makes me trust his map, at least. He knew we could've kept him, tortured him, *killed* him, if we wanted, but we didn't. And he didn't say squat for a while. He waited until he knew we weren't like Kurokawa or the goddamn League. You saw how Gravois reacted when I told him we knew about the German sub. It's real and it's out there. *Fiedler* volunteered that, potentially sacrificing a few of his countrymen so we wouldn't blame the rest, or him, for what it might do." He nodded. "So, yeah, I guess I kind of do believe him after all."

"I'd dearly love more detailed information about the League and its capabilities," Courtney mused, "and most particularly what constitutes its other problems, more pressing than us. We might make them more acute if we had an idea what they were."

"Probably exactly why he wouldn't go into it," Matt agreed.

"Then *why didn't* we squeeze him, as Mr. Silva put it?" Courtney asked, exasperated.

Matt pursed his lips. "Haven't you been listening? Because I'd rather have his voluntary cooperation. We've already had some, and I think we'll get more in time. Besides, he has to know we'll find out everything if we take Zanzibar. You don't think all the League personnel pulled out, do you? Gravois even said they still have an embassy there." He waved his hand. "And maybe Fiedler was uncomfortable enough about blabbing what he had that he wanted us to get the rest of the dope from someone else."

Courtney frowned. "That's not very principled."

"Maybe not. But it is human."

"He's no human—he's a Nazi!" Courtney flared. "*All* the League is fascist! How can we ever coexist with such as them? Any of them?"

"*Is* he a Nazi, Courtney?" Matt countered. "Did you ask him? He didn't even know who Hitler was, so even if he is one, he's not the exact same kind. The League's clearly fascist—Nazi, if you will—and Fiedler dropped hints that it may be just as bad as Hitler's Germany in some ways. Gravois's behavior, and *Savoie*'s before Gravois gave her to Kurokawa, tend to support that. But we've discovered principled men among our enemies before, remember." He leaned back on the rocker and took another sip of coffee. "I think, deep down, Fiedler's just a pilot who doesn't understand why his people have to keep fighting on a different world. Who knows how widespread that sentiment is in the League? And we're coexisting with *Halik*, for God's sake—so far—and he's a *Grik*. I'd say if that's possible, damn near anything is. Either way, I'm glad we didn't do anything to wreck Fiedler's goodwill—if we really have it," he qualified again. "It might come in very handy."

"Well, I'm sure you know best," Bradford said primly.

Matt set his cup down and rubbed his forehead again. "No," he said regretfully. "*I'm* not sure of that at all—regarding Fiedler or anything else."

Bradford looked taken aback by the sudden confession. Then he leaned back as well and cleared his throat. "So, you want my honest opinion?" he asked, and Matt glared at the Australian. "Very well," Courtney continued. "In that case, I disagree about the Fiedler issue. I think you *should've* squeezed him, as Mr. Silva so eloquently phrased it, for every drop of useful information, leaving him a dry, dead husk, if necessary." He nodded at Matt's surprised expression. "Indeed, I had a bit of an epiphany on my last adventure. The Shee-Ree have a simple philosophy: those who can't be trusted to live peacefully with others must go away. One way or another. And such are not considered people." He chuckled darkly. "It was somewhat disconcerting to find myself defending Mr. Silva—and *Chack*—from suspicions they weren't people, simply because they're so dangerous! I was distressed by that, at first. And though Chack, at least, is certainly a person by anyone's definition, the suspicion wasn't unfounded from the perspective of the Shee-Ree, and the *wisdom* of the concern converted me to their philosophy to a degree. I'm no longer quite the fuzzy, wobbly being I've been so long, and recognize things are now past the point that mere sentiment may be indulged." He sniffed. "That said, though I disagree about the Nazi, I'll support your decision in front of others, as always." Courtney frowned. "Not what you wanted to hear, I know, but there it is." He paused while Matt absorbed that. "I also know that's not what's troubling you," he added. "Your greatest fear, and why we're having this private chat, is that Lady Sandra's peril—yes, and all the others; you'd never allow yourself to worry so selectively—has influenced your planning for the upcoming operations."

Matt stared at him, wondering where this . . . different Bradford was heading.

"Well, I'm quite sure it has," Courtney stated. "The thing is, though I've never pretended to have a military mind, I was once quite the chess player. So I do have a minimal understanding of strategic"—he smiled—"principles. And having studied the plan alongside you, listened to all the arguments from those we trust, and based on what I know of Kurokawa and General Esshk, I believe your overall strategy and the plans you and your staff have prepared represent the only possible avenue to success. We're against the wall, so to speak, and can't simply wait for the enemy to come to us as before. Esshk's numbers are too great, if consolidated, and Kurokawa's potential combat power—most specifically *Savoie*, if he's allowed to bring it to bear at a time and place of his choosing—is too overwhelming. We *must* prevent them from doing those two things, and even more, we *can't* allow them to combine under any circumstances. It's as simple as that." He took a long sip from his own cup.

"Therefore, as I see it, the only option truly is to break the oldest rule in the book: to divide our forces in the face of the enemy, even though his dispositions remain mysterious. Often a recipe for disaster, to be sure, but it's succeeded rather spectacularly from time to time." He waved his hand. "So, your chief concern, that you're subordinating what you *should* do to what you *want* to do, is groundless. In this instance, what you want—to rescue your wife and destroy the maniacal Hisashi Kurokawa once and for all, while the rest of the entire Allied Expeditionary Force stands ready, waiting for the proper moment to assault Sofesshk unaware and unprepared—is not only the best option; it's the only one we have. So, rest easy, Captain Reddy, and do get some sleep. Just because you want to do it doesn't make it wrong."

"Why am I not overly reassured?" Matt asked, but his voice was dry, with a trace of humor.

"Because you're a man of principle," Courtney replied cheerfully, "who'll always question his decisions regarding life and death, at least when you're at leisure. I've never seen you display such uncertainty when fighting your ship. But that's immediate, instinctive. Planning ahead for operations that'll cost many lives touches your soul with its premeditation." Courtney grinned. "And also because we disagreed before. About Fiedler. You wonder why you should listen to me now. Well, the answer is that in both cases I gave you my honest opinion. *I* may be wrong about Fiedler," he confessed, "and it's quite difficult for me to be objective about Nazis, you know. I also admit I can't be entirely objective about you because you're my friend. But *as* your friend, I counsel you most urgently to lay your concerns about yourself aside because they can only benefit our enemies."

Matt stared back at his cup. "And if it all goes in the crapper?"

Courtney actually laughed. "It *always* goes in the crapper, doesn't it? Your greatest strength, Captain Reddy, and our most significant advantage over all our enemies in this war, above and beyond ships, guns, planes, and bullets, is how you always seem to wrench it back out again when it does. So rest easy. *Be* confident. I am, in you."

Courtney emptied his cup and poured more coffee for them both. When he spoke again, his voice was softer. "You know, despite my unwavering, reasoned Darwinism—and Sister Audry's resultant incredulity—I'm a religious man. All conscientious architects perpetually strive to refine their creations or adapt them to diverse applications, and the Supreme Architect of the Universe can be no exception. So I pray to Him each day for Lady Sandra, Adar, and all the rest. I pray for the success of our cause and all those we've lost. I hope you don't mind that I pray for you as well, because I know those losses weigh heavily upon you . . . some—quite naturally—more than others."

Matt knew Courtney was talking about Chief Gray now, and he was right. The Super Bosun, with all his faults and quirks, had been like a father to him—to the ship itself, in many ways, and certainly, by example, to the Amer-i-caan Navy as it was manifested on this world. And next to Sandra, Gray had been the firmest foundation for the confidence Matt needed so badly. He still missed him more than he could measure.

Courtney continued, choosing his words carefully. "Such personal loss causes the most excruciating pain imaginable, and can't—probably shouldn't—go away entirely. But it does fade. The Lemurian faith that the dead watch over us from the Heavens is quite attractive and I like to think it's true." He smiled ironically. "I'm not much given to proselytizing in matters of faith, but whether that's the case or not, I beg you to consider that the pain of loss also teaches us a lot about ourselves—focusing our concept of what defines us. Sometimes, at first, that concept can be distorted—I know *that* all too well—and not only to us, but to those who look to us for guidance and example." He shrugged. "And ultimately to those who passed, still hugely present in our minds and hearts, who I believe *do* watch us. They also grieve, to see us suffer, to allow what we've lost to define us, even for a time. Therefore, it's *what we have*, who we truly *are*—what *they* made us, to varying degrees—that we must strive to return to for their sake as well as ours, and for all who look to us for comfort."

There came a discreet knock on the bulkhead in the passageway forward, and Juan clomped in with a tray. Two plates slid precariously from side to side with his rolling gait but he made it to the table without dropping anything. He'd had a lot of practice in heavier seas. "Pleezy-sore steaks," he announced. "Medium rare," he said to Matt, laying a plate on the table. "And well-done." He sniffed disapprovingly at Bradford as he laid out the other. He paused a moment while the two men stood from their rockers and seated themselves at the long wooden table.

"Thanks, Juan. Smells great."

"Indeed," Courtney agreed.

Juan moved their coffee cups and added glasses of iced tea. The tea came from the Empire of the New Britain Isles. Most Allied steamers had freezers now, and ice—and refrigerated water—once unknown to virtually any Lemurian, was an accepted, beloved obsession. Juan stood for a moment while they dug in, but cleared his throat. Matt looked at him questioningly.

"I listen, Cap-tan," he said simply. "You know I do. I spread scuttlebutt, *true* scuttlebutt the hands need to hear from one of their own. You allow this because you know *I* know when to keep my trap shut." He shrugged. "I also know when not to listen, but sometimes I hear things by accident. The last part of what was just said was such a thing," he admitted. "So I'll tell you something about Chief Gray. He was a great man, a great destroyerman, but like the rest of us, was often afraid. He hid it well, but he *was*. How did he overcome that, you ask?" He shrugged again. "By looking to *you*, Cap-tan Reddy. As we all do. Because we know, no matter what or why"—he looked at Bradford—"when it all does go in the crapper, you will sort it out." He turned back to Matt, a smile on his brown face. "You always have before. And knowing that, your crew, your clan, the whole Alliance will always back you up." He nodded and started to turn away, but stopped and looked back. "And getting the Lady Sandra, your beybi, and all the rest back, is just as important to us as it is to you. We *owe* those *bobo gago* Japs, for this, and much, much more!"

CHAPTER 6

USS **Donaghey** *(DD-2)*
Mid-Atlantic
October 27, 1944

"My apologies to the Cap-i-taan, and please can he come on deck," came Lieutenant Saama-Kera's muffled voice from above, through the open skylight. Commander Greg Garrett had been fast asleep in a kind of gimballed hanging cot in the great cabin of USS *Donaghey*, but immediately tossed off the blanket, which had been made sodden and heavy by the humid night air, and came instantly awake in the fashion he'd learned to do. None of the usual noises of the ship—the groan of working timbers, the rush of the sea along her side, even the calls and whistles prompting the hands to adjust the sails amid squealing blocks and thundering feet—ever disturbed him. Those were normal, practically soothing sounds, no matter how loud or sudden. Anything out of the ordinary, however—a strange noise, even a different sway of his cot, brought him instantly awake and alert. He'd become such an integral part of *Donaghey* that he suspected part of his mind never slept, had become as much the ship's mind as his own. He was content with that.

Donaghey was the oldest ship in the American Navy on this world, aside from *Walker* and *Mahan* themselves. Older in *this* navy than *Santa Catalina*. But in spite of all the new construction he could've had his pick of, there was no other ship or assignment he'd rather have. His was the ultimate "independent cruise," far beyond the point that anyone they knew had ever ventured. He supposed he knew how Magellan must've felt, and by the time he reached the Caribbean, he would've circumnavigated the earth himself—if one combined this world with the last. He sat up on the cot and slid to the deck, reaching to pull on his shoes even as he heard the rumble of feet coming down the companionway forward. There was a knock on his door.

"Yes?" His voice was devoid of any inflection as he tucked in his shirt and plopped his hat on his head. He knew what the mirror would show him if he could see it in the dark, and frowned. Like Captain Reddy, he tried to keep himself well groomed, even to the point of shaving—which almost none of the old destroyermen did anymore. He'd set the precedent, and the hands expected it. It was harder for him, however. His black hair and beard grew so thick that his tanned face turned dark only a few hours after his razor passed over it. In addition, his Lemurian-made khaki shirt and trousers were available only in the most basic sizes. He was as tall as Matt but more slightly built, so to accommodate his long arms and legs, he otherwise looked like he was wearing a tent—impossible to keep from looking rumpled, even when he hadn't been sleeping in it. His steward was worse with a needle and thread than he was, and he refused to add to the sailmaker's toil. But he'd anticipated a call when he turned in, and hadn't wanted to skin down to his skivvies. According to his and Sammy's calculations, they'd raise Ascension Island sometime that night. Apparently, they'd been right.

Several 'Cats from the Republic of Real People accompanied them on this voyage, a token of Kaiser Nig-Taak's commitment to join the war against the Dominion. And the island of St. Helena had been right where they'd said it would be, according to charts they brought. Republic ships had sailed that far many times since SMS *Amerika* arrived in 1914 and revealed its existence. Nig-Taak loved maps and was obsessed with knowing where things were.

He'd commissioned what was probably the largest, most comprehensive world map of this earth in existence. It remained woefully incomplete, and vast areas of the globe were represented by approximate—at best—coastlines, but St. Helena had been painstakingly added. They'd stopped there, setting foot on dry land for the first time since Alex-aandra. They found the island, Napoleon's final address on another world, a charming, temperate, apparently safe haven, populated only by swarms of lizardbirds—none as dangerous as those on islands east of Madagascar—and huge, hard-shelled sea turtles that laid their eggs in crevices on the rocky beaches and apparently dwelt year-round in the adjacent depths. From his Tennessee point of reference, they looked like gigantic alligator snapping turtles, and he understood they were good eating if they could be caught. In addition, their shells were very durable and even beautiful when sanded and polished—like a dark, amber-shaded mother of pearl—and all sorts of decorative things were made from them. Like just about everywhere they'd been, flashylike fish lingered in the vicinity, but Greg supposed the aggressive, well-protected turtles had less to fear from them than most.

Still, though a permanent Republic outpost had once been attempted, St. Helena was probably one of the remotest islands in the world, and turtles alone couldn't justify the effort to keep it going. With the current crisis, Greg knew a garrison had been planned, but who knew when it would arrive? He'd strolled through the time-and storm-shattered remains of several buildings, while the hands pumped water to fill the empty casks in *Donaghey*'s hold from a well sunk long ago, and decided a garrison was probably a good idea. Not only was there evidence, old and new, that turtle hunters still came from time to time, but Doms had been there as well, erecting a stone marker claiming the island for their twisted pope. They might've even been the same ones Captain Laborde of *Savoie* let slip that the League was in contact with. And the League itself had also been there, judging by the number of rusting cans and other refuse scattered near old fire pits. That made him wonder what to expect when they reached Ascension Island, and he meant to approach with caution.

"Loo-ten-aant Saama-Kera's re-grets fer disturbin' yer sleep, sur," came the voice of a young Lemurian midshipman, "but could yer peese step up on deck? Dere's a st'ange light on de horizon."

"On my way," Greg said, snatching his Imperial-made telescope and following the 'Cat up the companionway and out on the broad quarterdeck. All around was utter darkness, and only the sharp, bright stars made it possible to tell where sea ended and sky began. Two shapes stood by the wheel forward of the mizzenmast, and others lined the starboard rail staring to the north. A brisk, steady wind on the port quarter swept *Donaghey* along at an effortless ten knots under plain sail alone. All this Garrett took in with little thought. It was the same when he retired, and he'd have felt a change. He stepped to the lee rail, joining the shape he somehow knew belonged to the white-and-brown-furred Saama-Kera.

Donaghey didn't have a "quarterdeck" in the traditional sense, any more than *Walker* did. Both were flush-decked from bow to stern. *Donaghey*, named for *Walker*'s chief machinist mate who died to save his ship, shared other similarities with the old four-stack destroyer. Both were outdated compared to their respective contemporaries, and both had seen more action of various sorts than any other ship in the Grand Alliance. *Donaghey* was the sole survivor of the first three frigates they'd helped the 'Cats build, and one of only a few dedicated sailors left. The rest were cargo haulers, transports, and DEs made from cut-down Grik Indiamen. With the introduction of steam power, even they were increasingly rare. Their range wasn't limited by fuel, but they were entirely dependent on the wind and required larger crews to operate. It meant that though *Donaghey* was held in similar esteem by the people of the Grand Alliance, and her crew of two hundred officers and enlisted was arguably the best in the fleet, unlike *Walker*, the ship herself had become somewhat . . . expendable. That, and her practically unlimited range, was why she'd been chosen for this mission in the first place.

Old, relatively speaking, and helpless against the wind she no doubt was, and smallish at only 168 feet long and around 1,200 tons, with her hull shape and sail plan, a clean bottom, and the wind where she liked it best, she could still log up to sixteen knots. Amazingly fast for any square-rigged ship Greg ever heard of, and faster than the new Scott class steam frigate DDs. And weak though she might be compared to them, she was far from helpless. There were twenty-four eighteen-pounders on her gun deck, four Y guns to launch depth charges off either beam, and a rack for the same weapons aft to discourage the enormous ship-eating mountain fish. Eight twelve-pounder field guns had been hoisted to the main deck from the hold and set on naval trucks the carpenters built to give her some light chasers—and slightly elevated grape or canister guns. She also had something no other Allied ship outside the Republic could boast: an even dozen water-cooled MG 08s—Maxims, as far as Garrett was concerned—and plenty of 7.92 x 57 mm belted ammo. None of the new copies of Browning MGs had been available when *Donaghey* set out. Maxims were still rare in the Republic, for that matter, having only recently gone into mass production. Inquisitor Choon and Kaiser Nig-Taak had lavished them on Garrett's ship in exchange (he suspected) for the loan of one of his Nancy floatplanes and its crew, and, even more, for his former captain, now major of Marines, Bekiaa-Sab-At. Bekiaa had remained in the Republic to teach Choon and General Kim what combat with the Grik was really like.

Of course, all these considerations hardly affected Greg Garrett. Particularly those concerning his ship's inadequacies. From rural Tennessee, just across the border from Corinth, Mississippi, he'd never been on the water in his life before joining the navy and coming to this world as *Walker*'s gunnery officer. Yet he'd become the most renowned frigate skipper in the Alliance—and loved the old *Donaghey* with all his heart.

"What've you got, Sammy?" he asked his XO, extending his telescope but waiting to be told where to point it.

"A light, Cap-i-taan. Lights," Sammy added more specifically, pointing due north; then he pulled his large Imperial watch from his pocket and stared at it in the gloom. Greg had long given up trying to match Lemurian eyesight, particularly in the dark, and took its superiority for granted now—a fact Sammy recognized, or he would've called Greg earlier. "Maasthead spotted 'em half an hour ago," he explained. "Most're still invisible from deck, but one is . . . rather curiously so."

Greg raised the glass and peered through it with his left eye, adjusting the objective. He grunted. "That, Mr. Saama, is a large fire, high above the sea," he said, still staring hard. "Stationary," he added significantly, "like a signal." He shifted his glass from side to side, but saw nothing else. "Damn strange. What about the other lights?"

"Maasthead there," Sammy called upward. "Report."

"Aye, sur," came the answer. "Dey's tree lights mebbee five de-gees east o' de high-up one: white, red, white. Low, hull down if it's a ship. T'other's west, mebbe fi'teen de-gees, an' movin' slow. Daat light's yellow, laak de high one. Dim, dough, laak a haze-fuzzy star on de horizon, but is movin'."

Greg rubbed his face and glanced around. The ship was utterly dark except for a couple 'Cats smoking pipes or PIG-cigs along the leeward rail, the red cherries glowing ridiculously bright. "The smoking lamp is *out*, and shade the binnacle light, if you please." He nodded upward. "I'm going aloft." High in the maintop, puffing from his climb, he extended his telescope again. He still couldn't see the moving light to the west, but was sure the first was a signal fire on an island, probably Ascension, and it was beginning to fade even as they drew closer. The other lights, however . . . Harsh certainty gripped him, and, tucking the glass in his waistband, he slid down to the deck by a backstay. "We'll bear away to the west-southwest," he said abruptly. "Helm, make your course two four zero."

"Two four see-ro," confirmed the 'Cat at the wheel, and even though there was no possible way the distant lights would hear him, Chief Bosun's Mate Jennar-Laan had caught his captain's sense of urgency that they remain undetected and called the hands to adjust the sails without using his whistle.

"What is it, Skipper?" asked Lt. (jg) Wendel "Smitty" Smith, *Donaghey*'s gunnery officer. Like Greg, Smitty was an original to *Walker*, having been an ordnance striker before the squall that brought them here. In his mid-twenties and already balding, he'd taken to muzzle-loading artillery easier than Greg, and, for *Donaghey* at least, was probably a better gunnery officer than his captain would've made. He'd come on deck with a "tribune" (basically, a major, the way the Republic Army reckoned such things), Pol-Heena. The Republic was strange in many ways, a more bizarre mixture of different cultures—from *different histories*—than anyone they'd met. They used some "normal," understandable rank structures, but sometimes added ancient, otherwise unused titles to differentiate seniority under various circumstances. For example, anywhere else Pol was just an ordinary major, or maybe prefect, depending on who addressed him, but as a tribune, he automatically had seniority over any other Republic major—or ship's master—he encountered during the course of his specific mission. And unless that officer was also a tribune on a mission of his own, he could compel his assistance. He'd better be able to show he really *needed* it, however. Only a legate (a similar title bestowed for similar reasons on colonels) or a general might supersede him. Greg likened the titles to commodore, as they were temporary in nature but meant to add authority for a given task and prevent confusion. It confused everybody else on *Donaghey*, though, and they didn't pay it any attention. The crew called Pol major or tribune indiscriminately. From a practical standpoint aboard ship, he acted as Marine Lieutenant Haana-Lin-Naar's XO, while she taught him how to fight Grik like a Marine. The main difference between what she showed him and what he already knew was an up-close and fiercely personal brutality he'd never imagined he'd need to learn. One of his Republic companions was Kapitan Leutnant Koor-Susk. He served as Sammy's sailing master, even though the Alliance had finally done away with that rank, as it didn't have enough sky priests to fill the role and required all officers to learn celestial navigation.

"I've no doubt that's Ascension Island," Greg answered Smitty, nodding a greeting at Pol. "You can see the rugged outline of the mountains against the stars, and I'm almost sure there's a steamer anchored in that little bay our old charts show just below Whale Point."

"What makes you think she's a steamer?" Sammy questioned.

"Electric lights," Greg told him. "The masthead light is bright white, and there's a red light lower down. A port-side running light," he added. "And a bright stern light, too. She's lit up like a Christmas tree without a care in the world."

"Sounds like a Leaguer," Smitty agreed. "Arrogant bastards. And either way, she wouldn't be lit up like that if she didn't think she could defend herself. So probably a warship," he deduced, echoing Greg's own thoughts.

"Yeah. We have to assume so, just as we have to assume they control Ascension. Damn!" Greg added, thumping the bulwark with his fist. "I wish we could tell somebody! It might at least get a garrison—and some guns—to St. Helena quicker!"

Sammy nodded in the darkness. They'd sailed in silence, on orders, since leaving the cape—not that they'd had anything to report. Now, even if sending a message wasn't too dangerous, they'd passed the point where they could realistically expect Alex-aandra to hear them. *They'd* heard a lot, from Alex-aandra's far more powerful transmitter. They'd still been close enough to learn of the defeat of the most recent Grik attempt to retake the Celestial City, and had picked through the increasingly weaker coded signals recounting the tragic losses north of Mahe. They could still piece a few bits together until about two weeks before. But if they couldn't hear Alex-aandra anymore, there was little chance anything they sent would be picked up. Particularly by anyone friendly. The next opportunity they had to communicate would be when they sailed into range of Fred Reynolds and Kari-Faask's tiny transceiver possibly still aboard the New United States ship *Congress* in the Caribbean. Hopefully by then, they could pass messages to Shinya and Second Fleet as well. But Fred and Kari, and certainly Second Fleet, were still a long way off.

"What are we going to do, Skipper?" Smitty asked.

"Stay away from Ascension, for one," Greg replied,

handing his telescope to the gunnery officer so he could see for himself. The masthead lights of the distant ship had been visible from deck for a short while. Now, with them turning away, they were receding again. "But we'll try to keep an eye on the other ship the lookout saw. I'm thinking the other lights, going slowly west, must've been the stern lanterns of a sailing ship, which means, most likely, she's a Dom. If that's the case, I'd love to know what they were doing at Ascension, talking to the League. And it might be a good idea to find out."

"Doms have steamers," Sammy pointed out. That was true; side-wheel sailing steamers like the Empire of the New Britain Isles had long relied on. And until recently, they'd been largely confined to this ocean to oppose what they must've considered the nearer, more dangerous threat—at least until they stirred the whole Alliance against them. That closer adversary was the apparently small but powerful navy of what Fred and Kari called the New United States. It was composed of various locals as well as descendants of US–Mexican War–era soldiers and sailors occupying much of what Greg and Smitty remembered as Texas, Oklahoma, Louisiana, Arkansas, and Alabama. *Have to add that to Nig-Taak's world map, once we're sure of the borders—and what lies beyond,* Greg reflected absently. *Maybe someday we'll get the whole thing filled in. But so far, we're probably sure of less than. . . what? Five percent of the globe? Silva and Cook explored more of* Borno—where our capital is!—*than anyone else from Baalkpan ever has. We've seen a lot of Pacific and Indian Ocean coastlines, mostly inhabited by enemies, and Nig-Taak was sure enough of some fairly odd Atlantic shores to record them on his great atlas, but most of those shores remain unknown. And we know almost nothing of continental interiors.*

"They do," Greg agreed with Sammy. "But why send one when we hammered so many west of the Pass of Fire? And they can't carry enough fuel to cross the Atlantic under power, anyway," he argued. "My bet is, she's a dedicated sailor like us, for the same reason: long legs and no longer fit for the line of battle." He barely saw thoughtful nods in the dark.

"So, if she *is* a Dom, do you mean to pursue her? To, ah, detain her?" Pol asked.

Greg looked at him. "Of course. We *are* at war with the bastards." He glanced at the dying fire on the distant island, now just the merest speck of orange light. "We'll try to keep the stern lantern in sight from the masthead, but crack on all night, staying to windward. I've no doubt we can get ahead of her. Grik Indiamen are better sailors than Dom galleons, by all accounts, and I've never seen the Grik we couldn't give half our sails with this fine breeze on our quarter."

"But if we're west of her when the sun rises, won't she see us before we see her?" Sammy asked.

"We don't know what her exact heading is, but my guess is she'll keep west-northwest. We should be able to stay to windward, slightly south, and take in topgallants before dawn." He snorted. "And if our 'Cat lookouts *can't* spot her first, I'll make sure they're transferred to the black gang on some tub of a steam transport—because they're going blind."

"But if the Doms resist us—they're very liable to, I understand—won't the League ship at Ascension hear the cannon fire?" Pol asked, concerned.

Greg grinned. "With this wind, even that Dom should make seventy, eighty miles before dawn. So unless the Leaguer follows, which is possible, I suppose," he confessed, "or gave the Doms radio, which is far less likely in my opinion, they'll never have a clue what happens."

"And if they *do* follow?" Sammy persisted.

"Then they should catch up by dawn and we'll see the lights they've been considerate enough to show. We'll bear away farther south, out of sight, then cross their wakes and continue on our way."

Smitty shook his head and almost shivered. "Well, I just had a weird thought. What if that ship, the one we're set to chase, *isn't* a Dom?" he asked suddenly. "What if it isn't anybody we know at all?"

Sammy blinked at him in a fashion mingling curiosity and dread.

Greg smiled. "Well . . . that would be interesting," he conceded, then shrugged. "And I guess it's even possible that whoever she is—Dom or not—the steamer isn't even a League ship either." Nobody really believed that, but they couldn't say it was impossible. "Either way, though," he continued, "that's what we're here for. To find out what's what."

"On deck!" came the cry from the masthead. "Sail, nort'-nort'wes!" Half a dozen Imperial telescopes rose along the starboard quarterdeck rail, pointed in generally the right direction and stabilized by elbows touching wood. *Donaghey* was sailing stiff with hardly a pitch under topsails and staysails alone, and the rail was rock steady. The sky above remained a light purple, with wisps of gilded clouds scudding along, but had begun to blaze bright orange in the east. The wind had strengthened, but the glass—the crude water barometer in Greg's cabin—remained unchanged. Soon, they could even pick out the distant sail from the deck, and Greg glanced impatiently aloft. The lookout should've been able to tell if the ship was alone by now. He certainly couldn't imagine a League steamer plodding along behind. But the longer he waited, the longer the target had to spot them—and react. Even if his plan went perfectly, they'd be seen very soon, and he wanted to be flying first.

"Just as you predicted," Saama-Kera said, blinking admiration. "Well done, Cap-i-taan."

"Just guesswork—and luck, Sammy," Greg said, his weathered face reddening. He stared intently at the lookout.

"What more do you see?" his exec demanded loudly, as impatient as Greg.

"Nuttin,' sur."

"Very well," Greg said. "All hands to make sail, Mr. Saama." He smiled, glancing at his bosun. "No need to whisper, now."

"All hands to make sail!" Sammy thundered, and Jenaar-Laan swept forward, blowing the corresponding series of blasts on his whistle. 'Cats that had been sweeping the deck clean fore and aft stowed their brooms and raced up the shrouds while others exploded from below, already carrying their hammocks. These they tightly rolled and stuffed in the netting amidships before racing aloft as well. Some, gunners and Marines or others unfit for duty above, went back for the rest of the hammocks. Greg raised his telescope again and studied the haze-fuzzed silhouette less than eight miles away. "Stand by to come right, to course zero two zero," he told the 'Cat at the wheel.

"Aye, sur."

Greg waited a moment longer, then said, "Execute." A flood of shouts and whistles followed his command, even as the wheel turned and a seemingly chaotic but carefully choreographed flurry of activity ensued. The mizzen sail loosed and the yards came around, the sails on the main and mizzen spilling their wind. The foresails pulled the ship around until the fore staysail started to flutter and the mizzen came up taut, far out to port, helping the ship complete her turn.

"Rudder's amidships!" shouted the 'Cat at the helm, and his call carried forward, repeated by the bosun and his mates. Immediately, 'Cats hauled on lines to reposition the yards and sheet the sails home—all to take best advantage of the wind based on the ship's current heading. Greg tried to keep his face impassive, but his heart bounded in his chest with love for his ship and the long-serving crew who knew her so well that all he had to do was give a course and say "execute." He doubted there'd ever been a skipper of a square-rigged ship with so little to do in that regard. "We'll have the forecourse and topgallants, Mr. Saama," he said, looking up. "And as soon as the target runs, we'll set the studding sails." The wind was nearly directly aft now, not *Donaghey*'s favorite point, and he wanted to close the target as quickly as he could. But the target didn't run. For long minutes, stretching to half an hour, while the range shortened to five, four, and, unfathomably, three miles, the target didn't respond at all. And anyone could see by now she was a Dom, with her faded red, almost pink sails, and the barbarously shaped golden crosses painted on them.

"I was going to send the hands to breakfast as soon as

the chase began," Greg told Sammy doubtfully, "but maybe we'd best sound general quarters and have the cook and his mates make a pile of sandwiches."

"Ay, ay, sur," Sammy said, equally confused about how the enemy could've ignored them so long. "Sound generaal quarters! Clear for aaction!" he said more loudly. "Cooks to make saamitches!" There wasn't much else left to prepare, and there was little further activity on deck. The ship had already been cleared for all intents and purposes. Gun's crews gathered closer to their weapons, helmets replaced Dixie cup hats, and armorers passed out pistol belts to gun captains and ensured the arms lockers between the guns had sufficient cutlasses and axes. Marines clambered up the shrouds with rifles slung, or lined the rails. There came a rumble almost beneath Greg's feet, and a gasp of gray smoke from a little exhaust pipe that snaked a short distance up the mizzenmast when the four-cylinder Wright-Gypsy-type generator engine, just like the ones used by Nancy floatplanes, whipped to life. It would power electric lights below, particularly in the magazine, where exploding case shot was kept, in the ammunition handling room where thick fabric-powder cartridges were stored in hundreds of robust Baalkpan bamboo pass box tubes, and in the wardroom, where the surgeon waited. The generator also powered the comm gear, which they wouldn't use unless things went very badly and Greg chose (and had the opportunity) to make a final report, hoping *someone* might hear, and the fire-control circuit, which they'd certainly use directly.

Donaghey had been the first Allied ship, besides *Walker* and *Mahan*, of course, to use electricity, originally in the form of a wind generator sufficient to power a crystal receiver and then a weak wireless set. She needed more juice for the firing circuit and needed it on demand, not on the whim of a capricious wind. Even though Allied storage batteries had improved, they still remained unreliable and drained quickly. Besides, a sufficient bank of batteries and capacitors for their purposes would take as much space as the generator and a fairly large fuel tank. The fuel tank, for the generator and floatplane, was below the waterline. But the generator produced more electricity than they needed, thus the electric lights.

Perhaps someone finally saw them, or maybe heard the insistent clanging of *Donaghey*'s alarm gong and the long roll of the Marines' drums thundering in the waist, because the Dom suddenly let fly her aft sheets and veered away, her staysails flapping in the wind. Greg raised his telescope and saw utter pandemonium erupting aboard the other ship: men running to and fro, a few beginning to climb the shrouds. A line of officers in large, lacy tricorns stared at them over the poop, as if amazed. A few gunports opened and guns ran out, but only a few. It seemed forever before the Dom shifted her yards and trimmed her sails in anything like an appropriate manner, and all the while *Donaghey* narrowed the gap. Even when the Dom seemed as squared away as she was able, running directly away to the northwest, *Donaghey* visibly gained—even without her studding sails.

Greg continued to study the ship, ignoring his steward, who snatched his hat off his head and tried to reach high enough to replace it with a helmet. Without thinking, he crouched to let the short Lemurian complete his task. He did notice when the little 'Cat buckled his cutlass and pistol belt around his waist, but never took his eye from the glass. He hadn't fought Doms before, and their ship wasn't actually what he'd call a galleon either. It had a quarterdeck and poop, but there was no ridiculously high stern castle like the word usually conjured in his mind. *Probably one of their heavy frigates,* he mused, and it seemed to roughly match the standard dimensions: 170′ x 50′, and about fifteen hundred tons. *Likely a crew of about three fifty,* he added to himself. It was handsome in a way Lemurians might appreciate, with gilded carving around the broad stern galleries and colorful paintings down its sides, fore and aft, above the gundeck. And the gundeck was a bit disconcerting. All the ports were open now, revealing sixteen heavy guns per side, probably twenty-four-pounders, and Greg had no doubt there were half again as many nine-pounders on the decks above. Considering their relative sizes and apparent power, he supposed the Doms must've run on instinct, surprised by the appearance of their foes. They probably hadn't been expecting to run into anything and their lookouts must've been dozing. *Wouldn't want to be them,* he thought with a chill, remembering the lurid accounts of Dom bloodthirstiness he'd heard. *Still, all those officers peering over the transom are glassing us as well now.*

"I wonder what they'll do now they've got a haan-dle on their confusion," Sammy said beside him. "An' realize they've got us outgunned. Oh! Here come the saamitches!"

Greg glanced up at the maintop—the "fighting top," now full of Marines with their Allin-Silva rifles—and Smitty Smith and a pair of ordnance strikers, already calculating ranges and clustered around the extremely crude but effective gyro Sonny Campeti had come up with. It was little more than a plumb bob in a wood-framed glass box, but it allowed Smitty to coordinate their salvos, or broadsides, and fire them as true as muzzle-loading smoothbore guns were capable of. Gunners would match his shouted elevations and train their weapons to lead the target as directed, and the guns would be fired electrically by a common circuit leading to primers in their vents—which would be closed at Smitty's discretion when his plumb bob swayed across a fixed point in the box. "They'll die anyway," Greg answered grimly, scooping a sandwich from the offered plate and taking a huge bite.

They'd closed the range to half a mile and were gaining quickly despite anything the Dom could do. He chewed and swallowed. "Run up the battle flag and give them a shot from one of the bow chasers," he said. "Who knows? Maybe they'll surrender." He doubted that. A few Dom ships had surrendered at Malpelo, completely surrounded and hammered into helplessness, or had been boarded and their officers killed. But quarter wasn't something expected in this war, by either side. The concept was utterly alien to the Grik, with a few notable exceptions, and just as unfamiliar to most Lemurians until recently. They *still* didn't quite get it. They'd only ever wanted peace, to be left alone, but if they had to fight it came with the instinctive acceptance that they had to kill whoever drove them to it or die themselves. *But maybe,* Greg reconsidered, *the Doms'll think we're a New US ship when they see our flag. They're kind of similar.* And they'd had reports from Fred and Kari that Doms would surrender to the "other Americans." He didn't know if it worked the other way around.

A huge cheer arose amid stamping feet when the Stars and Stripes swept up the mainmast to the very top and streamed away, reaching to the north-northwest. It was a very large flag, with all *Donaghey*'s major actions embroidered on the stripes in golden thread. *Walker*'s flag, similarly decorated, bore the most of those by far, starting with Makassar Strait and Java Sea on another world. But the record of the many bitter actions *Donaghey* had survived, usually victorious, infused her crew with a fierce satisfaction. To punctuate the cheers, the starboard twelve-pounder on the fo'c'sle barked over the headrails, its report somewhat flat with the wind aft. There was time for the breeze to sweep the smoke to the left before the shot plunked into the sea close enough to wet the officers on the enemy poop with the splash. Another cheer surged.

Almost immediately, smoke blossomed from two ports below the Dom poop, and a pair of splashes kicked up about two hundred yards short.

"She'll start hitting us soon," Sammy observed. "You want us to heat the chasers up? Fire like we mean it?"

Greg considered while he quickly finished his sandwich and washed it down with a swig from his canteen. *Donaghey*'s gunnery had reached such a state that soon she could yaw and deliver a concentrated salvo of a dozen eighteen-pound solid shot directly into the enemy's vulnerable stern. That was what she'd loaded first, for the range advantage solid shot had over case. But range hadn't turned out to be an issue. Even if it had, a much higher percentage of *Donaghey*'s guns would find their mark than the Dom could even imagine, supposing he hadn't been at Malpelo, which was a pretty good bet. The devastation would be horrendous as shot blew through windows and light bulkheads separating the officers' quarters from the gundeck—they'd been told Doms didn't remove those bulkheads during action—and shrieked its length, wounding masts amid shoals of wicked splinters, wrecking carriages, and overturning guns. Mere human bodies wouldn't noticeably slow them. Some might even exit the bow, making great, jagged holes. But if they didn't disable the Dom, he'd gain on them and it would take time to catch back up.

"By all means, Mr. Saama," Greg finally said. "Maybe we'll knock something important away and get this over quicker. Either way, when we have her right by the tail—within five hundred yards or so—we'll come left and unmask the starboard battery. We'll hit her as fast as we can, with two salvos of roundshot. If she strikes her colors, swell. If not, we'll follow 'em with a third salvo of exploding case."

"Risky," Sammy lamented. He blinked seriously, his tail swishing with apprehension. "I know you want to take the Dom ship in-taact. Not only for prisoners to question about its meeting with the League, but I can imagine all sorts of situations in which the ship itself might prove useful. Case might seriously daam-age or destroy it, 'specially if it sets her afire."

"True, but by all accounts, it's tough to make Doms quit. A few rounds of case ought to shake 'em up, maybe stun or demoralize the gun's crews enough to throw off their aim and let us get close enough to sweep her with chain, grape, maybe even our machine guns. Then, with the enemy's sails and rigging cut to pieces, we'll position *Donaghey* to rake her again and again with grape and canister while our Marines slaughter their crew with rifles." He frowned. "We'll see how much Doms can take before they throw in the towel." He looked intently at Sammy. "And we'll board her if we have to, but only as a last resort. The ship, and the information we might get, *is* worth some of us, but if I think the price is too high, I'll sink her without batting an eye."

Sammy grinned, trying to lighten Greg's darkening mood. "Mi-Anakka baat their eyes all the time, Skipper. And *this* crew may do so resentfully if you sink their prize!"

Greg's lips twitched upward. Ships that took prizes were getting bonus pay now. But that wouldn't influence his decision.

At the command, both twelve-pounders on the fo'c'sle

began banging away with a will. They were firing in local control, with friction primers, aimed by their gun captains, but Smitty was correcting their ranges and calling out when the keel was even. The gunners paid him little mind. They had plenty of practice at this and could *feel* when the moment was right to pull their lanyards. Soon, shot after shot was tearing home, spoiling the beauty of the target's stern gallery. The enemy chasers kept at it too, though noticeably slower. The ship shivered from an impact forward, above her starboard hawse, and the courses had a few holes in them now. A shot tore through one of the ship's boats stowed on the main hatch, sending a shower of splinters aft before it nicked the mainmast, struck the deck, and bounded over the rail. Greg had actually considered bringing his last Nancy floatplane on deck and assembling it, in case he had to look for the enemy. Now he was glad he hadn't.

"Good shooting, sur," observed the 'Cat at the wheel.

Greg was nodding, a little surprised himself, when the starboard quarterdeck 12-pdr gun captain, who'd been left out so far, snorted. "At dis range? I could hit 'em fum here, flickin' a musket baall wit' a spoo—" In that instant, a nine-pound shot struck him where his neck met his chest, nearly tearing his head off. The body pitched back, helmet flying, across the gun in a shower of blood. Blood spattered as far as Greg, spotting his khaki trousers red. Without a word, a pair of 'Cats rushed forward from one of the aft chasers and carried the body below. Greg's face turned hard as he watched them go; then he looked through his glass again. The range had finally closed to about five hundred yards, absolute point-blank for *Donaghey*'s guns, and he began to call the starboard battery to stand by and command the helmsman to turn—when he saw the *enemy* begin to yaw to port. "All hands!" he cried. "Down! Take cover!"

In another age, on his home world, such an order might've been appreciated, but would've been met with incredulity. Sailors and their officers were expected to stand, unconcerned, and take what was coming. Even here, in the thick of the fight, few would try to conceal themselves. It served little purpose, broadside to broadside, and the best way to make the enemy stop shooting was to shoot him first. But *Donaghey* would have to take this broadside head-on, delivered cold, and there was nothing Greg could do but present the smallest target possible, hope the rest of the enemy gunners weren't as good as her chaser crews, and pray his ship and people didn't suffer too badly before they could hit back.

The Dom ship grew larger, longer, turning quickly. Even before she had a chance to settle, a long, rolling broadside, starting aft and moving forward, erupted from her side, sending white smoke gushing over and away. Most of the big twenty-four-pound balls went high, shivering *Donaghey*'s sails and sending blocks racing down severed halyards to crash on deck. A fair number probably missed completely. One hit the muzzle of the portside chaser, shattering, and flipped the gun on its side. Screams arose on the fo'c'sle as 'Cats were crushed by the gun or flayed by fragments of the iron ball. More splinters sprayed aft from the shattered boat on the hatch, one hitting Greg's helmet that he'd providentially dipped. A couple crashed into the hull forward, shaking the entire ship. Then it was over.

"Starboard battery, stand by!" Greg roared. "Helm," he shouted, glancing at the wheel—only to see the 'Cat there was down, eyes clenched shut in agony, teeth showing bright. Something had fallen on him, probably breaking his collarbone. But the Republic sailing master, Leutnant Koor-Susk, had taken his place. "Helm," Greg repeated, "come left to three two zero! Execute! Make ready, Mr. Smith!" he called upward. "Commence firing at your discretion!"

"Range four-fifty," Smitty called down, estimating what it would be when *Donaghey* finished her turn. "Five degrees left!" The call was repeated and handspikes shifted guns to match the marks on the backs of the carriages with the ones on deck. "Prime!" Vents were pierced and primers inserted.

"Clear!" the gunners shouted as their crews stepped away.

"All clear!" cried *Donaghey*'s first lieutenant, Mak-Araa. "Baattery is ready!"

All this was accomplished in seconds, before *Dona-*

ghey's guns would even bear. Now the turn was complete and Koor called that the rudder was amidships. "Firing!" Smitty warned, staring at the plumb bob in the box. Just before it swung across the mark beneath it, he closed the firing switch. Electricity raced down the wires, igniting the primers in the vents, and the ship heaved as all twelve of *Donaghey*'s starboard eighteen-pounders spat orange flame and bright smoke simultaneously, backed by two twelve-pounders in rapid succession. There followed the ripping-sheet sound of heavy projectiles in flight, cut off by a staccato thunder of impacts. Younglings, holding tubular pass boxes and watching from the comparative safety of the companionways, erupted from below and ran to their appointed guns. Only Smitty, above the great cloud of smoke, could see the results, and he quickly called corrections. In fewer than forty seconds, Lieutenant Mak yelled, "All clear. Baattery is ready!" once again. Again, Smitty roared that he was firing. Another concussive blast shook the ship and shot pounded the Dom.

"Load case shot!" Greg shouted, even while the enemy remained invisible beyond the dense fog bank of smoke rushing down on her. Slowly, she began to emerge as the smoke dispersed. "God almighty," he breathed. Smitty's range estimates had been dead-on, but he may've led his target a bit much. Understandable, since *Donaghey* had never engaged a target so closely with her new fire-control procedures in place. Not that the result was a bad thing. At least for them. And to top it off, Greg's ship had never fired such densely patterned salvos in her life. It looked like every round had struck forward, battering three of the enemy's gunports into one, and the few that missed the hull seemed to have struck the foremast. It was still leaning far over to windward, the stays somehow holding it, but then they began to part, whipping high in the air, and the entire thing, practically from the fo'c'sle deck, crashed over the side into the sea. Men were seen jumping in the water, and Greg wondered how long they'd last. They hadn't seen many mountain fish, but the Atlantic seemed just as thick with other predators as elsewhere. The main topmast and topsail went with the foremast, settling like a shroud over the fo'c'sle, and the drag of the mast quickly brought the Dom ship around until she was bows on to *Donaghey*'s next broadside. "Belay loading case!" Greg shouted. "Those that already have, draw 'em out. Load grape! Helm, resume your original course." He turned to Sammy. "When we're within two hundred yards, we'll come left again and heave to."

"Aye, sur!"

Donaghey straightened, surging closer, then bore away once more, backing her foresails. For five long minutes, she punished the Dom frigate with grape shot, shredding fo'c'sle, sails, boats, and bodies down the length of her main deck. The forward bulkhead behind the shattered headrails became a sieve, and similar destruction must've been done all along the gundeck. Men taking cover behind cannon or in the waist might've survived the onslaught, but soon nothing moved amid the carnage they'd wrought.

"Cease firing!" Greg roared over the din, and his order quickly spread. Two more guns fired before there was silence, and Greg paced to the rail, taking a leather speaking trumpet his steward handed him. *Donaghey* was fewer than a hundred yards from the Dom's sagging bowsprit now, the wind blowing her down on the helpless ship. He glanced at the water churning with blue-gold shapes, tearing at corpses floating amid smoldering clumps of wadding from his guns. The bodies had either fallen or been thrown over the side of the Dom. *Not exactly flashies,* he thought absently. *Not as big, or quite as many as we'll probably find in coastal waters. But just as hungry. Maybe they follow ships?* He shook his head.

"Is anyone alive over there?" he shouted. "Your captain? Any officers?" A few shapes stirred slightly, unwilling to reveal themselves, but some obviously still lived.

"I doubt they speak English, sur," Sammy told him wryly. His blinking didn't match his tone, however, and it was clear he was sickened by what they'd done.

So was Greg, but he was more sickened by their own losses. "Uh," he said, racking his memory. He'd never heard Spanish in his life before going to the Philippines to join *Walker*, and hadn't been there long enough to pick up much. Then again, many Doms spoke . . . other languages, God knew what, and apparently only their officers used Spanish exclusively. "Smitty," he called above, "do you speak Spanish?" He'd had a Filipino wife—of sorts—in Cavite.

"Not a word, sir. Nothin' for *this*, anyway. My girl an' I never did much talkin', if you know what I mean. An' she jabbered in Tagalog mostly, probably to make sure I didn't catch anything."

Greg turned back to the ship.

"Sur," Sammy warned, "we're gonna run aboard her."

"Right. Shift the foresails and bring her around alongside." He raised the trumpet again while his order was obeyed. "Ah, surrendero immediato!" He shook his head. "No *fuego*, we no mato. Discardo *tu* armos!" Eyes appeared, peering from behind battered guns, and three men became visible from where they'd all somehow managed to cram themselves behind the mainmast. All looked at him like he had two heads.

"No! No!" cried a man, an officer, lying next to the broken wheel. His hat was gone and his long dark hair was matted crimson. His leg was obviously shattered and his white breeches were soaked with blood. *"¡Estan prohibos a renairse! Manténganse en sus cañones. Matadlos a todos!" Donaghey* was easing around, edging alongside the Dom that still wallowed there, dragging her foremast like a sea anchor. Most of her forward guns were smothered by wreckage, and few men could've been fit to serve them in any case. But three aft guns suddenly fired, one after another. A ball blasted through the bulwark not far from Greg, spewing a blizzard of splinters. Another struck lower. The third crashed through the bulwark forward, scattering several Marines and cutting the foremast shrouds at the chains when it blew out the other side of the ship. Without even waiting for the order, all *Donaghey*'s guns fired in reply. They were loaded only with grape, which couldn't much hurt those manning the belowdecks guns, not from abeam, but more bodies tumbled on the main deck and wreckage and splinters exploded away. Then, in the lull of the reload, most gunners calling for solid shot of their own accord, a man was seen rushing toward the fallen Dom officer. Marines shot at him, but he was too quick. As he reached the officer, he paused—

then brought a handspike down with all his might, smashing his head.

"Cease firing! Cease firing!" Greg bellowed, but he was probably the only one who hadn't seen the drama across the water. Instead, his eyes were fixed on Lieutenant Saama-Kera, his executive officer and friend, lying on the deck in a spreading pool of blood, a bright, jagged two-foot splinter protruding from his chest. He was quite dead.

"They struck their daamn colors *now*," Lieutenant Mak-Araa called, his tone bitter, practically regretful. "One of her crew tore their flaag down and threw it over the side."

"Very well," Greg said roughly. "Prepare grapnels. Inform Lieutenant Haana we'll lay alongside and board. All hands." He straightened. "Kill anybody who resists, but if they want to surrender we *will* let them. Make sure that's understood."

"Ay, ay, Cap-i-taan Gaarr-ett."

The Dom frigate *Matarife* was a charnel house. Shredded bodies lay heaped and scattered all over her main decks and it wasn't much better below. Shockingly, there'd been further resistance when *Donaghey*'s boarders leaped across—and *Matarife*'s survivors finally saw their foe. Greg had been right; though her officers must've seen his people through their telescopes, the majority of the enemy obviously thought *Donaghey* was a NUS ship. When Lemurian sailors and Marines swarmed aboard, many panicked at the sight of what they thought were genuine demons. Those wild-eyed unfortunates were promptly slain as soon as they lifted a weapon. Most who could merely fled belowdecks, though a couple actually jumped over the side. In spite of the senselessness of this further bloodshed, Greg was proud of his people. They were justifiably angry but showed remarkable restraint and no one who yielded was harmed. It took a little longer to convince those who hid below, but eventually they surrendered their arms—and wounded—when their own surgeon entreated them to. He did this after he saw *Donaghey*'s surgeon, a burly teddy bear of a 'Cat named Sori-Maai, and his mates immediately start trying to save the most horribly wounded Doms.

One of the more difficult obstacles, however, remained the apparent fact that neither side could communicate with the other, except by example in Surgeon Sori's case, and through laborious gestures. Greg's extremely limited Spanish was actually a hindrance, often causing gross misunderstanding. Tribune Pol-Heena's tortured Latin was probably of greater use, providing a few common words. A form of Latin had been preserved by Lemurian Sky Priests to interpret their Sacred Scrolls, but also lingered—from another obscure source—in the Republic. Greg hadn't learned if that source was Byzantine or came from a divergent history in which the classical Roman republic—or empire—survived beyond the tenth century. Unlike Captain Reddy, he wasn't a historian and had little basis for his opinion, but from what he'd picked up, the latter actually seemed more likely.

Establishing complete control over *Matarife* took longer than the fight, but, finally, her fewer than a hundred able-bodied men were secured below, her ninety wounded arranged along the gun deck, receiving care, and the 136 dead went over the side. Aside from her surgeon and a mate, the only surviving "officer" was a young boy, probably a midshipman or something similar. He was dressed as an officer, at least, and appeared so terrified of Lemurians that Greg himself took him aft and locked him in a cabin with food and water. He spent a little time poking through the shambles of other cabins, but *Matarife*'s stern had taken a terrible beating, and a thorough examination would take time. He'd approach the boy later and attempt communication when things were more settled.

"Our butcher's bill was seven dead, including Looten-aant Saama-Kera," Lieutenant Mak-Araa told Greg as they surveyed the damage to *Matarife*'s fo'c'sle. The foremast wreckage had been cut away before the stump could pound a hole in the ship, but then brought alongside. They were discussing whether it was feasible to fish the lower mast back together and reassemble the top. Probably, with additional reinforcing stays. Greg nodded, both at Mak's words and his sad blinking. "We have nineteen wounded," Mak continued, "six baad. Sori doubts three will live."

"Yeah," Greg agreed solemnly. Sori had worked under Karen Letts and came aboard expressly for this voyage with all the latest knowledge, tools, and medicines the Alliance had devised to care for two distinct species. Greg suspected he was probably better skilled and more experienced than any naval surgeon back home ever was. "I spoke to him a few minutes ago," he continued. "Thank God we have him. He's got the stamina of ten 'Cats, and he's going to need it." He looked at Mak. "You too," he added. "You're XO now, though you'll have to take over here for the time being, when—if—we get this tub underway."

"We will," Mak said, blinking assurance. "Hull daamage wasn't baad. The rigging's cut up, but it was a crummy rig in the first place. Have to change it to sail her understrength, anyway." He glanced at the sky, his tail swishing. "It'll stay fair. Long enough to reset her fore-maast an' get some headsails on her. Then we'll knot an' splice as we go—though I'd prefer a nice, protected anchorage to do it right."

"Me too, but no promises. And the more pressing problem is people," Greg said. Mak nodded. *Donaghey*'s complement was two hundred officers and enlisted. She actually carried more like two thirty, counting those who'd joined her from the Republic, and the many youngling "powder boys." That was more than enough to sail and fight her. And she didn't need nearly as many replacements as a similar ship in an earlier age, because so few succumbed to illness. But she'd just lost nearly thirty people, from a practical standpoint, and *Matarife* would need more to sail her than *Donaghey* did. *Fighting* both ships was practically impossible. At least one must be able to, however, and *Donaghey* was the better choice. So, though they'd already decided *Donaghey* would pose as the Doms' prize when they continued, *Matarife* would necessarily be extremely shorthanded. "Maybe," Greg began doubtfully, "some Doms have been cooperative once they figured out we're *not* demons. You might get a few extra hands from the prisoners in time," he ventured.

"I'd be more confident of that if we could talk to 'em," Mak agreed. "But I'll try."

They were interrupted by a small party of 'Cats suddenly standing before them in the midst of the chaotic labor. They had their hats in their hands and Chief Bosun's Mate Jenaar-Laan was among them. "Yes?" Mak demanded.

"Sur," Jenaar said to Mak, but clearly addressing Greg. "We got dead. We know we can't build a pyre, nor bury 'em on land." He blinked, dissatisfied. 'Cats generally preferred cremation, so their spirits could rise to the Heavens with the smoke, though a growing number of navy and Marine 'Cats had opted for burial in the human destroyermen fashion. "No choice but over the side wit' 'em, sewed in their haam-ocks an' smeared wit' grease so the flaashies don't get 'em . . . even Loo-ten-aant Sammy."

Greg nodded. He'd known this was coming and hadn't been sure how he'd deal with it. Apparently, his crew already knew. "I have to agree with you, Boats. It's a sorry situation, but there's nothing for it."

"Aye, sur. An' it's not like it aan't been done before. It's just . . ."

"What?" Mak asked.

"Well, we just want to make sure . . ." He was blinking rapidly now. "There's stories o' how *Waa-kur* buried her people with Jaap iron, shells that hit her an' didn't blow, when she first came here. . . ."

Greg nodded. He remembered it well. They'd already decided they couldn't spare the traditional projectiles—of their own, at least—and had sent his shipmates to their watery graves with whatever weighty objects they could spare. "What's your point?" he asked gently.

"Well, sur, it's just . . . not all believe you gotta have smoke for souls to rise no more, but some do. Always have. An' if our shipmates' souls *don't* rise, nobody wants 'em spendin' forever wit' a pair o' daamn *Dom* roundshot at their feet." He waved around, encompassing all the 'Cats. Many had paused in their labors to hear this exchange. "We talked this wit' ourselves before, an' . . . if it's okaay wit' you, sur, an' you think we have enough, we'd sooner have our *own* iron wit' us on the bottom of the sea. Not the iron that sent us there." He blinked exasperation, afraid his captain didn't understand.

Greg was surprised by the request, but quickly controlled his expression. After so long together, he couldn't possibly hide *his* "face moving" from *Donaghey*'s crew. And, perhaps oddly, he did understand. Mak, blinking impatience that they'd brought this up now, with so much to do, seemed on the verge of sending the delegation packing. He was a fine officer and would make a good XO, but he hadn't developed Sammy's patience with the hands, or his flexibility when dealing with awkward cultural issues. Sammy had been so good at it, they rarely even came to Greg's attention anymore—but when they arose, they had to be addressed. Greg touched Mak's arm to forestall his gathering rant and blinked acceptance. "Of course, Boats. I get it. And I'm sure we can spare the shot. I'd want the same myself."

"Thaank you, sur," the delegation chorused, and the toil around them resumed, the workers apparently satisfied. Greg looked at Mak. "Carry on. I'm going aft to have another look at the papers and such." He shook his head. "It's a mess back there, and stuff is scattered everywhere." He blinked frustration. "And I can't read anything I find anyway, so we still won't know what the Doms and Leaguers were up to at Ascension. Our best bet is to carry on with our mission. But there'll be no more casting about, exploring. We're bound straight for the NUS navy base on Cuba. It's even more essential we make contact as quickly as possible; let *them* tell us what they make of the papers and prisoners we took. We can't read them," he repeated. "Let's find someone who can."

CHAPTER 7

340 miles SE of Zanzibar
Alongside USS* Keshaa-Fas *(AVD-26)
October 28, 1944

Lieutenant (jg) Saansa-Belkaa dumped a parachute on the seat of her bobbing P-40E Warhawk, serial number 41-5304, before plopping down on it—atop the *other* parachute she already wore—and checking that the block extensions bolted to the rudder pedals hadn't shifted. Then she strapped herself in and looked up past the open canopy and black silhouette of the AVD at the sky. There was a hazy quarter moon overhead with a bright quarter halo washing the stars from the Heavens. Fortunately, however, the wind had settled to a virtual calm and the sea was much smoother now. When she'd set down alongside USS *Keshaa-Fas*—one of numerous armed seaplane tenders converted from *Dowden* and *Haaker-Faask* class steam frigates—the afternoon before, the sea had been fur-raisingly rough. Even worse than her first stop for fuel from AVD-11. And since no P-40 was ever designed as a seaplane, the bizarre contraption they'd created by "slaapin' a pair of Jaap floats" on number 41-5304 would've been difficult for even an experienced Warhawk pilot to get the hang of. That she, Captain Tikker, and the two others rated to fly the ship hadn't cracked it up already was considered a minor miracle, and she'd thought their (and particularly *her*) good luck was over the day before, when she almost flipped the thing.

Oddly, though, she was deeply devoted to the plane. It floated like a Nancy, so it could—theoretically—set down anywhere on the wild, predator-rich sea, and even with the weight and drag of the floats, it was faster than the new-model Fleashooters. She positively gloried in the sheer muscle of the big Aal-i-saan engine. She loved to fly anything and was very good, or she wouldn't have been chosen to fly the P-40-something, as it was often called. She certainly wouldn't've been picked for *this* mission. But nothing made her feel more powerful and free than to strap on the big, thunderous fighter and bolt through the sky at the three hundred miles per hour it could still achieve.

The propeller had been pulled through before they set her in the water, and she quickly performed the complicated start-up procedure. She cracked the throttle an inch, set the mixture, and switched the propeller to Automatic. Generator switch on, fuel boost pump on, she energized the starter. Five strokes of the priming knob, and she flipped the boost pump off. With the Mag switch on Both, she engaged the starter. The prop turned with a high-pitched whine and the engine fired erratically. Without thinking, she moved the mixture control to Auto-Rich and turned the boost pump back on, feeding the engine with the priming knob until it settled down to business and ran smoothly.

Exhaust swirled in the cockpit, quickly swept away by the roaring propwash, and after a glance at the oil pressure, she looked to her right when someone slapped her on the shoulder. "God go witchoo!" came a shout. She couldn't see the face in the dark, but knew her well-wisher was *Keshaa-Fas*'s air division chief, there to unhook the cradle straps used to lift the plane. P-40s didn't have built-in lifting points like Nancys, or even the giant Clippers. The chief's farewell was what gave him away, because she'd noticed before that he wore a wooden cross. *Lots more Chiss-chins these days,* she thought, not really troubled, just baffled. *Even with Sister Audry gone east, her Caato-lik . . . herd*—she shought that was the right word—*keeps growing.* She wasn't sure why. As far as she could tell, the fundamentals of Chiss-chinny weren't that different from her own faith in one Maker of All Things. But then someone told her Chiss-chins worshipped *three* gods: a father, his son, and a spook. That bothered her. Most Lemurians believed in ghosts who, for one reason or another, couldn't ascend to the Heavens. Captain Tikker—kind of—straightened her out, explaining the three gods were really one (even the spook), who combined to become a Holy Trinity. At least in Sister Audry's version. Other Chiss-chins, like some of the old destroyermen—and most of the Empire of the New Britain Isles—kept things simpler, it seemed, believing in one Maker who sent his son to save people from themselves. But they *killed* him! And it was *his* ghost that came and told everybody he still loved them before he went to the Heavens. Or something like that.

She actually found that rather comforting, that the Maker's own son—she thought he was Jeez, based on how often she'd heard that name called upon by hu-maans and Mi-Anakka—still cared for them, despite how he'd been treated. And she supposed she saw the attraction of believing that. A Maker of *love*, above and beyond the mere vaguely interested benevolence attributed to the Maker of *her* faith. She still found it odd there could be different kinds of Chiss-chins, but then, her faith was just as subtly different from the Aryaalans'. The fundamentals were the same, but Aryaalans thought the *sun* was the Maker, the moon His brother, and the Maker knew only what you did while one or the other was overhead. She believed the Maker *made* the sun and moon and was everywhere in the Heavens, watching all. The sun and moon were important, sure, as the most visible manifestations of His creation, and she faced them when she prayed. But she was no *sun worshipper* like those weird Aryaalans! Most Mi-Anakka shared one steadfast belief, however, that the stars in the Heavens were the souls of those who'd gone before. Why else would some gather in clan groups while others stayed to themselves?

She reached out and patted the chief's arm in return. "And the Maker watch over you!" she shouted back. Then, when she was sure the chief and the lifting straps had all been raised clear and her plane was pointed away from the dark side of the AVD, she slammed and locked the canopy and advanced the throttle. Quickly, the unlikely aircraft gathered speed until it finally bounced into the air and Saansa-Belkaa hurtled northwest in the black, lonely night. She saw the stars better now, above the low-lying haze, and as always they gave her great comfort. But she had plenty of time, and under the circumstances it seemed appropriate to let her mind wander among the various notions of the Maker—and her life beyond the coming sunrise.

An hour and a half later, at five thousand feet, what had been a dark smear on the graying horizon became the dawn-spangled shape of Zanzibar. They'd debated whether she should make a high-or low-level observation and finally decided *she'd* be observed either way. It would be best to make the most of it. And Kurokawa had to know they'd be looking for him. An overflight might raise his guard, but that couldn't be helped. And if the past was any guide, his paranoia might even move him to do something rash that they could take advantage of—if they knew about it in time. Besides, they had to learn what awaited them, and having a good, close look was the only way. Saansa glanced at the smooth board strapped to her leg, with a copy of the map the League Kraaut Fiedler drew, and was surprised to see she'd apparently made landfall near the northeast end of the island. *There's that Notion Isle,* she thought, *right where it should be.* She decided to continue on to Lizard Mouth Bay and then turn south. The island was only about fifty miles long, north to south, and if she followed the single road, she could check Tailbone Bay and still hit Lizard Ass Bay, where Kurokawa's primary facilities were supposed to be, before anyone knew she was coming. She began her descent.

She also pressed the Push to Talk button near the throttle and began describing what she saw to *Keshaa-Faask*'s radio operator, using the made-up place-names on the island along with apparently random, nonsensical words for the various features she confirmed, as well as their relative directions and distances from the place-names. They knew the League, at least, had learned Lemurian, and they could no longer use it to speak in the clear. In retrospect, doing it at all had been a terrible mistake, and they must always assume the baad guys were listening. At the same time, however, Saansa had to report in real time in case she didn't make it back. The easy answer was to use the apparent gibberish she'd been practicing for the last couple of days. The AVD wouldn't respond; the enemy might have radio-direction finding gear, and Saansa worried whether she was actually being heard. But "Kay-Eff" had been chosen as the closest picket because she had the very latest comm gear. She'd have to trust to that.

She reported shore batteries, poodles, that looked like the big hundred-pounders the Grik BBs used, covering the approach to Lizard Mouth Bay. And the next such emplacements she described would be "gri-kakka." After that would come "Dixie cups," "akka feet," and so on. The repair yard in the bay was a "grawfish," and the small tent city she picked out of the jungle, probably sheltering the Grik workforce or garrison, was a "soda straw," and it was "poot" (meaning to the south). Those names would change as well, following the list marked down the side of the map on her leg. Distances were the most difficult and would give the enemy the best chance to decode the rest, so she alternated her estimates in tails or miles, using preselected multiples. Obviously, the map must never fall into enemy hands, even if destroying it was the last thing she ever did.

The jungle was thick, but she picked out a well-worn trace meandering to the southeast and followed it down toward the gap between the "gut," which was a gently sloping mountain near the center of the island, and Tailbone Bay due east. About halfway to the gap was a fairly large Grik encampment, a "bowl of noodles," hacked out of the jungle. Tailbone Bay was a respectable anchorage, about five miles long and wide, and seemed better protected than the Mouth, but she saw only two ironclad cruisers—"six sticks"—there. Time to turn southwest. To her right, along the base of the gut, were more Grik encampments and, even though they were well hidden, a growing number of what had to be camouflaged industrial facilities betrayed by hazy oil smoke, as opposed to the cook-fire smoke hovering over Grik camps. When Lizard Ass Bay came in view at last, on the southwest coast of the island, she became very busy, describing all she saw—and trying to keep her excitement from throwing her codes out of order. Just as the map predicted, there were three distinct airfields and three large barracks buildings for most of the surviving Japanese sailors. There was also a lot of activity on the bay itself; at least a dozen cruisers were anchored, and a couple more were underway. None looked exactly like those she'd seen before either. More like what Mallory's 3rd (Army) Pursuiters observed when they rounded on Kurokawa's fleet that hit TF Alden so hard. She'd heard their top hampers had been reduced and they relied almost entirely on steam power—meaning Kurokawa must've improved their engines. She could confirm that now. Along the docks, several large shipyards were busy building or refitting some very big ships. They were too jumbled together to get a good count or determine precisely what they were, but at least two were becoming carriers. And *there* was the single large carrier she'd expected to see, moored near the center of the bay by one of the little islets they'd dubbed "the Turds," scattered from there, up around the point to the northwest. *Oh, how I wish I had just* one *bomb!* Saansa seethed to herself. Just sitting there, the carrier seemed helpless, and no one had fired a single shot at her.

That abruptly changed. A puff of white smoke appeared off her starboard wing, then another, and she knew her pleasant sightseeing trip was over. The Jaap-Griks were waking up. *And they've maybe built some plane-blaasting guns like the Allied DP 4"-50s,* she fretted. *But Col-nol Maal-lory didn't see anything like that on their carriers, so maybe it's* Saavoie? She banked toward the airbursts as she'd been taught, to foil corrective fire. She also dutifully reported taking flak "fleas," as opposed to "car keys"—whatever *those* were—that would've signified rockets similar to those defending Sofesshk. Swooping lower, northward and to the right, she saw *Savoie* at last, tied to a long dock on the upper end of the bay. The huge, light gray ship stood out sharply against the dark green jungle beyond. She wasn't as big as *Amagi* had been, but her lines looked more . . . aggressive somehow. More malevolent. And far less ascetic, she had to admit. Several flashes lit her sides, in her upper works, and *brown* clouds of smoke blossomed around her plane, shaking it with concussive blasts she heard over the engine. Bright tracers arced toward her as well, but there were only a couple streams and they fell well short. Still . . .

"Kay-Eff, Kay-Eff!" she said in her mic. "The fleas are new haatched. I repeat, *new haatched*! Goofy has his *own* fleas!" A burst below her plane rocked it violently and something struck it loudly. That was when she decided she'd probably seen as much as she'd get to, and it was probably time to go. *One last thing,* she decided. *Two,* she amended, banking hard to the east and diving. According to the map, Kurokawa's personal compound was near the dock *Savoie* occupied. If she confirmed that, it would corroborate virtually the entire map, and she'd send the coded phrase that meant it was reliable.

And there it is!

Immediately inshore of the east side of the dock, less than 150 tails distant, was a large, single-story structure much like the Japanese barracks, but wider and shorter, surrounded by a low wooden wall. Exactly as described. She was *so* tempted to strafe it, but they had no idea where Kurokawa was keeping his prisoners. They might be in there with him. Reluctantly, she continued on, turning southeast toward the central airfield she'd seen coming in. She wanted a better look. The airbursts turned white again—briefly—then quickly subsided as she flashed over a repair yard and one of the barracks buildings. There'd never been a *lot* of "aak-aak," which either meant she'd caught them with their kilts off or they had only a dozen or so weapons, aside from *Savoie*'s, that could engage flying targets with exploding shells. She hoped it was the latter, and they were just high-angle muzzle-loaders or something. She'd never seen one. Even if that was the case, though, they had to have a new carriage with better pointing and training features than anyone had seen before, not to mention some means of absorbing recoil. She didn't like it at all. *Good fire discipline too,* she thought, blinking worriedly, *means Griks aren't in charge of air defense—or Kuro-kaa-wa "Haaliked" his warriors as well.* That was certainly possible, and extremely concerning.

It was now universally accepted that though Grik were

born stupid, they weren't naturally doomed to remain so. They'd been kept that way by a wildly constrictive culture and God-on-Earth deity personified by their Celestial Mother. It was she—and her choosers—who decided which common Uul could live based solely on apparent aggression (a trait which, when pervasive enough, often resulted in youthful demise in any event), and by sending most others to the cookpots before they reached a mental maturity sufficient to allow something as simple as the concept of "Why?" to pop in their heads. General Halik—*no longer an active enemy of the Alliaance, thank the Maker*—had proven that older Grik *could* grow wiser, and if their instinctive obedience and late-blooming cognition was rewarded with benevolence, they might yield true loyalty, an undetermined, as yet, measure of initiative and genuine, selfless courage. They already knew General Esshk had "Haliked" a fair percentage of his army, at least, and equipped it on a material level similar to what the Allies had when they conquered Ceylon. That was likely to make the campaign for Sofesshk a bitter grind, completely aside from enemy numbers. But if Kurokawa trusted *all* his Grik with sentience—and better weapons—"Outhouse" might be an even tougher nut to crack than they feared.

Quickly, the jungle closed back in—but suddenly opened again, exposing the largest airfield on the island. There were two grass strips with crude, camouflaged hangers lining both from one end to the other. Many appeared empty, but at three hundred feet, Saansa saw the noses of a *lot* of planes poking out. She knew they'd hammered a good chunk of Kurokawa's air power when they sank two of his carriers, but he'd apparently been stockpiling more. Whether he had enough capable Grik pilots remained to be seen. On impulse, she pulled up and came around. Nobody was shooting at her now. Maybe they didn't have gun emplacements around the strip. But they'd *already* shot at her, and that pissed her off. She decided to exercise her discretion to raise a little chik-aash "if the risk is minimal." Lining up on one row of hangers, she watched the N3 sight reaching for it. Kicking the rudder slightly left, she squeezed the trigger.

The P-40-something had only two .50-caliber machine guns. Four had been removed, put back, then taken out again for this trip to save weight. There was some extra ammo for the guns Saansa had, however, and she saw no sense in taking it all back. Smoky Baalkpan Arsenal tracers converged on the hangers and debris immediately flew. Shredded foliage from branches and fronds placed on roofs exploded in clouds of dead leaves, disintegrating limbs, and whatever lay below. Figures ran in all directions, leaping into trenches or bolting for the jungle. A few just stood and stared. The third hanger erupted with an orange flare within a roiling ball of greasy black smoke and falling timbers. Saansa flew through the smoke, trigger still down, and was rewarded by another flash of fire from a second detonation that slammed her plane. Again, she felt it shudder when something struck the underside. Releasing the trigger, she pulled back on the stick. Blowing through the last of the smoke, she twisted around and saw something flit down the strip below. *A plane!* she realized. *At least one. Coming after* me*!* She reported the scramble with a *kack*ing double snort of derision by saying there were "bugs on the windscreen." Something tickled her mind, however, and she concentrated on what she'd seen. *Come to think on it, the plane didn't look like the others. It's bigger than the single-seat jobs, so like Allied Fleashooters, but not as big as Kuro-kaa-wa's twin-engine torpedo planes.* She wondered what it might be—and it dawned on her there'd been more, maybe five just like it, gathered on the downwind end of the southwest-northeast strip.

Standing the P-40 on its starboard wing, she came around, looking up to see what she'd done. She didn't see the weird plane anymore, or any of the others she *thought* she'd glimpsed. But more explosions rocked the jungle, involving perhaps a third of the line of hangers she'd attacked as flames began to spread. Grik were scurrying to push planes to safety, but with the prevailing wind she doubted they'd succeed. Particularly since the rough grass strip seemed to have caught fire as well. With any luck, the flames would leap across to the opposite hangers and she'd have erased an entire airfield with almost no effort at all. *A couple bombs would be nice,* she wished again, *in-cendi-aaries, to* really *get the fire lit. But I don't have any, and I've only got so many bullets and so much fuel.*

This was a scout, after all, not a full-blown attaack. The maap was pretty good, but it's more important now that I get back to tell anything that struck me than it is to shoot up a few more planes.

Enough, she decided. She wasn't concerned the strange aircraft she saw taking off might catch her, even if it made it in the air. *Nothing on this world can catch* this *plane—except another P-40E without floats dragging it down,* she amended. Still reluctant—her blood was up—she finally pulled up and away, quickly climbing to five thousand feet by the time she crossed the white sandy beach near "Head Point" on the southeast end of the island, heading out to sea.

"Kay-Eff, Kay-Eff," she said in her mic. "Am feet wet, and the Maker is good." The last was her confirmation that Fiedler's map was accurate. Now, combined with her coded observations and additions, they'd be better off from a planning perspective even if something still happened to her. That was a relief. Things *had* hit her plane after all, and it was a long way to the AVD. She eased back on the throttle to conserve fuel and shifted her rear on the double parachute cushion, settling in.

Tracers streaked past her canopy.

Saansa instantly knew what they were, but they came as such a surprise, all she could do for about two seconds was stare at the bright, arcing lines in the morning sky. And once in a while, situations arise in which two seconds can be an eternity—or make the difference between eternity and survival. This was one of those. An instant later, the big P-40 thundered with the impacts of bullets and she felt stunning blows on the armor plate behind her seat. Without further thought, she pushed the stick forward and opened the throttle wide. Her plane was hit, probably hurt, and likely leaking precious fuel. But she had to survive the next few moments to worry about the rest, and speed was her only chance. *More* tracers whipped past and, incredulous, she craned around to see her pursuer. It was still back there, keeping up—and there were at least two more! She rolled out and pointed her nose at the sea, mashing the Push to Talk button on the throttle.

"Kay-Eff! Kay-Eff! I'm attaacked by three planes *at least*

as faast as me! They big, too. Bigger than any Jaap-Grik fighters we seen!" Her English was slipping with the stress, and gone was any attempt to contemplate codes. Codes worked only when the enemy didn't know what you were talking about. Right now, no matter what she said, there'd be no doubt about the subject of her transmission. Best to describe her situation and the threat she'd discovered as carefully as she could, she realized. She eased back on the stick, looking up. Two planes were still above, odd zigzag markings on their wings, but one blew past, rolling left, with a red ball painted—over something else, it seemed—on the side of the fuselage. Her predatory instincts took over and she turned after it, greedily willing the gun site to get just enough ahead. . . . She pressed the button to talk. "They got no floats, an' wheels is up. Liquid cooled, an' pilot way back. Funny markings on the weengs, but there's a Jaap meatball on the side. . . ." She squeezed the trigger and two 50s roared. Large chunks peeled off the target and fluttered away. She kept firing, added more rudder—and black smoke belched from the plane, turning to a thick, steady trail. "Got *you*!" she snarled, still firing, and yellow flames burst from the long cowl in front of the cockpit.

"I got one!" she practically screeched as the strange plane rolled over and dropped toward the purple-blue water. But more tracers zipped past, punching through her right wing. Something made a terrible crunching sound and she fought the stick as the P-40-something tried to pitch forward to the right. That was when she saw one of her floats tumble away through the corner of her left eye.

"Shit! I in for it," she said, her voice tight with strain. The plane was suddenly very sluggish, trying to yaw. "They knock a float off. I think it hit the other, bend it up. I in for it now! Listen, Kay-Eff, these *not* Jaap-Grik planes. They *metal*, like Pee-Forties . . ." Another burst shattered the canopy, tore through her left shoulder, and riddled the instrument panel. Panic coursed in with the smoky gust through the broken, blood-spattered windscreen, but there wasn't any pain. Not at first. Her beloved Allison coughed, its mighty heart faltering, and more smoke burned her tear-filled eyes as she lost power. Still she fought to keep the plane from falling to the sea, but hope had nothing to do with it. There were still two enemy planes, at least, and she couldn't even look for them. Couldn't avoid them. Couldn't even *think* about them as the pain finally surged. But she'd never quit; it wasn't in her. And whichever Maker she was about to meet would have no cause to criticize her for giving up. The engine started rattling and she pushed the stick forward. It didn't matter. The battered plane was still trying to stall and there wasn't enough altitude left. . . . More bullets savaged the P-40 and the right wing folded up in a gout of flame just as the plane slammed into the sea with a fire-spewing splash nine miles off the southeast coast of Zanzibar.

***USS* Santa Catalina**
Nearing Mahe

"What the hell?" Matt demanded angrily, staring at another message form Commander Russ Chappelle had passed him. "What got her?" He was standing on *Santa Catalina*'s bridge with Chappelle, Bradford, Chack, and Lieutenant Michael "Mikey" Monk, Chappelle's XO and current OOD. The otherwise entirely Lemurian bridge watch was studiously performing its duties while doubtless straining to hear. Mahe Island loomed ahead, darkly silhouetted by the setting sun. One of the steam frigate DDs, USS *Tassat*—quickly patched after a brutal mauling in the fighting around the Comoros Islands—was coming alongside. She wasn't fit for independent patrols, still leaking too much to risk alone. Her bilge pumps never stopped, and the water coursing down from her scuppers had left dark stains. Matt knew her aggressive skipper, Jarrik-Fas, must be going nuts, his only consolation being that *Tassat* was next for *Tarakaan Island*'s attention. In the meantime, she could steam, and fight if necessary, and had sailed out to lead *Santy Cat* and the following battlegroup through the tricky harbor entrance, past the reefs. Right now, a motor launch was dropping to the water from her quarter davit.

"Probably sending a pilot over," Chappelle observed, distracted from Matt's question.

"Pilot is right," called the signal 'Cat on the bridgewing, watching *Tassat*'s flashing Morse lamp. "*Col-nol Maal-lory*'s comin' aboard!"

"It seems Mr. Fiedler didn't tell us everything he could after all," Courtney Bradford pronounced darkly, still focused on Matt's question. His tone was grim but somewhat self-satisfied.

Matt glanced at him. "We *knew* that. Just as we knew the League hadn't abandoned Kurokawa entirely. And it's possible these modern planes, whatever they are, showed up after Fiedler left."

"Convenient," Bradford muttered.

"Actually, his best guess is in the stack," Chappelle disagreed, waving another half-dozen sheets. "Third or fourth page down," he added. "Apparently, he left some notes—and a letter directly to you, Captain—stashed in the trimotor. The letter's been sent up by air. The notes detailed some assets Gravois might've arranged to be transferred to Kurokawa. One sounds like what jumped the P-Forty-something." Courtney harrumphed, but Chappelle leafed through the pages, selected one, and handed it over.

Matt quickly scanned it. "What's a Macchi-Messerschmitt?" he asked dubiously. Everyone knew what a Messerschmitt 109 was; they'd been the bogeymen of Air Corps and Naval aviation before the old war began. It was commonly believed the British Spitfire was better, and it had remained dogma in the Air Corps that Warhawks were better too—despite worrying reports from the Brits, who'd pitted export-model P-40s against 109s. In fact, the inexperienced flyers who first encountered Zeros over the Philippines thought *they* must be Messerschmitts, probably with Nazi pilots. Those who survived quickly learned the remarkably capable pilots shooting them down so easily were, in fact, Japanese—flying Japanese-made aircraft. Some survived long enough to learn P-40s were *still* better (in some ways), but they had to change the way they used them if they wanted to beat a Zero—and probably, a Messerschmitt. That Kurokawa might somehow have some of those was bad enough, but what did "Macchi" mean?

"Maybe we'll find out pretty quick," Mikey Monk temporized, nodding at the launch motoring toward them. He'd already ordered "dead slow." The coded-message traffic had been flying back and forth between Mahe and Grik City—the enemy knew they were on Mahe, after all—and *Santy Cat* had picked off and decoded everything. She couldn't send questions, though, since she and *Arracca*'s battlegroup had to remain silent. Comm discipline had been hard to adjust to, and instituting a mind-set of operational security among Lemurians in particular—naturally gregarious and prone to chatter—was no simple feat. 'Cats understood the problem, but preventing unintentional slips was a lot harder.

Courtney now believed that, despite their generally peaceful nature, Lemurians weren't *instinctively* pacifistic. They couldn't have survived long enough to accomplish their ancient exodus from Madagascar if that was the case, nor could they have become such good fighters so quickly. And the fact that isolated Lemurians still on Madagascar, such as the Shee-Ree, were decidedly *not* pacifistic only reinforced his new thesis.

They were talkers, though. Even among the Shee-Ree, spreading tales to other bands, tribes, even species, was their most lucrative export commodity. It was what it was, and everybody was doing their best, but it was hard to blame a 'Cat for backsliding in the stress of combat. Henry Stokes, trying to make the best of it, had even sent (with a code prefix specifying that the message be decoded only by Ed Palmer, *Walker*'s comm officer, and read by Matt alone) a suggestion that they try to use the inevitable lapses—which the enemy must be aware of—to their advantage. He hadn't suggested when or how because Lemurians were also helplessly curious and other comm.-'Cats probably *did* decode the message. Hopefully, the seriousness of its eyes-only nature would keep them from blabbing.

With the launch away, *Tassat* sped ahead, taking up position. She'd recover her boat from *Santa Catalina* after they anchored. Very shortly, Ben Mallory came huffing up the stairs. "Getting out of shape," he lamented, then grinned and saluted when he saw Matt; it had been a long time.

Matt grinned back and shook his hand. "I'm sure Colonel Chack'll be happy to let you train with his Raiders while they're on the island."

"Of course," Chack agreed, blinking amusement. "I thought pursuit pilots had to remain fit, to overcome the stress of their aarial acro-baatics?"

"Yeah, well, I've been more of an organizer than a pursuiter since I got here," Ben replied, evading the invitation. Chack's Brigade trained *very* hard. He looked at Matt. "I suspect—hope—my pen pushing is over."

Matt was nodding. "You did damn good work, Colonel," he said. "And I'm very glad to see you. The initiative you took after Kurokawa tripped his mousetrap north of here—hunting him down and getting in some licks of our own—is one reason we're in any shape to do anything but hunker down and wait for what comes next. The main reason, though, is how you kept your head and started organizing the mare's nest that landed here after the battle, before generals Alden and Rolak arrived."

"Thank you, sir," Ben said seriously. "Honestly, though, that was as much out of fear as anything. I didn't know if Alden or Rolak were even alive, and was scared to death I was *it*." He shrugged. "And somebody had to take charge. If Kurokawa came on with troopships, we were finished." He shook his head. "I didn't really think he *would*, but he could have. I started by getting the airfield sorted out. There were gas and bombs on *Tarakaan Island*, but we didn't have a single bullet or drop of fuel at the new strip." He scratched his nose. "And there were a lot of shell-shocked people just standing around, doing nothing. I figured I'd put 'em to work. I got the construction battalion busy improving the strip, shifting fuel and ammo and preparing for a *bunch* of people and planes. But then we learned *Sular* was coming in—that *all* the surviving troopships were coming here." He held out his hands. "So I got everybody, even *Tara*'s crew and engineers, laying out encampments and setting up field kitchens—the works. I didn't really know what I was doing on such a scale, but I had to try."

"You did well. Better than well." Matt smiled. "Pete's writing you an IOU for another medal—once we get around to making some." Everyone laughed. The subject of medals had been a running joke for years. No one wanted to divert even the relatively miniscule amount of labor and materials that making them would require from the war effort. But even Lemurians grasped how being recognized for martial accomplishments had an inspiring effect, and Adar once proposed that colorful ribbons be awarded for various acts. A census of the troops revealed that though they'd appreciate them, nobody would wear them and they'd just get lost. Most everyone liked the system that evolved: a commendation in front of one's mates, documentation of the deed in one's records, and the promise of a shiny medal one could wear—or be remembered by—after the war.

"Now," Matt said, smile fading, "instead of waiting the couple hours for us to anchor, I assume you came out—risking your neck in a little boat on water with fish in it that eat *ships*—to tell me what the hell a Macchi-Messerschmitt is? I was looking at Fiedler's description." He held up the message form. "He was very helpful," he added as an aside to Courtney. "But you know better what the specs mean for us."

"Yes, sir," Ben said, his grin sliding away as well. He lowered his voice so only Matt could hear. "And I scanned the letter he left you," he confessed, "as soon as the Nancy pilot handed it over. General Maraan had already opened it, so I thought, 'What the hell?'"

"That's fine, Colonel," Matt whispered back, "but I'd better have a look at it before we pass it around. If nothing else, we don't want the enemy to know we have it."

"Sure, Skipper," Ben said louder, handing over a leather satchel. Matt glanced inside, seeing a thick sheaf of rough Lemurian paper covered with handwriting. "It's in the section where he sketched out the history of the League—and even gave some background on the Confederation. . . ."

"Confédération États Souverains," Courtney supplied helpfully.

"Yeah, that," Ben agreed. "The outfit that became the League of Tripoli here. He obviously knew the League came from a different . . ." He shrugged, looking helpless.

"Progression of history," Bradford suggested.

"Ah, yeah," Ben agreed, blinking at the Australian. They'd surmised that, and Gravois confirmed it, blithely explaining that the League was initially composed of a large

Confederation task force and convoy headed for Italian Libya to conquer British Egypt in 1939. He'd refused to describe the composition of the task force, but they'd gleaned that even in that other world, the British Navy remained imposing, so the Confederation task force would've necessarily been robust. Matt wondered how the attack went after the convoy got . . . sucked here. He wrinkled his nose, disliking that description. *Maybe they called it off? But that's obviously why the League's so well equipped.*

"Anyway, Fiedler knew his world was similar to but different from ours, and tried to catch us up on *how* stuff is different. There's a *lot* in there about that," he said, nodding at the satchel, "and he must've been working on it quite a while before he blabbed." He pursed his lips. "I only focused on what he said about warplanes the triumvirate may send to Kurokawa, though." He frowned. "It isn't good."

"Spit it out."

"Some of this is guesswork," Ben defended, "piecing together things he didn't know we didn't know—or that we did. Macchi was an Italian aircraft company. Hispano Suiza was Spanish. That's the same. But apparently, they floated BFW—the company Willy Messerschmitt worked for—when a civil war cooked off in Germany about 1933. Makes sense. Old Willy had already come up with the basic design for his BF–One Oh Nine by then, and everybody wanted their hands on it. So whatever got our plane, this Macchi-Messer was probably a joint venture between Italians, Spaniards, and Krauts, with—it sounds like—most of the good points of a One Oh Nine. No way to know if it's *as* good. There might've been too many cooks spoiling the pot"—he paused—"but it might be *better*. The Eye-ties call it a Lightning." He shook his head. "*I* never will. That was the same name as our hottest new ship, the P-Thirty-Eight, and I never got to fly one. Anyway, they come with Hispano Suiza or Daimler-Benz engines, depending on whose they are. Kraut planes have DBs and are faster, but based on the reported markings, these were probably Italian, with the HSs." He considered. "Apparently, the French members of the League have planes of their own. On the other hand, the, ah, US in the world Fiedler came from had P-Forties, or was about to. He knew about 'em, anyway. And the Brits had Hurricanes. The bad thing is, the Macchi-Mess was considered a match for them. Maybe more than a match. They'd never tangled—yet."

Matt glanced at Courtney, his treatment of the German flyer apparently vindicated more quickly than he'd hoped. He looked at Ben. "So, what's the bottom line?"

"According to Fiedler"—Ben nodded at the satchel in Matt's hands—"performance-wise, they're probably on a par with my P-Forties. Similar speed and range, at least. We should be able to outrun 'em in a dive because we're heavier. And we've got six fifties. They have two, and a pair of seven-sevens in their wings. That said, it'll probably be like fighting Zeros because they're more agile. The good news? They can't get us here. They're not carrier planes either. The bad news? Our P-Forties can't get to *them* from here—and they'll chew our P-Ones and Nancys apart as easy as we tore up the Jap-Grik planes. Worse news? They've probably got at least five of 'em, not counting the one Saansa nailed. I've got *three* operational P-Forties. I might make it four, if I can fix one of our busted ships. I *could* make it six, if you let me order the two left at Baalkpan forward. But we can't fly 'em in, and getting them here might take longer than we have. I wish we'd known we needed them sooner; we could've shipped 'em out on *Madras*."

"We *can* get your Third Pursuit Squadron close enough to use them. P-Forties can fly off of carriers," Chappelle mused. "Hell, you've done it." He shook his head. "They just can't *land* on 'em, so that's a one-way trip. And not only are there five—or more—modern planes on Zanzibar to worry about, but the League obviously has enough of them to loan out. Should we risk *any* of our modern planes now?"

"Turn 'em back into hanger queens, you mean, while our Fleashooters and Nancys get creamed? No way," Ben said defiantly. "This is what they're *for*! Finally!"

"I agree," Matt assured him. "You said they hadn't tangled with P-Forties before? They will soon enough. But we've got to figure out how to get your planes there to support the operation." He smiled mirthlessly. "Operation Outhouse Rat has an appropriate ring, and should be suitably vague." They'd also learned to be careful about operation and task force names. "But how do we use them—that won't guarantee we'll lose them, along with you and your pilots? We'll get with Keje and figure out a better way to trap them on *Big Sal* than just stringing a big net across her deck." *Salissa* was equipped for that, but no one had ever tried it, considering it too dangerous and potentially damaging to the planes. But that might be the only answer. Matt rubbed his chin. "In the meantime, I wonder how good a *night fighter* this Macchi Messer is? Especially if Kurokawa's not expecting to need one."

"What are you thinking, sir?"

"Jumbo's Pat-Squad Twenty-Two has seven Clippers." He shrugged. "Well, six, until they fix the broken one. One's about to take Courtney to the Republic, and we're going to start bombing Sofesshk with incendiaries by night. We'll see how the Grik like it for a change. The good news, which I haven't told Jumbo or anybody yet, because it's almost as big a secret from our friends as it is to the enemy, is"—he looked around at the uncomprehending expressions—"since *everybody* wants the big mothers . . ." The quizzical blinking continued. "Oh, well, I guess I'd better spill it. Chairman Letts is sending the entire Baalkpan production of the newest Clippers here, to us, for the foreseeable future. Yeah," he said, gauging their suddenly glowing eyes and Chack's happy blinking. "Six more are on their way now, and we'll be getting three, maybe four, every two weeks. How does that sound?"

"To say 'swell' is a pretty big understatement, sir," Ben said excitedly. "General Alden's been dying for heavy bombers, and he's liable to . . . ah, urinate himself with glee—begging your pardon."

Matt grinned; then his face turned hard. "Good. And I hope the enemy pisses themselves with terror, because besides bombing Sofesshk almost every night, when our numbers are up"—he looked at Ben—"every now and then, we'll send Clippers to bomb Kurokawa as well. All of them. We won't do it often enough for them to predict us, and if the Clippers have trouble with fighters, we'll try sneaking *Big Sal* close enough to provide fighter cover. I bet even Fleashooters'll make pests of themselves against modern planes in the dark. If we're lucky, we might even get the Macchi-Messers on the ground. Not to mention *Savoie* and Kurokawa's other ships."

"But, Captain Reddy," Courtney said, alarmed, "won't that risk Lady Sandra, Chairman Adar, and the others? Not only to injury or death at our own hands, but to reprisals by Kurokawa?"

Matt sighed and closed his eyes. When he opened them, they were like green agate: opaque, but reflecting the sunset like they were aflame. "It might," he agreed softly, his voice rising as he continued. "But the campaign against Kurokawa *can't be just a goddamn rescue mission*! You encouraged me yourself that it's necessary, and I agree. But I can't—won't—let that crazy Jap bastard believe we'll hold anything back just because he has our people. That'll make him *really* test it, and . . ." His voice softened to a whisper that chilled his friends. "I honestly don't know how I'd handle a direct this-or-that challenge, with Sandra at stake." He looked at them helplessly. "I think I know. I hope I do. But I can't be *sure*." He took a deep breath. "Best not to give him the chance to make one," he said brusquely, then singled out Bradford again. "You're right. Bombing might put our people in danger from him, or, God help me, us. But probably less than if he gets the idea he can use them—her—to get what he wants. We all know he'll *try*. So I mean to slam the door on that notion as hard as I can."

He looked bleakly out the bridge windows at Mahe, its twin peaks looming larger now. "And if we *do* kill her," he said, his voice thick, "it's got to be cleaner than what *he'll* do." He looked back to hold each gaze. "I won't say it's what they'd want. Nobody wants to die. But given the stark choice between death and what Kurokawa might do to them to get what he wants, to make us waste the lives we've lost already and maybe lose the war, I know exactly what they'd all *prefer*."

Santa Catalina's bridge went utterly silent except for the usual creaks and groans of an old, hard-used ship, the muted rush of the sea, and machinery noises that traveled through the very fibers of her form. Finally, Ben Mallory patted his shirt pocket. "Oh," he said, his voice nearly as grim as Matt's. He fished a folded sheet from his pocket and handed it over. "The updated map of Zanzibar, based on Lieutenant Saansa's observations," he explained, while Matt opened it and looked at a map just like the one he'd seen before, only with written notations and new drawings on it. "She also said 'the Maker is good,'" he added, glancing at Bradford. He'd sensed the Australian's hostility toward Fiedler. "So we can probably trust it. We didn't hear Saansa's transmissions here," he continued. "Too far. But the AVD immediately dispatched its Nancy and it leapfrogged in. Just arrived before I headed out to meet you."

"The Maker *is* good, indeed," Chack agreed, peering around Matt's arm at the page. Now he could start to plan.

Matt was looking at the map and nodding. The positions of the features Saansa had described made sense, and he immediately saw potential opportunities. He'd discuss those with Pete, Rolak, and particularly Chack. The land assault would be his baby, after all. No doubt Chack would confer with Silva. "Just one thing missing here," he said sadly. "You think she went down southeast of this Head Point?" He put his finger on the bottom of the island.

"Yes, sir," Ben agreed.

"No chance she set down somewhere, that she's afloat?" Unspoken was the question of whether she might've been captured.

Ben tightened his lips and shook his head. "The last thing they heard was that she'd lost a float and probably damaged another. She was taking hits, then . . . nothing."

Matt nodded again, stung by mixed emotions. The loss of Saansa and the plane was tragic, but he was also relieved that the intelligence she'd gained was probably safe—and Kurokawa didn't have yet another hostage. He took a Lemurian-made lead pencil from his pocket and roughly scratched out "Head," and wrote "Saansa" next to it. "Kind of a crummy thank-you for somebody who died giving us so much. More than she'll ever know," he said, his voice tight with regret, "but it'll have to do for now."

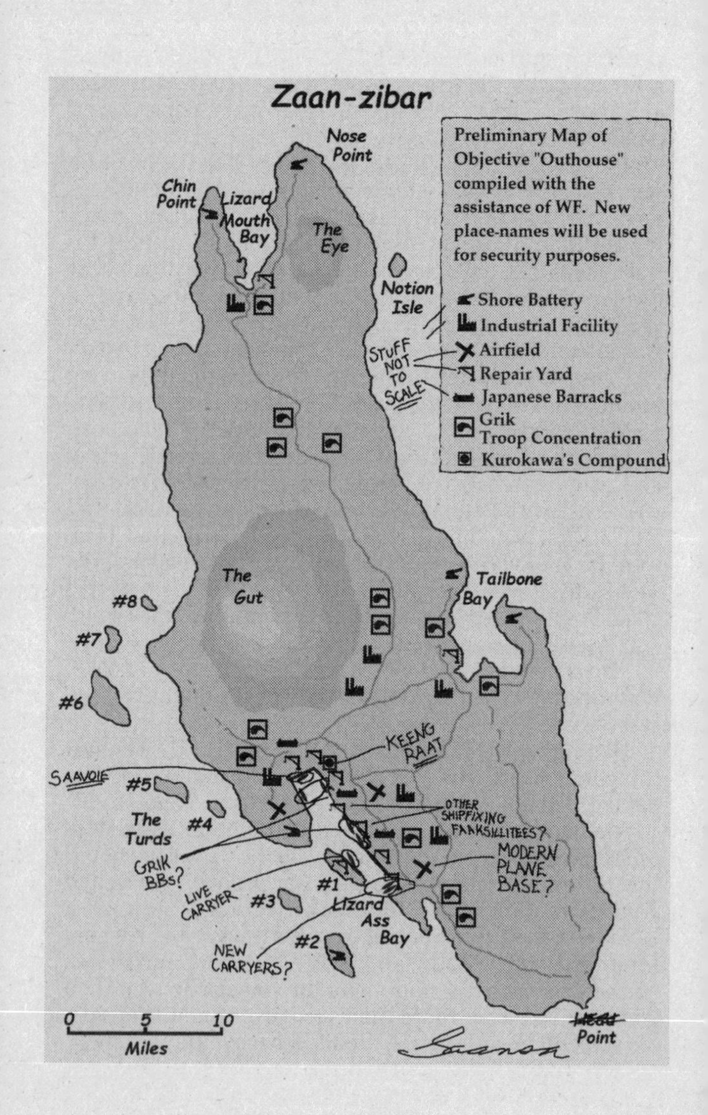
Zaan-zibar
Preliminary Map of Objective "Outhouse" compiled with the assistance of WF. New place-names will be used for security purposes.
Shore Battery
Industrial Facility
Airfield
Repair Yard
Japanese Barracks
Grik Troop Concentration
Kurokawa's Compound
STUFF NOT TO SCALE
Nose Point
Chin Point
Lizard Mouth Bay
The Eye
Notion Isle
The Gut
Tailbone Bay
#8
#7
#6
#5
#4
#3
#2
#1
SAAVOIE
KEENG RAAT
OTHER SHIPFIXING FAKKSILLITEES?
MODERN PLANE BASE?
The Turds
GRIK BBs?
LIVE CARRYER
Lizard Ass Bay
NEW CARRYERS?
0 5 10
Miles
Point

CHAPTER 8

Sofesshk
The Palace of Vanished Gods
Grik Africa

"We should have attacked immediately, while the enemy prey was indisposed," the Chooser, now Lord Chooser of all the Ghaarrichk'k, lamented again as he paced behind Lord Regent Champion Esshk, Guardian of the Celestial Bloodline and First General of all the Grik. The Chooser was still ridiculously plump compared to other males of his race, but his garish dress already fit looser than before they'd begun their ritual evening strolls. He hadn't dispensed with any of the odd adornments he'd decided befitted his exalted status, however, such as the short cape interwoven with tiny gilded bones that glittered as it swayed behind him, or the macabre "jewelry" suspended about his person. Nor had he stopped weaving his crest into a rigid fan atop his head, coloring his claws, and even staining the downy fur around his eyes and snout, in a blatant display of age-defying vanity.

Esshk was powerfully built and taller by far, standing nearly six feet—impressive for a male, even of the Blood. He was darker as well, yet with a lustrous, coppery hint to his otherwise dun and dark brown plumage—also a legacy of Celestial Blood. He still wore the fine, brightly burnished breastplate of a first general, but had added a longer, floor-sweeping version of the Imperial Red cape he'd always worn—his only outward concession to his new station.

Both were walking back and forth on the time-worn, slab-paved walkway before the high-arched, ground-level entrance to the Palace of Vanished Gods. The sky, struggling to release the final moisture of the rainy season, was gray and dull, edging toward night. A wall of lush green trees separated the palace from the rest of Old Sofesshk, and the grounds were bordered on the south by the mighty Zambezi, still often called Uuk-Arrg in the ancient Ghaarrichk'k speech. *The "scientific tongue" has claimed so many things, even our greatest river,* Esshk reflected, not yet replying to the Chooser's almost daily complaint. The Palace itself was a smaller, prehistoric version of the one in the Celestial City on Madagascar. It was old beyond imagining and time had eroded the dark granite smooth. Still, it remained an extraordinary edifice, second in size only to the palace in the Celestial City—and the Wall of Trees there, of course—of all known Ghaarrichk'k structures.

The walkway wasn't large or long, but Esshk and the Chooser briskly paced it many times for their daily exercise, weather permitting, surrounded at a discreet distance by Second General Ign's most slavishly loyal troops. And they *needed* the exercise. Both spent too much time cloistered in the Palace, dealing with all the multitudinous things required not only to rule the Ghaarrichk'k Empire, but also to maintain and continue assembling the impossibly vast land, sea, and air swarm they'd soon unleash to devour the enemies of their race. The troops weren't there to protect them from attack as much as ensure their privacy from interruption by the influential, pampered, even aristocratic Hij that dwelled on this side of the great Zambezi. This was Old Sofesshk, after all, where the illusion of some incomprehensible ancient empire, seemingly given more to other, forgotten priorities, besides expansion for expansion's sake, still remained. No one knew what truly constituted that forgotten society, how large it was, how governed, or even by whom. The most elemental, mystical remembrances suggested only that gods of some sort had ruled there in a time of prosperity, plentiful prey, and general contentment, and then went away.

Hints of that lost time endured in the carefully patched surviving architecture, mimicked by new construction. It was ageless, well considered, even vaguely ascetic, as if some half-imagined "flavor" of another era still manifested itself in the minds of the Hij who dwelled there. And many were like subregents in their own right, all supposedly of the Blood to varying degrees, so their views had to be considered. The Chooser, and even Esshk, had figuratively risen from their ranks, after all, even if Esshk and the previous Celestial Mother sprang from the same clutch of eggs laid by a long-dead Giver of Life. Esshk may have had a slight advantage as a result, with better teachers, but only ability brought him to achieve what he had.

In general, however, both were the result of one of the most singular privileges enjoyed by high-ranking Hij, and those of Old Sofesshk in particular: they could *pick* a hatchling from a crèche of offspring resulting from their union with a female of the blood, which was exempt from evaluation by the choosers—though choosers were often employed to make the selection. The only other examples of similar, if less official, accommodations were those afforded the houses of successful seafarers, artisans, and generals, so they might hone blood instincts among more likely pupils from the earliest practical age. But because of this, some Old Sofesshk Hij retained ancestral-blood claims to large tracts of land (and the Uul living upon them) within a broader regency. Few of those Uul came to the new army and navy Esshk was building, but they constituted the largest percentage of the workforce engaged in making advanced tools of war. Therefore, the support of the Hij of Old Sofesshk was necessary to Esshk's and the Chooser's plans and couldn't be ignored, but they mustn't be allowed to abuse their privileges either.

The other side of the river was like any other Grik city: a chaotic warren of mud and wood structures, congested beyond belief with more of their race than any cared to count, feeding as much on themselves as otherwise—at least before the military expansions of the last few years curtailed the cullings of the choosers. The riverfront was more orderly now, having been cleared to make room for great docks, warehouses, foundries, mills, factories, and the thousand other things required to end the threat of the prey they faced. *Kurokawa had been largely responsible for that,* Esshk confessed to himself as he walked. *It would have been better if that . . . ridiculously disagreeable creature had not allowed his ambition to run amok in India. Had I not* allowed *him the freedom to plot and scheme . . .*

Esshk glanced back at the Chooser. *And* he *had not been particularly helpful in regard to Kurokawa,* he thought with a trace of resentment. Of course, that was before they'd come to their *own* understanding. Now Esshk needed the Chooser's support as much as his cunning, something he hadn't even known the creature possessed when he'd been a member of the old Celestial Mother's court. *Further proof of its depth and breadth,* he supposed. The Chooser had become his most senior advisor—and only confidant. That was the *main* reason for their walks, in fact. It was the only time they could reveal their truest thoughts, away from even servants who might be in the employ of rival regents.

"The enemy was not as indisposed as Kurokawa led us to believe," Esshk reminded through long, clenched fangs. "I am not even positive he achieved a victory at all, as he claimed."

"Such is difficult to gauge," the Chooser huffed, reluctantly conceding Esshk's point as he tried to match his lord's longer strides, "particularly considering how long it took us to even learn of the battle. Time during which the forces around Lake Nalak were bombed, not once, but *twice*! If the enemy was as devastated as Kurokawa claims, could they have accomplished that? Would they still patrol the Go Away Strait, making it difficult to supply our secret"—he snorted—"forces sent to assail the Celestial City from the south? I think not. And it's only a matter of time before the prey bombs Sofesshk itself. I already warned what might happen then."

Esshk had to agree. For the moment, his and the Chooser's power was absolute—in the name of the newly elevated Celestial Mother, whom all knew wouldn't be fit to actually lead for a considerable time. Several years, at least. Both had decided that would *never* happen. *Their* lines, comingled with the Giver of Life, would hold supreme authority as Champions and Choosers behind the Celestial throne forever. Such "reform" was essential if their race, and any semblance of normalcy, was to survive the war—and all the other reforms they'd been forced to institute. Again, largely due to Kurokawa, Esshk had discovered what the Chooser's order had always known: there *was* no observable qualitative difference between hatchings, and his order had existed primarily as a means of population and thought control. They'd need that again, when the emergency passed.

But for a time, for the *first* time, rule of the Ghaarrichk'k Empire depended to some degree on the consent of its subjects. The regents, and even the Hij of Old Sofesshk to a lesser extent, might still combine against Esshk and the Chooser. And though the new army had been thoroughly conditioned for absolute loyalty to Esshk above all, even the Celestial Mother herself, it was more . . . perceptive than any similar number of the race had ever been allowed to become. That would be valuable on the battlefield, but afterward? Esshk firmly believed only he—and the Chooser—could deal with what came next. But the Chooser was most concerned about dissatisfaction among the Hij, perhaps to the degree Regent Ragak had displayed, if bombs fell on Sofesshk City. Particularly Old Sofesshk.

"We have already moved part of the army into the city," Esshk reassured patiently. "It *is* steadfastly devoted to me, and will tolerate none of the dissatisfaction that causes you such distress. And we have dispersed the transports as well. It is fortunate they can be dragged up upon the land."

"It is fortunate we moved them when we did, because the prey focused its bombs on the covered docks protecting them during their second attack."

"And accomplished nothing."

"True, but they knew something important must have been in them. Now they doubtless know whatever it was, it is gone! And the transports, made of green wood, cannot stay long upon the shore. They will not float when we need them to."

"It won't be long," Esshk stated more firmly.

"We should use them *now*," the Chooser urged forcefully, glad he'd spiked his crest. It would've fluttered with irresolution otherwise, and he'd made the same recommendation each time they spoke. He knew Esshk found it tiresome.

Esshk stopped pacing and turned with a deep sigh. "Must I explain again?" he demanded. "Must I *constantly* remind you which of us is the general? Very well." He held up a finger, the long talon like a shiny black sickle. "As you know, our advance force in the south of Madagascar was discovered and has . . . suffered setbacks. The local prey fights them, supported by weapons and advisors from the Celestial City. At the same time, as you say, that force grows more difficult to reinforce and supply. The enemy may have few ships in the strait, but they are sufficient to interdict our barge traffic and their lumbering tugs. There are now also flying machines patrolling for them as well. The advance force may never even survive to accomplish its mission. Certainly not with surprise, as planned. I think"—Esshk gently caressed his throat with his claws—"we may have to abandon *that* endeavor. It is pointless to keep wasting New Army troops and their precious equipment, most often destroyed before they even complete the crossing, on what increasingly appears a forlorn hope."

"All the more reason to launch the Final Swarm *now*, while some of that force remains to distract the prey!" the Chooser persisted.

"The enemy *is* distracted!" Esshk countered. "Not only by Kurokawa, but this other prey, the Dominion he told us of"—he sniffed—"at last." He considered. "But that does bring us back to communication. Since we can no longer dispatch ships from here to carry messages, we have relied on runners up the coast to take passage across the water between the mainland and Kurokawa's sovereign nest. That takes too long. I know *he* has a quicker way, but has never shared it," Esshk brooded. "I will not forget that," he added darkly. "I *will* quicken the process, however. Our swarm of airships is dwindling," he conceded, "and our raids on the Celestial City show little result. Perhaps . . . perhaps it is time we ceased those as well? I must consider that. But in the meantime, we will establish a relay between here and the main airship nest up the coast that the enemy has never found. Airships will, in turn, carry messages from there to Kurokawa's nest, shortening the time it takes to send and receive them to a mere two days! No longer will the General of the Sea be able to plead ignorance of our desires and intentions, or use that as an excuse for ignoring our commands. At least not if he wants to keep the oil and other material support he so desperately needs flowing from the mainland. And I will demand a further distraction from him soon," Esshk added. "*That* will be the time to act! When we can properly coordinate our actions."

"He is unfit to hold our trust!" the Chooser declared. "He has proven it time and again. Why do you persist in giving it to him?"

"That is very simple, Lord Chooser," Esshk explained resignedly. "Because we *need* him. I do *not* trust him, however. He is motivated only by survival and ambition—in equal parts, no doubt." He brightened. "He has been rewarded for returning to the Hunt, which will sate his ambition for a time, and even he must know at last that his fate is inextricably linked to our success. That cannot be more obvious, even to such as he. If we prevail without his aid, we will certainly destroy him next. If we do *not* prevail, the enemy can then focus all its might on him." He hissed appreciatively at the Chooser's expression.

"In the meantime, we have time. The weather will soon moderate—never have I seen such a lengthy rainy season!—and we have the luxury of completing all our preparations. We will continue to build our Swarm by drawing new army forces from across the empire. We already pulled much from the south, but can take more. It is still cold down there, and likely even wetter than here. The Other Hunters—the Republic, Kurokawa calls them—could not move against us even if they dared." He hissed again. "And no, I have not forgotten *them*. Their refusal to join the hunt will be repaid one day. In any event, we will soon have *six hundreds of ten hundreds* of warriors at our disposal, old and new, and the transports to carry them."

"Six hundred thousand!" the Chooser almost wailed, using the new way of numbers Kurokawa had taught him. "We cannot *feed* them! Why do we need so many?"

"Because we will not stop at the Celestial City, Lord Chooser," Esshk replied coldly. "We must be prepared to move immediately on India and beyond. We have a new army and fleet, but they must be invincible. They will both fight better than ever before, but only numbers can ensure success. Much has changed, but that has always been the Way, and numbers add the greatest measure of quality of all, beyond any training or weapons we can supply. That, at least, will never change. Do you doubt for an instant that even armed and trained as they always were, so many committed to any previous swarm would have prevailed?" He paused. "Of course not. And in the meantime, we will feed them what we must; keep the majority dispersed as long as necessary." He gurgled a laugh and jerked a diagonal nod. "Feed them Uul from across the river—or even here, if they become too 'dissatisfied.' One way or another, when the Final Swarm begins its hunt, *it will not be stopped*!" He glared at the Chooser. "I told you before, when we move, I want no 'perhaps,' no 'possibly.' Absolute certainty is all I will accept."

The Chooser hesitated a long time before speaking. "Lord, not all the mysteries of my order are . . . unfounded. You alone outside the circle know the truth. But you also know we actually can, on occasion, see certain potentialities. We can often even feel fairly certain about various traits—that a particular hatchling will make a fine warrior general, for example . . . such as yourself. But if any of us were commanded on pain of death to choose one hatchling based on *certainty* of any kind, we would condemn them all to the cookpots."

"What are you saying?" Esshk demanded. "You are the one who counsels haste above all."

"True, Lord, but only because I . . . I dread the word 'perhaps' as much as you. How can I not? And it is a word we cannot ignore, associated with any endeavor, regardless how much we would wish. That, above all, this particularly worthy prey has taught me. And no matter how diligently we prepare, the longer it takes, the larger 'perhaps' must loom. It is *always* thus with *this* prey, Lord," he stressed urgently. For just a moment, Esshk considered, and the Chooser thought he might have won his point at last. But Esshk's crest suddenly flared and he snorted with derision.

"No, Lord Chooser, even something as *dreadful*"—he used the word almost mockingly—"as 'perhaps' can be overwhelmed by the purity of the Way, when sufficiently beleaguered by the sheer numbers with which we will assail it."

The Chooser bowed, hiding the fear that flashed in his eyes. True fear, not just the ultimate outcome of "turning prey," was something he understood like few Grik did. He'd somehow learned to master it, however, and must never let it show. "Yes, Lord," he simply said.

It was almost completely dark now, and torchlight was glowing within the palace, illuminating the arch. Other lights began to flicker around Old Sofesshk, but the hive across the river was brightening even more, as fires were stoked beneath innumerable cookpots and the ageless scent of smoldering dung crowded the air. Esshk appreciated the more . . . refined airs in Old Sofesshk, but the other didn't disturb him. It was what he'd always known, and it smelled of normalcy. The faint addition of woodsmoke to the building fug reminded him of a swarm on campaign, however, and that quickened his blood. *The delays have been necessary, and still are if we are to succeed,* he thought. *I have sampled the bitter, ashy draught of defeat—mine and others—far too often. I will not taste it again. But what if the Chooser is right and delay is as much our enemy as the worthy prey across the strait?* He snapped his jaws in sharp objection, startling the Chooser. *No. Despite how keen I am to stir this greatest and most unique of Swarms to motion at last, the wisdom of the Way* must *still have meaning. Combining the quality of the New Army with the universal quality of numbers must be irresistible. The enemy still possesses formidable material advantages, but can never match my numbers. Delay only strengthens* me *in that respect. It is me whom time will aid! Any additional costs delay might bring will be insignificant to the final outcome.*

That was when he heard the deep, rumbling, droning sound, approaching from the east, and knew exactly what it was.

A spear of fire arced into the sky and popped, bright orange, over New Sofesshk. Another blinding streak followed the first, then another, as rockets lofted into the air to strike the enemy planes. Occasionally, one veered wildly, or began to tumble and tear itself apart in a smear of flame, but most now flew straight and true. He looked up as more orange flashes lit the sky, only now hearing the report of the first. Then, with mounting fury, he realized that not only had the enemy brought more than the one, then two planes, that came before—there must be at least four this time, probably more—but the rockets, improved as they'd been, and with better fuses and larger motors, were still utterly useless if their crews couldn't *see their targets*!

Frustrated rocket crews, commanded never to let enemy planes fly over the city unchallenged again, would be setting fuses for random elevations, pointing their rockets where it sounded like the planes would be. Esshk had just seen how pointless that was by how long it took the reports to reach him. The planes would be *past* where they sounded by the time the rockets reached that point, and could be higher or lower in any event. Still, as more and more rockets flew, exploding in the sky and sending hundreds of copper balls in all directions, it seemed increasingly impossible they all would miss. *Even if we fail to destroy a single plane, many might be hit and their crews terrified enough to flee. No,* he realized bleakly. *They are not like us. Like my warriors* used *to be. They have always had what my own army is just beginning to learn: this thing Kurokawa called courage. They will not flee.*

Flashes erupted on the ground several miles away, marching through the dense warren of New Sofesshk one after another, sending roiling balls of flame into the sky. The sound was muffled when it came to them, not like the cannon-blast detonations they expected, but more like the sound their own firebombs made. Another string of flashes lit the city, then another, each closer to the precious shipyards and warehouses on the other side of the river. There were five, all told, roughly confirming Esshk's estimate of enemy numbers, and they seemed as evenly spaced as the burning boils a tag'k beetle left on the skin beneath the fur, squirting its acid with every step. But these "boils" were huge, and each surely consumed hundreds in their fire.

"It is actually rather beautiful, is it not?" the Chooser quietly said beside him.

"Yes," Esshk replied absently. He was still furious, but knew what the Chooser meant. "As a general, I have always found war to be so. Particularly when fire is used. I confess I find it less beautiful when it is us and not the prey who burns beneath it." They watched for a while, long after the rockets stopped firing and the drone of engines receded in the night, and their customary time for exercise had passed. They were surprised to see the flames begin to spread instead of burning themselves out, as expected.

"Lord First General!" came the cry of General Ign, as he hurried toward them and flung himself on the paving stones at their feet. Ign had helped build the New Army and was second general of all the Ghaarrichk'k. Essentially Esshk's second in command, he was increasingly responsible for the day-to-day maintenance, training, and preparation of the entire Swarm. He alone could've approached without interference from the guards, and his use of Esshk's military title instead of Regent Champion meant he'd come to address a military matter.

"Stand, Second General," Esshk said.

Ign quickly rose. "Lord, the fires across the river are out of control. I have ordered that the ships close by the docks should pump water upon the warehouses that are threatened."

"Very well. But how can the fire spread? New Sofesshk is mostly made of earth."

"True, Lord, but the earth, the bricks—all are mixed with prairie grass. The flames are so hot that even they burn!"

Esshk narrowed his eyes. "It sounds as if you have taken appropriate steps. What else troubles you?"

"We can protect the waterfront, but with the prevailing wind, perhaps one part in ten of the city may burn."

"Why is that my concern? Has much of the Swarm been harmed?" At the Chooser's suggestion, they'd started quartering warriors in the city to make them easier to feed and shelter, and guard against unrest—of any sort.

"No, Lord. A few hundred were killed in the bombing. Others may have been killed when rockets malfunctioned. But the Uul in the city . . . Many are turning prey with fear."

"As I foretold," the Chooser said.

Esshk glanced sharply at him. "And as I prepared against." He looked back at Ign. "Go yourself, Second General. Control the fires, but, more important, control the Uul before the entire city turns prey. They are the workforce that supports the Final Swarm, after all."

"And those that have already turned?"

Esshk waved dismissively. "Destroy them. The New Army has been trained to fight a different way, but the old ways still have value. This will give them experience"—he paused and regarded the Chooser—"as well as easing our Lord Chooser's commissary concerns."

"At once, Lord First General!" Ign replied, and raced off.

The Chooser gathered himself. "Indeed," he said as ironically as he dared. "I feel *much* more confident about that now. But consider the damage done by just a few enemy planes." He waved across the river where the flames were gathering strength, pulsing and soaring, and glared at the smoky haze above. They'd be lucky if *only* a tenth of the huge city burned that night.

"I do, and will, Lord Chooser. But it was to be expected. We *did* expect it and acted accordingly." Esshk snorted impatience. "And they did not harm Old Sofesshk, so there is little to concern us."

"Of course, Lord Regent Champion," the Chooser said, now addressing him as the leader of all the Ghaarrichk'k. "But they will be back."

"Bloody gorgeous!" Courtney Bradford yelled, loud enough to be heard over the four big radials roaring practically overhead. He'd crammed his head up past Lieutenant Commander Mark Leedom's and was peering aft through the pilot's left-side window as their PB-5D Clipper headed south. Mark's brown-and-tan-striped Lemurian copilot, Lieutenant Paraal-Taas, snorted a laugh. They'd started some gorgeous fires indeed, and he seemed almost giddy. As did Courtney. "Bloody marvelous," he enthused again, witnessing the effect of the ton of incendiaries each plane dropped.

Mark Leedom was just as pleased, but wished Courtney would—literally—get out of his hair. Mark was COFO of the air defenses at Grik City, but led this raid because he'd already been over Sofesshk twice. That was how he'd rationalized it to Jumbo, anyway, who actually commanded Pat-Squad 22, the outfit his borrowed plane belonged to. He should've stayed out of the raid completely and carried Courtney straight down to Songze, but Courtney wouldn't countenance a special trip, and the risk of taking him along was deemed relatively minor—as long as they hit the city at night. Mark had personally experienced how effective the new Grik rocket batteries were when they could see you. As it turned out, they'd been right, and now Mark was looking forward to the chance of seeing his old friend Bekiaa-Sab-At. She could be anywhere in the Republic, but there was a chance they'd meet and have a chance to catch up. They'd shared a particularly rough time together, and were two of only a handful who survived it. Now if he could only put up with Courtney for another seven hours or so . . .

After they dropped their bombs, the other four planes turned northeast, back toward the Comoros Islands, but Leedom's ship still had eight hundred miles to go. Songze was the closest thing to a port city the Republic had on its east coast. It was *becoming* a port city, at least, a real one, from what Mark heard, sprouting large shipyards and heavy industry. The Republic had never dared grow too conspicuous on that coast before. The Grik had always dominated the littoral waters of the Indian Ocean, ranging ever farther and more boldly over the past two hundred years, and the isolationist Senate feared appearing too provocative—or tempting. That was over now, and the place was jumping, supposedly starting the first blue-water warships the Republic had built in at least a hundred years. (Maybe ever. That remained unclear.) Leedom was anxious to see for himself, but Songze was a long way off, and they'd be flying over a lot of land controlled by the Grik. At least it was dark. They might be heard, but never be seen.

Mark contemplated his Clipper. PB-5Ds were great, reliable planes, improved many times since the first variant flew. Their four engines had ten cylinders now, generating about 365 hp each. They could cruise at 120 miles an hour for almost 2,500 miles—about the same range as the old PBY flying boat that had inspired them. Range and speed should improve still more with the next planned variant, when they finally faired the engines into the wing to reduce drag. (Personally, Mark hoped they'd leave them be for now. He'd rather have a bunch more D models before they threw any curves at the assembly line.) Clippers had a crew of six and could carry eight passengers in relative comfort. More important to Leedom, they were armed with five .30-caliber machine guns and could carry a ton of bombs or two torpedoes. But having taken off from Jumbo's base on the Comoros Island of Mayotte, Songze was near the limit of their range, counting the run up the Zambezi to bomb Sofesshk, and Leedom was concerned about the quality of gasoline their Republic allies would use to replace what they burned.

"Marvelous!" Courtney repeated, still gazing back at the diminishing flames.

"Yeah, yeah, it was swell," Mark agreed sourly. "A real clambake—or lizard bake, I guess. And if they don't like that, wait till Jumbo gets more planes. He'll level the damn place." He shifted uncomfortably, but Courtney just wedged in tighter, trying for a better view. "Hey, I'm sorry, Mr. Bradford, but could you get off my neck? I'm getting a crick in it."

"Oh! Of course. Sorry." Courtney eased back but didn't leave the flight deck. Mark was suddenly glad, because he had a question maybe Courtney could answer.

"Say, what do you make of our mission orders? If all the top Grik brass was probably on the north side of the river, in that fancier part of the city, why not bomb there? We might've gotten lucky and cut the head right off the snake."

"Hmm. Yes. That was actually my suggestion, in point of fact."

"You don't say? What for?"

"Well, other than the possibility—I agree with—that the Grik leaders reside in Old Sofesshk, your own reconnaissance flight revealed little else of consequence there. No large troop concentrations, and all industry appears situated on the other side of the river. And, frankly, Commander, this is total war. Just as the enemy makes no distinction between our civilians and combat troops, we can't either. Their civilians support their war effort more directly and single-mindedly even than ours, so they're a legitimate target. A target that must've taken *severe* losses tonight, thanks to you and your mates in the Air Corps." He beamed, but then looked thoughtful. "And there's morale to consider. Even the new Grik warriors must have difficulty enduring punishment they can't reply to. Their Uul workers will find it more challenging still. Finally, on the other end of the morale spectrum, never forget what happened when Mr. Reuben killed their Celestial Mother at Grik City. You weren't there, but you must've heard."

"Sure. The little twerp chopped off her head and marched out of the Cowflop, where everyone, including the rest of their army, could see, and waved it around on a pole."

"I believe it was a spear, but essentially, yes. Did you hear what happened next?"

"Yeah . . . the Grik didn't like it much."

"That's a rather profound understatement," Courtney said, remembering. "In point of fact, the remainder of their forces that witnessed the spectacle, already beaten and in retreat, some even suffering the effects of Grik Rout, went absolutely berserk. Instead of showing them the futility of continued resistance and underscoring their defeat, Isak Reuben's actions inspired them to renew the fight." He paused. "It made little difference. By that time, we were in a position to slaughter them, both from land and the bay, but further casualties were sustained, more killed and wounded than might otherwise have been the case. It *wasn't* Mr. Reuben's fault," he stressed, "and no one blamed him. I expect in the heat of the moment I might've done the same after what he'd been through. We must assume the enemy's installed another Celestial Mother by now, however, who likely resides in what Hij Geerki translated as their Palace of Vanished Gods—the, ah, smaller Cowflop at Sofesshk. At this point, at least, we'd prefer not to give them more reason to fight than they already have, and instead of breaking their morale, we suspect that killing their new Celestial Mother might make them fight even harder. Does that make sense?"

"Yeah, I think so." Leedom frowned, but the expression turned into a huge yawn. He shrugged. "Take over awhile, Paraal," he told his copilot. "Keep this heading. I'm gonna get some shut-eye, so try not to run into anything, will ya?" He leaned back in his wicker seat and crossed his arms over his chest. "I suggest you go back in the waist and do the same, Mr. Bradford," he added, closing his eyes. "It's a long way to Songze, and there's not much to see below."

CHAPTER 9

Enchanted Isles
(Eastern Pacific)
November 9, 1944

High Admiral Harvey Jenks of the Empire of the New Britain Isles was Commander in Chief—East (CINCEAST) of all Allied forces fighting the Holy Dominion in the Americas. Yet since his 2nd Fleet was so badly mauled at the Battle of Malpelo, there hadn't been much he could do to directly influence the campaign. He and his deputy commander, Admiral Lelaa-Tal-Cleraan, *had* been fantastically busy, however. They'd made their headquarters at Elizabethtown, on Albermarl Island, not only the imperial capital of the Enchanted (Galápagos) Isles, but now the busiest Allied repair yard in the eastern Pacific. There were larger yards at Saint Francis, and the American Navy Clan yard at what they called San Diego might be even bigger someday, but its construction was on hold and most of its people were working here. The yards in Elizabeth Bay had been forced into a disproportionate percentage of the repair work, for which they were terribly unprepared in terms of labor, material, and facilities, because Albermarl was as far as many of the ships could make it after the battle.

Not only had Jenks and his staff, as well as the staff of Governor Sir Thomas Humphries, been overwhelmed arranging repairs to dozens of shattered ships, but they also had to import nearly everything to do it. Timbers, fasteners, strap iron, sheet copper, tools, new machinery—and workers, of course—had to be brought from across the vast expanse of an ocean empire. This while juggling a seriously depleted merchant marine and fleet of auxiliaries just as desperately needed to supply General Shinya's 2nd Fleet Expeditionary Force, his "Army of the Sisters." Shinya was trying to maneuver Don Hernan's Army of God into a decisive, crushing battle in the middle of, basically, a trackless jungle, before it could fall back on its own supply lines and reinforcements of loyal troops.

Adding to Jenks's frustration, though he remained CINCEAST, all the fighting in his theater was currently on land, and two heads of state were in the thick of it. His own Governor-Empress Rebecca Anne McDonald, and Saan-Kakja, the high chief of all the Filpin Lands, had stupidly, he thought, not only put themselves in harm's way, but their presence constantly deformed strategic planning. General Shinya was easy to work with; his sole priority was to bring Don Hernan to action and destroy him. In addition, the local contacts he'd made, opposed to Dominion rule, had eased his commissary requirements tremendously. That meant a larger percentage of freight could focus on troops, weapons, and ammunition. But with Rebecca's and Saan-Kakja's focus on the land campaign as well, they increasingly saw 2nd Fleet's role as one of support for Shinya. That was fine, even true to an extent, but they were losing sight of the big picture, as Captain Reddy so often described it. Even if Shinya's desperate end-around rush to block Don Hernan's retreat and smash him before he reached Popayan—and an open road to the Pass of Fire, or even back to the heart of the Dominion—was successful, the fleet would have to take the pass, and the fortified cities guarding it, before Shinya could press on.

Finally, Jenks thought, *Second Fleet may soon be ready to try.* He and Lelaa had just left a conference at the governor's mansion and were striding purposefully through the bustling streets of Elizabethtown toward the yard on the north side of the bay. *The people are certainly different from the half-starved scarecrows we met after the Dom siege,* he thought. Most were moving as purposefully as he and Lelaa, and though many appeared tired, even exhausted, there was a satisfied, almost excited air about them as well, a sense of purpose and resolve. Workers who saw them tipped their hats and even smiled, despite their fatigue, and soldiers saluted crisply, confidently. One reason for that was that, even here, still a distance from the waterfront, the great Allied aircraft carrier USS *Maaka-Kakja* (CV-5) was plainly visible over the rooftops of the city. And she was no longer the brutalized hulk that crept, coughing and smoking, into the bay two months before. She, at least, was almost ready for action. Her power plant had never been much hurt, and Chief Gilbert Yeager's snipes had put what little damage they'd found to rights. The ship's stout hull had taken a beating, but not enough to endanger her. Even so, it took an entire shipload of timber just to repair the hundreds of shot holes. Few penetrated every layer of diagonally laminated planks, but the wood around the holes had to be cut out and new wood spliced in. Without a dry dock, the ship had to be lightened enough to get at the damage below the waterline, and the hull work alone took a hundred workers almost a month. But the worst damage, and what rendered her almost useless, was the near-total destruction of her flight and hanger decks. Those had to be completely replaced. Fortunately, they were able to do that while other renovations were underway, and a lot of the timber came from the relatively nearby forests on the enemy coast, cut and dressed at the former Dominion city of Guayak, its surviving inhabitants now firm allies. *Regardless,* Jenks thought, *I hate to contemplate how many shiploads of timber went into those decks, and all the framing throughout.* Drawing nearer, he could still see the bright wood of the repairs, just now being covered by an odd new geometric paint scheme of contrasting grays.

"The other carriers, *New Dublin* and *Raan-goon*, are colored the same, I'm told," Lelaa said, guessing his thoughts. "Appaar-ently, we will see for ourselves tomorrow, at long laast," she added in a satisfied tone. She cocked her head as she walked. "It will be difficult to get used to," she confessed, "and it spoils her beauty, I think, but I understaand the purpose. The new paint job certainly distorts her shape, and even makes her seem more . . . menacing, somehow."

"That's because it looks so strange," Jenks said, absently twisting his long, braided mustaches. "Strange is always frightening."

"Then let's hope it scares the craap out of the enemy!"

Jenks chuckled. "I don't care what color they paint her, or any of our ships, as long as they're ready to fight." He paused. "Can you really put your air wing back together? I know what you told the governor, but it seems almost impossible."

"*If* I get Orrin Reddy and at least some of my planes and pilots back, the Third Naval Air Wing should be restored. *Raan-goon* and *New Dublin* are bringing sufficient crated air-craaft and pilots to bring it up to strength."

"*If* you get them back," Jenks agreed. "General Shinya needs close air support, and doesn't believe we can provide it. We *couldn't* for a while," he confessed. "But with three carriers offshore, shadowing his movements on land, I think he'll change his mind."

Lelaa was quiet as they drew nearer the docks. "You asked me; now I ask you. Will our surface element truly be so strong? It's hard to imagine."

"Five of our ships of the line, veterans of Malpelo, will be ready to sail as soon as *Maaka-Kakja*. That I promise. They include *Mithra*, *Centurion*, and *Mars*, which were all badly damaged, as you know. *Hermes* was the least affected. Others, I'm afraid, will take too long, or will need better facilities than we have here, but Captain Ruik's *Destroyer*, with its mixed crew"—Jenks smiled sadly—"will be ready for sea." The *Destroyer* had been the Dom *Deoses Destructor*, captured during the battle. Her new crew was made of survivors of Ruik's USS *Simms* and Lieutenant Parr's HIMS *Icarus*, both of which went down alongside her. Their two decimated crews, one Imperial and the other from the Amer-i-caan Navy Clan, had formed a tight bond and been combined. Ruik was in command, though still suffering from losing most of his arm, and Parr was his XO. "*Raan-goon* and *New Dublin* are bringing four more ships of the line," Jenks continued.

"That gives us nine." He took a long breath, watching a group of filthy, worn-out Imperial troops marching toward their camp outside the city. He nodded at them and they gave a halfhearted cheer. "We couldn't have done any of it if all the ships' crews, Marines, most of the troops assembled on the island, and virtually every able-bodied civilian hadn't been pressed into service as shipwrights." He chuckled darkly. "On the bright side, many who had none have now learned a trade. Like your people, however, they'll soon have to adapt again. I suspect it'll not be long before all our warships, at least, have iron hulls."

He shook his head, his thoughts returning to Lelaa's question. "We'll still be short of frigates"—he smiled at her—"I mean DDs, having only my old *Achilles*, as well as *Ulysses*, *Euripides*, and *Tacitus*. Some older DDs, converted to AVDs, are escorting the new carriers, but six of the latest class, similar to your Scotts but more heavily armed and armored, should be here within a few weeks. With smaller, better protected crews and a heavier punch, it's estimated they'll be even more formidable than ships of the line. There's nothing about them not to like. They're quite expensive, however, I'm told." He grinned at Lelaa. "It's well that, with the confirmation of the gold and oil deposits your people told us to expect near Saint Francis, the Empire's credit is quite strong just now. In any event, I expect them to arrive by the time we move against that accursed El Paso del Fuego."

"Which brings us to that," Lelaa said simply, stepping on the dock alongside *Maaka-Kakja*'s looming shape. Rope-and-plank scaffolds dangled down the side of the ship, covered with men and 'Cats plying paintbrushes. Raised voices attracted Lelaa's attention to her XO, "Tex" Sheider, who was arguing loudly with Gilbert Yeager. Something to do with boiler soot and fresh paint. She shut them from her mind.

"As you heard, Governor-Empress Rebecca wants us to take everything we have and smash directly through the pass. She won't order it, of course. Not after what happened to Task Force Eleven. But she's made her preference clear," Jenks said.

"I take it you dis-aagree?"

Jenks shook his head and spoke wryly. "I'm attracted by the boldness of the move, but, again, perhaps based on the experience of TF Eleven, I'm compelled to counsel against it. General Shinya's mountaintop wireless tower has established contact with Lieutenant Reynolds and Ensign Kari-Faask. We were all very relieved to hear that, but now we know, though the New United States fully intends to join in the destruction of the Dominion, their participation—expected *much* sooner—was delayed. In addition, though the dragons are fewer in the Pass of Fire than in the past—perhaps we've killed enough to make a difference at last?—it remains costly in aircraft and pilots to scout the defenses there. Perhaps the improved pursuit planes aboard the new carriers will simplify that?" He frowned. "But indications are that a powerful enemy fleet still remains on this side of the pass. It's not as large as the one we fought near Malpelo, but it's had time to prepare, to position and protect shore batteries. Who knows what else they might've done? We *must* not underestimate the enemy again. More disturbing, neither we nor the NUS know what waits on the other side of the pass. I agree we must break through, but we have to secure *this* side first."

Lelaa blinked thoughtfully, her tail swishing beneath her white kilt. She'd been thinking about something Orrin once said. . . . She shook her head. Now wasn't the time. "A careful, methodical approach, then. An unusual straa-ti-gee indeed," she murmured. Jenks started to bristle, then realized she was blinking irony. "And I aa-gree," she added. "We must also support General Shin-yaa—and Governor-Empress Rebecca and Saan-Kakja. Not knowing what lies beyond the paass, who's to say something won't prevent us from returning? That could make things . . . awk-waard for us, and do our ground forces no good. On the other haand, if we destroy the enemy at the paass and land troops there, they might support General Shinya's effort to stop Don Her-naan. If *he* caan't stop him, we might be the laast chance to cut him off from New Graa-nada. We caatch him between our forces, and he caan't run anymore. He'd have no choice but to fight or surrender. Either way, we could finally break his army and throw all the Doms into confusion."

"Yes," Jenks said, twisting his mustaches. "I'm almost tempted to suggest that General Shinya *let* Don Hernan escape for now, so we can do exactly that."

"But . . . we might fail," Lelaa said flatly. "What if we caan't take this side of the Paass of Fire and land troops?"

Jenks was nodding. "And that's exactly why Shinya must continue as before, trying to block the enemy while slowing him and herding him with Sister Audry's and Colonel Garcia's tiny TF Skuggik Chase."

"You mean *Major Blas's* taask force?" Lelaa had nothing against Sister Audry, but everyone knew who was really in command.

"Yes, I suppose I do."

"So, our plaan is?" Lelaa asked.

"When we've gathered our full strength, we'll move against the pass and destroy what remains of the enemy. We *will* not fail. Only once we have firm possession and can fully and sustainably support operations ashore will we try to push through. By then we should have aerial reconnaissance as well, and know what lies on the other side. Information the NUS might be grateful for. If we could then, *finally*, coordinate our efforts . . ." His voice trailed away.

"Then I only hope, in the meantime, Gener-aal Shinyaa gets his forces in place at Popayan in time to block Don Her-naan, for everyone's sake, but particularly Major Blas, Sister Audry, and the rest of their little force pretending to be an army." Lelaa's tone turned bitter. "I can only imagine what kind of chik-aash they're enduring, while we stand here, safe and sound, discussing how they should be used."

"Shinya's almost there," Jenks assured, trying to lighten her mood.

"Almost? Blas has what? Thirty-five hundreds of troops? Against forty *thousands*? More?"

"I think she has around five thousand now, counting the locals she's collected," Jenks said weakly.

"So many?" Lelaa snorted sarcastically. "And 'almost' will not help if Don Her-naan realizes he has a flasher fish on his tail instead of a mountain fish, and chooses to turn on it."

Jenks nodded sadly. "Indeed. But if Don Hernan does that, despite General Shinya's personal feelings, it will still give him more time—and serve his purpose just as well."

TF Skuggik Chase
Between Kotopaxi and Popayan
(La Frontera Horribles)
November 10, 1944

Major Blas-Ma-Ar, sometimes still called "Blossom" behind her back, waited tensely in the damp, drizzly, predawn dark. And it was unnaturally dark, deep in the dense, mountainous forest of the Horrible Frontier, as the locals described the almost trackless, foliage-choked wilderness between widely spaced villages in this part of the Dominion. And in addition to the thick overhead cover, there was no moon, and the stars couldn't penetrate the low-lying overcast. Blas wasn't alone, however, and heard the soft sounds of men to her right and 'Cats to her left. The men were Vengadores, former Dom soldiers converted to the "true" Christian faith by Colonel Sister Audry, whom they adored. Counting the recruits from Guayak, Puerto Viejo, and the Christian Rebels under "Captain" Ximen who'd joined them on the march, Colonel Arano Garcia's regiment of Los Vengadores de Dios had swelled to a brigade of more than three thousand men and women. The Lemurians belonged to Blas's own 2nd Battalion of the 2nd Marines. It had once grown to regimental strength itself, but had been whittled down in fierce battles to fewer than seven hundred, fit to fight. They had a few more men and 'Cats, from other units of the Army of the Sisters, mostly artillerymen and support personnel, and there was still a tiny remnant of twenty horse-mounted Imperial dragoons, primarily messengers back and forth to the new wireless station at Kotopaxi almost a hundred miles behind. They traveled the heavily trampled and hewn-down path that Don Hernan's large army, then Blas's TF Skuggik Chase, made in passing, but mounted scouts were useless for probing the enemy on the impenetrable flanks of the ragged trace. For that they had squads of Ximen's Christians and

Captain Ixtli's Ocelomeh, or "Jaguar Warriors." They'd lived in this dense, claustrophobic environment full of terrifying predators for generations, and knew every meager game trail well enough to give them names. Finally, the Ocelomeh also added nearly twenty-five hundred troops to the task force, armed with good-quality Imperial flintlock muskets and their own edged weapons.

Still, combined, Blas's and Sister Audry's force numbered barely six thousand against the possibly forty thousand Don Hernan still had. They'd made a brave front, impersonating Shinya's entire army in pursuit, nipping at the enemy's heels hard enough to make him stop and deploy from time to time. On each occasion, he'd taken bloody losses, inflicted by the Ocelomeh and local Vengadores who infiltrated through the forest and savaged the flanks of his ragged, dispersed battle line. But Blas *couldn't* make a frontal attack. She just didn't have the strength. So eventually, Don Hernan pressed on. Blas desperately wished she had better aerial recon, but most of COFO Reddy's planes were leapfrogging to new airstrips and lakes in preparation for supporting Shinya when he got to Popayan. And TF Skuggik Chase was a long way from the last Nancys at Puerto Viejo, beyond high mountains, and few planes could risk such missions. *It isn't all baad,* she reflected, looking around, finally able to discern vague shapes in the gloom. *We got plenty to eat, even if it's pretty weird.* Their native allies constantly brought wild game, strange roots, and unusual vegetables. She frowned. They also carried in baskets of bugs, little lizards, snakes, and some very unappetizing-looking fish they trapped in streams. She wasn't keen on any of those, but they *were* food.

On the other hand, all her scouts told her that Don Hernan's army was starving. That made it weak—and desperate. The problem was, the scouts also told her it had apparently grown desperate enough to do what she'd most feared: launch a major attack on *her.* They'd seen all the preparations, and reported troops massing in front of her. Don Hernan probably hoped to completely wreck her army so he could quicken his pace. Worse, he didn't have to make it all the way to Popayan before he did that either.

Blas now knew there was a tiny village about fifty miles south of it, with a road of sorts leading north. And it was only *thirty* miles ahead. Once the enemy no longer had to hack its way through heavy timber, it could race away.

Blas sent a pair of her precious dragoons to Kotopaxi with the news, to warn Shinya to pick up his pace and ask for any support he could give—a few planes, anything. She had no other means of communication. But it would take time for the dragoons to make the trip. Even if they survived the predators, which only numbers seemed to deter, they'd be lucky if their news arrived quickly enough to help Shinya. There was even less chance it would do her task force any good. Whatever happened today would be over long before Shinya heard of it.

Oddly, Blas wasn't particularly afraid. She knew it would be tough, and she'd probably die. She'd once endured a terrible violation that destroyed the youngling she'd been, and since then she'd seen more action than most. As a result, her mind and soul had hardened in a way she suspected few could understand. She didn't understand—or like it—herself. She *wanted* to live, and, in spite of everything, she loved life. But she'd become a different, damaged person, who'd come to literally *love* killing the enemies who tried to hurt those she cared about—particularly her 2nd of the 2nd Marines. That both excited and sickened her. She suspected it was normal to be proud and satisfied when she fought well, but to actually *crave* the killing, the primal release only the violence of combat gave her . . . She preferred not to dwell on it, but couldn't imagine a better way to die: in the midst of all that, doing what she loved.

So now they waited behind hastily erected breastworks across the track the Dom army made, as prepared as they could be for the attack they knew would come. Blas looked at the Marines materializing to her left as the black night began to gray, and in spite of the situation, managed a pang of amusement. She was aware they called her Blossom, and loaded the name with irony since they knew what a fighter she was. What they didn't know was that she *liked* the name the dead super bosun, Fitzhugh Gray, had bestowed on her.

"What aa-muses you so?" Sergeant Koratin asked in his gravelly voice, sliding up beside her. He'd been an Aryaalan lord, but despite being fully capable of leading this entire force himself, he had no desire to advance beyond sergeant. He had real power once, he often said, and wasted it. He didn't want it anymore.

Blas looked at him. "Nothing," she replied. "Just thinking. Where's the Col-nol?"

"Which one? Col-nol Gaar-cia is with his troops, on the right. Where he belongs. Sister Audry will be near him, no doubt, where she should *not* be."

"You still think she should stay back from the fighting?"

"Of course. She is all that holds the Vengaa-dores together."

"I hope you're wrong about that," Blas said darkly. "If their cause can die with one person, it's too fragile to rely on."

Koratin sighed. "Perhaps I am wrong. I hope so." He shook his head and blinked. "I believe I *think* so. I do tend toward a measure of cynicism from time to time. But given the faact she will not fight, even to defend herself, she has no place in the firing line." He shrugged. "So I caan't fight as I would wish, since it's my sworn duty to protect her." He grinned. "She *is* armed, with a pistol and cut-laass, at mine and Col-nol Gaar-cia's insistence, but I've never seen her draw either weapon. She caan't have any idea how to use them."

"Why would she need to, with you there?"

"But if I die? Today, that is not unlikely."

"Then someone else'll waatch her. You worry too much."

"And you do not? God keep you, Major Blas," Koratin said, then backed away from the breastworks before moving off to the right.

"That guy is so weird," said A Company's First Sergeant Spon-Ar-Aak, better known as "Spook," taking the place Koratin just left. The white-furred 'Cat had been a gunner's mate on *Walker*, but had followed Blas ever since. "Prob'ly could'a been a gen-raal. The Heavens know he can fight. You know he's a Chiss-chin, right?" Blas nodded.

"One o' the first o' our people to be one," Spook continued. "Now there's bunches of 'em. I don't know how folks can do that—just switch to a new Maker whenever they like. Gives me the creeps."

Blas waved around. "Half our humans are Chiss-chins, an' they fight just fine." She snorted and blinked impatience. "An' it ain't a new Maker, it's the same as ours. Even Adar said so. I got no problem with 'em."

A trumpet sounded dully in the gloomy woods ahead, followed by a terrible rumble of drums that echoed and reverberated through the trees and off the nearby mountains despite the mist. With warning from the Ocelomeh, she'd chosen this spot carefully. It wasn't exactly open, but the passing army had left a good killing ground. She nodded toward it. "I got no problem with *anybody* on our side today." Shapes began racing toward them, forest creatures of various sizes. Some were dangerous, and one Blas saw looked amazingly like a Grik. Their allies had told them those were solitary, territorial predators, and only a threat if they caught you alone or in small groups, unarmed. A few larger beasts, like rhino pigs but with different horns and strange armor on their heads, thundered toward them. All veered from the breastworks when they saw it, crashing into the woods on either side. One must've gotten too close, however, because Blas heard a muffled shot far to the right. *Somebody'll get reamed for that,* she thought. The drums grew louder.

"Here they come!" somebody hissed to her left. Through the mist-clouded morning, she saw them: rank on rank of men marching forward, muskets on their shoulders. Their lines grew confused as they avoided trees, but quickly reformed and pressed on. *This will be baad,* Blas thought. It still wasn't light enough to see the yellow of their coats, but if their facings had been white, she could tell by now. That meant these troops had *red* facings, and were the toughest, most ruthless soldiers Don Hernan possessed. Called Blood Drinkers, they were the personal, elite warriors of the Dom pope himself, so in their minds, they were God's own warriors. Rising, Blas stepped back a few paces, where a gun crew stood by its piece. They hadn't brought many cannon—they couldn't—and the two batteries they had were all the old, lighter six-pounders the Allied armies had used since the Battle of Aryaal. She knew there were even lighter guns now, little things called mountain howitzers that would've been perfect for this, but none had made it to her. She wondered if Shinya had them.

"Whistler," she said, calling her Marine signal-'Cat near. "Sound 'load canister,' then 'advance your pieces.'"

"Ay, ay, Major!" replied the 'Cat, raising his big brass whistle and blowing the sequence of sharp chirps to pass the command. Quickly, the cannoneers made their weapons ready and pushed them to the breastworks. She hadn't already placed them because she hadn't known how the attack would come. With the enemy moving straight back up the track like this, the guns would fight right alongside the infantry. "Standby mortars," she added. The mortar sections had been carefully situated where they could fire without hitting trees overhead. With a rising exhilaration, she prepared to "start the dance."

"Good morning, Major Blas," came Sister Audry's jarringly pleasant, strangely accented voice. Blas turned, blinking consternation, and saw the Dutch nun, dressed much as she was in helmet, combat smock, and tightly wrapped leggings. Her blond hair had been sawed off even with her jaw. A crucifix hung around her neck, and a white cross was painted on her helmet. Sergeant Koratin met Blas's searching gaze and he rolled his eyes to the Heavens, as if asking for assistance. Beside Audry was "Captain" Ximen, his gray beard almost covering his own wooden cross. Ximen wasn't a fighter, and rather frail in any event. His followers had joined Arano Garcia's Vengadores. Captain Ixtli retained direct command, under Blas, of his Jaguar Warriors.

"Get—" Blas snatched what she was about to say out of her throat. "Ah, I wish you'd get baack from here, Colnol. Those are *Blood Drinkers* comin' to kill us, an' we're about to open fire."

Sister Audry smiled. "Very well, Major. Don't mind me. I just thought you might enjoy some conversation during the battle. Perhaps you might step behind the secondary breastworks with me and describe the action as it unfolds?"

"But . . ." The implication was clear. Sister Audry didn't want Blas in the thick of it either. She looked to the front. It was almost time. The first volleys and initial blast of canister must be timed for maximum effect. "My place is here," she finished lamely, almost yearningly.

Sister Audry nodded seriously. "In that case, if you're certain, then here is where I belong as well, at your side." She smiled sweetly. "I *am* your commander, after all."

"But my Marines, they're used to me fighting with them."

"Your Marines, Major Blas, and Captain Ixtli and his Ocelomeh, consider you just as important as Sergeant Koratin insists I am to the Vengadores. It's true your presence in the line inspires them, but your recklessness unnerves them and they fear for you. It was they who asked me to encourage you to protect yourself." She nodded at the next line of stacked timber and deadfall. "It's only a short distance. They will hear your orders quite well."

Blas was stunned. She hadn't considered that. Most important, however, Sister Audry meant what she'd said. If Blas stayed, so would she, and her death would be Blas's fault. After a final glance at the enemy, now little more than a hundred tails away, pausing, preparing for the command to raise their own weapons, she looked Sister Audry in the eye. "Commence firing!" she roared. Even in the misty morning, her voice carried in that singular way Lemurians had, and the command was immediately repeated by officers up and down the line. Rifle and musket companies fired crashing volleys and the twelve guns of her two batteries slammed out buzzing swarms of canister amid great, choking clouds of dense white smoke. Screams echoed back from the enemy. "Cap-i-taan Aalis," Blas shouted to her XO of the 2nd, "carry on. I'll be just back here behind the fallback line, chaatting with the col-nol."

"Ay, ay, Major!" The voice sounded triumphant. A heavy returning volley of musket balls churned the damp earth, sent splinters flying from the barricade, and caused a few screeching cries of pain. Most *vroop*ed by overhead. With all the mist and lingering smoke, their position would be as invisible to the enemy as the Doms now were to them. Through it all, Sister Audry never flinched, her smile never faltered. "Okaay, Col-nol," Blas said stiffly. "After you."

Volley after volley thundered in the tight forest track, and even after the sun burned the mist away, choking smoke hid the combatants from one another. Blas imagined that if a plane did fly over, the battle would be easy to mark, simply by the rising smoke. The noise, unable to disperse, was tremendous, and her ears ached with the steady, cracking pressure of the heavily charged six-pounders. The mortars were behind them and they popped and popped, their bombs whooshing high in the air before falling so close. Screams accompanied their detonations—they'd been ranged and sited well—and many exploded in the trees, spraying blizzards of splinters into the enemy. But the Doms just stood and took it, maintaining a withering fire in return. Blas had expected them to charge almost immediately, to overwhelm the breastworks with sheer numbers, but that hadn't happened. It made no sense.

Teniente Pacal, one of Garcia's company commanders whom Blas considered a friend, hurried to join them, running low. Their hiding place, as Blas regarded it, was near the center of the line and had become, essentially, the division HQ—if one could describe a small group huddled in the damp soil behind fallen trees in such a way. Pacal saluted as he slid to his knees in front of them. "Capitan Garcia's adoration, *Santa Madre* . . ." he began.

"Stop calling me that!" Sister Audry interrupted.

"Of course, *Santa Madre*. Capitan Garcia begs to report: our weapons do not miss fire as much, now the mist is gone, but the ammunition, it runs low. He wonders if this might be part of the enemy's plan."

Captain Ixtli joined them as well, walking upright. He was very young, probably twenty, but very self-assured. He seemed to be having the time of his life—and maybe he was. His Ocelomeh had suffered terribly at the hands of the Doms, and now to kill so many so easily made his eyes flash with satisfaction. He barely seemed to notice when a musket ball snatched at his tattered sleeve. "We are not so low on ammunition," he said. "My people are not as well trained as yours." He nodded at Pacal. "But this is not what I expected," he confessed.

"I've begun to ask myself the same as Teniente Pacaal, Col-nol," Koratin admitted to Sister Audry. "Like the Grik have done, they sacrifice warriors to leave us defenseless."

Blas had been peering over the breastworks, as far as she thought she could get away with without earning a gentle reprimand. It was true they were using a lot of precious ammunition they couldn't easily replace, and her 2nd Marines, with their breech-loading Allin-Silvas, were almost dry after nearly two hours of constant firing. *Two hours* . . . So, Koratin's theory made sense—if the enemy knew how far out on the logistical limb they were. But if they knew that, they also had to know how small their force was. Why not just mob them under? She could *see* Doms out there as the smoke eddied, still roughly a hundred tails away. Gaps constantly opened in their lines and bodies were literally heaped at their feet. But the gaps closed and they continued firing. They were taking a grim toll in return and there were many dead and wounded behind the breastworks, but it *seemed* insane . . . She turned to Ixtli. "And our scouts still see no evidence the Doms are sneaking through the woods on our flaanks, like we've done to them?"

"No, Major Blas," he said, bowing respectfully. He treated her with the same reverence the Vengadores showed Sister Audry, mostly because of what she and her people *looked* like. That made Blas uncomfortable.

She looked at Sister Audry, speaking loudly over the battle. "Don Her-naan wouldn't waste his finest troops just to soak up bullets," she said, thinking her way through it. "He'd use reg-laars. They'd take it awhile, then break, an' he'd send up more until they did the same. If he was just tryin' to empty our guns, he'd do that, *then* send Blood Drinkers to wipe us out. But Blood Drinkers'll stand from start to finish until we kill every daamn one, if they're told. Why waste 'em?"

Koratin's eyes widened. "*Because* they're the only ones who'll staand that long. And perhaps because they're the only ones there! They do not sacrifice their lives for our bullets, but for *time*!"

Blas's mind whirled. "This *isn't* a major attaack! It's a

rearguard made to *look* like one. They can't charge because they'll spend themselves up, an' we'll see there's nothin' behind 'em!" She barked a laugh, barely audible over another blast of canister, but there was no humor in it. "They've done the same thing to us we've done to them—slowing us with a small force—the Maker knows how long. Now they try to stop us in our traacks *just one more day. . . .*"

Sister Audry's benign expression finally faded. "What must we do?"

Blas stood, oblivious to enemy fire, blinking determination. "We kill 'em until our ammunition's almost gone, then attaack. It'll be bloody," she cautioned. "Blood Drinkers fight up close with the same resolve that keeps 'em staandin' there, takin' all we've thrown at 'em for two daamn hours. But we're in a hurry now, an' have to know how long we've been sloggin' along behind a reflection of ourselves." She looked at Pacal, then Ixtli. "An' that means prisoners. When we have 'em, we'll leave it to you to find out what we need to know."

"Major Blas . . ." Sister Audry began, her voice stern.

Blas blinked at her emphatically. "We leave it to *them*, Col-nol! I know your ways work on people"—she glanced at Pacal—"but these're *Blood Drinkers*. You might convert a few over months, but we got *no* time—an' lives're at stake! Maybe the whole daamn war!"

When Blas predicted it would be bloody, she hadn't really known how grimly inadequate her description was for the true horror to come. She'd fought Blood Drinkers before, but always with an advantage, from defensive positions. Never on the open ground, bayonet to bayonet. And despite Sister Audry's objections, she didn't stay behind when her Marines, the Ocelomeh, and the Vengadores followed their last loads of canister over the breastworks. She couldn't abandon them for that, and if Koratin was right and the bulk of the Dom army was long gone, this last fight and what they discovered would be the task force's final purpose. Charging and yelling with bayonets fixed, her Lemurian Marines yipping and howling in that terrifying way that unnerved even the Grik, they slammed into the brutalized Dominion line. The sheer magnitude of the slaughter they'd already wreaked hindered them then, as they had to climb or wade through bodies before they could even come to grips with Dom soldiers more lethal than any Grik. And they were at least a match, in terms of training, for Marines and veteran Vengadores. For the rest—the new members of Garcia's force and the Ocelomeh in particular, despite their courage and rage after generations of abuse—it was a slaughter.

The Jaguar Warriors might be the finest rough-terrain, woodland guerrillas in the world—Blas knew nothing of the Khonashi—but they were hopelessly outclassed in this kind of fight. It was as if they were fighting her own Marines, and the Doms' bayonet work was professional, and just different enough that even her Marines had trouble adjusting. Many died in that first, frantic embrace, amid flashing bayonets, jetting muzzle flashes, the clash of steel, defiant roars, and shrill, unearthly shrieks. And despite the slaughter the Doms had endured, there were still plenty of them. Blas lost her rifle, knocked away by a finger-numbing blow, and immediately drew her pistol and cutlass. She'd become an artist with both, under the tutelage of such as Chack, Silva, and Gray, and inside the reach of Dom bayonets, she hacked, slashed, and shot her way through the line and started cutting men down from the sides. Others did the same. Finally, ultimately, it was technology and determination that turned the tide.

These Doms were still encumbered with plug bayonets, making it impossible to fire their muskets once they resorted to their blades. On its face, on some procurement bureaucrat's ledger, it might seem a minor thing, but in practice, the tactical disadvantage was devastating. Blas suspected the *next* Dom army they met would be better equipped, but in the meantime, her people, with their offset, socket bayonets, could still fire when they got a chance to load, and that didn't take but a few seconds for her Marines with their breech-loaders. And then there were the pistols, like her Baalkpan Armory copy of a 1911 Colt. At bayonet range, they were overwhelming. All her Marine officers and NCOs had them, and their sharp *pop! pop! pop!* joined the other sounds of battle. She'd hack a man with the cutlass in her right hand and shoot another with the pistol in her left. When it was empty, she'd push the magazine release with her trigger finger, thrust her cutlass in the ground when a moment came, and insert another magazine from the pouches on her belt. It took only seconds. Then she was back to hacking and shooting. Soon, all her Marines had broken through the center of the Dom line and begun sweeping to the left, killing as they went, joining the Ocelomeh.

And that was where the determination came in. Outmatched as they were, the Jaguar Warriors didn't fall back. They kept up the pressure—and the enemy's attention—even as they died in droves, and the 2nd of the 2nd rolled the Doms up in an irresistible sweep of lead and steel. By the time the last cluster of exhausted, broken, mostly wounded Blood Drinkers were surrounded on the far western side of the artificial clearing, triumphant shouts came from the Vengadores on the right, having achieved the same result on their own.

"Prisoners! Prisoners!" Blas shouted, gasping for air, her voice cracked, throat feeling like she'd swallowed hot sand. Others took up the call somewhat belatedly, and slowly, reluctantly, the killing began to ebb. It was only then she realized she was limping, and glanced dazedly at her right leg beyond the hem of her filthy, blood-soaked smock. *How'd I get that?* she wondered, seeing the deep puncture in her calf, blood flowing freely to mix pinkly with the foamy sweat slicking her fur. The rush of combat was beginning to fade, as if it were leaking from her wound. She felt faint.

"Corps-'Cat!" First Sergeant Spook bellowed, suddenly beside her. He looked worse than she did, with all the blood soaking his white fur.

"You do it," Blas croaked, sitting heavily on a Dom corpse and fumbling at a pouch on her belt for a battle dressing. Her hands were shaking so badly, she let Spook get it out. "Healers are busy enough," she managed to say, "an' it's just a little poke. Prob'ly a bayonet got me. By the looks of it, one of ours." For some reason, that amused her. "How 'bout you? You look awful."

Spook shrugged, uncapping the vial of polta paste and

smearing it on her wound; then he started to apply the bandage. "I'm too daamn sore to tell, but I don't think I'm hurt," he answered at last. "That was tough," he added, in classic understatement, tying the dressing in place. Then he raised his voice at the milling Marines and Ocelomeh. Many—those not still menacing the surrounded Doms—seemed utterly spent, almost in a state of shock. "Some o' you dopes, gimme a haand with the major!"

Captain Ixtli himself, nose and lips smashed and bleeding from several superficial cuts, suddenly appeared and helped Blas to her feet. More of his people gathered, their haggard expressions radiating something like awe at the sight of her. "If I had any doubt before, Major Blas, I have none now," he said softly. "We did our best"—his eyes strayed across the many, many dead as they filled with tears—"but we are mere pretenders. You and your people, your Mi-Anakka, gave us victory today! You are the *true* Ocelomeh!"

"Naah, Cap-i-taan Ixtli," Spook said. "We're just Maareens. Your people can do as well, once they're armed an' trained right."

Blas said nothing as they helped her to where the shattered Doms waited. Sister Audry and Colonel Garcia joined them. Both looked terrible, and even Sister Audry's smock was dark with blood. She saw Blas looking at it. "Captain Ximen tried to join the charge," she said softly. "He never even made it over the barricade before he was shot down."

"And Teniente Pacal," Garcia added, knowing he was Blas's friend.

"Daamn." Blas shook her head, then looked at them. "Did you get anything from your prisoners?"

"We have barely tried as yet. We wanted to check on you. Sergeant Koratin has remained to speak to them through one of my men."

"Then let's see what *these'll* spill." Blas nodded forward.

"Certainly," Garcia agreed, "but be warned; they do not consider themselves prisoners. They have not surrendered, and likely won't."

"We'll see." Blas stared at the Doms within the ring of

leveled rifles and muskets. There were probably fewer than two hundred in this bunch. Those who could were standing, glaring with defiance. "Ask 'em who's in charge."

Garcia did, and a man dressed the same as the others except that his red facings were piped with gold lace stepped forward. His hat was gone and there was a bloody bandage around his head. He snapped something lengthy in response. "He's their *teniente.* Their sole surviving officer."

"What else did he say?"

"Only that we may as well kill them and send them down to, ah, Heaven. We may have won the fight, but lost the battle."

"Then it's just like Koratin suspected," Blas said grimly. "Ask him where Don Her-naan is."

When Garcia complied, the Dom laughed and spoke again. Garcia gasped. "He says His Holiness left the army even as they were 'cleansing' Kotopaxi." ("Cleansing" meant "exterminating the people" there.) "And the main army force-marched away shortly afterward. As *you* said, we have pursued a mere reflection of ourselves for weeks!"

"But he doesn't know that. He is gloating," Sister Audry said with a frown. "As far as he knows, we *are* our main army, trapped in the wilderness. He also cannot know how quickly we can get word to General Shinya."

"Not quick enough," said Blas, blinking disgust as she looked at her bulky Imperial watch. She was amazed to realize it was already late afternoon. How long had that final assault taken? How long had they fought for their lives? Ordinarily, such things seemed to last much longer than they actually did. This time, apparently, it was the reverse. For her, at least. "Another day lost with this fighting, another to get word to Koto-paaxi an' send a message. Even with air-craaft, who knows how long it'll take Generaal Shin-yaa to shift gears, find an army that isn't where he expects it to be, then change direction, if he can."

"There is another concern," Sister Audry said. "Quite obvious, actually, that the enemy officer told us without our even asking." She looked at their questioning, blinking faces. "With Don Hernan gone, the enemy has had another commander for some time, obviously more talented, and therefore more dangerous. We were confident what Don Hernan would do: continue to flee to save his life. This other may do something entirely different. He's likely already past Popayan, and may be moving to join their forces at the Pass of Fire. Or . . ." She paused, stricken. "If he somehow discovered it with his scouts, or even civilian rumors, he may be preparing to attack General Shinya's army!"

"Then we have not a moment to lose!" Garcia cried. "We must send couriers back to Kotopaxi at once."

"Send six," Blas agreed. "We can't risk this message with less. We'll send the rest—all of 'em—forward to scout. Straight up the path the enemy left. They should be safe enough now," she added, blinking bitterness. "We'll follow."

"Why?" Garcia asked. "Shouldn't we return the way we came? We're almost out of ammunition. And what of our wounded?"

"We're a lot closer to Popay-aan. Hopefully, even if the Doms learned Shin-yaa was coming, they just beat it anyway, glaad to get past him. We'll meet him there, an' our wounded'll get quicker care."

"And if that is not the case?" Sister Audry asked.

Blas shrugged. "We're screwed."

"What about them?" Ixtli asked, gesturing at the Blood Drinkers. "We will get no more from them than we have already learned or guessed."

"Kill 'em, for all I care," Blas said coldly.

"No!" Sister Audry said, glaring at Blas. "Such an act goes against God, the Maker of All Things. He will *never* forgive it, or you. They are our prisoners!"

Blas returned her glare with a steady gaze. "You say we do the Maker's work, an' I think so too. Would He forgive a *useless waste of troops* doin' His work?"

Garcia looked torn. "With all my adoration, *Santa Madre*, Major Blas may be right. The Blood Drinkers will *not* surrender and we will have to disarm them by force. People will die. How many lives is that worth?"

"As many as it takes!" Sister Audry insisted. "Or have we become like them? What if mercy had been denied *your* people, Colonel Garcia?"

Garcia recoiled as if slapped.

"I won't ask the Ocelomeh to fight more today, to no purpose," Ixtli stated flatly. "They have suffered enough."

Arano Garcia recovered himself and sighed. "Very well, *Santa Madre*," he said sadly. "The Vengadores will do it. We remember the mercy and grace *we* received. But none of us were Blood Drinkers," he cautioned, "so do not be disappointed if fewer than we lose subduing them are ever brought to the light."

Sister Audry placed a hand on his shoulder, a sad smile on her face. "My dear Arano, don't you see? Any we lose in the effort will be tragic, but not to *try* would be a terrible sin. And if only *one* is brought to God, if a hundred die to do it, it will be a victory."

"That's some daamn weird reckoning, you ask me," Spook whispered in Blas's ear.

But Blas had been strangely moved, and suddenly felt . . . ashamed. "Shut up," she hissed back.

CHAPTER 10

Ostia
Republic of Real People
Southern Africa

"I don't know how you staand it here," grumped Major Bekiaa-Sab-At, former captain of USS *Donaghey*'s Marine contingent, as she and her Republic aide, Optio (basically "lieutenant") Jack Meek, threaded among disinterested humans and Lemurians in the rough-hewn, smelly, and uncomfortably *cold* city of Ostia. Most people paid them little heed, but a perceptive few stopped to gawk at the unusual pair. Bekiaa habitually wore field garb, even at official functions with Republic leaders, in order to—she told herself—impress them with her seriousness for the task at hand. In reality, she probably did it subconsciously to shock: to jolt them into taking the coming campaign more seriously. Today, however, she wore her Marine (combat) dress uniform over her brindled fur. It consisted of a dark blue kilt and tunic, and bright white rhino-pig armor over chest and shoulders. No dress headgear had been prescribed for Allied Marines, so her mottled, battered, "doughboy" helmet contrasted starkly with the rest—as did the blood-and powder-stained cartridge-box strap and pistol/cutlass belt. The ornately tooled black leather sling on the 1903 Springfield that Colonel "Billy" Flynn had given her was new. It was the same sling issued to all Repub troops, minus the tooling, and was a gift from Inquisitor Choon. He'd also given her warm, form-fitting knee boots, better suited to the often muddy, sometimes snowy land she was in. Republic shoe and bootmakers had centuries of practice making all-weather footwear for humans and Mi-Anakka. *Kon-Choon's been paying me a lot of attention lately,* Bekiaa reflected with mixed feelings, *an' not all's been strictly professional.* She shook it off.

"I *don't* live 'ere, Cap'n," replied Optio Meek with a tolerant grin that made him look like his father, despite further narrowing of his oriental eyes. His father, "Leftenant" Doocy Meek, was British, serving as the Republic's liaison to Captain Reddy. Bekiaa had never seen his mother, but figured she must be of Chinese descent. Meek wore standard "undress" attire for Republic noncoms, with a polished bronze cuirass and helmet—oddly reminiscent of those once used by Grik officers—over an ordinary dark yellow-brown woolen tunic and trousers. His black boots also reached his knees, and his pistol belt, supporting a large revolver, was black as well. He carried no rifle or sword, and constantly appealed to her—in vain—to follow his example. "I've lived all me life near Alex-aandra, as ye know. An' can't get used ta the *heat* hereabouts," he goaded.

Bekiaa rolled her eyes. Despite her fur, she was used to the equator. Unlike Grik, however, her people could function perfectly well in the cold, as long as they dressed appropriately. That didn't mean she liked it. And though this was considered a pleasant spring day by the locals, before *Donaghey* rounded the cape and brought her to the Republic, she'd experienced fifty degrees only when she'd flown. Her primary duty in the Republic, as Inquisitor Choon described it, was to represent the other allied powers and advise him, Kaiser Nig-Taak, and, more specifically, General Marcus Kim. She considered it just as important to advise Captain Reddy, via wireless, on the true state of the Republic's preparations for war. Second to that, she'd done her best to ensure it was ready to make a useful contribution when operations finally began. After what had been, in some ways, a tediously delayed mobilization, enforced by the League battleship *Savoie* in Alex-aandra harbor, the Repubs were frantically making up lost time to open the second front their allies so desperately needed.

Historically, the Republic's approach to any hypothetical conflict with the Grik was to rely on superior firepower. They'd apparently been on par with the Empire of the New Britain Isles, militarily, for about two hundred years, and had been equipped with decent artillery and flintlock muskets. But the Grik had now passed that point themselves. Since the late-nineteenth century, however, and certainly since SMS *Amerika*'s arrival with early twentieth century Germans and British prisoners of war, the Republic had changed amazingly. Ostia, bordering the huge Lake Taa-Hu, was a prime example. In sharp contrast to the architectural opulence of Alex-aandra, Ostia was rough-hewn and angular, a wilderness city surrounded by a mixture of prairie and dense forests of tall trees with high, chaotic branches. Until the last few decades, low-lying Ostia had been a small, picturesque village blessed with moderate winters, where wealthy merchants and government officials often retired. There'd always been modest timber, and, to a lesser extent, iron production there; the unpretentious mills and puddling furnaces reminiscent of eighteenth-and early nineteenth-century Europe, fueled by coal from Nicaeaa and strong rivers that formed and fled the lake. Over the past twenty years, however, as the Republic experienced a true industrial revolution, Ostia's and nearby Cosaa's abundant resources and central location had turned them into lumber-and metal-producing powerhouses.

Little actual manufacturing occurred there, but huge stone buildings housing smelters and foundries were erected. Bremen joined Nicaeaa to provide coal for the new furnaces, and steam power had largely replaced the rivers. More iron ore—and now manganese—came from dozens of little mining towns that had sprouted to the west. Other raw materials like copper, lead, tin, and zinc came for processing, from Colonia on the west coast, and left as refined ingots, as well as brass and bronze. Much of Ostia's and Cosaa's output went south to the steel mills of St. Peter and St. Paul, where new open-hearth and Bessemer process furnaces stood side by side, the first making less, but more specialized, steel; the latter making more, for less critical applications. But Nicaeaa and Bremen, little different in appearance from Ostia, had burgeoning steel mills as well, and took more of the trade each year. Heavy manufacturing and shipbuilding, as well as armaments factories, were still largely centered in Augustus and Trier on the west coast, but Derby, Whitby, Emden, and now even Ostia itself were beginning to test those waters—except for shipbuilding, of course. Derby was farthest along, despite its location on the frigid highland steppe, in the production of high-quality heavy ordnance. This was because it had a fine river of its own, the newest, most modern facilities, and possibly because its workers never complained about the heat they had to labor in.

But Ostia was nearest the very center of the predominately human/Lemurian Republic of Real People, encompassing all of southern Africa up to latitude 260 south, and slightly farther in the west. The boundary wasn't political, established through negotiations with the Grik, but had been arrived at after centuries of coexisting with the malevolent species to the north. The Grik simply didn't seem comfortable crossing it, and comfort was apparently the prime consideration. The moderate to downright cold climate in much of the Republic had been its greatest protection across the ages. This defense was reinforced by a network of road-connected forts along the frontier, none of which could've long withstood a concerted attack, but each theoretically supportable by garrisons from the others—with sufficient warning.

And there'd never been any delusion that the Grik weren't their enemy. Parties of them did occasionally venture south in the summertime, killing and eating anyone they found, and their mass hunts sometimes drove great packs or herds of destructive or carnivorous beasts south of the frontier. Indeed, numerous Republic expeditions had traveled north over the years, in search of exotic game or resources (iron, copper, and coal were plentiful in the eastern mountains), or even attempting peaceful contact with the Grik. Few returned. Finally, though the Republic never courted all-out war, the Grik had made it plain that the Republic was next on their list for conquest. That made the Republic and its people *reasonably* glad the alliance with the United Homes and the Empire of the New Britain Isles had given them an opportunity to deal with the long-standing threat.

Fortunately, the Republic hadn't been entirely unprepared. For nearly a decade, they'd been making fine, breech-loading field pieces called Derby guns, after the new city where they were manufactured, based on something they referred to as a French 75. They'd been making powerful, single-shot, bolt-action rifles in 11 mm even longer, and now a respectable number of Maxim-inspired machine guns in 7.92 x 57 mm were being manufactured in Augustus. They also had other, quite interestingly lethal devices, but Bekiaa's appreciation of them was tempered by her indignant annoyance at having to learn yet *another* unit of measurement.

She'd quickly learned a yard was virtually identical to a tail, and it took three feet to make one. Feet were . . . okay, being about the same length as two average Lemurian feet, with their toes turned up. An inch was basically a finger width. From that, smaller decimal measurements were based on tenths, hundredths, and ten hundredths. But the metric system here, with nothing ready at hand to compare it to, drove her to distraction. Particularly when her misunderstanding made her look foolish in the eyes of troops she was trying to train. That impression rarely lasted once her pupils got to know her.

Besides being breveted major by Safir Maraan, she'd been made legate of the 1st's and Kim's personal legions. Essentially, legate equated to a Republic colonel—which no other colonel outranked. She thought that was weird, but it helped cut the red tape when she was temporarily assigned to instruct other legions. Choon had finally convinced the kaiser that superior firepower alone couldn't defeat the Grik or even keep them at arm's length where they could bring it to bear. They needed her advice in retraining all their troops, even more professional legions like the 1st, to fight as their allies did: face-to-face, with the bayonet. And few Allied warriors had as much intimate experience doing that as Bekiaa-Sab-At. She wished she had more help, but she *had* made a difference—as had other Allied "trainers" *Donaghey* left behind, such as one of her Nancy floatplanes, with its flight and ground crew. The Nancy was serving as a pattern for Republic engineers to copy, and the flyers, though young and untested in combat, were helping train the fledgling air arm of the Republic. Despite their inexperience, they were excellent pilots and had received good instruction. In fact, their relatively recent education probably made them better teachers for beginners than more hardened veterans might've been. Even so, Bekiaa didn't envy them their task.

The Republic *Fliegertruppe*, or Air Corps, consisted of only a handful of interesting if complicated-looking biplanes called Cantets. Named after black, skuggik-size lizardbirds Optio Meek simply called crows, they were loosely based—she was told—on recollections of something called an Albatross B-1. The first had flown nearly ten years before and numerous improvements had been made, but the utility of aircraft had never been fully appreciated by the Republic until now. As far as she knew, fewer than twenty had existed before she arrived, but the country's burgeoning—frankly astonishing—industrial capacity, barely visible at Alex-aandra, had already doubled that number in the past few months. And after examining the Nancy, they were incorporating further improvements, modest at first, but paving the way for an entirely new model, possibly a monoplane. She hoped the planes would help, but with the go date perhaps only days away, they probably wouldn't make a significant difference. Yet.

"Heat. Ha," Bekiaa said dryly. "Spend time in *Waakur*'s fireroom, *any* fireroom, then complain to me of heat."

Meek chuckled. "Nah. Unlike me da', I'm content ta make me life in the legions, an' spurn the fearful sea! Remainin' a meager optio is good enough fer me." He paused and grinned. "There's one, didja' hear? A fetchin' verse!"

Bekiaa looked at him, knowing that, like Dennis Silva, Jack was far more than a meager optio, and his simple-soldier act didn't fool her. He obviously worked closely with Inquisitor Choon and clearly understood there were often advantages to being underestimated.

"You aas-tonish me, Optio," she said sardonically, eyes drifting back to his bouncing flap holster as they hurried along. Like Republic rifles, their pistols were also 11 mm, though the cartridges were only half as long. *What's wrong with calling them forty-three caal-iber?* she asked herself. *And why not go with an honest .45 in the first place? Or .50, like our Allin-Silvas? Now,* there*'s a nice, round number. An' 75 mm guns! Why couldn't they just call 'em three-inchers? It takes a lot of stupid, wasted time to sort that out in my head, and the Maker knows I have enough to keep track of as it is.* "We're late," Bekiaa added, still cursing millimeters in her mind as they hurried along the wooden walkway. The main road through the city to the station was baked brick.

"Aye," Jack replied soothingly, "through no fault o' yers—or mine. 'Twas that sodding—beggin' yer pardon, Legate—that . . . useless reserve colonel 'oo wouldn't b'lieve ye, a fine, *foreign* lady, could possibly be a act'yal legate, till ye showed 'im Gen'ral Kim's letter! Ha! 'Is eyes near spit outa 'is 'ead! 'Specially when 'e read you was authorized ta *shoot* 'is fat arse if 'e didn't get it movin'!"

Bekiaa ignored the latest jab at her choice of dress, but one of her tasks in Ostia had been to personally deliver movement orders to a reserve legion gathered outside the city. Orders had been sent by telegraph but not acted upon. To her consternation, Bekiaa had seen a lot of that: a general reluctance of local commanders to leave their comfortable headquarters, usually luxurious villas, and actually head for the front. The standing legions impressed her with their professionalism, if not overall preparedness, for what they'd face, but some of the reserve units . . .

"We may not've been here to meet the train, but it'll not bolt off wi'out ye," Jack consoled. "It must change cargo 'ere, an' take on fuel an' water, o' course."

"That's not what I'm worried about. The maan we're to meet . . ." She sighed very deeply. "He's brilliant, of course, but with that often comes distraaction. I expect he's already jumped from the train and lost himself by now, if he didn't do it somewhere along the way, for a better look of some strange beast."

"Not ta worry, Legate," Meek assured. "They're prob'ly

guardin' 'im careful as a hooker tendin' her nest." Hookers looked like miniature Grik—with claws like long fishhooks for catching prey; thick, bristly fur; and the temperament of a jackal.

"It may not matter," Bekiaa murmured grimly.

In the event, she was mistaken. The long military train—Bekiaa looked upon Republic railroads with fervent greed—hadn't been there long, and no one was exiting the passenger cars behind the coal tenders yet. The pair of surprisingly compact—by naval standards—engines were still venting excess steam, and Gentaa stevedores were just moving forward to begin their work.

Gentaa are weird ducks, Bekiaa considered again, barely aware of what a duck was, but equally uncertain about Gentaa and the legend surrounding them. Word was they were a hybrid mix of humans and Mi-Anakka. *And they do* look *like crossbreeds,* she confessed, *built a little like both, with big eyes, but less furry than 'Caats. And shorter tails, of course.* Like most true humans in view, they wore jackets or coveralls. The 'Cats wore more clothing than Bekiaa was accustomed to as well, but also grew longer fur. Still, Bekiaa didn't know what to think about Gentaa. They didn't go for soldiers, though some slipped off to join the Republic Navy. And apparently, they actually *did* have to sneak away from their people to do so. Mostly she just saw them at labor such as this or on the docks in port, and knew they worked in the steel and timber industries—anything involving heavy, manual toil. By all accounts, they loved and supported their country, but had gained such an organized monopoly over relatively unskilled labor that they commanded considerable collective political power. They were even excused from military service and deemed essential to the economy. Particularly now. Bekiaa understood that, but wondered why so few ever broke ranks from their class. As far as she knew, though every race in the Republic was uncomfortable with the official origin story of the Gentaa, only the Gentaa themselves seemed intent on keeping their people so insular. She shook her head.

Behind the engines, on the folded iron rails and wooden ties paralleling the road through the city, were scores of flatcars heaped with everything from limbered guns to ordnance, casks of salt meat, tentage, even penned animals. Most of the animals were horses, remounts for the excellent Republic Cavalry already scouting past the mountains beyond the frontier. Bekiaa wouldn't put Repub Cav on a par with Maa-ni-los and their dangerous me-naak mounts, but they were good.

There were also quite a few suikaas, stoically awaiting their fate—and food. Suikaas were large gray-furred beasts that Jack said his "da" told him looked like a cross between a camel and a giraffe—whatever those were. A generally passive—if disagreeably slobbery—draft animal, they were used like the other Allies employed more temperamental paalkas. Suikaas, quite contentedly it seemed, drew heavy wagons and artillery with apparently boundless energy, as long as they were properly fed. They grew recalcitrant at the least shortage of fodder, however, and seemed quite aware of times when they should be awarded more than usual, after extra exertions.

Beyond the flatcars were countless boxcars, vanishing around the bend. The doors had already opened and hundreds of troops, dressed like Optio Meek, minus the armor, were hopping down. *Supposed to be another whole brigade, or legion, just on this train,* Bekiaa mused. An Allied brigade consisted of two (sometimes more) regiments of around a thousand troops each. A division was composed of at least two brigades, but usually five or six, and Allied cavalry and artillery assignments were made by division commanders. A corps was built around two or more divisions.

Republic legions were supposed to be self-contained, however, and were composed of about 3,500 troops, including support personnel. Each had its own "cohort," roughly a battalion, of cavalry and artillery. This arrangement worked well when legions merely protected a section of the frontier, but few had ever trained or maneuvered together as a larger force. One of Bekiaa's greatest challenges still was convincing Choon and Kim, and ultimately the Kaiser, how important it was that their admittedly competent regular legionnaires, not to mention the reserves and new recruits, learn to cooperate seamlessly in larger concentrations. Equally important, the legions needed to surrender their personal packets of artillery and cavalry so they could be massed as needed, as well. A confusing compromise had been reached, by which each legion surrendered half its artillery and cavalry to form legions of their own, under the direct control of Kim's general staff. Bekiaa supposed that was better than nothing, but remained concerned about how it would work.

She continued to watch the new arrivals. Still so far from Fort Taak, on the far eastern frontier, they'd been raised and organized under the old system, and it was largely her and her growing staff's job to sort them out, as she'd tried to do with all the others when they arrived. But time was short. The Grik were concentrating, Captain Reddy was planning something big, and they might get the go order any day. *And we'll* need *these guys,* she reflected sourly. *Ready to go; ready to fight.* Regardless how much work had been done to prepare for the campaign, besides her, possibly only Choon had any real idea what they were getting into. The Republic had gathered more than sixty thousand troops near Fort Taak, but there were reportedly *several hundred thousand* Grik at Sofesshk. And they'd have to fight through more to get there.

Motioning Jack forward, they strode past the engines toward the foremost passenger car. Republic officers, human and Mi-Anakka, spilled down the stairs amid the swirling steam, jabbering loudly and grateful to stretch their legs. Behind them, peering excitedly at the bustling city, was Courtney Bradford. Bekiaa hadn't seen him for a very long time and her first impression was that he'd aged. Humans' fur grayed as they got older, starting around the face, just like Mi-Anakka, and Courtney had grown a beard—almost white—since last they met. The enormous eyebrows he often moved so dramatically, to the amused delight of many, were graying now as well. She couldn't see his balding head beneath the bizarre hat he wore. He'd replaced his broad sombrero with a furry, pointed cap, complete with a bell with an enclosed rattler at the peak. Long ear warmers extending to the collar of his fur-lined parka were furnished with more bells, like she'd seen on suikaa bridles. She suspected Courtney's keepers had given him the specially accoutered garment for the same reason suikaas wore the bells: to make them easier to keep track of. Bekiaa entirely approved. The ruddy face beneath the near-white fur looked the same, however. There were no new lines around his youthfully inquisitive eyes, and he seemed just as energetic as she remembered when he bounded down the stairs at last, followed by another pair of keepers. He saw her then and beamed.

"My dear Bekiaa!" he boomed, sweeping forward to embrace her. She endured the hug with a smile, then stepped back. "Just *look* at you, my dear!" he gushed, and she glanced down self-consciously, expecting to find a muddy blotch on her brilliant armor. "Such a welcome sight for these old eyes," he quickly clarified. "A veritable recruiting poster for the Marines! I've missed you so, I may embrace you again at any moment."

Bekiaa smiled more broadly, blinking genuine pleasure, but took another step back. "It's good to see you as well, Minister Braad-furd. Or should I say Mr. Am-baas-ador?"

He waved it away as he might a bothersome insect. "Between us, it must always remain Courtney, of course."

Bekiaa gestured at her aide. "This is Optio James Meek. Doocy Meek's son," she added significantly.

"Jack, sir, if ye please," Meek said, shaking the hand Courtney extended. "How's me da?" he asked anxiously.

"Busy, as are we all these days. But thriving. He particularly asked me to pass his warmest regards, should we meet. He knows you've been assigned to assist the, ah, legate." He smiled at Bekiaa. Courtney spent the next several minutes introducing the officers he'd traveled with from Alex-aandra. Most had heard of Bekiaa and were anxious for her views. A few looked resentful, and she knew Jack would remember which they were.

"How was your journey?" Bekiaa asked. "I'd hoped to see you sooner, at Fort Taak."

"I know, my dear, but the trip was more tedious than expected. After the Clipper brought me to Songze, I viewed the new Republic shipyards. You can still see the

Dark from there, you know. It's utterly fascinating!" The Dark was a perpetual, ship-killing storm that lingered off the cape, kept alive by the collision of warm/cold sea currents and the cold winds from the south crashing into warm, moist air gusting from the equator and across Madagascar. *Donaghey* was the only sailing ship known to have survived the passage, traveling east to west, and she'd been severely battered. For decades, the Republic's most powerful warships, now antiquated twin-turret coastal monitors of the Princeps class, had protected its southern and western ports, but they were terrible sea boats with a low freeboard and couldn't have survived a passage in either direction. After its embarrassment by *Savoie*, the Republic had—at long last—commissioned a blue-water navy better suited for warfare against the Grik, Doms, and perhaps the League. The first ships, supposedly a type of protected cruiser with heavy guns, tentatively the Imperator class, had been started at Songze in the east, and Trier and Augustus in the west. One of Courtney's first promises as plenipotentiary at large had been technical assistance from Baalkpan's engineers.

"From Songze, we flew to Lake Taa-Hu—here—where the Clipper left me. COFO Leedom was sorry to miss you, and sends his regards, by the way. I believe he intended to take a daylight observation of General Kim's proposed line of advance before turning into the Go Away Strait for a rendezvous with a waiting tender." Courtney spread his hands. "I'd *so* hoped to behold one of the great, woolly sauropods, but there was no time, alas, and I was immediately whisked south and west on a heavily laden train bound for St. Peter. From there I went to Kaava-la in an equally packed steam lorry—which looked strikingly like an undertype Super Sentinel to me—pulling several other cars along a remarkably smooth, if very hilly and windy, road." He frowned. "That stretch was the most excruciating, in terms of time, due to frequent stops for fuel and water, and took as long—nearly three days—as the rest of my trip combined. From there, I traveled west in a coach with a six-horse team and finally reached Alex-aandra the following day. Such a city!" Courtney enthused. "Quite like Constantinople, I must say, flavored by dashes of Peking, ancient Rome, even Athens! And a great deal else, entirely unlike anything I've ever seen. Remarkable!"

Bekiaa nodded. She'd spent far too much time there, in her opinion, and had no appreciation for his comparisons, in any event. Alex-aandra was a weird, showy dive, though, that was certain. "Did you speak to Nig-Taak?" she asked.

"Immediately, and at great length," Courtney replied with satisfaction. "There was no waiting about, cooling my heels. He seems most sensible to the need for haste, at last, and made a most positive impression. I saw no lingering trace of shyness for the fray, and believe his Assembly, his Senate, was most responsible for that. Even they are convinced at last that the Republic may not simply ride this out, and hope to survive. For all the other trouble *Savoie* has caused, she helped in that, at least: making it abundantly clear the Republic needs allies. Some remain unconvinced the Grik pose an immediate threat, but know they must help destroy them if they don't want to face a suddenly more hostile world all alone."

He paused to watch the Gentaa laborers, mildly satisfied. "Despite our lengthy consultations, I did find a *few* moments to explore"—Bekiaa glanced at the bells on Courtney's hat and blinked sympathy at his keepers—"and I'm quite satisfied that the myth of the Gentaa is precisely that: a legend, a fable, a fabricated folktale, perpetuated most vehemently by the Gentaa themselves. They are, in fact, an entirely separate species. Perhaps they arrived much like we, from another earth in the distant past. They maintain their position here, quite lucratively—particularly now, when you consider the sums being devoted to logistical preparations—by playing on the societal guilt of both their parent species!" He chuckled. "I can't help but admire their enterprise, if not their cultural veracity. Some are quite wealthy, you know, in quiet, inconspicuous ways, and all are cared for in their retirement. This, while the poorest humans and Lemurians are reduced to begging in the streets."

"That's no real secret," Optio Meek said lowly, glancing around, "but it's simpler ta 'believe' the myth, as ye call it, than confront the buggers. If we tried ta break their monopoly, it'ud shut the country down."

Courtney pursed his lips. "Well, I suppose you're right, as things now stand. But I'm personally gratified to have *one* of my theories about this world borne out."

"That's all very interesting, Mister Braad-furd," Bekiaa said, her tone growing impatient, "but what did you an' the Kaiser talk about? When do we shove off?"

Courtney nodded at a Lemurian officer returning from the station office and lowered his voice. "*That* gentleman bears dispatches commanding General Marcus Kim to begin his advance as soon as we arrive." Bekiaa shot a meaningful glance at Meek. They were *out* of time. Hopefully, Kim was smart enough to save the new arrivals as a reserve, or replacements, they could instruct on the march. "Inquisitor Choon rolled up quite the network of human spies, you know," Courtney continued. "From the wretched League. But he can't have gotten them all, and the telegraph is particularly suspect. So, as not to alarm the League and possibly give them the opportunity to alert others, the go order is being carried by hand." He smiled rather wistfully. "Very soon, we'll all board that train together and proceed to Fort Taak. As quickly as possible after that, we'll open yet another front in this dreadful war and more people will begin to die. Please God it will herald the final campaign."

CHAPTER 11

Mahe Island
November 11, 1944

Purple clouds stood against a golden horizon as dawn swept across the crowded anchorage on the east side of Mahe Island. Ships of every description, large and small, had collected there, some tied to brand-new docks, with others "docked" to them. More were moored away from shore, and a few were even secured to the several ship-size islets jutting from the waters of the cramped lagoon. Half of the eight PTs in Lieutenant Nat Hardee's MTB-Ron-1 were motoring about, transferring people and supplies, while the other half served as mobile channel markers. With the new boats that came aboard the SPD, there were eleven in theater, but Nat left three to patrol off Grik City. And as crowded as the little harbor already was, with *Salissa*'s, *Tarakaan Island*'s, and *Sular*'s massive shapes, USNRS *Arracca* and USS *Santa Catalina* still lingered there. The latter two, along with their flock of escorts, now constituted TF Bottle Cap and were preparing to steam south and take station off the mouth of the Zambezi. *Santy Cat* and the battlegroup would protect *Arracca* while she added her planes to the air attacks on Sofesshk and the heavy Grik ships nearby.

Before they left, however, they'd have to find a bit more room. The brand-new fleet carrier USS *Madras*, exactly like her sunken sister, *Baalkpan Bay*, except for the dazzle paint scheme she'd been given—like *Sular*, *Arracca*, and even *Big Sal* now wore—was creeping into the anchorage. She'd refuel from the large storage tanks that had been hastily built and concealed from the air. She and *her* battlegroup, as well as *Sular*, would await orders to embark I and III Corps, head down to pick up II Corps, then launch the invasion of Grik Africa.

When all that would occur depended largely on reports from Jumbo's Pat-Squad 22, Bekiaa-Sa-At, and now Courtney Bradford, with the Armies of the Republic of Real People. The latest word was, the Repubs had begun their offensive but something was screwy with it. Basically, so far, they hadn't found any Grik. So the newest tweak to the strategy was that the First Fleet Expeditionary Force had to cool its heels and hold its assault until the Repubs were thoroughly "noticed" by the Grik. The enemy was already massed at Sofesshk, so the Repubs *had* to be the first diversion. Nobody was happy about that, but it made the most sense. The only consolation was that it couldn't take the Grik too long to discover they'd been invaded. . . . Could it?

Behind *Madras* was a string of new fast transports, again, basically Scott class steam frigates built lighter and beamier to accommodate I'Joorka's 1st North Borno. Part of Rolak's I Corps, Major Simon "Simy" Gutfeld's 3rd Marines had embarked aboard *Santy Cat* and *Arracca* and her auxiliaries in case Tassanna and Russ Chappelle wound up needing troops for any reason, including low-risk, irresistible opportunities to cause mischief for the enemy. The 1st North Borno would occupy the camps the 3rd Marines left behind.

At the moment, however, nearly every human and Lemurian in sight of the anchorage was focused on USS *Tarakaan Island* as she slowly flooded down, almost two weeks to the day since she'd taken *Walker* aboard. Water flooded into the repair basin, swirling, scouring, retreating in waves topped with floating wood debris, pumicelike torch slag, and oily, multihued tendrils. More water poured in as the SPD settled lower. Then, starting on *Tarakaan Island* and spreading to ships nearby, a great cheer mounted and echoed in the anchorage. Observers farther away couldn't see anything but knew what it meant and joined the tumult. USS *Walker* was afloat.

A cable had already been secured to *Walker*'s baby sister, USS *James Ellis*, the tops of her funnels hazed with smoke. Slowly, the new DD took up the slack. The cheers redoubled and steam whistles sounded when *Walker*'s freshly painted fantail probed the harbor. Her aft deckhouse, dominated by the dual-purpose 4″-50, was crowded with 'Cats, mostly "yard dogs" (and the irony of that term, once explained, remained a source of hilarity throughout the fleet) who were waving and cheering back. Spanky was there, trying to look severe as 'Cats capered around the auxiliary conn, but even he leaked a grin now and then. Soon *Ellie* had eased *Walker* entirely out of the repair bay and, so close to each other for the very first time, they looked virtually identical from a distance—even down to the bold, white 163 painted on both their bows. This because the campaign against Zanzibar might require *Ellie* to impersonate *Walker*, as *Mahan* had once done. Maybe not, but they wanted to be ready. Presently, however, the two ships, stern to stern, resembled a mirror image.

Walker slipped the tow cable and it slithered wetly up between *Ellie*'s depth-charge racks, where 'Cat sailors coiled it down as it ran off the steam winch. Slowly at first, but gathering speed, *Ellie* moved away with another resounding blast from her horn. Smoke was already streaming downwind from *Walker*'s funnels as well, her hot heart beating again. Water foamed around her propeller guards and she twisted nimbly away from *Tarakaan Island*. Smoke chuffed insistently and she swung around toward a place at the pier that Jarrik-Fas's USS *Tassat* had just cleared. Once there, she'd begin taking on more fuel, provisions, and ammunition from stockpiles unloaded from the SPD as soon as she'd arrived. Later that day she'd steam out of the harbor, theoretically ready to fight, but the purpose would be to make some high-speed runs and put her through her paces to see what they might've missed. No one had any illusions that she was as good as new; there simply hadn't been time for a complete refit, and a close inspection would reveal that her plates, newly riveted in many places, were still dented and washboarded beneath the thick, fresh paint. Few of her once-sharp angles remained quite as crisp as they'd been, and despite all their efforts, she still leaked a little. Small streams of water were already starting to spurt from her sides as bilge pumps sucked it from below. But a great deal had been accomplished in the little time they had. She'd *never* be as good as new, but hopefully, the repairs had made her good enough to face what lay ahead. Almost immediately, as soon as *Walker* was clear, *Tassat* began creeping toward the open stern of the SPD, anxious to begin her own repairs.

Captain Reddy had the conn and was personally steering his ship to the pier, his hands feeling the living machinery through the familiar burnished brass of the wheel. As always, he was amazed by the people's enthusiasm for his old destroyer. *Well, she's damn sure earned it,* he thought, *surviving when no one thought it possible, time and again, and performing what must seem like martial miracles to many watching.* He deeply appreciated their gratitude and approval, but knew better than anyone how truly miraculous some of those victories had been. *And they'll expect more,* he thought, *from Walker . . . and me. It isn't fair, but it's true. All I can do is pray that, critical as this old ship's been to the survival of the Alliance and the new nation it spawned, she—and I—are no longer indispensable. Neither of us'll last forever, and I don't want all we've done—and lost—to be for nothing.*

And it won't be, he consoled himself. *I have a lot of responsibility, but I'm not* necessary *to the degree Alan Letts, Adar, Saan-Kakja, Rebecca McDonald, even Keje and Courtney Bradford have become. Not anymore. I'm not even essential to the continuation of the American Navy Clan. There might be some rough patches if I buy it, but it'll go on. The traditions we've established with so much blood'll see to that.* He did wonder how his ship, or whatever battle killed him, might fare if he was lost, but the thought of Spanky gave him peace of mind. *Spanky's a diminutive, gnarled red oak who naturally inspires confidence and obedience, loyalty and respect. He might have little interest in the big picture beyond the ship, but he can fight her as well as I ever have, and knows every rivet in her. If something happens to me,* Matt thought, Walker *and her people will be in good hands.*

It never occurred to him, of course, that all of that—while possibly even true—would never have been the case if his example hadn't formed the Alliance, the Union, his Clan—even Spanky and the rest—in the first place.

"How does she feel, Skipper?" asked Bernie Sandison, *Walker*'s torpedo officer, tipping his hat up on his dark hair. Even this early, sweat was trickling down his temples.

Matt forced the grim thoughts from his mind and managed a cheerful tone. "Pretty good, as a matter of fact. A lot of the shaft vibration's gone, and the rudder responds like it should again. We'll know better when she stretches her legs. Minnie?" he called behind him to the tiny Lemurian bridge talker. Min-Sakir didn't really look like Minnie Mouse, except for size, maybe, but her voice was just as small, and that was what earned her nickname long ago. She was a good talker who kept her cool, and her little voice inspired a measure of amusement that seemed to help others do the same in times of stress. "Anything from Tabby yet?"

"She on her way up now."

"Dead slow ahead," Matt called to his first officer, Chief Quartermaster Patrick "Paddy" Rosen. Rosen was technically the OOD, but just as Matt had taken the wheel, Rosen stood by the lee helm, the engine order telegraph.

"Dead slow ahead, aye," Rosen replied, moving the levers on both sides of the EOT to the desired position amid a clash of bells. Almost instantly, the bells rang again and the pointers matched. "Tabby's girls are on the ball." Rosen grinned. Most of *Walker*'s snipes were female now, Lemurians and former Imperials. Spanky's early objections to any female aboard, let alone in "his" engineering spaces, had long ago given way to grudging acceptance. And engineering was Tabby's and Isak's concern now. Tabby had seen the trouble many females of both species had in the deck divisions, where stature and physical strength were often more important, and had been the driving force behind the change. "Broads're plenty strong an' can take the heat," she'd explained. As far as anyone could tell, Isak Reuben—not much bigger than Tabby, and one of the few males still in her division—didn't care one way or another.

Chief Jeek's bosun's call squealed on the fo'c'sle, echoed by whistles aft, and 'Cats gathered with lines in their hands. "Dead slow astern," Matt said, turning the wheel as the ship nosed toward the dock where line handlers waited. Slowly, the old destroyer quivered to a near stop, barely inching forward as her screws reversed. "All stop," he finally said, and moments later, the sailors on the fo'c'sle tossed their lines. "Secure the engines," Matt instructed, "but we'll keep the steam pressure up to break the boilers in, and I want to go for a run in two hours." He stepped away from the wheel and smiled, noting that Tabby had joined them. "Mr. Rosen, you have the deck again."

"Aye, aye, sir. I have the deck."

"So," Matt asked Tabby, "what do you think?"

The gray-furred 'Cat shrugged noncommittally. "Is okay, I guess. Ever-thing *seems* good, but anybody can putter aroun' a pond like we just done. We'll see better later."

"You're right, and we will. In the meantime, I'm going ashore. I'joorka's First North Borno is coming in. General Alden, Chack, Silva, and Lawrence are waiting to meet them, but I'd kind of like to see 'em for myself." He shook his head. "A regiment half made up of people who look like Grik—on *our* side. It's bound to be interesting, and I want to see what I'joorka's like. Pass the word. . . . Oh, there you are, Mr. McFarlane," he said, seeing Spanky climb the metal stairs aft. "You can come along."

Pam Cross, *Walker*'s surgeon, joined Matt and Spanky as they tromped down the gangway as soon as it slid out the entry port on the quarterdeck. Matt started to ask what the pretty, dark-haired girl from Brooklyn needed ashore, but bit his lip. When duty allowed, Pam could come and go as she pleased, and it was well-known that she was helplessly, probably stupidly, in love with Dennis Silva. Knowing exactly where he'd be, for once, she was going along. *Silva's only been aboard one time since we came to Mahe on* Santa Catalina, Matt reflected, *and then only to help tie the ship's guns back into the director after they were relined and reinstalled. Granted, he's been busy scheming with Chack and helping get his Raiders ready, but except for a brief reunion at Grik City, he's been away from Pam a very long time. She's probably annoyed that now they're so close to each other again, he seems to be avoiding her.* He considered. *Then again, I'm not sure Silva's just avoiding Pam. He's just as devoted to* Walker *as anyone. Probably more than most. She's the only home he's ever had. But he's been aboard only once since Chief Gray was killed.*

In a way, he understood. He could certainly sympathize with Silva's loss; he felt it every day himself. And now it had been magnified a hundredfold by his fear and uncertainty regarding Sandra's fate. But he couldn't let it overwhelm him or even look like it might. Each day was a struggle to stay calm, focused, even positive, for the sake of the hands. Pretending to be cheerful would be impossible, and he'd never pull it off. His crew knew him too well. But he must never let his inner turmoil influence him or those around him again. *That's probably how Silva feels,* he realized. *Gray was more a father to him than anyone, and Silva knows he . . . left things for him: his hat, pistol, his chief's coin. It isn't much, but Silva can't afford to break down any more than I can, and if he spends too much time aboard, those things—and the memories—will draw him to them.*

Matt, Spanky, and Pam continued along the bright, fresh-cut dock, gathering generals Alden and Rolak as they walked. "So," Pete Alden asked, "what do you think of your repairs?"

Matt pursed his lips. "I'm as happy as I can be, I guess, given where we are, the time we had, and what we had to start with," he qualified. "The guys on *Tara* did a helluva job. They stopped most of her leaks, replacing about two thousand rivets—"

"Damn rivets," Spanky grumbled. "Nothin' but trouble with 'em from the start. Sorry, Skipper," he apologized, realizing he'd spoken aloud, interrupting.

"No, you're right. There's always been something different about the iron that accelerates corrosion. Particularly when they're used to refasten the ship's original plates." Matt smiled grimly. "And all the beatings haven't helped."

"She'll be in better shape to dish it *out* now," Spanky

said, trying to be optimistic. "Her guns're like new, for one thing. The liners are softer than the ones she came with and won't last as long, but, God willing, they won't have to. Right now, the rifling's fresh and crisp. Won't be near as many fliers," he assured. "And I'm glad to have the new quadruple-torpedo mounts. They're a tight fit alongside the aft 'stack, but we're only two fish shy, per side, of the six we used to have. And Bernie says the new fish're better too. Swears the Mark Sixes are a big improvement over the Fours. They've got their own little turbines and can run thirty knots. Longer range too, though Bernie thinks six thousand yards is more realistic than the ten thousand Baalkpan Nav-Ord claims."

"Still better than the *maybe* two thousand we could count on from the Mark Fours," Matt said, thinking more about how the improved torpedoes might stack up against the League's than against anything the Grik—or Kurokawa—had. Kurokawa's new aerial torpedoes didn't explode at the end of their runs, and they'd found one floating near where *Baalkpan Bay* went down. They were *good* fish, if small, but their size and resultant fuel capacity probably limited their range to about a thousand yards. That didn't mean Kurokawa didn't have bigger, better fish—he'd certainly started with better torpedo technology. They'd probably find out soon enough. But the League *definitely* had big, heavy, shipborne torps. They'd seen the launchers on *Leopardo*. The question was, How good were they? The scuttlebutt before their old war was that the Japanese had practically copied the Italian torpedoes. That could be very bad indeed. He shook his head. He couldn't worry about that now.

"Yeah," Spanky agreed. "We don't have as many as I'd like, though. *Tara* brought some, enough to fill all the tubes of everything we've got that can use 'em, plus a few for the PB-5s, I hope. About a dozen spares. The rest went down on one of the ammo ships. We'll get more," he encouraged. "Mr.—*Chairman*—Letts'll make sure of that."

Matt nodded, certain Alan Letts would do all he could, but he couldn't perform miracles. It would take time to replace all the torpedoes—and everything else TF Alden lost. He nodded forward, indicating they'd reached the point where Chack, Risa, Lawrence, and Silva were waiting. Silva, with Petey drooping, asleep, over his shoulder like a fuzzy rag, looked uncomfortable at the sight of Pam, but as they often did, his lips were moving as he sang some—usually inappropriate—little song to himself. The fast transports were tying up, and their anxious, seasick, long-confined "cargoes" were lining their rails, practically bursting to get ashore.

"Look at all them weird-lookin' critters!" Silva said, pointing at the nearest ship, its gangway sliding across to the dock. "Look, Larry! Now you ain't the only lizard in the Army." He narrowed his brows. "Which you're in the Navy, though, so I guess . . ."

"Oh, shut up, you!" Pam snapped. "Not even a 'hello' or a 'howya been'? What a jerk!"

"Hiya, doll," Dennis said evenly, looking directly at her for the first time. "What call've you got to get all rared up at me?"

"Stow it," Matt said. "You can tear each other's heads off later. Right now we've got company." He nodded at a large Grik-like form, obviously Major I'joorka, striding down the ramp. The newly promoted Captain Abel Cook, looking much older than his seventeen years, and a short, wiry, dark-haired, dark-skinned man with file-sharpened teeth followed behind him. Cook was familiar to them all, despite his changes, but Matt had never met the Khonashi war captain turned major in the Union Army before. He was bigger than Lawrence, but, like the rest of his party, dressed in the same tie-dyed smock and camo-painted leather armor that was standard issue for all Allied ground forces. The armor wasn't universally worn by foot soldiers anymore because it interfered with properly shouldering a rifle. Some infantry kept it, with the right shoulder segments removed, because the tough rhino-pig hide came in very handy when things got close. Most officers, cavalry, and artillery still used it.

The feathery fur on I'joorka's face, arms, and legs was dark rust streaked almost black, more similar to the color of Keje-Fris-Ar's pelt than Lawrence's orange-and-brown tiger stripes. And his head was bigger, the teeth in his jaws more intimidating. At the bottom of the gangway, he straightened to his full height, his feathery tail brushing the dock, and saluted with his companions.

"'Ajor I'joorka, 'Urst North 'Orno, regorting to duty, sir!"

Everyone returned the salute, and I'joorka smiled in that rather frightening way his people had, revealing far too many teeth perfectly designed for tearing flesh. "You know Ca'tain Cook," he continued, "and the other is Lieutenant N'shoosh. Ca'tain Rassey is join us soon. He's in another transtort." He gestured toward one of the other ships tying up. I'joorka's English was interesting. Where Lawrence often omitted sounds he couldn't make, I'joorka made free use of substitutes.

"Glad to have you, Major," Matt greeted him sincerely. "I believe you know Lieutenant Cross, Chief Silva, and Lawrence?"

"Yes. I know they all good," he agreed, nodding with apparent pleasure at the three. "Us kill lotsa Jaaphs together."

Matt motioned to Pete, then Chack and Risa. "This is General Alden, commander of all Allied armies and Marines, but your immediate superior for the coming operation is Colonel Chack-Sab-At. His sister, Major Risa, and the Imperial Major Jindal, command two regiments of his First Raider Brigade. The First North Borno will join that brigade as its third regiment."

"Us are honored." I'joorka bowed his head. "Chack's 'Rigade has earned great reskect." He regarded Silva, Pam, and Lawrence. "Are you in Chack's 'Rigade too?"

Silva snorted, then grinned. "Not *us*, ol' buddy, but me an' Larry, at least, will be around. Hiya, Mr. Cook! Good to see you . . . sir." He focused back on I'joorka. "Don't worry, though. I bet we'll get to play together again before it's over."

"Major Risa will show you around," Chack said, "and help get your troops settled. We'll begin sorting things out immediately, and tomorrow you'll start training with the rest of the brigade. You have much to caatch up on, and little time."

I'joorka nodded, but Cook spoke up. "Excuse me, sir, but we brought some new equipment along, and you might want to examine it directly. It's, ah, possible that *your* troops may have a bit of catching up to do as well."

Chack looked at Cook and grinned, blinking anticipation. "Truly? Very well, I'm aan-xious to see what you brought." He looked at Dennis. "Chief Silva, will you and Lawrence join us at the training ground?"

"Sure thing, in a bit."

"I think I'll stay with Chack a little while and see what Mr. Cook's talking about, Skipper," Spanky said.

"Very well. Carry on," Matt replied. More salutes were exchanged and Matt, Pete, Pam, Silva, and Lawrence left Spanky and Chack talking with I'joorka, while Risa formed dockworkers into details to help coordinate the disembarkation of the Khonashi troops. Strolling back the way they'd come, Silva had started humming the same tune as before, very low. It was an annoying habit, but sometimes endurable because it usually meant the big man was thinking. Whether his thoughts were pertinent—or appropriate—wasn't always clear. Matt spoke. "One last thing, Silva, before you run back and play commando with Chack."

"Sir?"

Matt looked at Pete, then back at Dennis. "A Nancy off one of our AVDs steaming close along the African coast spotted another Grik zeppelin flying just inshore, following the coastline. That's three in the past week. The first two were heading north-northeast toward Zanzibar," he added significantly. "This time, the Nancy shot the damn thing down, but it was apparently on a *return* leg." He shrugged. "The pilot probably should've followed it. Might've found where that base, at least, is located. But it may work out better this way. We already knew Kurokawa and the Grik must've made up, but this means even if Kurokawa still hasn't given his allies radio, they're in direct, relatively prompt communication, most likely trying to coordinate their strategies."

"That's not good," Silva said thoughtfully.

"No," Matt agreed. "I don't like any cooperation between our enemies. But . . ." He studied Silva's expression. "It's already given you the same idea it gave me, hasn't it?"

"If you mean that Griks are stupider than we ever

thought to trust that crazy Jap again, then yeah," Silva said, then paused, letting his captain roll his eyes before that disconcerting, gap-toothed grin spread across his face. "Course, I'm *also* thinkin' that if lizards're *already* flyin' zeps back an' forth to Zanzibar, the Jap-Griks there might not take much notice if we used *my* zep in some interestin', apparently un-threatenin' way. . . ."

"That's more like it," Pete ground out.

"Now, wait just a minute," Pam suddenly flared. "You're not talkin' about that heap of junk you *crashed* at Grik City, are you? Is *that* your zeppelin?"

"Sure. We fixed it up good as new," Dennis defended. "Mostly. It'll fly." He looked at Matt. "I figger maybe a dozen, includin' the aircrew. An', ideally, a few fresh-dead Grik if we can rake 'em up. That'd put icin' on the cake."

Pete nodded. "We should be able to arrange that, complete with current Grik gear. We'll get word to Colonel Miles an' his irregulars, dogging the Grik force south of Grik City." He grinned. "Might have to hurry, though. Word is they're bogged down in a swamp on the edge of that big band of jungle, and the bugs an' critters are getting them faster than Miles. If he can get us some bodies, alive or dead, maybe we can fly 'em up here in that trimotor Fiedler left. Leedom's already used it to take a load of weapons and ammo down. Says it's airworthy."

"Who would you need for aircrew?" Matt asked. Silva waved his hand. "A couple o' the same ones as before, if they'll volunteer." He shrugged. "Me an' them Shee-Ree're the only ones checked out in Grik zeps, anyway. As for the rest, I guess I can make do with Larry an' maybe eight or ten of I'joorka's guys." He looked thoughtful. "I wonder if he's got ol' Pokey with him."

"Okay," Matt agreed. "I'll have Mr. Palmer put it all together and send the request to General Maraan. We'll get it in motion." He saw Pam practically boiling, but holding her tongue. "Come on, Pete," he said. "Let's leave Chief Silva and *Walker*'s esteemed surgeon to . . . talk things through."

Dennis sighed heavily when Matt and Pete were gone. "Go give Risa a hand, will ya, Larry?" he asked his friend, then finally turned to Pam. "Okay, doll. Let's have it out."

Instead of launching into the expected tirade, Pam suddenly burst into tears.

Silva's eye went wide with alarm. "No! No, damn it! You can't do *that*! What the hell's the matter with you?"

"You are," Pam confessed miserably.

Dennis was at a loss. "Well, sure. I know that. An' I *warned* you too. I'm no good."

Pam shook her head violently, tears pattering on the dock. "Oh, don't start that again. We both know different. But I thought we understood each other. I wouldn't push you—an' I haven't—but *you'd* stop pushing me away."

"There ain't no understandin' *you*, doll, an' I been a mite busy."

"Not too busy for *Risa*," she said caustically, and Silva's expression hardened. There'd always been rumors about Silva and Chack's sister, which neither had done much to squash. They'd been soul mates when it came to their unconventional personalities, and out of sheer amusement had never confirmed or denied that their great, obvious friendship might've involved "experimentation" from time to time. Not even to Pam. But Pam was like a sister to Risa and had even participated in the joke to the extent of fueling further prurient speculation. But Risa finally tired of the game as the war made her more serious, and, besides, everyone—except maybe Silva—knew that Silva belonged to Pam.

"Risa's my pal," Dennis stated simply, definitively. "I knew her before you an' me ever met, when you were off on *Mahan*. An' we been *workin'* together, gettin' ready for this next push. Don't lay that crap on me."

"And *I'm* not your pal? At least? I was worried sick about you while you were running all over Madagascar. Didn't know if you were alive or dead for weeks. Then you came back—an' that was great—until I shipped out for here." She shook her head. "Okay, that's the breaks. But then you show up on *Santy Cat* an' I think my guy is here—only he isn't, far as I'm concerned."

Dennis scratched the whiskers on his chin, thinking. "Look, doll," he finally said, his tone softer. "I am yer guy, always will be, though God knows why you want it that way. I even practically threw you at Colonel Mallory once, remember? He's here. You should'a looked him up."

"No."

"Okay," Dennis agreed, "but here's the deal, same as before. I am what I am, an' the war is what I *do*. More important, the Skipper needs me." He grimaced. "Maybe more than ever. That Jap havin' Lady Sandra an' the rest is tearin' his guts out, but does he let it show? Can he? Hell no. I don't know how he does it." He looked directly in Pam's eyes. "If they had *you*, I'd say the hell with everything an' do what I had to to get you back. No waitin', no plannin'—an' we'd prob'ly lose the damn war. He feels the same, wants the same, but he's *stronger* than me, see?" He laughed bitterly. "I'm so weak, I do my best to push you away—even outa my mind, so if somethin' happened to you, it wouldn't hurt me like he's hurtin' now; wouldn't run me crazy, just killin' an' killin' till they take me down. You know that's what he *wants*. Me an' him ain't all that different, down deep. But his top layer's thicker, stronger, *smarter* than mine, an' it's spread a lot wider too. When it comes down to it, he just . . . gives a damn about more than I do. He's carryin' whole countries on his shoulders, thousands o' troops an' sailors, maybe a couple hundred ships, all told." He snorted and thumped Petey on the head with his thumb. "All I have on mine is this dumb-ass little lizard, the double handful o' folks I've learned to care about, an' my two simple little missions in life: kill anybody who threatens them folks—an' not let the Skipper down."

Pam blinked. Then, as hard as she could, she punched him in the center of his left bicep with her sharp knuckles.

"Ow! Goddamn!" Silva snapped.

"Goddamn!" Petey shrieked, still groggy from the blow on his head that woke him.

"That's for bein' a jerk," Pam told him. Then, without warning, as soon as he lowered his right hand from briefly massaging the spot, she punched it again.

"Ow!"

"An' that's for bein' stupider than your pet lizard. I guess Chack an' Risa, Lawrence an' Tabby—way more than a double handful—are people you care about too, aren't they? You don't avoid *them*. Why do you have to treat me different?"

Silva wiggled his arm and flexed it a couple of times. "I told you. 'Cause you can hurt me more."

"That didn't hurt you. What you've been doin' hurts *me*."

Silva held up his hands. "Okay, okay. Sorry. Damn. Women. Buncha harpies. Get mushy with 'em an' try to tell 'em how you feel, an' they take to beatin' on you. Did you ever think maybe I been steerin' clear out o' self-defense?"

"No."

Dennis looked at her, furrowing the brow over his good eye. "Is that your new favorite word?" He scratched his chin again, considering. "Tell ya' what. I'll come a-callin' this very evenin', when I'm done out at the trainin' ground."

Pam's eyes went wide in mock bashfulness. "Why, Chief Silva! Are you askin' me out?"

"Well, sure. I guess. Not many fine restaurants hereabouts, an' I don't think there's any good pictures showin'. But there's usually music, chow, an' a little dancin' at the airfield, even if they're always dousin' the lights whenever somebody thinks they hear a plane."

Pam seemed to consider it. "Okay, you big dummy. One last chance. But don't do this to me anymore. Let's quit hurting each other, okay? An' if one of us gets it—probably you, with this next idiot stunt—that's just the way it goes. But we can't just quit livin', waiting for it to happen, see?"

"Sure."

Pam frowned. "One last thing. Lawrence is the sweetest lizard I ever knew, but you'd better tell him to find something else to do with himself tonight—and don't come get me with that *other* lizard wrapped around your neck!" She stepped closer and smiled, looking up at him. "Just you an' me, babe, an' I'll *prove* that 'no' ain't my favorite word."

Petey, now fully awake, cocked his head and peered seriously at her with his big eyes. Then he nipped Silva on the ear. "Eat," he said flatly. His morning feed was long past due.

CHAPTER 12

The Plain of Gaughala
Grik Africa
November 14, 1944

"Well?" demanded General Marcus Kim, of no one in particular, his oriental features set in a deeper frown than usual. "Where are they? I must say, it's rather embarrassing when you attack an enemy you have feared for centuries, and they do not even notice." Bekiaa said nothing; Kim already knew she believed most of the local Grik had been sent across to Madagascar or summoned to Sofesshk. Many of Kim's other advisors were afraid to credit that. Inquisitor Choon tended to agree with her, however, and was staring fixedly at the map on the field table, his large, pale blue eyes intent. Courtney Bradford stood beside him, absently fanning himself with the huge sombrero he'd reclaimed since they'd moved north into lower, warmer climes.

He'd seen his woolly sauropod at last—more than one—and his eyes now greedily absorbed a herd of massive, browsing beasts beyond the field fortifications. The standard trench-and-berm perimeter defense the Republic always erected was sprouting a permanent palisade, complete with gun emplacements, as Fort Melhausen became the primary forward supply depot more than a hundred and fifty miles into Grik Africa. The shriek of a train whistle drew Bekiaa's attention. Much to Courtney's surprise, the Republic offensive had actually begun months before when their cavalry ensured there were no Grik in the cold mountains north of Fort Taak, and heavily protected engineers had begun laying track through the passes even while Alex-aandra was menaced by *Savoie*. No one was much surprised by the lack of resistance at the time; both sides of the frontier were usually sparsely populated, particularly in winter. But it was spring now, and the real offensive had begun at last. The result, so far, was . . . anticlimactic.

The same engineers had followed the initially cautious progress of the army, laying temporary track as it went. Here, at Fort Melhausen, they'd continue improving the rail line, assemble fresh troops, munitions, victuals, and all the cornucopia of war, while the bulk of the army moved on. For now, Kim's corps-size 1st Army remained encamped in its orderly rows of yellowish tents, still conspicuously separated by cohorts and legions. A third of Kim's entire force, 1st Army consisted of nearly twenty-five thousand men and 'Cats, thousands of horses and suikaas, hundreds of freight wagons, and a hundred Derby guns. Two other corps, though they called them 2nd and 3rd Armies, had taken alternate routes of advance up dirt tracks they'd discovered through the low hills and gullies blemishing the lowland Plain of Gaughala that lapped against a belt of heavy timber their meager maps called the Teetgak Forest.

Bekiaa gazed around her. The senior officers of nine of Kim's twenty-six infantry legions, as well as the new artillery and cavalry commanders, were gathered under the huge command pavilion, their aides outside beneath the afternoon sun. The scene struck Bekiaa with a number of contrasts. The pavilion was a dark, muddy color, and the uniforms were the usual dull yellow-brown with dark-painted helmets and black leather accoutrements. All would've normally provided fair concealment in most terrain if many of the officers hadn't been wearing their polished cuirasses and helmets. The cavalry was the worst, adding short capes reflecting the colors of their legion's standard. General Taal-Gaak, the Lemurian cavalry legion commander (whom Bekiaa had to admit looked particularly dashing), had explained that horsemen were easy enough to see already; no sense trying to hide. And perhaps they'd intimidate the enemy. Bekiaa knew that was nonsense, but also a pointless argument compared to others she'd raised.

Besides Taal-Gaak and his cavalry men and 'Cats, the surrounding prairie presented the sharpest contrast of all. It was almost as flat as the table Choon leaned against, and except for the distant hills and blue line of the Teetgak Forest far to the north, a vast sea of riotous flowers of every imaginable color rippled in the breeze as far as the eye could see. And flitting among them in great, heaving swarms were broad-winged insects just as vibrant, and apparently benign, as the flowers they so manically attended. She knew the land was cut and gouged by ravines and draws, but none were visible from where she stood. It was beautiful, and unlike anything she'd expected to find in the land of the Grik. Herds of enormous animals, similar to others she knew but much, much larger, grazed on the colorful plain. Most paid little heed to the invasive host. There were some frightening creatures, to be sure—large predators like Borno super lizards—but even they avoided the army for the most part. Bekiaa suspected their instinctual memory had taught them to avoid swarms of hunting Grik, and that was an advantage. It should also have served as a warning to her comrades, but they were content with the fact and unconcerned by the implications. Most interesting and frustrating of all, however, regardless of the abundance of life on the Gaughala prairie, was that they'd encountered very few Grik.

"We have looked, Gener-aal," Taal-Gaak said almost plaintively. "We have looked *everywhere* and found no concentration of the enemy beyond Agut." He blinked. "Other villages have been located. Quite a few, in fact. Most are along the coast, discovered by Third Army, but Second Army, paralleling our march to the west, has found some as well." He paused, blinking consternation. "All were praac-tically empty," he added, "with the exception of some, ah"—he looked at Bekiaa—"Griklets, I believe they've been termed. Naasty little brutes." He continued looking at Bekiaa and Courtney. "There was considerable evidence of death, however. Much blood was splashed about, but few corpses were found."

"They'll have dragged the dead along as rations, I shouldn't wonder," Courtney stated grimly.

"Indeed," Taal agreed, blinking disgust. "The clear impression was that the Grik departed in a hurry and slew all who couldn't travel. That suggests, despite our diligence at Agut, they know we are coming."

General Kim grunted. It also implied that there couldn't have been a great many Grik left in the area in the first place. He looked at Bekiaa and Courtney as well. So far, their assessment, based on Courtney's observations in Madagascar and communiqués from the distant Cowflop at Grik City, had been borne out, and they'd pushed the combined Armies of the Republic, now numbering almost seventy-five thousand troops, all the way to Agut—the first real Grik city they'd expected to find before they met any opposition at all.

There *had* been Grik at Agut, perhaps as many as five thousand, living in a typical, sprawling adobe warren. And there'd been a garrison of sorts, numbering about a thousand. Taal's cavalry quickly enveloped the village in an impressively professional manner, and very few of its inhabitants could've escaped. But when General Bahadur's 9th Legion, leading Raakel's 18th, with two more legions in reserve, were tasked with taking the town, it hadn't been the walkover everyone expected. Bekiaa got to see two batteries of the Republic's vaunted artillery in action for the first time, and it was very impressive, but the Grik returned fire with a handful of guns of their own—with exploding case shot that no one had known they had. Worse, when the 9th and 18th, already thinned by the Grik artillery before it was finally silenced, rolled in to sweep away the depleted defenders, they'd been slammed by volleys of *musket fire*. The muskets were only smoothbores, but they'd taken an unexpectedly fearful toll before the Repubs, still remarkably unshaken, finally came to grips. That was when everything changed. For the first time, besides Silva's and Courtney's escapade in Madagascar, Allied troops came face-to-face with what could only be described as professional Grik *soldiers*. Most terrifying of all, they fought like defending soldiers—until Repub numbers tipped the scale. Then, to the horror of the uninitiated Republic troops, they reverted to fighting like Grik that wouldn't run away.

The 6th had the worst of it, and lost more troops in the melee of slashing teeth, claws, bayonets, and sickle-shaped swords than they already had to that point—until a reserve legion raced to reinforce them and the 9th wheeled and slammed the defenders from the flank and behind. All the holdouts were killed at last, except a couple hundred that rampaged through the city, destroying the noncombatants—who had apparently gathered to *offer* themselves for slaughter! Bekiaa and Courtney had seen that before. They tried to explain, to get more troops sent in to prevent the massacre, but Kim didn't understand at first. The exhausted and shaken men and 'Cats who'd made the assault saw what was happening but were too dazed and shaken by what they'd endured to intervene without orders. And, frankly, they couldn't care less what happened to the rest of the Grik in Agut as long as they didn't have to fight them anymore. When it was over, and the 9th and 20th finally occupied the city, the 18th had been decimated, and only a few Grik, all warriors, were left to kill.

No other survivors were discovered except the usual crazed Griklets their own kind couldn't catch. Warrior Grik began their training from birth. Those destined to be Uul laborers were penned and fed, growing utterly dependent on their masters. Some, destined to be upper-class Hij, essentially ran wild until "domesticated," again by offerings of food they didn't have to hunt or scrounge. That was when they were taught a trade. All Griklets were dangerous, and only Isak Reuben, *Walker*'s chief engineer, ever—briefly—tamed one. No one here, except possibly Courtney, had the inclination to duplicate Isak's feat, and Courtney didn't even suggest it. The Griklets at Agut were shot on sight.

The fierce action served as an eye-opening baptism for the Armies of the Republic, at least for some, and that was a good thing, Bekiaa supposed. But it involved only a fraction of Kim's forces. Other legions had heard about it but hadn't *seen*, so it still wasn't real for them. And, of course, they hadn't found another live Grik for a hundred miles. Bekiaa already saw signs that the trauma was fading, and other legions that hadn't been there even spoke contemptuously of those that had, implying their losses—heavier than the Grik, counting the wounded—must've been the result of incompetence or poor performance. Most distressing to Bekiaa, since there'd been no more fighting, disdain for the enemy was beginning to take root. She looked at General Kim. He *seemed* capable but had no experience at this, and Bekiaa didn't think he'd done enough to combine his armies into one focused force—or quell a growing conceit. Confidence was good, but arrogance could be disastrous.

"I wish Gener-aal Rolak was here," she whispered to Courtney.

He looked at her, seemingly following her train of thought precisely. "Why Rolak in particular?" he murmured back, his voice softened by the general hubbub surrounding the apparently concentrating Kim.

"Because he's like these people in some ways, but he *knows*. And he'd also know how to straighten them out. Gener-aal Maraan would piss everybody off and they'd dig in their heels." She grinned and shook her head. "And they'd resist Gener-aal Aal-den, because he'd make 'em all think he wanted to be the *Kaiser*, just by the way he takes charge of everything in sight."

"Quite possibly," Courtney agreed with a fond smile. "But none of them are here, nor will they be until they land with objectives of their own. I fear it's up to you and me for now."

Bekiaa nodded, and reluctantly raised her voice. "Gener-aal Taal," she said, and the talking dwindled to a murmur. "You say you've looked everywhere. How far forward? Did your scouts penetrate the forest to the north? It's what, about fifteen miles ahead?" She paused, raising a lip over a sharp canine, doing the mental math. She hated math. "I mean, twenty-something killo-meters," she added in exasperation.

"Twenty-five," Taal said, amused; then his tone turned serious. "No, I ordered them not to press too deeply into the Teetgak." He glanced at Kim. "Perhaps I should not have, and I confess it concerns me deeply. But cavalry is useless—and nearly helpless—in that maze. There *are* roads of a sort, but we did not explore them for any great distance. Large numbers of the enemy could remain undetected, and even a few could do disproportionate harm to my scouts. Ambush is to be expected, but to probe farther without support invites annihilation to no point. It might confirm the enemy is *there*, if no scouts return, but I already suspect that, and we'd learn nothing more, despite the sacrifice."

Courtney frowned. "I'm no military man," he said, "and don't mean to seem insensitive, General Taal, but isn't that a risk all scouts must face? With no better intelligence than we possess, we can only blunder forward into a meeting engagement the enemy might control. How do we seize the initiative? Even a costly ambush might tell us something."

Bekiaa looked at Courtney, blinking surprise. She happened to agree, but was startled to hear him make such a ruthless assessment. She reminded herself that he'd seen a lot since they last met, including some fairly intense combat with the very type of Grik they now faced. "The Aambaas-ador is right," she said. "Just as we have to aassume warning has preceded us, we must also expect the enemy will meet us in places, on ground, of his choosing." She looked around. "I know what many think: the Grik run from us, or all their troops from this region have been sent to Mada-gaas-gar." She nodded at Bradford. "The latter may even be true. And maybe the civilian Grik *do* flee. But we know countless Grik gaather near Sofesshk. Many likely came from here. And whether they know we're coming or not, we'll eventually caatch up with some, at least. And that'll probably happen when we least expect it." She paused and took a breath. "I have . . . some experience in these matters. The Grik aren't stupid. At least their leaders aren't. And Agut—and other events—show they've learned to fight as soldiers, not just a mob. You *must* remember that!"

"What do *you* advise?" asked Inquisitor Choon, genuinely curious.

Bekiaa blinked conviction. "We must hasten our advance,

force a baattle, *make* the enemy notice us. If they don't, we're useless as a diversion and can only help Gener-aal Aalden by joining him when he attaacks Sofesshk. At our current pace, that could take *months.*" She shrugged. "At the same time, we must be cautious, guard against over-confidence, and be prepared for the enemy to appear at any time, any place. This is their land, remember, and they know it better than us."

Choon gestured at the map. "Then where do you think they will be? Where will we meet them at last?"

Bekiaa hovered over the map. It was crude, compiled from the few overflights they'd managed to arrange and an atlas of sorts, painted on the wall of what was likely the southern regent's palace. It had been a dismal place, but the largest building in Agut by far. Features depicted on the regent's atlas, even a few place-names for a change, including rivers, the plain they occupied, and the hundred-mile-wide band of forest ahead had been added to Kim's map. It helped, but as usual in this war, they were campaigning in places they barely knew. "I'll bet, if they've had waarning—which we must presume," she stressed again, "the closest forces moving to join the horde at Sofesshk will round on us as we reach the forest. It's the perfect place to stage an attaack unobserved. Yet with their new army, dense cover will hinder their movement and combat power as much as ours." She stabbed the map with the long, sharp nail on her finger. "Here, at the *edge* of the Teetgak, is where they'll mass." She looked at Kim. "I know I just counseled haste, but the object is to *win* the battles we force. We should take time to combine our armies and approach as a united force. General Taal is right to fear the forest," she said, smiling at the attractive cav-'Cat. "But we *must* scout ahead." She glanced at Kim. "In the meantime, the other armies should meet us here." She tapped the spot on the map again.

Kim looked thoughtful. "It would leave our flanks exposed."

"Gener-aal," Bekiaa began, then paused, blinking apology. "Right now your armies have *six* flaanks the enemy can exploit. They invite defeat in detail." She blinked regret at Kim, realizing how sharp her criticism must feel, then smiled at Taal again. "Combine the armies and secure the flaanks with the bulk of our cavalry." She shook her head. "I've grown spoiled by air reconnai-saance. I wish we had some now."

Choon brightened, after an annoyed—possibly jealous—blink at General Taal. "I have good news in that regard, at least. Soon we will have it." He waved outside. "Even now, a strip of the colorful ground cover is being cleared and the first operational squadron of our *Fliegertruppe* is en route. The flying machines will arrive today or tomorrow, in fact. When they are assembled, we will have eyes in the sky at last."

"Today or tomorrow," Courtney grumped. "More delay. Do we wait for them?"

"No," Kim suddenly stated. He raised his voice. "And the legate's . . . somewhat scathing counsel is well taken. I won't send our cavalry into the forest, but the armies will converge here"—he pointed at the same spot on the map Bekiaa indicated—"just short of it, and await our flying eyes to see beyond us. If the enemy is not already there, our planes should sight them moving through the trees to meet us. A large force cannot remain entirely undetected, even in heavy timber, I should think. If the Grik are waiting, we will allow them to deploy and receive their attack in the open, where we should have the advantage. If Ambassador Bradford and Legate Bekiaa are correct, we will be conceding to the enemy's new strengths as well, but I see no alternative. On the other hand, if nothing awaits us, we shall make a forced march through the forest to the open land the map depicts beyond, and prepare to cross this"—he paused, staring closer—"this Ungee River." He glanced up. "*There*, my friends, is where *I* expect to meet our first, fiercest resistance. There is where the Grik will likely notice us at last—to Captain Reddy's satisfaction," he added ironically, then paused, his deep frown returning. "And we must expect resistance to grow fiercer still from there to Sofesshk. Hopefully, the Grik will have other concerns by then."

CHAPTER 13

Sovereign Nest of Jaaph Hunters
Zanzibar

The dusty little compound holding Sandra, Dania, Adar, Lange, Gunny Horn, and two Lemurian sailors was roughly thirty yards square, situated on a peninsula on the southwest coast of Zanzibar. Surprisingly true to his word, Kurokawa had confined them together with an illusion of open space, and a wonderful view of the world around them. There were numerous blue-green islands strung up and down the coast and a tall, rounded mountain in the distance to the north. To the east was the anchorage, about two miles wide, and stretching possibly ten miles diagonally down the shoreline. Another lump of an island stood near its center.

Their vantage point gave them a wealth of intelligence about the enemy; they saw factories, shipyards, even a number of thoughtfully placed shore batteries armed with heavy Grik guns. There had obviously been an early attempt at camouflage, but the scope of Kurokawa's presence on Zanzibar and the fleet he'd assembled had made that impractical. A lot probably remained hidden, but there were many things that simply couldn't be. They even had a good idea where three enemy airfields were (one was less than a mile to the north) from watching planes come and go. Ominously, Grik zeppelins flew in and out every few days as well.

Savoie's sinister shape was still secured to the dock on the north end of the anchorage, not far from where Sandra, Diania, and Adar had been dragged for the meeting that resulted in their new quarters. Unfortunately, their quarters within the compound consisted only of a small shack Gunny Horn and Becher Lange had been allowed to build, and it, surrounded by ragged blankets rigged out for shade, was their only protection from the merciless sun. So their wonderful view and slightly looser confinement didn't come without a cost.

Still, every day they busied themselves gathering information and concocting schemes to escape with it. So far, none seemed very promising. Sandra had been right that there was no barbed wire; Kurokawa probably had more important uses for his limited steel. The Allies had a different perspective. Barbed wire could've made the difference between survival and defeat for their forces on several occasions. Instead, the compound was surrounded by densely spaced, sharpened stakes woven together with vines as tough as any wire, in the absence of an ax or heavy blade to cut it. And beyond that was a genuine moat, connected by a swamp to the sea. Low tide left it shallow enough to wade across, but their Grik guards baited it with the offal of their grisly meals, keeping it stirring and swirling with the local version of flasher fish. It would be next to impossible to cross. A gate on a little land bridge was the only way in or out of the compound, and the Grik guarding it were unusually diligent and well armed with smoothbore percussion muskets, obviously copied from the ones the Allies used when they invaded Ceylon. Those had only recently appeared, as had the gray leather armor uniforms the sentries wore, and the prisoners guessed they'd been supplied by the Grik on the mainland. Kurokawa obviously had at least a few new automatic weapons, and his Japanese went armed with Arisakas they must've taken from *Amagi* when they abandoned her, but this was the first time the prisoners had seen Grik equipped with anything more modern than matchlocks. Beyond all that, however, even if they escaped the compound, they were on an island infested with enemies. How on earth could they ever get off and away?

Sandra stepped to a cistern near the gate that the Grik kept filled with hot, greenish water. Her clothes were filthy rags and her hair was a frazzled, grimy, knotted mess. Her skin had turned to old, dark leather, and her lips were cracked and covered with sores. With a glance at the Grik guards beyond the gate, she filled a battered cup with water and gulped it down. It tasted horrible, but hadn't harmed them so far. She scooped another cupful and carried it to the shack where Adar lay in the shade. He'd gotten a little better—Kurokawa wasn't exactly starving them—but his recovery was slower than Sandra would've liked. She knelt beside her friend and held the cup to his lips. The fur on his face around them had gone white.

"I can manage just fine," Adar objected, reaching for the cup. "I'm not a helpless youngling."

"Could've fooled me," Gunny Horn said, joining them. He was followed by Lange and the other two Lemurians. Both were Repub crew-'Cats off SMS *Amerika*. One was Ru-Fet, and the other was Eaan-Daat. Horn had long ago dubbed them Ruffy and Eddie, and if either resented the humanizing nicknames, they'd grown to accept it. The third Lemurian sailor had died anyway, giving sad credence to Sandra's excuse for moving them. Only Diania remained outside for the moment. It was their only way of allowing the ladies a little privacy at the slit trench serving as their latrine. The Grik could watch, of course, as could anyone else, but the prisoners didn't care about them. Only their friends were people with sensibilities worth protecting.

"I will soon be fit," Adar disagreed. "But you should not exert yourself," he scolded Sandra, nodding at her abdomen. Even as she'd thinned, her belly had finally begun to noticeably grow. "You are—what?—five months along now? If I'm not mistaken, that is more than halfway there. If you were Mi-Anakka, it would be nearly time to begin the birth rites." Lemurians were born after about seven months and their infants were almost as helpless as humans. Utterly hairless, they even looked much the same—with tails, of course. But the final two months were considered critical to the health of the mother, particularly from a nutritional standpoint, and she was often confined and even ritualistically fed. The final rites of welcoming the gift of life from the Maker were performed by a Sky Priest. Adar blinked regret. "With so little to eat, I fear for you and your youngling, and . . . if you allow me the honor, I'd much rather welcome your new life to a place of freedom."

"Nobody but you, Adar," Sandra assured, then forced a smile. "You're the only Sky Priest around." She shook her head. "And we'll be out of here before then. Besides," she added dryly, "I eat pretty good. There's nothing like 'goop soup' twice a day, with a few bones thrown in to chew on." Goop soup was what they called their daily, unchanging fare. For all they knew, it was the same thing the Grik ate—made of Grik. They preferred not to think about that. Diania stepped into the shack with an embarrassed glance at Gunny Horn. That was their cue to return outside. The sun was falling toward the horizon, and it was time to take their meager bedding down.

"He's not doing so hot," Horn whispered, following Sandra out. Lange was behind him. Both men had grown long black beards, but Lange's had a lot of gray. They'd become much thinner too, though Horn's muscles hadn't faded as much. Like Sandra, Diania, and the surviving 'Cat sailors, he tried to keep in shape. They all hoped eventually they'd get their chance to make a break. When it came, they had to be ready. The exceptions were Adar, of course, and Becher Lange. Lange was a strong, brave man, but the destruction of his ship and the *way* she'd died had almost destroyed him. He hated himself for not dying with her—and Kapitan von Melhausen, whom he'd loved like a father—but his hatred for their murderers was even more intense. Instead of pushing him, however, it was consuming him. Still, though his strength might be ebbing, his mind was sharp.

"Chairman Adar is fine," he said dismissively, crouching with a stick to draw in the sand. "Now, I have been thinking about the antiaircraft guns that fired at your swift scout plane that observed the bay." One of those guns was very close, just a few hundred yards away, but remained hidden from view by a dense band of jungle. "I believe they're large Grik muzzle-loaders, perhaps hundred-pounders, taken from the ironclads being rebuilt as aircraft carriers.

That would give them quite a few." He scratched in the dirt. "I imagine interesting, complicated carriages, perhaps a type of barbette, which would not only facilitate rapid pointing and training at a high angle, but also absorb their recoil. They might also allow for rapid reloading, if they can depress the muzzle between shots."

Horn studied the sketch in the fading light. "Might be possible. 'Complicated' is right, though. Recoil and elevation would be the trick, muzzle-loaders or not. I wonder how they do it. Some kind of twisted-rope torsion arrangement like Grik bomb throwers use? 'Hydropneumatic' means 'heavy machinery, with tight tolerances.'" He shrugged. "But they're building airplane engines, so they've got that. Still, I think you're right. They were shooting pretty fast, but not as fast as a breech-loader." The AAA was just one of many things they'd speculated on since the P-40-something was seen. They believed its pilot had done some serious damage to one of the airfields, because they'd watched the distant column of smoke for two entire days. But they'd also seen the *modern* aircraft Gravois must've arranged rise and give chase, so they feared the "something" might've been caught. Particularly when the planes, minus one, returned so quickly.

Most of all, they couldn't help wondering if the P-40 pilot might've seen them, dancing and waving, and somehow reported it. The plane passed fairly close at one point. But Kurokawa hadn't summoned Sandra, as she'd expected, to discuss what it meant, so they might never know. Kurokawa hadn't spoken to any of them, in fact, since the move, and the only notable visitor had been a dark-haired League major named Rizzo, who stayed very briefly and seemed interested only in their living conditions. That surprised them all, and they wondered if Kurokawa had forgotten them.

More likely, he was busy with *Savoie*. Without binoculars, all they could see on her was a lot of Grik activity—mostly trainees learning to operate her, apparently. But she hadn't moved, and even her great gun turrets remained still. If Kurokawa was training a crew, it didn't look like he'd gotten to gunnery yet. That was both encouraging and a little unnerving. Then again, everything about their situation was unnerving. They had no idea what was happening, how their friends were, how the war progressed, or what twisted purpose Kurokawa was saving them for. Most unsettling of all, perhaps, were the groups of Japanese men who came to stare at the women. Given how distracting the "dame famine" had been to Matt's destroyermen, the same issue here, prolonged far longer, must be growing difficult for Kurokawa to control. Sandra remembered Muriname's declaration of loyalty to his lord, but had also seen the naked lust in his eyes. He couldn't be the only one driven half-mad by the total lack of women for so long. Unless they'd all resigned themselves to becoming warrior monks, that issue alone might eventually overthrow Kurokawa when nothing else could. Not that *they'd* benefit. His "protection," for whatever reason, was probably the only thing keeping them alive. It was certainly the only thing keeping the women unmolested. Some of the men who came to watch were boisterous and mocking, shouting insults and throwing sticks and rocks over the moat, laughing among themselves. Others were silent and intense. Gunny Horn seemed most concerned about the latter, and everyone knew he'd die before such a group got their hands on Sandra or Diania.

Lange stood, grunting, his drawing in the dirt fading as the light quickly left them. As usual, so near the equator, night fell abruptly. He kicked the sand with his shoe. "Not that it matters," he said grimly. "Nothing we observe will do our side any good."

"It will," Sandra insisted, "when we get away." Lange snorted. "We *will* escape," she stated defiantly, unequivocally. "In the meantime, it gives us something to do."

Diania had joined them, and suddenly cocked her head to one side. "Tss!" she said sharply. "What's that sound?"

All talking abruptly ceased and they strained to hear. At first it was hard to discern over the hiss of the nearby surf, but soon even Horn, with the worst hearing of them all, held up his hand. "It's planes," he said definitively. "Lots of them—or fewer, with multiple engines. Still, more than one."

They all stared at the near-black sky. Even Adar had managed to rise and, with Ruffy's help, stepped outside the hut, looking up. "Ra-diaal engines," Adar said, silver eyes flashing in the growing starlight. The Japanese planes all used radials, and the League Ju-52 had boasted three. But these were different, with a distinctive sound. "That new Clipper that brought Hij Geerki down to Liberty City"—Adar still called Grik City that—"was one of the first of a new class; the first of many Cap-i-taan Reddy hoped to get. It had staacked ra-diaals that sounded like that, but there *is* more than one!"

They all looked at the anchorage, awash in the gleam of hundreds of lamps and even torches burning from one end to the other, as workers prepared to slave through the night on the many projects. "What a target!" Horn almost whispered. The drone grew louder.

"I see them!" Ruffy cried, pointing with his free hand. "Exhaust flares! Blue! Very high. They block the staars as they paass!"

The others stared again. They believed him but couldn't see what he did. That was probably a good thing. Grik fought in darkness but preferred not to. Their night vision was poor compared to that of Lemurians or even humans. So if Ruffy was the only one to see them, the Grik certainly couldn't, especially through the glare surrounding the anchorage. A bright flash lit the harbor, near where the ironclad BBs were becoming aircraft carriers. Another quickly followed, then a whole string of eruptions, totaling ten or twelve, boiled up in the air, followed by distant *whump, whump, whump* sounds. Balls of orange fire rolled into the sky and spread along the docks or the surface of the water. Moments later, more firebombs marched across Kurokawa's harbor facilities. Then a third cluster fell, much closer, near where the HQ compound stood. A couple even fell on *Savoie*, lighting up her afterdeck and possibly marking her for further attention. Flames soared in the distant forest, in the vicinity of the airfield the P-40 set alight, and another string of explosions seared the ground very close, just a few hundred yards to the north near that other airfield. They weren't loud explosions, just deep-throated, whooshing thumps of heavy Allied incendiaries, but the shouting excitement they aroused in the compound was very loud indeed.

"Why are you all so happy?" Becher Lange demanded. "They might hit *us*!"

"Yeah, they might," Horn agreed gleefully, "but that just puts us back in the fight, doesn't it?"

Lange shook his head. Despite his depression and frustrated rage, Horn's enthusiasm and disdain for his own skin was lost on him. A loud roar bellowed from the antiaircraft gun they'd been discussing. A streak of sputtering light arced into the sky, followed by a flash and a dull boom. A couple other guns went off in the distance, but then the marching explosions got louder as well, as other planes apparently dropped big, new, ship-killing bombs, heavier than they'd ever seen. There weren't as many of those as the others, but a fair percentage fell near *Savoie*, raising towering, luminescent waterspouts. It didn't look like any hit, but there were some very near misses. Maybe they did some damage.

"Look!" Diania cried, pointing at the bay. A huge fire was building in the distance, roaring and roiling skyward from the vicinity of the carrier-conversion projects. And just as they gazed at that, another string of waterspouts marched relentlessly toward the one operational carrier. The last bomb in the cluster of six—probably all the big planes could carry—hit the carrier on the forward flight deck, sending smoldering debris and shattered timbers far and wide.

"Yes!" Horn and Sandra chorused, and Horn, beside himself with excitement, snatched up Diania and spun her around. The bay reverberated with the thunder of dozens of big guns now, and *Savoie*, her fantail still aflame, spat dazzling tracers at the sky. The darkness overhead snapped and flashed with exploding shells, though no one could tell if they were coming close or even how the gunners could tell how high the bombers were. Still, one shot at least must've gotten lucky, because a bright red-orange flare unexpectedly scorched the sky. It carried on for some distance, curving slowly away to the west, then south, before suddenly growing much more intense—and shattering into a spray of flashing smears of fire that tumbled to the sea like burning confetti.

"Damn!" Horn muttered, setting Diania down. "They got one."

"But out of how many? At least ten, maybe a dozen," Sandra said, her tone more sober but still excited.

"I think maybe sixteen, seventeen," Ruffy said. "They go now." Sandra didn't know how he could tell. The ack-ack was still firing wildly, the night still flashing with lurid thunderclaps as the fused shells burst. But the bombs *had* stopped falling. They looked back at the bay.

Kurokawa's new carriers were engulfed in flames, the tinder-dry timbers left baking beneath the equatorial sun burning too fast and furiously for anything to quench. And the flames were eating the facilities around them as well. A great crane, its legs quickly withering, fell across the raging inferno amid an explosion of swirling red sparks. Quite a few other ships, cruisers mostly, had gotten underway. They'd dodged the bombs and some were moving toward the burning ships, probably to bring their hoses to bear. It was no use. Both the conversions were clearly doomed—and Kurokawa wouldn't like that at all. Perhaps worse, his sole surviving carrier had taken a hit as well. A mall flickering fire still marked her forward flight deck, but it was shrouded with steam as hoses beat it down and it looked like her crew had it under control. Still, it might be a while before she could operate aircraft. That was something.

The same was true for *Savoie*. None of the bombs had pierced the armor beneath her wooden deck, and all the planks could burn entirely away and it wouldn't hinder her combat power. Certainly not her main armament. In any event, she seemed to have her fire under control as well, and they were too far away to see if the near misses had any effect, whether her bilge pumps were discharging more water than usual. They all remained excited, however. A serious blow had been struck. Yet even as they celebrated, they couldn't help wonder what the cost would be to them. Within an hour, they got their first answer.

A group of about twenty Japanese appeared on the earthen bridge, talking loudly among themselves. Some were in uniform, while others wore the simple coveralls of overseers in the shipyards and elsewhere. A few looked hurt or scorched by fire, and several wore bandages. None seemed happy. The two Grik guards confronted them, their muskets at the ready, bayonets fixed. In addition to keeping the prisoners confined, they apparently had orders to prevent something like this. The crowd hesitated, but then there was a shot and a Grik fell back and splashed in the moat. Almost instantly, the flashies swarmed and the guard screeched in agony. The other Grik lowered his bayonet and charged forward, only to be hacked down by several men with swords. Together, bolder and committed, the men rushed forward and slammed the gate aside.

"Get back!" Gunny Horn snapped at Sandra and Diania, stepping in front of them, immediately joined by Ruffy, Eddy, and Becher Lange. Even Adar moved slowly into the line, defying the intruders, who suddenly paused again. Several had rifles and they pointed them at the prisoners. Ignoring Horn's command, the two women joined him, one on either side. None held any kind of weapon, but Sandra had one hand behind her, fumbling at her waistband beneath the ragged, untucked shirt. One of the men yelled something at them, then exchanged his rifle for a heavy wooden staff. He pointed it at the women and yelled something else, glaring at Horn. "*Please* step back, ladies," Horn ground out through clenched teeth. "I think he wants to make this man-to-man."

"*Animal* to *unarmed* man, you mean," Sandra hissed. She pointed at the staff. "Why don't you give him one of those? Are you afraid to face a half-starved, helpless prisoner? Are you that big a coward?"

Maybe the Japanese sailor understood a little English, or maybe the meaning of her tone was universal. Either way, he grunted and snapped something at a comrade. An instant later, another staff sailed through the air and landed in the sand at Horn's feet. The Japanese sailor confidently twirled his like a propeller and took a step forward. "Whatever happens . . ." Horn said to the others, stooping for the staff. He never got a chance to finish. The sailor raced forward and slammed his weapon down on Horn's shoulder. Obviously expecting it, Horn rolled with the blow and came up, the heavy staff in hand. He twirled it himself, experimentally, grinning at his adversary. "You know, I was always pretty good with one of these, you dumb-ass

Jap," he said. He spun it again, but then, in the blink of an eye, stopped the rotation and slammed the hardened end into the other man's belly. He quickly recovered to follow the blow with an overhand swing, but that was as far as he got before the other Japanese, now behind him, surged forward and grabbed his arms. The first man, still gasping, viciously rammed his own staff into Horn's belly, making him double over in pain. Then he started beating Horn as hard as he could about the head and shoulders. Sandra's hand found the grip of the Colt, and she knew everyone around her was tensing to surge forward.

Three shots popped in the darkness, the muzzle flashes blinding. For an instant, Sandra though she'd done it herself without realizing it, but her hand was still behind her. To her amazement, Hisashi Kurokawa himself strode through the knot of men, leading Maggiore Rizzo and a squad of musket-armed Grik. "How dare you!" he shrieked, his purple face and bulging eyes reflecting the light of the distant fires. "If I wanted them dead, I would have killed them myself. Release that man at once."

Hesitantly, almost rebelliously, his sailors dropped Gunny Horn to the ground. The last couple of blows had been telling and he only groaned. Kurokawa turned to the man with the staff and shot him in the chest. With a little cry that turned to a bubbling moan, he collapsed in the sand. Kurokawa leveled his Nambu pistol at the others. "Now throw this ungrateful *traitor* in the moat, before I feed you all to my guards. I may do it, anyway. *Such treachery!*" Without the slightest hesitation, the Japanese sailors snatched up the body and did as they were told. Maggiore Rizzo, the highest-ranking League representative left on Zanzibar, stepped to stand by Kurokawa. With the water seething and splashing around another body, the sailors waited, eyes lowered. Kurokawa holstered his pistol. "Let them through," he shouted at his Grik. "I will decide what to do with them later. Half of you will remain here tonight, to make sure nothing like this happens again. The rest will escort Maggiore Rizzo and me back to my quarters." The Japanese sailors bolted, and with a harsh command from their captain, NCO—whatever—ten Grik, uniformed just like their guards had been, arrayed themselves at the far end of the land bridge. Sandra stooped beside Horn and began examining him. She wished she had a light, but feeling his head, at least it wasn't bashed in.

"You may tend him in a moment," Kurokawa said. "Follow me." He turned to walk where they'd all stood watching the raid on the harbor. Rizzo followed him. "Help him," Sandra whispered to Diania, and stood, hitching up what was left of her trousers, feeling the weight of the Colt. She almost drew it out at last. Now would be a perfect time to kill Kurokawa, and Rizzo as well. She and her friends would surely die, but at least the snake before her would be dead at last. *Maybe in a minute,* she decided. *I'll see what he has to say. And I don't know enough about Rizzo to decide if killing him's a good idea or not.* When she joined the two men, their faces now easier to see, she thought Kurokawa looked unusually controlled. Rizzo, on the other hand, his fingers absently stroking the large, dark mustache on his face, seemed to be pleading with his eyes. *For what? Forgiveness?*

"So," Kurokawa said at last, "another debt you owe me. That is the second time I have saved one of your people, not to mention you, from perhaps worse than death." He smirked.

"Why did you kill that man?" she blurted. "One of your own?"

"To protect you, as I said." He shrugged. "And as an example. Events such as the one tonight, an unexpected attack where we felt most secure, tend to encourage . . . impulsive behavior. Now, perhaps, I won't have to kill the others."

"But even one . . . You can't have many of your old crew left, and with so many probably engaged in manufacturing, training, flying some of your planes, commanding ships . . ."

"I have more than enough that I can kill any who disobey me," Kurokawa said flatly.

Maggiore Rizzo glanced at him, incredulous, then looked pleadingly back at Sandra. "Signora Reddy," he said, "I fully understand if you do not wish to share certain particulars regarding your, ah, martial dispute with General of the Sea Kurokawa. And I believe you may have even told him all you knew at the time of your interview.

But the happy coincidence that brought us here in time to intervene in this unpleasant business occurred at *my* request," he continued urgently, waving at the bay. "I must appeal to you as a representative of a power *not* at war with your Alliance. Signora, please. After tonight, what do you believe your *marito*, Capitano Reddy, will do?"

She turned to Rizzo. "After what *Savoie* did, under League control, and then after giving her to him"—she nodded at Kurokawa—"how can you still imagine we aren't at war?"

"I imagine—and pray for—a great deal, Signora," Rizzo said quietly.

Sandra nodded, but looked at Kurokawa. "Very well. In that case, I remain morally certain that Matt will kill you all—and everyone on this island."

"Like this?" Kurokawa demanded scornfully. "From the air? Our aircraft will be ready next time."

"In the dark?"

Kurokawa made no reply to that. "But he has *begun* his attack," he countered. "You said he wouldn't bother with us—with me—until he is ready."

"Maybe he *is*. I haven't had any information since my companions and I were taken hostage. If I knew what's been going on, I might advise you better."

"Do you take me for a fool?" Kurokawa demanded.

No, Sandra thought. *A madman, yes. Not a fool.* "I told you he wouldn't let my presence here influence him, and tonight I was proven right," she said instead.

"How so?" Rizzo asked.

"Because we were as much at risk as anyone else on the ground. Bombs fell very close. If they were dropped a few seconds earlier or later, we might've been killed. That would . . . hurt my husband, but he'd accept it." She appeared to consider, and she was, but she was trying to think of something to say that would be obvious to them, yet appear as if she truly was revealing her inner thoughts. "With the means to do so now, he'll keep bombing you. Maybe only now and then; maybe every night. But even that won't mean he's coming for me. It just means he wants you dead. If he can do it like this, that's fine. But how many more nights like this can you take? It looks like you lost all your carriers, so if you want air cover, you're stuck to the vicinity of Zanzibar. That may be good enough for him in the short term." Then she remembered *Savoie*, just sitting there all this time, and spoke before she had a chance to think about it. "Wait! You're *afraid* he's coming soon! Before, you were going to use me as bait, to lure him into a one-sided duel with *Savoie*. You *wanted* him to come. But not now. Why?" She answered her own question. "You're not ready, are you? Tonight's raid did a lot of damage, but you've still got a fleet of cruisers, Grik BBs, and *Savoie*. . . . But you don't have *Savoie*, do you? You can't crew her! You've been so busy trying to pick your duel, you forgot to load your pistol!"

Kurokawa took a deep breath and regarded her stiffly. "I have *many* pistols, *Lady* Sandra, and *Savoie* will be ready." He took another calming breath before continuing briskly. "You will not be molested by my men again. If your husband kills you, as you say, I cannot prevent it. Otherwise, you'll be safe . . . for now." He nodded at the dark shapes gathered around Diania, kneeling next to Horn. "See to your man." He tugged at the tight, ornate tunic under his pistol belt, then wrinkled his nose. "I had no idea you were living in such squalor. I will have fresh clothes sent over immediately." He bowed his head. "As before, this conversation has been quite enlightening." He started to stride away, then stopped. "You are most observant, most astute, but *if* Captain Reddy still lives"—he reminded her of that uncertainty with evident satisfaction—"he can come whenever he likes. Tomorrow or a year from now. It makes little difference to me. When he does, he will still find you in my power, and we may well discover the strength of his resolve. Either way, I *will* destroy him. Good evening." With that, he turned a final time, and his round form disappeared into the night.

"A word of advice, Signora," Rizzo said as he passed. "I *beg* you. Do not antagonize him. He is most dangerous when he appears most reasonable." He touched his hat. "*Buona notte.*"

"What did Roly-poly-san and the Eye-Tye want?" Horn asked moments later when Sandra knelt beside him. Adar had finally lowered himself to the sand, exhausted, but the others had formed a protective circle around him and Diania.

"How are you feeling?" she asked instead, as Eddie handed her what was left of his T-shirt, soaked in water from the cistern.

"I've felt worse after a night on the town in Shanghai," Horn replied. "Damn Jap hit like a girl." His teeth shone bright in the dark. "No offense."

Sandra chuckled. She could see black blood streaming down the China Marine's face from a cut somewhere on his scalp, and his hair was matted with it. But he seemed able to move, so he was probably telling the truth. There was danger of a concussion, though, so they'd have to watch him.

"He was *very* brave," Diania said quietly, tenderly, dabbing at his head with part of her shirt she'd torn from around her slim midriff. There was clearly no doubt in her mind where the confrontation had been headed, and what it would've meant for all of them. In the end, probably none of them would've survived. But Horn had tried to protect them. Protect *her*.

"I was an idiot," Horn objected. "I should've just held back and watched you ladies kick their asses. But what did the bigwigs want?" he pressed.

Sandra sighed. "I don't really know. I don't think it was to gloat, for once." She thought about it while she squeezed water from Eddie's shirt over Horn's head and let Diania mop it away. She had a vial of polta paste in her precious bag, and a needle and thread. She'd stitch the wound when she could see it better. "I think Matt really hurt them," she said at last, "and maybe now *would* be a good time for him to come." She shook her head. "It was so weird. Rizzo seemed almost panicky, and Kurokawa protected us, and then said we'll get new clothes. It was like . . ." She snorted. "Like the condemned man on the gallows, bobbing his head and trying like crazy to dodge the rope, but still so arrogant, so slippery about it, you could hardly tell."

Maggiore Rizzo joined Kurokawa on the seat of the rickshaw, even as Kurokawa snapped at the two Grik holding the poles to proceed. The rickshaw jerked into motion and their guards fell in, trotting alongside. It was five miles back to Kurokawa's residence, and would take about forty minutes to get there at this pace. It was a good thing they'd been closer, at Riku's ammunition factory, when the enemy attack began. They'd been able to see a great deal from there, and telegraph reports from around the harbor and the surrounding facilities had given them a more complete picture. In spite of his rage and frustration, it had actually been Kurokawa who guessed what might happen at the prison compound. Rizzo did beg him to intervene, but decided he'd meant to from the start. Still, when they set off, Rizzo wasn't entirely sure Kurokawa didn't mean to do exactly what his men attempted: kill the prisoners in retaliation for the raid, and rip his greatest vengeance from the women. Not getting an answer, Rizzo had reasoned with him, then threatened to depart—with his planes—if anything was allowed to happen to them.

Though a dedicated fascist and firm supporter of the League, he was unhappy with what Gravois had set in motion. Surely an accommodation could've been reached with the Alliance instead of this madman. They were half a world apart, after all, and need not come into direct conflict for decades, if ever. Who knew what the future might bring? But the policy of encouraging the warring parties to tear each other apart had been set in motion long ago and had succeeded quite well. Peace between any of them was clearly impossible. Best to make the most of it. But he'd personally been horrified by what Captain Laborde and *Savoie* had done to *Amerika*, and then by the treatment of the survivors brought here. The League had treated its own prisoners, human and otherwise, abominably, as it systematically subjugated the Mediterranean. Laborde had participated in that, was a product of it. Suspicions regarding his support for the pre-Revolutionary regime in France had probably made him even more zealous than others to prove his commitment to the League. But Rizzo liked to hope that one day, when the hard work of establishing civilization on this world was done, they might rebuild a measure of humanity to populate it.

That was what made him increasingly desperate as the

rickshaw approached the prison compound. Kurokawa had said nothing as Rizzo threatened and cajoled, his demeanor merely shifting from manic fury to that unnerving, icy resolution. Rizzo still hadn't known what Kurokawa meant to do, even as they strode toward the confrontation in the compound, and if things had gone as Rizzo feared, he wasn't sure what *he* would've done either. That Kurokawa's behavior had surprised him was an understatement. He wondered if it signaled a return to sanity, or had merely been a fragile bubble of reason and humanity rising through the swamp of madness, only to pop at the surface. Hesitantly, he decided to test it.

"She was right, of course, as you know," he said. "Besides Laborde and Dupont, only a tiny handful of *Savoie*'s crew remained behind. They have taught your Grik to make steam, handle ammunition, even fire her guns. But to teach them to maintain her, to repair critical damage, will take much longer. Old as she is, she is infinitely more complex than any of your other vessels."

"Don't you think I know that?" Kurokawa spat. "That's why I add my own people to each division. *Amagi* was far more advanced than *Savoie*. They will make the difference."

"But will it be enough? I have seen. And the simple fact that your people are used to more—and less—sophisticated equipment makes *Savoie* difficult for even them to master. Then, as Signora Reddy guessed, you have very few men available not already occupied with critical tasks. Dumb Grik must operate equipment that takes *men* many months to learn."

"My 'dumb' Grik are smarter than you think now, and even the stupidest can learn anything by rote."

"But rote can quickly vanish in battle. How can they cope with the unexpected? With damage? With the loss of their precious few supervisors with the understanding they need?" He paused, knowing he was about to tread on dangerous ground. "And what will you do for fire control? Without it, *Savoie* is much like your ironclad battleships. Far more powerful and better protected, but little better able to strike a target."

Kurokawa seethed. "I should *kill* Laborde for allowing

his lieutenant, Morrisette, to savage her fire-control equipment!"

When Kurokawa's fleet returned from the battle north of Mahe, *Leopardo* and her oiler had already sailed and Gravois had departed. But he'd been entranced by Gravois's "gift" of *Savoie*. It was in that mood that he received Sandra for their first meeting, even before inspecting the great battleship. That Morrisette, apparently under Gravois's orders, had taken a party and utterly disabled the ship's primitive but still quite effective fire-control equipment, had come as a terrible surprise. Even the critical level/cross-level mechanism had not been left him. It was simply gone. Perhaps removed and taken aboard *Leopardo*, or even thrown over the side. It had probably been Gravois's final way of leveling the playing field one more time.

"Laborde and Dupont had no idea," Rizzo said. "Or opportunity. I had placed them under arrest. I didn't know Gravois would give them the choice to remain with you, to redeem themselves. Had they known what Morrisette would do, they might've chosen otherwise."

"If I thought *you* had anything to do with it . . ." Kurokawa muttered menacingly.

Rizzo, driven beyond fear, simply laughed. "Do you think *I* would have stayed, had I known? Not counting Laborde and Dupont, who have been abandoned, I remain the ranking League representative—and I only stayed because my countrymen, in my planes, are here. And one of those planes has already been lost. It's fortunate I moved them to a different airfield, or more would've been destroyed tonight. If your enemy continues to bomb us, can your aircraft defend the airfields? In the dark?"

"Not as well as yours," Kurokawa confessed. "Your planes must protect us!"

Rizzo laughed again. "I only have five left, and little more than the ordnance they brought with them! Your aviation fuel is terrible and bad for their engines. More ammunition for their guns will arrive with the submarine, but no parts, no more aircrew."

"Then place the submarine under my control!" Kurokawa demanded. "With it, I could seek out and destroy the rest of the enemy's carriers, at least!"

All expression vanished from Rizzo's face. "Honestly, General of the Sea, I would *never* do that, even if I had the authority to do so."

Kurokawa actually gasped with fury, his eyes bulging beyond the point that Rizzo thought they must pop out of his head. Practically flailing with his hands, Kurokawa groped for the pistol at his belt. Rizzo saw what he was doing, but only sat straighter in his seat, turning to look directly ahead. "If you kill me, you may as well murder my pilots. They will never fly for you. Some of your people might use my planes, but not well. Nor will you get the ammunition the submarine is bringing. And there will be no further aid of any kind from the League."

Breathing hard, Kurokawa slouched back, as if his fit had exhausted him. Finally, when he spoke, his voice had lost all inflection. "Then your planes—and pilots—had better make themselves useful, Maggiore Rizzo. The next time Allied bombers come, *I want them opposed*. Discuss how best to do that with General of the Sky Muriname." He pursed his lips. "And as you say, the *Lady* Sandra may be right about the rest as well. The damage we sustained tonight will trap us here for a time, and might prompt Captain Reddy to focus on the Grik at Sofesshk." He smirked. "General Esshk has been under heavy bombardment as well, and the airship couriers imply that he *must* soon launch his offensive against Madagascar. He desires that we join him, of course, and I've assured him we will. But my . . . sudden inability to do so can't be held against me. Esshk's offensive should *force* Captain Reddy's attention away from here, long enough for us to repair *Akagi*, at least," he smoldered, "and then we can, perhaps belatedly, join the attack and destroy whatever the Grik were unable to, whether they're successful or not." He smiled at the thought, but just as quickly his expression turned grim once more. "And if Captain Reddy comes sooner rather than later, we will destroy him with what we have. *Savoie*'s secondary batteries are more powerful than anything Reddy has, and my Grik can at least fire her main battery in local control. Not ideal, of course, and many shots will miss—but *one* hit on whatever he brings against me will be quite enough. We still have the advantage."

CHAPTER 14

On the Plain of Gaughala
Grik Africa
November 16, 1944

"What a foul, unnatural, bloody place!" Optio Meek observed, eyes squinting in the sharp light of the sun, rising over the mist-shrouded depths of the Teetgak forest. "I don't fancy a stroll through *there* a'tall."

"Careful, Optio," Bekiaa said, blinking mild amusement. Their banter over survivable habitats never stopped. "It looks a lot like many lovely places *my* people live." The Teetgak was extremely dense, practically a jungle, composed of tall, narrow trees resembling ships' masts, knotted together with concentrated, vinelike limbs. These were clotted with broad, ferny leaves from near the ground to the very top, almost a hundred feet high. And the abrupt distinction between forest and plain reminded Bekiaa of many islands within the Malay Barrier.

"Aye, p'raps," Meek conceded, "but that there's prob'ly full o' Grik. An' it's so bloody *straight*-like," Meek continued, "like they done it a'purpose."

Bekiaa briefly pondered that. He might be right, but her mind was mostly elsewhere. It had taken two whole days for First Army to advance the twenty-five kilometers to the edge of the forest. The snail's pace was less the result of renewed caution than the sheer amount of baggage the army brought, much to be dispersed among the other armies when they gathered. Third Army had been less than a day's march away and quickly moved within sight to the west. Second Army had to negotiate some treacherous ravines in order to rejoin, however, and not only did that cause serious delay, it clearly illustrated how impossible mutual support would've been in an emergency. Finally, all three armies had converged about where Kim intended, roughly a kilometer from the sharply, perhaps artificially, defined boundary of the ominous wood. Now, still distinctly separated by cohorts, legions, even armies, Kim's entire force presented a formidable—if possibly fragile—front, more than four kilometers long. And at least Taal's limited scouts had discovered that all the woodland roads and paths seemed to emerge somewhere before it.

Bekiaa had marched with the newly arrived 23rd Legion, trying—again—to pass her knowledge to the raw Republic troops. Most listened solemnly to the war wisdom she shared, but the colonel, Lok-Fon, a haughty, red-furred 'Cat from Augustus with near-black fur on her face that surrounded blue eyes, darker than Choon's, appeared disinterested in her lectures. She seemed more concerned that her personal baggage wagons, groaning under a truly stunning quantity of expensive wine from Colonia, nestled among other luxuries, not be excessively jostled. Bekiaa made several attempts to engage the colonel, but despite her unusual status, she'd been rebuffed. Most annoying, the snub was accompanied by the utmost courtesy. Bekiaa doubted its sincerity, but had no grounds to complain. Instead, she focused her attention on Lok-Fon's officers and noncoms, most of whom were anxious to learn how to stay alive.

"I'd wager it *is* artificial!" Courtney enthused, surveying the abnormally straight line of trees with his Imperial-made telescope. He'd quietly joined the 23rd shortly before dawn, as if drawn to Bekiaa by a sense of what lay ahead. Ever since the darkness faded, he'd been studying the swarms of lizardbirds swooping and surging above the distant treetops. Occasionally, they darted out en masse to scour away thousands of the butterflylike insects that hovered among the flowers. "It's likely a boundary between regencies! Perhaps the inhabitants of the plain are devoted to hunting the great beasts upon it, while those in the forest engage in other pursuits?"

That seemed possible to Bekiaa, but she couldn't summon much interest. She was far more anxious for the two brand-new Cantet biplanes to return from their flight over the forest. Choon had been right, and the first four aircraft of the *Fliegertruppe* had arrived at Fort Melhausen the day before. They were odd-looking things, she'd thought, when they roared swiftly overhead and vanished into the raucous clouds of lizardbirds and the haze rising from the damp ground beneath the trees. They were the first biplanes she'd seen, which made them appear awkward and complicated compared to Nancys or Fleashooters, but their coloration, a kind of jagged, checked pattern of earth tones, made sense if someone was looking for them from the air. And despite carrying two people, a pilot and an observer/gunner, with a machine gun on a swivel aft, they were fast. Their engines were liquid cooled, like Nancys, but apparently more powerful for their size. She was impressed. But they'd disappeared almost an hour before, and she couldn't wait to find out what they might've discovered.

A human Repub officer named Bele, the legion's senior cohort commander, or prefect, stamped up to join them and slapped his polished breastplate in salute. Bekiaa had noticed all the officers of the 23rd, and many other legions, wore their dress armor. It was light but strong, work-hardened bronze, and apparently didn't hinder their movement. She actually approved. In open-field combat where concealment didn't matter, any kind of protection might be useful. She even caught herself wishing for shields. More than once, her Marines had discovered they'd discarded theirs too soon. Inspired by Bele, she'd dressed in her best rhino-pig armor. She wondered briefly if it might single her—and all the officers—out as targets, but decided the risk was worth the possible morale boost to the untested troops.

If the Grik met them here.

So far, there was no sign of that, and despite the hit her credibility might take, she was relieved. Notwithstanding

Kim's attempts at compromise, she remained concerned about the basic organization of the Armies of the Republic. She returned the prefect's salute in her way, fingers to her helmet, and smiled. The man towered over her. He was also as black as Safir Maraan's fur, and must've been two and a half tails tall, yet the respect he showed seemed sincere. She'd seen enough brown humans that their difference from the nearly all-white but deeply tanned original crews of *Walker*, *Mahan*, and *S-19* hardly registered. But for the first time in the Republic of Real People, she'd seen people as black as a starless night and finally realized hu-maans came in nearly as many colors as her people did.

"Prefect Bele," she acknowledged.

"Each soldier has been issued another twenty rounds of ammunition and all canteens are full," Bele reported. "As you, ah, advised."

"And the artillery?" she asked, referring to the six-gun battery, a "century" in itself, that the legion retained as its own.

"At the rear, but ready to be deployed as needed."

"Very well." Bekiaa paused. "Have you reported to Colonel Lok-Fon?"

"No, Legate," Bele said, nodding at the command tent that had been erected to the rear as soon as the legion took its place in line, his expression inscrutable. "She remains . . . indisposed."

"I see." Bekiaa glanced to the front, at the dense trees beyond the bright plain. "No matter. I for one am glaad General Kim seems to have been right about where the enemy would first maass against us, and my concerns were unfounded."

"You know the Grik better than we, Legate," Bele said, then gestured at the army to either side. "We'll have to move through the forest close enough to support each other in any event. It would be impossible if we'd stayed spread out."

Courtney harrumphed. "I can't imagine pushing seventy-five thousand troops through *that* in any kind of order." He sighed. "But at least, perhaps, we'll be allowed to attempt it unimpeded."

Suddenly, as if to expressly deny their hopes, the deep

roar of one of the new mechanical Grik horns blared from the dense timber, its bass rumble seeming to shiver the very trees. Immediately it was answered by another, and another, until the great forest seemed alive with the strident moan. Lizardbirds swirled more insistently, their flocks convulsing outward in response to apparent movement below.

"Daamn," Bekiaa said absently. "Sometimes I hate being right."

"Aye," Optio Meek agreed, his young features grim.

Clusters of distant figures bolted from the trees, quickly forming into squads. Others followed, swelling the growing ranks with amazing speed. It appeared chaotic, but Bekiaa saw the Grik troops—for troops they were, dressed and armed exactly as Courtney had described: dark leather armor and crossbelts over light gray smocks, iron-plated leather helmets, and bright muskets with socket bayonets held high and tight above their narrow shoulders against their necks—knew exactly what they were doing. Squads gathered into companies, companies became battalions, then regiments, brigades . . . and still they streamed from the woods. An engine roar rose above the horns and the Cantets, widely separated now, abruptly appeared, flying back toward the Armies of the Republic. One flashed directly over the 23rd before following the other in a wide turn to land near Kim's pavilion about a quarter of a mile away. A strip had been cleared even as the pavilion was erected, the gap in color doubtless visible from the sky. "I wonder what they saw?" Courtney mused, his tone tense. The answer struck Bekiaa as self-evident.

"Thaat, I'll bet," she stated dryly, pointing at the army emerging to meet them. Long serpentine flags were appearing now, probably regimental colors. All were at least partially red, something common to every Grik flag they'd seen, but these all had distinctive patterns painted on them. They'd noticed unusual flags over Grik ships from time to time, but never over land forces. It was something else new to ponder. She looked from side to side, gauging the size of the growing Grik force. Kim's 1st Army was in the center of the Republic formation, and the 23rd was on the far left of its line. A twenty-yard gap separated it from 3rd Army's 10th Legion farther to the left, and others existed between *every* legion, no matter where they were. "Runner!" she called to one of the cavalry century's riders. The cav-'Cat approached and saluted. "I'm sure Generaal Kim'll send word about what the planes saw," she said quickly, "but go to him, as fast as you can. Tell him the legions *must* close the gaaps between them! And with the enemy armed with muskets, a more open formation would be ideal, but I doubt we can manage it now." She glanced at the enemy. The Grik had apparently already matched the length of the Republic line, and their ranks were thickening by the moment. She was stunned to see them forming up, shoulder to shoulder.

"Just as they did when Mr. Silva, Colonel Chack, and I—and the Shee-Ree, of course—engaged them at the river crossing in Madagascar," Courtney told her, reading her thoughts again. "Probably First General Esshk's latest account of our armies was when we struck at Ceylon." He nodded grimly forward. "You'll recall, armed with smoothbore muskets ourselves at the time, we were quite wedded to linear tactics. They've copied what they learned rather amazingly, don't you think?"

Bekiaa nodded. That was good—and bad. Good because now armed with rifles—and vast experience—Union and Imperial forces had adopted more effective tactics. Bad because, despite her warnings, the Republic battle line was also arrayed shoulder to shoulder, which would make even muskets more effective than they should've been, but the Grik would surely exploit those idiotic gaps if they got close enough. "We have to dig!" she suddenly blurted to the cav-'Cat, still waiting for her to finish. "General Kim must order everyone to dig for their lives! Throw up breastworks with whatever they caan! There's no time to lose! And tell him to close those *goddaamn gaaps*!" she stressed again.

"At once, Legate!" The cav-'Cat thundered off.

Bekiaa turned to Prefect Bele. "Bring up the guns. Place a section in the gaap on either side of us, for now. Thaat'll help. And bring up all the waagons too, on the double. We'll make a wall of 'em. Have the legion's maasheen guns sited around the waagons when they're in place." She was suddenly, desperately, wishing for portable mortars like her people had. The Republic had mortars, and howitzers too, but they were large, heavy monsters designed for fixed defenses, protecting their ports. The very biggest were still muzzle-loaders. They'd focused perhaps too heavily on their excellent, modern, breech-loading Derby guns.

Bele was already gone. Bekiaa turned to Meek. "Take charge of erecting the breastworks. You know what I want. If any puffed-up centurions object, tell 'em they can do as they're told—or you'll replace 'em with their optios in my name. Clear?"

Meek grinned. "Aye, clear as can be!" He started to turn.

"And, Optio," Bekiaa said, "get a rifle. You'll need it."

"But, Legate, aides don't carry rifles!" He slapped the pistol at his side.

"They do today. *You* will, at least, or I'll find another aide. I'll have to, because you'll be dead."

"Aye, Legate." He hurried off.

Within minutes, shredded flowers and dirt began spewing forward of the line in front of the 23rd as men and 'Cats, recognizing the wisdom of Bekiaa's order, started digging like maniacs. Wagons trundled forward and were tipped on their sides. Bekiaa noted that the legionnaires in the 10th, to her left, and 5th, to her right, were already following suit. Unhappy suikaas, interrupted from their morning feed, dragged the legion's six Derby guns up, and their crews unlimbered three on either side. Bekiaa prayed that just as they were apparently giving the enemy time to prepare, the Grik would allow them time as well. *How weird,* she thought, *to hope the Grik will fight fair!*

"What are you doing!" came a screech behind her. "Those are *my* wagons!" Bekiaa turned to see Colonel Lok-Fon rushing up behind her, buttoning her tunic, eyes flashing with fury. "Stop them this instant!" the colonel shouted at her.

"I won't. They're following my orders."

"Your *orders* . . ." Lok-Fon choked. "You!" She grabbed the arm of Prefect Bele as he rushed up. "Arrest these meddlesome foreigners at once. *Both* of them! They're destroying Republic property." She stared in horror as a decoratively painted wagon tilted on its side with a wet, grinding crash. The sharp-sweet smell of Colonia port overpowered the scent of flowers. "You . . . you . . . *savage*!" she seethed at Bekiaa.

Bele tried to whisper something urgently in his colonel's ear, but she shook him off. "I don't *care* if they've foolishly chosen to call her a legate! She's nothing but an uncouth barbarian, pampered far too long. Don't think I haven't heard how she"—she glared at Courtney—"and that bizarre man with her presume to talk down to their betters, even General Kim himself!" She suddenly paused, blinking. "Whatever is that dreadful racket?"

"The *real* savages, Colonel," Bele said stiffly, physically pushing her forward to see the growing Grik force. "And thank God ours is a *real* legate!"

Lok-Fon's fur bristled with a fear her sudden, spastic blinking confirmed. "I . . . I must g-go to Gener-aal Kim at once!" she stuttered. "To, ah, consult with him." She took a shaky step back and then turned, almost running toward where the cavalry's Gentaa horse holders were gathered.

"I doubt we'll have further interruptions from *her* today," Courtney quipped, taking the Krag from his shoulder and opening the loading gate to check the magazine.

"I expect you're right, sir," Bele said, blinking humiliation in the Lemurian way.

Almost inexplicably, the Grik *did* give the Armies of the Republic considerable time to throw up breastworks and counter their initial panic. Of course, they were new to this type of warfare as well, and considering the inevitable confusion associated with forming dispersed and jumbled ranks to their apparent satisfaction, and compared to their old tactics of simply rushing to the attack, they got their "shit in the sock" quicker than Bekiaa would've believed. Their newfound patience and discipline was disconcerting. Courtney had seen it before, of course, but his usually placid, even cheerful expression was grim.

"Probably expected us to just march right into the forest," Bekiaa said darkly. "They could've jumped on us pretty hard then. Now?" She considered. Orders had quickly come back from General Kim, putting her in official, temporary command of the 23rd Legion. Colonel Lok-Fon didn't return. Kim also instructed all his forces to do most of what Bekiaa suggested. The first good news was that the best estimates of the enemy force, reinforced by observers in the Cantets, suggested the Armies of the Republic actually outnumbered the enemy by ten or fifteen thousand. That was something Bekiaa wasn't used to. She'd never been part of any force bigger than the Grik it faced. *Maybe it'll be okay,* she prayed. *Maybe.* The horns were still braying in the woods, a different tone from before. She supposed it was some kind of assembly call. Behind her legion, limbered guns from the 1st Army artillery legion rattled by, moving to bolster 3rd Army, somewhere. The planes must've seen something else she couldn't. To her eyes, there seemed just as many Grik in front of her as elsewhere.

"I wonder why we haven't commenced firing? Our friends' artillery will easily range a thousand meters," Courtney said, staring at the distant Grik line. It was firm now, still, and eerily silent when the blaring horns suddenly tapered off. There was no chanting or clash of weapons, yet the tension was somehow greater than Bekiaa ever felt it, as if the entire host was coiling, setting its feet, preparing to spring into motion. Courtney seemed to sense it too, and nodded at the single-shot bolt-action rifle slung on Optio Meek's shoulder. He'd obeyed Bekiaa's order, returning just moments before. "I'm told Republic machine guns and even small arms are somewhat effective at this distance."

Bekiaa lowered her telescope. "Kim's probably waiting to make sure all the Grik are deployed, to kill as many as he can when we do open up. That makes sense," she replied. "I think they're all here now, though I only see a few artillery pieces. They obviously brought *them* up the roads. And if this force was moving to join another, as I suspect, they may not've had much artillery to begin with." She looked at Courtney. "We'll probably get the word very soon."

The Grik got it first.

Great clouds of white smoke, perhaps twenty or so,

blossomed up and down the Grik line. That was apparently all the artillery they had, but it was sufficient to do some damage. Geysers of earth rocketed up, short of the breastworks, but several white puffs snapped overhead, sleeting musket balls and hot shards of iron down on the defenders. Men and 'Cats began to scream. Bekiaa was surprised—and alarmed again—to see how well the new Grik fuses worked. Another tone sounded from the Grik horns, and the tightly packed formations suddenly loped forward through the smoke, keeping their alignment. Trumpets trilled down the Republic line, slipping the leash on the Derby guns. Dozens cracked at once, sending exploding shells among the advancing infantry or probing for their Grik counterparts. Dirty gray-brown thunderclaps erupted among the enemy, throwing soil and colored confettilike vegetation high in the air. Shrapnel clawed at their ranks. Bekiaa and Courtney were closest to the section on the left, and watched three guns fire as one. Spades at the rear of each carriage dug deep, locking them in place, as the barrels leaped back and then slid forward, just like Bekiaa had seen *Walker*'s bigger weapons do. Mechanical brakes applied to the wheels further stiffened the platform, and these guns' crews had their own pointers and trainers as well, already turning wheels to adjust windage and elevation while their first projectiles were still in flight. They knew they had to compensate for the sudden change in elevation caused by the burrowing spade, but subsequent shots would require less adjustment, as long as they engaged the same target.

Most amazing was how fast they fired! As soon as the tubes returned to battery—it took about a second—gunners stepped forward and twisted handles. Empty shell casings arced back on the trails with smoky clangs, and loaders slammed new shells in the chambers. They barely had time to get their hands clear before the gunners closed and locked the breeches, taking up dangling lanyards. Pointers and trainers raised their hands, indicating they were satisfied, before crouching behind a protective shield attached to the front of the trail. Lanyards snapped taut and the tubes recoiled again, with a tremendous, earsplitting roar. It dawned on Bekiaa that just those three guns, little larger than the twelve-pounder muzzle-loaders she was used to, could dish out as much destruction per minute—as long as they had ammunition—as *fifty* or more Union or Imperial Naa-po-lee-aans.

And it was taking a terrible toll. Great gaps had already opened in the Grik line, advancing at a trot beneath the falling curtain of dirt, debris, and parts of Grik. Somehow, they maintained their orderly ranks, however, closing the gaps and continuing on. But by the time they'd crossed a third of the distance between the two armies, they had to have lost a quarter of their force. Another trumpet call, muffled and indistinct, wafted from the right, chased by clattering machine-gun fire and rifle volleys. The 23rd's own trumpeter picked it up. Prefect Bele glanced at her and she nodded. "Twenty-third Legion!" Bele roared. "Set your sights at five hundred meters! Front rank, present." Six hundred troopers in the first of three ranks leveled their weapons, aiming offhand or resting their rifles on overturned wagons. "Take aim!" Bele shouted, staring to the front and shielding his eyes from the sun with his hand, looking almost as if he was saluting the enemy. "Fire!"

Six hundred rifles crashed with barely a stutter, the black powder in their 11 mm cartridges making a dense, white, impenetrable cloud, even as the 10th and 5th Legions fired as well. But the thunder didn't stop. The rapid-fire bark of six Maxims spaced along the front of each legion, set to fire in a traversing arc, perpetuated the racket. A Grik case shot exploded in front of the line, shattering a wagon and flinging half a dozen troops to the ground in a flurry of planks and splinters, their shrieks rising shrill and distorted amid the roar of battle. "Second rank! Take aim!" The second rank had already leaned forward, their rifles over the shoulders of the men and 'Cats in front. They had precious little to aim *at*, however, because they could barely see the gray mass drawing closer. That was sufficient, for now. "Fire!" Another volley crashed. "Third rank, take aim!"

The first rank would be finishing loading by now. Bekiaa could only marvel at the firepower of the legion, and when it struck her that it was surrounded by *two dozen* more, it was easy to understand why the Republic had anticipated an advantage over the Grik. The enemy had narrowed that advantage more than anyone here, aside from Courtney Bradford, perhaps, had expected, and there was no longer any question in her mind that this force, at least, had observed their advance. If that was the case, they'd *known* they were outnumbered, and it would've taken time and thought to prepare this reception in this place. No doubt they were terribly surprised by the lethality of Republic weapons, but they'd adapted and were moving quickly to limit their exposure before they could get in range of their own, and perhaps come to grips. Even so, they'd *initiated* the battle, and Bekiaa found it hard to believe they were just coming on in the same old way without a reason. Between the sharp rifle volleys, the bark of 75 mm guns, and the clatter of Maxims, Bekiaa's ears were in a state of shock. Somehow, though, she managed to perceive a different horn call from the distant woods. She stepped forward, closer to Lok-Fon's overturned wagon of comforts. Off to the right, to her amazement, the firing was beginning to slacken off.

"They run away!" a 'Cat in the first rank cried triumphantly, followed by roars of satisfaction from his mates. Bekiaa had raised her glass. The trooper was partly right; the Grik *had* broken into a run, about three hundred tails to their front. But they weren't running *away*. They were slanting forward, to Bekiaa's left, trying to focus all their remaining forces against 3rd Army. That was when she knew exactly what the Grik commander planned. She spun. "Give 'em everything you've got!" she roared. They'd be harder targets for her riflemen, running from right to left, but they had little choice but to simply fire into the mass in any event. "Maa-sheen gunners! Hose 'em! We have to whittle 'em down. Optio Meek! Go to General Kim. I don't know what's happening in front of him or in front of Second Army, but every Grik *we* see is about to hit the Third. Kim must *charge* them before they can maass, or Third Army, at least, will be destroyed! Go!" she shouted at his stunned, blinking face.

"I—I can't leave ye!" Meek protested. "Me duty's here, with you!"

"Your duty's where I say it is!"

"Charge them?" Courtney asked after Meek reluctantly trotted to the rear. His voice was milder than she would've expected.

"Yes, daamn it. Don't you see what he's done?" she demanded. By "he," Courtney suspected she meant the Grik commander. She immediately confirmed it. "We deployed, thank the Maker, so he didn't get to hit us on the march, or all scattered out—but by comin' out across our whole front, he fixed us in place! We're so spread out, Second Army can't shift over to support the Third. Even if they got no fightin', they're a mile an' a half away!" As usual, in times of stress, Bekiaa's careful English was beginning to slip. The firing on the left was reaching a fever pitch, louder even than the fighting where they stood. And they hadn't been forgotten by the enemy either. Close enough to Third Army to suit many charging Grik, and now only distinguishable from it or any other legion by the section of guns between, thousands of Grik were coming at them.

The tight, careful formations were gone, yielding to confusion at last, but the mass of the enemy was no less dense—and they were finally shooting back. Musket balls tore through overturned wagons and, often, bodies behind them. Splinters sprayed in all directions, blinding men and 'Cats. The troopers of the 23rd were through with volleys, though, and were firing as fast as they could. Maxims still chattered insistently, sweeping away great swathes, but each time one stopped to reload, more Grik surged closer, eyes wide with terror or anticipation, sharp teeth gnashing, shooting, reloading, roaring like the hellish fiends they were. The Derby guns slashed at them, muzzles depressed, blasting scores with every shot. They were using canister now, something they'd never expected to need, so there wasn't much in their limber chests. Runners raced between the guns and caissons farther back, each with as many rounds as they could carry.

The wagons bulged inward with the press and many troops had to stop firing just to push back against the horde. One by one, however, the wagons tipped over, back on their wheels, crushing defenders underneath. Grik took advantage, leaping up and over, jumping down behind their thrusting bayonets. Most were quickly shot down, but they paved the way for more. Bekiaa was shooting now, firing her Springfield at gray-clad shapes in the smoke. She paused to insert another stripper clip and noticed Courtney standing beside her with his Krag, calmly killing Grik with unhurried shots. How he'd changed!

"We can't hold them, Legate!" the third cohort senior centurion named Tinaas-Kus told her desperately. Tinaas was the only female officer in the legion, aside from Lok-Fon.

"Where's the prefect?" Bekiaa demanded, eyes searching for the tall black man.

Tinaas motioned at the thickest fighting with her head. "He led the reserve cohort forward. We *must* form square!"

A musket ball *vroop*ed past so close that Bekiaa felt it cut fur on her cheek. A defensive square was a common formation in the legions, and in the open, with a single legion, it might be the right thing to do. Here they'd have to contract away from the 10th and 5th to pull it off, and they couldn't shoot toward them either. She remembered when Greg Garrett formed a desperate square on a little beach on the coast of Saay-lon. It held barely long enough that there were still survivors when help finally came. Here, a square might save the 23rd, but would totally shatter the line. "Never!" she snapped. "Send runners to the artillery sections. The one on the left'll stand by to wheel forward an' to the left. The one on the right'll wait to advance with the legion. Then bring up everyone you can find—cooks, horse holders, I don't care! General Kim *will* charge, and so will we! Trumpeter!" she shouted. "To me." She looked back at Tinaas. "Spread the word as fast as you can." She pointed toward 5th Legion, where the fighting was less intense. "And tell them to charge with us—or be destroyed after we're dead!" She paused perhaps two seconds, staring at Centurion Tinaas, who blinked back in incredulous terror. "*Now*, Centurion!" she roared. Tinaas raced off.

Courtney had opened the loading gate of his Krag. "You'll forgive me, I hope, my dear," he said, as if speaking to the cartridges he dropped in the magazine, "if I can't tell if you hate all this or love it."

Bekiaa looked at him. He knew how . . . tough her time had been in Saay-lon, then Indiaa. But had her time in *Donaghey*, away from the fight, been any better? She looked past him. Prefect Bele and his reserves had pushed the breakthrough back, but now her troops and the Grik were trading fire across the wagons almost muzzle to muzzle, and men, 'Cats, and Grik were blown down with every shot. That couldn't go on. She was more certain than ever that the Republic hadn't been ready for this war, but there was no doubting the courage of its people. "You'll forgive *me*, Mr. Am-baas-ador, if I wonder how you stay so calm. I think I'm gonna shit myself."

Courtney laughed. "I doubt that. As to the other, I suppose—if nothing else—Mr. Silva's taught me how to behave in desperate situations. Whether the calm you think you see is courage or resignation to my fate, I can't say. Part comes from my faith in you, however, because whether you hate it, love it"—he closed the loading gate and chambered a round, then gently touched her arm—"or fear it, you can still *lead*. And that's what we need right now: a decision, *action*, right or wrong."

She touched his hand and smiled. "Then my first decision is to order you to the rear. Get a horse an' ride to Gener-aal Kim." She pressed on even as Courtney's face contorted and he blinked violent objection. "If he hasn't already ordered a charge when you get there, you gotta persuade him. He's listened to me on occasion, and he'll listen to you coming from me—from here." She blinked sadly. "I'll be dead by then, if he hasn't, and so will the Twenty-third Legion. But he might still save Third Army."

Stinging with a sense he was running away, but realizing Bekiaa was right and that one more middle-aged rifleman could make little contribution to her desperate plan, Courtney hurried to borrow a horse from the Gentaa teamsters conscripted to hold the cavalry's animals while their riders ran to join Bekiaa's charge. He nodded at the enigmatic man/Lemurian who seemed so unconcerned by events, and awkwardly swung into the saddle. Higher now, he had a better view of the battle. Bekiaa had been right. Almost the entire Grik force had concentrated against 3rd Army, and the fighting there was frantic.

Unfortunately, the 23rd and, to a lesser extent, the 5th Legions had fallen under that avalanche as well.

As he turned to kick the horse toward Kim's distant pavilion, he recognized another terrible weakness of the Republic military organization, besides its outdated formations. Though the Republic had wireless technology and a respectable telegraph network between its cities—a line had even followed Kim's HQ—they hadn't deployed *field* telegraphy. Certainly nothing like the new field telephones their allies were using. Courtney supposed they'd considered it impractical, in view of the traditional, independent role of their provincially separated legions. They'd ordinarily have access to local telegraph stations in any event. But even though they weren't separated now, they were still too spread out for instant communication.

He rode as fast as his inexperienced horsemanship allowed, seeing there was indeed very little fighting in front of the rest of 1st Army, and many of its troops were cheering what they thought had been an easy victory. His chest clenched with dread as he heard the trumpets behind him signaling the charge and knew the 23rd, at least, was launching itself into a meat grinder the rest of the legions weren't even aware of. Or maybe not . . . Directly in front of him, a couple hundred yards away, a large cavalry force was thundering his way, surrounded by clouds of colorful flower petals thrown up by galloping hooves. A constant trumpet was sounding, calling all cavalry cohorts within earshot. The cohort of the legion he was passing—he thought it was the 9th—was already forming up to join the coming formation as it passed. He finally recognized the leaders riding out front. One was General Taal-Gaak, his short cape flowing behind him. Most surprising was the sight of Inquisitor Kon-Choon riding awkwardly beside him in his usual stylish civilian kilt, waistcoat, and frock. He reminded Courtney of a small, extremely furry Scottish gentleman—with a tail. The intensity of his pale blue eyes and the carbine slung over his shoulder erased any humor Courtney might've found in the image. Abruptly, he turned his own horse to join the charge.

"Bekiaa?" Choon cried as Courtney was swept along.

"Charging, even now, to save Third Army," Courtney gasped back.

"I *knew* she would not wait," General Taal snapped, annoyed—and admiring. "Trumpeter!" he called. "General Kim's preparatory notes, if you please, on his orders. Then sound the charge! A *general* charge, to follow us!" As commander of all the armies, Kim's personal audible prefix would oblige everyone who heard it to obey the signals that followed. Taal glanced at Courtney and Choon. "I only hope we're not too late!" They wheeled around the 9th Legion into the void left by the 5th—which must've followed the 23rd after all—and dashed into the heaving, thunderous maelstrom of smoke and flashing rifles, muskets, and blood-darkened bayonets ahead.

The battle on the Plain of Gaughala, on the edge of the Teetgak Forest, dissolved largely into chaos. There was no help for it, really, and if the Grik had possessed significant reserves it could've gone far worse. Only 2nd Army, at Kim's specific orders, refrained from joining the melee that ensued, and it deployed into a block formation to move to support the 3rd and 1st. All but the leftmost legions of 3rd Army and Kim's own 1st Legion poured into the attack behind General Taal, but by the time most of them got there, there was little left to do; the damage was already done. Very few Grik survived, aside from isolated companies and battalions that were probably late to their jump-off points. Those melted back into the forest to fight another day. Some of the guns disappeared as well, farther down the roads than the cavalry was willing to pursue, but probably more than half were captured. It was interesting and ominous that most of the guns had been spiked or otherwise rendered unserviceable by their crews—who fled in good order as well. It would later be calculated that of the roughly fifty thousand Grik that formed at the edge of the forest, possibly fifteen thousand died during their initial advance. Fewer bodies littered the ground after they shifted into their stunning, oblique charge, and that left more than thirty thousand to slam into the roughly eighteen thousand men and Lemurians of primarily the 7th, 8th, 10th, 14th, and 15th Legions.

The Republic troops fought very well. It was their first real battle and they gave as good as they got. Unfortunately, that ratio couldn't be sustained and they simply hadn't been prepared for the savagery of their enemy. At close quarters, the Republic's superior weapons gave them little advantage, and all five of the Grik's "target" legions, as well as the 23rd and 5th (of the 1st Army) and the 16th and 21st (of the 3rd), were gutted in the vicious hand-to-hand fighting that ensued. Even Bekiaa and Courtney couldn't have prepared them for the discipline they'd faced, combined with the determination to, even outnumbered, inflict the greatest possible damage they possibly could. They'd seen the latter before, to a degree, but never the former to such an extent. That had been frighteningly new to them all. Now all that remained was to count the cost and decide what to do next.

General Marcus Kim and his staff rode carefully, grimly, through the abattoir where perhaps a quarter of his 3rd Army had died. Its commander, another human named General Modius, stood wearily to meet them as they approached the growing lake of wounded being carried from where the worst fighting had been. Modius's pale face was anxious, his hands clasped before him. "I—I don't know what . . ."

Kim held up his hand. "It wasn't your fault, General. Continue your work here, caring for our wounded." Modius bowed his head, and Kim and his staff moved on. Around the toppled barricade of wagons, the bodies were so thick on the ground that they were forced to dismount. Most of the dead were Grik, lying in bloody, disemboweled heaps, and the stench was overwhelming. Details were removing the Republic dead and wounded, and had been for some time. The Grik wounded were bayonetted or shot and then dragged into great mounds of ragged, oozing flesh. Kim had ordered that some be taken prisoner, if practicable, but apparently enough men and 'Cats had died or been wounded in the attempt that it was universally deemed *im*practicable to continue. Kim wouldn't push it. None among them spoke Grik, and the behavior and equipment of the enemy probably told them as much as they'd learn by questioning them. His eyes lit on a group of officers near the breastworks where they'd gathered, exhausted and covered with blood, in a space cleared of bodies. Healers moved among them or brought mugs of something to refresh their parched throats. He was amazed to find several people he'd never expected to see alive again.

"That's *enough*, you carrion-clawing buggers!" cried Courtney Bradford. Inquisitor Choon, bloody and coatless, was helping Optio Meek, his left arm in a red-splashed sling, hold Courtney facedown on a blanket. General Taal, also steeped in blood, appeared to be supervising. Kim was particularly surprised to see Meek. The young optio had delivered his message and bolted directly back to the fight so quickly that he'd forgotten the rifle he'd brought to the pavilion. Courtney heaved and cursed again, fighting their efforts to restrain him while a healer and his assistant worked on the Australian's right upper calf. Bekiaa-Sab-At, her once-white armor now a dark black-red, stood a little apart, leaning on an equally red-stained rifle, its bayonet encrusted, lumpy, and dark. Beside her, dwarfing her, was a tall black prefect. Both were watching the operation, but occasionally glanced over a shattered wagon at the distant trees.

"It's just a damned, bloody *scratch*!" Courtney ranted, his face buried in the blanket. "I'm sure there are others who need your torment more than I!"

"'Bloody scraatch' is right," the gruff Lemurian healer growled. "And you could bleed to death for all I care, but Gen'raal Kim might be annoyed if the am-baas-ador from our allies died of obstin-aacy. Now quit squirming so I can finish—and get to those who *do* need me more!"

Chastened, Courtney fell silent, but turned his head and saw Kim approach. "General!" he said.

Choon and Taal both moved to rise, but Kim motioned them to continue what they were doing. "No! Don't let him up. The healers may not catch him again." He glared at Courtney. "You had no business in the middle of the fight, Ambassador Bradford," he scolded lightly.

"Well, I wasn't really in the *middle*. A damned Grik shot a musket ball through my leg and killed the horse I was riding, poor creature. A *musket ball*," he repeated, lowering his voice to an indignant murmur before he continued. "The horse laid down on me and kept me quite immobilized through the fiercest fighting. I did almost nothing and was hardly noticed by the enemy. It was rather frightening, however, I must say. Lying there as helpless as a babe, with Grik running to and fro!"

"He wasn't as helpless as he claims, General," Choon stated. "He kept a grip on his rifle and killed many Grik, even while trapped. I saw it myself."

"Several might've done for me if not for that big bloke with Legate Bekiaa," Courtney added.

Kim shifted his gaze back to Bekiaa and Bele. It was then he noticed how . . . protectively the prefect hovered near the Allied Marine. Bekiaa herself seemed utterly void of expression. Her face was slack with exhaustion, with good reason, but her eyes betrayed nothing and she didn't even blink a greeting. "I sent the charge as quickly as I could," Kim told her, but looked away. "Still my fault, the whole disastrous mess. You warned me to reorganize our legions—and I did, but not well enough. I tried to compromise and it only made things worse. It was *all* my fault," he repeated.

Bekiaa seemed to break out of her trance and regarded him skeptically. "What will you do now?"

"Our first priority is to reform the armies, obviously." He shook his head. "Third Army was almost destroyed."

"It *was* destroyed, as a fighting force," Bekiaa snapped. "Send the badly crippled legions to Fort Melhausen, escorting the wounded, but keep the rest. Integrate them into First and Second Armies."

"It's not that simple," Kim objected. "Nor is it certain we can continue. I must consult Nig-Taak, hear his views."

"It *is* that simple," Bekiaa stated. "*You* command and *must* continue, moving faster than ever before!" She gestured around. "Other plans were set in motion when you began this caampaign. They all depend on you. If you stop now, you invite the destruction of your allies. Just as bad"—she waved around again—"all these people will've died for nothing. If you don't push after the Grik that got away—stay close behind them—word of this baattle will get too far ahead and we'll face another army sooner than we would have. Sooner than we have to. Now is the time for your forced march through the forest, supporting Gener-aal Taal's scouts."

"The Grik will oppose us. Some got away."

"Sure, but not many. We'll brush 'em aside and keep going." She looked at Taal for support. The cavalry commander was blinking thoughtful agreement.

"But our supply lines . . ." Kim protested. "They will not be secure in the forest, with raiders on our flanks."

"They can be strengthened by sea, when we reach the Ungee River," Courtney suggested tightly as the healer wiped at his wound. "Songze, and certainly Fort Taak, are far enough north that at this time of year they're rarely affected by the blasted Dark. Move supplies from them by sea."

General Kim seemed to consider. "That might work. It's not as easy as you make it sound, but might be possible—if we can get the ships completed in time, or your people can supply them." He glanced around, then back at Bekiaa. "I'll at least do part of what you suggest and send the wounded to the rear immediately, escorted by the crippled legions." He paused and met Bekiaa's gaze. "What of the Twenty-third?"

"What about it?"

"It's your legion now, you know."

"Mine?" She was surprised. She'd expected it to be a temporary command.

"Shall it go to the rear as well?" Kim pressed.

"No, sir," Prefect Bele interjected. "Our losses were heavy, but not crippling. We can continue." He looked at Bekiaa. "With *her* in command."

"Perhaps we can experiment with her notions," Choon suggested. "Let what remains of the Tenth Legion be absorbed into the Twenty-third. It will be a start," he explained to his doubtful general. "The survivors of the Tenth will resent it, of course. I do not blame them. But if anyone can combine two legions—from two armies—into one, it is her," he added with certainty.

"I caan," Bekiaa insisted, stepping forward. "And I'll do it on the march—if we march at once, together."

Kim wavered. "Very well. We will try that." He gestured around once more. "It will take time for the rest, but I finally understand the difference between your system and ours. I did not see it before. Your First, Second, and Third Corps can operate independently, as do our armies with the same names. Except your corps, no matter how diverse, were always trained to work and fight together, as part of the *same* army. Even our legions, perhaps equivalent to your regiments or brigades, do not truly consider themselves part of a greater whole. Perhaps after today, and with the example you will set with the Twenty-third"—he sighed—"along with other changes I must make at last, the Armies of the Republic will begin to see themselves, *itself*, as the Army of the Republic. . . . If we continue the advance." He looked at the carnage once more, hand rubbing his perpetual frown. "I truly never imagined . . ." He shook his head and stared at her. "You told me this was a terrible war, but most of us didn't even know what war was until today. God help us if we suffer another defeat such as this, even farther from our homes."

Bekiaa barked a laugh that sounded almost hysterical. "Defeat?" she said harshly. "I've *seen* defeat, General. Bloody as this was, and despite our mistakes, today was a *victory*. How do I know the difference? Because enough of us remain to ponder whether we won or lost." She laughed again at his expression.

"She's right, you know," Courtney Bradford said, rising to his elbows, the eyes beneath his bushy brows deadly earnest for once. "And now you've had a taste. You may not've known what you were getting into, but you've got a *bloody* good idea now. Get used to it, General Kim, or you may as well go home after all." He grimaced as the healer cinched the bandage tight around his calf, then regarded Kim with sad compassion. "Not that it'll save anything. If you retire, your armies will split and your legions return to their provinces. You can't keep them together long, doing nothing. And after your allies, *our* people"—he said, nodding at Bekiaa—"have lost the war, which we will without your participation in this campaign, the Grik will finally come and snap your legions up in penny packets. You know it as well as I."

"Indeed, Gener-aal," Choon said, standing. After glancing distastefully at the blood that had spoiled his fine shirt, he looked at Kim. "I must agree with the Am-baasador. More importantly, though the Senate may not, the Kaiser certainly will. This has been a costly first encounter, yet we learned much about the enemy; perhaps more than our allies now know. The Grik have a *real army*, with real soldiers and a sharply focused cause—our destruction. We must similarly redevote ourselves. Consider that the enemy likely initiated this battle fully aware they couldn't win. They hurt us more grievously than they should have, and there were numerous reasons for that, but most revealing was that they were willing to sacrifice their entire force merely to destroy a portion of ours. That implies a dedication to their cause like none of us has seen, as well as an understanding that this war will be decided by a *series* of battles, not only one." He bowed to Bekiaa. "You are used to that idea, but have you ever known the *Grik* to accept such a notion?" He looked back at Kim. "Only one thing hasn't changed: there will always be more Grik, and the longer it takes us to defeat them, the more there will be." He paused and blinked down at Courtney. "And from a purely political standpoint, we *must* press on. Even if our allies were not so exposed, what additional assistance could we ever expect from them if we—as they might say—took one punch and quit?"

Courtney snorted and glared up at Optio Meek. "Don't just stand there gawking! Help me up, damn you." When Meek complied, Courtney, leaning on the younger man, controlled a grimace. "Couldn't've said it better myself, Inquisitor," he granted, then looked at Kim. "So, let's get cracking, shall we? You can reshape your army, General, but do it on the march. Use this victory to weld it together. And make sure your people *know* it was a victory. I'll warrant they already know how much worse it could've been—and why. They'll want change now. Let's give it to them, and push on until the end!"

General Kim nodded, his expression hardening as decision came. "Very well," he agreed. "So be it." He held each gaze a moment and then nodded once more. "Until the end."

CHAPTER 15

Southwest of Zanzibar
November 17, 1944

Rough-sounding Grik-made engines *blaaapp*ed loudly in the predawn dark as the dirigible bucked the chilly, quartering crosswind at around three thousand feet. Their altitude was a guess; there was no altimeter, nor was there a light in the forward gondola, and Dennis Silva could barely see the shapes of the aircrew flying "his" zeppelin. There'd been light below earlier when they crossed the phosphorescent wakes of (probably) Allied AVDs, steaming closer to the south coast of Zanzibar than ever before. Their planes wouldn't scout the island itself, but would continue making sure Kurokawa's fleet hadn't sortied, and start cutting the supply line to the mainland. Now there was nothing, not even the glimmering wave tops reflecting the sparkling stars. At some point, they'd crossed the African shoreline, and the stars had disappeared behind a hazy overcast. Only occasional flares of Silva's Zippo over his pocket compass kept them aimed at their objective.

Dennis felt a prickly sensation on the back of his neck and automatically reached up to thump Petey on the head. But Petey wasn't there. He'd left him with Isak and Tabby. Pam would've devotedly watched him right up until he left, then pitched him out the nearest porthole. She couldn't stand him. Silva wondered why *he* could. He'd never wanted him, and on his *best* behavior the little lizard was an obnoxious, annoying pest. *Kinda like me,* he thought. But Petey was also a constant reminder of Sandra, and the Governor-Empress Rebecca Anne McDonald. Particularly the latter, when she'd merely been a scared little girl he called Li'l Sis. Petey took Dennis back to a cherished time when a little girl saw nothing but good in him, looked at him as an indestructible protector, and gave him her unqualified trust. That had changed him at least as much as Chief Gray's example and Captain Reddy's confidence that he'd do what had to be done, no matter what. He took off his helmet and scratched his head. *Well, I guess if anything happens to me, ol' Petey'll be okay, at least. That dopey creep Isak always wanted a pet.*

"You ne'er go this long wi'out talking," Lawrence said. "You're not scared, are you?"

Instead of his usual bluster, Dennis chuckled. "What's to be scared of? We're flyin' a string o' gas turds in a paper bag, patched together with balin' wire an' gum, toward what're likely the best-trained, best-armed Griks we ever met, led by Japs with modern fighters an' a battleship. An' our mission is to *crash* in the middle of 'em all an' run around spyin' an' reportin' what we see. Oh yeah, an' rescue the Skipper's pregnant wife in our spare time. I'm dozin' on my feet."

Lawrence nodded seriously and Silva noted he could see him better now as the sky began to gray. "You say it like that," Lawrence said, "it does sound kinda dull. It'll get greater exciting 'hen the 'ig show starts, I think." They laughed together, Lawrence's sounding like a leaking steam line. The three aircrew, all Shee-Ree, looked at them like they were nuts, and as the light improved, Silva could see them better. The 'Cats were dyed and dressed as Grik, just like Lawrence. They wouldn't fool anybody in daylight, but might in the dark, at a distance. It was better than nothing. They'd rely on Lawrence and Pokey (the only real Grik they had) to do any talking. But Pokey, despite his obvious glee at seeing "See-va" again, still struck Dennis as retarded, even for a Grik.

Maybe it's just how he acts around me, he considered.

The Khonashi troops in the aft gondola might actually be more problematic. Their rust-colored plumage was darker than the average Grik and they'd had to be lightened with stuff that might wash off if it rained. And then there was Silva and Captain Stuart Brassey, of course. Dennis knew the young Imperial officer I'joorka sent to command his detachment of Khonashi very well, but neither looked like Grik in daylight or dark. Hopefully they'd pass as Japanese, though Silva, at six foot two, would be a very unusual—and memorable—Japanese sailor. There couldn't be many, if any, like him, and they'd be very well-known. Maybe there were still some Leaguers around? Their best bet was to remain undetected.

"Is dat it?" asked the 'Cat behind the tall, upright tiller controlling the rudders and elevators aft. He was nodding northeast over the open rail at a dark, distant shape beginning to firm up. It lay across a broad ocean gap from the mainland below.

Dennis strode forward and extended the Imperial telescope in front of his good eye. "Guess so," he said. "It's about the right time." He aimed the glass down at several ships in the strait. A couple were old-style, square-rig Grik Indiamen, the growing day separating their dingy white sails from the purple-black sea. One ship looked like the double-ended steam tugs they'd seen pulling troops and supplies up the West Mangoro River on Madagascar. The barge behind was stacked with barrels. "Steer for the island," he ordered, still staring at the barge. The sun peeked over the horizon like a molten ball, battering the filmy overcast and spraying them with light. "Ever'body but Larry, remember to stay back from the rail," he warned. "Pass the word aft." Through the telescope he began to see multicolored streamers in the water, trailing the barge. He grunted. "Oil barrels. Leaky. Fuel oil for Kurokawa. Just like we thought, he's done with coal. At least for his ships. An' he has to have oil to make gas for his planes. Those casks're so leaky, though, I bet I could burn the whole thing just by droppin' a lit cee-gar." He shrugged. "Oh, well."

Brassey climbed down the ladder from the envelope above, the only way between the two gondolas. He stepped beside Silva and peered over as well. Silva glanced at him. Brassey was about the same age as Abel Cook and looked a lot like him, except for his dark hair. The two were best friends and young enough that they probably hadn't even finished growing. Yet they were already captains who'd earned the rank. Still, even though he was technically the senior officer, Brassey understood this was Silva's mission and would follow his lead.

He nodded at the dark island ahead, its prominent features reflecting the rising sun. "It's fairly obvious we're heading the right direction. Kurokawa must get all his supplies from the mainland."

"An' he's gotta have tank batteries for all his oil somewhere close to the harbor. I'd love to find those."

"We will," Brassey assured. "I'll prepare my troops. It won't be long now."

"Nope. An' be sure to arrange them nasty dead Griks around. I know they stink, but we can't afford for 'em to find the damn things still wrapped up like mummies."

Brassey frowned but nodded, and climbed back up the ladder. "The rest of us better ease back now," Dennis said, as much to himself as the others. "Except you, Larry. Time to put your new artistic skills to use."

Lawrence had discovered that he loved to draw, and had often used sticks on the ground or rocks on rocks. Now, with his rifle-loading claws filed away, he'd learned to hold pencils and brushes. He stepped to the forward rail in the gondola, wind whipping the crest on his head, and prepared to make additions to his already updated copy of Fiedler's map. He'd call out any changes so Silva, now crouching near the tiller, could mark them on his own map. They'd decided to make for the central airfield closest to Kurokawa's HQ, suspecting that was where the Grik usually went. But they also knew it had been hammered, both by the P-40-something and the big night raid. They'd veer off, crossing the anchorage a second time, and head for the strip on the northwest side of Lizard Ass Bay before "losing power" and apparently falling prey to the prevailing wind. That would be when things would get interesting—unless they were already shot down for flying over something Kurokawa had ordered other Grik to avoid. That was Silva's main concern: that there was only one acceptable approach. He hoped if there was, under the circumstances, Kurokawa would let his desire for news from Esshk overrule his pique.

"We're crossing o'er nunder three island now," Lawrence said. "I don't see anything there. Nunder one is co'ing ut." There was a long pause while the airship bucked the morning breeze, now beating on its starboard bow. "There's cranes and things," Lawrence finally reported, confirming what they already knew. Then his voice grew more excited. "There's the carrier that got a'ay! It got hit in the raid! They're 'orking on the launching deck! And o'er at the great docks, south-southeast, it's all gone! 'Urned a'ay!"

"So we burned out all the new carrier conversions too," Silva muttered gleefully, scribbling on his map. "Kurokawa'll be one unhappy Jap—if the fit it musta gave him didn't croak him."

Lawrence's monologue continued as the sun climbed, beginning to glare inside the gondola as they swept across the docks, over one of the Japanese barracks—exactly where it was supposed to be—and neared the central airfield. As expected, it was gone. The scorched remains of the strips were clear but surrounded by burned-out hangers, charred fragments of aircraft, and a two-mile-wide blackened hole in the jungle. And what looked like some kind of factory complex east of the airfield had burned as well. All that remained were rusting heaps of metal, which might've been heavy machine tools of some sort, amid fallen, fire-blackened timbers.

"Turn us around," Silva told the 'Cat at the tiller, handing him his compass. "Head due west."

"Ay, ay," the Shee-Ree said, using the term he'd heard so often now. He was clearly nervous but trusted those he was with, and their methods, to see them through. After what happened on the Mangoro River crossing, he had good reason for his faith, though the scope of that action was miniscule compared to what likely lay ahead. They flew back over the bay, and all of them half expected to come under fire at any moment, but nothing happened. A couple of Jap-Grik fighters, so similar in appearance to the Allied Fleashooters, roared past in formation, but after a cursory glance, banked away to the south.

"There's *Sa'oie*," Lawrence said, his tone relieved, as he moved to the starboard side of the gondola. "Still on the north end o' the anchorage. She's got stean."

"Steam's up," Silva repeated to himself, thinking. "Maybe they're trying to move her. How far's the other airfield?"

"Two or three 'iles," Lawrence replied.

Silva knelt beside him and poked his head over the edge of the rail, chancing a look. "I see it. Looks like the bombs came close, but didn't get it." He nodded a little to the left. "What's that?"

"Another shore 'attery, the 'ap says. Is it antiaircra't guns?"

"Not that. I mean the clearing between the airstrip and the battery. It ain't on the map." He started to slide the telescope over the sill.

"Hey," Lawrence protested. "They'll see the glint. Griks don't ha' telescokes."

"Relax. Ever'thing's shiny in the morning." Silva adjusted the resolution. "Jumpin' Jehosephat!" he exclaimed. "There's a couple *'Cats* down there, inside a fence surrounded by water! There's a little shack inside too, an' . . . some other folks may be stretched out under awnings." He stared a moment longer, then eased back and closed the telescope. "Larry, ol' buddy, I think we found our people."

"Did you see Lady Sandra?" Lawrence asked excitedly.

Silva looked at him incredulously. "Sure. An' she has a mole on her cheek I never noticed," he snapped. "Hell, no, I didn't see her! I couldn't tell them others was *'Cats* from here, without their flippy tails. What's the matter with you?"

Lawrence shrugged. "I got excited, I guess."

"Yeah? Well, me too," Silva admitted. "I *hope* she's there. It'll make things a lot easier if they're all in one place. We'll find out quick as we can." He looked back at the crew-'Cats. "Okay, it's about time to play busted duck, anyway." In response to their confused blinking, he elaborated. "Make like we're coming in to land at the strip, but when I give the word, we'll kill the engines on the port side, see?" He looked at the Lemurian at the tiller. "It'll get tough for you, an' I doubt you'll have to pretend how hard it is to keep 'er under control. Larry, you'll have'ta guide us in. Too many eyes'll be on us in a minute for me ta' show my purty face. You know where we wanna set down. Just sing out if it looks wrong when we get close."

"Rong?"

"Yeah, you know: big rocks, trees, ten thousand lizards waitin' underneath us. That sorta thing." His eye rested on the three Grik corpses secured in the forward gondola. "Get ready to peel 'em," he said.

From the ground, the dingy, hard-weathered airship must've looked like it had seen a lot of action. Perhaps it had survived numerous raids over Grik City? Several large patches were evident, specifically where Silva once painted *Walker*'s number, DD-163, so they wouldn't be shot down by friendlies. But as it descended toward the airfield, turning into the wind, and Grik line handers began to assemble, two engines on the port side suddenly clattered and died. Immediately, it veered left as the thrust of the starboard engines and the breeze took it. The rudders slammed hard over, and the throttles controlling the starboard engines were quickly cut, leaving only the centerline motor behind the forward gondola. More a steering engine than anything, however, it just wasn't enough. And too much hydrogen had already been vented for the airship to rise again, so it kept descending as it drifted swiftly westward.

The young Japanese sailor only recently promoted to officer and who had the duty at the airfield sprang into action. He quickly ordered a telegraph message sent to HQ that they had an airship in distress and raced off on foot, leading a dozen Grik security troops. They ran as fast as they could through the dense jungle separating their post from the sea, but before they'd made it a mile down the narrow, winding path, they saw a ball of bright orange fire roll into the sky through a gap in the cover. Black smoke gushed away to seaward. Picking up their pace and panting as they went, they covered the final mile to the coast. It was all over by the time they arrived; there wasn't even much smoke anymore. Through heroic effort, the crew of the airship had apparently managed to crash-land on the broad, blindingly white beach before they were blown out to sea, but whatever caused the engines to malfunction—whether they overheated or their fuel lines burst, there was no telling—must've started a fire. Constructed almost entirely of wood and fabric, the very cells containing the volatile hydrogen saturated with a highly flammable sealant, and with the heaviest weight aboard being fuel tanks, Grik zeppelins, once ignited, burned as quickly and thoroughly as nitrated paper. All that remained were scattered engines, a frail, collapsing skeleton, and the two gondolas, still smoldering.

"Check inside!" the Japanese officer shouted, waving his Grik forward before he bent over gasping, hands on his knees. The skeleton crumpled with a sparkly crash, nearly catching a couple of his Grik, but they ventured forward again to peer inside the gondolas.

"Su'ete no shisha!" one of the Grik reported in his best butchered Japanese. He held up three clawed fingers on each hand. Six bodies; no survivors. The officer sighed and sank to the sand. "We'll wait until the wreck cools, then see if any dispatches survived." Those were usually in thick leather satchels or wooden tubes and may have escaped the fire. The Grik gathered round and squatted in the sand around him.

"Well, we're here," Silva whispered, peering from the jungle shadows nearby. Lawrence was putting the brass-framed Remington MK III flare gun that ignited the zep back in his pack. He took out a thick paper box of hardtack "heart attack" crackers and offered them around. Brassey took one, biting into the thick, dark square, and munched quietly. Silva nodded at the Khonashi sergeant who stuck to Brassey like glue. "Quick work covering our tracks, Sergeant . . . Oolak, right?" The fierce-looking Khonashi nodded. "I doubt they'd've noticed 'em, the way they charged right up, but who knows?" He slithered back and leaned against a tree, gazing around at his, Brassey's, and Lawrence's ten Khonashi and three 'Cats. "My poor zep," he lamented. "It was the best one in the whole damn Air

Corps!" He held up his canteen in salute and took a solemn sip.

"I believe it was the *only* one," Brassey observed wryly.

"So?"

"And next?" Lawrence asked.

"Next we check the radio an' Morse lamp; make sure we didn't bust 'em. But don't transmit," he warned the two Khonashi comm-*tokeks*, as Silva called them (after the little house geckos in Java), burdened with big packs on their backs. Inside one was a hand-crank generator, folded up, that weighed forty pounds. The other contained the smallest radio they'd made yet, the same short-range set they were putting in the P-1C Mosquito Hawks, as well as a small Morse lamp. Built tough by necessity, together they weighed close to *sixty* pounds, and both troopers still had to carry their Allin-Silva rifles and ammunition. Their rations and other equipment had been split among the others. Dennis had most of his usual arsenal of tommy gun, .45, cutlass, and '03 bayonet, as well as his odd flintlock pistol. At the last minute, he'd decided to leave his beloved Doom Stomper behind. It was too long and cumbersome for what they had in mind, and he'd made up the weight with extra ammo and a haversack full of grenades. He'd always liked grenades. "Then we get comfterble," he continued. "Take a nap. It's been a long night an' mornin'." He waved at the beach. "Those guys look like they'll stick around awhile, but I doubt it'll be too long. We'll hang here till dark an' try to signal our offshore support. Tell 'em we made it, an' what we seen so far." One of the converted AVDs (seaplane tenders), with a Nancy aboard, was supposed to steam close enough to receive their Morse lamp report sometime around midnight, then head southwest toward the African coast, and south again before repeating it by radio.

Interestingly, it and several other AVDs had been further modified as DMs, or mine layers, as well. Silva had seen the new mines that arrived with *Tarakaan Island* and heartily approved of them. They didn't look much different from depth charges, but had enough buoyancy to float just under the surface and were studded with contact exploders. Weights kept them anchored in place. A keen eye would probably see them in daylight, in anything but the roughest sea, but when it came to mines, sometimes it was better when the enemy knew they were there. Dennis wished they had more of them, but most were lost in another ship in the battle north of Mahe, and they'd never get replacements in time to use them right. But they had enough for an . . . interesting scheme the Skipper cooked up. It might cost them all their AVD-DMs sometime over the next few days, but if it worked, it could give them an edge against Kurokawa's fleet.

"So just relax," Silva said, pulling his helmet down over his eye. "The next few nights'll be mighty busy, once we start pokin' around."

CHAPTER 16

TF Bottle Cap
***USS* Santa Catalina**
Go Away Strait
November 18, 1944

Commander Russ Chappelle took a paper box from his shirt pocket and knocked out a PIG-cig. His trusty old Zippo flared to life and he sucked the acrid-tasting smoke. Somehow he didn't even grimace. *Getting used to the damn things, I guess,* he thought, stepping farther out on *Santa Catalina*'s starboard bridge wing and staring past the 'Cat sailors by the pelorus and Morse lamp. Beyond, on the late-afternoon waters of the Go Away Strait, was the massive USNRS *Arracca*. She still looked weird in her new dazzle paint scheme, after all the time she'd just been brown, then gray, and he wondered why. *Santy Cat* had the same paint job and didn't look weird anymore. He glanced at the nasty-tasting cigarette between his fingers and shrugged. *Boils down to what you're used to.*

Mikey Monk sauntered out of the old ship's armored pilothouse and joined him. Russ offered him a PIG-cig, but Monk took an exaggerated step back and shook his head. "Not me, Skipper! I can't stand those damn things. Make my mouth taste like old socks . . . ah, *probably* taste."

Russ laughed. "So that's your secret, Mikey! Maybe I'll try chewing old socks to get the taste *out*." Monk chuckled too and they stood companionably for a while, talking about little of consequence. All the while, they stared at the ships around them, the purpling sky past the single, smoke-streaming funnel above and behind the choppy, marbled sea, and the distant dark smear of Africa beneath the setting sun. Below them, 'Cats practiced loading the big twenty-foot, ten-inch rifle mounted on the foredeck. It was the salvaged breech section of one of *Amagi*'s main guns, and combined with her 5.5″ secondaries and cluster of machine guns, *Santy Cat* was still the most powerful ship in the Alliance. She'd remain so at least until USS *Gray* commissioned. Her current mission was to guard *Arracca* against any Grik heavies that chose to poke their noses past the mouth of the Zambezi. So far, none had tried.

There was a metallic rumble on the stairs behind and they turned to see Lieutenant (jg) Dean Laney's overstuffed form rising to join them. Looking up, he saw them watching and scowled, perhaps self-consciously, but kept coming. "God," Mikey murmured, expecting the worst. Laney had always been an asshole, and hardly a day went by that he didn't find something to complain about. There'd been a time when he was a match for the mighty Dennis Silva, and they'd been associates and competitors in a number of escapades over the years, but Laney had gone to seed since they came to this world—physically and spiritually. Where Silva thrived, Laney faltered, and being engineering officer of *Santa Catalina* was probably his last chance in Matt Reddy's Navy. Fortunately, he really was an excellent engineer and seemed to have found his place at last. His skill, if not personality, was sufficient to win the admiration of his division. Now, if only he wouldn't bitch so much . . .

"Skipper," Laney said. He didn't speak to Monk, but that was normal. He and *Santy Cat*'s XO didn't like each other very much.

"Laney," Russ acknowledged, then sighed. "What's the problem?"

Laney looked confused. "I, ah . . . nothin', Skipper. No

problems to report." He seemed to think about it. "I wouldn't mind if the bunkers were topped off. We've done a fair amount of high-speed steamin' lately." Russ and Monk both stared at him. "High speed" was kind of relative for their ship, her top end being barely twelve knots, with all the extra armor and armaments she carried. But she had to keep up with the carriers and sail/steam DDs, all of which could make fifteen when they had to. And with their position known to the enemy, they'd been burning a lot of fuel dodging Grik zeppelins at night. *Arracca*'s Mosquito Hawks tore the formations apart and kept them off their backs, but a few always got through and they had to evade their bombs. So far, there'd been very little damage. A few near misses were the worst. And there hadn't been any suicider bombs. *Maybe training their pilots had always been a Kurokawa thing. Or maybe even the Grik down here are training them for something else now.* Russ wondered. *At least the bombings at Grik City have stopped, giving Second Corps and Leedom's flyboys a break—not to mention maybe keeping the Grik from getting wise when First and Third Corps come down. And we're finally narrowing down where some of the Grik air bases must be. We'll get 'em soon.* Russ didn't understand why, but finding and eliminating those bases had suddenly—briefly, he was assured—become a lower priority than before. He shook his head, still staring at Laney. That their fuel state was all he could come up with to gripe about today was . . . phenomenal. Was it possible he was straightening out at last, finally looking beyond his own narrow priorities? Using his own real knowledge and skill to sort things out in his division without demanding someone *tell* him to? Could he have actually discovered constructive *initiative*? Russ hoped so.

Chief Bosun's Mate Stanley "Dobbin" Dobson stepped out of the pilothouse and it occurred to Russ that, except for Surgeon Commander Kathy McCoy and Major Simy Gutfeld of the 3rd Marines, every human aboard *Santy Cat* now stood together. And Kathy had only just left, possibly sensing Laney was coming. Laney had been ineffectually, somewhat sulkily, sweet on her for a long time. As far as anyone could tell, Kathy flat wasn't interested.

There'd once been a lot more humans on *Santa Catalina*, but most had gone to new construction and some were lost at Second Madras—along with James Ellis. *Not many of us left,* Russ reflected.

"The strike's coming in," Dobbin told them, nodding back at the pilothouse. "Bridge talker just got it from the wireless shack."

Russ raised his rare, precious binoculars and looked west, the glare of the setting sun making his eyes water through the glass. "Very well," he said. "Pass the word to the quartermaster. We'll ease closer to *Arracca* and take our usual station. Sway out the motor launch and have the recovery crew stand by."

"Aye, aye, sir." Dobbin stepped back in the pilothouse, relayed the command to the OOD, then walked briskly back past them, blowing his bosun's pipe. The loudspeaker crackled and the bridge talker's voice echoed through the ship: "All haans! Staan by for re-cov-ry maan-oo-vers! Line haanlers an' marksmen, report to you stations! Aan-tiair baat-ries, maan you guns!"

TF Bottle Cap had started hitting Sofesshk and the military and industrial centers beyond it every day. Whenever the airstrikes returned, every ship of the nearby screen prepared to recover flight crews as fast as they could, in case damaged planes or wounded pilots missed their landings on the carriers. There was little they could do for P-1s that went in the water, except send the motor launch and try to get their pilots out before the voracious flasher fish—or other things—did. Nancys always landed on the water, but if they were badly damaged, they'd set down alongside *Santa Catalina* so they wouldn't clog recovery operations around the carrier. *Santy Cat* still had her cargo booms aft and would take the crew aboard, then lift the damaged plane whether it would ever fly again or not. They could always salvage parts. And Kathy and her large medical team were there to treat injured flyers. Picked riflemen from the 3rd Marines prepared to discourage larger predators like gri-kakka. There were a bunch of those in the strait, big ones, and different from what they'd ever seen. But there was little evidence that rifles bothered them much. The machine guns did a better job, but were also manned in case some kind of enemy attack followed their own planes in. After the Battle of Mahe, they'd never assume anything again.

They prepared to do much the same each night, after the big boys, the PB-5D flying boats, went in. Clippers carried heavier bomb loads but were also more vulnerable to Grik defenses. Whereas the Nancys and Fleashooters went after specific targets they could see in daylight, the Clipper's job, for now, was area "terror" bombing of the Grik capital city—though still not Old Sofesshk across the river. So far, the Clippers had been amazingly lucky. Several had limped in to land alongside *Santy Cat* for quick repairs or gas, after losing fuel from punctured tanks, but they'd lost only two of the big planes and their crews. One, badly damaged and smoking, set down too far away for any ship's launch to reach before it burst into flames and sank. The other had simply disappeared. But Jumbo had eighteen now, with more arriving all the time, and a dozen dedicated to the bombing effort.

"This assignment's been a grind so far," Russ admitted, watching Fleashooters land on the carriers, tail hooks snagging the arresting cables and jerking the planes to a stop. They were always first, being the shortest on fuel. He lowered his binoculars. "But the raids are giving the Grik fits. Commodore Tassanna says her Nancys have blown the hell out of a lot of industrial sites they've identified along the river. Sunk some big ships too. Those new Grik BBs are tough customers, by the way. Heavier armor and fewer guns—but the fore and aft guns're *big* mothers, behind sponsons. Probably on barbettes. It'll be hot work with 'em when they come out, if our air doesn't get 'em all first. Tassanna thinks there's bound to be more ships and industry farther upriver, past that big-ass lake, and maybe up the other river running north. Maybe that's where all their transports are too. Planes still haven't seen much along those lines, but they're concentrating on what they *know* is there for now. With things so stirred up, Jumbo's afraid to risk Clippers on more long-range daylight scouts past all those rockets, and likely into more."

"The rockets are bad news," Monk agreed. "And as many as they shoot off, you'd think they'd run out."

"Nah. Damn things're so simple, they can probably

crank 'em out as fast as we make shells. It's almost humiliatin', they're so effective," Laney said, startling Russ and Monk that he'd taken an interest in something beyond his engineering spaces. He seemed to notice their surprise and continued, a little defensively. "They're just wooden tubes with fins an' black powder motors, for Chrissakes. A lot of 'em probably blow up when they light 'em. But I looked at one o' the early contact-fuse types we found at Grik City. Japs must've designed the motors an' fuses for 'em, but from what the flyboys say, the *new* fuses scare me most. It took a while for us to come up with good time fuses for our guns, an' *we* had some to look at." He shrugged. "Maybe they did too. But they gotta light 'em different with a rocket. Maybe there's a hole up the middle of the motor." He thought about it. "Or they redirect the exhaust at the nose somehow, when they shoot 'em off. Have to get a look at their launchers."

Russ and Monk looked at each other, then back at Laney. Russ took another drag on his cigarette. "Whatever they're doing, however they make 'em, those stupid rockets are getting too many of our planes and people. Only a few each day, but it adds up."

"Put enough musket balls, or whatever they use for shrapnel, in the air, and it doesn't matter if it's on the way up or down. You're liable to run into some sooner or later," Monk said. Russ watched the second-to-last Mosquito Hawk coming in astern of *Arracca*. By his count, most had made it back. When the pursuit ships were all down, the carrier would slow almost to a stop and begin recovering Nancys. Russ suddenly raised his binoculars again. The very last fighter descending toward *Arracca* was smoking, coming in too low and slow. Even as he watched, it struck the aft edge of *Arracca*'s flight deck and burst into flames. The smoldering engine tore away and cartwheeled forward until it snagged in the net rigged across the deck, even with the conn tower. The rest of the flaming wreckage dropped in the churning wake of the huge ship, the spreading fuel fire bright against the darkening sea.

"Damn," Monk murmured grimly into the silence on the bridgewing.

"Staan by the sea-plane re-cov-ry detail!" came the

voice on the loudspeaker again. "We got two hurt Naancys, gonna land alongside wit wounded aboard." They immediately felt the ship begin to slow. Russ stayed where he was. To interfere might be seen as a lack of confidence in his officer of the deck, and this had all become routine. He did glance up and spot the damaged planes as they left the circling formation above, headed for his ship. He also thought he heard the distant, higher rumble of the flock of PB-5Ds heading in for their night attack. Still flying from the Comoros Isles, they used the task force as a way point. *But if our friends can see us, so can the enemy,* Russ thought. His greatest fear was always that Grik zeppelins would hit them *now*, when they could still see their targets, and before *Arracca* could get sufficient pursuit ships turned around to respond to what the CAP or the task-force screen spotted coming in.

"I wonder," Laney said. Russ and Monk both looked at him again. "The transports," Laney continued. "What if they ain't got any? What if the Grik ain't comin' at all?"

"They're somewhere," Russ disagreed. "We haven't sunk near all their BBs. Like I said, they're tough. And they have other stuff too, that we already know of. More cruisers, at least." He looked back at the dying fire on the water. "Those are *offensive* weapons, and can't just sit in port an' take what we've been giving them forever. And their huge army's in the city now too. Probably safer, even in the rubble, than it was out in the open, but troops can't sit there and take it forever either." He scratched his chin. "No, they're still coming." His eyes hardened. "It's what they *do*, remember? How they do it or when, I don't know, but whatever happens, it's liable to be something we don't expect. Again."

The Palace of Vanished Gods
Old Sofesshk

Sofesshk was burning—again—and Esshk and the Chooser paced in their usual place, each alone with his thoughts, brooding and forming his own ideas of what must be done.

As had become the norm, the small enemy planes had come and done their worst in daylight, concentrating on factories and warships. Then the big planes followed with the night, raining fire indiscriminately on the teeming city across the river. The rocket batteries had small successes, occasionally damaging or destroying an enemy plane, but they did considerable harm to the city themselves, exploding on the ground, flying erratically and detonating where they struck, or sometimes the fascinating new fuses malfunctioned, until they fell from the sky. Even the scores of balls they blasted away when they worked perfectly had to come down somewhere, and many on the ground were injured or killed by those. But none of that compared to the destruction the enemy brought. Great sections of the city had become a charred, shattered wasteland, and more surged with living, spreading fires tonight, pulsing and shimmering, leaping and roaring, beneath the great pall of smoke they made. Esshk didn't much care about the toll among the city's Uul, too stupid to seek shelter or even flee in the right direction from the rampant, greedy flames. But the losses his Final Swarm, his *army*, was suffering, though still miniscule in comparison, were no longer trifling. And the damage to its carefully cultivated discipline and sense of purpose could not be measured.

"It is good that they do, but why does the enemy still avoid bombing Old Sofesshk?" the Chooser wondered aloud, breaking the silence.

"I have no idea," Esshk grated back. Then he considered. "Perhaps the previous Celestial Mother was right, in a way: they *dare* not harm it. Even they must know by now that it is the most ancient, holiest cradle of civilization. It's possible, I suppose, that she was only mistaken in her certainty that its protection extended to the Celestial City—and her—on the island the enemy calls Mada-gaas-gar."

"Perhaps," the Chooser reflected. "The tree prey—'Lemurians'—originated on Mada-gaas-gar. The Celestial Palace was an invasion of *their* most sacred home, and could not be holy in their eyes."

Esshk snorted frustration, confused thoughts mingling

with the vapor that sprayed from his snout. "As much as we learn about this enemy, we still know far too little. I must ask Kurokawa about that in the next dispatch."

The Chooser looked at him. "Indeed. And we must find our answers soon. To that and other things. Though they've suffered no personal harm, our esteemed Hij delegates from the various old houses of Old Sofesshk see the holocaust across the river and imagine it on their heads. Their respect for, and fear of, you remains strong, but they will not support us forever in the face of this." He waved across the water.

"They urge me constantly to do something about it," Esshk agreed sourly. "I argue with them—and myself," he confessed, "that, in the broader scope of things, it's just as well the enemy concentrates his attention here. The material loss in ships and facilities to make them—as well as all the other things the Final Swarm requires—has not been negligible, but is not crippling either. More ships and industry lie beyond the enemy's apparent sight." He took a deep, long breath and his crest lay flat. "But as you so often warn, I've waited too long for more and more troops to arrive from the far corners of the empire. We had enough to reconquer the Celestial City long ago. Only my ambition to sweep the enemy away entirely, in a single stroke, stayed my hand. Now, if the rumors of a battle beyond the Teetgak Forest, on the Plain of Gaughala, and General Ign's reports are to be believed, weakening the frontier with the Other Hunters to the south was yet another error." His crest rose again. "That, at least, I can remedy at once." He gazed at the Chooser, eyes flickering with reflected fire. "My army is suffering, and one way or another, the time has come to move it." He considered. "The threat in the south cannot be grave. We know little of the creatures dwelling there, only that they *are* hunters of similar races to our other enemies. But just as we cannot abide their frigid climate, they cannot possibly thrive in ours. The farther they come, the weaker they must be. They strike now only because *they* sense weakness. That is my fault," he confessed again. "Had I not stripped our warriors from the frontier to cross the strait or gather here, they would have never dared attack. So. We will turn *all* the troops we took from that land back, to face them at Soala, on the Ungee River." He hacked a laugh. "If any survive to reach that place, we will destroy them."

"And the rest of the Swarm?"

Esshk was quiet a moment. "That has become more problematic," he said. "No matter what we do, the enemy will see our movements and know when we are coming. All we can do is shorten the warning they have. Fortunately, *Lord Regent* Kurokawa"—he spoke the title with heavy sarcasm—"is preparing to amuse the majority of the enemy fleet in some final way. I do not know what he intends, but if we can coordinate our attack with his, all we should have to face is the smaller fleet that lies off the coast."

"Our great warships should make short work of it," the Chooser agreed, his enthusiasm growing.

"Indeed. But that is the dilemma as well. Our transports—and the Swarm they will carry—cannot fly across the strait. Not only are they dreadfully slow; they are fragile as eggs. We built them in their hundreds, using designs of the earliest human prey we overcame because of their simplicity, but also in the certainty we would strike with surprise. Now we cannot even gather them here, let alone load them, without giving the enemy air attacks *days* to destroy them, lined up, immobile. We must find another way."

"Send our fleet to destroy the enemy! Then they could not harm our transports."

"Sadly, Lord Chooser, I do not think that will work. If we amassed all our warships, making a larger fleet than they can imagine, the enemy will see that too. They will attack it, even sink some of it, and when it sails, what will the enemy do?"

"They will die!"

Esshk shook his head. "No. They will *continue* to attack from the air, sinking more and more, while avoiding direct ship-to-ship combat. Our fleet, powerful as it is, cannot match their speed. Nor can it reconquer the Celestial City, or any land, by itself. We would lose many ships to no purpose—without the *lure* of the transports to make the enemy oppose us directly!"

"But you just said—"

"That we cannot assemble the transports or the Swarm where they can see it, and we will not." Esshk clacked his toe claws on the burnished stone walkway decisively. "Beginning this very night, we will start to disperse the Final Swarm away from New Sofesshk. It will be arranged by full crews and companies appropriate to the capacity of the transports, and each detachment will march toward where a specific vessel lies hidden. It will be difficult to coordinate," he conceded, "and there will be much confusion, but I see no other choice."

"But, Lord Regent Champion! Such a thing has never been attempted! The transports are scattered far and wide! To organize something so complex, so . . . *independent*, without proper leadership for the hundreds of detachments you describe . . ." The Chooser was struck speechless.

"It will be even more complex than you yet know," Esshk said. "The detachments detailed to transports across the river must bring them here under cover of darkness. And some of those are hidden *quite* far away. Yet those troops might have the easiest task, able to use the water to reach here—as long as they're not seen by day. Others detailed to fetch transports from this side of the river will have to carry them."

The Chooser finally found his voice. "*Carry* . . . But why? And to what point?"

"You've seen the transports. Their full complement is perfectly able to carry them if they must. Slowly, I admit, and the terrain might pose difficulties, but for whatever reason, the enemy is clearly reluctant to attack Old Sofesshk. We will use that to our advantage in three ways. First, we will stage our transports here, on *land*, with their crews and troops ready to rush them to the water and move with the fleet at a moment's notice. The enemy will know we gather our battle fleet, but will not know what to make of our intentions. When it sails, probably at night, it will do so in company with the transports, quickly launched all at once, and the enemy cannot know they're coming until dawn reveals our entire force already in the strait. We may lose many transports then," he said, "to air attacks, most likely. But they will remain dispersed, difficult targets. More than enough will get through, and the enemy fleet will *have* to fight. Second, it is time to fully involve our 'loyal' Hij in the war effort. They and their servant Uul will help hide the transports in the city, covering them from view from the air, and helping feed and quarter the troops who must also not be seen. Those who object . . . will wish they had not."

The Chooser's crest was fixed in place but his tail plumage flared in admiration. "And so the *third* thing you accomplish is total control, far more quickly that we ever planned! And with the Swarm—*your* devoted army—around you, pleased to be out from under the bombing, glad to be doing something, and enraptured by the comforts of Old Sofesshk that *you* granted them, no one can possibly oppose us." He picked at something between his teeth with a painted claw. "But again, what you envision will take even *more* time."

"True, but not as much as you believe. My army is quite different, you know, and I have every confidence the detachments will accomplish their tasks. In the meantime, the enemy will continue bombing across the river, thinking they accomplish much, when all they really do is feed our army!" He snorted again in satisfaction. "It is unfortunate, in a way," he reflected, "that when all is done, most of the wondrous army we have made will have to be destroyed if we mean to remake the world, as we must."

"Indeed," the Chooser agreed. "But I've little doubt that battle will accomplish that end. Some survivors may join us in ruling the new empire as regents, I suppose. We will need new ones, you know. But those we do not need will end with the satisfaction of what they helped achieve."

Esshk's eye caught movement near the entryway to the palace and he was surprised to see the new Celestial Mother herself venturing out to view the fire across the river. Her relatively small entourage consisted of the few remaining sisters Esshk rescued that she hadn't been forced to fight to the death. None could ever take her place now; only hatchlings of her body could do that. But her sisters would always have status at court, and only breed with the finest Hij. And as long as the Celestial Mother lived, they'd stay in the luxury of the palace. For that reason, she couldn't have better bodyguards, and that was what they were training for. Their training, like hers, was far from complete, however, and though no one could actually say no if the Celestial Mother chose to take a stroll, Esshk was stunned that she'd exercised the will to override the strong objections she must've faced. He paced quickly toward the group of females.

"Giver of Life," he greeted her humbly. "You should not be out here. Danger lurks from the sky and . . ." He glanced around. "Other directions." She turned to him and regarded him, her large eyes and coppery plumage also reflecting the distant flames. She was already larger than she'd been at the time of her elevation, practically obese even compared to her sisters. *Ripe for breeding,* Esshk thought. He couldn't help himself. The faintest scent surrounded her, signaling she'd soon be ready. But Esshk could control himself. *He* could wait. That smell would be enough to drive any Uul mad, however, and he glanced around again.

"My Lord Regent Champion," she said. "Please explain. Why does fire fall from the sky?"

"You have no reason to concern yourself with such things."

"I want to know. Is that not reason enough?"

Esshk was taken aback. *Already so sharp, so innately imposing! Her mother's blood runs thick in her.* "Of course," he finally replied.

"Is it a natural thing? My tutors say that fire can spout from the ground beneath us. Can it also fall from the sky?" She closed her eyes. "I seem to recall another time, before I came to this place, when there was much fire. Much fear. But the memory is elusive."

Esshk was surprised again. Few females elevated at her age could remember anything before the rites and their education began. "You know the purpose, the principles underlying the Great Hunt?" he asked.

"Of course. We pursue prey across the world until it is all our own. When that day comes and all prey are vanquished at last, the Vanished Gods will return and smile upon us. A new time, like that which was lost, will begin."

"Yes. Well, occasionally, in the course of the hunt, we encounter prey that hunts us in return. Worthy prey, but also hunters in their own right. They seek to deny us our destiny and must be destroyed. Such contests between more equal hunters are called wars. So in that sense, yes, what you see is a natural thing, just as is the fire that spouts from the earth."

She waved at the burning city. "And such as they have poured fire upon us?"

"Yes. They have been . . . most obstinate."

"Will they not join the hunt? Tie their destiny to ours?"

"No, Giver of Life." Now wasn't the time for a history lesson, to describe why this particular prey would never do that, why such things had never really worked. "They seek to destroy us entirely."

"But . . ." The young Celestial Mother rapidly licked her bright, fresh teeth. "You will not let them?"

"Never fear. I will personally lead your Final Swarm to bring them down."

CHAPTER 17

USS* Donaghey *(DD-2)
Mid-Atlantic
November 20, 1944

"Goddamn snakes are *everywhere*!" Lieutenant (jg) Wendel "Smitty" Smith snapped with a grimace and a noticeable quaver in his voice as his shore party clambered up the ship's side and reported to Captain Garrett. *Donaghey* and *Matarife* had enjoyed fine weather for another week and a half, pleasantly slanting northwest while they repaired the damage they'd inflicted on each other, but the southern edge of a fierce tropical storm finally caught them. It sped them along amazingly for a while, but eventually hammered them severely in exchange. *Matarife*'s foremast survived, though not without some very concerning sounds and a tendency to lean alarmingly with the wind. Only the heavy hawsers they'd rigged had saved it, and possibly the ship. She'd labored particularly hard as well, opening seams in her bow and stern, both of which had taken a beating in the fight. As she took on water, she worked ever harder and Lieutenant Mak was finally forced to set his prisoners pumping to relieve his exhausted crew. To his surprise, they'd been happy to help in spite of their fear of their captors. Then again, they'd been locked in the hold up to that point—with an immediate appreciation of the amount of water the ship was taking, and the peril they were in—and were anxious to lend a hand to save themselves.

When the storm swept past and the two ships came within hailing distance, Greg decided they must stop and make more concerted repairs if they didn't want to abandon their prize. Raising an active, smoky Martinique Island with a clear dawn, they'd approached the eastern shore with care. In their world, Martinique had been French, and it was possible the League had already occupied it. There'd been no sign of anyone as they approached, however, and all they saw as they entered a picturesque bay on the northeast coast and dropped anchor at last was a jagged, mountainous isle covered in dense forest. Two of the mountains sullenly smoldered, but there was no recent evidence of more boisterous behavior.

"God, I *hate* snakes," Smitty continued. "I was raised in Baltimore and never even *saw* one from then till now, an' they still give me the willies. Must've seen too many jungle pictures an' Westerns, I guess. Always bitin' somebody or squeezin' 'em to death. Anyway"—he nodded at the shore a hundred yards away—"they're thick as maggots workin' in meat over there!"

Greg Garrett could sympathize with Smitty's discomfort. He'd seen snakes, big timber rattlers, and didn't like them any more than his gunnery officer. And there hadn't been any to speak of within the Malay barrier, or almost anywhere else they'd been. Too many things on this world would gulp a snake like a worm.

"An' lizards!" Bosun Jenaar-Laan added emphatically, blinking yellow-green eyes. "Big as skuggiks, but with haands, an' runnin' on two legs. They look laak little spiky-back Griks, with scaly fish bodies." He grinned at Smitty. "Least they eat the snakes. I seen one snaatch up a snake an' eat it, even while gettin' bit."

"Immune to the poison," Surgeon Sori said with interest, having joined them with so many others, anxious to hear what lay onshore. "Or the scales protect them."

"You saw nothing else?" Greg asked. "No sign that *anyone* might be around?"

"Nothin', Skipper," Smitty confirmed. "No fire pits or chafing marks on trees near shore where a boat might've tied up. Not even a beer can. I bet the snakes keep 'em away," he added significantly.

"Or the smoking mountains," Sori speculated. There were a lot of *those*, with a long history of violent activity, where he came from. The worst recent example had been Talaud Island, but several volcanoes on Jaava and Sumatra always seemed on the verge of "pulling a Talaud." "We know the Doms an' new Amer-i-caans sail this far."

"As has the Republic," Leutnant Koor-Susk defended, though it had been forty years or more since any of his people came here. The final known visit was made by a swift little topsail schooner, exploring beyond St. Helena. No one knew if she'd run into Doms, a NUS ship, or someone else, but whoever it was had fired on her, probably to induce her to heave to. She ran instead, easily leaving her lumbering pursuer in her wake. No one had returned since—till now—and all depictions of shores beyond the easternmost windward isles of the Caribbean were based on charts older than memory, or brought to the Republic by SMS *Amerika*.

"They probably have more important islands—to them—to fight over," Greg speculated, referring to the NUS and Dominion. "Any outpost this far out would be too hard for either to protect." He snorted. "I bet they do come to the west side of the island from time to time, just to tip over each other's flags and plant their own." That produced a few chuckles. "I'm sorry, Smitty," he continued. "Snakes or not, we need to get *Matarife* and *Donaghey* squared away. That means stopping the prize's leaks, if we can get at 'em, and replacing her lower foremast, if there're suitable trees ashore. We also need water and fresh food of some kind—if, again"—he grinned—"there's anything besides snakes and lizards."

Repairs came first, of course, but though provisions had held up well (there was plenty of salt meat, fish, biscuit, and dried polta fruit), they'd grown less appetizing with every mile. And *Matarife*'s stores weren't even considered edible by *Donaghey*'s crew. "I *hope* we can count on the NUS for help with more comprehensive repairs and such," Greg said, "but all our information about them comes through Fred's and Kari's eyes. How free have they been to meet with more than just a few handlers? We have no idea. The NUS could be worse than the Doms for all we really know, so we have to be ready to fight *whoever* we come across when we continue west. We may not get another chance to do the work we need." He frowned. "That said, it's about time to start transmitting on Fred's frequency. Starting tomorrow, we will. We likely won't hear back for a while; Fred's set is a short-range job, out of a Nancy, but he should hear us." *As may the League,* he added darkly to himself.

Greg hated the Grik. They were nightmarish monsters that'd killed a lot of people he cared about. The Doms were just as bad, and probably even more evil from a moral standpoint. But of all their adversaries in this goofed-up world, Greg Garrett probably despised the League most of all. He considered the Grik to be predators, pure and simple: murderous reptilian jackals with an almost hivelike pack mentality. Intellectually, he knew that was a simplistic view. There was more to it than that, and from what he understood, their leadership was pretty perverted. Maybe General Halik and Hij Geerki had proven even Grik could learn to behave, to rise above what they'd been conditioned to be, but, generally, Grik remained dangerous animals as far as he was concerned—like snakes. They were a plague, a pestilence, vermin that would tear you apart and eat you. They were easy to hate.

The Doms had *descended* to embrace a barbarism equal to the Grik, and were a culture that placed no more value on life. But Greg's Dom prisoners were people, ordinary seamen, impossible to hate. They'd done as they were told, as they'd been conditioned to do, fully believing it was God's will. And even those who fired into his ship after receiving mercy did so at the command of their "evil leadership": a possibly deranged, wounded officer. The impression he got now, reinforced by Mak's report of their prisoners' behavior during the storm, and the fact no Blood Priests were taken alive, despite spending the battle belowdecks—was they were more afraid of what their own people would do to them for having been taken, than of their "demon" captors.

The young midshipman had ridden out the storm aboard *Donaghey*, and though they still couldn't communicate with him, the boy seemed little more than a terrified child. Greg knew what Doms were capable of, what they'd done elsewhere and how they treated *their* prisoners. He didn't doubt they were the enemy and they were bad. But so far, *Matarife* embodied his entire personal experience with them, and in spite of Sammy and the others he'd lost, he hadn't come to *hate* the Doms like the Grik—or the League.

A submarine belonging to the League of Tripoli had sunk two Allied ships without warning or mercy, ships crammed with people he knew and supplies desperately needed to fight the Grik. The League, represented by *Savoie*, also basically incarcerated *Donaghey* and prevented the Republic from joining the war against the Grik on schedule. *Savoie* then destroyed *Amerika*, also packed with what Greg considered his people, including Adar and Sandra Reddy. Adding insult to injury, the League then gave *Savoie* and her prisoners to Hisashi Kurokawa, arguably the Allies' most uniquely dangerous enemy of all. So despite the fact they weren't technically at war with the League, Greg hated it—and certainly *felt* at war with it.

Then, as if his dark thoughts had summoned the devil in his heart, a cry came from the masthead: "On deck! A ship! A *steamer*, baar-een one two seero! Is hull down, but comin' faast. About eighteen tous-aand tails—I mean, yaads!"

Greg whipped his telescope to his eye but saw nothing over the choppy sea beyond the placid little bay. Tucking the glass in his waistband, he scrambled up the ratlines to the maintop, followed by Jenaar–Laan. There he paused and looked again.

"No sails," he gasped significantly at the Bosun, who wasn't even breathing hard. "A dedicated steamer, for sure." He stared harder, trying to improve the focus of his glass. Then his heart quickened. The thing *looked* like an old British destroyer, a four-stacker like *Walker*, but with a raised fo'c'sle. Gray smoke streamed downwind, so it was an oil burner. A *Brit* oil burner. *What if . . . ?* Then it dawned on him. "Crap," he said sharply. "The Spanish Alsedos look like that, and there's Spaniards in the League. No way to tell if it's the same ship *Matarife* met, but it's likely." He paused. "Or is it? If so, where'd she go between then and now? I wonder what her range is. Maybe the Doms met her tender or some other ship coming to take possession of Martinique. Either way . . ."

A furious determination seized him. "Come on," he said, and he and Chief Laan slid down the backstays together and Greg started barking orders as soon as he hit the deck. "Let our anchor cable out another ten fathoms," he said, looking at the prize, "and stand by to pass a line from our stern to *Matarife*'s hawse. We'll take it in until her bowsprit stands right over our taffrail. In the meantime, I want a boat to carry an anchor out from the prize's stern with a spring in the cable to bring her around parallel with the beach, nose to tail with us. See?" He looked at Smitty. "Back in your boat. I want cables secured to shore. The tide'll soon start to ebb, and I want us to maintain position when it does."

Smitty glanced nervously at the beach and nodded. "Aye, aye, sir."

"What will you do?" Tribune Pol-Heena asked.

Greg turned to him. "I'm pretty sure that's a League DD out there, coming this way. If my memory of her class serves, she's a little smaller than *Walker* but with similar armament." Pol's eyes went wide and there was an explosion of excited chatter.

"Silence fore an' aaft!" Laan roared.

"Maybe she hasn't seen us yet, with the island behind, but she will soon enough. And I think she's coming in the bay, anyway." Greg snorted ironically. "We may have to fight *before* we sail west."

Pol's eyes went even wider, if that was possible. "How can we?" he demanded. "It is said your *Walker* has destroyed *hundreds* of Grik ships—vessels not so different from ours. And you just told us the intruder is not unlike her in its capabilities. Surely we must try to talk to them, even perhaps . . . contemplate surrender?"

Greg glared at Pol-Heena, amazed. "You're kidding, right?" he snapped, voice rising. "I hope to *God* I didn't trade Bekiaa for a pack of cowards. If that's really who's coming in, I *will not* be a 'guest' of the goddamn League again. Do I make myself clear? And who's to say, after what they did to Lady Sandra and Chairman Adar, they won't just give us to the Doms? No, sir. You'll find your courage, Tribune, and obey my orders as you swore to do, or I'll throw you over the side myself. Is that understood?"

"Ah . . . yes, of course. I didn't mean . . ."

Greg spun to face Lieutenant Haana-Lin-Naar. "Get all your Marines over to *Matarife* as quick as you can and acquaint Lieutenant Mak with the situation. He'll need you, and we don't have much time at all. I'll try to send more of our topmen."

"Aye, sur. But what *is* the situation? What're we gonna do?"

Greg smiled grimly and quickly laid out the plan that had suddenly bloomed, fully formed, in his mind. It was a long shot, and depended on a number of things falling their way, but it was probably the only chance they had. "We'll wait until we're absolutely certain she's a Leaguer—and nobody does anything until I give the command," he stressed. "But, fortunately, one Spanish word I'm pretty sure of is *ayuda*. It means 'help.'"

Antúnez was indeed an Alsedo class destroyer, as Greg Garrett guessed, renamed in honor of a nationalist officer who'd supported the coup ushering Spain into the fascist alliance with Italy and France. She was 283 feet long, displaced 1,300 tons fully loaded, and was quite similar to USS *Walker* in performance, armament, and even general form. The most pronounced differences were her raised fo'c'sle, lack of a large aft deckhouse, and that her aft three funnels actually seemed to decrease in height. Those, and a lack of the generally battered appearance *Walker* seemed doomed to wear despite her frequent repairs, set her quite apart. And, of course, in addition to the naval jack of nationalist Spain, she also streamed the fascist banner of the Confédértion États Souverains, which had carried over to this world as the flag of the League of Tripoli.

Capitan de Cobeta Francisco Abuello Falto stared out the bridge windows of his ship, hands clasped behind his back, his pink, fresh-shaved face festooned with tiny pieces of bloody tissue. Occasionally, the breeze took one and a seaman quickly tracked it down. Capitan Abuello Falto didn't like to see the little specks again after his steward applied them. Ahead lay Galion Bay, smaller on this world than his charts depicted, but better protected. It would make a fine anchorage for a League station in the western hemisphere one day. Beyond the bay lay the rugged, heavily forested island of Martinique, and Abuello Falto was entranced by its beauty, despite the smoldering mountains. He was deathly afraid of volcanoes for some reason, though he'd never seen one erupt. Perhaps he was haunted by childhood tales. The focus of his attention at present, however, was the two square-rigged ships moored in the bay.

"The one is certainly the Dominion *fragata* that rendezvoused with that Italian *idiota*, Contrammiraglio Oriani, at Ascension, Capitan," said Teniente Casales Padilla, the destroyer's executive officer, gazing through binoculars.

"And the other?" Abuello Falto asked mildly.

"She *must* be the Allied/American *fragata* we were sent to intercept as she crossed the Atlantic. She's exactly as described, and flies the Old World flag of the Estados Unidos, with its many stars and stripes"—he coughed with amusement—"and the Dominion rag with its heretical cross flies above it!"

"An end to our primary mission, then," Abuello Falto said with evident relief. "Now we can get on with the rest." He hadn't relished returning empty-handed, which he'd begun to fear would happen. *Donaghey* was a very small ship on a vast ocean, after all, and they'd had only the vaguest notion of her course. He was slightly disappointed, however. Catching the elusive American ship himself, after it so humiliated that French royalist, Laborde, would've been delicious. And of course there was a pang of queasiness over how *Donaghey*'s crew had probably already met their end. He'd heard tales of Dominion Blood Priests. . . . He would've treated the *Americanos* and their *hombres simios* properly, with as much courtesy as he could. It was the least he could do—before turning them over to Oriani and his OVRA reptiles. OVRA had been the Italian Organization for Vigilance and Repression of Antifascism and had become the chief party enforcement arm of the League on this world. Each national faction retained its own military intelligence branch, which often competed with or even targeted the others. The OVRA had been granted exceptional powers by every member, understanding there had to be a supreme, coordinating authority when it came to quashing dissident elements and compiling intelligence. And, sadly, given the way this cruel world turned, the OVRA used methods not terribly distinct from those attributed to the Dominion when it came to extracting information. He supposed they had little choice.

"What do you make of them, Alferez?" the captain asked the young ensign on the starboard bridgewing in a louder voice. Alferez Tomas Perez Moles wasn't quite twenty, and was slightly built with blond hair and a fair complexion. He'd been a mere first-year officer cadet when the entire Confederation task force suddenly found itself on this . . . different Earth. Since then, he'd progressed rapidly, and Abuello Falto had high hopes for him. He was an excellent seaman and the men respected him despite his youth. If he had a single flaw, it was perhaps a lack of fervency for League ideals. But that might change, and avoiding politics was always best for younger officers.

Tomas was also straining his eyes through a pair of binoculars, trying to make out details of the ships now less than 1,200 meters away. "*Matarife* seems to have suffered worse than the American. Both are torn by battle and storm, but though the American seems little hurt, *Matarife* was clearly raked. Her bows have been dreadfully abused and she must've lost her foremast. It's been crudely repaired."

"Damage consistent with eagerness to close with the enemy and board," Abuello Falto murmured, nodding. "That's how they took her, no doubt. *Donaghey*'s crew was not reputed to be large. What else do you see?" he called.

"A signal for assistance," Tomas replied. "But all the cannon on both ships are run out, and pointing . . . generally at *us* as we approach," he added with a concerned glance at his captain. Abuello Falto stepped out on the wing and raised his own binoculars.

"She has suffered cruelly indeed," he agreed. "Do not mind the guns, Alferez. Why should they threaten us? We are now allies of the Dominion, are we not?" He said the last with a grimace, still dwelling on the Blood Priests. He shook his head. "It's in the nature of primitive ships of that sort that all their guns point to the side. There's nothing they can do about it. Fear not. No doubt the guns are run out to air the deck and make room for repairs. And look: there are hoses discharging water through the gunports, and they toss debris through them as well. Look again, Alferez, they wave! They welcome us!" He paused and considered. "Though there *are* dreadfully few of them. The fighting must have been horrific. It's a wonder they managed to sail both ships, and through a storm as well." He lowered the binoculars at last. "Of course they request assistance. We will stand in and render it."

Antúnez slowed and crept into the anchorage. The entrance was guarded by dangerous reefs, and she took her time. All the while, Tomas continued to study the ships, still slightly on edge despite his captain's assurance. And his eyes kept going back to the guns. Their size—the Americans' looked to be 130 mm or so, and there were twelve of them to a side, not counting a few lighter ones on the main deck. If anything, *Matarife*'s looked even bigger: sixteen on the gundeck and eight smaller ones above. At least thirty-six guns were pointed at them, all larger than the three 102 mm guns in *Antúnez*'s main battery. Granted, his ship's weapons were far superior—at a distance—but they were getting very, very close. And though all *Antúnez*'s weapons were manned, none were trained out, their crews lounging around them unconcerned. He squinted. Was it just his imagination, or did it seem like all those guns were somehow . . . tracking *Antúnez*? Continually shifting, ever so slightly, to adjust their aim? He hesitated to mention it because he couldn't see anyone moving them, past the gunports, and Capitan Abuello Falto seemed so sure. It *had* to be his imagination. He refocused on the deck.

The capitan was certainly right that there were very few people in view. Only a couple still watched their approach as *Antúnez* made a leisurely turn to come alongside, now less than a hundred meters distant. They were officers, apparently, judging by the old-fashioned hats on their heads. One wore a coat, but the other was in shirtsleeves, as though he'd been helping with the work. That seemed odd. Dominion officers wouldn't stoop to manual labor any more than his officers would. And something else struck him. Every single man working on the ships appeared to have his back turned and his head covered, and almost seemed to be . . . crouching a bit. All he could see over the ship's bulwarks was their shoulders and heads. Then he noticed the strangest thing of all: not a single soul was aloft, working on the rigging.

"All stop," came the order within the pilothouse. "Drop anchor. Prepare the launch."

"Capitan," he said hesitantly, his voice strengthening as conviction grew. "Capitan, something is wrong."

The anchor splashed and Capitan Abuello Falto looked at him questioningly. Then Tomas saw his eyes widen in stunned disbelief, and he turned just in time to see the Dom flags on both ships suddenly stream away and fall into the bay, their halyards slashed. Instantly, the Stars and Stripes raced to the top of *Matarife*'s mainmast.

"*Surrendero*!" cried the harsh, determined voice of one of the officers through a speaking trumpet. "Surrender *now*, damn it! Touch a gun and we open fire!"

The capitan said nothing, utterly frozen where he stood. A heartbeat later, Teniente Casales Padilla raced to the aft bulkhead and activated the general alarm. "Battle stations! Battle stations! Action starboard. All guns, commence firing!" he shouted over the shipwide circuit, his voice thundering outside and screeching with feedback.

Capitan Abuello Falto blinked, then rushed to push his executive officer away. "No!" he shouted over the raucous alarm as he reached for the switch. "It's *too late*—we're too close! We must surrender, even as we send a distress signal. We will not be—" He never finished. One of the ship's two 47 mm antiaircraft guns spoke, its distinctive voice reaching them over the noise. Perhaps its crew had been as skeptical as Tomas, or maybe they were simply better trained, more prepared than others. And their weapon was easier to bring to bear than the rest of the ship's arsenal, in any event. Just as the *capitan* already knew, however, resistance was pointless, and his XO's reaction, though perhaps laudable, had doomed his ship.

No more than six or seven 47 mm shells exploded against *Donaghey*'s sides. None penetrated her stout timbers, but each did as much surface damage as *Matarife*'s roundshot—before *Donaghey*'s twelve portside eighteen-pounders fired as one, double charged and double shotted. Such a load didn't lend itself to accuracy, and the added recoil strained the gun's breechings and heaved *Donaghey* over several degrees. At little more than a hundred yards, however, hardly a shot could miss. A couple did, both hooking into the sea, while at least twenty struck savagely home, tearing gaping holes through the destroyer's thin sides like BBs through a beer can. One shot swept so close by Tomas's head, the pressure wave sent him staggering and left him momentarily stunned. Not so much that he didn't see the same ball spatter both Capitan Abuello Falto and Teniente Casales Padilla all over the aft bulkhead, gouge its way through the equipment there, and punch out through the port side of the pilothouse. The hellish thunder of impacts ended—for almost three seconds—before *Matarife*'s rolling broadside, carefully aimed by *Donaghey*'s Marines and everyone else she could spare, continued tearing *Antúnez* apart. A great explosion shook the ship, and Tomas suspected a boiler had blown. Screams tore forward through a gush of steam, and the 47 mm went silent as the sound of small arms joined the cannonade. Two shots, in quick succession, blasted through the aft part of the bridge where the ship's electronic gear, her sonar, and radios were stationed. The alarm bell instantly fell silent, but that just made the other sounds more intense.

Matarife's cannon kept firing, quite deliberately, and *Antúnez* shook with each impact. It already seemed an eternity since Tomas called for his captain's attention, but he realized this horror had taken only seconds to engulf them. *Donaghey* hadn't even finished reloading yet. Trying the blood-sprayed shipwide circuit, the microphone dangling from a bundle of twisted electrical conduits, he found it dead. Snatching a dented speaking trumpet from the deck, he staggered out on the bridgewing, expecting a bullet or cannonball to find him at any moment. Nothing came at him. The forward gun crew was all either dead or hiding behind the gun mount. And as long as they made no effort to continue traversing their weapon, no one shot at them. He looked aft. Little was visible through the smoke, but for the first time he realized the ship was already listing to starboard. *The boiler,* he thought. *Probably tore out the bottom. And as she leans, more water comes through holes in the hull, open portholes . . .* With a chill, he considered the hungry denizens in the water. Raising the speaking trumpet, he shouted aft through the turmoil. "Cease firing! Prepare the rafts and lifeboats!" They couldn't fight and they couldn't run. Only one alternative remained. "Stand by to abandon ship!"

"My God," Greg Garret murmured, watching the Alsedo lean farther onto her starboard side. What had been a proud, trim fighting ship just moments before was already a sinking wreck. "Cease firing! Bring the boats around." All *Donaghey*'s and *Matarife*'s boats had been secured on the landward sides of the ships. 'Cats quickly jumped in them and took in their lines, grabbing oars. The motor launch was already speeding around *Donaghey*'s bow with a couple of armed Lemurians aboard. Two of the destroyer's boats splashed into the sea, and a raft fell on top of one of them. It was chaos over there, Greg realized, and men were going to die in their panic to save themselves. "Be careful!" he called to his boats through the trumpet. "Don't let them swamp you!" More boats were coming around *Matarife* and there'd be more than enough for everyone on the sinking ship, but only if they got there in time and her people could control themselves.

"Well done," came a high-pitched voice behind him, sounding quite satisfied. Greg turned, surprised, and there was the little Dom midshipman—holding a rifle pointed at Greg's belly. The weapon looked huge in his hands, but steady as a rock, and the boy shrugged. "One of your demons was kind enough to unlock my door before the action, just in case. I suppose she feared I might drown if things went poorly." He shrugged again. "I killed her with my dirk and took this." He raised the rifle slightly. "No one ever searched me for weapons, you know. How careless of you."

Marines were quickly gathering now, pointing their rifles at the boy, shouting for him to drop his. Greg held up his hand to quiet them and took a deep breath, somehow not surprised the boy spoke English after all. "Why do you say 'well done'? My impression was that you and the League are friends now."

The boy snorted. "Hardly friends. They're weak, like you, and unknown to the God of this world. That may change," he added thoughtfully, "but for now they're merely useful tools." He smiled. "Far more so after what you just did."

"You just said they're weak. Why would that benefit you?"

"Weak in spirit, not in arms. You saw their ship and knew what it was capable of. That's why you did as you did. It was your only hope. But such a convenient encounter will be difficult to arrange again and they have *many* more ships, some quite near." He nodded at the Alsedo, now lying on her beam ends. "And that was probably the least capable of them all."

"Then what makes you think they'll be your tools and not the other way around?"

"As I said, they're weak. They're afraid of this world and do not possess the spiritual strength to survive—without our guidance. Some even know that already."

Greg felt a chill, imagining the result of a marriage between League fascism and technology and Dom fanaticism.

"You and I, however, will not live to see it," the boy continued. "You've served our purposes well today. Your act will bring the League even closer to us, closer to God—susceptible to direction and our understanding of His will." His smile turned almost blissful, lighting his childish face. "I must now do *my* part." Reaching up with his small thumb, he cocked the hammer back. Instantly, his head exploded when at least two rifles fired at once. The rifle clattered to the deck, followed by the thump of the corpse, its legs kicking spastically.

For a long moment, Greg could only stare. "Talk about demons," he whispered. "Somebody throw that rotten, twisted little shit over the side. Damn!" he said emphatically, his skin crawling with horror and relief. "I'm gonna have *nightmares* about that punk."

"Which was probably his intent," Pol-Heena said gravely, stepping forward. The Allin-Silva rifle in his hand wisped smoke from the muzzle as he approached.

Greg nodded at him, blinking a mixture of apology and

appreciation. It had rattled him more than he could show, that a seemingly innocent little boy could not only try to kill him, but be so filled with evil. "Most likely. What a creep. All right," he said, raising his voice, "let's get those people out of the water!"

Antúnez lay on her side for half an hour, her undamaged port side holding air long enough for her people to gather on her hull and calm to return. Some had jumped into the sea and not many of those survived. The few who did were plucked out almost as quickly as they hit the water and some had some ugly bites. The blue-gold flashies were just as attentive to the dinner bell as their cousins in other seas. No doubt some men had been trapped below, and there was nothing they could do for them, but the boats brought away more than fifty of her eighty-four officers and men. Outwardly deserted, *Antúnez* finally blew out her air in a long, dying shriek, settling by the stern on her side. Nothing was left above the surface but a spread of oil and floating debris. That was just as well. Somebody would find her eventually, running up on her if nothing else, but Greg would've had to blast her superstructure and masts apart if they'd been left sticking up. The sole surviving bridge officer was a blond ensign, the looped strand of braid on his left coat sleeve torn and dangling. His young, blood-spattered face was suffused with fury when he was brought before Captain Garrett.

"Do you have any idea what you have done?" he seethed, perfectly understandable but with a heavy accent. "How dare you! You killed half my crew. War, sir! There will be *war* after this! We will be avenged."

"Are you finished?" Greg demanded harshly. "How dare *you* expect any less? *You* fired on us *first* and we defended ourselves. This after your goddamn League committed act after act of war against *us*, including sinking a hospital ship full of helpless wounded. Spare me the pretense of innocent outrage."

The young officer paused. It was pointless to deny that *Antúnez* opened the action, not that it would matter, and he was apparently aware of the events Greg cited and unable to find an argument. Perhaps a touch of shame even darted across his face? It firmed again, however, and he stood straighter. "I am Alferez—Ensign—Tomas Perez Mole, the senior surviving officer of the Nationalist Spanish destroyer *Antúnez*. Who do I have the . . . honor of addressing?"

"Captain Greg Garrett, United States Navy, commanding the American Navy Clan ship USS *Donaghey* for the United Homes."

"I cannot speak to the allegations you make," Tomas said stiffly. "I am merely a junior officer in a single ship and have little knowledge of events elsewhere, nor can I—or my crew," he stressed, "speak to the policies of my government. But for our present purposes, regardless who fired first—I cannot say for certain who did so," he qualified, glancing slightly away, unwilling to openly concede the point, "the fact remains that you sank my ship and killed many of her people." He glanced at his crew, gathered in *Donaghey*'s waist under guard, and Greg looked at them too. Many seemed angry; others subdued. Some were wounded, and Sori and his mates were attempting to examine them. Most who could shied away, though not with the terrified expressions of the Doms. Their hesitation seemed more like a desire not to accept help from an enemy. Or was it a racial response? "We are your prisoners," Tomas stated simply. "What are your intentions?"

For the first time, Greg seemed unsure of himself and unconsciously swept a hand across his face. "I can't leave you here," he began, noting Tomas's sudden hopeful expression when he realized that he and his people wouldn't simply be killed. *Stupid kid,* he thought. *Why would we rescue them, just to bump 'em off?* Then he saw belated disappointment touch the ensign's face. Clearly he'd expected a quick rescue, if they were marooned, by other League ships. "Besides being a dumb move on my part, I'm told there're deadly snakes all over the place," he expanded. He looked at *Matarife*. "I guess we ought to cram you aboard her. There're already a couple hundred Doms in her. Some are even helping out." His face darkened. "Not sure that's a good idea. We had one of their midshipmen aboard, only a little kid, and he just tried to kill me—

after murdering one of my Marines." He looked thoughtful. "I bet your leaders would be interested to know how he saw the relationship between his country and yours."

"I . . ." Tomas hesitated, his face genuinely concerned. "I'd much prefer that my men not be mingled with Dominion sailors."

"Yeah," Greg said, thinking. "That might be awkward," he added, for reasons of his own. "I guess we'll have to keep you all aboard *Donaghey* for the time being. Your wounded will be treated, but I'll have to keep you locked below." He glared at Tomas. "One false move by anybody, and we *will* cram you in with the Doms," he warned.

Tomas frowned. "In chains, belowdecks . . . I don't suppose I can convince you to accept our parole? My parole?"

"Not right now. We'll have a chance to get to know one another, and maybe that's the best way for us to avoid things like this in the future," he said, nodding at the bubbling, flotsam-covered sea. "But your ship came steaming in here and shot at us just as soon as we ran up our own flag. For all I know, she was hunting us specifically." He paused and studied Tomas's face. *Interesting. That's what I thought. Poor kid looks like I caught him with his hand in the cookie jar. At least he has a conscience. We might learn a lot from him if I handle this right.* "And so far," he continued, "we haven't met a solitary Leaguer who didn't try to kill us or help somebody else do it. As far as I'm concerned, your League is just as screwed-up as the Dominion. You'll forgive me if I'm not feeling too trusting right now."

Without waiting for a reply, he turned to Lieutenant Mak. "Put the prisoners below." He glanced at Tomas. "We don't keep irons in our ships—never needed them—so your people won't be shackled; they'll be secured and guarded in a storeroom. If they try anything, though, there'll be hell to pay." He looked back at Mak. "The wounded will be treated here first, and any seriously wounded will be moved to the orlop. We'll rig a secure sick bay." He raised his voice. "As soon as that's done, we double up on repairs and get the hell out of here. Tribune Pol-Heena, take charge of Ensign Mole and lock him in the cabin that psycho kid was in. Talk to him all he wants and assure him we won't eat him." He frowned. "That reminds me. Boats, please have a detail bring the Marine the kid murdered on deck and prepare her for burial." He looked back at Tomas. "We'll bury her in the morning, along with any of your people who don't make it. Hopefully, she'll go down alone. There's been enough dying today."

CHAPTER 18

Sovereign Nest of Jaaph Hunters
Zanzibar
November 20, 1944

"They've *mined* the entrance to the anchorage!" cried Commander Riku, Kurokawa's chief of ordnance, as he burst into the parlor of his lord's headquarters residence without waiting to be announced. Kurokawa and his flag captain, Hara Mikawa of the improved cruiser *Nachi*, General of the Sky Muriname, Signal Lieutenant Fukui, Maggiore Rizzo, Contre-Amiral Laborde, Capitaine Dupont, another man, clearly one of Rizzo's pilots, and several more were standing around the great desk. They'd been peering at a large map unrolled atop it, but all looked at Riku as he belatedly paused and saluted.

"I'll have *no more* of your outbursts, do you understand?" Kurokawa roared at him. "Can't you see we're busy here? How can we concentrate if you are always charging in, yelping about this or that? If you can't control yourself, I will *have* you controlled. Is that clear?"

Riku gulped and lowered his eyes. "Yes, Lord."

"What about mines?" Muriname asked forcefully, gazing intently as he adjusted the spectacles on his nose. Kurokawa glared at him but said nothing. They'd met in response to another air attack, accompanied by some kind of surface raid in the bay. They were trying to decide what the attacks meant and what to do about them. The air raid had been smaller than before—just a few planes—and accomplished little more than relighting fires along the dock and burning some empty jungle near the northern airfield. Muriname was convinced the airfield had been the target and even sortied planes in response, including two of Rizzo's Macchi-Messerschmitts. The results were mixed, at best. Four of Muriname's fighters had been lost in the air. Two collided in the dark and fell into the sea. Two more were shot down by either the bombers or friendly ground fire—both were equally possible. They'd learned the bombers had defensive machine guns, and the antiaircraft batteries around the city were much better at throwing a lot of metal in the air. Searchlights on the cruisers gave gunners brief glimpses of shapes to shoot at as well, but *Savoie* had been forbidden to light her own more powerful lights, for fear of drawing attention to herself. Finally, four more of Muriname's fighters were damaged landing in the dark. After so many planes and pilots were lost in the attack on TF Alden, he was increasingly disturbed by the rate of attrition.

One of his engine factories had been destroyed in the first raid. He had another, and quite a few engines were already stockpiled, so he could still build planes, but it took time. And what of the Grik craftsmen he'd lost? What of the pilots? Training either took much longer than building the planes. He and his XO, Lieutenant of the Sky Iguri, had been pushed beyond endurance by that endeavor alone. Muriname smirked darkly. At least Iguri wasn't quite as enamored with Kurokawa as he'd been. For that matter, despite their recent victory, a growing percentage of all the dwindling Japanese were finally losing faith in Kurokawa. Their impotence in the face of the Allied bombing and, frankly, Kurokawa's inability to find them women after so long only added to their disillusionment. And the incident at the prison compound, whether most would've done the same or not, reinforced that issue. Lastly, despite all they'd done for him, all their suffering and sacrifice, it wasn't lost on anyone that their leader was now constantly and exclusively surrounded by *Grik* guards.

Rizzo's modern fighters managed to destroy one seaplane/bomber and possibly cripple another, but the ground fire prevented them from pressing their attack, and the enemy formation apparently split after its run. The one confirmed kill had been alone, flying low. And then even Rizzo's planes were almost wrecked trying to land in the dark. They, however, gave the first warning of a small squadron of enemy ships approaching from the south.

"Four targets were identified as sailing steamers of the enemy's latest class by searchlights on the cruisers that rushed to meet them," Riku reported. "They're normally heavily armed with large-bore guns and were a match for our cruisers—before we improved them. But their fire, while spirited, was not as heavy as we've seen in the past. And the searchlights allowed our commanders to observe objects splashing into the sea in the enemy's wakes."

"Fewer guns, to accommodate mines," Muriname guessed.

"Apparently," Riku agreed, "though this wasn't understood at first. The enemy steamed up across the South Channel, trading effective fire with eight of our cruisers, making for the center isle and the North Channel."

"What happened?" Kurokawa demanded. "We saw nothing from here because of the island, and only heard that the small force was repulsed."

Riku gulped again. "It was, Lord, but as I said, their fire was effective, and some damage was sustained by our ships as they turned to pursue the enemy around the island. I should add that the new forward-firing guns were quite effective at this point, destroying one enemy ship and likely damaging the rest—but, suddenly, one of ours just . . . exploded and sank. Moments later, another did the same. The enemy couldn't fire directly astern, so our ships *must've* struck mines."

"And then?" It was Contre-Amiral Laborde's turn to demand.

Riku looked at him resentfully, but continued to his lord. "The rest of our ships continued the pursuit, scoring multiple hits. Finally, making smoke, the enemy turned and fled to the west. Sadly, their vessels remain swifter than ours and the smoke choked the searchlights. They escaped."

"But they didn't mine the North Channel?" Kurokawa demanded.

"No, Lord. It is clear. The six cruisers reentered the bay in line abreast to make sure."

Kurokawa made a pouting expression. "Very well. A good report, Commander. But do contain yourself better in the future."

"Of course, Lord."

Kurokawa looked at the others. "This practically confirms what we've surmised. Captain Reddy will concentrate on Sofesshk, for now. He pricks us with his bombers, and now attempts to contain us with mines. We'll try to clear those in daylight, but for the present, we'll focus our defenses on the North Channel. We can't allow him to block that as well."

"I understand your reasoning, General of the Sea," Rizzo said, almost cautiously, "but Reddy's actions do not necessarily preclude a serious attack here."

Kurokawa slammed the desk, not as much in anger as frustration. "Of *course* they do! The mines prove it. They would prevent him from entering the bay just as surely as they'd keep us from leaving." He sighed and looked at Laborde. "If *Savoie* was ready and had even the most rudimentary fire-control capability, and if *Akagi*'s repairs were complete, this would be the *perfect* time to break out and attack the Allies in the rear. As it stands, you will have a little longer to make *my* battleship ready for action. Use that time wisely, Contre-Amiral. When we do sortie, I want *Savoie* able to smash any Allied vessel from twenty kilometers away—is that understood?"

"It's not *possible*!" Dupont objected. "To make a level/cross-level device, not to mention the necessary fire-control equipment, in mere days or weeks! Your machining capacity is impressive," he allowed, "but we have no blueprints. Even then, it would take time."

"You have manuals," Kurokawa countered. "Make use of them. *Extrapolate* dimensions if you must, and use whatever and whoever you need. This project has priority over all others." He sneered. "The enemy has employed an effective, if crude, fire-control system for his *smoothbore muzzle-loaders*!" he said, his voice rising to a rant. "We have now done the same, so *do not* tell me it can't be done! With all my industry at your disposal and a well-equipped machine shop on your ship, you *must* not tell me you can't contrive some way to coordinate *Savoie*'s main batteries! If that's the case, what *possible* use do I have for you?"

"To lead the French crew who remained loyal to us, and are now her only experienced officers. And to fight *Savoie*, when the time comes," Laborde said simply.

"All *eleven* Frenchmen!" Kurokawa chortled savagely. "Really, Contre-Amiral, the loyalty you inspire is staggering. And are you saying *I* cannot fight her?" he challenged, his face purpling. Muriname had noticed how easy it was to get him to lose his temper again. For a while, almost a year, he'd controlled it. Now, particularly since the first bombing—and he went to see the prisoners—it seemed always on the loose.

"Not at all," Laborde appeased. "But you're our General of the Sea, a fleet admiral. Why should you concern yourself with operating a single ship that others, Dupont and myself in particular, are more accustomed to, who know her every quirk, how she handles in any sea, and what her strengths—and limitations—are?"

Kurokawa fumed. "Indeed," he finally acknowledged. "But don't disappoint me," he warned.

"We will not," Laborde assured. "Given enough time," he qualified more quietly.

"Such a shame the mine layers couldn't complete their task," Captain Stuart Brassey murmured, lowering his telescope. He'd watched the whole thing with Silva from their hidey-hole, a patch of dense jungle east of the prison compound. From a blind they'd erected in a tall tree on a slight rise, they could see a great deal. They were able to watch the prison compound and confirm that Sandra, Diania, Lange, Horn, Adar, and two other 'Cats were indeed present, all together. They could see *Savoie* to the northeast and watch her preparations, and they'd made an exact count of enemy ships in the anchorage. Besides

Savoie, there were still two unaltered ironclad BBs moored near her, and two more to the south, though they hadn't seen much activity aboard them. They weren't sure if that meant they'd been relegated to a secondary role or were ready in all respects for battle. A fifth had apparently been altered into an armored oiler. They guessed that by the number of ships that periodically went alongside it, and that, in the days they'd watched, three of the double-ended barge tugs arrived to replenish it.

That meant at least some refining was taking place on the continent, which stood to reason, since the Grik had been making a gasoline/ethanol mix for their zeppelins for quite some time. But oil barrels also went ashore, and Lawrence guessed they were going wherever more specialized aviation fuel was made. Frantic work continued on the damaged aircraft carrier, still lying inshore of the island in the middle of the bay, and it looked almost ready for action. Equally concerning, they'd counted a total of twenty of the formidable ironclad cruisers after a couple more arrived, probably from other harbors around the island. *Eighteen, now,* Silva reminded himself, *all startin' to bunch up in the vicinity of the North Channel, free of mines. They've worked on those cruisers,* he thought. *Reduced the sails, which means they must've improved their engines. They're still not fast, but they've raised the armored bulwarks amidships. Maybe added some guns.* They'd always been vulnerable from the air or to plunging fire, but were tough to crack at close range, from the surface. Even *Walker*'s guns had trouble punching through their armor and the heavy scantlings backing it. *An' maybe they've armored their decks now too,* Silva speculated. *They've got less weight in masts, so they're more stable, but lie lower in the water, so they're heavier.*

"A shame, sure," Dennis replied absently to Brassey's statement.

"Just another mile and a half, and the mine layers could've sealed the North Channel as well! I hope Captain Reddy disciplines their commanders."

"Not sure they deserve it. One went down," Silva defended, inwardly shuddering at the fate of its crew. Even if their pursuers were inclined to rescue survivors, the voracious sea wouldn't have left many—and their captivity would've probably been worse than the horrible but quick death the fish gave them. He glanced toward the compound, unseen in the dark. *Or would it? Either way, it's just as well none of 'em survived to blow. Prob'ly knew going in that they couldn't let that happen.* He shrugged. *Just like us.* "They were getting' pretty beat up, Mr. Brassey," he said. "I think they did enough. Quit worryin' about it."

Brassey regarded him curiously in the dark, wondering what Silva knew that he didn't. Quite a bit, he suspected. For operational security, nobody but Silva, and maybe Lawrence, needed to know everything. They heard a hiss below, and Lawrence scrambled awkwardly up the tree.

"Finally back, huh?" Dennis asked.

"As you see," Lawrence replied dryly.

"Sneaky booger. Finally found somethin' yer good at. Didja get the message off?"

"Aye. Ca'tain Reddy should soon know all us has learned." A ship had appeared as scheduled, offshore from the burned-out zeppelin. They didn't know if it participated in the mining or not, but it didn't matter, and Lawrence flashed a rather lengthy report by Morse lamp. He and Brassey's Khonashi had been roaming practically at will all over the southern part of the island. They'd been seen many times, but no alarm was ever raised and they hadn't been forced to "eliminate" anyone. Apparently, just as it took the Allies too long to realize their enemies had learned Lemurian, compromising their communications, and that the Doms and League had spies in the Empire and Republic—probably everywhere—it hadn't dawned on Kurokawa that the Allies could have Grik-like scouts ashore on Zanzibar. One group, led by Lawrence, had explored the harbor defenses and industrial sites. Sergeant Oolak, with Pokey posing as his superior to do any talking, had ventured east around the mountain called the Gut, toward Tailbone Bay. Together they'd assembled a remarkably good picture of what Chack's Brigade would face. They'd ignored the north, beyond the Gut. There were a lot of Grik up there but no airfields, so it shouldn't be an immediate factor in the coming action. There were plenty of Grik in the south too, however, maybe twenty thousand or so. But many were laborers, sailors, dock and factory workers. Most were probably trained soldiers as well, but they were dispersed. It would take time to gather, arm, and organize them into an effective defense—if Chack's Brigade ever made it to the beach in the first place.

"How much longer now?" Brassey suddenly asked, the slightest tension in his voice for the first time.

"Not long," Silva replied thoughtfully. "The Jap-Griks may not have mine sweepers, but it won't take 'em more'n a few days to clear the South Channel if they get on it. They may not try, figurin' they're safe from that direction, an' preferrin' ta' wad up an' defend the North Channel against another mine layin'."

"So . . . just a few more days?"

"I expect."

"Then why not free our people *now*?" Brassey pleaded. "They've suffered enough, and I want them under our protection. Who knows what might happen to them if we wait too long? We could bring them here and hide them. Their escape might even cause confusion, and a useful diversion among the enemy."

Silva frowned in the dark. "I'm sure you're right about the diversion, an' I know how you feel, believe me. But the ruckus we'd kick up ain't the kind we need. For one, what if it *ain't* just days? What if it's a week? Two weeks? I know our friends look scrawny as hell, but they *are* bein' fed. We can't feed 'em that long. We'll be outa rations before then ourselves. An' I don't think we could hide 'em *anywhere* after we poked that ant bed. The only reason we ain't been found is 'cause nobody's lookin' for us. We swipe our people back an' Kurokawa'll have *ever'body* combin' the whole joint for 'em. Yeah, that'd cause a helluva distraction, but crazy as he is, Kurokawwy ain't a idiot. He'd know somebody helped 'em, which means somebody's runnin' around *spyin'* on him too."

"Which means he might change his entire disposition, all his plans, right when we need him most complacent," Brassey completed Silva's point with resignation in his voice.

"Aye," Lawrence agreed, reaching out to touch the boy

with his fully clawed left hand. He knew how he felt as well. Sentimentality had once been a great mystery to him, particularly directed at things. He'd pretended to be excited when *Walker* was raised after the Battle of Baalkpan, because everyone else seemed to be and he'd been desperate to fit in. But he'd already been devoted to certain people: Rebecca Anne McDonald first, then (oddly) Silva, who'd shot him on sight. Ultimately, many others—hundreds—had joined the list of people he esteemed. And even as the concept of friendship, *family*, matured in his heart, he eventually caught himself experiencing attachments to things, such as *Walker* and weapons, which had served them well. Finally, ideas—such as honor, duty, even country, so influential to his friends—became important to him as he began to understand how large a part they played in making his friends, and, by association, himself, who they were.

Dennis Silva hadn't always been a patient teacher, or even a clear-cut example for him to follow. But Captain Reddy—and Lady Sandra—had. To him, to his heart, as his friends referred to the sentimental part of his being, rescuing Lady Sandra and the rest was the most vital part of their mission. But they couldn't succeed without victory, and a premature rescue might shatter any chance for that. He patted Brassey's arm. "As Dennis says, Ca'tain 'Rassey, quit 'orrying. In days, or a little longer, us *are* going to get they out."

CHAPTER 19

***USS* Walker**

SS *Walker*, DD-163, bounded through the wind-whipped, white-capped sea north of Mahe with an exuberance she hadn't shown for a long time. Gray smoke from her aft three funnels quickly vanished and pure white foam sluiced across her fo'c'sle, parting beneath her bridge, when she knifed through the waves at fifteen knots. Each time, she rose to expose the round curve of her bow beneath the boot topping like a soggy greyhound shaking itself off. The fresh wooden deck strakes in the pilothouse creaked snugly against their new fasteners, and the machinery rumble they transmitted to Matt Reddy's feet was . . . tighter, less labored, than he thought he'd ever felt. He was sitting on his captain's chair, drinking real coffee from a small supply that Juan had triumphantly secured on his own—and even he hadn't managed to destroy—as he contemplated the frenzied, relatively brief overhaul.

It hadn't been the most comprehensive refit she'd undergone by any means, but it might've been the best. Her first rebuild after the Battle of Baalkpan saved her, but had also been a scratch learning experience for yard workers who'd never had anything like her in their hands. The same was true, to a lesser degree, of her refit in Maa-ni-la. Steel hulls and complicated machinery had been as alien to

Lemurians as their diagonally laminated wooden hulls had been to Matt's human destroyermen. But Lemurians were quick learners, and with the plans they'd drawn during her rebuild, they'd almost immediately begun copying *Walker*.

Whole new industries and occupations sprouted to support that. All were necessary for other endeavors, but repairing and maintaining *Walker*—and making others like her—had been the test bed and driving force behind so much else. Her first two "daughters" took a long time to make, while furry workers and engineers honed their experience with near-constant practice, all the while making boilers and engines for wooden warships. They were different engines, in different hulls, but the new skills still applied. Often, they reinvented methods even their teachers couldn't show them, or came up with entirely new ideas. Aside from the first boilers built to power Baalkpan's infant industries, all newer ones were near copies of *Walker*'s. Some were larger, a few smaller, but—particularly now that the "tube crisis" seemed under control—all seemed uniformly *better* as well, incorporating improvements Spanky had long yearned for, or the 'Cats came up with by themselves. Just as important, interchangeability of parts and assemblies had been stressed throughout Lemurian industrialization. Standard units of measure were quickly adopted, and things like calipers, yardsticks, and tape measures had been among the first items mass-produced—even during the frantic effort to arm the 'Cats against the first Grik swarm. Ancient, wildly variable Lemurian measurements almost instantly vanished from use. Some still used the term "tail" instead of "yard," but they were so similar, there'd been little difficulty defining both as 36 inches.

It helped that Imperial inches, feet, and yards were the same in principle, even if other weights and measures were screwy. But as Allied designs for things went to the Empire, so did Allied calipers and other measuring devices. Interchangeability had been *so* heavily stressed that innovation sometimes suffered, with manufacturers occasionally disdaining improved designs for various parts simply because they wouldn't exactly fit existing assemblies that otherwise worked just fine. One example was Baalkpan Arsenal's refusal to replace the brittle flat mainsprings in its rifle locks with new, improved coil springs—because then they'd have to change the tumblers as well. Instead, they attempted to improve the flat springs and sent out lots of spares. Things like that were understandable in wartime, Matt supposed. Design changes caused production delays they could ill afford, and the obsession with interchangeability didn't much affect the development of new weapons or prevent qualitative innovations. For example, *Walker*'s new shaft packing that so reduced vibration was identical to what she was built with, but the materials, the naturally creosoted trees in northwest Borno, were better. Innovations of that sort left him confident that now that Lemurian inventiveness had been unleashed, they'd never be hopelessly shackled to the tried and true once the pressure of "good enough now is better than perfect later" was eased.

And interchangeability was a wonderful thing. *Tarakaan Island* had carried entire extra boilers. If they'd had time, they could've installed a new one where *Walker*'s old number one used to be. They'd never removed the stack above it, after all. Not only was it useful for venting the forward fireroom when the need arose, but Adar once convinced him that it would diminish the appearance of his ship in the eyes of his people—make her look incomplete, less capable somehow. Matt conceded, still hoping to someday replace the boiler, but, honestly, even he hadn't relished the image of the gap-toothed silhouette that would result. Still, even if they had all the time in the world, with three healthy boilers, Matt wasn't sure he would've replaced the fourth. It would cost them the fuel bunker they'd installed in its place, and the extra few knots might not balance the range penalty. He'd reassess all that if he ever *did* have time—and if he and his old ship lived long enough. That returned his thoughts to the action ahead and he frowned as he set his cup down and lurched to his feet.

Raising his binoculars, he watched a pair of Mosquito Hawks from *Salissa*'s Combat Air Patrol complete the northern leg of their pattern and then turn south. There were Nancys up there too, farther out, watching for anything approaching the task force. They'd heard the engine drone of the big PB-5Ds before dawn, heading back to

Mahe after another raid on Zanzibar. Two were lost this time, and he grieved for the planes and pilots. *They have it awful tough,* he reflected, immediately turning around at the Comoros Islands after missions over Sofesshk, to fly all the way up to Zanzibar via Mahe. Now they'd go back. He was asking a lot of the big seaplane bombers—and their crews—and Sofesshk had been anything but a cakewalk. The strange Grik rockets were knocking planes down as well, as the enemy's aim, and possibly the rockets themselves, improved. Fortunately, as promised, replacements from Baalkpan continued to make up for losses. So far. The latest raid on Zanzibar had focused on the southernmost airfield, so at least Matt felt confident it hadn't killed his wife, now that he knew about where she was. The thought that she might die due to actions undertaken at his orders had tormented him beyond words. And it was possible she still could. There'd be one final raid, and then who knew what would happen when the full attack commenced? But to know she was still alive *now*, thanks to Silva's report, was a tremendous comfort.

He directed the binoculars to the right. Far across the heaving sea, about six miles to the east, he occasionally caught glimpses of USS *James Ellis*, apparently matching *Walker*'s renewed vivacity, as the two practically identical destroyers screened ahead of the plodding task force. For just a moment, in spite of everything, the sight let Matt peel back the years; wash away all the blood, anxiety, and crushing responsibility; and pretend it was *Mahan* over there, or *Pope* or *Stewart* or another old comrade *Walker* had paced in similar fashion in another place, before another war. But *James Ellis* wasn't one of those other ships, Matt remembered with regret, and was, in a way, far more distant than a mere six miles of boisterous sea. She was separated from *Walker* by a quarter century and another world.

Shaking his head, he stepped out on the starboard bridgewing. Nodding at the Lemurian lookouts, he stared aft, past the wisping funnels, the amidships deckhouse, the searchlight tower, and the aft deckhouse, with its gun crew exercising the tall 4"-50 on its DP mount. The roiling wake churned white and peeled back and away, leaving a broadening, darkening V that shattered on the following waves. About three miles back was his little fleet, arrayed in two columns. USNRS *Salissa* was on the right, its massive form seeming almost motionless, the brisk sea barely affecting it. As he watched her, he suspected Keje was probably looking back. They'd been through so much together, and he wished, unreasonably, he could be on *Walker* beside him. Keje's gruff but irrepressible personality rarely failed to cheer him and always helped keep things in perspective.

But Keje's duty was to his carrier, his Home, and that was where he belonged. Her forward flight deck was cluttered with Mosquito Hawks, ready to escort the PB-1B Nancy floatplanes that would attack with bombs beneath their wings. Behind them, Ben Mallory's four operational P-40Es were securely strapped to the deck. They'd take off last, ready to react to whatever went after the others. Nobody was happy about the recovery procedures, and even if they all made it back, they might still lose them. *If Chack's Brigade can overrun one of the Grik airstrips . . .* began the thought, but Matt shook his head. They couldn't count on that. One way or another, the next few days might mean the end of almost all their carefully hoarded modern fighters. *If that's the case, we'll manage,* he decided. *And if there's such a thing as fate, maybe this is what they were for all along.*

He looked at the almost equally massive USS *Tarakaan Island*. She carried half their assault force and one of the few aces he had to play. He hated that they had to take her so close to danger; she represented their only means of repairing serious battle damage and might be very busy when this was over—if she survived. Behind the two biggest ships were a large number of oilers and other auxiliaries. Alan Letts had moved Heaven and earth to get as much to them as he could, after TF Alden's losses, but could only replace so much, so fast. And if they lost more, there was no telling how long it would take to replace the ships, crews, and cargos. Pete, Rolak, and Safir might have to go on the defensive at Grik City after all. Matt smiled. Letts had *tried* to send the new cruiser, USS *Fitzhugh Gray*, but she flat wasn't ready and Matt forbade it. Fully complete and worked up, she would've been very welcome, but untried and unfinished, she might not even make it there, and waiting for her would impose an unacceptable delay. There'd be more than enough for *Gray* to do when the time was right.

Surrounding the task force in a wide semicircle to port were the sail-steam DDs of Des-Ron 6, including Jarrik-Fas's *Tassat*, Muraak-Saanga's *Scott*, and Naala-Araan's old *Nakja-Mur*. To starboard were *Clark*, *Saak-Fas*, and *Bowles* of Des-Ron 10. All were veterans, and a couple, like *Tassat*, were barely seaworthy even after extensive repairs. Still, only *Nakja-Mur*, the oldest ship in the task force besides *Walker* and *Salissa*, and one of their very first steamers, seemed to be having trouble keeping up. Her engine had been very hard-used over time, and even with every stitch of canvas she could carry, she was sagging behind. Mentally comparing what he had to fight with against what they knew Kurokawa had, Matt needed every ship. But if *Nakja-Mur* couldn't keep up, he'd have to send her back to Mahe. Grimly, he turned and stepped back in the pilothouse, but almost released a snort of amusement when he saw the embroidered cushion on his chair again. Someone had slipped in and secured it during the refit. Perry Brister's chair in *Ellie* had one, and it must've been decided that he—and *Walker*—needed one too. His amusement was fleeting, however, and the frown returned as he sat.

"Good morning, Skipper!" Lieutenant Ed Palmer said cheerfully, suddenly standing by his chair. Matt let the frown slide off his face and looked at the young signal officer. The reversion to signal designation from comm just seemed more appropriate now, since they used signal flags, Morse lamps, and rockets just as much as radio and CW. More, actually, for line-of-sight communication. And in addition to Henry Stokes in Baalkpan, Ed was responsible for formulating and distributing new codes, as well as trying to break them. He spoke some French, and he'd had some success with League voice codes—before they changed them again. Undaunted, he'd started again.

"Good *afternoon*, Mr. Palmer," Matt said, glancing significantly at the Imperial chronometer secured to the aft bulkhead. It was 1222. "I believe you're late. You were on the watch bill as OOD for the afternoon watch." Matt wanted all his officers able to conn the ship, and Ed had always been reluctant to assume that responsibility, not trusting his seamanship.

Ed's smile vanished. "Aye, sir. I apologize. It won't happen again. I was going over the command codes for Outhouse Rat, and got, ah . . ." He stiffened. "No excuse, sir." He glanced at Tabby, who'd had the conn since 0800, and she grinned back at him. When Matt said every officer, he meant it, and Tabby's engines and boilers were doing fine.

"Then you'd better get to it. I'm sure Tabby's anxious to check things out below."

"Aye, aye, sir." Ed turned to Lieutenant Tab-At. "I, ah, I'm ready to relieve you, sir."

The 'Cat at the big brass wheel chuckled behind Tabby as, just as formally, she replied, "I'm ready to be relieved. Course is tree one seero, fifteen knots. Wind's outa the north-northeast, an' the sea's runnin' about six feet, but moder—gettin' less. *Ellie*'s on station six miles east, an' the taask force is tree miles aft, makin' ten knots, an' zigzaaggin'. We're due to alter course an' exchange positions with *Ellie* in"—she glanced at the chronometer—"twenty-five minutes." At preselected times, but seemingly at random, *Walker* and *James Ellis* converged and passed each other to take the other ship's position in the screen. Not only did the maneuver allow the task force to keep up, but *if* there was a sub out there, it might shake it up and help detect it.

"Thanks, Tabby—I mean, I relieve you, sir!"

"I staan relieved," Tabby replied. "Attention in the pilothouse: Lieuten-aant Palmer has the deck!"

Self-consciously, Ed took her place and, clasping his hands behind his back, peered out over the plunging, bucking fo'c'sle.

Spanky McFarlane chose that moment to join them. He had his own cup of coffee and seemed enormously pleased with himself. He tapped the deck with his shoe. "She sure feels fine, huh, Skipper?"

"That she does," Matt agreed. "Another big job ahead, though," he added.

"Sure, but that's nothing new."

"No, but the stakes . . ." Matt shook his head. "I keep

running the plan through my mind, trying to find flaws. It's not all that complicated, but a lot can go wrong."

"Stuff *always* goes wrong," Spanky told him gently. "You know that." He waved back at the little fleet behind them. "And everybody knows what to do when it does. Chack's got better intel than we've ever had before jumping on a beach, the minelayers did what they were supposed to before they got chased off, an' that idiot Silva knows where they're keeping our people. His reports on *Savoie* are kinda weird, though. Don't know what to make of that. But if everybody does their job, we got a better than even chance o' pullin' this off." He chuckled. "Since those're better odds than we ever had before, I'd say it makes this stunt a sure thing!"

Matt tried to smile. Ordinarily, he'd agree. But this time they were dealing with Kurokawa himself. A stab of worry burned his chest. *What'll he do when he figures out what's happening? He will, at some point, no matter what we do. And when he does, what'll he do to Sandra? So much depends on Silva! Not only my wife—if she's still alive by then—but* everything. *So much of what we think we know has come from him.* He bit his lip. Silva had always been dependable when it came to getting things done, but not always the way you expected, or even *wanted.* That could cause confusion, and confusion was deadly. The knife of apprehension twisted in his chest. *I have to put it away!* he thought forcefully. *Put it way back in my mind. I don't have the luxury—the right—to focus on Sandra.*

Spanky looked at him oddly. "You're thinkin' about Silva?"

Matt started, surprised. "How did you know that?"

Spanky shrugged. "You're not the only one. Somehow or other, I bet just about everybody goin' into this fight is thinkin' of him." He grinned. "Good thoughts an' bad. I know he's on Chack's mind and I'joorka's, thinkin' about how many Grik he counted. Ben has to be wonderin' if he got the best dope on the airfields. Keje an' Tikker'll be wonderin' that too. Then there's *Savoie* an' all those Grik cruisers. Will they still be where he said? What if they're not? I just came from the wardroom"—he held up his coffee cup—"an' Pam's a nervous wreck, figurin' Silva'll do somethin' stupid an' get himself killed." He took a sip. "And he might. Sooner or later, he *will*. It's the law of averages, an' the fact is, he's pushed his luck too damn far." He gulped down the last of his coffee and smacked his lips. "We all have, I guess, but Silva takes the cake." He looked out to sea, forward. "I called him an idiot, an' he is—in some ways. But not in ways that matter for this. He'll do *somethin'* weird, you can count on it, but it'll probably make some sort of sense. And he'll probably raise a lot of hell, right when we need it most. More important, if anybody can get our people out in one piece, it's him—and Larry. You can also count on that." Spanky's rough voice turned uncharacteristically soft. "They're *his* friends too, see? He *will* die to save Sandra if it comes to it, an' not just for her—though she'd be enough. They're not five years apart, but she's probably more a mother than he's ever had." He shrugged. "I know—kinda weird. But it's true. When *she* scolds him, he listens." He looked back at Matt. "Still, mainly, he'll do it for you, because you *trust* him to." He shook his head. "Chief Gray saw it before I ever did. Saw something in that big goon before anybody else, I think. That's why he left him his hat an' coin. His *legacy*." He held up a hand. "Don't get me wrong, Silva'll never be Super Bosun of the Navy! But if he lives, he might wind up something else, maybe just as important someday. I think, in the end, what Gray figured out was that Silva never had a cause before this ship—and you—came along. Now? He'd set himself on fire an' wallow in fuel oil before he let you down."

"But . . . why?" Matt asked, almost whispering, genuinely mystified by Spanky's observations.

Spanky rolled his eyes. "You still really don't know, do you? He'd do it for the same reason I would, an' thousands of other humans an' 'Cats on this screwed-up world. Because of who you are, what you are, an' what you've made of the rest of us. Simple." With that, he scratched his chin under the reddish beard. "Simple," he repeated softly, then took a deep breath. "C'mon, Tabby," he said to the gray-furred Lemurian who'd watched the exchange, blinking amazement. "Let's go watch your hot new boilers an' listen to the steam sing!"

CHAPTER 20

Operation Outhouse Rat
November 23, 1944

It was pitch-dark, without even stars, when the first act of Operation Outhouse Rat began. Clouds had moved in during the night and, because of concern about the implications for air operations, the go order had been delayed. The experience of the Sky Priests, many of whom had joined together in a meteorological section aboard *Big Sal*, had finally made the difference. Unfamiliar as they were with these seas, they'd spent their lives observing the weather and had concluded, though it might storm a bit, it should be a relatively short, mild blow. The whipping wind and occasional pulses of lightning to the north seemed to contradict their prediction, but not only were they the best resource for such things, a *little* storm might be advantageous, preventing the task force's discovery. And it would be discovered if it lingered long. They had to go now, or bear away and wait another day at least. Another day for Kurokawa to change his dispositions, possibly move his hostages, or even discover the task force with a scout plane and make preparations far costlier to overcome. And the bombing raid was going in, anyway. If they delayed, the whole plan might have to be retooled. Finally, Matt himself gave the order with a simple "Commence OOR" flashed from *Walker*'s Morse lamp.

Colonel Chack-Sab-At was accompanying the Imperial Major Alistair Jindal's 21st Combined Regiment. It consisted of 'Cats and humans from the 9th Maa-ni-la and 1st Respite. His sister, Risa, was with Major Enrico Galay's 19th Baalkpan, and the 1st of the 11th Imperial Marines. Galay had been a corporal in the Philippine Scouts in another war, and had grown into an enterprising officer with many talents. It was he who'd taken the first aerial photographs of Sofesshk, in fact. Too bad they hadn't been able to do the same here, but anything capable of carrying a pilot and photographer over Zanzibar in daylight could never survive. They still had to rely on Fiedler's map. Fortunately, because of Silva and a very brave pilot, the map had been much improved.

"I suppose it's time," Jindal said, twisting his long, dark mustaches as he peered over *Tarakaan Island*'s side at a capering, forty-foot motor dory packed with troops. *Tara* was half-flooded down, but the dory—and the deadly, boisterous sea—still seemed at the bottom of a high cliff. Dozens more ghostly dories bobbed and pitched erratically nearby, and some motored in circles a short distance away. As busy as it seemed in the huge ship's lee, it was even more chaotic behind them inside the great repair basin, where nearly seventy more dories waited impatiently to join those in the rougher water outside.

Chack shifted the sling of his trusty Krag on his shoulder and flashed teeth at his Imperial friend. "Should I lower you down with a rope?"

Jindal glared at his commander but managed a small smile. "I can manage."

"Then it *is* time. After you, Major." Together, they descended a cargo net down to the dory. Chack hopped lightly across, and well-meaning 'Cats guided Jindal's feet, nearly causing him to fall. Finally, he was safely aboard and the coxswain steered away from *Tara*'s side. It had begun. Barely seen, except for the phosphorescent wakes they kicked up, eight torpedo boats of Lieutenant Nat Hardee's MTB-Ron 1 burst from *Tara*'s open stern and fanned out in a protective arc. Almost immediately, the first cluster of dories, packed with Grik-like members of I'Joorka's 1st North Borno, rumbled into the offshore swells at a more sedate pace and turned for the invisible shore of Zanzibar. They'd be the first to land. With any luck, sentries would think they were Grik, performing some predawn exercise they hadn't been expecting, and I'joorka himself, leading the first wave, would achieve a toehold on the beach west of Saansa Point before the enemy knew what was happening.

The first flotilla disappeared in the gloom, followed by the second, carrying the human Khonashis. They wouldn't be separated from the rest of their clan for long. As soon as they passed from view, the rest of the brigade began to spread out and head for shore. They traveled more slowly, pacing larger barges loaded with light artillery and paalkas to pull them. Heavy mortars were already set up in the pitching boats, ready to rain shells behind the enemy, if necessary. Their fire couldn't be very effective until they got ashore, but it might be unnerving. Finally, they'd brought some other surprises. Instead of the flamethrowers they'd used in the past—which everyone hated and were nearly as dangerous to them as to the enemy—they had twenty of what Matt called mountain howitzers. They were very small 12 pdr muzzle-loaders weighing only about five hundred pounds, which could be quickly moved and operated by very small crews. They were too light to fire solid shot but could deliver exploding case to a range of a thousand yards. More to the point, they also fired a devastating load of canister from their stubby little barrels, consisting of *three hundred* half-inch balls. Between them and the light machine-gun sections attached to each company, they should be in good shape—unless opposed by enemy machine guns and dug-in artillery. Bringing up the rear, in four even larger barges, was their final "surprise," but Chack still believed he'd be more surprised than the enemy if they were actually of any use.

They never heard the big Clippers pass high overhead; their own engines and the sound of the sea drowned them out. But new, sharper stabs of lightning, about fifteen miles to the northwest, joined the more distant, natural sort flickering on the horizon. Orange flashes popped, unheard, in the sky over Lizard Ass Bay. There were quite a few, Chack realized, and he wondered if enemy planes would rise as well. Strobing pulses of fire outlined the jungle treetops ahead and he knew those must be the bombs hitting the ground, hopefully burning ships, planes, and Grik. So far, none of the ships offshore had opened fire. They'd be completely invisible from the beach and wanted to stay that way as long as possible to aid I'joorka's surprise. There'd be covering fire for a while, if asked for, but even then it had to be done with care, and its effectiveness would be questionable. With their own people in contact with the enemy, they had to shoot cautiously long, and couldn't keep it up for any length of time, even if asked. *Salissa*, most of the auxiliaries, and the sail-steam DDs had already departed for other positions, and *Walker*, *James Ellis*, and the MTBs had specific places to be before dawn. *Tarakaan Island* must be gone by then as well. With no protection, she'd be a sitting duck. The ground-assault force of Operation Outhouse Rat would be on its own.

"Major I'joorka should be landing now," Jindal observed, putting his watch back in a pocket he'd sewn to his combat smock. Chack doubted he'd seen what time it was, but thought he was probably right. Long moments went by and nothing disturbed them but packets of spray dashing back from the blunt bow of the dory. They could see the darker black outline of the jungle against the sky, still silhouetted by distant bombs, antiaircraft fire, and flames on the ground or sea, but the first-and second-wave dories remained invisible. The first, at least, must be ashore. The problem was, Grik-like though they appeared, albeit dressed somewhat strangely, none of I'joorka's Khonashi actually *spoke* Grik. Confused or not, sentries wouldn't put up with being ignored for long. Conversely, Chack was also concerned about I'joorka's Grik-like Khonashi being accidentally shot by friends. The different dress should help, but ironically, he suspected more such mistakes from veterans than newies. They were used to identifying enemies more by general shape and how they moved, not by what they wore. Grik had only recently begun making widespread use of anything resembling a uniform.

This train of thought shattered when the orange tongue of flame from a rifle or musket lit the beach ahead, much closer than Chack expected. Perhaps he'd been expecting breakers or something to define the beach, but there was nothing. The shot was answered by another, then several at once. Immediately, he suspected sentries. The second wave, humans also Khonashi, were the *least* likely to fire on their own. But very quickly, the flashes became continuous.

"I'joorka's troops are either very excited or ran into more than just a few lookouts," Chack shouted at Jindal. Just then, a great gash of flame lit the shore and muffled screams arose from boats somewhere ahead as the pressure of the muzzle blast hit them and thunder rolled from the woods beyond the beach. "Shore baat-tery!" Chack yelled at the closest boats alongside. "Paass the word! Step on it! We must get ashore as quickly as we can." He turned to Jindal. "A red signal rocket, if you please."

Jindal had already opened the waterproof wooden box and was selecting a rocket from the right side. In the darkness, colors were indistinguishable. He placed the guide rod in a hole bored in the bulwark and lit the fuse with a borrowed Zippo. With a gout of yellow-red sparks and a great *whoosh*ing sound, the rocket leaped into the air. It burst high above them moments later and a bright red ball appeared like a tiny comet, trailing sparkling streamers downwind. Another gun boomed in the woods beyond the beach, spraying grapeshot or canister into the running shapes the muzzle flash lit. Almost immediately, nine impossibly bright, white-yellow spears of flame lit *Walker*, *James Ellis*, and *Tarakaan Island* as they commenced firing with the three guns aboard each ship that would bear. The MTBs had nothing to contribute and had probably already dashed off in the direction of their next assignment. Chack heard the harsh shriek of shells whip overhead before they impacted in the trees past the shore. Yellow flashes erupted in the limbs and on the ground, geysering brief images of earth and splinters in the air, or scything hot iron and more shards of wood on the foe. A huge splash alongside nearly swamped his dory, and another wide pattern of grapeshot smote another to his left, leaving it spinning and sinking in a welter of blood and screams. Mortar bombs thumped in the air from heaving barges, their explosions adding to the chaos ashore, but Chack doubted they did much good.

Salvo after salvo flashed from the ships, churning the jungle with brilliant strobes of light, but cannon still snapped back at the landing force, on the beach and beyond.

"How many guns can they *have* here? And *why*?" Jindal yelled. Chack had no answer. He'd personally chosen the spot, close enough to the harbor that they could reach it quickly, yet far enough not to require a shore battery to protect it. And it *wasn't* really a shore battery. The cannon firing at them were comparatively light; "standard" Grik nine-or sixteen-pounders like they'd faced many times. They were using more effective munitions than usual, however, which was relatively new to Chack's experience and a complete surprise to most. And though the guns were incapable of seriously damaging the ships offshore, they were perfectly suitable against an amphibious assault. Apparently, Kurokawa had seen the same vulnerability as Chack and prepared accordingly.

His dory roared up on the beach at last, and 'Cats of the 9th Maa-ni-la poured out onto the sand. Machine guns were stuttering now, and white tracers probed the trees and bounced manically away in the night. A disorganized line of riflemen was lying in the sand, fully exposed except for the shallow depressions they'd scooped or scrunched under themselves, firing back at the sparkling flashes of Grik muskets as fast as they could. Chack followed Jindal out of the dory and they strode among the whizzing bees of musket balls, calling for I'joorka. A Khonashi rushed up, keeping low, but sprawled on his face before he could report.

"Who's in charge here? Where's I'joorka? Mr. Cook?"

"Get down!" yelled a human Khonashi lying nearby. "They all dead! Griks kill us all!"

A dory slamming up the beach just a dozen yards away was shattered by another Grik gun, parts of it and its occupants twirling in all directions, wounded troops spilling out the sides and writhing in the surf. Two lines of tracers converged on the muzzle flash and sparkled as they ricocheted amid a chorus of unearthly Grik squeals.

"They certainly *will* kill you if you lay there and let them. Get up, daamn you!" Chack roared back at the cringing soldier, reaching the line at last. It was quickly becoming a huddled mass, a perfect target, as more troops raced ashore, stopping at the growing obstacle made by their hesitant comrades. A green signal rocket popped overhead, launched from somewhere to the right. It was the signal that the beach was secure and the ships offshore should proceed to their next objectives. Of course, the beach *wasn't* secure, but the fire support might be doing more harm than good, Chack realized. Somebody else must've thought that too. *The baarrage's probably killing Grik, but nobody wants to run toward it either. For safety's sake, the ill-aimed, exploding hell in the jungle is too far inland to affect the closest defenders, and might be doing more to staall the assault than the enemy.* A few more rounds landed in the trees, but the sea was dark again. Somewhere out there, the task force would be securing its guns and steaming away, even though they doubtless saw for themselves that the fight was just getting started. Captain Reddy would guess exactly why whoever fired the green rocket did so, dooming the brigade to win or die. He might've even thought it was Chack himself. *No maatter,* Chack thought. There'd been no choice and he completely agreed with the decision. *We all knew "win or die" was the deal from the start.*

The lifting barrage didn't mean it went quiet, and the Grik fire redoubled, but the first howitzers were up now, sending heavy doses of canister slashing to the front, and the stutter of Blitzerbugs and the crackle of rifles resumed. "Major Jindal," he shouted, pointing to the left, "organize those troops and prepare to advance." Jindal nodded and raced away. Chack took the Krag off his shoulder. "Fix bayonets!" he bellowed, latching on his own.

"Sur," came a distinctive, toothless voice beside him, and even in the dark Chack recognized Sergeant Major Moe. He was an ancient 'Cat who'd made his living hunting the wilds of Borno. Despite his unremembered but extraordinarily advanced age, he was apparently simply too tough to die and had advanced from scout to militia sergeant, then from first sergeant to sergeant major of the

1st North Borno, even though he was the only Lemurian in its ranks.

"Sergeant Major," Chack greeted him. "Where are I'joorka and Mr. Cook?"

"To de right," Moe said, waving. "Dey was first ashore an' got pinned down. Shit get baad wit-out nobody see-um, but Risa's M'reens git ashore an' sweep far anuff up to un-pin 'em. Dey send me to tell you dey's gonna ad-vaance."

Chack looked behind him. More dories were still coming through the withering fire, followed by the four larger, flat-faced barges. Facing that, there probably weren't more than five or six hundred defenders—yet—with maybe six or eight cannon left. But more would be rushing to the sound of the guns and they had to secure the beach and break through before the defense grew strong enough to stop them. After that, there'd probably be a ten-or twelve-mile running fight to the harbor. If they moved fast enough up the wide pathway Fiedler drew and Saansa confirmed, they should roll the Grik up in squad and company packets before they reached the only other place they could establish a proper defensive line: at the edge of the harbor itself. "Very well. Tell Major I'joorka we're about to push forward as well. Whoever moves first will be the signal for the rest."

Moe touched his brow and scampered off in that weird, bow-legged gait he had.

Musket balls whickered overhead or struck the ground and spewed clouds of sand. Others slapped flesh, raising cries of pain. The last wave of dories was landing now, and suddenly enemy tracers started chewing at them. *Maa-sheen guns!* Chack raged. *The Grik have maa-sheen guns!* "Suppress that fire!" he shouted, and rifles and Blitzerbugs hammered at the source of the flicking lights. A heavy blast, almost directly to their front, revealed another cannon, and its shot struck one of the four barges right at the waterline. It quickly filled, its heavy load taking it down just thirty yards from shore. The other barges were drawing a lot of fire as well. Being larger and coming up last, the Grik must've thought there was something particularly dangerous or worthwhile about them. Another Grik machine gun opened up, spraying the next barge as it touched shore.

"Everybody up!" Chack shouted, his voice carrying above the sound of battle. "Sound chaarge!" NCOs raised their whistles and blew one long burst. *"Up and aat 'em!"*

With a roar that sounded as terrified as it was savage, the hundreds of Respitans, Maa-ni-los, and Khonashis gathered near him leaped to their feet and raced ahead, firing as they went. Mortar bombs still fell in the woods, and there'd been enough fiery attention there that a few trees had begun to burn. Chack's troops had targets now in the flickering light, and less ammunition was wasted. Grik, rising behind their breastworks to shoot at the barges, tumbled back, stitched by yammering Blitzerbugs or clutching terrible wounds inflicted by the .50-80 Allin-Silvas. One machine gun to their front redirected its fire and dozens of Chack's troops fell screaming. Something snatched at his smock and he felt a stunning blow on his helmet, but he rushed forward, gasping, his feet heavy in the deep, soft sand. The front of the mob—for that was what it had become—swept up and over the Grik position, shooting and stabbing, their bayonets flashing in the flickering light of growing flames.

Most of the cannon crew, still trying to load another stand of grape, fell sprawling and flailing. Chack shot a Grik in the face, blowing its bottom jaw away, then stabbed another in the side with his bayonet. It nearly yanked the Krag from his hands, raking spastically at the barrel and stock with vicious claws, but the press of stabbing and shooting attackers carried it away. Suddenly in the chaos, a *man* stood in front of Chack beside a strange-looking machine gun, its belt of ammunition protruding rigidly to the side in a curious fashion. Chack thought his face was vaguely similar to Tomatsu Shinya's, with the same narrow eyes and an expression just like Shinya made when he was utterly focused. He also had a two-handed sword, cocked back, ready to strike. For an instant they just stood like that, staring. Then the man's eyes darted down at the bayonet-tipped muzzle of Chack's Krag, held low but aimed unwaveringly at his chest. His eyes came up again, wider, desperate, face twisting, posture stiffening. Chack pulled his trigger and the man cried out, toppling to his side. Blinking harshly, Chack pressed on, thrusting at another Grik with his bayonet. In the frenzied, kaleidoscopic, ear-numbing moments that followed, the fight reached a terrible crescendo of furious, blood-spattering, flame-and-steel-flashing, shrieking, squealing death. And then, with a stunning abruptness, it was over . . . there.

Chest heaving to suck smoky air in his lungs, Chack hopped on the breastworks they'd overcome and looked east. "Re-form!" He gasped. "We'll attaack to the right and roll up the enemy in front of I'joorka and Risa!" The charge on the right was stalling, machine-gun bullets and canister tearing at its front. Behind, however, the bows of all three remaining barges slid to a stop in the shallows, dropping heavy ramps in the sand. Amid a thunderous roar of exhaust, their burdens pitched down into the surf and rumbled forward, shedding water from churning tracks and heavy, riveted plates.

Taanks, Chack thought. *Stupid daamn things. Only four in the whole world—three now,* he corrected. *And we'll never squeeze them through the trees to get them to the road beyond.* The word "road" was something of an exaggeration. As reported, it was little more than a game trail through the jungle. *Probably have to leave them here,* he expected, *even if they make it up the beach.* Then his eyes narrowed and he reconsidered. The three iron, smoke-jetting monstrosities were having no difficulty with the sand and they came on with a thunderous air of invincibility. This was underscored by the fact that they seemed to have drawn the fire of every Grik still defending the beach, and they shrugged it off as if oblivious. Musket balls and tracers *spang*ed off the big machines, and machine guns in sponsons began spitting tracers back, chewing at the source of incoming fire. Even roundshot clanged loudly against them, warbling off in the night, but the tanks kept coming.

"Huh," Chack said aloud as the storm of roundshot, grapeshot, musket balls, and tracers increased—practically ignoring his infantry now—and ricocheted off the creeping, armored vehicles. He imagined the noise inside must be incredible. The engines were loud enough, more than 150 tails away. Combined with the battering they were taking, the crews must be deaf by now. Another sound grew louder too: the vengeful roar of his Raiders. Teetering on the verge of annihilation moments before, they swept forward again, shouting, shooting, getting close to the breastworks. A big ball, maybe a sixteen-pounder, possibly even double-charged, based on the tremendous report and spreading fog bank of smoke, must've found a weak spot, and one of the tanks rocked with the impact and lurched to a stop. A figure leaped out the hatch on top and jumped to the ground. Another crew—man, 'Cat, lizard; Chack couldn't tell—tried to escape, but was consumed by a gush of flames that spewed out the hatch. An instant later, a dull explosion shook the tank and burning fuel spilled out the back onto the sand.

The tank's death didn't make any difference. In the time Chack took to watch it, the other two crawled over the breastworks, accompanied by battle-crazed troops who slew everything in their path. He saw many Grik run away, panicked by the relentless charge and the iron monsters they couldn't stop. "Maybe there's something to taanks after all. Stick a little caannon in 'em and they might *really* do something," he muttered to himself, unheard by the roaring, cheering troops around him. They'd gathered for their flank attack, but it looked like it wouldn't be necessary.

Major Jindal joined him, breathing hard, his left arm hanging useless, and stabbed his bloody sword in the sand. "That was . . . brisker than I'd've liked," he hissed through pain-clenched teeth. A corps-'Cat was following him impatiently, and now that he'd stopped, the 'Cat slit his sleeve and soaked away blood with a battle dressing so he could see the wound in the flickering light of a burning tree. "I'm shot," Jindal snapped irritably at the corps-'Cat. "But I'll live—if you don't kill me with your infernal poking." He tried to move away. "I don't have time for this."

"Yes, you do," Chack told him. He'd learned wounds better than he'd ever wanted and could see that Jindal's was bad. "Whistlers!" he shouted. "Sound recall!" NCOs promptly blew the proper sequence of loud chirps. The firing had all but stopped, and he tried to imagine how long the sharp fight lasted. Thinking back, it probably seemed much longer than it was. He'd acquired a feel for such things and figured it hadn't taken half an hour from the moment the first shots were fired. He looked back at Jindal and continued in a low voice. "We have to press on and leave the wounded here, as plaanned. Just as important, we'll have to send back any who're wounded along the way. If we succeed, they should all be evaac-uated by the end of the coming day." He didn't add that if they *didn't* succeed, there probably wouldn't be anyone left to evacuate anybody, but Jindal knew that. He blinked regret, but doubted Jindal saw. "I'm sorry, old friend, but I caan't lose you, and you'll die trying to keep up. You have to take chaarge here and com-maand the company of Respitaans detailed to defend our injured."

Jindal looked away to hide the wetness on his cheeks from the light. "You're right, of course. I'd just be a hindrance."

Chack smiled. "*Never*, Aal-ist-air, and that's the problem. You'd just drop dead before you ever allowed it." They both looked up as Risa and Galay joined them, followed by I'joorka, Abel Cook, and Moe. Risa and, oddly, Moe, were the only ones not covered in blood, but none looked hurt. With all the shooting and Jindal's wound, he'd felt a growing fear for them. Risa in particular.

"There was a field tele-graaph over there," Risa warned.

Chack nodded. It had been inevitable. They'd hoped against it, but expected it. Even Gravois had confirmed that Kurokawa wouldn't give wireless technology or radio to the Grik on the mainland, but there might be telegraphy in Sofesshk by now, matching the advantage of their own field telephones. Something else for Pete Alden to worry about.

"They'll know we're coming. All the more reason to move before they get their shit in the sock," Risa urged.

"I is sorry, Colonel," I'joorka blurted.

Chack was taken aback by the change of subject. "For what?"

"For the actions of the First North Borno," Cook said for his commander. "They froze up under fire and nearly cost us the landing."

Chack waved it away. "It was their first baattle," he said, "and a confusing one at that. We have always had trouble with landings, and this one was unusually well opposed. Besides, your troops were leaderless for a time. It's normal," he added grimly.

"But it *wasn't* their first battle, Colonel. Not for most. Many fought the Japanese from *Hidoiame*. All the NCOs did."

"Okay. But that was at home. This was not. This was a shore they never even knew existed and they fought *very* well once they overcame their uncertainty." He looked at I'joorka. "That uncertainty is gone now and will not return. You have no reason to be ashamed of yourself *or* your troops. I am not."

"Thank you," I'joorka said, looking down.

"Now," Chack said briskly, sharing a relieved glance with his sister, "we must pursue the enemy. I don't expect serious resist-aance until we near the harbor, but there may be aam-bushes. We'll pull two sections of the mountain howitzers before us on the trail, supported by a company of Maa-reens with Blitzerbugs and a maa-sheen gun section. We have to move swiftly," he reminded, "and it should be very difficult for the enemy to block that much firepower on a narrow trail."

"What about the taanks?" Risa asked. "I like 'em!"

Chack considered. "If they can make it, they can come. But they'll have to bring up the rear. We can't take the chance one will break down or get jaammed and block the trail." He looked grimly at his officers and the troops gathering round, the crackling of damp, burning trees and moans of the wounded the only sounds. "We're ashore," he said. "Now the haard part begins. We have a long way to go before daylight, and a great deal to do when we reach our objective. Let us proceed."

CHAPTER 21

Kurokawa's HQ

The bombing woke Kurokawa, as it had before. He didn't leap from bed this time, however. There was nothing he could do and it was already too late to run outside and dive in the muddy, protective trenches. His Grik had taken to using them as latrines, in any event, damn them. Muriname would flush the fighters—*Not that they'll do much good*, he thought bitterly—and the antiaircraft artillery was already booming. It was better to stay where he was. If a stray bomb found him, his worries would be over. If it didn't, at least his people might interpret his actions as unconcern, and wouldn't see the terror that had begun to torment him.

Considering all he'd been through, it rather amazed him that he'd never realized he was a coward. He'd always been able to blame his failures on others and rationalize his escapes, to define his behavior as the courage to survive and continue fighting in the face of adversity, to strive for the destiny awaiting him on this world. But then he'd seen *real* courage in the eyes and actions of the defenseless pregnant wife of his most hated adversary. Not only were she and her friends entirely in his power, helpless to resist if, on a whim, he chose to snuff them out, but regardless of their position and the fear they surely felt, they still had faith in Captain Reddy and their cause—and an absolute certainty they'd be avenged. And it wasn't just bravado; *he'd* used that enough to recognize it when he saw it. They were so *sure* that *he* was doomed that it shook Kurokawa to his core.

He knew his people relied on him and obeyed him. His Grik practically worshipped him. But it wasn't faith that drove them, only fear. Fear of his power and anger, as well as the enemy he'd constantly provoked, perhaps disastrously this time. The latter had bound them together against a common threat, and since none could expect more mercy than he, they'd still fight to save themselves. But the former hadn't inspired loyalty, faith, or even true respect, and most had probably judged him a coward long ago as he squandered their lives to preserve his own. It was as if a light of reason had flickered to life in his long-deluded mind, and even as he'd tormented the small woman with his words at their first meeting, he'd reluctantly realized he *admired* her—and grown ashamed of himself.

His first reaction had been denial. He'd *show* her—he'd wreck the cause she fought for, destroy the puny ship that thwarted him at every turn, *kill* the man she loved, his most implacable foe that . . . And then it hit him. Captain Reddy was the enemy he had *made*. There'd been the old war, of course, and that couldn't be ignored. It even still seemed reasonable that they should've continued their battle here. But the Grik had perverted that purer cause, and by aligning himself with them, he'd lost any honor a victory might give him. The reason he'd regained admonished him that he should've made peace with Captain Reddy, worked with him, allowed him to conquer this world, the Grik, and now the League at his side. With Captain Reddy's ability to inspire, to raise armies and alliances, and Kurokawa's beloved *Amagi*, nothing could've stood against them. But somehow he doubted Reddy would've been as ruthless as required. *I could always have removed him later, when the time was right.* He shook his head as the bombs exploded closer and he trembled. *No,* he realized. *I am what I am and Captain Reddy would never have joined me. I would've had to join* him, *support* his *vision, and that was never possible.*

A sharp rapping on the door to his bedchamber brought him upright and he tried to compose himself. "What is it?" he demanded harshly.

"General of the Sea!" came Signal Lieutenant Fukui's anxious voice. "I just received a telegraph message from the garrison on the southern point of the island!"

"Well? What did it say? Did they see a plane go down?" he asked hopefully.

"No, Lord," Fukui said impatiently. "Lord, may I come in?"

Kurokawa sighed loudly, hoping it sounded exasperated and not afraid.

"Very well. Bring a lamp. I will dress."

Fukui thrust the door aside and entered, already holding a lamp, while Kurokawa pushed the mosquito netting aside and shifted to the edge of his leaf-stuffed mattress. "Hand me my shoes," Kurokawa ordered imperiously.

"Lord!" Fukui insisted. "The enemy has landed in force and swept away the garrison. It can only be assumed they are coming *here*."

Kurokawa goggled at him. As fearful as he'd become, he'd also grown complacent, actually *believing* Sandra Reddy's hints that they had more precious time. He shook himself and quickly dressed, pacing into his office where Muriname, Iguri, Riku, Hara Mikawa, Maggiore Rizzo, Contre-Amiral Laborde, and Capitaine Dupont already waited. "They are coming," he said simply.

"No, Lord," Muriname corrected, "they're *here*. The final confrontation you've craved so long is upon us," he added somewhat dryly.

Kurokawa jerked a nod. "So be it," he said, gazing at the map on his desk. "Their objective is plain. They'll attempt to reach the harbor by land, but those troops did not swim here. We can expect a concerted attack by sea and air at dawn." He looked at Laborde. "Prepare *Savoie* to get underway." He glanced at Mikawa. "The rest of the fleet as well. I will likely go aboard *Savoie* myself, but have *Nachi* stand by in case I change my mind."

"Of course, General of the Sea," Mikawa said.

"You mean to meet them at sea?" Laborde asked, surprised. "Surely it would be better to wait for them in the harbor. They can't attack through their own minefield, so that leaves only the North Channel. We can concentrate all our firepower there."

Kurokawa regarded him with contempt. "You clearly do not understand. If they're coming, they'll do so with what they consider sufficient force to succeed. That means they've brought one carrier, at least. Would you rather sit immobile while agile aircraft bomb and possibly torpedo *Savoie*, or do you prefer room to maneuver?"

"How dangerous can their little planes be?" Dupont asked derisively. "Our antiaircraft weapons will swat them from the sky."

"I hope you're right," Kurokawa said, "but you haven't faced their little planes before. I have. Do not underestimate them." He looked around. "Our fleet will sortie at dawn and seek theirs." He looked at Muriname. "I want scouts—torpedo planes with radios—in the air at once."

"And *my* planes?" Maggiore Rizzo asked, his voice laced with irony.

"With the dawn, with the rest of the fighters, prepare to pounce on the enemy air attack." He regarded Fukui. "It may take too long for them to arrive, but send an urgent message to all ground forces on the island to converge here, prepared to fight. We must *stop* the enemy before they reach the harbor." He waited expectantly. "You have your orders," he shouted, and the room quickly emptied. Rizzo stopped to stare at him a moment, blocking Fukui, with an unreadable expression on his face. Finally, he turned and left. "One more thing, Fukui," Kurokawa said as the communications officer tried to follow. "Send a message to the airfield near the prison compound." It was the last intact airfield they had. "In addition to preparing for operations against the enemy, the commander will send a detachment to bring Sandra Reddy to me." He hesitated, then took a deep breath. "The rest of the prisoners have no value now. They will be executed at once."

Fukui gulped. "Lord . . ."

"At once!" Kurokawa roared.

* * *

The Prison Compound

It had been another lovely bombing raid, coming much later (or earlier, depending on your perspective) than usual, and Sandra, Adar, Diania, Horn, Lange, Eddy, and Ruffy all came out to watch. Fires spread in the dockyards and at least one fuel-oil storage area was engulfed, pushing a gratifying toadstool of orange-red flame into the sky. No more surface-based machine-gun fire was wasted on the high-flying bombers, but a few tracers speared the cloudy darkness above as enemy planes went after them. Exploding shells burst overhead with impressive regularity. The Grik triple-A crews had continued to improve and twinges of apprehension accompanied each detonation, but there'd been no resultant smear of falling fire. They couldn't tell if the raid hit much that previous ones missed, other than the tank battery, but no doubt it infuriated and inconvenienced Kurokawa, Laborde, and all their enemies here. Anything that accomplished that was a source of satisfaction. Their *only* satisfaction lately, other than Adar's slow recovery.

He spent more time moving around, goading Lange into doing the same, but remained very weak. They were *all* weak, for that matter, and the exercises most performed were necessarily less strenuous. There'd been no more abuse or even visits from jeering Japanese sailors, but their already meager rations had been cut. Sandra suspected everyone on the island was doing with less, judging by the gauntness of their guards—which occasionally, unnervingly, eyed them with a different hunger than the Japanese—and she wondered if Matt's ships or planes from his AVDs were interdicting shipments from the mainland. It made sense.

The lively fireworks show of the raid finally began to ebb without the apparent loss of a single bomber this time, and they began drifting back to their bedding. Diania suddenly stiffened. "What's that?" she asked, pointing far to the south. They all stared. Distant flashes glittered on the horizon past the bay, near where they assumed the southern end of the island must be. They couldn't hear them but they came like lightning, sharp and swift. Most faded instantly but a few lingered, sputtering intensely, even casting a faint glow against the high clouds.

"Would'ja look at that?" Horn said softly.

"Maybe one of our planes got hit after all and crashed down there?" Sandra murmured doubtfully.

"That's no plane crash," Horn stated unequivocally. "That's gun flashes—naval rifles—and mortars too, maybe. Plenty of cannon and rifle fire," he added darkly, "and tracers shooting two different ways. If you look hard you can see 'em bouncing up, like sparks from a fire." He took a deep, long breath. "I guess I've been in enough night actions to know one when I see it."

"Then that means . . ."

"I believe your mate comes for us at last, Lady Saandra," Adar said, his strong, confident voice belying his persistent frailty.

"And that's just the start of it," Horn agreed. "Whatever happens next'll probably be big, creative, and hopefully unexpected. The question is, what're *we* gonna do?"

"We can't stay here," Sandra reminded them definitively, "and we don't have a lot of time. They've probably already sent somebody for us." They'd long agreed that when this moment came, they had to make a break. Kurokawa *would* try to use them and that simply couldn't happen. Even if it cost them all their lives. She glanced worriedly at Adar, but spoke to them all. "Is everybody ready for this?"

"We ha' nae choice," Diania agreed, putting a hand on Horn's arm. It was a simple gesture, but full of meaning for them—and Sandra. She prayed they'd come through okay, have a chance to explore their feelings, perhaps even find what she and Matt had discovered. She frowned, and laid her hand on her belly. She wouldn't just be fighting for herself, and, as Adar had said, she ought to be taking it easy, but she'd do what she must. Obviously, without her, the child had no chance at all. Helpless and unknowing, it risked as much as any of them. The thought chilled her and filled her with a deadly resolve.

"It's settled, then," Lange said. He and the two 'Cat sailors hurried to dig up their weapons. They weren't much. Over the weeks, they'd removed an assortment of the sharpened stakes around their stockade, carefully re-weaving the bindings so their absence wouldn't be noted. Then, at night, they sharpened them further with stones the Japanese sailors had thrown, before hiding them for the day. Moments later, Lange and his companions returned with the sandy wooden spears and quickly distributed them. Sandra's, Adar's, and Diania's were thinner, lighter, than the others, but Fitzhugh Gray had taught them what to do. Horn's, Lange's, and the other 'Cats' were longer and heavier, and Horn had showed them how to handle them like rifles with bayonets. There were only two guards, as usual, and against normal Grik their odds would be good. But these had muskets with *real* bayonets, swords, and armor. Of course they also had the terrifying teeth and claws every Grik was born with. Armed with spears and determination, the prisoners should still have a slight edge, but it was unlikely all, or even most, of them would survive.

Sandra hesitated. "I should use the pistol," she said. She'd kept it secret, even from her friends, for quite a while. What they didn't know they couldn't spill. But when they'd started making weapons and planning what to do when the time was right, she'd revealed the little Colt and suggested it might give them an advantage.

"You could," Horn hedged, "but how effective will a few rounds of three eighty be against two armored Grik? And what about the noise? There's *gonna* be noise—nothing we can do about that—but screaming never seems to get much attention." Grik fought among themselves all the time—at least *these* Grik did—and sometimes, for reasons they barely understood, one of their guards might be tossed in the moat. There was plenty of screaming then. "Shots're different, though," Horn continued, "and might raise alarm when nothing else will."

"Agreed," Adar said, looking intently at Sandra, "and re-gaard-less how the breakout goes, I will feel better knowing you have a final defense, for you and your youngling."

"That's settled, then," Horn said, and with a last glance at the distant fighting, as if for inspiration, he grasped his spear more tightly and nodded at the others. "Let's get it done."

Quickly, most of them hid behind the stockade on either side of the gate, relying on the Grik's poor night vision for concealment. Then, standing in full view, Lange and the two women began to scream at one another. Ordinarily, the guards wouldn't care. But Lange's experience as a tramp merchant sailor in the Far East, before joining the Hamburg-America Line, and some recent polish speaking with Toru Miyata, gave him enough Japanese that the guards—subject to Japanese orders all the time, and commanded specifically to keep Japanese sailors from the compound—should react. They wouldn't know how a Jap got past them, but their first inclination—it was hoped—would be to get him out. Sure enough, illuminated by torches at the end of the land bridge, the guards turned to stare. When they did, Sandra and Diania began to fight Lange and scream more desperately for help. The "fight" consisted of exaggerated pushing and shoving, but the guards probably didn't know why the Japanese had wanted in so badly in the first place. They only knew they weren't supposed to be there. Together, they trotted over the land bridge, opened the gate, and rushed inside.

"Now!" Horn roared, jumping up and thrusting his spear as hard as he could. To his horror, the sharpened tip touched a square of iron sewed to the leather tunic and turned. The blow slammed the closest guard into the second, however, and there was a moment of confusion while the rest of the prisoners attacked, instantly realizing what had happened, and aiming their spears for necks, eyes, armpits. But the guards were good. They battered the thrusts away, apparently unsure how to react. Sandra recognized their predicament at once. "They're here to keep us from escaping, but also to protect us!" she shouted, driving forward with Lange and Diania. "Don't give 'em time to decide which is more important!"

Apparently, they already had. One knocked Lange's spear away and slammed a musket butt in his chest, doubling him over with a gasp. Sandra's and Ruffy's spears found its neck just as it spun and drove its bayonet in Eddie's side. The 'Cat shrieked horribly but wrenched at the musket as he fell, tearing it away from the Grik—which was also squealing as twisting spears in its throat ground savagely deeper and Adar's spear probed for its eyes. Horn had launched himself at the other Grik, pounding it to the ground. Both had ahold of the musket, and Horn was pushing down. He wasn't trying to choke the guard as much as keep its snapping jaws from tearing out his face and throat—all while kicking and squirming to stay inside its flailing back legs and the claws that could rip him open. Diania, fearful of stabbing Horn, had finally positioned her spear in the armor gap down the guard's side and lunged forward with all her surprising strength, piercing its belly.

It roared in agony, flailing even more madly, almost launching Gunny Horn. Somehow he held on, but yelled in pain when a wicked back talon raked his thigh. Diania, screaming too, her small voice a piercing wail of rage, worked the spear inside the Grik, slamming it back and forth with the speed and force of a steam piston. Blood jetted up the shaft, ruining her grip, and frothy, ghastly smelling blood sprayed Horn's face. Slowly, the guard's struggles began to ease, but its hand somehow found the wrist of the musket, its finger the trigger. The percussion cap exploded brightly in Horn's face when the musket fired, the tongue of flame at the muzzle actually scorching the other guard in the back. Its spine turned to exploding salt and it dropped as if the big lead ball had severed the strings of a reeling, screeching marionette. Lange, still gasping loudly, had retrieved the other musket from Eddie's corpse and rammed the bayonet in the throat of the Grik still snapping feebly at Horn's face. It finally convulsed and lay still, and Horn rolled off in the sand. Instantly, Diania was kneeling beside him, her tears dropping on his face.

"No! Adar!" Sandra said, her voice rising in alarm, almost panic. "No!" she shouted. Horn scrambled to his feet and he and Diania joined the rest, already gathered around another form lying in the sand.

"It seems I've finally fought my first—and last—baattle,

my dear," Adar's distinctive voice met them. Still so calm, so gentle, but painfully strained. Sandra had bunched up his battered robe and was holding it against his chest.

"The ball that killed that one passed through and hit Adar," she explained, visibly calming herself, but her voice was brittle. "It's probably not deep; was nearly spent."

"Good," Lange said, getting his breathing under control. "We must leave at once. We can carry him."

Horn leaned hard against him. "Just shut up, you," he hissed. "We have a couple minutes. Not like we need to pack. We got these muskets. Let's strip the Grik for ammo and other weapons."

"No," Adar told Sandra, and coughed. It was like she was the only one with him now. "I've always studied anaatomy as well as the Heavens. My friendship with Courtney Braad-furd increased my interest in the first to the extent . . . It grieves me to say that I feel . . ." He coughed again, more raggedly, and blood darkened the fur on his chin. "The baall went deep enough." He raised his hand and touched the tears streaming down Sandra's cheek. "It does *not* grieve me to die, you know. I will soon join my friends, my aan-cestors who've gone before, high in the Heavens. And have no fear: I *will* share the final victory with you, watching from above." He managed a smile. "I only grieve for you and *your* pain, because I know you'll miss me. As will Cap-i-taan Reddy and my brother Keje. Alaan Letts is my son, his daughter mine as well. Remind him, remind *everyone* of my love, my thoughts for them. You know the rest as well as I, and . . . There is not time to name them all." His hand dropped to her belly. "I may meet this one before you, my dear. I think I hear him whispering to me even now." His silver eyes glistened in the torchlight from across the bridge. "Yes, *he*," Adar pronounced confidently, "though it might be a female—with Cap-i-taan Reddy's voice. But it saddens me I will never *hold* him until the day he joins us all in the sky. Still, I can perform a final duty."

Sandra couldn't speak, couldn't even tell *him* not to speak, to hold on, to save his strength—all the usual platitudes. None mattered now, because he was right. Hot blood was washing across her hand behind his back and the ball *hadn't* been spent until it knocked the spear from her hands. If it hadn't hit Adar first . . . The tears and darkness clouded her vision and she desperately wanted to see him clearly one last time. She shook the tears from her eyes but it didn't help.

"Maker of All Things," Adar began, staring upward now, his voice growing thicker, weaker. "We thaank you for this life you gifted us, this soul you made and gave a fraa-gile form. As you instructed it to do good in your name while among us, so shall we remind and admonish it, so that when it returns to you, its maker, you will be pleased with what it has become." He looked back at Sandra and managed a real grin. "Thaat's it," he said. All Lemurian prayers were very brief and to the point; something he and Sandra had discussed before. She snorted wetly. She'd echoed the prayer with her own and was amazed how equally well it applied to this good person lying in her arms as it did to the life inside her.

"Thank you," she murmured. Weakly, Adar reached for her face again and she clasped his furry hand and held it to her cheek.

"It doesn't hurt a great deal, and I'm sure you could save me under . . . other conditions." Adar's voice had become a whisper she could barely hear. "As it is," he continued, "I will ask a final favor. You know I have few real differences with my esteemed colleague, Sister Audry, and her Chiss-chin faith. One is fairly profound, however, the one about vengeance. I believe the Maker has more to occupy Him than righting the wrongs His people do, at least until they stand before Him. I still believe He brought *you* to us to help with that, but then, as always, He left it to us to present the evil ones for His judgment. So I ask you to avenge me, avenge *Amerika* and the helpless ones aboard her. And my last request to you and . . . Cap-i-taan Reddy . . . is to . . . finish . . ."

Adar was gone. He hadn't completed what he wanted to say, but Sandra knew what it was: finish the job, win the war, make the world safe for his people—of whatever race and species. It was all he'd worked for, almost since the day they met. Gently, she laid him in the sand and straightened. "You'll have your revenge, Adar," she told him. "We all will. And somehow, some way, we *will* finish the job!"

Diania touched her, breaking the spell. "We haftae go, Lady Sandra!" she insisted. Sandra nodded, covering Adar's pathetically frail, lifeless form with his tattered robe. "We'll be back for you," she murmured. Then, standing, she strode toward where the others had gathered behind the stockade, just inside the gate. Horn was peering out.

"I should've used my pistol," she said to no one in particular.

"Maybe. Maybe not. Let's go."

"Wait!" Ruffy warned, pointing at the woods where the trail leading to the compound disappeared. A double line of torches was approaching at a trot. "More Grik!" he said. They'd waited too long. There were at least twenty of Kurokawa's personal guards coming for them, just as they'd expected, and no way they could bolt now without being seen.

"Well, shit," Horn said, quickly loading the musket. It was the one that killed the Grik—and Adar. Lange's was still loaded. "How many rounds in that little three eighty?" he asked Sandra.

"Seven."

"You pretty good with it? I mean, can you wing a few? Between me an' Lange, we might knock down a few more. Give you and . . . I mean, *us* a chance to make a break."

"I'll try," Sandra said, knowing what he'd started to say. She also knew it was hopeless. The Grik were in the open now, halfway to the gate. The leader had noticed the guards were gone, the gate stood open. He snapped something and the column stopped.

"Get ready!" Horn said, voice tensing as he slid the bloody musket over the palisade.

The clearing roared with the up-close, thunderous crack of rifles and the frantic stutter of several automatic weapons firing at once, and the tree line to their left lit up with bright muzzle flashes. The Grik danced and jerked as bullets tore them apart. Bodies dropped and sprawled on the ground, some flailing, others still, amid a downy haze of blood spray, clattering weapons, and scattered torches. In seconds it was over, except for a few quick bursts that stilled moving, moaning forms. To everyone's surprise, the first rescuers that appeared, kicking through the dead, looked like more Grik, even down to their dress. Then they saw a couple of Lemurians and two humans trotting toward the compound, weapons ready.

"You there, Gunny?" came a distinctive, inimitable voice.

"My God! Silva!" Horn exclaimed, standing up. In the light of the torches on the land bridge, Dennis's face split into that particular gap-toothed grin that defined his personality so well—and that few enemies ever survived.

"I ain't a *god*, Gunny. Leastways, not that I know of. An' nobody ever *called* me one before." He paused, apparently considering. "Unless you count—"

Sandra stood. "Chief Silva." She managed a smile at Stuart. "Mr. Brassey, and Lawrence as well, of course. We're *very* glad to see you," she said earnestly. "You could've come at a slightly better time . . . but I'm grateful and won't complain, as long as you stow your banter for later. I assume we need to move?"

"Yes'm," Silva agreed. "Right smart too. Griks yonder at the airfield'll be closest with the mostest, but even if we can take 'em, we don't want them tangled up. There's a few more projects on my wish list tonight—I mean, this mornin'."

"Which way?" Sandra asked.

"Right down the throat o' the snake," Silva said, pointing at the trail the Grik emerged from. "It's the right direction, an' except for these lousy boogers"—he kicked a dead Grik in the snout—"anybody else's liable to be headed the other way, toward the harbor. Shouldn't meet much till we get near it ourselfs." The rest of the prisoners had stepped out to join them, those without weapons gathering the Grik's.

"We have a couple extra Blitzers for you ladies, if you'd like," Stuart Brassey said, his young voice cracking in an attempt to sound mature and gallant.

"Thank you . . ." Sandra peered at the bars sewn to his collar. "*Captain* Brassey! Congratulations. And your troops?"

"The First North Borno, ma'am, under Major I'joorka—which, along with Chack's Brigade, is landing in the south as we speak."

Sandra and Diania took the offered weapons and they started to move.

"Hey," Silva asked. "Where's ol' Adar, an' the other 'Cat? We sneaked up close enough to see 'em yesterday evenin'."

"Dead," Sandra replied hollowly. "That's why your timing could've been better. Ten minutes earlier . . ." She shook her head and patted Silva's arm. "*Thank you.*"

Silva hung back with Horn just a moment while Brassey led their team and the prisoners toward the trail, Lawrence, with Pokey trailing, already casting ahead. Dennis would bring up the rear in case of pursuit, but for a moment he stared at the compound. "In there, huh?"

Horn nodded, unseen. "Yeah."

"We heard a shot. I should'a known you'd make a barehanded break, like a dumb-ass, when *you* of all people should'a known we'd come get you when the time was right."

"It was Lady Sandra's idea."

"No shit?" Dennis sounded offended. "*She* should'a known, even more than you!"

Horn snapped back. "Yeah? Well we *didn't* know, see? How could we? You don't know what it's been like."

"Okay, okay," Silva said, looking back at the compound. When he spoke again, his voice was . . . different, rougher somehow. "I'll swan. Ol' Adar now too. I'll swan," he repeated, then seemed to shake himself. "Let's go. It's a damn bad start to a busy day—an' it ain't even started yet!"

"What's the plan?" Horn asked as they turned and jogged after the others.

"It's a doozy. You'll love it," Dennis replied, giving Horn a handful of ship's biscuits to munch on. Horn stuffed one in his face.

"So, as usual," he mumbled, spilling crumbs, "you're making it up as you go?"

"Kinda."

"Works for me," Horn agreed, swallowing. Then he

chased the dry food with a swig from Silva's canteen. "Especially since I may have an idea or two you haven't thought of. Call them preconsiderations to the inexpressible."

"You an' your weird words," Dennis complained. "Okay, spill 'em."

"At least my weird words are real," Horn retorted.

Eventually they caught up with the others and jogged with Brassey, Sandra, Diania, and Lange, who'd hung back with the Khonashi rear guard. Lange was already gasping, taking deep gulps from a canteen someone gave him, but the rest were bearing up. Of course, they'd only just begun a near-five-mile run.

"What's the plan?" Sandra asked, echoing Horn's earlier question.

"It's a doozy. You'll love it," Silva repeated.

Horn snorted. "*I'm* going for *Savoie*—and that goddamn frog admiral, Laborde. He'll be on her, guaranteed."

"I don't think . . ." Brassey began.

"What for?" Dennis interrupted.

"I assume Captain Reddy intends to lure her out?" Horn asked. "Well, even if he has a plan to deal with her, she's an iron bitch. Literally. She'll kill a *lot* of our guys. I think in the confusion, with help from some of Captain Brassey's Khonashis, I can get aboard."

"Then what?" Brassey demanded, suddenly intrigued.

"Get in one of her gun houses. There's no way they can pry us out." Horn shrugged. "Then maybe blow her up."

"Shit!" Dennis grinned. "Sounds fun, if you can pull it off—then get off her."

"I agree," Brassey said between breaths. "Horn and I can try to pass ourselves as Japanese. We'll make the attempt, along with half the Khonashis, and perhaps Pokey. He speaks the language."

"And I," Becher Lange said on a gasp, "have my own score to settle with Laborde. But we needn't pass as Japanese. A few of her original crew remained, and I speak excellent French."

"Okay. Sounds like a good preconsideration," Dennis agreed.

"What about us?" Sandra demanded.

"You, *Lady* Sandra, an' Miss Diania too, are gonna

find a nice, safe hidey-hole while me an' Larry, our Shee-Ree kitties, an' what Khonashis Cap'n Brassey leaves us raise as much hell as we can." He patted the satchel bouncing at his side. "I got a whole poke full o' grenades—my very favorite kind o' fun! Who knows? Maybe we'll catch Kurokawwy before he boards *Savoie*."

"As good a plan as any, I suppose," Sandra agreed. She was also starting to breathe heavily, weakened by lack of food and the unaccustomed weight she carried in her abdomen. "Except for one detail," she added. "I'm not sitting this out."

"Nor I," snapped Diania.

"But . . ."

"No buts, Chief Silva," Sandra said. "I'll let you and the rest do the heavy lifting, I promise." She added quickly, "But don't you see? That maniac meant to use me as a weapon against my husband, our cause. If in any way my presence helps you prevent that—and I can already think of several ways—I have to be there. Do you understand?"

"Maybe," Silva grudged, mashing his sweat-soggy eyepatch to drain it before its weight made it sag off his face. "But if I let anything happen to you, the Skipper'll keelhaul me on *Big Sal*. An' I'd have it comin' too."

"Don't worry, Chief Silva. I believe we have a couple of excellent plans, and we *will* make them work."

Breathing hard, but otherwise accompanied only by the rattle of weapons, the soft clatter of accoutrements and ammunition magazines, the dull clinking of .50-80 shells in cartridge boxes, and Silva's incessant humming, the enlarged team hurried on with a more specific and deadly purpose.

CHAPTER 22

Lizard Ass Bay

It was pitch-dark as eight PT boats of Lieutenant Nat Hardee's MTB-Ron-1 thundered north at twenty-five knots, their light hulls planing and bouncing in the choppy sea between Island Number 3 to the west and Number 1 to the east. Occasional lightning still flashed from the overhanging clouds, providing some visibility, but also creating an ominous atmosphere that Nat found hard to ignore. By most definitions, even Lemurians', he was still just a kid, but he'd seen and done a lot since arriving on this world aboard the old *S-19*. He'd been back aboard *S-19* when she was rammed and sunk by a Grik dreadnaught and had to escape—almost straight up—through a torpedo tube with only a few feet of the sub's bow remaining above the surface. He'd participated in a night torpedo attack at the Battle of Grik City, and experienced eerie combat on a jungle river against savage and rarely seen attackers. Still, tested as he was, he remained just a teenager, and having command of the entire squadron had been an unexpected—terrifying—thrill.

He felt no terror now that the waiting was over, however, and he was leading his little "mosquito fleet" into battle. Perhaps a measure of anxiousness persisted about what lay ahead, and that was wholly understandable. They were charging full speed aboard frail little boats, into a stirred-up hornet's nest with what was probably the highest concentration of overwhelming firepower any Allied force had ever faced. What was more, his squadron was all alone.

The strait was only about four miles wide, and Nat couldn't see Island Number 3 at all. He barely saw Number 1 because it was highlighted by the dockyard fires left by the bombing raid. It was enough. His veteran Seven boat, *Lucky Seven*, had the best crew in the squadron, and her XO, Lieutenant (jg) Rini-Kanaar, was a wonder. She'd studied to become a Sky Priest before the war and still hoped to be one someday. She'd make a good one, with her uncanny memory of images and knack for mentally superimposing charts or scrolls she'd seen upon the sea around her, automatically calculating where their speed, course, leeway, sea conditions, even the currents (when they knew them) would put the boat at any given moment. Her dead reckoning was dead-on to a degree Nat hadn't imagined possible. With her steering the Seven boat, the rest of the squadron had only to follow its frothy, phosphorescent wake exactly where they needed to be. And as soon as they rounded the north end of Island Number 1, they'd have a fine, fire-lit view of the anchorage beyond, while the same light marking the enemy should hide them as they approached. Nat reminded himself not to stare at the flames, to protect his night vision. *But when we are seen . . .* came the sudden, seditious thought.

"I'm sure glaad we ain't goin' at that daamn *Saavoie*. Her big guns give me the creeps!" Rini shouted at him, probably talking to settle her nerves. That was fine. Nat's nerves had spiked a bit, thinking about the ex-League battleship.

"Me too," he agreed. "And she doesn't even need her biggest ones. Her *secondaries* can shred us farther away than our torpedoes will even go."

"Yaah. We still gotta get past all them kroozers, though," Rini reminded.

"We do," Nat acknowledged. "But they'll be surprised, trying to hit smaller, faster surface targets than they've probably ever seen—with muzzle-loading cannon." Nat didn't *think* any Grik cruisers had ever faced *Walker* and survived, so sufficiently leading anything fast shouldn't come naturally to any of their gunners. He might be wrong, he supposed, but they *would* be surprised—especially when only a few boats actually attacked them. The rest had other business.

Finally, the mouth of the North Channel began to open before them. Rini eased her helm over and they roared through the entrance, little more than a mile wide. The question now was shore batteries, and the hairs on the back of Nat's neck stood up. They knew the batteries were there, but would their crews see the little flotilla speeding between the peninsula and Island Number 1? Maybe they were still scanning the skies, watching for planes. The PTs would certainly *sound* like planes from shore. Even if the enemy spotted them, they wouldn't see them well, and any hits they achieved would be pure luck. Probably *catastrophic* luck, given the size of their guns—and possibly catastrophic whether they hit or not, since the batteries would alert their targets.

Maybe they're distracted, Nat hoped. *I don't think they can see the fighting to the southeast—I can't anymore, with the island blocking the view—but maybe they've received word? Perhaps they're watching out to sea for another landing force?* A wry smile touched his lips. *No one would be insane enough to run a few little boats into a harbor full of powerful warships.* "Steady as you go," Nat told Rini as the bow aimed directly at the center of the channel. He took a step and turned the switch that activated the clattering alarm bell for a few seconds, calling his crew to their battle stations. It wasn't really necessary. Everyone had been in place since the shoal of MTBs spilled out of *Tarakaan Island*. A pair of 'Cats were forward, behind the new splinter shield protecting the water-cooled .30-caliber machine gun. Two were stationed at the torpedo tubes, one on either beam, and three stood behind Nat and Rini, ready to operate their second machine gun on whichever side of the cockpit they were directed. They'd also be ready to take Nat's or Rini's place if either got hit. Finally, two 'Cats sweltered and shed fur in the hot motor room, between the big six-cylinder Sea Gypsy engines mounted side by side.

I'm responsible for ten people on my boat, Nat thought. *Eighty-seven in the squadron.* He didn't count himself. *Lord, don't let me make a hash of it!* Without realizing it, he bared his teeth as the squadron passed through the narrowest part of the channel, where they were most likely to be noticed. The minutes ticked by and his white-knuckle grip on the coaming began to loosen. Before them lay the fire-lit upper end of Lizard Ass Bay, cluttered with a flock of moored Grik cruisers. *They're lethal-looking things,* Nat conceded, *even somewhat elegant, with their bows sweeping up and aft, away from underwater rams. Silva was right about the top hamper and bulwarks as well.* Those gave better protection for more guns amidships and sleeker, flusher lines. Anchored as they were, practically served up for him, it was tempting to have at them, despite his orders. But he had bigger frogs to gig. Beyond them, in the distance, a bright white spotlight flared to life and stabbed first at the shore battery on the peninsula, then swept outward, where the boats had been. It was *Savoie*, but even if she saw them now, she had no shot with the cruisers stacked between them.

"Lucky Handy!" Nat shouted at Rini, referring to Lieutenant (jg) Haan-Dar, commanding the Four boat, leading 16, 20, and 21. Only they would attack the cruisers. His Seven boat, leading 13, 15, and 23, would soon veer off.

Something else flashed, reflecting off the spray sluicing back from the bow. Then, when a great, bright column of water erupted behind his boat and a huge roundshot bounded up over him, splashing again in the sea ahead, he realized they hadn't completely fooled the shore batteries after all. They could've already fired several times, for all he knew, their reports drowned by the roar of engines. It was probably their shooting, in fact, that alerted a lookout on *Savoie*. "You're too late!" he shouted backward. "Your nap lasted just a *bit* too long!" Several more waterspouts stitched their wakes, well back now. "Signal Handy to have his fun!" Nat told one of the 'Cats in the cockpit. A Morse lamp flashed and Haan-Dar's section peeled off to the left and surged ahead, toward the brooding cruisers. "Come right to one two zero," he told Rini.

"One two seero, aye!" Rini spun the wheel, staring at

the small, lamp-lit compass binnacle below the coaming in front of her. "My course's one two seero," she proclaimed. Nat glanced behind again to watch his consorts follow his turn. As planned, they were fanning out in line abreast on his port beam. Two miles ahead lay a pair of the huge, four-stack, ironclad battleships, secured to a pier, one in front of the other. Nobody knew if they were operational or if Kurokawa was preparing them for conversion to something else, more carriers perhaps, but either way, they had to go. From Silva's reports, there were two more in the harbor, and another converted to an oiler, recently shifted near *Savoie*, but they were a job for the Naval Air Corps. These two were in a unique position to prevent the final detail in Captain Reddy's plan.

At about 2,800 yards, Nat crouched slightly and glanced through the crude sights on the coaming. They aimed their torpedoes by aiming the boat—which could be difficult when the sights kept jumping around and the target was underway—but the Grik BBs were just sitting there, presenting an easy shot. In theory. Nat hadn't used the new Mk-6 torpedoes yet. They were supposed to be good to 10,000 yards, but Bernie Sandison, burned so often by what torpedoes were *supposed* to do, told them to count on half that distance. Nat's boats had only two tubes and no reloads. As long as they weren't taking fire, he wanted to get close enough to stab the enemy in the gut. He'd use one fish on the BB to the right, as would the Twenty-three boat. The other two boats would launch at the one on the left. All were supposed to save their last fish for something else. "A point to the right!" he cried to Rini. "Steady! Ready number one!" he added louder to the torpedo crew to starboard.

"Number one's ready in aall respects!" came the response.

A blossom of orange flame lashed out from the side of the behemoth ahead, removing any doubt about its operational status. Several more followed sporadically; then the whole side of the ship's armored casemate erupted at once. Iron shrieked overhead, splashing far astern, and Nat was mightily tempted to shoot back at once, but wanted a few seconds more. Thirteen and Fifteen didn't wait, and flashes lit their starboard sides as impulse charges hurled their brass-bodied fish into the sea and they creamed away, little faster than the boats that launched them. "Just a little closer," Nat crooned. The other BB fired a full broadside of hundred-pound shot that churned the sea in front of the Thirteen and Fifteen boats before they could turn. All the massive iron balls may have skated, but one did for sure, opening the bow of the Thirteen boat like a banana. The boat bounced up, standing on its tail, pointing straight at the sky. It actually left the water and briefly flew through the air before slamming down on its side and cartwheeling across the waves in a shattering welter of ragged fragments and phosphorescent spray. It came to rest in seconds, upside down, torn apart, swiftly sinking. The Fifteen boat was turning frantically now, and Nat shouted at his torpedo crew. "Fire one!" He closed his eyes to the flash and with a loud *thwump!* the deck jolted beneath his feet. "Come right, thirty degrees! Make your course two one zero, and let's shake our tails!"

"Makin' my course two one seero—an' wavin' so long!" Rini's tail swished rapidly behind her. The Twenty-three boat matched their course, its fish on the way as well. Nat wondered if the torpedoes would hit before the Grik could reload their monstrous guns. "Look, Skipper!" one of the 'Cats on the foredeck shouted, pointing right. A heavy explosion rocked the bay as one of the cruisers arched its back amid a tall spear of foam, then settled, its bow and stern already rising independently. "Broke her baack!" Rini cried, satisfaction in her voice. Another cruiser was already burning, but several were firing now, stabbing the darkness with tongues of flame. Nat watched bitterly as a ball of fire rolled away from a low, swift shape, and it quickly wallowed to a stop, burning gasoline spreading fore and aft, lighting the sea around it. Another cruiser heeled hard over, pushed by a tall column of green-glowing water, but several were underway now, probably cutting their anchor cables. One smashed into the burning wreck with its underwater ram, lifting it until it came apart, its flickering wreckage swept aside by the bow wave, tossing and smoldering in the churning wake. Then they heard heavy detonations aft. Everyone but Rini turned to watch as two hundred-foot feathers of spume rose alongside the target that killed the Thirteen boat. Seconds later, one, then another, geysered up beside Nat's target as well. "Four for four!" one of the machine gunners cried happily, almost hopping with glee. Fire broke out aboard Nat's BB, glowing hungrily behind the open gunports. It might've been Nat's imagination, but both ships already seemed to be listing toward them.

"Taar-git ahead! Mebbe . . . four thousand tails!" Rini shouted, snatching their attention back to what they were really after. Barely visible in the gloom was another huge, dark shape, not as tall, but just as long as the Grik battleship it once was. The higher freeboard and elevated deck made it seem even bigger. Washed by distant flames and the lightning still rippling in the clouds, no doubt fully alert and preparing every defense, was their primary target: Kurokawa's last aircraft carrier. Nat looked to his right and saw that the Fifteen boat had rejoined the line as they roared southwest, perhaps fifty yards apart. "We oughta shoot *now*—we in range," Rini prompted.

"We only have three fish left between us," Nat reminded, "and I think the target's moving." He was right. Like the cruisers, still shooting at the rest of the squadron zooming between them, the dark apparition was gathering way. A firing solution now, with no idea how fast the thing could accelerate, would be nothing but a guess. At 2,500 yards, a pair of searchlights snapped on aboard the carrier, probing at the darkness, sweeping back and forth. One swung across them, blinding bright, then fastened on the approaching boats. The other light joined it, glaring like a pair of small suns.

"Shoot them out!" Nat yelled at his gunners, and tracers immediately arced away, reaching for the lights. More tracers from the other boats joined in, but then, at 2,000 yards, so did those of the enemy.

"Maa-sheen guns!" Rini cried indignantly, as if it wasn't fair that the enemy had made their own.

"Their planes have them. Why not their ships?" Nat ground out. "Two points to starboard!" The enemy tracers were still wild, falling sharply as they neared, but they *could* reach. They felt and heard occasional thumps and clatters as bullets hit the boat. Nat tried to concentrate on his sights as two streams of bullets converged on them and one of the 'Cats on the foredeck tumbled back amid sleeting splinters and rolled over the side with a silent splash. The torpedo-'Cat on the starboard side raced to replace him, but sprawled facedown on the deck. The two Lemurians at the gun kept up a relentless fire as bullets hammered the shield, shattering on impact and cutting their exposed legs and feet with tiny, scything shards of lead and copper. The gunners in the cockpit watched in frustration. There was nothing they could shoot at until the boat turned away.

"The Fifteen boat's fired!" Rini shouted over the gunfire, roaring engines, and pounding sea. Nat glanced to the right. The Fifteen boat was roaring away to the north, chased by a searchlight and two strings of tracers. A great waterspout—from something—erupted in her wake; then another landed in front of her, swamping her with foam. Even as the bullets settled down to the terrible work of chopping her to bits, another shell of some kind punched through her side and exploded against an engine. The boat disintegrated in a shower of flaming fragments, just as tracers from the Twenty-three boat snuffed out one of the searchlights. The sea heaved and tossed, rising in great stalks around the last two PTs, drenching the 'Cats at their stations. Explosions began ripping the air above them as well, spattering the sea with hot shards of iron. Nat stared through his sights, trying to keep the picture clear enough to estimate his lead, loudly calling corrections to Rini. At barely more than a thousand yards, bullets slammed through the coaming, and Rini reeled back. Without a thought, Nat took the wheel and shouted over the din, "Fire two!" The portside fish coughed into the sea, and Nat turned hard left. "Make smoke!" he yelled. Two of the 'Cats behind him had mounted their machine gun on the starboard side of the cockpit and began firing at the last light, even as the third twisted a lever feeding light oil into the fuel line. Almost immediately, thick, blue-white smoke gushed from the exhaust stacks and started piling up in their wake. Possibly thinking they were finished, all the fire now concentrated on the Twenty-three boat, which had also launched and turned to follow. A glare lit up behind them like a flare on the water and slowly died away. They couldn't tell through the smoke whether it signaled the end of the Twenty-three boat or not.

The former prisoners and their rescuers finally emerged, gasping and spent, from the jungle trail near the northwesternmost shipyard in what Silva called Lizard Ass Bay. Explosions and cannon fire still boomed on the water, but all their attention was immediately taken by the looming, malevolent form of *Savoie*. Her searchlights were lending illumination to other lights on the cruisers, questing for targets on the surface, and Silva told Sandra and the others about Nat Hardee's attack. *Savoie*'s alarm bell was also sounding loudly in the dark, and shapes were running aboard, up a long gangway from the pier. There was surprisingly little activity right around them, though, and the time had come to split up.

"Sure you wanna do this, Arnie? Mr. Brassey?" Dennis asked. "Bad guys catchin' you is only half your problem. Come daylight, everything we got's gonna be doin' its damnedest to *sink* that ship yer so hot to sneak aboard. Maybe we best stick together."

"The decision's made, Chief Silva," Brassey said. "If we can disable her somehow, it might make all the difference. You have business of your own, and unless we merely hide and wait for events to unfold—something none of us is disposed to do—we stand a better chance if we separate. A group as large as ours can't move unnoticed and is sure to attract attention." He nodded at Horn, Lange, Pokey, and the five Khonashi who had volunteered to join them, and then motioned toward the ship. "If we're going to get aboard, now is the time, while the confusion is at its height. We must be off."

"Just one second, Captain Brassey," Horn said. He stepped to Diania, and with the utmost tenderness that probably embarrassed him and definitely stunned Silva, he reached up and caressed the woman's cheek. Right then, he didn't give a damn what anybody thought. Even more surprising, Diania closed her eyes and leaned her face into his hand.

"Do be careful, Gunnery Sergeant Horn," she said softly. "Arnold," she added, speaking his given name for the very first time.

"I will," he assured, taking the bayonet from the musket he'd been carrying and sticking the long blade in his waistband. The other members of Brassey's party, realizing his purpose, did the same. They'd have to leave their rifles behind. Brassey and the Khonashi all had pistols, however, and a couple who'd be going with Silva and the others passed theirs to Horn and Lange, along with extra magazines. Horn glanced at Silva. "Never had much reason to watch out for myself before, and I've pulled some stupid stunts. But for the first time, I'm thinking past what I'm doing right now." He fumbled around his neck and handed a sweat-rotted leather thong to Dennis. On one end was a tooth that appeared a good match for the one missing from Silva's mouth. "I'm not giving it to you," Horn warned. "Just hold on to it, in case something happens. If it does, you can have it back. Glue it in or something." It still remained a mystery how Horn wound up with one of Silva's teeth, a long time ago on another world, but no one doubted it had been a memorable adventure. "Now give us some of those grenades from your bag."

"Sure," Silva said, raising the satchel and opening the flap. Brassey, Lange, Horn, and the rest all took one and either hooked it on their belts or stashed it in a pouch. "Plenty for all." Dennis held up the tooth. "I'll keep this for ya, an' make sure you get it back. I got no use for it now, an' you damn sure earned it."

"We *must* go," Brassey insisted.

"Yeah, us too," Silva agreed. "So long, Arnie. Mr. Cook." He looked at Pokey, the little Grik they'd captured at Aryaal so long ago, whom he remembered as barely bright enough to pick up their spent brass. He'd obviously flourished in the 1st North Borno. "So long, Pokey."

"So long, See'va!"

"Good luck, and godspeed," Sandra said.

"And you, Lady Sandra," Brassey replied.

"One last thing," Horn said. "What's that stupid tune you've been humming?"

Silva grinned. "Just a little ditty I learned as a kid.

Kinda catchy, ain't it? Can't remember all the words, but the ones I do go, 'You wanna chase the devil, you wanna have fun. . . . You wanna smell hell. . . .' He shrugged. "Seems kinda fittin'."

With that, the broken party went its separate ways—Brassey's toward the long gangway, Silva's around the outskirts of the shipyard, toward Kurokawa's compound.

It was bizarre, in a way, how easily Horn, Brassey, Lange, Pokey, and their five Khonashi companions boarded the bustling ship on the port quarter and boldly made their way across to the stair beside the number three turret. There were Grik all around, still racing aboard as they were, but no humans in sight. "What about this one?" Brassey hissed, gesturing at the closest turret.

"Well, if all we do is knock one out, maybe we should get one up forward, most likely to be shooting at our people," Horn countered.

Brassey grimaced. "Perhaps, but I dislike the thought of strolling half the length of the ship, surrounded by enemies!"

"It'll be a cinch. Just scowl a lot. And Mr. Lange can holler French at anybody who gets in our way. As long as we don't meet a *real* Frenchie, we should be okay."

Lange and Horn led the way, pretending to know what they were doing. At least they were somewhat familiar with the ship and didn't have to go belowdecks. That would've made it more likely they'd come face-to-face with someone who knew they had no business there. They made their way briskly past the mainmast, then the barges and lifeboats underneath the pair of great cranes flanking the aft stack. There were antiaircraft guns on either side of the deckhouse beneath the empty seaplane catapult, and the number of Grik they saw increased as they passed the forward superstructure. Obviously, as they'd hoped, the Grik must've thought they were French or Japanese. They probably couldn't tell the difference. They *did* see several Japanese officers, waving or leading Grik to their stations, but in the gloom, and seeming to move with a purpose, Horn and Lange were apparently taken for Frenchmen doing the same. Under the chaotic circumstances, paced by obvious "Grik," any notion that they were strangers there to sabotage the ship didn't occur to anyone. For the first time perhaps, the enemy's sense that the species they surrounded themselves with left them immune to infiltration might just bite them on the ass as hard as it had the Allies on occasion.

Trooping around in front of the armored fighting bridge, they arrived underneath the massive, overhanging rear of the number two turret gunhouse. Two large, thick hatches, just a few feet apart, hung open underneath it. Dull yellow light splashed down on them as they gathered around a pair of ladders. "Okay," Horn whispered. "I spent some time in the old *New York* when I first joined the corps. That was another life, back in 'thirty-five. . . ." He shook his head. "Doesn't matter except, to look at, this ship might've been copied from her—or vice versa. Chances are the layout in there"—he nodded up at the gunhouse—"isn't too different. And these hatches aren't buttoned up, so the turret's probably not fully manned. We split: half up one hatch; half up the other. Get in and kill whoever you see as fast and quiet as you can. With all the ruckus on the bay, we might get by if they holler a little, but try to keep it down—and don't add to it. Just get on them and keep sticking"—he glanced at a Khonashi—"or slashing until they quit squeaking. And *no* shooting," he stressed. "But no matter what, we have to kill them all before they raise an alarm, and that means some of us have to get all the way to the gun pit below and shut the hatch down there. Once we secure that and these two, we'll *have* the joint, and there isn't much they can do about it, savvy? Then we'll do what we came for." He paused. "Ready?" There were nods, and Stuart Brassey positioned himself under the left hatch, pulling the bayonet from his belt. Taking a deep breath, Arnold Horn did the same and stood under the hatch on the right. "Let's go!" Brassey said, his young voice cracking, and he and Horn led the rest inside the monstrous turret.

For such a large structure, the interior was incredibly cramped. A heavily armored bulkhead separated the two guns, and only an equally heavy hatch allowed access from one side to the other. The space Horn entered was crammed with the enormous breech of a 13.5″ naval rifle and all the lifts, rams, levers, and trays required to load it. To Horn's surprise, the first being that turned, unconcerned, was a Frenchman. The expression on his face quickly changed to surprise, then terror. Horn was already pushing him back, banging his head against the optical range finder and slamming him against the hard steel side of the turret officer's booth. He'd been stabbing the triangular bayonet into his chest from the instant they touched. Blood sprayed back and coated the first Khonashi leaping up behind him to pounce on a Grik near the rammer operator's station. That one had just enough time to voice a startled hiss before the North Borno trooper slashed its throat and stabbed it in the top of the head. More blood all over the bright brass shell tray—and a third Khonashi that dove past a Grik near the breech of the huge gun and down into the gun pit. Horn couldn't see, but he heard muffled shrieks and thumping sounds from there, and from the other side of the armored bulkhead. The hatch was open, and ignoring the Grik by the breech for the moment—it seemed immobilized by shock—he peered around and through the hatch. Becher Lange met him, bayonet raised, eyes wide and wild.

"Goddamn!" Horn cried. "It's me!"

Lange's madness faded slightly and the bayonet, dripping blood, began to shake. "One bit me," he murmured, and gestured at his other arm, badly torn, pattering blood on the deck.

The sound of fighting had already stopped, punctuated by the heavy *clang* of the gun-pit hatch, but a fairly loud voice was yammering in Grik. Horn thought it was Pokey. Even though he'd known the little Grik as long as Silva, he'd only heard him say a few words. To his astonishment, the Grik near the gun breech seemed to relax and stand back, as unthreateningly as possible, his crest lying flat. "What the hell?" Horn hissed, pulling the belt off the man he'd killed with a flapping sound. He started to wrap it around Lange's arm. Brassey's head joined the German's in the hatchway. "All secure?" he asked.

"We've got one left," Horn said.

Brassey pushed his head past Lange to see. "Ah, well. He probably heard Pokey's harangue and chose to change sides. Kurokawa's Grik are apparently old enough to reason with."

"What?"

"Never mind, Gunnery Sergeant. Something our friend Lawrence discovered not long ago, when an entire fireroom full of the buggers surrendered to him." Horn was amazed by that, by how short the fight had been, and by how self-assured young Brassey suddenly sounded. The boy frowned. "We lost one on this side, but two have surrendered. Are you hurt?"

"No, but Lange is."

"Medic," Brassey called over his shoulder, and a Khonashi appeared, its Grik-like face giving Horn a start, and began tending Becher's wounded arm.

Boy, have I got the jitters! Horn thought. *Too long out of the fight, not enough to eat, out of shape*, and *probably thinking too much about what's next.* The *clang* of the other hatch under the gunhouse reminded him to shut the one by his feet. He pulled the lever that raised it up and shakily dogged it. *Nobody's getting in now unless they crawl up the shell or powder hoists, and I never saw a Grik that could do that. A 'Cat probably could, but . . .* He shook his head. *We've done what we set out to, but now we're trapped if anybody comes to check or take his battle station. Just one thing left, and we can* go. *Damn it, Diania! I wish we could've . . .*

A raucous alarm began to sound, making him jump again; then a loud voice came from a speaker on the bulkhead. He caught only a few words; they sounded French. But then the message was repeated in Japanese, which he couldn't speak, but had learned to understand fairly well as a POW in the Philippines. Becher Lange, sitting on a stool in the booth and talking through clenched teeth as the Khonashi medic worked on him, interpreted vaguely what Horn thought he heard. "Contre-Amiral Laborde is calling the ship to battle stations and it is getting underway immediately. An air attack is imminent, and the ship must be prepared for evasive maneuvers."

"Well, that's just *dandy*," Horn snapped. "No chance *at all* of getting off this bucket now." His plan had been to pull the pins on half a dozen grenades and drop them down the powder hoist, into the upper handling room. With ready ammunition stored there, the resultant explosion would at least temporarily disable the turret. With real luck, grenades or flames might make it down to the lower handling room, and that would *wreck* the turret. Maybe worse. Of course, if somebody had carelessly left the armored hatch to the forward magazine open—not a ridiculous stretch of the imagination with a crew largely composed of untrained Grik—they might even destroy the ship. In any case, they had to get out of the gunhouse, the last man out dropping the grenades, and run like hell. Realistically, even if the scheme worked, they probably wouldn't have made it. But at least there'd been a *chance.* Now there was none.

"Then we'll just have to make the most of our opportunity," Brassey said reasonably. "You sounded somewhat familiar with the operation of the equipment here. Can you tell us what to do?"

Horn looked dumbly around and blinked. "Yeah, I think so."

Brassey strode to the dead French sailor and took off his hat. He looked inside at the sweatband. "Kapitan Leutnant Lange, your name is now Chartier, and I suspect you command this turret. I'm sure they'll try to communicate with you at some point. If someone asks why you don't sound like Chartier, tell them your throat is sore from yelling at your gun's crews."

"Why are the hatches shut?" Lange demanded, immediately understanding Brassey's play. "They might ask."

"You shut them so your cowardly reptiles won't flee their stations in battle."

Lange seemed to consider that. Ironically, almost immediately, there came muted thumping at the hatches below. "Why won't I let the rest of my crew in?"

"After hearing Lady Sandra's theory, I doubt they have enough human crew members to put more than two in here. If another of those want in, we'll let him—and overwhelm him. Otherwise, your entire crew *is* present. You don't know why those others think they belong in here."

A slow grin seemed to crack Lange's gaunt, stony face. It was the first time Horn had ever seen him smile. "We will try it!" Lange said with something akin to satisfaction.

"Try *what*?" Horn demanded.

"Please just show us what to do, Gunnery Sergeant Horn," Brassey said, his face too intense for one so young. "With our prisoners, we already have three who know."

"You're staying here, Lord?" General of the Sky Muriname asked, amazed, when Hisashi Kurokawa stepped briskly down the gangway from the great battleship. Immediately, the gangway was pulled ashore and Grik started taking in lines. "I assumed you'd prefer to be aboard your new flagship today."

Kurokawa avoided answering the question directly. "The cruiser *Nachi* remains my flagship," he said instead. "For now. That may change as the day progresses. At the moment, a large air attack is coming. *Savoie*'s radio operator informed me that a number of enemy *carrier aircraft* were sighted by one of your scout planes—before its transmissions abruptly ceased."

"Yes, Lord. Fukui received the same transmission. I immediately ordered all our remaining planes to respond. They'll be rising at any moment." He paused. "Fukui also told me that the telegraph station on the extreme south end of the bay reported that the land assault has already advanced that far. It made no other transmissions and we must assume it was overrun."

For a long moment, Kurokawa didn't speak. He simply stared at the burning ships in the bay. Two of his last four dreadnaughts had been destroyed, and there were flames in the distance near where his precious carrier *Akagi* had been docked. A number of cruisers were also smoldering closer by. Who knew how many of his remaining Japanese had already died that terrible morning, with the sun not even up? All he'd accomplished, all he'd prepared for, was systematically being destroyed around him. Panic lingered on the edge of his consciousness but he knew that was what Captain Reddy hoped to achieve; what his whole plan was aimed at inspiring. *But I'm not finished yet,* Kurokawa decided. *Not nearly so. Despite recent losses, I still have more and better aircraft, even without Rizzo's. No more than five thousand enemy troops could possibly be ashore, and I've already directed that my nearly* thirty thousand *begin moving to meet them. Granted, they're scattered, but many, perhaps half, will arrive before the day is done. They'll be enough to hold the invaders until the rest come and finish them.* "What of the torpedo boats that caused so much damage?"

"All destroyed," Muriname said. "Or gone. The bulk of our cruisers remain unscathed, as do two of the ironclad battleships. And there is still *Savoie*, of course."

"Indeed. I still have *Savoie*. With the cruisers to screen her, she can still destroy whatever naval forces show themselves. But at present we must allow our ships to avoid their planes, while yours swat them from the sky." He paused, his protruding eyes narrowing against the stinging smoke. Shapes beneath the burning pyres were becoming more distinct. When daylight came, he'd have a better grip on the situation. "But this plan of the enemy's has only begun to unfold," he said. "Something important has not yet been revealed. Until it is, my place remains here, focused on the air and land battle we face. When we know more, if my main enemy and his pitiful ships appear, my fleet will deal with them. If I can't still shift my flag to *Savoie*, I'll join the battle aboard *Nachi*. Laborde will have to manage. He has every reason to distinguish himself—and knows the consequences for failure. Even better, after what *Savoie* did to *Amerika* under his command, he can expect less mercy from the enemy than he can from me."

He paused again, as the dark shapes of aircraft began to roar overhead. The clouds still blocked the rising sun, but they were breaking, and occasional spears of light flashed across the small, deadly planes. Sometimes he saw hints of his beloved Hinomaru on the wings or fuselage, no longer defiled by the modifications Muriname once made to inspire their Grik allies. The Grik, as a whole, had actually adopted that version for several reasons. They'd never had a single flag before and it reflected their revered, imperial red. It had also come to symbolize strength. *Strength I gave them,* Kurokawa inwardly seethed, *as I've always taken it from the* proper *Hinomaru.* He knew part of him still tried to justify what he did here as service to his emperor on another world, though he rarely consciously considered it anymore. More and more, the red roundel had come to symbolize *his* will, *his* destiny. He took a long breath and coughed smoke. No matter what happened today, whether his appreciation of the balance of power was flawed or not, he believed, *hoped*, he still possessed a final, insurmountable advantage over Captain Reddy. "Has the detail I sent to bring Sandra Reddy returned?" he demanded suddenly.

"Not yet, Lord."

"Ensure she is brought to me at once when it does."

Muriname hesitated. He'd had his own . . . designs on Sandra and her servant, impossible though they might've been from the start, but he never would've physically harmed either one. Their mere existence as living proof there were still females on this terrible world had been enough to keep the worst of his madness in check. But the pretty servant would be dead now, at his Lord's command, and there was no telling what Kurokawa meant to do with Captain Reddy's wife. But what could *he* do? "Of course, Lord," he said.

"Holy shit! There the sumbitch is!" Silva hissed, staring through his telescope. He, Sandra, Diania, Lawrence, the three Shee-Ree, the Repub 'Cat named Ruffy, and their five Khonashi had hidden in the jumbled, fire-scorched debris of a bombed-out warehouse halfway between where *Savoie* was edging away from her dock and where Kurokawa's compound was. They were about a quarter mile apart, which meant Silva was trying to identify an individual he'd never seen at over two hundred yards, in the dark. But it wasn't *that* dark. Dawn was near and the fires on the bay helped. Besides, it was as if his one good eye had taken up some of the slack and it was *really* good. "Least I think it's him," he corrected glumly. "Never saw the bastard before. But he's actin' the part, talkin' to another Jap. Taller, skinnier."

"Is he short? Round?" Sandra demanded.

"Yeah."

"That's him," she said bitterly. "I haven't seen another fat Jap on the island. Can you hit him from here?"

"Sure I could, with my ol' Doom Stomper." Silva raised the Thompson. "Prob'ly not with this."

Sandra turned to the Khonashi troops. "Can any of you hit a man at two hundred paces?"

"Us *all* can, Lady Sandra," their corporal stated confidently.

"Woah! So could Larry," rebutted Silva sharply, "but *nobody*'s shootin' that bastard now, from here."

"I'm the senior officer, *Chief* Silva," Sandra seethed, "and it's my *order* that you take that man under fire at once!"

"No way."

Sandra opened her mouth but couldn't speak. Silva had *never* disobeyed a direct order from her, and to do so now, with such a chance . . . She simply couldn't believe it.

"Here's the deal," Silva continued quickly before she could recover herself. "You know my rule: last, highest-up order. Well, the one I'm followin' now came from hisself, your hubby, Cap'n the All-Powerful Reddy. Far as I'm concerned, Union or not, there *ain't* no higher-up orders. Now, he told me I could have all the fun I want *after* I got you an' the other pris'ners secured." He shook his head. "I wadn't quick enough for ol' Adar, an' that's on me. If Horn an' Lange wanna go play with Mr. Brassey, that's on them. They can help, an' they're grown-up men." Sandra formed an angry retort, but Silva cut her off. "I know yer a hellcat in a fight, both of ya, so don't go on about that. It ain't *about* what wimmen can or can't do—except for the part about babies, I guess." He nodded at Sandra's abdomen. "I damn sure can't do *that*. Even so, gen'rally pertective as I may be, I'd say, hell, let's go play. We'll kill that damn Jap, an' you can pull the trigger. Poke his eyes out an' pull his guts out his nose, for all I care. But you got that baby, see? The *Skipper's kid* to worry about." He pointed out to sea. "He's out there now, fixin' to fight. An' you know what? He'll know in his bones that I got you, an' that'll help him fight clear-headed. He's gonna need that. But if Kurokawa's goons get you back—which they will, dead or alive, if we take to shootin' at 'em now—they can still use that against him, against *ever'body* out there!" He leaned back.

"Now, this here's a pretty safe place, and it's my intention to leave you with these Shee-Ree to watch over you. They can't just run loose either once the sun comes up. They got Blitzers an' ammo. You an' Miss Diania got Blitzers too. If you keep quiet an' don't go blastin' away, you should be fine till things get sorted out. Give your *word* to sit tight, an' me, Larry, an' these Khonashis can go raise a lotta hell that might save lives—might save *the Skipper's* life—if we're not worried about you. If you won't stay put, I'll stay here an' *sit* on ya. Swear to God. So right here, right now, you gotta pick which is more important: you an' that kid we all risked our asses for—doesn't matter whether this fight was already comin' or not; that's why *we* came an' done what we done—or your own personal revenge. Me an' Larry'll get that for you, in spades, I promise."

Sandra's glare was visible now, in the light seeping through the charred ceiling beams that had collapsed during a previous raid. The sound of airplane engines became more distinct, as did the patter of machine guns they were firing at one another.

"We can do a *lot* with this goin' on," Silva pleaded.

Sandra finally nodded. "All right, damn it. Go. And you'd better keep your promise!"

Silva and his companions were already weaving their way through the wreckage. He stopped and grinned back at her, the gap in his suddenly bright teeth telling her all she needed to know. "You bet," he said. Then he was gone.

CHAPTER 23

The Seven Boat
Lizard Ass Bay

"Cease firing!" Nat yelled. "Our tracers are pointing right *back* at us." The machine guns stopped and smoking oil streamed away from blistering hot water jackets. Except for the roaring engines and distant explosions, there was a skittish silence that seemed unreal after the last few minutes. "How's Rini?"

"She's gone," came the simple, stark reply, and Nat's heart felt like a stone wall had collapsed on it.

Just then, through the smoke, about where the carrier ought to be, came a deep, wet blast—then another! A third! A *fourth*! The last was so intense that Nat felt it through the deck beneath his feet, even in his teeth. Abruptly, he eased the throttles back and craned his neck around. Through the thick smoke hanging over the entire bay, the night almost vanished as an enormous sheet of fire lit the haze. Seconds later, an ear-pounding wave of pressure slammed the boat hard enough to rock it. "*Got* her," he grated, his voice like a stranger's to his abused ears. He was relieved they'd succeeded, but amazed how little satisfaction he felt. Rini was dead, and for all he knew, so was every other crew in his squadron. "Keep a sharp lookout," he added, easing the throttles down still more, diminishing their wake. "Secure from making smoke; there's plenty already." There was still a lot of shooting in the north end of the bay, but nothing came at them. *The enemy might even be shooting at each other now in the confusion,* he thought, turning to starboard just a bit. Slowly, engines idling down to a burbling rumble, the Seven boat crept toward the southern end of Island Number 1, a little more than a mile southeast of the shipyard that had been repairing the carrier. Oddly, no shore batteries had been reported there, guarding the South Channel. The one on the outer Island Number 2 was better placed to cover that entrance to the bay, but with four miles of water between it and the main island, it was simpler to evade in darkness. Finally, uneasily, he steered toward land. That was when he realized he could actually see the black outline of the bow, the forward gun, and the 'Cats gathered around it.

It was humid enough to mist and it wet his face and dripped from his helmet. Strange blue lightning still fluttered in the sky, but beyond the thick smoke and clouds, dawn was ending the long, hellish night. He wondered if the day would be any better, and squinted hard ahead. *Who knows?* he thought. *Maybe it will be.* Lying very near the island, right where she was supposed to be, was USS *Walker.* She'd snuck in the back door, right through the minefield they'd sown, from the one direction the enemy *knew* they couldn't come. What they hadn't known, and couldn't without sweeping up the mines and examining them—far more difficult than blowing them in place—was that those dropped in the very center of the channel never had their safety pins removed. *The passage must've still been somewhat unnerving,* Nat thought, *probably more than ours, beneath the shore batteries. But* Walker *never could've slipped through there, and every ship and gun in the harbor probably would've focused on her, exclusive of anything else. Instead, they had my squadron to focus on. But we had a chance, at least, and landed some very shrewd blows. I just hope my boat isn't the only one left.* Finally managing a bitter smile, he eased his battered *Lucky Seven* toward the old destroyer. *Now,* Walker—*and Captain Reddy—can do their part. If those cruisers were surprised by my little attack,* Nat thought, *I wonder what*

Kurokawa will think when Walker *comes steaming up, blasting away behind him.*

Nat called down to the motor room to disengage the shafts as they drifted alongside, and one of the 'Cats on the foredeck caught a line thrown down from *Walker*'s quarterdeck. Climbing over the splintered coaming and stepping out on the foredeck, Nat watched a pilot ladder unroll down *Walker*'s side. He jumped across, grabbed the ropes, and scrambled up the wooden rungs. To his surprise, Captain Reddy himself was waiting by the entry port.

"Sorry, no side party," Matt said, grabbing his hand and helping him the rest of the way up. "You deserve it after what you did, but since the ship's at condition two, you'll just have to settle for me." He waved around, grinning. "And a few Marines." *Walker* always had a contingent of 'Cat Marines now, every member rated to perform various shipboard duties, particularly in action, just as her entire crew was proficient with small arms, to assist the Marines when needed. For this operation, they'd embarked an extra two dozen Marines in case Chack—or Silva—needed a hand at an opportune moment or, God forbid, they had to repel boarders again. It had happened before.

"I'm honored, sir," Nat said, saluting as soon as he had his hand back.

"The honor's mine, Lieutenant," Matt countered. "Your squadron did a fine job."

Pam Cross appeared with a couple of assistants. "Wounded?" she demanded in her brusque way.

"Yes. Some splinter wounds, I think. My XO is dead," he added miserably.

Pam nodded, and she and her party climbed down the pilot ladder.

"Could you see . . ." Nat began, but paused.

"We saw a gallant attack, carried home with determination," Matt assured him, then waved around at his ship, "which not only got us in, but also took out its priority targets." Visibility was quickly improving, and they saw the carrier burning and listing steeply to starboard about two and a half miles ahead. Across the bay, one of the ironclad BBs had sunk at its moorings. The other, a roaring inferno, would soon join it. The water around them blazed with burning fuel.

"My . . . my squadron?"

Matt frowned. "It was hard to tell, but the lookouts saw at least four destroyed. With any luck, the rest made it out, or, like us, hunkered down along the shore."

"They might be seen," Nat said. "*We* still might be seen."

Matt glanced at his watch, then up at the brightening sky. "The enemy will have plenty to distract them again in a few minutes."

Juan Marcos clomped up and thrust a cup of coffee—real coffee—into Nat Hardee's hand. "Good morning, Mr. Hardee," he said, his tone full of respect.

"Ah, you too, Juan," Nat replied, as the Filipino turned and stumped toward the companionway leading down to the wardroom. He was muttering, "Earl Lanier has his nasty battle sammitches, if the lieutenant wants to poison himself, but there are real sandwiches below." Nat looked dully down at the cup, savoring the aroma, afraid to trust it.

"It's real," Matt assured him.

"I, ah . . . What do we do now, sir?"

"For just a little longer, you and I will watch and wait, Lieutenant. We'll reload your torpedo tubes, if we have time. If not, the extra fish we brought go over the side. I can't have them on deck when we fight." Likewise, the ship's Nancy floatplane had gone over to *Big Sal*, to get it off the ship as well. "Eventually, the Jap-Grik *will* sortie, what's left of them, when we dangle the final bait. Kurokawa won't be able to help himself. When they do . . ." He stopped and smiled, but his eyes had turned as remorseless as the sea. "Eat," he said instead. "Call your guys aboard to eat something too. We'll handle the reloads." He stopped and cocked his head to the side, listening. The firing had finally stopped once the cruisers saw there was nothing left to shoot at, but a new sound was rising over the gentle roar of the blower and the nearby surf. Planes. The clouds were starting to dissipate overhead, the lightning moving east. The haze would thicken for a while as the rising sun cooked moisture out of the jungle, but then it would become another typical equatorial day: unbearably hot, humid, and mostly clear. Matt raised his binoculars and stared northwest, studying gaps in the columns of dark smoke blending with the sky. "Enemy planes, rising from the airfield on the peninsula." He looked northeast. "Some coming up from the one east of Kurokawa's compound, too. Look like those twin-engine jobs. But they're too far away to hear." He scanned southeast and bared his teeth. "More planes. Ours. Good old Keje. His strike's right on time." He looked at Nat. "We may be about to witness the first fairly evenly matched dogfight between prepared participants this world has ever seen."

"I hope it's not *too* evenly matched, sir."

"I said 'fairly.' I fully expect Colonel Mallory and COFO Tikker to mop them up. Now go eat. You need to get back on your boat pretty quick, and I need to be on the bridge. We might be here for two hours or ten minutes, but when the time comes for us to move, things'll happen in a hurry."

"Aye, aye, sir."

"Good luck, Mr. Hardee," Matt said, and shook the boy's hand again. Then he bounded up the metal steps to the bridge.

"Cap-i-taan on the bridge!" Minnie shouted with her squeaky voice.

"As you were," Matt said.

Spanky was waiting for him, watching through an Impie telescope. "Tikker's Fleashooters're goin' for the enemy planes. Nancys are followin' with bombs."

"Any sign of Ben?"

"No, sir. But there wouldn't be."

Matt nodded. For several moments they watched the formation of thirty P-1C Mosquito Hawks off USNRS *Salissa* sweeping northwest toward the growing swarm of enemy planes. Even with a combined closing speed of somewhere around 450 mph, they seemed to creep toward one another. White puffs of smoke blossomed in the sky as antiaircraft batteries lit up, and some were washed in gold as beams of sunlight played across them. Dark brown puffs, almost black, joined in, probably rising from *Savoie*. Matt didn't know how they'd keep from hitting their own planes. *Maybe they won't even try,* he snorted. *It's been a long night for them too, and they're bound to be on edge. But their day's just going to get worse and worse, if I have anything to say about it.* He raised his binoculars to watch as well, noting the leading edges of the two formations were about to overlap. *They'll be shooting now,* he thought, and just as he did, several enemy planes and at least two P-1s tumbled out of the sky. Some were smoking; others burning. One just fell, spinning out of control. And then, as the airborne enemies became enmeshed in a terrible embrace, he was stunned by how rapidly streams of smoke appeared, crisscrossing the sky, and aircraft started plummeting into the bay or impacting the shore with rising balls of fire. The furball—that was the only word for it—began to expand as pilots chased specific targets, their tracers, invisible from this dawn-lit distance, sawing at wings, engines, control surfaces, pilots. Greasy smears of fire erupted, drawing dark lines through the exploding shells. Most planes that caught fire fluttered apart before the fuselage, engine, and pilot hit the ground, leaving smoldering wing or tail fragments to tumble down behind them.

"Goddamn it!" Spanky grouched. "Beggin' your pardon, Skipper, but I can't tell what the hell's goin' on. Who's winnin'? The planes look too much alike from here an' I can't see *crap* though this smoke."

"Which means the enemy'll still have a hard time seeing *us*," Matt reminded, "particularly with their attention elsewhere." He knew Spanky's greatest frustration was that he wanted in the fight. It wasn't in him to stand and watch. Matt felt the same, but possibly for the very first time in his experience, everything seemed to be going according to plan. Maybe it was because they'd prepared so carefully and everyone was on the exact same page for once. Or maybe, having faced Kurokawa so many times, they knew him well enough to predict his reactions. Matt hoped so, but did that mean Kurokawa knew him just as well? The thought bothered him.

"Hold on. What's that?" Spanky asked. Even as the air battle raged above and the Grik cruisers crisscrossed the upper bay, sometimes shooting at planes but mostly trying to avoid them, two of the monstrous ironclad battleships were getting underway—and so was *Savoie*. Matt wondered if they were moving solely to avoid the planes or had already smelled the bait past the North Channel. It was still a little early, but Kurokawa obviously had scouts in the air. Matt's speculation shattered when Spanky continued. "I see three—*four* modern planes swooping down. I think they're goin' for our guys! Jeez . . . They're tearin' 'em up! One pass knocked *three* P-Ones out of the sky!" He turned to look at Matt. "Those damn Macchi-Messers, Skipper."

Matt looked for himself. "Anytime now, Colonel Mallory," he said tensely. "Have Mr. Palmer pipe the Third Pursuit Squadron chatter up here," he told Minnie. "I want to hear it."

There was bright sunlight at seven thousand feet, and the four P-40Es of Colonel Ben Mallory's 3rd Pursuit Squadron seemed all alone. The lightning storm still lingered to the west but visibility was good—until one looked down at Lizard Ass Bay. Smoke piled high and the haze made it difficult to see what was going on. There was a helluva fight underway, though, in the air and on the land. Flitting, burning, wildly maneuvering shapes soared over the haze about three thousand feet below, and clouds of gray-white smoke rose from the land about ten or twelve miles northwest of Saansa Point, where Chack's Brigade and the 1st North Borno were driving fast, fighting hard. Down below, Ben suddenly saw four particularly fast planes almost as big as his P-40s, with strange, mottled, camouflage patterns, swoop in from the north and tear a swathe through *Salissa*'s P-1Cs. It was like a blowtorch boring through a swarm of moths and, caught unaware, they never had a chance. Several enemy planes fell burning before them as well. With their dark green paint and bright red "meatballs," the Jap-Grik planes were clear to him even at this distance. The indiscriminate slaughter wreaked by the Macchi-Messers hardened his heart against them even more.

"Flashy Lead to Flashies Two, Three, and Four. Tallyho!

Tallyho! League fighters, nine o'clock low!" Ben hollered in his microphone over the roar of the big Allison. "All Flashies, follow me!" He tightened his grip on the stick and pushed it forward. Down below he saw the League planes split, two breaking right, two left, whipping around for another pass through the furball. "You're with me, Flashy Four," he called to 2nd Lieutenant Niaa-Saa, better known as "Shirley." She was one of the shortest Lemurians Ben ever saw, and one of the best pilots. "We'll go for the two turning west. Flashies Two and Three, take the ones breaking east."

"Wilco," came Lieutenant Conrad Diebel's stoic, Dutch-accented voice. He was Two. Lieutenant (jg) Suaak-Pas-Ra, "Soupy," didn't respond, but Ben saw him edge away in his mirror, sticking to Diebel's wing. They were screaming down, all probably trying to find their targets with the N-3 gunsights in front of them.

Ben put his illuminated crosshairs in front of one of the enemy planes. "Let's see how *you* like it, you bastards!" he said aloud. P-1 pilots, expecting their appearance after the League fighters showed themselves, were careful to stay out of their way. The Japs and Grik had no such notion. A couple shot at them as they blew past, just as the P-1s probably had at the enemy, but they were diving too fast. There were a lot of them, though, and trying not to collide with any was distracting Ben's attention from his target.

"Soupy's hit!" Diebel shouted, more emotion in his voice than Ben had ever heard. "He lost part of a wing and is going down!"

Damn, Ben swore, *he probably hit one of these stupid planes. What an awful way to go after all we've been through!* "Stay on your targets," he said harshly. The targets must've seen them or sensed they'd suddenly become the prey, because they started jinking. They were still too low for anything fancy, however, and Ben put his crosshairs in front of a plane now less than a hundred yards away and pressed the trigger. The P-40 shuddered violently as all six lovingly maintained .50-caliber machine guns in its wings poured tracers in a tight, converging stream just in front of the enemy. In the next instant, the plane and hundreds of heavy bullets met. Amid a glittering confetti of shredded aluminum, the Macchi-Messer coughed black smoke, then fire, and nosed down to scatter its burning fragments across the northwest end of Island Number 1, a few hundred feet below. "I got one!" Ben shouted triumphantly, pulling up. After all this time, it was his first victory over an "equal" aircraft.

"I got one," Diebel reported, his voice strained, "but the other rolled in behind me! They are rather good at this, I think."

"Head up, Col-nol!" Shirley cried. "I winged mine, but he's turnin' aaf-ter you!"

Ben glanced at his mirror as he roared east over the bay. Everything down there, including *Savoie*, seemed to be shooting at him. "I see him, Shirley! I can't shake him. Try to brush him off, wilya?"

"Yaah, hold on!"

"Ha!" Diebel shouted. "I got him! He didn't expect *that*!" Ben wondered what Diebel did to turn the tables. No doubt something he'd learned flying Brewster Buffaloes against far better Japanese planes. Tracers whipped past, a couple of bullets tearing into Ben's right wing. *No time to ask him now.*

"Break leff, Col-nol!" Shirley shouted. He did so without thought. In his mirror, he saw the Macchi-Messer blur by, tracers spraying. Then, right in front of him, was a Jap-Grik plane, coming straight on, two guns twinkling in its wings. Bullets hit his plane—not hard, he thought, compared to the Macchi-Messers—and he fired back. The green plane with red roundels exploded into fragments.

"Whaa-wee!" Shirley cried. "Got 'im *thaat* time! He's . . . Ha! He craash into daamn Grik Bee-Bee! Don't think he done much to it, though," she added, disappointed.

"Colonel!" came Diebel's urgent call. "There is a *fifth* League plane! It must have been flying cover for the others! It is coming down. . . ." The transmission broke, but Ben saw what happened. Flashy Two had been climbing over the eastern docks when the Leaguer Conrad Diebel warned about swooped down, above and behind. He never had a chance. He was probably killed by the concentrated fire that shredded the canopy, because his plane just stood on its tail and fell from the sky, impacting south of Kurokawa's compound. "Damn it, Conrad!" Ben whispered. There was a loud clatter as Ben's M plane flew through a burst of machine-gun fire. He whipped the plane right and pressed his trigger again, blasting another Jap-Grik from the sky. His engine coughed and he quickly scanned his instruments. "God*damn it*!" he shouted. "My engine's starving. Fuel lines must be shot up. I'm losing Prestone too, overheating. . . ."

"Get out o' here, Col-nol," Shirley's little voice, full of anger and resolve, came to him. "I *get* thaat baas-tard thaat get Con-raad!"

"I know you will, Shirley," Ben said, his engine running rougher by the moment. Another green plane came for him, but a P-1 took care of it. "I'll never make it to *Big Sal*. I never trusted Tikker's scheme for trapping us, anyway," he added, trying to keep his tone light. Suddenly, there was a familiar but unexpected voice in his earphones. "Flashy Lead, Flashy Lead, this is CO, OR-One. Do you read? Over."

OR-1? Holy crap, it's Chack!

"Roger, CO, OR-One. I read."

"We are at Objective Baker," Chack said, meaning the south end of the bay, almost across from *Walker*, "and are securing Objective Chaarlie as we speak. There *is* fighting there, but if you come in east to west and don't hit a hole, you should aar-rive among friends."

"Thanks OR-One, I'll give it a try. Did you hear that Shir—I mean, Flashy Four?"

"Aye. But I'm a little busy." Her voice was strained with G-forces and concentration. "I'll see you there, Lead."

Ben said nothing more, hopeful Shirley would prevail, one-on-one. She'd always been the best. Now she was the last. Crossing the docks over a pair of burning, sunken Grik BBs, he tried to coax a little more altitude out of his ship before the engine crapped out entirely. "See you in a minute, CO, OR-One," he said, as his poor, beloved P-40E began to buck. Behind him, except for Shirley's duel with the Macchi-Messer, little activity remained over the bay. The pursuit ships had fought themselves out. He thought *Big Sal*'s squadrons got the best of it, but it was hard to tell. Either way, those that remained would be regrouping to escort the Nancys with their bombs. In just a few minutes, it would be over for him—one way or another—but the battle of Lizard Ass Bay was about to kick into high gear.

Maggiore Antonio Rizzo caught up with Kurokawa, Muriname, and their Grik guards beside a shattered, burned-out warehouse. There they stood while the drama played out overhead. Kurokawa and Muriname had been ecstatic when their planes first confronted the enemy's, but their elation quickly turned. Muriname's AJ1M1c fighters (the M in *their* designation standing for "Muriname") might've been better than the Allies' P-1s, but not the new C model, and their pilots, even the Japanese, weren't even close. They simply didn't have the experience, nor had they been taught by trained pursuit pilots. The massacre in the making was delayed by Rizzo's Macchi-Messerschmitts, which took a terrible toll that seemed to please the Italian, but then the P-40s came. That had been a very close match between aircraft and pilots, but now they'd essentially wiped each other out, and the remaining P-1Cs quickly finished or chased away the last of Muriname's planes. His torpedo bombers and a final squadron of escorts were up somewhere, but their target—the enemy carrier—hadn't been found. Now more planes were coming: the little seaplanes with their bombs.

"We must sortie the fleet!" Muriname pleaded. "I cannot protect it in the harbor anymore!"

"*Anymore*," Kurokawa scoffed sarcastically.

"Yes! My air force has been *destroyed* trying to protect your fat, slow targets! They must put to sea at once. The enemy light bombers will be above us momentarily."

"They must get close to harm our ships, and their new defenses will slaughter them!" Kurokawa stated, his face already red. Had Muriname actually *defied* him?

"The enemy is *already* close!" Muriname shouted, unable to contain himself. "Their planes have torn ours from the sky." He glared at Rizzo. "*All* of them. And his ground forces are less than five miles away. All that remains unseen is their fleet, and it will come at *Captain Reddy's* pleasure, not yours! Don't you understand? We're *finished* here. If not today, tomorrow. All that's left is to save what we can. *Again*," he added bitterly.

For the barest instant, Kurokawa seemed to comprehend, but then his face contorted with rage. "Control yourself, General of the Sky! How *dare* you speak this way! *Nothing* is finished . . . except the enemy. His fleet has already come; mere torpedo boats are all he can spare, and we destroyed them. His air attack is a final gasp, his puny invasion easily countered once our forces are assembled. And if Captain Reddy somehow sends more against me . . ."

"General of the Sea!" cried Signal Lieutenant Fukui, racing up to join them.

"How dare you approach me so!" Kurokawa screamed. "How often have I warned you? No more! This time you have pushed too far!"

"But, Lord!" Fukui insisted, pointing past the north entrance to the bay. "The enemy fleet is here! Our scout planes have seen it, just around the peninsula! It's nearing the extreme range of our shore batteries. They confirmed the sighting by telegraph as well!"

Kurokawa glared. Antiaircraft guns began firing again as thirty-odd Nancys appeared over the bay, clawing through shell bursts, growing inexorably closer. Some peeled off, probably to support the ground attack, but the rest came on. "I see nothing!" Kurokawa snapped, squinting west, ignoring the planes.

"It lies offshore, around the peninsula," Fukui repeated impatiently. "Ten of their heavy sailing steamers, several of which are those they converted to seaplane tenders, with fewer guns. And . . ." Fukui paused. "*Walker* is with them, Lord! It is confirmed. She waits for you! Captain Reddy has come for his woman, as you predicted! Now you can destroy him at last!"

Muriname's brows furrowed. "I don't like this, Lord. You shouldn't go out."

Kurokawa rounded on him. "You were just telling me I *should*!" he shrieked, spittle flying, his face a purple moon. The sky, briefly blue and clear of all but smoke, was filled once more with bullets, bursting shells, and the ungainly looking but surprisingly nimble blue-and-white enemy attack planes. Bombs fell from the first Nancys, exploding in the water among the speeding, erratically turning cruisers. Tracers arced up to meet them, as did exploding shells and blizzards of high-velocity canister. Kurokawa was right; their close-in defenses were formidable, and the cruisers were better protected from the air. Not only had their armored bulwarks been raised, but they'd also been inclined inward. Combined with their tumblehome, their vulnerable deck was a smaller target, and falling bombs and plunging projectiles were more likely to glance off. Some attacking planes immediately staggered and fell or retreated, trailing smoke. But in quick succession, more bombs fell on and around *Savoie*, blasting deck timbers and tall columns of water in the air, even as a pair of Nancys fell to her guns, crashing beyond her on the dock she'd stood away from. That focused their attention.

"Captain Reddy is here now," Kurokawa murmured to himself, then turned to Fukui. "Signal the fleet to sea! *Everything* will pursue the enemy beyond the channel mouth. The cruisers will precede the battleships." He looked hotly at Muriname. "You were right *and* wrong, General of the Sky," he seethed. "Right that we can't simply cower under this onslaught, but wrong to counsel we do so now, particularly with victory in our grasp!"

"I already took the liberty of hoisting the sortie signal, Lord," Fukui announced.

Kurokawa glared at him again, but let it pass. "As you knew I would order," he conceded. "Quite right."

"Do not go, Lord. I fear a trap!" Muriname pleaded.

Kurokawa paused, his expression softening slightly. "It was concern for me, then. I am touched." His bulging eyes hardened. "But my enemy is *there*," he said, pointing west. "The fleet is in danger and *must* sortie." He paused, the word "trap" clearly moving behind his eyes. As usual, the innate caution that had kept him alive so long, despite his madness, attempted to assert itself. Muriname could actually *see* the struggle on his face, harder than ever to heed. His enemy *was* there, practically helpless, *daring* him to come—and that was just too much. But the word "trap" might've made him wonder if the bait was a little too tempting as well. "Except for *Nachi*," Kurokawa finally added, flinching when a tank battery exploded nearby. "She lies closest to my offices. When Sandra Reddy arrives, I will take her aboard *Nachi* and join the battle." He looked at Fukui. "Where *is* the woman?" he demanded. "She should've been here by now!"

"I will find out," Fukui promised, "and send a squad to hurry her escorts."

One of the cruisers, already steering for the passage, was straddled by bombs before it took a direct hit forward of its stack. The bomb must've penetrated the lightly armored deck and exploded near the magazine. In an instant, all that remained was a spreading cloud of smoke, steam, and splashing debris. Kurokawa took a deep, calming breath. He had only ten cruisers left underway, but they were more than a match for the enemy frigates. Walker *will not engage them,* he decided. *She must save all her guns and torpedoes for my two battleships—and* Savoie. "Very well," he said. "I will wait for Captain Reddy's wife in my office, but we haven't a moment to lose. Ensure that Contre-Amiral Laborde knows that I do not want *Walker* sunk until I can see it—and Captain Reddy can see who I have!" With that, he spun and marched through the mounting destruction around him, quickly attended by his guards.

"Were you really concerned for him?" Rizzo asked Muriname, almost casually, just as a bomb exploded near the dock, spraying them with muddy water. The thin, balding Japanese removed his spectacles and wiped them on his sleeve. "No," he replied. "But I *do* think it's a trap. After today, most of my people still alive will be those aboard *Savoie*, and they might fare better under Laborde than my Lord Kurokawa. As you must have seen, he is . . . not being realistic." He took his own calming breath. "I fear none of us are, if we expect to survive."

"But with Signora Reddy," Rizzo said, "perhaps we will bargain for our lives?"

Muriname faced him with contempt. "*You* might," he snapped. "I have other plans to save myself, and as many of my people as I can." Straightening his tunic, he marched away to the north, past one of the smoke-wreathed antiaircraft batteries, and disappeared.

"As do I," Maggiore Antonio Rizzo said quietly to no one. For the moment, he was alone, watching the chaos of a fleet in a panic it was struggling to control, gravitating into a ragged column headed for the North Channel. The two great ironclads and *Savoie* brought up the rear amid continued splashes, beneath a swarm of angry hornets.

Sandra and her companions had watched the entire exchange from just a few yards away in the warehouse wreckage. The temptation to spray them all with their Blitzerbugs was almost overwhelming. They might even get away with it, with all the explosions and chaos. Only when one of the Shee-Ree got through to her that *Walker wasn't* waiting out there, offering herself for destruction, did Sandra's growing, murderous tension ebb. *Matt knows what he's doing,* she decided. *Silva said so. Anything I do might screw everything up*. Nancys were attacking furiously, but, with a few exceptions, seemed to be accomplishing little, all at great cost to themselves. Their bombs couldn't penetrate the armor upgrades Kurokawa had obviously made, and had no more chance of badly damaging *Savoie* than *Walker*'s 4"-50 guns would have. There was an increasing likelihood the bombs would hit *them*, however, if they lingered this close to the dock, and, still watching Rizzo, it dawned on her that there might be something she could do after all. Another tank battery exploded, and she suspected it was Silva's doing more than the bombs. She looked at Diania, wondering if she should risk her friend further—but they *were* in danger here. The Shee-Ree were still wearing Grik armor, their fur dyed. They might pass at a distance in the bedlam outside. "We have to get out of here," she whispered urgently. "You'll be our Grik guards. If anybody looks our way, treat us rough, see?"

"They caatch us!" one hissed back, blinking something Sandra hadn't seen before. These were the first Shee-Ree she'd ever met and she didn't know anything about them.

"We'll be killed if we stay here," she said simply. "We

have to find Chief Silva and tell him where Kurokawa is. My guess? He'll see us before we see him, and we won't be in sight for long."

All three Shee-Ree nodded solemnly. "You right at thaat," one said. "See-vaa see *ever-teen*, wit' ony one eye! We go!"

Sandra was surprised by the quick change of heart and wondered what Silva had done to make these strange 'Cats trust him so much. "Fine," she said. "Just one last thing. See that man out there?" She pointed at the Italian major. "We need to catch him first."

Together, they squirmed through the fallen, blackened timbers, smearing charcoal all over themselves, until they emerged behind the building. It was deserted there, with nothing but jungle beyond. Big wooden cranes and other repair facilities, still undamaged, stood beside the ruined structure, and they gathered behind a great, cold boiler. Two 'Cats immediately bolted. "Wait!" Sandra called after them.

The one that remained held her back. "You say 'caatch 'eem.' They caatch 'eem," he said reasonably. "Us stay here. See-vaa *skin* us, you lay-dees hurt. He make us into furry haats!" The 'Cat shook his head. "Not waana be haat!" Even as he explained, to Sandra's amazement, Maggiore Rizzo appeared around the boiler, pushed by the muzzles of two Blitzerbugs. Diania whipped out a bayonet and crouched, even as Rizzo's perplexed expression turned to one of relief at the sight of them.

"Dear Signora Reddy! Signorina Diania!" he exclaimed over the sound of an explosion uncomfortably close to where they'd been hiding. "I'm so glad to see you both safe!"

"Why? So you can bargain for your life?" Sandra demanded harshly.

"Of course not! As always, I merely suggest reasons to *others* not to harm you." He gestured around. "A most exciting day, and somewhat perilous, I admit. But I have my own plan to remove myself. I need not, nor would I ever, endanger you to that purpose."

"Sure," Sandra snorted. "So, you're about to run? Not so fast."

Rizzo spread his hands at his sides. "This is not my war, Signora, and I do not want to die."

"It *is* your war!" Sandra growled. "You and that bastard Gravois helped make it what it's become." She nodded at the 'Cats behind him, and one roughly snatched his hands together while another bound them behind his back. "You're *my* prisoner now, Maggiore, and you're going to sing like a canary about your damned League when this is over. For now, if you make a peep"—she nodded at Diania—"I'll let her *gut* you."

"So dramatic," Rizzo objected. "As I said, I'm neutral here. You have nothing to fear from me."

"Sure. And those modern planes we saw were neutral too. Somebody shut him up." Ruffy quickly made a gag and thrust it in Rizzo's mouth, tying it around his head with a bandanna.

Lawrence suddenly appeared, followed by two Khonashi, who tried to herd them into a tighter circle behind the boiler. "Us *seen* you!" Lawrence snapped at Sandra, the first time he'd ever spoken harshly to her. "Others could. You su'osed to stay hidden!"

"We can't," Sandra retorted, waving at the ruins. They'd caught fire again. "Besides"—she glanced at Rizzo—"we have information Chief Silva needs."

"Okay," Lawrence agreed doubtfully. "Let's go, try to locate he. I don't know at, though." He shook his head disapprovingly. "He's al'ays running around on his own. Rags La'rence, *I* do it! Asshole!"

"Take us to Kurokawa's compound," Sandra ordered. "That's probably where Silva and the others are, anyway. You'll pretend to be our guards."

"*Are* your guards," Lawrence reminded forcefully. "I ask you *hard* to do as I say!" Sandra was amazed that someone as fearsome-looking as Lawrence, with all his razor-sharp teeth, could look so vulnerable.

"We will," she assured, then looked at Rizzo. "And if *he* causes any trouble, feel free to tear his throat out."

CHAPTER 24

***USS* Walker**

"They goin' out!" Minnie cried, holding her earphones so they wouldn't fall down. Her helmet made it hard to keep them in place. Matt looked at her. "Lookout in the crow's nest says the Grik cruisers are paassin' the point, headin' troo the channel. Grik BBs are followin' 'em out, with *Saavoie* bringin' up the rear. Mr. Paal-mer says the Naancys've dropped all their bombs an' Keje's recalled 'em to *Big Sal*. They'll rearm for strikes against the Grik fleet or to support Chack's Brigade, as directed."

"Very well," Matt said. "If the fighters have the fuel, ask them to do a sweep around *Ellie* and the DDs to the west, for enemy torpedo bombers. But I think *Big Sal* and *Tara* need their protection more. I want rearmed Nancys at Chack's disposal for close air support." Matt almost wished he had some of the big Clippers, armed with torpedoes, but to use them against *Savoie* in daylight would be suicide. They'd all gone back to Mahe after the night raid, to linger until they knew whether they'd be needed again tonight. If they were, it would probably mean the plan had failed and saving Chack's Brigade was all that remained. "Tell Ed to send 'well done,'" he added, hoping it *had* been. They'd lost an awful lot of planes and the 3rd Pursuit, and their precious P-40s were used up. Ben and

Shirley had survived their landing on the Grik airstrip, but there was no word about their planes. *At least Kurokawa's air force seems out of the fight,* he thought. *But was the Nancy attack worth the price?* He straightened his shoulders. *It kept the enemy occupied and their attention away from us. Now it's up to* Walker—*and* me—*to make sure it was worth it,* he realized.

He looked at Chief Quartermaster Patrick "Paddy" Rosen, who, as usual before a fight, had taken his place at the big brass wheel. His helmet was tilted back and sweaty red hair poked over his freckled forehead. Ensign Laar-Baa-Ra, a gray-and-brown-striped Lemurian, stood behind the lee helm, ready to transmit engine orders below. He was still training to become a bridge officer in addition to being a pilot for the ship's Nancy. With the plane gone, he had nothing else to do. The pilothouse was fairly crowded, mostly by Lemurians, of course, but Commander Bernard Sandison was working on the port bridgewing, checking the torpedo director with his assistants.

'Catfish, Matt suddenly thought, amused. *Bernie's torpedomen are mostly 'Cats now. Torpedo-'Cats, fish-'Cats: 'Catfish.* Like Silva, he often came up with nicknames in his mind but rarely voiced them, letting such things originate elsewhere. He might have to mention that one, though. He raised his binoculars again. Through patches of lighter smoke, he saw the Grik column steaming through the channel. Perry Brister was out there in USS *James Ellis*, with *Walker*'s number painted on her bow. He'd support the sail-steam DDs they'd raked up, then stand away, inviting the heavies to go for him. And Matt expected Perry had hoisted *Ellie*'s big Stars and Stripes battle flag on the foremast. *Just another little barb to goad the enemy on.* "Stand by," Matt said, glancing at Ensign Laan and Paddy Rosen. "Try to keep us in the smoke of the burning carrier as long as you can, but don't take us close enough to blister the paint. Besides, the damn thing's liable to blow up." He glanced at the sky, the leaning columns of smoke, the bandannas around the faces of the number-one gun crew. "The wind's come around out of the west-northwest. The smoke should hide us long enough. Bernie?" he asked, looking at Sandison.

"The Seven boat's torpedo reloads are complete. We tossed the other six fish over the side." They'd hoped to reload three more boats, but as far as they could tell, only Nat's Seven boat survived the PT attack. "Our fish are primed and ready in all respects, Skipper."

"Good. Train the tubes out thirty degrees. I'll give you straight shots if I can, but we might have to rely on internal guidance and shoot from the hip."

"It'll be fine, Skipper," Bernie assured confidently. "These new fish *work*. They'll go where we tell 'em." He grinned. "It's *so nice* to have torpedoes we can count on, short legs or not!"

Matt grinned back as much at Bernie's enthusiasm as anything. "Okay. Minnie, pass the word to the Seven boat to shove off. Mr. Hardee will follow in our wake." When the confirmation returned that the Seven boat was clear, Matt sighed and clasped his hands behind him, willing his nerves to obey. "Here we go. All ahead one-third, Mr. Laan. Sound general quarters," he added to Imperial Marine Corporal Neely, without looking at him. "And then run up our own battle flag, if you please."

"Ay, ay, sur," Laan replied, ringing up the engine-room repeater. "All ahead one-third." Neely raised his bugle to his lips and turned the switch on the aft bulkhead to the shipwide circuit. It was possible, even likely, that the Grik in the nearby shipyard aft of the drifting, burning carrier heard the piercing notes of Neely's bugle, amplified around the ship. Many might've seen her for the first time then, as she surged away from the jungle-shrouded shore and gathered speed. A few of the shore batteries might've engaged her, but likely by the time their crews realized what she was and tried to bring their guns to bear, she would already be plowing into the denser smoke of the burning ship. Even if they had wireless contact with their ships or Kurokawa's headquarters, there'd be no time for a warning to be acted upon. Juan Marcos clomped up the stairs aft, and in a ritual they'd repeated more times than either could remember, buckled Matt's sword and pistol belt around his waist, then exchanged his hat for a helmet.

* * *

"God*damn* it!" Earl Lanier roared when the distinctive bugle call blared from the loudspeaker on the bulkhead. The cook's voice was thunderous in the otherwise empty aft crew's head. "Goddamn bugles. Goddamn war. Goddamn shitty flour they make me cook with! I stay bound up tighter'n a rubber on a jackass half the time, an' whenever I finally settle down for a nice, satisfyin' shit, somebody always decides to throw a goddamn *battle*!" He was acutely conscious of the fact that many of the hands considered the head his "battle station" because, somehow, battles always seemed to catch him there. *Not my fault,* he brooded. *My guts is sensitive.* And the strangely pumpkin-flavored flour the Lemurians provided seemed to clog him up worse than anything. He tried frying everything he used it with, hoping honest grease would . . . smooth the process, but though that seemed to help, the crew complained and said he'd fry ice cubes from the freezer if he could get away with it. Chances were, he would. But the perception that he went to the head to escape danger actually stung. *I ain't afraid o' nothin'! An' it ain't like it's safe here. These thin walls wouldn't stop a shell or bullet or anything much heavier than a spitwad. The overhead's maybe a tad thicker, to support the number-four gun, but it damn sure won't stop a bomb. I'm cursed,* he thought bleakly as he quickly finished and drew his cavernous, greasy trousers up and buckled his belt over his expansive gut. *A victim o' circumstance . . . an' not enough fried fish,* he decided.

It never occurred to him that he was truly a victim of his abrasive tyranny over his division—and a certain peg-legged Filipino. One of the most closely guarded secrets in the entire Alliance was the tasteless laxative powder Juan Marcos hoarded, acquired in Baalkpan, and supplied to Lanier's long-suffering assistants and mess attendants. Driven to distraction by Lanier's petty nagging, complaints, and extra work details, the only justice they could enjoy—short of murder—was the occasional "doctoring" of his food to aggravate his condition. And they didn't *want* to murder him; they didn't even hate him. He was what he was. So they used the powder and kept mum.

"Gaad," he said, choking on smoke as he stepped outside. 'Cats in the 25 mm gun tubs on either side of the empty Nancy catapult stared as he raised the bottom of his filthy T-shirt over his face to filter the smoke. His huge, hairy belly was marred by a crooked tattoo with some very respectable scars running through it. The tattoo was no longer identifiable; the scars saw to that. *They also prove I'm no coward*, he thought, glaring back at the inscrutable 'Cat eyes, blinking nothing and peering over bandannas that hid their noses and mouths.

"Look, fellaas," one 'Cat yowled—it was impossible to tell which, with their faces covered. "This fight's already over. Earl's outa the head!"

"Yeah? The hell with you!" Earl snapped. "You come for a battle sammitch, just think o' me usin' your bread to wipe my ass!" Fuming, he stalked past the searchlight tower and between the new quad-tube torpedo mounts, their crews already turning the big wheels that trained them out over the side. Spanky went by at a jog, heading for the auxiliary conn aft. He saw Lanier but didn't stop. He only rolled his eyes and shook his head. Earl made a gesture at his back but continued on, passing the number four funnel and looking up at the gun's crews on the deck above his galley. They were training out as well, probably reporting to Sonny Campeti on the fire-control platform over the bridge that the number-two and-three guns were "maaned an' ready." He looked to port before stepping under the open end of the galley deckhouse. The big Jap/Grik carrier was lying almost on its side, flames shooting up through collapsing sections, close enough, it seemed, to blister his flesh with the searing heat. A huddle of Grik clutched the sloping flight deck aft, trying to keep from sliding into the terrible sea. Others dangled lifelessly over the rails of the conn tower, or "island." They'd all probably cooked or suffocated. "Serves 'em right," he mumbled, but the image stuck in his mind. *Back home, if your ship's done, you can always jump in the water. You take your chances with drowning and sharks, but there's a* chance. *Here, if you can't get in a boat or raft, you might as well cook or choke. The water might be a quicker death, but nobody wants to get ate*. In the shadow of the deckhouse, his eyes settled on a large, red rectangular object that shouldn't be there: his beloved Coke machine.

"What the hell's that doin' here? It should'a been struck down below!" he bellowed. Two 'Cat heads popped out of the galley over the battered stainless-steel counter.

"Aaaw, c'mon, Earl!" one said. "Is busted agaan, anyway. Even when it's runnin', you don't put nothin' in it! Why you keep it for?"

Earl summoned his resources to continue his rant, but stopped. Then he removed his filthy hat and scratched his head. "You know? Damned if I know. I used to, but not anymore." He shrugged. "The hell with it. Leave it. Let it take its chances with the rest of us." The two 'Cats looked at each other, their pose and rapid blinking so hilarious that he laughed out loud. Just then, they heard the deep roar of mighty guns. Of the three, only Earl had ever heard anything so big go off. He quickly waddled into the galley, snatched a sandwich, and stuck it in his mouth. "*Savoie*'s opened up, fellas," he mumbled around it. "C'mon, we got work to do." He nodded at the platter of sandwiches for the crew. "Not near enough there. Let's get stackin'."

USS James Ellis

"*Savoie* has opened fire!" announced Lieutenant Jeff Brooks. Ordinarily *Ellie*'s sound man, he'd relieved the bridge talker so he could *see* what was going on for a change. He wouldn't be able to hear anything underwater for a while, in any event.

"Hard not to see it," replied Commander Perry Brister in his rough, scratchy voice, raised over the roaring blower, *shoosh*ing sea, and the wind whipping in from the bridgewings as his ship sprinted at thirty-two knots. He still looked like a kid, but ever since the Battle of Baalkpan he'd sounded like a seventy-year-old chain smoker. Two huge splashes spewed skyward back near the ten DDs and AVDs of Des-Rons 6 and 10, currently steaming in line of battle as Des-div 2, under Captain—acting Commodore—Jarrik-Fas in USS *Tassat*. Two more fell in the same general area but were surprisingly haphazard, and it seemed as if only one of *Savoie*'s turrets was firing. Perry wondered why. *Ellie* was racing down to lay a smoke screen between Des-div 2 and the equal number of armored Grik cruisers making for them.

Ellie was out of range of the Grik, but everything *Savoie* had could reach her. The first two salvos, though wild, missed long, and her secondaries would soon come to bear. *Ellie* could hit back, but probably couldn't hurt her. All she had that might do that were eight torpedoes, and they were for the Grik BBs. Hopefully *Walker* would take care of *Savoie*. For now, *Ellie* could at least try to hide Des-div 2 from the heavies until the battle lines embraced, and maybe she could do a little more. "Tell Mr. Stites to commence firing the main battery to port, targeting the cruisers," he rasped. "We'll start with the first and work our way back. A salvo of AP into each. Let's try to beat 'em all up a little before we turn 'em over to Commodore Jarrik."

Almost at once, the salvo buzzer rang and three guns barked. Tightly spaced splashes rose in front of the leading Grik cruiser, and Perry had no doubt the next salvo would be on target. "Stand by to make smoke," he said, raising the Impie telescope. "Execute." Thick black smoke piled high in the air from *Ellie*'s four stacks. Equally thick gray smoke streamed aft from smoke generators on either side of her aft deckhouse. The huge, dark cloud she left was stunning to behold and hard to imagine it could be created by something as small as she. All the while, the numbers one, two, and four 4″-50s banged away with metronomic precision. More huge splashes rose around *Ellie*, still strangely wild, but smaller ones were joining them, much closer, tighter. There was a blast aft, near the Nancy catapult.

"That one took out the cat," Brooks reported, "and the starboard twenty-five-millimeter mount. About a dozen casualties," he added.

Perry winced. A dozen *friends*, hurt or killed. He raised his glass and saw that a couple of cruisers were starting to lag a little and one had a fire aft of its funnel. "Very well. They've got our range. Come about to a heading of zero four zero. Main battery will continue to target the cruisers once we clear our smoke. Stand by starboard tubes. Torpedoes will target the Grik BBs." Even as *Ellie* turned, a flurry of 5.46″ and 3″ shells churned the sea around her. One hit the side under the port torpedo mount, knocking it askew in a flashing explosion and spilling its fish into the sea. Steam gushed up the stack and out the gaping hole the shell punched in the hull. Another shell hit the back of the charthouse, shredding the forward stack and sending fragments sleeting through the bridge.

Perry stood, shaking his head, ears roaring. His white uniform was suddenly blackened and smoldering in several places and there was blood on the back of his right hand. Jeff Brooks was down and screaming, trying to gather his guts off the splintered deck strakes. There was no one at the wheel. Lemurian corpses lay beside it and the lee helm both, their blood spattered on the windows. Oddly, only one window was broken, but the steel around them looked like it had taken a giant shotgun blast. Perry quickly grasped the wheel, looking at the compass. He tried to spin the wheel but his hands slipped on the blood that painted it. Taking a firmer hold, he completed their turn. More shells exploded in their wake, but even as he coughed on the smoke they'd made, he was profoundly grateful for it.

"For-waard fireroom outa aaction!" came a shout loud enough to clear his damaged hearing. He glanced back to see the ship's Lemurian cook, Taarba-Kaar "Tabasco," standing in the talker's place. Jeff wasn't moving anymore. Usually, Tabasco spoke better English than any human aboard, but the stress was showing. "Portside torpedo mount's outa aaction too. Caa-shultees there, on the gaally deckhouse . . . an' here. Loo-ten-aant Paarks says all the snipes in the for-waard fireroom is goners." Paul Stites dropped down the ladder from the fire-control platform. He was wounded in the arm but his eyes looked worse, taking in the carnage in the pilothouse. Immediately, he moved to take the wheel from Perry, who stood back, breathing hard. "Loo-ten-aant Ronson—I mean, Rodriguez—aasks should he take the auxiliary conn aaft," Tabasco added.

"Thanks, Tabasco. Please tell Mr. Rodriguez that won't

be necessary. I have the conn. Replacements and corps-'Cats to the bridge, on the double. And please tell Mr. Parks to give me as much steam as he can. Maybe he can restore at least one boiler in the forward fireroom. If we can't maintain speed when we clear the smoke, we've had it."

"We *have* to clear the smoke, Skipper?" Stites asked.

Perry nodded. "How else are we going to put our starboard fish in the guts of those bastards over there?" 'Cats scrambled up from aft, some taking stations from the wounded and dead, others tending the ones that were replaced. Perry was just beginning to realize that somehow, he and some of the 'Cats around the starboard torpedo director were the only ones in the pilothouse not seriously injured—or killed. The scything fragments had missed them, just as they'd missed the glass. A Lemurian quartermaster's mate suddenly appeared beside Stites at the wheel. "Return to your post, Mr. Stites. You'll have plenty to do again shortly. As soon as we clear the smoke, open up on *Savoie* instead of the cruisers. Concentrate your fire amidships. We can at least raise hell with her secondaries, and they shouldn't have it all their way. Then, as soon as we fire our torpedoes at the Grik BBs, we'll make more smoke and go back for the cruisers, clear?"

Stites nodded, for the first time seeing something of Captain Reddy's damn-all determination on Commander Perry Brister's boyish face. "Aye, aye, sir," he said.

USS Walker

"*Savoie*'s commenced firin'," Minnie reported. "Lookout says," she added. Matt only nodded; he'd seen it himself: a great pulse of bright light beyond the smoke. Then he heard it, of course. *Walker* wasn't being fired on, probably hadn't even been seen. *Savoie*'s targets were *James Ellis* and the other ships beyond the channel—all in easy range of the battleship's guns. "Caam-peti estimates range at fifty-five hundreds, but is *only* a guess until he see better."

"Very well. We need to get moving," Matt told Rosen and Laan. "Increase speed to two-thirds. I'd go faster, but it would be pretty stupid if we smacked something in this smoke. We wouldn't be good for anything then." *Walker*'s fantail crouched in her wake and she rapidly accelerated to sixteen, seventeen, eighteen knots. She left the carrier's smoke at last, but there was more, just a haze, but enough to blur her shape. At least Matt hoped so. Ahead, equally hazy, the Grik ironclad BBs were passing from view around the island into the channel, and *Savoie* loomed massive and seemingly unstoppable. She was probably only making six or eight knots, to keep from running down her consorts, but her short fo'c'sle and forward-raked fighting top made her seem to lean toward the sea she shouldered aside.

"Taar-get range, forty-eight hundreds!" Minnie called out, repeating Campeti's new, firm estimate. "Course, two tree seero! Speed, seven knots." She waited a moment, listening. "Range, forty-five hundreds. Caam-peeti requests can he commence firin' main baatt-ery."

"Request denied. Mr. Sandison?"

Bernie was crouching behind his torpedo director, staring through the sights, turning knobs. "Anytime, Skipper!"

Savoie's forward guns fired again and again at targets beyond their view. So did her forward secondaries. Then flashes lit her port side, amidships, and four tall waterspouts erupted in front of *Walker.* Three were right in line; the fourth wild. "They've seen us," Matt said, "and were pretty quick on the draw. too. Inform Mr. Campeti he may commence firing after all," he told Minnie. "Mr. Sandison? Fire the port-side torpedoes."

"Aye, aye, sir! Number two mount," he cried into his microphone, making final adjustments, "stand by. . . . Fire two! Fire four! Fire six! Fire eight!"

Matt heard the first two impulse charges, punctuated by the report of the numbers one and two 4″-50s firing in salvo. He felt the third and fourth fish leave the ship as he forced his way past Bernie's "'Catfish" to look over the port rail. Bernie was already scampering to the opposite bridgewing and the torpedo director there. Five splashes straddled the ship and one shell hit just under him, leaving a long furrow and skating off to explode when it hit the water a hundred yards away. "Right full rudder!" he shouted. "All ahead full!" He searched the sea for the torpedo wakes while *Walker* heeled. There! One was heading for the island, lancing straight away from the tube, but three had dutifully made their turn and were streaming toward *Savoie*. "Left full rudder!" he said, leaving the rail and returning to his place as the deck leaned again. Six splashes, tightly clustered, fountained where *Walker* would've been without the radical turn. Three of her own guns slashed back, and he watched the tracers arc in and explode, one in front, two behind *Savoie*'s aft stack. Boats and deck timbers exploded into fragments and a small fire started. Less impressive but more numerous waterspouts started chasing *Walker* as who knew how many quad-mounted 13.2 mm Hotchkiss machine guns sprayed at her. Hard, clattering sounds told him when they caught her, but they were still too far to do much harm—to anything but Matt's people. *Walker*'s own machine guns remained silent, but the port-side twin 25 mms opened up with a quick *bamm, bamm, bamm*!

"Turn Nat loose," he told Minnie. The Seven boat had followed *Walker*'s twists and turns, but there was no point taking her closer to the machine guns. "Tell him to duck back in the smoke and try to work closer along the island shoreline. The enemy'll probably stay focused on us and he should get a chance to use his fish."

"Ay, ay, Cap-i-taan. Range, thirty-eight hundreds!" Minnie repeated.

Splashes rose all around *Walker* and she staggered under two solid hits: one aft and the other forward, in the crew's berthing space. *Savoie* had lots of secondaries, and shore batteries had probably joined them by now. Wounded would be flowing to the wardroom, where Pam and her assistants were fighting their own battle to save lives.

"Skipper?" Bernie prompted.

"We'll get around behind her, where fewer of her guns will bear," Matt replied. He didn't need to add that there were four 13.4″ rifles pointing that direction. So far, though the ones forward had remained busy, the aft two turrets hadn't even tried to engage the jockeying destroyer. They probably couldn't resist when she showed up right in front of them, though. "Right full rudder, make your course three five zero. All ahead, flank!" A light shell, something like a three-incher, hit the aft deckhouse and exploded inside. Matt raised his binoculars and saw the people on top, including Spanky, get up, just as the number-four gun fired. He wondered briefly if Earl had been in the head. A forest of splashes rose behind them, confirming he'd been right to increase speed when he did. On impulse, he swung his binoculars in the direction of Kurokawa's HQ. He couldn't see it through the haze and burning docks; wasn't exactly sure where to look. But he knew if Kurokawa wasn't on *Savoie*, that was where he'd be. And he could damn sure see *Walker* now. He prayed Sandra was safe. Was she watching too? *Walker*'s guns barked more hate at *Savoie*, each salvo punishing his ears. "How much longer on the torpedoes, Mr. Sandison?" he asked.

"Looky there! *There*'s my girl!" Silva exclaimed to his two Khonashi companions. They were hiding in a burned-out gun position, the great blackened iron tube pointing at the sky. He was impressed by the ingenious—if crudely made—mount. And it was tough too, probably not even really damaged. But its crew and all the ready ammunition had been immolated together at some point, last night or days ago. It didn't matter; the pit was empty now. But he'd glanced up at the sound of *Savoie*'s main battery firing at the invisible squadron to the west, and that's when he saw USS *Walker* lunge out of the smoke on the far side of the bay, spilling curling eddies behind her, her own smoke and huge battle flag streaming aft. A smaller shape, little more than a hazy speck hiding in the tall-sided wake, must be one of the MTBs, Silva thought. He felt something akin to what he supposed anxiety must be like, at the thought of his ship, his captain, his girl, his *home* rushing to confront the iron behemoths in the channel. There was pride too; he knew what *that* felt like, but also a vague sense of shame that he wasn't out there where he belonged. "Well, that just means I gotta do *this* right," he muttered, though his companions couldn't know what he meant.

Lawrence suddenly jumped in the pit with them, head darting back and forth. He almost got a bayonet in his guts.

"What're you doin' here?" Silva demanded.

"The ladies didn't stay," Lawrence reported. His tone implied they never should've expected otherwise.

"What the hell? Where are they now?"

"They're all on the east side o' Kuroka'a's HQ, next to the . . . 'all."

"The wall?" Dennis prompted.

"Yeah. They had good reason to not stay, though. Their hide catch sphire." He shook his head. "Also had to tell *us* they caught a Leaguer—and Kuroka'a didn't join *Sa'oie*, e'en a'ter she sailed. He's in his HQ!" He nodded at the lone cruiser by the dock. "He go on that"—he pointed at the battle—"there or . . ." He waved away. "Get gone. Again."

"Izzat so?" Silva growled, looking around. There weren't many Grik left in the area. Most had gone south to confront Chack's Brigade. More troops were probably coming from other parts of the island, but none were passing through just now. The sound of fighting was increasingly intense—and close. A few Grik remained here and there, and with the air attack over, most just stared at the battle in the bay, where splashes were starting to fall around *Walker*. Dedicated yard or dockworkers, they probably weren't particularly dangerous. The only exception was the dock beside the last armored Grik cruiser, where there was quite a bit of purposeful activity. "Well, we can't have that, can we?" he said, looking speculatively at Lawrence and one of his Khonashi. "You'll do."

"Do?" Lawrence asked warily.

"Sure, you'll both pass for fine, low-crouchin' specimens o' Grik lizardyhood. 'Specially in all the ruckus." He laid his Thompson aside and took Lawrence's Allin-Silva rifle. He knew it was dead-on. In return, he handed Lawrence his bag of grenades. He'd been fairly busy during the Nancy attack and there weren't many left. He pointed at the cruiser. "Looky there. See those tall mushroom vents forward? Not the gooseneck ones by the funnel; they're for the fireroom."

"Yeah. So?"

"So . . . those're vents for the *fuel bunkers*. Better pertected from smolderin' shit fallin' *in* 'em, see? You toss a couple grenades in there, the ship won't blow, but it'll burn mighty pretty—an' fast. Me an' Sergeant Oolak'll cover you from here, anybody gets wise—or chases you when you haul ass."

"You co'er us," Lawrence asked doubtfully. "Not do so'thing else?"

"I won't take a *single* eye off ya," Silva promised loftily.

"You only *got* one eye, and it gets easy distracted," Lawrence accused.

"Quit bitchin'. Have I ever let ya down? Besides that one time, I mean. An' here's your big chance to finally make somethin' o' yerself, do somethin' *useful* for a change."

"You! Hands up!" screamed Lieutenant of the Sky Iguri, leading a squad of Grik guards around the corner of the northeast wall of his master's compound. He looked bedraggled, as well he might, after crash-landing his fighter at the destroyed central airstrip. Hearing from Fukui that their prisoners were missing, and fully understanding how important they might be to their survival, he gathered some Grik troops to search for them himself, after he reported to his lord. There was nothing else to do. If there were any planes left, they were five miles away on the peninsula strip. As he neared the HQ, however, he'd been stunned to discover the very prisoners he sought poking their heads over the far side of the stockade to view events in the bay. There was no mistake. He clearly saw the bleached-out sandy-brown hair and delicate features of Captain Reddy's wife. Without stopping to go inside, he went to investigate. "Your hands! Now!" he screamed again, rigidly pointing his pistol at the group.

Corporal Tass of the 1st North Borno stood, still clutching his rifle, looking just like any other Grik. "I and One squad catched these, tryin' to get gone," he said excitedly, waving the other Khonashi to their feet. The Grik troops with the Japanese officer probably didn't understand him, but visibly relaxed. With the slightest hesitation, but grasping his intent, Tass's Khonashi comrades rose, leaving Sandra, Diania, Ruffy, and the three Shee-Ree sitting by the stockade.

Iguri looked at Tass with red-rimmed eyes, unsure. Something wasn't right. Perhaps he'd never heard a Grik speak English so well or he recognized Maggiore Rizzo, bound and gagged. Maybe he realized there were too many Lemurians and not enough . . . That was when the "prisoners" raised their Blitzerbug SMGs and opened fire with a clattering roar. The first shots were ill aimed and some of Iguri's squad was able to shoot back, but Iguri's suspicions ended when a .45-caliber bullet spun through his left eye and blew out the back of his head. It was all over in seconds, hopefully little noticed over the roar of battle quickly approaching and the deadly duel at sea, but their small victory didn't come without a cost. . . .

Savoie
Number Two Turret

"Whatever you do, don't close that firing circuit!" Gunnery Sergeant Arnold Horn shouted down in the gun pit. He was back in the turret officer's booth, staring through the range-finding periscope. The number one turret in front of them had already fired three times—six rounds—somewhat wildly missing their targets: ten lightly armored wooden frigates, their sails brailed up tight, steaming swiftly for the line of ironclad Grik cruisers. The four-stacker destroyer had made a pass at the cruisers, shooting them up with her 4″ guns before laying a heavy smoke screen in front of her friends. Then she raced behind the smoke, hopefully avoiding long-range fire from the two Grik BBs and a blizzard of shells from *Savoie*'s secondaries. Silva had told him that was *James Ellis* out there, not *Walker*, but the enemy wouldn't know. And it was clear she was trying to bait Kurokawa's heavies away from the impending frigate/DD-cruiser fight. Somewhat to Horn's surprise, it seemed to be working. The smoke screen was dispersing now, but the Allied frigates would be masked by the cruisers and *Ellie* would be the only target for the mighty guns of two Grik battleships—and *Savoie*.

"Us not!" came the indignant roar from a Khonashi in

the gun pit, awkwardly seated on the trainer's stool. "Are us gonna shoot? Hoo at? How co' us e'en load the dan' guns?"

The loading procedure would've been comical if it hadn't been so urgent and terrifying. As soon as the command for all guns to load and commence firing came over the speaker, a bell rang, signifying that a shell was in the hoist. After a frantic search by Horn and Lange—the first looking for a familiar lever switch; the second trying to read tiny brass plaques in the low light, while bleeding all over everything—they found the proper control, and a massive shell appeared in the hoist, nose down. What came next was intuitive to Horn, since USS *New York* had handled her shells the same way. He showed Brassey how to rig the brass loading tray and position the cradle to place the shell on it. "Wait!" he'd cried. "Pull the lift key in the base of the shell. Twist it out and throw it in that chute behind you." Brassey did so, mystified. "Now everybody stand clear. Push that big lever there, Mr. Brassey." A heavy, greasy chain ram clanked forward and pushed the huge shell into the breech. "Ease it in," Horn almost whispered. "Okay, now reverse the lever." Two big powder bags, together the size of an acetylene bottle, appeared in another chute, and the "prisoner" Grik, in apparent exasperation, hopped the tray and helped Brassey roll them on it. So intent on what he was doing, Brassey wasn't even alarmed when the strange Grik joined him.

"There will be two more!" Lange had called. He'd gone to the other side to supervise the same effort beyond the partition. Horn had wondered how he knew, then realized the German sailor probably remembered quite a lot about the specs, if not the operation, of this class of ship. From their old war. The Grik prisoner helped push the bags forward, then joined Brassey in rolling two more into place before returning to stand by the breech. That was when Brassey realized how close he'd just been to a Grik that would've shredded him without thought minutes before. Lawrence had told him that older, smarter, "technical" Grik would surrender if given time to think about it. They might even cooperate. They had no idea if "combat" Grik would do so. Still, despite what Brassey told Horn earlier, this had been his first up-close experience with the phenomenon. Hands suddenly shaking, he'd used the ram to push all four bags behind the shell.

"Secure everything!" Horn had shouted, heading back to the turret officer's booth. With a sympathetic glance back at Brassey, he added, "Undo everything we just did." With the ram retracted and the tray folded down, their Grik slammed the breech and locked it.

"We loaded them because we're going to *use* them," Captain Stuart Brassey now shouted into the gun pit. "And they won't keep sending ammunition if we don't."

Lange and even Pokey were shouting over the comm in reply to strident calls from the bridge. Becher took his hand off the Press to Talk switch. "We cannot keep this up much longer. They demand to know why we're not firing. First I told them our gun's crews were frightened by the blast of the number one turret and we were trying to return them to their duty. Then I told them we haven't received any instructions from fire control. That's when they became mistrustful." He hesitated. "There *is* no central fire control for the main battery! The secondaries have their own directors, but not us. Something has happened to it, and I—whoever Herr Chartier was—would've known we must fire in local control! I pretended to be flustered—not difficult—and Pokey, posing as my assistant, assured them all is now in order, I think, and we'd commence firing presently, bu—" He listened to the rant over the speaker a moment more. "Fire the guns at once, Mr. Horn," he urged. "They are suspicious and suspect Chartier of cowardice, at least. They may send a party to relieve him. If they cannot enter, they will certainly cut off our electricity, and we can do nothing more. Miss your targets, but *fire the guns*. Only that will give us time to do what Mr. Brassey intends. I don't think missing will earn greater reproach than is being heaped upon the crew of the forward turret. They're not doing well either. But they *are* firing. So must we."

"Okay, damn it," Horn said, staring through the eyepiece. "Crap. I never actually did *this* part before!" He turned a knob until *Ellie*'s magnified shape became as clear as the haze would allow; that was how the range finder worked. Far beyond her, above the coast of Africa, dark clouds still loomed, laced with lightning. The wind had shifted, and he wondered if the storm would return. He shook his head and checked the numbers. He wanted to make sure they missed over. "Okay," he said in the voice tube to the gun pit. "Range is about six thousand yards. Make your elevation . . . hell, say five degrees. Belay that! Shit, this is all in meters, I guess. What the hell's a meter? Uh, make it four degrees. That should be plenty." Brassey looked at him anxiously, his self-assurance flagging slightly as the gunhouse rumbled when the huge, coarse-threaded screws under each breech turned. Horn continued. "Trainer, aim to hit *behind* our people. If you try to miss forward, you're liable to lead them just enough to hit!"

"Okay," came the doubtful reply, and the gunhouse lurched to port. "Whoa," Horn yelled, watching *Ellie* edge out of his vision. "Not that far. They'll know we missed on purpose!" He sighed. "Aim right at her. We *can't* hit, then." The huge steel contraption eased right a little, still tracking slightly, the crosshairs in Horn's periscope bisecting the distant DDs stacks. "Okay, damn it. God help us. Fire!"

With a noise like God beating the armored turret top with a hammer the size of a truck, both guns recoiled inward. Horn watched though his optics, guts twisting, as the two shells converged toward *Ellie*, but then she edged away and it was clear they'd fall far behind and beyond. The muzzles gushed smoke as the guns were blown out, and they lowered themselves to their reload angle. "Reload!" Brassey yelled, slamming the brass tray in place after their Grik opened the breech and jumped over to join him. Horn glanced at Lange, who gave him a strained grin and an uncharacteristic thumbs-up sign. "Now they only complain that we did not hit," the German said. "Apparently, this turret has the most advanced range finder and should have performed better. Possibly why they were so annoyed earlier."

"They'll be a great deal more upset in a moment!" Brassey swore.

In less than a minute, the reload was complete, and Horn found *Ellie*'s range again. She'd turned toward them, becoming a smaller target. The guns elevated and turned. Then, suddenly, Horn called his Khonashi trainer to center the turret. It rotated quickly, as if to engage the frigates now exchanging a furious fire with the Grik cruisers, but Horn settled his crosshairs on the Grik battleship directly in front of them, less than five hundred yards away. "Elevation, minus one!" he called. "Right a little . . . Stand clear! Fire!"

The two huge projectiles that spat from fiery brown clouds were HE (high-explosive) rounds, not armor piercing. HE was all Contre-Amiral Laborde had expected to need. Nothing facing them had any appreciable armor, certainly not the frustratingly agile little destroyer. A direct main battery hit almost anywhere might destroy her, and even near misses would cause hull damage and flooding. The only things on the water that day that might've been somewhat protected against such large HE shells—at a very great distance—were the Grik battleships. At a mere five hundred yards, however, though their improved armor would turn a hundred-pound roundshot with ease, it made no difference at all when two 13.4″ shells weighing about a thousand pounds apiece and traveling close to 3,000 feet per second struck the rear casemate of the battleship, close to the weather deck that was almost awash. The entire thing blew open like a pecan hull, and the weather deck over the fantail was shoved forcibly down. Even as the sea rushed up, over, and into the gaping chasm, the forward casemate bulged outward as boilers burst and exploding magazines blew what was left all over a square mile of choppy gray sea.

Through Horn's range-finding periscope, the explosion of the Grik BB happened practically simultaneously with a gout of gunsmoke that momentarily blinded him, and it was several moments before he saw what they'd done. They all felt it, though; the underwater pressure slamming the ship, then the pieces, some huge, began raining down. Incredulous shrieking was already rattling the speaker from the bridge, and Kapitan Leutnant Becher Lange was yelling *"Je suis desole!"* over and over. He looked pale and weak but was grinning like an idiot, and his apology didn't sound very sincere.

"Reload!" Stuart Brassey yelled. "As fast as we can before they shut us off!"

They could feel the ship turning to starboard, to avoid the sinking wreck ahead, and Horn tried to get the other BB in his sights. Smoke was everywhere, and something large and jagged was lying on top of the number one turret in front of them, but the last Grik BB was still steaming, apparently unconcerned, about 1,500 yards off the port bow. He tried to keep it in the crosshairs as the turn suddenly sharpened, and for a moment it was clear. "How's the reload coming?" he shouted. Just then, three tall waterspouts, probably 150 feet high, marched down the length of the ironclad battleship, one after another. He blinked. "Jesus!" he roared. "*Ellie* just put three fish in the other heavy!" The eruption of cheers was cut off by a sudden, terrible jolt that slammed those in the gunhouse against the hard, unforgiving objects around them. Horn fell away from the eyepiece and smacked his head against the back of the booth; blood streamed down his face from a split brow. The lights dimmed but came back. "I think we just collected a fish or two ourselves," Horn said muzzily, leaning forward again. He wiped blood away, but still could hardly see.

"Lords!" shouted their pet Grik. "Look! Look!" He was staring down the barrel of the gun. Brassey jumped over to join him, looked up through the right-hand spiral of rifling, and turned to face Horn. "We're pointing directly at one of the number-one turret's guns," he said simply. "It must've trained left as we turned but stopped, for now, possibly while its crew recovers from whatever landed on top of them, and then jolted us."

Horn wiped away more blood and nodded. "Then we better hurry before they shake it off."

"We will shoot the other *gun*?" Lange asked, uncertain.

"Why not?" Horn looked through the range finder again, surprised he could see a little better. He was also surprised the ship was still turning as sharply as before and the shore of the peninsula was creeping into the right side of his field of view. "What the hell?" he murmured. The ram shoved a shell in the breech, then pushed four bags of powder after it. Just as their Grik slammed the breech shut, all power went out in the turret and near-total darkness descended.

"They shut us down," Pokey said through the hatch to the other gunroom. Though still distinctive, his voice sounded amazingly human.

"And they no longer even rant at us," Lange almost complained.

"I still shoot!" came their Grik's triumphant shout. Just as it dawned on Horn that, like *New York*'s, *Savoie*'s primers had a backup percussion feature, the gun roared and recoiled inward with a blast louder than anything Horn had ever heard, and a concussion that tossed him completely off his stool. There came another blast a few minutes later, possibly even worse, but Horn hardly noticed.

CHAPTER 25

***USS* Walker**

The Grik battleship steaming a quarter mile in front of *Savoie* suddenly erupted like a volcano, blowing bits of itself, large and small, in all directions. To Matt, watching through his binoculars, it almost seemed as if *Savoie* herself . . .

"Taar-git's turnin' to starboard!" Minnie cried.

"Bernie?" Matt called, knowing the target angle would change the torpedo solution.

"Just a few seconds, Skipper," Bernie answered nervously. "One might still hit."

The wait was agonizing. *Walker* was sprinting past *Savoie* now, directly astern, crossing her T at about two thousand yards. The fish weren't much faster than she was and had farther to go; still, they should be there *now*. The salvo bell rang and *bam!* three shells converged on *Savoie*'s fantail. Just before they hit, two 13.4″ rifles fired back. Both projectiles splashed short and one exploded, throwing up a huge column of water. The other shell skipped and tumbled, clearly visible because of its size, regardless of how fast it came. Splash, splash, splash, the geysers got smaller, but closer—and drew a straight line at *Walker*. Unconsciously, Matt gripped the back of his chair. There was a terrible crash forward and the whole ship shook beneath his feet. *Raaaa! Bam!* Only two shells flew this time. The crew of the number-one gun was scattered on the deck around it, trying to stand. "Damage report!"

"Waard-room reports, Skipper!" Minnie said, and Matt had a quick mental image of shredded wounded, and Pam Cross lying torn and bleeding on the deck. "Ever-body's shook up," Minnie said, to his relief, "but the shell must'a hit sideways, right at the waterline. Punched clear through both sides o' the for-waard berthin' spaces. We takin' waater pretty faast."

"Secure the watertight doors and rig pumps and hoses up through the fo'c'sle hatches."

"Chief Jeek's on it."

"Left full rudder. Time to bring our starboard tubes to bear." Matt glanced back at *Savoie* and saw her big guns fire again. She'd overcorrected and the shells rumbled high overhead. There was an impressive fire on her fantail now, the smoke slanting back at them, hopefully blocking the enemy's sights. He'd already decided *Savoie* must be firing her main battery in local control, though he didn't understand why. Splashes leaped up near the starboard bow, shore batteries this time. "Rudder amidships," he called as his ship pointed right at the enemy, making her the smallest possible target. The number-one gun fired alone. "Stand by, starboard tubes!"

A tall jet of water spurted up alongside *Savoie*'s port quarter. An instant later, another rose high in the air almost directly under the aft flagstaff, tearing away the incongruous Rising Sun flag she flew.

"Yes!" Bernie cried. "*Two* hits!"

The ship was still turning and her starboard secondaries lashed at *Walker*. Another shell hit aft, knocking *Walker*'s mainmast and plane-handling boom over to crash across the starboard 25 mm mount.

"Auxiliary conn is out!" Minnie reported, "but the number-four gun's still up."

"Spanky?" Matt asked anxiously.

"He make the report," Minnie assured. "He's cut up a little. Lotsa guys are, but nobody killed." Machine-gun fire raked the ship again, clattering off the battle shutters over the windows and the light armor they'd added to the front of the pilothouse.

"Starboard tubes?" Matt demanded.

"Ready in all respects," Bernie reported, staring though his sights and flinching as bullet fragments and paint chips sprayed around him. "But . . . Skipper," he shouted, "look at *Savoie*!"

Matt did. "I'll be damned," he said. "Left standard rudder. Put us back on her tail."

"Sir?" Paddy Rosen looked at him questioningly as he spun the wheel. There was blood on his face. A bullet had shattered the glass in front of him, through the slit in the shutter. Ensign Laar was down behind the lee helm, unmoving, and another 'Cat had taken his place, tail whipping back and forth. *Later,* Matt thought. *I'll think about Ensign Laar—and all the rest—when this is done.*

Walker's bow came left slower than before, heavier. She was getting logy with the weight of water forward. "*Savoie*'s still turning," Matt said simply. He swept his view to the white sandy beach of the peninsula, marred only by the scorched wreckage of a burned-out Grik zeppelin. "If she doesn't pull out of it in the next couple minutes, she'll run hard aground!" He stepped outside with Bernie, oblivious to the bullets still clattering around him, and looked through his binoculars.

"I don't think she *can* turn, Skipper!" Bernie said excitedly. There was blood on his face too, from spattered lead and copper. He was lucky he hadn't lost an eye. "I bet we jammed her rudder!"

Matt nodded. "I think you're right," he agreed, lowering his glasses. His eyes were hard, uncompromising. It was an expression Bernie had seen before, and it always made him uneasy. "She's going aground," Matt said. "Nothing she can do." He stared directly at Bernie now, his teeth bared in a feral, humorless grin. "Secure torpedoes," he snapped. "Minnie, have Ed tell the Seven boat to belay her attack. Make sure Nat understands he's to *hold* his fish! Mr. Campeti!" he shouted above at the fire-control platform. "Cease firing the main battery, but I want every machine gun on board mounted to starboard, hosing that bastard down. Concentrate on the secondary gun positions, then on anything that moves. Marines'll take small arms. *Everybody* but the bridge watch will take small arms!"

"Sir?" Campeti shouted back, voice confused. It also sounded unnaturally loud. That was when Matt realized the shooting had all but stopped. A great cloud of white gunsmoke and the darker smoke of burning ships roiled around the distant surface action between the Grik cruisers and Des-div 2, now joined by *Ellie*'s precision sniping that gutted one cruiser after another. A high, broad haze drifted away over Zanzibar from the middle of the smoldering shipyard where Chack's Brigade had advanced, blasting its way forward with the little mountain howitzers and assisted by occasional dipping planes. But *Savoie* and the shore batteries had stopped shooting, and everything else was too distant to be more than a dull rumble over the wind and sea. It was like everyone was steeling themselves to watch the great battleship slam ashore. It was also Matt's first real look at the big picture for a while, and for the first time he could think about something besides fighting his ship. He could consider the future.

"I want *Savoie*, Mr. Campeti!" Matt snarled. "We're going to need her. And when she grounds, we're going to *take* her!"

Near Nachi

"I wish they'd hurry the hell up," Silva murmured, watching Lawrence and the Khonashi trooper move aboard the Grik cruiser tied to the dock. He was following them through the sights of Lawrence's rifle, and Sergeant Oolak was doing the same. "They've singled up lines, fixin' to get underway, an' our guys're just sankoin' along. They need to quit walkin' so slow, actin' like they got nothin' to do. Sure as shit, somebody'll try to give 'em a chore. Then where'll they be? An' that Jap officer just went up the gangway. I bet he's the skipper."

"You . . . concerned at La'rence?" Oolak asked.

"Concerned? Me? Nah. Little turd wouldn't be worth thinkin' about, he didn't hang around buggin' me all the time."

"He hangin' around you kill *Hidoia'e* Jaaphs 'ith Khonashi, 'ith King Scott."

"You were there? Well, sure. I didn't say he hadn't been doin' it awhile."

"You let he, he let you. You . . . 'riends."

"Maybe. So?"

Oolak bared his wicked teeth in a grin. "So nothing."

Silva tensed. "Look. They're makin' their move." Lawrence and his companion were walking to the mushroom vent, passing through busy Grik preparing the ship to get underway. The Khonashi acted like he was checking the vent, making sure the cover was secure, when he was really poking under it to check for mesh. Lawrence was sniffing around the edge, but then reached in the bag slung over his shoulder. A Grik Hij officer suddenly stopped in front of them, shouting something. Lawrence nodded, talking back, but the officer only got more agitated, gesturing at the bag. Lawrence, still nodding, pulled his hand out—with a pistol—and shot the Grik officer in the face.

"Crap! That's done it!" Silva snapped, and fired. Two Grik fell together when the big, 450-grain bullet punched through one and killed another. Oolak fired too. Suddenly, Grik were taking cover behind the bulwarks, ignoring the saboteurs, thinking all the fire was coming from shore. Lawrence and his companion each seized a pair of grenades from the pouch, pulled the pins, and stuffed them under the lip of the vent. Then they ran. They made it all the way to the gangway before the apparent captain rose, shouting and pointing a pistol of his own, and shot the Khonashi in the back. He fell down between the ship and dock with a splash. Lawrence hesitated, looking back, then bolted. Silva had already reloaded, and raising Lawrence's rifle, quickly shot the officer. The man tumbled back, but popped off five rounds as he went down. Lawrence stumbled but kept running.

The grenades went off. The top of the mushroom vent blew off and twirled high in the air like a huge, flying hubcap. The rest of the vent and a fair portion of the fo'c'sle deck followed in a spray of splinters. For an instant, that was it. Then a gout of flame roiled up from the gaping hole and pandemonium broke out. Grik sailors and a few Japanese surged for the gangway, but it quickly clogged and few could pass—particularly after Silva snatched his Thompson and stitched the packed sailors with a full twenty-round magazine. Flames raced up the tarred rigging of the foremast and caught the brailed-up sail. It didn't matter. Every vent and seam was already spitting fire. Lawrence reached the burned-out gun pit, gasping, starting to limp, and sprawled down on top of them. That was when the surging flames must've found a magazine and the forward part of the ship was obliterated in an ear-shattering explosion. Oolak started to look, but Lawrence held him.

"Stay down!" he growled as debris began to fall. Silva rolled on his back and stared up, figuring if anything big enough to worry about landed on them, it wouldn't matter if they were curled in a ball or not. An entire cannon and carriage crashed to earth just a dozen yards away. "Wuu-aaah!" he said, and shuddered. "Wouldn't o' mattered *at all.*" He rolled over. "Where you hit, Larry?"

"In the hiph, here," the Sa'aaran said, groping for the wound with the clawed fingers of his left hand.

"In the ass, you mean." Silva snorted. "Lucky."

"The other, not lucky," Lawrence lamented.

"Nope."

Silva pulled a field dressing from a pouch on his belt and tore it open. The new ones had a lacquered wooden tube of polta paste rolled up inside. He opened it, smeared it on the wound, then mashed the dressing on the bleeding hole. "Hold that," he said, rising and looking at the ship. Amazingly, it was still afloat, the stern nearly intact. But the bow was just . . . gone, down to the waterline, and the whole thing was a roaring, crackling inferno. He sat back and took a chew.

"Hear that?" Lawrence said, stiffening.

Dennis shook his head. "I can't hear nothin', buddy."

"*I* do. Is shooting . . . !" He pointed back toward Kurokawa's compound. "*Lots* shooting!" Oolak thought he'd heard some a few minutes before, while Lawrence and the other Khonashi neared the ship, but it lasted only a few seconds and most sounded like Blitzerbugs. There hadn't been anything they could do at the moment, and figured whatever the girls and their guards had run into, they'd handled it. Apparently not—or they'd found more trouble.

"Wimmen," Silva sighed, and glanced south. "How far

you reckon Chackie's an' I'joorka's guys are?" he asked. "I can't hear shit."

Oolak held up one finger, then two. "'Iles," he said.

"Maybe a couple miles. Huh. An' there might be Grik runnin' back this way ahead of 'em." He shrugged. "Well, I guess our little hootenanny ain't quite over yet. I got a dooty ta' finish, anyway. Can you move with that hole in your ass, Larry? Or do we have to leave you here?"

Savoie slammed ashore at six knots. The engines had been reversed, but just as it took time to accelerate twenty-five thousand tons to the eight knots she'd achieved, it also took time to stop it—unless it met something immeasurably larger and immovable. In this case it was the white sand on the gently sloping beach of Zanzibar. Even then, though *Savoie* slowed rapidly, she didn't stop at once as her bow gouged into the sand and rode up toward shore. Few things can remain stationary on any moving object that rapidly quits doing so, and anyone without a handhold went sprawling. Guy wires supporting the aft funnel parted with a sound like cannon shots and whipping metal serpents, and the funnel tilted forward, crashing on the seaplane catapult in a swirling cloud of sparkling soot and smoke. But the sand was soft and loose and the bow had pushed to within a few dozen yards of dry land before it came to rest.

Two hatches dropped open under the number-two turret and battered, bloody men and Khonashi half climbed, half fell into the shaded daylight below. There they sat, panting in what seemed luxuriously cool air. They hadn't realized how hot it had become in the turret, and the day, already past eighty degrees, felt like half that in comparison. At present, they were alone, and Stuart Brassey roused himself first, examining Becher Lange while Gunny Horn watched. The German sailor was in bad shape. Already weakened by captivity, the long night march, and now a serious wound as well, Horn thought he'd probably had it. Their solitude lasted only a few moments before Grik started running past, heading forward.

"What the hell?" Horn mumbled. His lips were broken and he still felt dazed from . . . whatever happened in the turret. He remembered trying to shoot at one of the forward guns, but not much after that. The deck was swarming with running shapes—Grik, for the most part, but Japanese as well, dashing for the fo'c'sle. None paid them any heed and some just leaped over the side, possibly hoping the surf would break their fall and that the flasher fish had either retreated from the disturbance of the grounding or already abandoned the shallows for their deeper daylight haunts. Others, more thoughtful, tried to secure lines to stanchions and lower themselves down. Many were pushed over by the crush. Their two remaining Grik—the other was killed when he fell down in the gun pit on his head—scrambled to their feet to join the rest, but Pokey shouted at them. They paused and jabbered back. Pokey spoke again and they seemed to relax slightly. "What was that about?" Horn asked Pokey. Instead of answering, Pokey spoke to Brassey in Khonashi, which the boy captain translated.

"The Grik want off because they expect the ship to sink. They've learned to fear torpedoes, and no Grik ship can survive them." He pointed at the last Grik BB rolling on its side, still barely a mile away, and Horn remembered seeing *Ellie*'s torpedoes hit her. "That only adds to their panic."

That doesn't explain the Japs in the mix, Horn thought. *They know better. Our torpedoes aren't* that *powerful, and even disabled,* Savoie *could—probably—soak up several more. Besides, she's aground and can't sink even if she fills.*

What Horn couldn't know was that a tipping point had been reached. As far as the Japanese were concerned, *Savoie* wasn't their ship, their *home.* She was a French *League* ship, filled with Grik. She flew their flag, but even that now symbolized more what they'd lost than what they'd accomplished. The Emperor wasn't on this world, and Kurokawa—whose mad, single-minded pursuit of personal power and revenge had only led them to misery and grief—could never replace him. The closest thing to home they had was the island they were touching; that they'd been *returned* to as if fate had twisted the great ship's rudder. Few knew why they were fighting anymore, but if they must keep on, their home was a better place to die than the foreign ship that had just become a helpless target.

Adding to this perception was the hit in the flank that had opened an engine room and shorted a distribution panel, cutting electricity to half the ship. A well-trained crew would've restored power in moments, but *Savoie* didn't have one of those. Even cooler heads found themselves in the dark, unable to fight the vengeful old destroyer rushing toward them, already spitting a torrent of machine-gun fire and possibly preparing *more* torpedoes. That was the final straw that sent most of the Japanese running for the fo'c'sle. Crews around the secondaries were swept down by the grounding and the bullets. Even if their captains returned to their posts, they found themselves with crews that were dead, wounded, or already fled. They fled too, for the bow—and land.

"Well, what did Pokey say to make them stay?" Horn asked.

Brassey shrugged. "He told them the ship won't sink. Other than that, he said they're on our side now, and we're winning."

"Hmm. I hope he's right. How's Lange?"

Brassey's reply was cut off by the clatter of bullets striking the armored gunhouse in front of them, then a whole flurry of slugs slashing into the Grik and men in their growing hundreds, bunching together on the fo'c'sle.

"I suggest we move to better cover, more to starboard," Lange said, speaking for the first time since they fell from the turret. "Actually," he added, standing with great effort, "I have a better idea." Awkwardly, he pulled the pistol from his waistband and looked at it. Only then, somewhat surprised, did Horn remember they were armed. Lange continued. "Now, in the confusion, strikes me as an excellent time to find Contre-Amiral Laborde. What do you think? I suspect under the circumstances—if we're not accidentally shot by our friends, of course—we might move fairly freely."

Horn's brows furrowed. "Get Laborde. Okay, I'm game. What the hell? But are you up to it? I'm not sure *I* am, and I haven't had my arm half chewed off."

"I will manage that, if nothing more," Lange said, his pale face tightening in determination. "I have a debt to settle."

The throng on *Savoie*'s fo'c'sle made an easy target, and *Walker*'s machine guns were mowing them down. Panicked before, even the steadiest Grik and most experienced Japanese sailors threw themselves over the side. Fortunately, there actually weren't many flashies in the water, and those who weren't drowned or killed by the fall—or when someone else landed on them—finally dragged themselves to the beach. Most were surprised by how many they were. But that left few to defend *Savoie* when *Walker* surged in from astern, machine guns still clattering, and disgorged her boarders onto the battleship's fantail. With her flooding aft and her bow aground, they actually had to jump *down* onto the huge ship's charred deck. A surge of water had washed over the fire, and the planks only steamed and smoldered wetly now.

Matt, his Academy sword in one hand, 1911 Colt in the other, led almost seventy sailors and Marines. They'd been quickly organized into six squads of ten, with Matt, Campeti, and Jeek commanding two squads each. Even-numbered squads were Marines, mostly armed with *Walker*'s '03 Springfields; odd-numbered were sailors, with Blitzers, Thompsons, and two precious BARs. *Walker* had stopped shooting, and it was eerily quiet as the boarders quickly fanned out around the aft gunhouses. The four huge rifles protruding from them still seemed menacing, even in their immobile silence. With Spanky in command, *Walker* stood away, but her guns remained ready to protect her people as they moved forward. Matt looked at her for a moment, at all her new damage, and felt sick at heart.

"Can't keep anything looking nice around here," Campeti said, guessing his captain's thoughts.

Matt forced a smile. "No, and we just got her out of the shop too." He pointed to starboard. "You take Third and Fourth squads. . . ." He stopped. "What the hell are you two doing here?" he demanded when he saw Earl Lanier and Isak Reuben. He'd seen Pam Cross as well, but it was pointless to argue with her—and she had a reason to be there. Isak and Lanier were a different story. So was Petey, coiled around Isak's skinny neck, looking around like he really didn't want to be there.

Isak shrugged, and Petey chirped irritably. "You need a snipe who's been in a big wagon like this to lead a party below," Isak stated reasonably in his reedy voice. "Hell, somebody might be puffin' a pipe in a magazine right now, fixin' to light a fuse. An' I fought Grik in tight places before," he reminded.

"An' I ain't just a cook!" Earl snapped. "I'm a by-God *destroyerman*, same as anybody!"

"Cook!" Petey countered emphatically. "Eat!" he added with unusual solemnity.

"Shut up, you! I *ain't* just a damn cook!"

Matt shook his head. If Lanier was arguing with *Petey*, something had him extra touchy. "Fine," Matt told Isak. "You're right. *You* take Fifth and Sixth squads, and clear her out belowdecks. Chief Jeek, go with Mr. Campeti instead." He looked at Lanier. "You go with Isak—if you can keep from killing each other."

Isak glared at Earl, still mad about a certain episode with *another* pet. . . . "I won't kill 'em," he mumbled, "but he's bringin' up the rear. Ship keeps floodin', we'll all drown, he gets his fat ass stuck in a hatch."

"Third and Fourth squads will sweep up the starboard side with Mr. Campeti and Chief Jeek," Matt repeated. "First and Second'll go with me to port. We'll meet on the bridge, clear? Nurse Lieutenant Cross, you're with me as well. Let's move."

"Aye, aye, Skipper." Campeti led his squads to starboard, between the gunhouses.

"Pack Rat?" Matt gestured the Lemurian gunner's mate Pak-Ras-Ar and his BAR forward. "First squad, take point."

Not all of *Savoie*'s crew had abandoned her, and some, Japanese and Grik, retained very old-fashioned views about fighting to the bitter end. As soon as they mounted the companionway alongside the number-three turret, they came under fire from forward, among the remains of shattered boats, launches, and the toppled funnel. Musket balls blew splinters from the deck and 6.5 mm Arisaka rounds cracked past. Pack Rat hosed the boats with his BAR and they charged forward, shooting as they went. Two 'Cats spun and fell, helmets clattering and rolling away. Pam grabbed a sailor to help her drag the wounded under cover. "Go!" she shouted. Matt, Pack Rat, and seventeen 'Cats went. A man and two Grik lunged from behind a large locker, bayonets leveled. Matt shot the man with his .45, but both Grik pinned a screaming 'Cat against a bulkhead before they were shot and bayonetted down in turn. More fire came from around the funnel and a fierce fight erupted to starboard when Campeti's sailors opened up with Blitzers. Another 'Cat fell to a shot from the superstructure.

"Half the Marines take cover and stay here," Matt shouted. "Watch for snipers up high and keep us covered." They pushed on under a withering exchange of shots. The forward funnel loomed, and they clattered up the closest companionway. Six 'Cats followed Pack Rat to the next level while Matt and the rest covered Campeti and Jeek, who'd been slowed by a mad rush of two dozen Grik and Japanese.

"Did you see Pam?" Matt yelled at Campeti as the gunnery officer charged up the matching starboard companionway.

"Aye, sir. I left two more riflemen with her. We had some wounded too. These Jap-Grik bastards're fighting *nuts*."

Pack Rat's BAR hammered above, spilling Grik from the upper levels. Hot brass showered down. "Let's go!" Matt urged.

The battle for the forward superstructure turned into a chaotic nightmare, like fighting through a mazelike jungle gym with enemies around every turn. To the Marine marksman, the analogy was probably even more apt, Matt thought, as bullets *whaang*ed off the rails from above and below. *We must look like a bunch of monkeys fighting through a huge steel tree.* One thing quickly became clear: for whatever reason, whether to compel any remaining League officers or defend against Grik insurrection, here was the core of Kurokawa's last-ditch support on the ship, and their opponents were increasingly Japanese. Fortunately, though surprisingly well armed, they didn't seem to have any automatic weapons or grenades. The BAR, Thompsons, Blitzerbugs, and '03 Springfields that picked off those who exposed themselves to fire down on the assaulting squads finally crushed the defense.

The price was high, however. Another five 'Cats were

killed and eleven wounded. Campeti took a 6.5 slug through his forearm, probably breaking the ulna, but quickly wrapped it and pressed on. That delay was probably why Matt, his uniform now grimy and spattered with blood, was first on the bridge. He approached the pilothouse with his battered Academy sword at arm's length, probing, freshly loaded Colt held back, elbow bent, sights clear in front of his eyes. He'd discovered that no one could resist taking a whack at the sword as it came around a corner, making them an easy target for the .45. Pack Rat, Campeti, and Jeek crowded in behind him, trying to squeeze past and protect him, but when they saw what awaited them through the final hatch, they knew their fight was over and couldn't rival what had happened here.

Blood was everywhere, and bodies lay in heaps. It even looked like Grik had fought one another, tooth and claw. Kapitan Leutnant Becher Lange, his once-robust frame now thin and wasted, lay atop a pudgy corpse in a blood-soaked white uniform. The man's eyes seemed to stare at the overhead, astonished, from a face bearing a thin, dark mustache. Just beyond them on the bulkhead was a bronze plaque with the raised letters of the word HONNEUR upon it. Another white-uniformed man with a bloody leg wound sat on a chair, staring at Gunnery Sergeant Arnold Horn, who, almost as thin as Lange, was sitting on the deck, leaning on the engine-order telegraph with a pistol in one hand. His face was filthy, smudged dark with powder smoke and drying blood. Two pinkish tracks ran down his cheeks because his other hand supported the head of Captain Stuart Brassey, lying across his lap. It was impossible to tell how much of the blood Horn sat in was his and how much Brassey's, but Horn at least was alive. One of the Grik suddenly whimpered and tried to crawl toward Horn. Matt raised his pistol.

"No!" Horn cried. "That's *Pokey*! One of ours." Apparently, Horn, Pokey, and the French naval officer were the only survivors on the bridge.

"My God," Matt breathed. "Pack Rat, get Lieutenant Cross up here on the double. Chief Jeek"—he pointed at the Frenchman—"secure that prisoner."

"Ay, ay, Cap-i-taan."

"Capitaine Reddy?" the man asked, apparently surprised, as the bridge filled with 'Cats and Matt went to Horn.

"Yeah," Matt snapped back. "How are you, Gunny?" he asked Horn.

"I'm okay. Pretty beat." He glanced down at the still, young face, and absently brushed a lock of hair aside. "He was a *good* kid, sir. A good officer. All he wanted to be." He nodded at Lange. "He got what *he* wanted too, I guess. Revenge for *Amerika*. That's Admiral Laborde under him. He had a pistol. Shot Captain Brassey when we charged in. Lange's pistol was empty by the time we got here, but he soaked up the rest of Laborde's bullets until I could get a shot." He glared at the wounded Frenchman. "*He* shot poor Pokey and a couple of our Khonashis. Winged me too—not bad—before I popped him in the leg. I guess he's out of bullets." Horn waved his pistol. "I got one left."

"Capitaine Reddy, I am Capitaine Dupont, of the League of Tripoli. I demand—"

Matt spun to face him. "You! Shut your *goddamn face*! As far as I'm concerned, you're a pirate and a murderer, in no position to *demand* anything. Chief Jeek, if that man speaks again before I want him to, you will not hesitate one single second to blow his head off. Is that clear?"

"Aye, sur."

Horn was chuckling. It seemed painful.

"What?" Matt asked.

"Nothing, sir. I just don't think I ever heard you cuss like that."

Matt's blazing eyes softened slightly. "I'm sorry to disappoint you, Gunny, but I guess I do sometimes. I'll try to watch it in the future. Where are Sandra, Diania, Adar—and Kurokawa?"

Pam pushed her way in the pilothouse and flung her medical bag on the deck. "And that idiot Dennis," she added anxiously, yanking the bag open.

Horn looked down as two 'Cats gently eased Stuart Brassey away. "See to Pokey first, ma'am. He's hit worse than me. Mine's clean, in and out over the hip." He looked at Matt. "Chairman Adar's dead, sir. Died breaking out of the camp." Matt's eyes went hard again. "But the ladies were fine when we split off from Dennis," Horn assured. "Him and Lawrence went to raise hell ashore and hopefully catch Kurokawa there. He's not aboard." He shook his head. "Might've boarded something else, but that's what Dennis meant to stop, I figure."

Matt, stung by the news about Adar, squeezed Horn's shoulder and stood, moving aside so Pam could work. Stepping out on the port bridgewing, he saw *Walker* idling just a hundred yards away. She didn't seem any lower by the head, so she must've gotten her flooding under control. Far beyond, *Ellie* was steaming closer, the battle between Des-div 2 and the Grik cruisers apparently over. *That had to have been a hell of a fight,* he imagined grimly, *but it served its purpose—to draw away the torpedo-soaking screen.* He couldn't tell how many ships had survived—friend or foe. They were all jumbled up—except for a couple drifting away, burning out of control. He glanced forward, and for the first time noticed that one of the guns in *Savoie*'s forward turret had burst just past a deep indentation in the barrel, like it had been hit hard by something big and they fired it anyway. *Have to remember to ask Horn if he knows how that happened.*

"Captain," Campeti called, "report from Chief Reuben: belowdecks is secure. They didn't run into much resistance and only have two wounded." He snorted. "One's Earl. Fell down a companionway and sprained something, seems like. There's flooding aft," he added, "but there's steam. Isak wants some firemen to help tend the boilers so he can get more pumps online. Anyway," he said, and took a long breath, "looks like the ship's ours."

Stepping to a Morse lamp, Matt signaled *Walker* to come alongside. "Very well, Mr. Campeti. Get that arm looked at, but you're in charge here. Keep squads combing the ship for holdouts and see if the comm gear is working. Get the word out, if you can. We have a lot left to do, and the sooner started . . ." He looked aft at the mainmast, where another big Rising Sun flag flew. "And get somebody to rip that damn thing down. I've got to go back aboard *Walker* and get ashore. I'll send one of our big battle flags across first, though. Run it up high, where everyone can see it."

CHAPTER
26

Chack's Brigade

POOM–POOM, POOM–POOM went two sections of little mountain howitzers, spraying 1,200 half-inch balls at a battalion of Grik trying to form in front of them. Machine guns sprayed the tree line as still more of Kurokawa's army tried to join the defense. 'Cats and Khonashi fanned out to the sides and hit the deck or crouched behind dockyard equipment damaged in the bombings and opened fire. More Grik fell. A comm-'Cat near Chack was shouting in a microphone hanging from a companion's heavy pack by a woven fabric wire. He was wired to yet another 'Cat, lugging heavy batteries.

"Make daamn sure they know where we are this time!" Chack shouted bitterly at the comm-'Cat as a pair of Flea-shooters roared overhead. There'd been a few . . . incidents.

"Ay, ay, Col-nol!" the comm-'Cat replied. "Akka Lead, Akka Lead, this is OR-One, over!"

"OR-One, dis is Akka Lead," crackled the response from the headset, through the comm-'Cat's fur. "Whaat can I do fer you?"

"You can hit the goddaamn *enemy* this time!" the comm-'Cat snapped, blinking impatience with the pilot's cocky tone.

"Roger daat," came the deflated reply. One of the earlier incidents had been very costly. It hadn't been a pursuit squadron that did it, or even planes off *Big Sal*. Two Nancys from a pair of AVDs had dropped their incendiaries in the wrong place, killing or severely wounding nearly forty raiders. Realistically, it wasn't their fault either; the fighting had been close, intense, and almost impossible to understand through the thick jungle from the air. Worse, a company of the 1st North Borno had accidentally marked its position with red smoke instead of green—at the same time Risa marked a *target* with a red smoke flare and called a strike on it. The planes were already diving and there hadn't been time to unscrew the mix-up. And it *was* just a stupid accident, but now Risa was devastated and fighting like she didn't care whether she lived or died, I'joorka was hideously, almost certainly mortally, burned, and nobody trusted their air support anymore. Chack shook his head.

"Make red smoke on the taar-git. Repeat *red*," the pilot said.

Chack rolled over to the comm-'Cat. "Give me thaat," he ordered, gesturing for the microphone and headset as sand and splinters showered him, sprayed from the debris around by musket balls. "Akka Lead, this is Col-nol Chack-Sab-At, OR-One Commaand," he transmitted. "We *caan't* get smoke on the enemy from here. There's a clearing a hundred tails across between us. No more trees, no cover. We're in the ship-yaard now. The enemy is forming behind a large, fallen crane, lying di-aag'naly southwest to northeast, using it for a barricade. Do you see it?"

There was a pause. "Aye, Col-nol. Near de ass end o' dat sunk baattle-waagon, beside the dock?" Akka Lead asked uncertainly.

"Yes! I need you to strafe thaat position. And I could use some incendi-aaries *directly* to the east of the point of the crane, south of thaat big undamaged building. Some attention to *it* would be nice. All enemy forces seem to be coming from those two places."

"No smoke," the pilot said hesitantly. Apparently, the flyers had caught the caution too.

"Follow the crane in from the southwest," Chack said

patiently. "Get bombers to follow you in an' drop their loads on the building."

"Aye, Col-nol. Akka Lead out."

Chack hunkered down to watch. The nightly bombings had been far more effective at disrupting Kurokawa's shipyard activity than imagined, but the primary result, from his brigade's perspective, was more junk for the enemy to hide behind. Now would've been a good time for their last two tanks—his opinion of them was much improved—but one had broken down and the other was still stuck in the trees behind. They might come in *very* handy in the open terrain around Sofesshk. He glanced left. The PT attack must've gone well; two Grik dreadnaughts lay on the bottom beside the pier. One still burned furiously, but the other was only smoldering now. Across the bay, the last enemy "flaat-top" had sunk on its side in shallow water, its port side still spewing flames.

The two Fleashooters bored in, one after the other, bullets spitting from their wings, throwing up fountains of sand and plenty of charred splinters of their own. Grik fell, squirming and screeching as the planes pulled up and away. Moments later, three Nancys with *Salissa* markings roared down. Incendiaries—still basically big barrel bombs full of gimpra sap and gasoline—tumbled from the first even as tracers rose to meet it. The enemy had apparently been saving one of their machine guns for Chack's final charge but decided the planes were the most pressing threat. They were right.

The target plane staggered, rolled inverted, and slammed into the big warehouse, just as the incendiaries from the following planes fell through the roof. Orange fire and oily black smoke seared Grik warriors and mushroomed up from the fallen crane, but a huge explosion blasted the warehouse apart. A second explosion, even bigger, sent a massive cloud of white smoke high in the air and pummeled Chack's Brigade with smoldering timbers and other debris. *"Maker!"* Chack hissed. "The joint must've been full of munitions!" He scrambled to his feet. Flames roared all along their front, and few Grik could've survived the bombing and resulting explosion. Wiping his eyes, he spied a gap between the burning crane and shattered warehouse. "Gener-aal advance!" he shouted at the comm-'Cat, still trying to hide under his helmet. "Send it now! All units forwaard, no stopping!" He raised his voice. "First Raiders! Up an' aat 'em!" He snatched up his Krag, bayonet already fixed. "Follow me!" he roared.

Very little fire met them as upwards of six hundred Raiders raced across the clearing. A few 'Cats fell, but the Grik musketry was sporadic and rushed. The fight for the downed crane itself, the parts not burning, was some of the bitterest Chack had seen. With such a narrow front, just a few dozen Grik made the Raiders pay dearly, but they couldn't hold for long and the desperate work of bayonet, cutlass, teeth, and claws lasted only moments before the surviving Grik pulled back and the Raiders poured through. They were about halfway up the bay now, almost even with the north end of Island Number 1. *Soldiers,* Chack thought a bit grudgingly. Real *soldiers, even better than the Grik we fought on the Western Maangoro River. And those were rear-area troops, for the most part.* He knew these Grik were different from what they'd face at Sofesshk. *Trained different, fighting for a different reason, but are these better—serving Kurokawa—than the Grik at Sofesshk will be, fighting for their own capital, their Celestial Mother, their* God*?* Either way, it was going to be tough. And it wasn't finished here. The Grik were running, but not running *away*, like the old days. They were looking for another place to stand.

The section of comm-'Cats caught up with him, puffing under the weight of their burden. "I got Akka Lead again," the talker said. "He waanna know what else he can do."

"Look at *daat*!" someone yelled, pointing out to sea. Chack looked. About six miles away, around the point of the western peninsula, *Savoie*'s tops could just be seen over the intervening jungle. Even at this distance, the huge Stars and Stripes of the Amer-i-caan Navy and Marine Clan was plainly visible, streaming from the mainmast aft. What's more, *Walker* was steaming around the point, laying punishing shell fire into shore-battery positions that had opened up on her again as she headed back into the bay.

"Maker above," Chack murmured in wonder. "Cap-i-taan Reddy has taken *Saavoie*!" he roared, his voice carrying above the din of battle. Feral cheers from Khonashi and Lemurians mounted in response. The force was growing rapidly as the rest of the brigade moved up. He looked at the comm-'Cat. "Tell Akka Lead to hold on. We'll holler if we need him. We're about to get mixed up pretty thick with the enemy." He raised his voice again. "Onward, First Raiders! Aat 'em, First North Borno! Let's finish it!"

Kurokawa's Compound

Musket balls flailed the wooden pickets of the stockade surrounding the compound, spraying them with splinters. Sandra picked one out of the skin of her upper arm and glanced at Diania. The girl was rocking back and forth on her knees, eyes clenched shut—in pain, not fear—as she held her shattered hand to her breast. A musket ball had smashed it during their wild, brief exchange of fire with Iguri and his Grik. None of the enemy survived, but between that and now this firefight with Kurokawa's guards, only Sandra, Diania, Corporal Tass, Ruffy, one Shee-Ree named Minaa, and Maggiore Rizzo were alive. And only Sandra, Ruffy, and Rizzo weren't seriously wounded. Tass had been hit in the leg and face. The leg was useless and his jaw had been shattered by a ball. He looked dazed, his mouth hanging open at an unnatural angle, bloody drool stringing down, but he still fired over the stockade as quickly as he could load his Allin-Silva rifle. Minaa was hit in *both* legs. He and Ruffy, with their Blitzers, were on either corner, guarding against a flank attack. Sandra had done all she could for the wounded and the jungle beyond the palisade beckoned, but Tass and Minaa weren't going anywhere and she couldn't leave them to die. Instead, she removed the magazine from her Blitzer and looked at it.

"Only a few rounds left," she told Diania. She'd already taken her friend's magazines, since the Impie girl could barely hold her weapon. "I doubt Ruffy and Minaa have much ammo either." The result of their expenditure was clear to see in the courtyard between them and Kurokawa's HQ, through gaps in the stockade: twenty Grik guards lay dead, and just as many were crawling, moaning, or squealing in pain. They'd all been victims of an impetuous charge straight at them through the door. Bunched up, they were impossible to miss. The fire galling them now came from the windows, the heavy timber frames giving the shooters better protection than the spindly palisade offered. "Do you think you can crawl over there and get his pistol?" She nodded at Iguri's corpse.

"Aye'm," Diania said, her voice strained. "An' p'raps some Grik muskets."

"Good girl. Just stay low."

"Go! Us hold!" Corporal Tass slurred, proving once and for all that much of the human speech Grik-like beings managed came from their throats and the backs of their tongues. His broken jaw never moved.

"No way, Corporal," Sandra stated flatly.

"We came for you," Minaa pleaded. "Get *hurt an' dead* to save you. Don't let us fail!"

"We'll be okay," she snapped irritably. "Chack'll be here soon. Listen: the fighting's only a few hundred yards away."

"Runnin' Gaa-reiks'll get here quicker," Minaa objected.

"He is right," Ruffy reluctantly agreed. "They came to save us. They have done all they can. My kaiser would expect me to get you to safety."

Rizzo had finally spit the gag out of his mouth. "Do as he says, *signora*," he begged, his expression at least looking sincere. "You have a chance to escape. Take it!"

"Shut up, you!"

Corporal Tass tumbled back, the top of his head and right eye a pulped wreck. The ball that hit him whined into the trees and struck one with a loud *thwok!* "Damn!" Sandra swore, and fired a few precious rounds over the palisade. To her surprise, there was no answering fire. A moment later, however, there came a voice—one she knew and hated.

"Your position is hopeless, Mrs. Reddy," Kurokawa yelled. "You have—what? One or two companions left? You will soon be surrounded, overwhelmed by my army. Surrender now and you will not be harmed!"

Sandra barked a laugh. "How ironic," she called back. "If we get surrounded by your army, that's running from the fight. Even more ironic is that you think your position's better than ours. *You're* about to be surrounded by *my husband's* army!" She twisted the knife. "I guess you saw your getaway ship go up in smoke, and your whole damn fleet is done!" She only hoped the last was true, as she was unable to see past the bay with the building blocking it. But the cruiser's fate was obvious. "I'll tell you what," she countered. "If *you* surrender now, I give *my* word you won't be roughed up too much—before you're hanged."

The laugh that returned was maniacal, and Grik troops suddenly filled the doorway, rushing out, bayonets fixed. Sandra rose and shot one before her bolt locked back on an empty magazine. A few shots came from Ruffy and Minaa, dropping a couple more, before they were also empty. Ruffy dove for Tass's rifle, but a staccato clatter of musket shots chewed through the palisade and sent him sprawling. Ten Grik remained and they bounded toward them.

This is it, Sandra thought, almost relieved. She groped for the little .380 in her waistband and stood, prepared. Diania rose to stand beside her. To her astonishment, so did Maggiore Rizzo.

"Stop!" Kurokawa shrieked. "Stand down! Keep them covered—nothing more!" Briskly, he strode through the door, and the Grik parted before him. He stopped on the other side of the splintered pickets, pointing a Nambu pistol at Sandra's belly. "Maggiore Rizzo. What a pleasant surprise," he said, then glared at Sandra. "Not *running* troops," he snapped, continuing the argument as if there'd been no interruption. But he spoke as if trying to reassure himself. "My reinforcements are on their way."

"Keep telling yourself that," Sandra replied. She knew she was shaking but couldn't help it. Her adrenaline was spiking and all she could think was that if he shot her *there*, her and Matt's baby would die. Of course, she was about to die anyway. "You just don't get it!" she shouted suddenly, surprising herself. "You're beaten!" She pointed south with her left hand, using his distraction to get a firm grip on the little Colt. Running Grik were visible now, very close but not coming this way; they were running for the trees, chased by muzzle flashes and puffs of smoke. "That's *Chack's Brigade*," she said harshly, "the best light infantry in this whole crappy world, and those're probably your reinforcements on the run! You're *finished*, General of the Sea!" She laced the title with as much contempt as she was capable of. Oddly, instead of shooting her in a rage, as she expected, Hisashi Kurokawa only smiled.

"Perhaps you are correct, to a degree, *Lady* Sandra," he retorted with his own sarcasm. "But what you don't understand is that I can never be beaten as long as I have you. Whether you believed what you told me or not is immaterial; you were wrong. Captain Reddy came after all, risking everything to save you. Don't you see? He would *lose the war* to save you." He shrugged. "He may already have. Even while he is here—with the bulk of his fleet, no doubt—General Esshk mounts his Final Swarm to overwhelm Madagascar and roll back every gain you've made. So while I may have lost all I achieved, so have you."

Without warning, the pistol in his hand barked twice, three times.

Sandra blanched, expecting the pain to come, but there was nothing. Instead, Maggiore Rizzo gave a small, surprised cry and slowly sank to his knees. Then, utterly lifeless, he fell face-first against the palisade and slid to the ground.

"You're insane," Sandra whispered.

"Possibly," Kurokawa agreed, his face oddly troubled. "But I'm also quite valuable. Even more so now that *he* is dead. I know a great deal about the League of Tripoli. I also know more about the Grik than any man alive and can help against General Esshk as well." He pursed his lips. "Many of my people, made prisoner over time, have been released in the Nippon of this world. It is one of your allies in the war, but no matter. I and the rest of my people can make a place for ourselves there, just as that *traitor*"—he flared—"Sato Okada did." He calmed himself. "More important, however, to that end, though I've never met Captain Reddy, I *know* him quite well. By all accounts, including yours"—he glanced disdainfully at Rizzo's corpse—"and his, based on League intelligence, Captain Reddy is a man of honor and keeps his word. If I surrender you unharmed in exchange for assistance against your enemies and safe transport"—he paused and lifted an eyebrow—"home, your husband's *honor* will never let him harm me."

Sandra was shocked. She'd never seen Kurokawa so rational, and most frightening of all, he could be right. It *was* very possible Matt would let him live now that he was out of the war, if that was the price of her life. And on his own, in this world's Japan, he'd be free to continue to plot and scheme in pursuit of his own agenda, just as he'd done during his association with the Grik. They'd *never* be free of his treachery. *It can't happen,* Sandra decided. *I can't allow it, even if it costs—*

Her thoughts were shattered by the familiar, rapid stutter of .45 ACP rounds spraying from a Tommy gun, a 1911 Colt, and at least one Blitzerbug. Sandra knew instinctively what they were because despite shooting the same round, each weapon had its own distinctive sound. A storm of lead came from the very doorway Kurokawa had just left, and Sandra grabbed Diania and dove for the ground, even as Kurokawa turned to face the threat behind him. Guards spun and fell, some performing macabre, boneless, blood-spraying dances as slugs tore through them and warbled away. Kurokawa raised the Nambu, an expression of surprised outrage purpling his face, but cried out in pain and fell atop a pile of writhing, shrieking Grik. A few managed to fire their muskets, but most went down before they even knew what was happening. There was a slight pause accompanied by the metallic *click* and *snik* of magazines being replaced, and the firing resumed. Sandra kept her head down, tight against Diania's, mumbling, "Don't move, don't move," over and over. No bullets came close, but splinters gusted down on her back amid a cloud of the feathery Grik fur that drifted through the few inches between her wide eyes and the earthy sand.

Finally, except for the nearing roar of battle, there was no more shooting, and she raised her head and peered through a gap in the stockade. There, standing over the writhing, mewling heap of Grik, oil smoke streaming from the hot barrels of their weapons, were Dennis Silva, Lawrence, and the Khonashi Sergeant Oolak. Sandra blinked alarm at the expression on Silva's face. She'd never seen anything quite like it there, not even that time on Billingsly's ship. Silva was usually so easygoing, even in battle, that regardless how grim things sometimes got, he could always summon a grin, find something to amuse him. His wit was often quite dark indeed, but it was always there. He showed no humor now at all, not even satisfaction, and his one eye reflected a pool of hatred deeper and blacker than death itself.

Sandra actually shivered. *Whatever we do,* she thought, *we have* always *got to keep that man on our side, and focused on the real enemy.* Then she coughed and spat Grik fuzz out of her mouth. "*There* you are, Chief Silva," she said. "Lawrence. Sergeant Oolak," she added, then helped Diania up. The change that came over Silva's face was remarkable and swift, the relief flooding across it like surf scouring shattered sand castles on a beach.

"Aye," he managed. "We was a tad de-layed. A few needed killin' out front." He gestured, then hesitated. "You *knew* I was comin', right?" he asked anxiously.

"Of course," Sandra lied, though upon reflection, she *should* have. He always did. She watched his expression soften even more.

"We need to get you ladies inside quick as we can. Chackie'll be here any minute, but we need defensible cover in the meantime." Silva's eye narrowed when he pointed at the pile of Grik with his Thompson. "Got an old pal here to deal with, though," he added.

"In a moment. First, help me get Minaa and Diania inside." Lawrence and Oolak knocked the spindly remains of the palisade over and carried the Shee-Ree through the door. With a worried glance at Sandra, Diania followed. When they were gone, Silva and Sandra knelt together in front of Hisashi Kurokawa. He hadn't spoken but appeared only lightly wounded, lying with his dead guards, clutching a bloody upper arm. His pistol was in the sand a few yards away and he glanced at it occasionally, diverting his gaze from their remorseless stares. He licked his lips.

"I can be very useful to you," he said, voice strained. "More useful than you can imagine."

"Are you *begging*?" Sandra asked softly. "Sounds like it."

"I am *not*!" Kurokawa spat.

"Pity," Sandra said. "That might've actually done you

some good." She looked at the Grik. "You shot a lot of them in the back, Chief Silva," she said, her tone mock scolding.

"Yeah, well, their backs was at us, an' they should'a looked over 'em from time to time. Just like him." He poked Kurokawa hard in the belly with his Thompson. "Didn't shoot *him* in the back, an' only winged him too, case you hadn't told him off enough."

"Thank you. There *is* something else I'd like to say." She looked intently at Kurokawa. "You're a monster," she said simply. "An evil, evil man, with no honor at all, who's only ever thought about himself. I respect the Grik more than you, because they're just doing . . ." She shrugged. "What they do. You're similar in that regard, but the difference is, *you know better*!" Her voice was rising. "You can't trade me now, but you might be right about my husband. He'll use whatever advantage he can find to *save* lives, *win* the war, and thwart the League, because—like I told you—he's fighting for a cause bigger than himself. A *good* cause, which too many have already died for. You just might convince him not to kill you—for their sake."

Sandra stood, and a look of relief began to spread across Kurokawa's face, along with something else: a kind of triumph. "So," Sandra said, "I think it's best all around if we don't put my husband in the position of making that decision. God knows he's had enough to worry about, largely because of you." For the first time, she displayed the little .380 Colt. "You know, I had this all along and could've used it whenever I wanted. I probably should have, a time or two, but better late than never."

Kurokawa's eyes bulged. "Lady San—" he began, but never had a chance to finish. When the pistol was empty—*Annoying how the slide doesn't lock back to let you know,* she thought absently—she started to toss it on his bloody chest. Reconsidering, she put it back in her waistband and scooped up Kurokawa's Nambu. Then she glared at Silva.

"Anything to say?" she demanded.

"No, ma'am," he replied, taking a chew and then digging a rusty snuff can out of a pouch. "Cain't imagine how hard it was to rake this up," he said conversationally. "Never used snuff myself, dippin' er snortin' either one, it bein' a womanish habit by my lights. One o' the boys on

Tarakaan Island, offa *S-19,* said this was his granny's—sent him candy in it—but I don't believe him. Had ta' trade him *two* pouches o' good, sweetened chew for a empty damn can." Reaching down, he opened Kurokawa's perforated shirt, twisted the lid off the can, and dumped what looked like little horns on the blood-seeping wounds. Closing the shirt, he suddenly pounded the spot several times with the butt of his Thompson.

Sandra watched it all, as the shakes began to take hold once more, but no regret touched her. "What was that about?" she asked. Then she remembered their time on Yap Island and her eyes went wide. "Was that . . . ?"

"Oh, just a little idea the Skipper gave me. Had another, maybe funner prank floatin' around in my head, but this'll do." He paused, gauging the battle. The fury of the fighting seemed to be dying away as it neared. "Reckon Chackie'll be here quicker than I thought. Let's get inside." He pointed at Kurokawa. "Might wanna put up a sign warnin' folks not to go pokin' around the little garden that sprouts here, directly."

Hisashi Kurokawa wasn't dead, and he watched through the searing waves of agony as the one-eyed man and that murderous, ungrateful woman stepped into the HQ building. *His* HQ! His chest and stomach where the bullets hit were a sea of pain he could hardly bear, but whatever the one-eyed man had dumped on him was worse. It burned like fire, quickly spreading outward from his wounds until it felt like flames would flare from his fingertips. Oddly, though, even as the pain mounted, so did his ability to discount it, ignore it, to think clearly and plan. Soon the pain, while just as excruciating, simply didn't matter anymore. The only real inconvenience was that he didn't seem able to move. Even his eyelids no longer obeyed. That didn't matter either. *The fighting will end and someone will find me, tend me, heal me. Captain Reddy will understand how indispensable I am. And I* shall *help! I'll prove my loyalty over and over, until the last doubts fade away. Then again, my time will come. . . .*

But it wouldn't. Even as he lay there, scheming to the end, hundreds of tiny filaments probed his capillaries, luxuriating in the nourishing blood, questing deeper, faster, releasing the toxins that made their host so cooperative. In a matter of days, they would have fed enough to provide a firm foundation for the swiftly crawling kudzu-like plant that would burst forth from the rotting corpse.

One final time, the fighting surged around Kurokawa's HQ compound as Chack's Brigade made its push, but any Grik trying to shelter there took fire from within. They quickly fled or were cut down. The Brigade flowed past, shooting as it went.

"Hey, Chackie!" came a familiar voice, calling from the bullet-pocked building. "About damn time you got here!"

Chack paused, looking for the voice. When he saw a helmet rise from the other side of a bullet-riddled windowsill, followed by a one-eyed, grinning face, he snorted a laugh. "Major Risa, with me!" he ordered his sister, who was bounding past. She took a few more running steps before glaring back, blinking resentment before she could cover it. "Bring a squaad to investigate this building," Chack told her. "I believe there are friends inside. Captain Cook!" Abel Cook was acting CO of the 1st North Borno. "Continue the pursuit, if you please, but keep a raa-dio close at haand."

"Aye, sir," Cook replied grimly, and sprinted on.

"Friends," Risa said woodenly as she joined him.

"Yes," Chack told her definitively as Silva appeared in the doorway. He was followed by Sandra, Diania, Sergeant Oolak, and finally Lawrence. "*Good* ones," Chack stressed, "worthy of our sacrifice this day."

"But Major I'joorka . . ."

"Is a soldier, and a friend as well. With the Maker's help, he may recover. Most important, his injury was not your doing. It was the fault of the war. Just as our reunion with *these* friends is made possible by the war." Silva was with them now. He pounded Chack on the back and swept Risa up in his arms.

"Hey!" Silva asked Risa in alarm. "What're you cryin' about? Ain't you glad to see me? I'm *damn* sure glad to see *you*!"

"Yes," she whispered against his neck. "Yes," she said louder. "Very glaad!"

"Colonel Chack," Sandra said. "We have wounded inside and I need assistance."

"Corps-'Cats!" Chack called. His summons was answered by a pair of Grik-like Khonashi with medical gear.

"Inside," Sandra repeated gratefully. "The building is secure." She raised her voice for Minaa's benefit. "Khonashi coming in!" After what they'd been through, there was no sense in scaring Minaa to death—or getting Khonashi medics shot. But now that she had that out of the way, she looked hesitantly at Chack, as if terrified of the question foremost in her heart.

Chack knew what it was and didn't make her ask. "*Waa-kur* will be alongside the dock momentarily," he said. "I saw her coming in and sent troops to meet her. She looks a little baattered, as usual," he warned, "but I *spoke* to Cap-i-taan Reddy on the raa-dio before our last push through to here. He will be here shortly, Lady Saandra."

To Chack's consternation, the pregnant woman embraced him with surprising strength, considering how frail she looked, and then kissed his furry cheek. "Thank you," she murmured. "Thank God."

Walker came to rest against the charred, battered pier south of where a sunken Grik cruiser's protruding parts still smoldered. The air was sodden with moisture and heavy with smoke. Water spewed over the old destroyer's side from hoses secured to stanchions on her fo'c'sle, snaking up from below. More water jetted from her sides as bilge pumps labored to keep ahead of the flooding, caused mostly by the single 13.5″ shell that hit her sideways, punching a pair of holes large enough for a 'Cat to step through. Otherwise, her damage and casualties were remarkably light, under the circumstances. Particularly considering what she'd faced. She'd certainly had it easier than *James Ellis* and Des-div 2, and reports concerning their condition were still coming in.

It started raining hard, lashing steam from fires burning up and down the harbor. The storm swirling to the west throughout the night and morning had finally fallen apart, but the sky remained moody, noncommittal, all day.

It finally settled for an afternoon squall, which seemed to add an exclamation point to the battle, and more or less ended the fighting on Zanzibar.

As soon as the gangway was rigged, Matt Reddy, Bernie Sandison, and Pam Cross rushed up from the pier, surrounded by a squad of Chack's Raiders, and approached the compound from the west at a trot. Matt was almost breathless when he saw Sandra, but that wasn't why he couldn't speak when his eyes took in her thin, bedraggled, barely recognizable form, made more shocking still by her bulging belly. The concern—and relief—on his face was obvious for all to see, however, and for the longest time he merely held her, despite the rain. Silva roughly embraced Pam as well, but shooed her inside with a muttered, "Later, doll. I'll make it up to you. Promise." Oddly, this time she knew he really would and obeyed without complaint. Silva still belonged entirely to Captain Reddy for the moment. She'd get him when his duty was done.

Neither Matt nor Sandra seemed to notice, even as his soiled whites and her tattered rags became soaked and Sandra's hair turned to a stringy mop. "Never again," was all she said.

"I sent you away to *protect* you," Matt replied, furious at himself, what she'd endured, and how close he'd come to losing her.

"Never again," Sandra repeated forcefully, looking up into his eyes. Even as the rain washed the tears and grime from her face, it also seemed to scour away the ordeal they symbolized. It would take far more than a little rain to loosen the pain, rage, and sorrow that held her heart and soul in its viselike grip, but it was a start. With great effort, she managed a smile. "You're stuck with me until the end, sailor. I won't leave you again, no matter what, so you'll just have to change your silly rules about mates aboard ship."

"Maybe I will," he hedged, already thinking, *No way will I risk her—and the baby—aboard in a fight.* He didn't mention it then, though. "In hindsight, on this world, in this war, it was kind of a stupid rule to start with," he said instead.

"Yeah."

Together, they stepped inside Kurokawa's HQ, through

the same door Sandra first entered a thousand years ago, it seemed. They were followed by Chack, Silva, Risa, and Lawrence, who'd remained outside to watch over them from a discreet distance.

Diania met them, holding her bandaged hand, her face clouded with worry. "Beggin' yer pardon, Cap'n Reddy. On the ship—*Savoie*—what of Gunnery Sergeant Horn?" she asked.

Matt frowned. "Horn's fine," he assured her. "But he and Pokey are the only ones left. Becher Lange, Captain Brassey, and all the Khonashi died taking the bridge. Without them . . ." He shook his head. "Horn secured a prisoner, though, a Capitaine Dupont." He nodded to himself when he saw Sandra's and Diania's faces both harden. From his brief encounter with the man, he hadn't expected Dupont had behaved in a way that would ingratiate him to the people *Savoie* brought here. He *wanted* to hang him, but might have to settle for some kind of deal in exchange for information about the League. That reminded him. "Kurokawa?" he asked simply.

"He's dead, Skipper," Silva piped up with a quick protective glance at Sandra. "Plumb layin'-on-the ground, starin'-at-the-sky, tongue-hangin'-out, *eye-witness* dead this time." He jerked a thumb out back. "I told Minaa I'd hold him up so's he can piss on him later. Them Shee-Ree are weird like that. Course, it might be good for morale if we lined up ever-body to"—he glanced at Sandra and Diania—"uh, relieve theirselfs on his dead ass. Water the bushes, as it were," he added cryptically.

Matt nodded. One less thing, then. He'd get the details later. His greatest personal enemy was finally dead and they'd never even met. It was probably for the best. The war had become personal enough without the dramatic face-to-face confrontation that madman had craved. Now he could focus all his attention on their bigger problems. Looking around the room at his friends, the wounded Shee-Ree, and then back at Sandra, a dam collapsed and a wave of sadness finally gripped his heart. "Gunny Horn told me about Adar," he managed. Sandra hugged him again, tight enough to hurt, but whether she was trying to take his pain or relieve her own, he couldn't say.

CHAPTER 27

"I will miss you, my brother," Admiral Keje-Fris-Ar said heavily, the white-streaked, rust-colored fur on his face damp with tears. He stood with Matt, Sandra, and hundreds more on the northern tip of Island Number 1. As many people as they could briefly spare from recovery operations had come to the funeral, and the only ones Matt saw who didn't look anxious to get back to something important were Ben Mallory and the tiny female Lemurian lieutenant beside him. Shirley's plane, stripped of everything they could take out and carrying a belly tank, would fly to Mahe when they brought enough fuel ashore. Ben's *might* fly again—if they cannibalized enough parts off the plane they left behind—but the 3rd (Army) Pursuit Squadron was no more. Ben took his duties seriously, though, and wouldn't wait for his plane. He was only waiting for another one to carry him to Grik City, where he'd take over coordinating all air operations against Sofesshk.

The island was on fire again, this time with the pyres of those they'd lost, the flames and smoke carrying their spirits to the heavens. Adar's pyre was in the center so he could rise with the rest, guiding them in death as he'd always done in life. And for the first time, the spiraling sparks carried the spirits of every member of the Alliance: Lemurians from as far as the Filpin Lands, Imperial humans from Respite and the New Britain Isles, Khonashi, Grik-like, and human. The Republic of Real People was represented by Becher Lange and his three loyal sailors, the third exhumed for the purpose. Even a few Grik, whom Horn pointed out, were placed on the pyres beside their former enemies. As always, it seemed, a few more of Matt's dwindling original destroyermen had been lost as well, mostly aboard *James Ellis*. Perry Brister seemed particularly affected by Jeff Brooks's death. And every sailor, soldier, pilot, and Marine killed in the Battle of Lizard Ass Bay joined Adar on his journey above, because there'd be no graves on Zanzibar.

Kurokawa's corpse had already sprouted, but no one was much concerned that a single killer kudzu plant would overwhelm the island anytime soon. There were still plenty of Grik there, though, and no reason to waste lives hunting them. They'd stay only long enough to complete necessary repairs and salvage what they could before destroying what remained and steaming back to Mahe. As Perry Brister said, they "wouldn't leave anything there they ever needed to come back for." Perry was on *Tarakaan Island*, his ship already in her dry dock, while *Tara* and *Salissa* waited for high tide to try to pull *Savoie* off the beach. If they were successful, they'd tow her to Mahe even while repairs to *James Ellis* continued.

"We all will, Keje," Matt said, putting his hand on his friend's furry arm. He cocked his head in thought. "But he *did* prepare us for this. He groomed Alan Letts to replace him, almost as if he'd always known he'd have to, and he made a lot more out of Letts than I ever could."

"A better chaar-man for the Alli-aance, the Union, than Adar himself could be," Keje agreed sadly. "But though he left a noble legaacy, his loss is no less painful."

"I know."

"Will *Waa-kur* be ready for sea?" Keje asked, concerned. "*Ellie* may be more sorely hurt, but I caan't agree she should've been repaired before your ship."

"*Walker*'ll be fine," Matt argued. "There was plenty of plate steel stockpiled here. We covered her big holes before we started loading the surplus. As long as we don't push her, the patches'll last until *Tara* spits *Ellie*'s out. Other than the plate steel, the hardest things to haul off are going to be Kurokawa's surviving heavy machinery for making guns, engines—things like that. At least we have plenty of labor." Two hundred Japanese and nearly three thousand "yard" Grik had surrendered. The Japanese, with the exception of a few officers, had been granted amnesty and transport to the Shogunate of Yokohama. As far as the Grik were concerned . . . Matt frowned at the three remaining DDs of Des-div 2—and their four seaworthy prizes. Six frigates and AVDs had survived the sharp action with the cruisers, but only because *Ellie* intervened. Three of them, including *Tassat* at last, were so far beyond repair that they'd been scuttled. The cruisers surrendered, under *Ellie*'s guns, when a cease-fire was arranged and Lawrence motored out in the Seven boat to "reason" with their crews. Matt didn't trust them enough to leave them in their ships, despite Lawrence and Horn's assurance that they'd do their duty as long as they were treated well and fed, but the ships were relatively undamaged and might come in handy. Still . . . "I'm worried how vulnerable *Tara* and *Big Sal* will be without a proper screen."

Keje's gaze had returned to the towering column of smoke, the only blight on the cloudless blue sky. "You worry about the planes that got away," he said. Their best estimate, partially confirmed by a Japanese signal officer named Fukui, who actually seemed relieved his side had lost and Kurokawa was dead, was that two squadrons of the twin-engine torpedo bombers and at least one squadron of fighters—almost thirty planes—had flown west during the battle. Whether Esshk could make weapons for them was unknown, but he could probably fuel them. All Kurokawa's raw fuel had come from the mainland. Fukui hadn't known if there was an airstrip in Africa, but the planes were designed for unimproved fields, so they probably found a place to land. Just as interesting was a *third* type of plane that was spotted.

"Sure," Matt said. "One of our AVDs in the strait saw 'em, but even if her Nancy hadn't been over the harbor, it wouldn't've had a chance." He waited while a Sky Priest spoke some of the words for the dead. "And a Type Ninety-five floatplane was seen. Fukui said it was the same one that bombed Baalkpan so long ago, and Muriname—their air force commander and Kurokawa's XO—has been hoarding it. It's likely he flew it out."

"Muriname's a . . . complicated person," Sandra said, frowning, her eyes narrowing. "I think he had honor once and would like to have it back." She glanced at Diania, a short distance away with Gunny Horn, his arm protectively around Diania's shoulders. Her hand was still wrapped—it would never work right again—but for the first time in a long while she seemed content. "He protected us, after a fashion," Sandra continued, "but I never figured out if it was for honor or himself." She shrugged. "He actually told me he'd gone insane when we first got here, but I don't know if it's true. He's not as crazy as Kurokawa, at least." She shuddered. "Or Gravois. *That* guy may be even crazier than Kurokawa was." She frowned. "That reminds me, though. Rizzo."

"That League Major who Kurokawa shot?"

"Yes. He kept saying it wasn't his war and he had his own way out."

Keje looked at her. "I understand some of his ground crew was captured."

Matt nodded for his wife. Between Dupont and six others taken aboard *Savoie*, and the twenty-odd pilots and mechanics, they finally had plenty of Leaguers to squeeze, giving them a plausible means of obtaining the same information Fiedler left him in his private letter. He'd kept it private too, except for Ben and Safir, who'd read it already, not only so it couldn't "spill" and possibly compromise his source, but also because everyone already had enough to worry about. The pertinent parts came toward the end, detailing much of what the League had in terms of ships, planes, armor, and manpower, not to mention the murky political situation and barbaric methods the League used to fortify its position in the Mediterranean. He'd read that part often enough to memorize it, and it was daunting indeed. He considered the final lines:

> *You understand honor, Kapitan, and know why I am torn between assisting your cause and my conscience. Yet your humane treatment of me after all you've endured at the hands of the League has convinced me that my honor cannot allow me to sit by*

and watch those who have none destroy your people. I will pass what information I may, to help you defend against League schemes—yet I cannot help should it ever come to open war between our people. To that end, I close with a plea: no matter the provocation, you must never allow yourself to be lured into direct conflict with the League. Not only could I no longer aid you, but you cannot possibly hope to prevail. The disparity of forces is simply too great. Please do not be insulted when I say, no matter how valorous the mouse, it cannot slay the wolf.

With their new prisoners, Matt could finally share the letter and the list of ships that, to the best of Fiedler's recollection, composed the League fleet—not that he was certain even now that was a good idea. But when the squeezing started, they'd learn, anyway. He mentally shook himself. "There were no League planes left," he said.

"Then how did Rizzo mean to escape?" Keje asked.

Sandra shrugged and Matt said nothing. *According to Fiedler, there'd been at least one more League sub in the Indian, or "Western," Ocean. If that was true, where did it fuel? Where is it now?* That was another reason Matt was anxious about *Salissa*'s and *Tara*'s screen. *Maybe we'll get it out of Dupont. . . .*

The funeral was winding down and the usual big drunk that normally followed had been postponed until they returned to Mahe. Dozens of boats were waiting at the dock, ready to return the attendees to their duties. Matt was surprised to see Spanky step ashore from the Seven boat, which must've brought him across. He'd skipped the funeral because of repairs to *Walker*, but now he was here, wearing a very grim expression. Sandra took a sudden sharp breath and clutched Matt's arm.

"Esshk is out, isn't he?" Matt demanded, throwing out the worst possible scenario he could imagine.

"Uh, no, Skipper," Spanky said, taking a message form from his pocket and unfolding it.

My God, Matt thought, *how I hate the very sight of those things!* He glanced to the side and saw Keje, Bernie, Tikker, Silva and Pam, Horn and Diania, Jarrik-Fas, and dozens of others watching. "But it's bad enough that Ed asked you to bring it?"

"Bad enough I took it from him," Spanky countered. "He already thinks you hate looking at him."

"Not *him*," Matt sighed.

"I know." Spanky held the message out.

"Just tell me what it says." Matt waved around. "Tell us all."

Spanky cleared his throat. "Esshk isn't *out*," he stressed, "not exactly. But a flight of Nancys off *Arracca* on a dusk raid must'a caught 'em by surprise. The Grik're *getting ready* to come out, sure enough. Their fleet's assembling in that lake west o' Sofesshk, and the Nancys spotted hundreds of oared galleys on shore, bein' carried down close to the water—goddamn *galleys*, for Christ's sake—practically floatin' on Grik, rarin' to go."

"Galleys," Matt said, shaking his head.

"Hundreds were seen. There may be *thousands* of 'em," Spanky pointed out. "If you think about it, galleys make perfect sense. Not too many troops stuffed in fewer, bigger ships, an' they can move against the wind, tide, an' current. There're barges too, big ones, probably ready for towin' by Grik BBs or little tugs, like we've seen before. Either way, there's no stoppin' 'em. We can bomb the crap out of 'em now while they're wadded up or as they come downriver, but once they hit the strait they can scatter an' cross wherever they want, land wherever they want. We can kill 'em all the way to Grik City an' never get a tithe of 'em."

"What will we do?" Keje demanded. "We must go at once!"

"What good will *that* do?" Matt asked sharply, bitterly. "*You* could go, but we really need *Salissa* to tow *Savoie*. And neither *Walker* nor *Ellie* is in any shape for a high-speed run to the strait. Even if we made it, we couldn't fight our way out of a wet paper sack when we got there." He shook his head, his hand tightening on Sandra's. "We'd do more harm than good." He added, "So. We have to stick to the plan: repairs and evacuation here, but kick it into high gear."

"And Esshk is free to swaarm our base at Grik City with hundreds of thousands of troops!" Keje growled.

"No, sir," Spanky said bleakly, "not if Russ Chappelle's plan works." Hundreds of expectant eyes were on him now and he shifted uncomfortably.

"What is Commander Chappelle's plan?" Matt asked in the sudden silence.

"He's goin' in," Spanky said. "Takin' *Santy Cat* up the Zambezi to block the river—with her sunk carcass, if he has to."

"My God," Sandra murmured.

"*That's* the style, Russ!" Silva exclaimed admiringly.

"What an asshole!" Pam snapped at him. Then she saw Matt's face. "Wait a minute! *You* can't let him do *that*!"

"Lettin's got nothin' to do with it," Spanky countered. "He's *gonna* do it. Tassanna's backin' his play with *Arracca*'s planes. She'll probably back him with *Arracca* herself if she has to."

Keje looked devastated. "Of course she will," he murmured softly, blinking rapidly, his tail lashing like a whip.

"Okay," Matt grated, his voice like hot iron. "Like I said, we pick up the pace on repairs. Meanwhile, First and Third Corps on Mahe will embark aboard *Sular* and *Madras*, and steam for Grik City to pick up Second Corps. *Everything* on Mahe goes, including anything that'll float and anybody who can hold a weapon. Clear? And every single thing that flies will start hammering the Grik choked up behind *Santa Catalina*. If Russ's stunt and air attacks can't stop the Grik, Generals Alden, Rolak, and Maraan will deploy at Grik City to defend against the biggest bunch of Grik we ever saw. But if the stunt *works*, the entire Expeditionary Force will follow *Santy Cat* up the Zambezi and land behind her. They'll never expect that"—he suddenly grinned—"because it's crazy. But that's open country. If Pete gets ashore with his whole force, all his artillery and every machine gun we can get him, and gets *dug in*"—Matt shook his head—"he'll kill Grik like cutting wheat."

There was murmured approval, but Matt held up his hand. "Either way, two more things have to happen. First, Courtney Bradford and Bekiaa-Sab-At need to get General Kim to kick his Army of the Republic in the ass and keep it moving toward Sofesshk from the south. Second"—

he looked around—"I know we just had a helluva fight, and the smoke over there will remind us what it cost if anybody starts to forget. But we need to get patched up good enough to *fight*, not just show up, and do it faster than we've ever done anything in our lives. *Santy Cat*'s going to buy us time. We won't waste a minute of it, and we *will*, by God, get there before *she* runs out."

EPILOGUE

Army of the Republic
South Bank of the Ungee River
Grik Africa

"Oh my," Courtney Bradford exclaimed, gazing through the telescope General Kim handed him. "I've never seen such birds before—and so *many*! They carpet the river in their multitudes. Quite like geese, the way they bob about, but with long, toothy jaws—for snatching fish, I'm sure!"

"Oh my, indeed," General Kim growled sarcastically. "But you might also, incidentally, note the multitude of the enemy massed on the *far* side of the river."

Courtney blinked. "Well," he replied primly, "that goes without saying. But I've seen large numbers of Grik quite often, you know."

Bekiaa-Sab-At rolled her eyes and flicked her tail in amusement. Just because Courtney had devoted his life to defeating their enemies didn't mean he'd forsaken the pleasures of discovery, and she considered that a good thing. She, Courtney, General Kim, Inquisitor Choon, General Taal, Prefect Bele, and Optio Meek were standing behind a low adobe wall on the north end of the city of Soala. Like all Grik cities, the place reeked of filth, rot, and excrement. They'd also found it utterly abandoned when they finally emerged from the Teetgak Forest. The reason was obvious: the Grik clearly meant to contest their crossing of the Ungee and hadn't wanted their backs to the river. The strategy was disconcertingly sensible.

"It's well we marched as fast as we did, or the enemy would be stronger still," Inquisitor Choon remarked, then sighed. The passage through the forest hadn't been pleasant and they'd faced ambuscades, small and large, by Grik musketeers—or huge, terrifying monsters—on an almost daily basis, but they'd actually maintained a better pace than Choon expected. That was largely because General Kim had applied the lessons learned on the Plain of Gaughala and built a real, united army at last, an army of toughened, realistic veterans who knew they could lose—but also knew they could win. The transformation had been profound.

"Still, their force is quite formidable enough for my taste, and we must find a way through or past it with all haste," Choon reminded. They'd received word of Captain Reddy's victory at Zanzibar with satisfaction, but close on its heels came the rest: the Grik were stirring, TF Bottle Cap would try to stifle their movement in the nest, and if successful, General Alden would land his army ahead of schedule. That meant the Army of the Republic had to churn forward without pause, regardless of resistance, across another hundred miles of enemy territory. On the upside, *if* they secured a crossing—and a depot—at Soala, their supply situation would improve dramatically, by land and sea, and the growing *Fliegertruppe* would have a base of operation. In addition, the closer they got to Sofesshk, the more support they might expect from Allied aircraft. The ultimate question no one could answer was whether the two-pronged attack would help them defeat the enemy in detail—or invite the Grik to do the same to them.

General Kim retrieved his telescope from Courtney and snapped it shut, eyeing Bekiaa. "What do you think?" he asked.

Bekiaa blinked, then flattened her ears, looking behind them at the army still spilling from the forest in the distance, spreading out, forming up. The tawny uniforms were faded now and the army wasn't as pretty, but it finally *acted* like a proper army, deploying, positioning artillery, erecting tents, and throwing up breastworks, all without a word from General Kim. The Grik had already done much the same on the other side of the river, and there were more of them. But even if the quality, armaments, and determination of their individual troops had improved, they still weren't . . . *people*, with all the imagination, initiative, and personal awareness of "why we fight" that the term implied. And they didn't have machine guns, breech-loading rifles, rapid-firing artillery. . . . She looked back at Kim. "I think it's gonna be chick-aash—hell—gettin' across," she said slowly. "An' even worse pushin' on to Sofesshk. But we'll do it." She shrugged, blinking determination. "We got no choice."

General Tomatsu Shinya's HQ
Popayan

Major Blas-Ma-Ar flung the tent flap aside and marched inside the command HQ with Sister Audry, Colonel Arano Garcia, and Captain Ixtli in her wake. When their bedraggled, much-depleted column eventually joined Shinya's X and XI Corps, the full "Army of the Sisters," in the high mountain village of Popayan, they'd been cared for, fed—and left cooling their heels for a week. All while rumors of a fierce battle to the *east*, at the Quito road and Camino Militar crossroads, flashed through camp. None of the army's senior commanders were present, and Blas couldn't get a straight answer out of anyone. Finally, the day before, Generals Shinya and Blair, Governor-Empress Rebecca Anne McDonald, and Saan-Kakja arrived, looking exhausted. When there was still no summons, and growing increasingly furious and frustrated, what remained of the leadership of TF Skuggik Chase marched, en masse, to Army HQ, bypassed sputtering guards, and burst in on what was apparently a fairly heated staff meeting, judging by the loud voices they heard outside.

Blas blinked as her eyes adjusted to the canvas-filtered light, but soon recognized Shinya, Blair, Rebecca, and Saan-Kakja. There were others too that she didn't know, but whatever was going on, she was immediately certain it *was* their business—at least Sister Audry's—and they had a right to the unvarnished version.

"Ah," Shinya said with a glare at a standing officer in the old-fashioned uniform of the Imperial lancers. "The very people we were discussing. I apologize for not greeting you sooner, but things have been rather hectic, as you may have gathered, and we"—he nodded at the other commanders—"were attending a conference with High Admiral Jenks at Quito when the . . . unpleasantness commenced. Making it here was somewhat tedious, I'm afraid. Please make yourselves comfortable." He blinked genuine, relieved pleasure to see them. "Would you like a refreshment?"

Blas was taken aback. "Ah, sure. What *about* us?" she asked, taking a cold mug of beer an Impie steward offered.

Shinya gestured at the lancer. "This gentleman, Colonel Lassiter, believes you should've more quickly detected that the force in front of you *wasn't* Don Hernan's entire army, and a more timely warning might've allowed us to prevent the . . . situation that arose as a result."

Blas bristled.

"I cannot see how that might be," Sister Audry stated coldly, leveling an expression of distaste at the lancer. "Given our limited resources compared to what we *all* believed was Don Hernan's main body, not to mention the very specific orders we were constrained to obey"—she bowed her head to Blas—"the major, in tactical command of our force, did all anyone could expect. She followed orders precisely, kept pressure on the enemy to the best of her ability, and used initiative and daring to discover the ultimate unpleasant truth. She behaved with honor and courage, and I will *not* hear her performance—or that of Colonel Garcia—disparaged. In fact, I will recommend them both for recognition and reward."

"Hear her," Saan-Kakja stated flatly, her gold-and-black eyes flashing at Lassiter.

"I still maintain that had we—"

"Silence," Rebecca McDonald said softly and sighed, her little-girl voice somewhat incongruous in a council of war, but her tone brooked no argument. "Perhaps some context is in order, to familiarize our friends with recent events?"

Shinya scowled. "Indeed," he agreed, looking at the visitors. "I think we can confirm your intelligence that Don Hernan no longer commands the Army of God. One reason is the skill with which whoever does disengaged from your pursuit without even our native allies"—he nodded respectfully at Ixtli—"discovering it. Another is how he turned a beaten rabble back into an army and wasn't content to merely escape. As you may have pieced together, he carefully planned his, ah, redeployment in such a way, and with sufficient time and preparation, to land a devastating—some might say humiliating—blow on a *third* of our army, strung out, in column, on the march." He glanced at the lancer. "Our dragoons, in particular, were handled very roughly."

"My God," Sister Audry whispered. "We knew something was wrong, but not *that* bad."

"No one knows, yet," Rebecca said. "*We* didn't know the full extent until we collected General Blair on our way here. Communications have been spotty, and couriers have apparently fallen prey to enemy raiding parties."

"That third of the army, troops under *my* command, for the most part, were not annihilated," General Blair said, but his tone wasn't self-congratulatory. "They gave a good account of themselves, in point of fact, once the initial confusion was contained. But they were—*I* was—soundly beaten." He nodded at the lancer. "Our dragoons, cut off from the start, very nearly *were* wiped out. Only timely air support prevented that." He rubbed his chin, thoughtful. "This new commander does have talent, as your warning proposed, Major Blas. And even if your dispatches arrived more swiftly, I'm not sure we would've prepared appropriately, given our preconceptions." He sighed.

"So you see," Saan-Kakja said, "*all* of us were deceived, with dreadful consequences. Laying blame on anyone in particular is counterproductive and corrosive when the real blame lies with our *collective* conviction that, not only would Don Hernaan continue in command, but after its defeat at Fort De-fi-aance, his army itself could no longer fight. I now suspect, given a competent commaander, the Doms will prove a far more formid-aable foe."

Blas glanced at Lassiter and saw, for the first time, how tired and sick at heart he seemed. "After what you endured, Col-nol Laass-iter, I understand your laashing out." She looked at Sister Audry. "I've done it myself before."

Lassiter waved a hand. "My apologies, Major Blas. High Chief Saan-Kakja is right. There's sufficient blame for all. *I* should've been more careful."

"Enough, both of you," Rebecca said. "The question now is what do we do?"

"We must halt, reconsolidate . . ." Blair began thoughtfully.

"No!" Shinya snapped. "That will only complete their victory, and it's exactly what they want." He stood and strode to the painted map pinned to the canvas wall. "Our reconnaissance reports that the enemy is moving north, for the Pass of Fire instead of the Temple at New Granada, and probably means to reinforce the garrison there." He glanced at Rebecca. "The *Navy*'s next objective."

"What do you suggest?" Rebecca asked.

Shinya stabbed the Pass of Fire with his finger. "We follow him there and attack, in conjunction with an amphibious assault by sea. Admiral Jenks's original plan, in fact. It will be costly," he conceded. "The cities around El Paso del Fuego are loyal to the Dominion, by all accounts, and quite a few Grikbirds remain to counter our air power. They've had time to prepare for us, emplace shore batteries, and possibly armor their ships. With forty or more thousand troops added to the defense . . ."

"There's no way to prevent them from reaching there?" Saan-Kakja asked.

Shinya moved his finger east. "We could march on the temple ourselves. We couldn't possibly reach it without support—it's too far—but the enemy might pursue *us* then, particularly with our supply lines at his mercy. That might prevent his reinforcing the pass, and it's possible we could arrange a decisive meeting." He shrugged. "Or we might all starve in the jungle."

Rebecca frowned. "I doubt it would work, in any event. We must give the devil his due, my friends. Based on what we've seen, I doubt *this* Dom commander would cooperate."

Shinya nodded agreement.

"So," Rebecca mused, "there seems little choice, and I suppose it's past time we combined all our leaders, all our forces, in this theater once more." She sighed. "Sister Audry, Saan-Kakja, my *sisters*, please stay. We may want to consult High Admiral Jenks and Admiral Lelaa further, but for now, the sisters whose army this is must discuss this. The rest of you, please excuse us."

All but the three females filed out of the tent. In the shade of the fly, Shinya stopped Blas. "You did very well, by the way. No one could've imagined . . ."

"I know," Blas interrupted. "We *did* do well." She shook her head. "Don't put me in a spot like that again."

"I'll try."

Blas gestured at the tent. "What do you think they'll come up with? They won't have us march east, will they?"

Shinya shook his head. "No. That's ridiculous. They'll order an attack on the Pass of Fire, from land and sea. Admirals Jenks and Lelaa, General Blair, and myself—and you, Major Blas—will plan it as carefully as we can." He frowned. "And it'll be the biggest, bloodiest mess we've ever seen—on *this* side of the world." Then he smiled rather ruefully. "But it makes the most sense, and a lot more than what I had you doing. Besides, it's all there is, and it's *time*." He shrugged. "Hopefully, it'll even work."

USS* Donaghey *(DD-2)
South of Cuba

USS *Donaghey*'s comm-'Cat didn't contact Fred Reynolds until the day before the two battered frigates, carrying more prisoners than crew, would've made Santiago Bay. It was good he finally did, because lower sea levels had choked the narrow entry and the bay didn't exist where they thought it should. There was only a pleasant, scenic lake, made brackish by storm and tidal surges, and the land around it was only sparsely inhabited by farmers growing something similar to sugar beets and real tobacco.

The "actual" Santiago Bay, founded by the Dominion and now the largest NUS naval station in the Caribbean, was in south-central Cuba, where Manzanilla Bay would've been. Their understandable mix-up corrected, *Donaghey* and *Matarife* altered course, and the heavy NUS steam frigate *Congress* was dispatched to meet them. After another night of favorable winds carrying unusual but welcome island smells, *Donaghey*'s lookout spotted a sail, then two, then quite a few smaller ones on the brightening horizon.

"The larger are probably NUS warships," Greg told Pol-Heena. "They're flying their weird, five-stars-and-stripes flag from every masthead, probably so we won't think they're Doms. Sparks said the little one's a corvette that *Congress* invited to join her." He grinned. "There're two of us, and who's to say *we're* not Doms, trying a trick?"

"Everyone must be careful these days, it seems," Pol agreed, glancing at Greg. He didn't blink, but his tail betrayed a trace of nervousness. He tended to dwell on his behavior prior to their encounter with the League destroyer. As far as Greg was concerned, Pol more than made up for it by saving his life. But he'd been less talkative since, except to report on his conversations with the young League ensign. Greg had invited Ensign Perez Mole to a Spartan dinner with *Donaghey*'s officers, but Mole hardly spoke and it wound up an awkward affair. Yet he seemed more open with Pol-Heena alone. Maybe he sensed that Pol had been against a hostile confrontation, or perhaps still hoped the Republic was an uneasy member of the Alliance—something he'd confessed his superiors believed. Or maybe their appearance was enough to make people perceive Lemurians as less belligerent, more sympathetic creatures in general. They were comparatively small and furry, with long, plush tails and big eyes, after all. Mole wouldn't be the first human to make that mistake. Citizens of the Empire of the New Britain Isles found it difficult not to *pet* them . . . before they saw them fight.

Come to that, maybe Pol-Heena remained tense because of the nuggets he gleaned from Mole. Greg had no idea what Captain Reddy might've discovered about the League in his absence, but they'd always assumed it must be large and powerful if it could send *Savoie*, a submarine, and now a destroyer and its armed tender—at least—to far-flung places, solely for the apparent purpose of stirring up trouble. (Tomas *had* warned them not to tangle with *Antúnez*'s tender, the *Ramb V*, which was apparently armed similarly to the Allies' *Santa Catalina*.) The reason he named and described the ship was undoubtedly to spare his own captive crew in the event of a meeting. And one of the last, fragmentary, cautionary messages Greg received from Captain Reddy, via Alex-aandra, had been to watch for a powerful League ship named *Leopardo*. Perez Mole refused to elaborate on her or itemize the League's resources, but confirmed with conviction that the Alliance hadn't seen anything yet. This had been the universal contention of every League officer they'd met.

"If they're so damn powerful, why don't they just finish us off?" Smitty had demanded, as frustrated as the rest.

"For the reason they *always* give," Pol had replied. "They're preoccupied elsewhere. They expect us all to weaken ourselves sufficiently, fighting one another, to minimize any threat we might pose."

"Yeah," Greg agreed, then asked, "But what are they preoccupied with? Another enemy? Internal strife? Sealing their hold on the Med? Or just a lack of resources, like fuel, for instance?"

"Whaat-ever it is," Lieutenant Mak-Araa had said, "it must be less bothersome than before, based on recent aactions." His point had caused gloomy blinking around *Donaghey*'s wardroom table.

Now there was an air of excitement, however, as *Donaghey* and *Matarife* closed with *Congress*, her consort, and half a dozen small sloops, apparently curious fishing boats. Soon, the NUS ships were near enough to see clearly, and Greg was impressed. They were amazingly similar to the Allies' Scott class, but he couldn't tell how many guns they carried. Their sides were painted black, their gunports closed. Both ships took in their sails, closing under steam, with blue smoke wafting to leeward.

"Back the foresails," Greg told Mak. "Signal *Matarife* to do the same. We'll heave to." He was about to order the cutter over the side when *Congress* lowered a boat from a quarter davit. Men climbed in, along with a small figure with a tail that could only be Kari-Faask. Greg's heart quickened with pleasure at this confirmation that their friends were safe. "Stand by the side party," he told his Marine lieutenant. Haana-Lin-Naar called her people and they stood easy at the gangway as the boat rowed across. Greg quickly surveyed his ship. A few remnants of her battles remained: shot-gouged decks and bright new timbers along the bulwarks, not yet painted. And he could only imagine how dingy *Donaghey*'s white stripe between her gunports must look. But the crew had done him proud with respect to squaring everything away as best they could. The boat came alongside, and Jenaar-Laan raised his whistle.

The first man up the pilot's ladder was short and portly, with large muttonchops and a hawk nose. A wide smile covered his face, and he wore a dark blue shako and double-breasted coat. Laan blew his whistle, and the Marines saluted. To everyone's approval, the visitor saluted the Stars and Stripes before facing Greg and rendering another open-palm salute. Greg returned the gesture, palm down, and the Marines crisply returned to order arms.

"Captain Ezra Willis," the man said, extending his hand. "Honored to command the New United States frigate *Congress*. Beg permission to come aboard."

Greg beamed and shook the hand. The pleased expression seemed out of place on his youthful but careworn face. "Permission gladly granted, Captain Willis. I'm Captain Greg Garrett, United States Navy." He paused, then added ironically, "Commanding the American Navy Clan ship USS *Donaghey* for the United Homes."

Willis chuckled. "Indeed, indeed. The world's full of surprises. A very few, like this, might still be pleasant from time to time." On the tail of his comment, Ensign Kari-Faask hopped on deck, grinning hugely and blinking fast enough to blur her eyelids. She also saluted the colors and Greg, then embraced him. Greg was taken aback. He knew *of* Kari, but they'd never met. She'd joined *Walker*'s special air division after he already had *Donaghey*, and with her and Fred's capture by the Doms, escape, and continued activity with Second Fleet, they'd been half a world apart ever since. That didn't seem to matter to her. Finally, she stepped back and simply said, "Is good ta' be home, sur, with my own claan."

"Glad to have you, Ensign," Greg said sincerely. "You've done *very* well." He grinned. "My orders were to arrest you or hug you—at my discretion. We've already sorted that out. But where's Lieutenant Reynolds?" Greg remembered Fred as the youngest member of *Walker*'s crew, joining her at the advanced age of seventeen. He doubted he was twenty yet.

"He's aboard *Ol' Zaack*, the Nussies call her," Kari said offhandedly. "Their flaag-ship. Playin' with his raa-dio. Gen-raal Shinya has a raa-dio tower in the mountains at Chim-bo-raazo, er some such, an' there's traaffic all the time. Stuff's goin' on," she added significantly, then shrugged. "We'll tell you all about it when we get to Saan-ti-aago."

Willis smiled at the meeting as several of his crew came aboard, mostly dressed as he, but a couple wore straw hats and white roundabouts. Then he nodded aft at *Matarife*. "Speaking of pleasant surprises, seeing that villainous brute apprehended is certainly one. Like many of the latest old-style Dom frigates, she can show our steamers her heels with a favorable wind. Steamers're rather heavier, you see, and screw propellers make them somewhat crank when not engaged." He pursed his lips. "Lieutenant Reynolds says *your* sailing steamers aren't so handicapped," he probed. "Perhaps a matter of design?"

"That may be, Captain Willis," Greg admitted noncommittally, "but I can't speak from experience."

Willis didn't press. "And *Matarife*, in particular, has behaved rather badly," he said, returning to the subject of the prize.

"By consorting with representatives of the League?" Greg probed.

Willis frowned. "So you know. Having taken her, of course you do. Yes, that—and other things." He gazed about, apparently pleased by what he saw. "Your ship's a beauty. The very pinnacle of the last age—I mean no offense!" he hastened to add. "I often yearn for the days before those hot, smoky machines filled our ships! And *you* caught *Matarife* quite handily, avoiding a mauling as well."

"*Donaghey*'s a fast sailor, sir, and my heart agrees with you. But in a world of steamers . . ." He shrugged. "We didn't have to catch *Matarife*, though. She sort of sailed into our arms. I don't think she expected us," he added wryly. "The same with the League destroyer *Antúnez*."

Willis looked surprised. "We've heard of that ship," he allowed, "though we didn't know her name. Fishermen reported her haunting the windward isles a few weeks ago, and I understand she's astonishingly fast. From their description, Mr. Reynolds declared she's much like your *Walker*. But . . . however did you escape? She's never fired on any of our ships, but I'm given to understand your Alliance and the League are not on the best of terms."

"We sank her," Greg stated simply.

Willis blinked, incredulous. "Did you? By God!"

"Yes," Greg declared unequivocally, eyes narrowing at Willis's tone. "And come to find out, she was looking for us all along, to keep us from meeting you. We've got about fifty of her people aboard, and *Matarife*'s surviving crew is secured below her decks. I'd ask if you might take custody . . . if I knew what would happen to them."

"Sank her," Willis mused, shaking his head, disbelief swept away by Greg's straightforward manner and the mention of prisoners. "How . . . ?" He stopped himself. "That is to say, may I ask how you accomplished that?" He took a long breath, realizing he may have offended, and reproduced his engaging smile. "Answer or not as you please. I didn't mean to question you. It seems Mr. Reynolds and Miss Faask," he said, bowing to Kari, "actually understated your resourcefulness. Not that I doubted them, in all honesty." He seemed to shake himself. "In answer to your request, I'm afraid I can't commit my government in regard to your League prisoners. They're not our enemies, and please God that remains the case." He frowned. "I suppose we might harbor them, as a neutral." His expression brightened once more. "But the Doms we'll certainly take. Their officers will be exchanged, if they desire. It's the only way to save any of ours in enemy hands, though it's fairly unusual and difficult to arrange. And their desire for exchange often passes, upon reflection. The ordinary seamen are usually decent fellows, wholly ignorant of anything beyond the duty they're raised to perform. And quite amazingly, beyond their fear and its representatives and capricious brutalities, they know little about the abominable cult that rules their lives. Once they recover from the shock that *we* won't mistreat or kill them, they often find employment in our fisheries or merchant marine. A few even join our navy, though they know better than most what will happen if they're captured." He looked at *Matarife* once more. "What will you do with your prize?" he inquired. "I only ask because I can imagine several ways she might be wonderfully useful, and I'm sure my government would be delighted to purchase her."

"She's not for sale," Greg replied, "but I've had a few ideas myself. Between us, I bet we can come up with something interesting to use her for."

Captain Willis smiled, recognizing that Greg knew he might *sail* both ships without assistance, but couldn't *fight* either if he did. At the same time, he wanted to keep a controlling interest in his prize. After a lifetime dealing with the bureaucracy of his own navy, he could only applaud the young officer's prudence.

"So, what now?" Greg asked, eager to proceed.

"If you please, we'll steer for Santiago. Commodore Semmes awaits you there, and we look for Admiral Duncan to arrive any day with the entire Caribbean squadron." He glanced fondly at Kari. "Your countrymen have convinced us that a golden opportunity lies before us, to crush the evil Dominion at last, and the consensus of *my* navy, sir—finally, I must say—is that there is not a moment to lose."

CAST OF CHARACTERS

(L)—*Lemurian, or Mi-Anakka*
(G)—*Grik, or Ghaarrichk'k*

Operation Outhouse Rat

Lt. Cmdr. Matthew Patrick Reddy, USNR—CINCAF (Commander in Chief of All Allied Forces).

First Fleet Elements

USS *Walker* (DD-163)

Lt. Cmdr. Matthew Patrick Reddy, USNR

Cmdr. Brad "Spanky" McFarlane—XO, Minister of Naval Engineering.

Cmdr. Bernard Sandison—Torpedo Officer, Minister of Experimental Ordnance.

Lt. Tab-At "Tabby" (L)—Engineering Officer.

Lt. Sonny Campeti—Gunnery Officer.

Lt. Ed Palmer—Signals.

Surgeon Lieutenant Pam Cross

Chief Quartermaster Patrick "Paddy" Rosen—First Officer.

Chief Boatswain's Mate Jeek (L)—Former crew chief, Special Air Division.

Chief Engineer Isak Reuben—One of the original Mice.

Gunner's Mate Pak-Ras-Ar, "Pack Rat" (L)

Earl Lanier—Cook.

Juan Marcos—Officer's Steward.

Wallace Fairchild—Sonarman, Anti-Mountain Fish Countermeasures (AMF-DIC).

Min-Sakir "Minnie" (L)—Bridge talker.

Corporal Neely—Imperial Marine and bugler assigned to *Walker.*

USS *James Ellis* (DD-21)

Cmdr. Perry Brister

Lt. Rolando "Ronson" Rodriguez—XO.

Lt. (jg) Jeff Brooks—Sound Man, Anti-Mountain Fish Countermeasures (AMF-DIC).

Lt. (jg) Paul Stites—Gunnery Officer.

Lt. (jg) Johnny Parks—Engineering Officer.

Chief Bosun's Mate Carl Bashear

Taarba-Kaar "Tabasco" (L)—Cook.

Salissa Battlegroup

Admiral Keje-Fris-Ar (L)

USNR *Salissa* (*Big Sal*, CV-1)

Captain Atlaan-Fas (L)

Lt. Sandy Newman—XO.

1st Naval Air Wing

Captain Jis-Tikkar "Tikker" (L)—Commander of Flight Operations (COFO), 1st, 2nd, 3rd Bomb Squadrons, 1st, 2nd Pursuit Squadrons, 1 x P-40E floatplane.

USS *Tarakaan Island* (SPD-3)

In self-propelled dry dock.

Frigates (DDs) Attached

Des-Ron 6

USS *Tassat***

Captain Jarrik-Fas (L)

Lt. Stanly Raj—Impie XO.

USS *Scott****

Cmdr. Muraak-Saanga (L)—Former *Donaghey* XO and sailing master.

USS *Nakja-Mur**

Lt. Naala-Araan (L)

Des-Ron 10

USS *Bowles****

USS *Saak-Fas****

USS *Clark***

MTB-Ron-1 (Motor Torpedo Boat Squadron Number 1)

11 x MTBs (Numbers 4, 7, 13, 15, 16, 18–23)

Lieutenant Nat Hardee

Assault Force

1st Allied Raider Brigade—Chack's Raiders or Chack's Brigade

Lt. Col. Chack-Sab-At (L)

Major Risa Sab-At (L)—XO, Chack's sister.

21st (Combined) Allied Regiment

Major Alistair Jindal (Imperial Marine)—1st, 2nd Battalions of the 9th Maa-ni-la, 2nd Battalion of the 1st Respite.

7th (Combined) Allied Regiment

Major Enrico Galay—Former corporal in the Philippine Scouts; 19th Baalkpan, 1st Battalion of the 11th Imperial Marines.

1st North Borno

Major I'joorka—Respected warrior and "King" Tony Scott's friend.

Brevet Captain Abel Cook—1st Battalion.

Brevet Captain Stuart Brassey—2nd Battalion.

Sergeant Major "Moe" the Hunter

Independent Assignment

Chief Gunner's Mate Dennis Silva

Lawrence "Larry the Lizard"—Orange-and-brown tiger-striped Grik-like Sa'aaran.

Pokey—"Pet" Grik brass picker.

Land-based Air

Mahe Field—Army/Navy Air Base Seychelles

Colonel Ben Mallory

3rd (Army) Pursuit Squadron (5 x P-40Es, 4 serviceable)—Remnants of 4th, 7th, 8th Bomb Squadrons, 5th, 6th, 14th Pursuit Squadrons

3rd Pursuiters

Lt. (jg) Suaak-Pas-Ra "Soupy" (L)

Lt. Conrad Diebel

2nd Lt. Niaa-Saa "Shirley" (L)

S. Sergeant Cecil Dixon

At Grik City, Mahe, and Comoros Islands

USS *Madras* (CV-8)—8th Naval Air Wing.

USS *Andamaan*—Protected Troopship Converted from a Grik BB.

Frigates (DDs) Attached

DES-Ron 9

USS *Kas-Ra-Ar***

Captain Mescus-Ricum (L)

USS *Ramic-Sa-Ar**

USS *Felts***

USS *Naga****

AEF-1 (First Fleet Allied Expeditionary Force)

General of the Army and Marines Pete Alden—Former sergeant in USS *Houston* Marine contingent.

Leftenant Doocy Meek—British sailor and former POW (WWI). Liaison for the Republic of Real People.

I Corps

General Lord Muln-Rolak (L)

1st (Galla) Division

General Taa-leen (L)

1st Marines, 5th, 6th, 7th, 10th Baalkpan

2nd Division

General Rin-Taaka-Ar (L)

1st, 2nd Maa-ni-la; 4th, 6th, 7th Aryaal

II Corps

General Queen Safir Maraan (L)

3rd Division

General Mersaak (L)

"The 600" (B'mbaado Regiment composed of "Silver" and "Black" Battalions); 3rd Baalkpan; 3rd, 10th B'mbaado; 5th Sular; 1st Battalion, 2nd Marines; 1st Sular

6th Division

General Grisa (L)

5th, 6th B'mbaado; 1st, 2nd, 9th Aryaal; 3rd Sular

1st Cavalry Brigade

Lt. Colonel Saachic (L)

3rd, 6th Maa-ni-la Cavalry

"Maroons"

Colonel Will

Consolidated Division of "Maroons," Shee-Ree, and Allied Advisors

III Corps

General Faan-Ma-Mar (L)

9th & 11th Divisions

2nd, 3rd Maa-ni-la; 8th Baalkpan; 7th, 8th Maa-ni-la; 10th Aryaal

Hij Geerki (G)—Rolak's "pet," captured at Rangoon, now "mayor" of Grik POWs at Grik City.

Land-based Air

Lt. Cmdr. Mark Leedom—Commander of Flight Operations (COFO) at Grik City.

Lt. Araa-Faan (L)—XO.

Lt. Walt "Jumbo" Fisher—Pat-Squad 22, Comoros Islands.

TF Bottle Cap

***Arracca* Battlegroup**

USNRS *Arracca* (CV-3)

Commodore Tassanna-Ay-Arracca (L)—High Chief, 5th Naval Air Wing.

USS *Santa Catalina* (CA-P-1)

Cmdr. Russ Chappelle

Lt. Michael "Mikey" Monk—XO.

Lt. (jg) Dean Laney—Engineering Officer.

Surgeon Cmdr. Kathy McCoy

Stanley "Dobbin" Dobson—Chief Bosun's Mate.

Major Simon "Simy" Gutfeld—3rd Marine.

Prisoners of Kurokawa

Adar (L)—Former Chairman of the Grand Alliance (COTGA) and High Chief and Sky Priest of Baalkpan.

Surgeon Commander Sandra Tucker Reddy—Minister of Medicine, and wife of Captain Reddy.

Kapitan Leutnant Becher Lange—Former XO of SMS *Amerika*.

Diania—Steward's Assistant and Sandra's friend and bodyguard.

Gunnery Sergeant Arnold Horn USMC—Formerly of the 4th (US) Marines.

Ruffy and Eddie (L)—Republic sailors.

The Republic of Real People

Kaiser Nig-Taak (L)

General Marcus Kim—Military High Command.

Inquisitor Kon-Choon (L)—Director of Spies.

Courtney Bradford—Australian naturalist and engineer; Minister of Science and Plenipotentiary at Large for the Grand Alliance.

Captain (Brevet Major) Bekiaa-Sab-At (L)—Military liaison from the Grand Alliance and Legate under General Kim.

Optio Jack Meek—Bekiaa's aide.

Prefect Bele—Bekiaa's XO of the 23rd Legion.

TFG-2 (Task Force Garrett-2)

(Long Range Reconnaissance and Exploration)

USS *Donaghey* (DD-2)

Cmdr. Greg Garrett

Lt. Saama-Kera "Sammy" (L)—XO.

Lt. (jg) Wendel "Smitty" Smith—Gunnery Officer.

Lt. (jg) Mak-Araa (L)

Chief Bosun's Mate Jenaar-Laan (L)

Surgeon Lt. (jg) Sori-Maai (L)

Marine Lieutenant Haana-Lin-Naar (L)

Major Tribune Pol-Heena (L)

Leutnant Koor-Susk (L)

Alferez (Ensign) Tomas Perez Mole—League prisoner (Spanish).

In Indiaa and Persia

Allied Expeditionary Force (North)

VI Corps

General Linnaa-Fas-Ra (L)

5th Maa-ni-la Cavalry

Detached Duty, shadowing General Halik

Colonel Enaak (L)

Czech Legion

The Czech Legion, or "Brotherhood of Volunteers," is a near-division-level cavalry force of aging Czechs, Slovaks, and their continental Lemurian allies, militarily—if not politically—bound to the Grand Alliance.

Colonel Dalibor Svec

At Madras (Indiaa)

USS *Mahan* (DD-102)

Repairs have resumed, with the arrival of a floating dry dock.

At Baalkpan

Cmdr. Alan Letts—Chairman of the United Homes and the Grand Alliance.

Leading Seaman Henry Stokes—Formerly of HMAS *Perth*; Director of Office of Strategic Intelligence (OSI).

Cmdr. Steve "Sparks" Riggs—Minister of Communications and Electrical Contrivances.

Lord Bolton Forester—Imperial Ambassador.

Lt. Bachman—Forester's aide.

Surgeon Cmdr. Karen Theimer Letts—Assistant Minister of Medicine.

Pepper (L)—Black-and-white Lemurian keeper of the "Castaway Cook" (Busted Screw).

Among the Khonashi (North Borno)

"King" Tony Scott

Eastern Sea Campaign

High Admiral Harvey Jenks—CINCEAST.

Enchanted Isles

Sir Thomas Humphries—Imperial Governor at Albermarl.

Colonel Alexander—Garrison commander.

Second Fleet

USS *Maaka-Kakja* (CV-4)

Admiral Lelaa-Tal-Cleraan (L)

Lt. Cmdr. Tex Sheider—XO.

Gilbert Yeager—Chief Engineer, one of the original Mice.

3rd Naval Air Wing

2nd Lt. Orrin Reddy—Commander of Flight Operations (COFO), 9th, 11th, 12th Bomb Squadrons; 7th, 10th Pursuit Squadrons.

The wing is currently badly understrength and operating from shore near Puerto Viejo.

Sgt. Kuaar-Ran-Taak "Seepy" (L)—Reddy's "backseater."

USS *New Dublin* (CV-6)—6th Naval Air Wing.

USS *Raan-Goon* (CV-7)—7th Naval Air Wing.

Line of Battle

Admiral E. B. Hibbs

9 Ships of the Line, including HIMSs *Mars*, *Centurion*, *Mithra*, *Hermes*, plus:

USS *Destroyer*—Former Dom Deoses Destructor.

Cmdr. Ruik-Sor-Raa (L)—One-armed former commander of USS *Simms*.

Lt. Parr—XO; former commander of HIMS *Icarus*.

Attached DDs

HIMS *Ulysses*, *Euripides*, *Tacitus*

HIMS *Achilles*

Lt. Grimsley

USS *Pinaa-Tubo*—Ammunition ship.

Lt. Radaa-Nin (L)

USS *Saanga*—Fleet oiler.

USS *Pucot*—Fleet oiler.

2nd Fleet Allied Expeditionary Force Army of the Sisters

General Tomatsu Shinya

Saan-Kakja (L)—High Chief of Maa-ni-la and all the Filpin Lands.

Governor-Empress Rebecca Anne McDonald

Lt. Ezekial Krish—Aide de Camp to the Governor-Empress.

Nurse Cmdr. Selass-Fris-Ar (L)—Daughter of Keje-Fris-Ar.

**Sister Audrey* is considered one of the "sisters," but has an independent command.*

X Corps

Total 8 Divisions with artillery train

General James Blair

4 regiments Lemurian Army and Marines, 4 regiments Frontier troops, 10 regiments Imperial Marines

Colonel Dao Iverson—6th Imperial Marines.

Lt. Anaar-Taar (L)—C Company, 2nd Battalion.

Lt. Faal-Pel "Stumpy" (L)—A Company, 1st Battalion, 8th Maa-ni-la.

XI Corps and Filpin Scouts

General Ansik-Talaa (L)

Pursuing Don Hernan (TF Skuggik Chase)

Colonel Sister Audry—Nominal command; Benedictine nun.

"Lord" Sergeant Koratin (L)—Marine protector and advisor to Sister Audry.

Major Blas-Ma-Ar "Blossom" (L)—2nd Battalion, 2nd Marines.

Colonel Arano Garcia—"Los Vengadores de Dios," a regiment raised from penitent Dominion POWs on New Ireland.

Teniente Pacal—Garcia's XO.

Spon-Ar-Aak "Spook" (L)—Gunner's Mate, and 1st Sgt. of A Company, 2nd Battalion, 2nd Marines.

Captain Ixtli—Commander of the Ocelomeh (Jaguar Warriors).

Captain Ximen—Commander of the Christian rebels.

In Contact with New United States Forces

Lt. (jg) Fred Reynolds—Formerly Special Air Division; USS *Walker*.

Ensign Kari-Faask (L)—Reynolds's friend and "backseater."

Enemies

Japanese

General of the Sea Hisashi Kurokawa—Formerly of Japanese Imperial Navy battle cruiser *Amagi*; self-proclaimed Regent and Sire of all India; currently confined to Zanzibar.

General of the Sky Hideki Muriname

Lieutenant of the Sky Iguri—Muriname's exec.

Signal Lt. Fukui

Cmdr. Riku—Ordnance.

Grik (Ghaarrichk'k)

Celestial Mother (G)—Absolute, godlike ruler of all the Grik, regardless of the relationships between the various Regencies.

General Esshk (G)—First General of all the Grik, and Regent Champion Consort to the new Celestial Mother.

The Chooser (G)—Highest member of his order at the Court of the Celestial Mother; prior to current policy, Choosers selected those destined for life—or the cookpots—as well as those eligible for elevation to Hij status.

General Ign (G)—Commander of Esshk's new warriors.

In Persia

General Halik (G)

General Shlook (G)

General Ugla (G)

General Orochi Niwa (Japanese)

Holy Dominion

His Supreme Holiness, Messiah of Mexico, and by the Grace of God, Emperor of the World—"Dom Pope" and absolute ruler.

Don Hernan de Devina Dicha—"Blood Cardinal" and commander of the "Army of God."

League of Tripoli

At Zanzibar

Maggiore Antonio Rizzo (Italian)

At Grik City

Capitaine de Fregate Victor Gravois (French)

Oberleuitnant Walbert Fiedler (German)

Aboard *Savoie*

Contre-Amiral Raoul Laborde (French)

Capitaine Dupont (French)

SPECIFICATIONS

American-Lemurian Ships and Equipment

USS *Walker* (DD-163)—Wickes (Little) class four-stacker destroyer. Twin-screw steam turbines; 1,200 tons; 314′ x 30′. Top speed (as designed): 35 knots. 112 officers and enlisted (current), including Lemurians (L). Armament: Main, 3 x 4″-50 + 1 x DP 4″-50. Secondary, 4 x 25 mm Type 96 AA, 4 x .50 cal MG, 6 x .30 cal MG. 40-60 Mk-6 (or equivalent) depth charges for 2 stern racks and 2 Y guns (with adapters). 2 x 21″ quadruple-tube torpedo mounts. Impulse-activated catapult for PB-1B Nancy seaplane.

USS *Mahan* (DD-102)—Under repair at Madras. Wickes class four-stacker destroyer. Twin-screw steam turbines; 960 tons; 264′ x 30′ (as rebuilt). Top speed: 25 knots. Rebuild has resulted in shortening and removal of 2 funnels and boilers. Otherwise, her armament and upgrades are the same as those of USS *Walker*.

USS *James Ellis*—Walker class four-stacker destroyer. Twin-screw steam turbines; 1,300 tons; 314′ x 30′. Top speed: 37 knots. 115 officers and enlisted. Armament: Main, 4 x DP 4″-50. 4 x .50 cal MG, 6 x .30 cal MG. 40-60 Mk-6 (or equivalent) depth charges for 2 stern racks and 2 Y guns (with adapters). 2 x 21″ quadruple-tube torpedo mounts. Impulse-activated catapult for PB-1B Nancy seaplane.

USS *Sular*—Protected troopship converted from Grik BB. Twin-screw, triple-expansion Baalkpan Navy Yard steam engine; 18,000 tons; 800′ x 100′. Top speed: 16 knots.

Crew: 400. 100 stacked motor dories mounted on sliding davits. Armament: 4 x DP 4″-50, 4 x .30 cal MG.

USS *Tarakaan Island*—(*Respite Island* class SPD in self-propelled dry dock.) Twin-screw, triple-expansion steam; 15,990 tons; 800′ x 100′. Armament: 5 x DP 4″-50, 6 x .30 cal MGs.

USS *Santa Catalina* (CA-P-1)—Protected cruiser; formerly general cargo. 8,000 tons, 420′ x 53′, triple-expansion steam, oil fired. Top speed (as reconstructed): 12 knots. Retains significant cargo/troop capacity, and has a seaplane catapult with recovery booms aft. 240 officers and enlisted. Armament: 6 x 5.5″ mounted in armored casemate. 2 x 4.7″ and 5 x 4″-50 DP in armored tubs. 1 x 10″ breech-loading rifle (20′ length) mounted on spring-assisted pneumatic recoil pivot.

Carriers

USNRS (US Navy Reserve Ship) *Salissa* (*Big Sal*, CV-1)—Aircraft carrier/tender, converted from seagoing Lemurian Home. Single-screw, triple-expansion steam; 13,000 tons; 1,009′ x 200′. Armament: 2 x 5.5″, 2 x 4.7″ DP, 4 x twin-mount 25 mm AA, 20 x 50 pdrs (as reduced), 50 aircraft assembled, 80–100 in crates.

USNRS *Arracca* (CV-3)—Aircraft carrier/tender converted from seagoing Lemurian Home. Single-screw, triple-expansion steam; 14,670 tons; 1009′ x 210′. Armament: 2 x 4.7″ DP, 50 x 50 pdrs. Up to 80 aircraft.

USS *Maaka-Kakja* (CV-4)—Purpose-built aircraft carrier/tender. Specifications are similar to *Arracca*, but it is capable of carrying upward of 80 aircraft, with some in crates.

USS *Madras* (CV-8)—Purpose-built aircraft carrier/tender. Second of 4 smaller fleet carriers (850′ x 150′, 9,000 tons). Faster (up to 15 knots) and lightly armed (4 x Baalkpan Arsenal 4″-50 DP guns—2 amidships, 1 each forward and aft). Can carry as many aircraft as *Maaka-Kakja*.

USS *New Dublin* (CV-6) and **USS *Raan-Goon*** are virtually identical.

Frigates (DDs)

USS *Donaghey* (DD-2)—Square-rig sail, 1200 tons, 168′ x 33′; 200 officers and enlisted. Sole survivor of first new construction. Armament: 24 x 18 pdrs, 8 x 12 pdrs, 12 x MG 08 "Maxim" 7.92 x 57 mm MGs, Y gun and depth charges.

***Dowden class**—Square-rig steamer, 1,500 tons, 12–15 knots, 185′ x 34′; 218 officers and enlisted. Armament: 20 x 32 pdrs, Y gun and depth charges.

****Haakar-Faask class**—Square-rig steamer, 15 knots, 1,600 tons, 200′ x 36′; 226 officers and enlisted. Armament: 20 x 32 pdrs, Y gun and depth charges.

*****Scott class**—Square-rig steamer, 17 knots, 1,800 tons, 210′ x 40′; 260 officers and enlisted. Armament: 20 x 50 pdrs, Y gun and depth charges.

Corvettes (DEs)—Captured Grik "Indiamen," primarily of the earlier (lighter) design. "Razeed" to the gun deck, these are swift, agile, dedicated sailors with three masts and a square rig. 120–160′ x 30–36′, about 900 tons (tonnage varies depending largely on armament, which also varies from 10 to 24 guns that range in weight and bore diameter from 12–18 pdrs). Y gun and depth charges. Nearly all of these, as well as many DDs, have been converted to AVDs (Destroyer-seaplane tenders).

Auxiliaries—Still largely composed of purpose-altered Grik "Indiamen," small and large, and used as transports, oilers, tenders, and general cargo. A growing number of steam auxiliaries have joined the fleet, with dimensions and appearance similar to Dowden and Haakar-Faask class DDs, but with lighter armament. Some fast clipper-shaped vessels are employed as long-range oilers. Fore and aft rigged feluccas remain in service as fast transports and scouts.

USNRS—*Salaama-Na* Home—Unaltered, other than by emplacement of 50 x 50 pdrs. 1014′ x 150′, 8,600 tons. 3 tripod masts support semirigid "junklike" sails or "wings." Top speed: about 6 knots, but capable of short sprints up to 10 knots using 100 long sweeps. In addition to living space in the hull, there are three tall pagodalike structures within the tripods that cumulatively accommodate up to 6,000 people.

***Woor-Na* Home**—Lightly armed (ten 32 pdrs) heavy transport; specifications as for *Salaama-Na*.

Aircraft

P-40E Warhawk—Allison V1710, V12, 1,150 hp. Top speed: 360 mph. Ceiling, 29,000 ft. Crew: 1. Armament: 6 x .50 cal Browning MGs, and up to 1,000-lb bomb.

PB-1B "Nancy"—W/G type, in-line 4 cyl 150 hp. Top speed: 110 mph. Max weight: 1,900 lbs. Crew: 2. Armament: 400-lb bombs.

PB-2 "Buzzard"—3 x W/G type, in-line 4 cyl 150 hp. Top speed: 80 mph. Max weight: 3,000 lbs. Crew: 2, and up to 6 passengers. Armament: 600-lb bombs.

PB-5 "Clipper"—4 x W/G type, in-line 4 cyl 150 hp. Top speed: 90 mph. Max weight: 4,800 lbs. Crew: 3, and up to 8 passengers. Armament: 1,500-lb bombs.

PB-5B—As above, but powered by 4 x MB 5 cyl, 254 hp radials. Top speed: 125 mph. Max weight: 6,200 lbs. Crew: 3, and up to 10 passengers. Armament: 2,000 lbs bombs.

PB-5D—4 x 10 cyl, 365 hp radials. Top speed: 145 mph. Max weight: 7,800 lbs. Crew: 5–6, and up to 8 passengers. Armament: 5 x .30 cal, 2,500 lbs bombs/torpedoes.

P-1 Mosquito Hawk or "Fleashooter"—MB 5 cyl 254 hp radial. Top speed: 220 mph. Max weight 1,220 lbs. Crew: 1. Armament: 2 x .45 cal Blitzerbug machine guns in wheel pants.

P-1B—As above, but fitted for carrier ops.

P-1C—Third variant, with a 10 cyl, 365 hp radial. Top speed: 275 mph. Max weight: 1740 lbs. Crew: 1. Armament: 2 x .30 cal Browning MGs in wings.

Field artillery—6 pdr on stock-trail carriage; effective to about 1,500 yds, or 300 yds with canister. 12 pdr on stock-trail carriage—effective to about 1,800 yds, or 300 yds with canister. 3″ mortar—effective to about 800 yds. 4″ mortar—effective to about 1,500 yds.

Primary small arms—Allin-Silva breech-loading rifle (.50–80 cal), Allin-Silva breech-loading smoothbore (20 gauge), 1911 Colt and copies (.45 ACP), Blitzerbug SMG (.45 ACP). M-1917 Navy Cutlass, grenades, bayonet.

Secondary small arms—Rifled musket (.50 cal), 1903 Springfield (.30–06), 1898 Krag-Jorgensen (.30 US), 1918 BAR (.30–06), Thompson SMG (.45 ACP). A small number of other firearms are available.

MGs—1919 water-cooled Browning and copies (.30–06). 41 lbs without mount, 400–600 rpm, 1,500 yds.

Imperial Ships and Equipment

Until recently, few shared enough specifics to be described as classes, but can be grouped by basic size and capability. Most do share the fundamental similarity of being powered by steam-driven paddle wheels and a complete suit of sails, though all new construction is being equipped with double-expansion engines and screw propellers, and iron hulls are under construction.

Ships of the line—About 180′–200′ x 52′–58′, 1,900–2,200 tons. 50–80 x 30, 20 pdrs, 10 pdrs, 8 pdrs. (8 pdrs are more commonly used as field guns by the Empire.) Speed: about 8–10 knots. 400–475 officers and enlisted.

Frigates—About 160′–180′ x 38′–44′, 1,200–1,400 tons. 24–40 x 20–30 pdrs. Speed: about 13–15 knots. 275–350 officers and enlisted. Example: HIMS *Achilles*, 160′ x 38′, 1,300 tons, 26 x 20 pdrs. New construction follows the design of the Scott class DD.

Field artillery—The Empire of the New Britain Isles has adopted the Allied 12 pdr, but still retains numerous 8 pdrs on split-trail carriages—effective to about 1,500 yds, or 600 yds with grapeshot.

Primary small arms—Allin-Silva breech-loading rifle (.50–80 cal), rifled musket (.50 cal), bayonet. Swords and smoothbore flintlock muskets (.75 cal) are now considered secondary and are issued to native allies in the Dominion.

Republic Ships and Equipment

***Princeps* class monitors**—210′ x 50′, 1,200 tons. Twin screw, 11 knots, 190 officers and enlisted. Armament: 4 guns in two turrets, 4 x MG08 8 x 57 mm (Maxim) MGs on flying bridge. The Republic has finally begun construction of blue-water warships, though details are scant.

Field artillery—75 mm Quick Firing breech-loader influenced by the French 75. Range: 3,000 yds with black powder propellant and contact fuse exploding shell.

Primary small arms—Breech-loading bolt-action, single-shot rifle, 11.15 x 60R (.43 Mauser) cal. **Secondary small arms**—M-1898 Mauser (8 x 57 mm), Mauser and Luger pistols, mostly in 7.65 cal.

Republic military rank structure—A combination of ancient and new, with a few unique aspects. An army, commanded by a general, is ordinarily composed of 6 legions. Each legion, commanded by a colonel, has 6 cohorts. The senior cohort commander (and XO) is the prefect, and roughly equivalent to a major. The remaining cohorts are led by senior centurions (captains), who still command one of the 6 centuries in the cohort through their senior optio (2nd lieutenant), who has a junior optio (like an ensign) as his assistant. Other centurions are roughly equivalent to 1st lieutenants. The Republic also has provisions for temporary, special-purpose rank appointments. A military tribune may be given specific tasks requiring them to outrank all prefects and below, as well as single-ship captains. A legate may supersede the colonel of any legion for a specific purpose, unless countermanded by the general of the army the legion is attached to. Likewise, legates act as commodores at sea.

Enemy Warships and Equipment

Grik

***ArataAmagi* class BBs (ironclad battleships)**—800′ x 100′, 26,000 tons. Twin-screw, double-expansion steam. Top speed: 10 knots. Crew: 1,300. Armament: 32 x 100 pdrs, 30 x 3″ AA mortars.

***Akagi* class CVs (Aircraft Carriers)**—800′ x 100′, 12,000 tons. Twin-screw, double-expansion steam. Top speed: 14 knots. Crew: 1,100. Armament: 10 x 3″ AA mortars, 10 x Type 89 MG (copies) 7.7 x 58 mm SR cal.* 40–60 aircraft.

***Azuma* class CAs (ironclad cruisers)**—300′ x 37′, about 3,800 tons. Twin-screw, double-expansion steam, sail auxiliary. Top speed: 12 knots. Crew: 320 Armament: 20 x 40 or 14 x 50 pdrs. 4 x firebomb catapults.

Heavy "Indiaman" class—Multipurpose transport ships and warships. Three masts, square rig, sail only. 180′ x 38′, about 1,100 tons (tonnage varies depending largely on armament, which also varies from 0 to 40 guns of various weights and bore diameters). The somewhat crude standard for Grik artillery is 2, 4, 9, 16, 40, 60, and now up to 100 pdrs, although the largest "Indiaman" guns are 40s. These ships have been seen in diminishing numbers and are apparently no longer made.

Tatsuta—Kurokawa's double-ended paddle/steam yacht. It was also the pattern for all Grik tugs and light transports.

Aircraft—Hydrogen-filled rigid dirigibles or zeppelins. 300′ x 48′, 5 x 2 cyl 80-hp engines. Top speed: 60 mph. Useful lift: 3,600 lbs. Crew: 16. Armament: 6 x 2 pdr swivel guns, bombs.

AJ1M1c Fighter—9 cyl 380 hp radial. Top speed: 260 mph. Max weight: 1,980 lbs. Crew: 1. Armament: 2 x Type 89 MG (copies) 7.7 x 58 mm SR cal.*

DP1M1 Torpedo Bomber—2 x 9 cyl 380 hp radials. Top speed: 180 mph. Max weight: 3,600 lbs. Crew: 3. Armament: 1 x Type 89 MG (copy) 7.7 x 58 mm SR cal.* I torpedo or 1,000 lbs bombs.

*Note: No MG of any type is available to any Grik as yet, other than those under the command of Hisashi Kurokawa on his ships, or the island of Zanzibar.

Field artillery—The standard Grik field piece is a 9 pdr, but 4s and 16s are also used, with effective ranges of 1,200, 800, and 1,600 yds, respectively. Powder is satisfactory, but windage is often excessive, resulting in poor accuracy. Grik field firebomb throwers fling 10- and 25-lb bombs, depending on the size, for a range of 200 and 325 yds, respectively.

Primary small arms—Copies of Allied .60 cal smoothbore percussion muskets are now widespread, but swords and spears are still in use—as are teeth and claws.

League of Tripoli

Savoie—548′ x 88′, 26,000 tons. 4 screws, 20 knots. Armament: 8 x 340 mm, 14 x 138.6 mm, 8 x 75 mm. 1,050 officers and enlisted.

Leopardo—Leone-class Exploratori (destroyer leader). 372′ x 34′, 2,600 tons. Twin screw, 30 knots. Armament: 8 x 120 mm, 6 x 20 mm, 4 x 21″ torpedo tubes. 210 officers and enlisted.

Holy Dominion

Like Imperial vessels, Dominion warships fall into a number of categories difficult to describe as classes, but again, can be grouped by size and capability. Despite their generally more primitive design, Dom warships run larger and are more heavily armed than their Imperial counterparts.

Ships of the line—About 200′ x 60′, 3,400–3,800 tons. 64–98 x 24 pdrs, 16 pdrs, 9 pdrs. Speed: about 7–10 knots. 470–525 officers and enlisted.

Heavy frigates (cruisers)—About 170′ x 50′, 1,400–1,600 tons. 34–50 x 24 pdrs, 9 pdrs. Speed: about 14 knots. 290–370 officers and enlisted.

Aircraft—The Doms have no aircraft yet, but employ "dragons," or Grikbirds, for aerial attack.

Field artillery—9 pdrs on split-trail carriages—effective to about 1,500 yds, or 600 yds with grapeshot.

Primary small arms—Sword, pike, plug bayonet, flintlock (patilla style) musket (.69 cal). Only officers and cavalry use pistols, which are often quite ornate and of various calibers.

LOOK FOR THE NEXT THRILLING
DESTROYERMEN ADVENTURE,

RIVER OF BONES

AVAILABLE IN HARDCOVER AND E-BOOK
FROM ACE IN JULY 2018

Taylor Anderson continues his thrilling* New York Times *bestselling alternate history series as the crew members of a World War II destroyer in a strange new world face their greatest challenge yet.

When the USS *Walker* and her captain, Matt Reddy, were mysteriously transported from the Pacific to another world, they became involved in a never-ending conflict between their Lemurian allies and the vicious Grik. They may have destroyed a maniacal general and captured a mighty battleship, but victory came at a terrible cost.

Virtually the entire Allied fleet in the West has been sunk or severely damaged, and the Allies' most elite strike force has been badly mauled. Now the Final Swarm, an unprecedented horde of ravening Grik, is coming to slaughter the weakened Allies.

Alone against this relentless tide stands the armored freighter *Santa Catalina*. Her skipper has only one hope: stall the Grik with a mad, suicidal dash upstream to block the river until help arrives—and he'll do it with the corpses of his ship and crew, if that's what it takes.

With enemies on all sides, Matt Reddy's destroyermen and their friends will need to fight as they've never fought before—or face utter extinction.